STANDARD NOVELS.

N° LXXXIV.

"No kind of literature is so generally attractive as Fiction. Pictures of life and manners, and Stories of adventure, are more eagerly received by the many than graver productions, however important these latter may be. APULEIUS is better remembered by his fable of Cupid and Psyche than by his abstruser Platonic writings; and the Decameron of BOCCACCIO has outlived the Latin Treatises, and other learned works of that author."

THE INHERITANCE.

COMPLETE IN ONE VOLUME.

LONDON:
RICHARD BENTLEY, NEW BURLINGTON STREET;
BELL AND BRADFUTE, EDINBURGH;
J. CUMMING, DUBLIN.
1841.

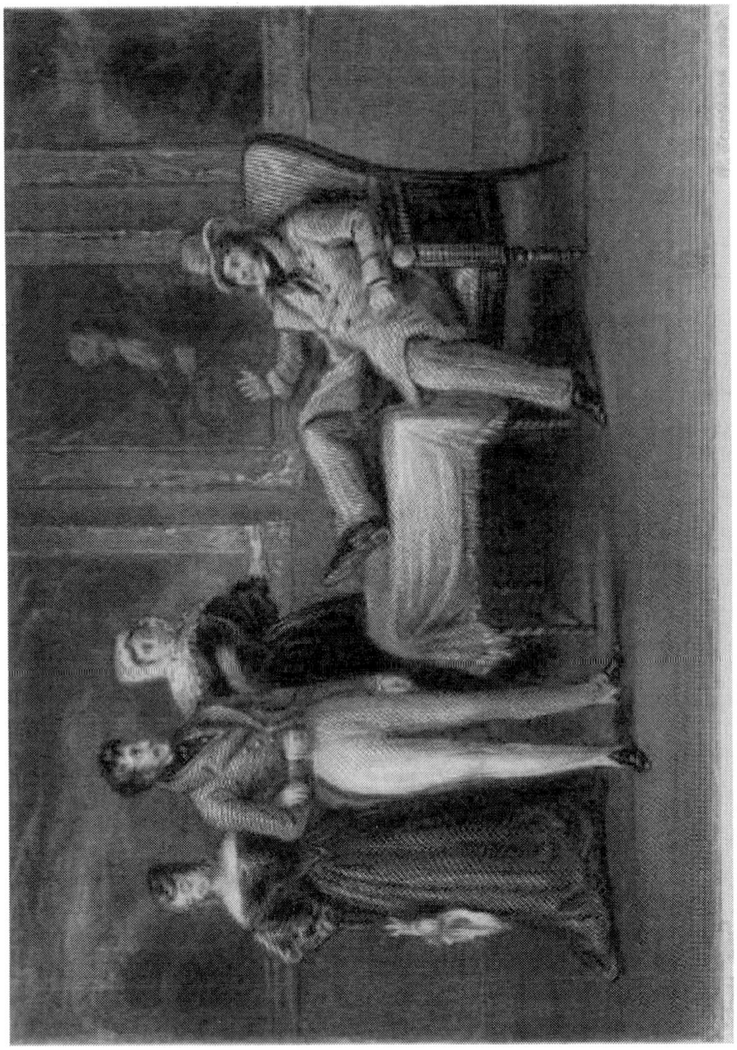

THE

INHERITANCE.

CHAPTER I.

Strange is it, that our bloods
Of colour, weight, and heat, pour'd all together, Would quite confound distinction, yet stand off In differences so mighty. All's Well that Ends Well.

It is a truth universally acknowledged, that there is no passion so deeply rooted in human nature as that of pride. Whether of self or of family, of deeds done in our own bodies, or deeds done in the bodies of those who lived hundreds of years before us — all find some foundation on which to build their Tower of Babel. Even the dark uncertain future becomes a bright field of promise to the eye of pride, which, like Banquo's bloody ghost, can smile even upon the dim perspective of posthumous greatness.

As the noblest attribute of man, family pride had been cherished time immemorial by the noble race of Rossville. Deep and incurable, therefore, was the wound inflicted on all its members by the marriage of the Honourable Thomas St. Clair, youngest son of the Earl of Rossville, with the humble Miss Sarah Black, a beautiful girl of obscure origin and no fortune. In such an union there was every thing to exasperate, nothing to mollify the outraged feelings of the Rossville family; for youth and beauty were all that Mrs. St. Clair had to oppose to pride and ambition. The usual consequences, therefore, were such as always have, and probably always will accompany unequal alliances, — viz. the displeasure of friends, the want of fortune, the world's dread laugh, and, in short, all the thousand natural ills that flesh is heir to when it fails in its allegiance to blood. Yet there are minds fitted to encounter and to overcome even these — minds possessed of that inherent nobility which regard honour as something more than a mere hereditary name, and which seek the nobler distinction, open to all, in the career of some honourable profession. But Mr. St. Clair's mind was endowed with no such powers ; for he was a man of weak intellects and indolent habits, with just enough of feeling to wish to screen himself from the poverty and contempt his marriage had brought upon him. After hanging on for some time in hopes of a reconciliation with his family, and finding all attempts vain, he at

B

length consented to banish himself and the object of their contumely to some remote quarter of the world, upon condition of receiving a suitable allowance so long as they should remain abroad. The unfortunate pair, thus doomed to unwilling exile, retired to France, where Mr. St. Clair's mind soon settled into that state which acquires its name from the character of its possessor, and, according to that, is called fortitude, resignation, contentment, or stupidity. There, too, they soon sunk into that oblivion which is sometimes the portion of the living as well as the dead. His father's death, which happened some years after, made no alteration in his circumstances. The patrimony to which he expected to succeed was settled on his children, should he have any, and a slender life annuity was his only portion.

The natural wish of almost every human being, the weakest as well as the wisest, seems to be to leave some memorial of themselves to posterity — something, if not to tell how their fathers thought or fought, at least to show how they talked or walked. This wish Mr. and Mrs. St. Clair possessed in common with others; but year after year passed away, and it still remained ungratified, while every year it became a still stronger sentiment, as death seemed gradually clearing the way to the succession. At the time of his marriage Mr. St. Clair had been the youngest of five sons ; but three of his brothers had fallen victims to war or pestilence, and there now only remained the present Earl and himself, both alike childless.

At length, when hope was almost extinct, Mrs. St. Clair announced herself to be in the way of becoming a mother; and the emigrants resolved upon returning to their native land, that their child might there first see the light. Previous to taking this step, however, the important intelligence was communicated to Lord Rossville, and also their intention of immediately proceeding to Scotland, if agreeable to him; at the same time expressing a wish that he would favour them with his advice and opinion, as they would be entirely guided by him in their plans.

Lord Rossville was a man who liked to be consulted, and to overturn every plan which he himself had not arranged; and as Mr. St. Clair had spoken of taking shipping from Bourdeaux, where they then were, and going by sea to Scotland, Lord Rossville in his answer expressed his decided disapprobation of such a scheme, in Mrs. St. Clair's situation, and in stormy winter weather. But he enclosed a route by way of Paris, which he had made out for them with his own hand ; and directed them, upon their arrival there, to signify the same to him, and there to remain until he had resolved upon what was next to be done, as he had by no means made up his mind as to the propriety, or at least the necessity, of their returning to Scotland. The packet also contained an order for a sum of money, and letters to some friends of his own at Paris, who would be of service to

Mrs. St. Clair. So far all was kind and conciliating; and the exiles, after much delay, set forth upon their journey, according to the rules prescribed by the Earl—but, within a day's journey of Paris, Mrs. St. Clair was taken prematurely ill, and there, at an obscure village, gave birth to a daughter, which, as Mr. St. Clair sensibly remarked, though not so good as a boy, was yet better than nothing at all. As the salique law was not in force in the Rossville family, the sex of the child was indeed a matter of little consequence, save in the eyes of such as are sturdy sticklers for man's supremacy. Its health and strength were therefore the chief objects of consideration ; and, although prematurely introduced into life, it was a remarkably fine thriving baby, which Mrs. St. Clair, contrary to the common practice of mothers, ascribed entirely to the excellence of its nurse.

They had been fortunate enough to meet with a woman of a superior class, who, having recently lost her husband and her own infant, had readily adopted this one, and as readily transferred to it that abundant stock of love and tenderness which those dealers in the milk of human kindness always have so freely to bestow on their nursling for the time. Mrs. St. Clair's recovery was tedious, and her general health she declared to be so much impaired that she could not think of encountering the severity of a northern climate. Instead of prosecuting their journey, therefore, they retired to the south of France, and, after moving about for some time, finally settled there. This was not what the Earl had intended; for, although pride still opposed his brother's return to Scotland, he had, at the same time, wished to have the family somewhere within the sphere of his observation and control, — the more especially as, having lately separated from his lady, his brother's child might now be regarded as presumptive heiress to the family honours. He had purposed, and indeed pressed, to have the little Gertrude transmitted to him, that she might have the advantage of being trained up under his own eye; but to this Mrs. St. Clair would not consent. She declared, in the most polite but decided manner, her determination never to part with her child; but promised that, as soon as her health was sufficiently re-established, they would return to Britain, and that Lord Rossville should have the direction and superintendence, if he pleased, of the young heiress's education. But some obstacle, real or pretended, always arose to prevent the accomplishment of this plan, till at length Mr. St. Clair was struck with a palsy, which rendered it impossible for him to be removed. Dead to all the purposes of life, he lingered on for several years, — one of those melancholy mementos, who, with a human voice and human shape, have survived every thing human besides.

At length death claimed him as his own, and the widow lost no time in announcing the event to the Earl, and in craving his advice and protection for herself and daughter. A very polite, though long-winded reply, was received from Lord Rossville, in -which he directed that Mrs. and Miss St. Clair should immediately repair to Rossville Castle, there to remain until he should have time and opportunity fully to digest the plans he had formed for the pupillage of his niece. This invitation was too advantageous to be refused, even although the terms in which it was couched were not very alluring either to the mother or daughter. With a mixture, therefore, of pleasure and regret, they hastened to exchange the gay vineyards and bright suns of France for the bleak hills and frowning skies of Scotland.

CHAPTER II.

Hope well to have, hate not past thought;
For cruel storms fair calms have brought:
After sharp showers the sun shines fair,
Hope comes likewise after despair. Richard Alison.

Many years had elapsed since Mrs. St. Clair had left her native land, and those who had known her then could scarcely have recognised her now, so completely had the tout ensemble changed its character. The blooming hoyden, with her awkward habits, and provincial dialect, had been gradually transformed into the beautiful woman, graceful in her movements, and polished, though elaborate in her manners. Though now long past her meridian, she was still handsome, and to superficial observers could be captivating ; but the change was merely outward, proceeding from no innate delicacy of thought or ennobling principle of action. It was solely the result of nice tact, knowledge of the world, and long intercourse with foreigners. The mind ' remained the same, although the matter had been modified.

In her early days her pride and ambition had been excited by making what was considered a splendid alliance ; and it was not till her understanding was thoroughly ripened, that she made the mortifying discovery that high birth, when coupled with personal insignificance, adds no more to real distinction than a showy sign does to an ill-kept inn. It was this disappointment which, operating on a naturally proud and violent temper, had brought into play all the worst qualities of her nature, and made her look upon the world as indeed a stage, where all the men and women were merely players. To act a grand and conspicuous part, and regain the station her husband's pusillanimity had lost, was therefore now her sole aim.

It rarely happens that one artificial mind can succeed in forming another — we seldom imitate what we do not love. There is something in human nature which recoils from an

artificial character even more than from a faulty one; and where the attempt fails, the revulsion generally produces a character of a totally different stamp. Mrs. St. Clair had spared no pains to render her daughter as great an adept in dissimulation as she was herself; hut all her endeavours had proved unsuccessful, and Miss St. Clair's mind remained pretty much as nature had formed it — a mixture of wheat and tares, flowers and weeds. There existed no sort of sympathy or congeniality of mind between the mother and daughter — there seemed little even of that natural affection which often supplies the want of kindred feeling, or similar tastes, and which serves to hind together hearts no human process ever could have brought to amalgamate. Without any point of resemblance in their characters or ideas, there was consequently little interchange of thought; and when Gertrude did address her mother, it was more from the overflowings of an open heart and buoyant spirits than from any reciprocity of feeling.

" How I wish I had Prince Houssain's glass," exclaimed she, as they drew near the borders of Scotland, "that I might take a peep at the people I am going amongst — a single glance would suffice to give me some idea of them, or at least to show whether they are the sort of persons it will be possible for me to love."

" You have formed very high and somewhat presumptuous ideas of your own powers of discrimination, it seems," said Mrs. St. Clair with a disdainful smile; " but I should numbly conceive that my knowledge and experience might prove almost as useful as your own observations or theories are likely to do."

" I beg your pardon, mamma, but I did not know you had been acquainted with the Rossville family."

" I am not personally acquainted with any of them —I never was — I-never would have been, but for you. It is upon your account I now stoop to a reconciliation, which otherwise I would have spurned as I have been spurned." She spoke with vehemence ; then in a calmer tone proceeded, " It is natural that you should wish to know something of the relations with whom you are henceforth to associate, since there is nothing more desirable than a previous knowledge of those whom it is necessary we should please. It is only from report I can speak of the Rossville family, but even from report we may form a tolerably accurate idea of people's general character. Report then says, that Lord Rossville is an obstinate, troublesome, tiresome, well-behaved man; that his sister, Lady Betty, who resides with him, is a harmless, dull, inquisitive old woman: then there are nephews, sisters' sons, to one of whom you are probably destined : there is Mr. Delmour, a weak, formal, parliamentary drudge, son of Lord Somebody Delmour, and nephew to the Duke of Burlington; and his brother, Colonel Delmour, a

fashionable unprincipled gamester ; and Mr. Lyndsay, a sort of quakerish, methodistical, sombre person, —all, of course, brimful of pride and prejudice. Nevertheless, beware how you contradict prejudices, even knowing them to be such, for the generality of people are much more tenacious of their prejudices than of any thing belonging to them ; and should you hear them run out in raptures at such a prospect as this " (pointing to the long bleak line of Scottish coast), " even this too, you must admire ; even this cold shrubless tract of bare earth and stone walls, and yon dark stormy sea, you will perhaps be told (and you must assent), are fairer than the lilied fields and limpid waters of Languedoc."

Miss St. Clair remained silent for a few moments contemplating the scene before her ; at last she said, " Indeed, mamma, I do think there is something fine in such a scene as this, although I can scarcely tell in what the charm consists, or why it should be more deeply felt than scenes of greater beauty and grandeur ; but there seems to me something so simple and majestic in such an expanse of mere earth and water, that I feel as if I were looking on nature at the beginning of the creation, when only the sea and the dry land had been formed."

" Rather after the fall, methinks," said Mrs. St. Clair with a bitter smile, as she drew her cloak round her; " at least, I feel at present much more as if I had been expelled from Paradise, than as if I were entering it."

The scene was indeed a dreary one, though calculated to excite emotions in the mind true to nature in all her varied aspects; and more especially in the youthful heart, where novelty alone possesses a charm sufficient to call forth its admiration. The dark lead-coloured ocean lay stretched before them ; its dreary expanse concealed by lowering clouds, while the sea-fowl clamouring in crowds to the shore announced the coming storm. The-yet unclothed fields were black with crows, whose discordant cries mingled with the heavy monotonous sound of the waves, as they advanced with sullen roar, and broke with idle splash. A thick mist was gradually spreading over every object— an indescribable shivering was felt by every human thing which had bones and skin to feel— in short, it was an east wind; and the effect of an east wind upon the east coast of Scotland may have been experienced, but cannot be described.

" This is dreadful!" exclaimed Mrs. St. Clair, as her teeth chattered in her head, and her skin began to rise into what is vulgarly termed goose-skin.

" You do look ill, mamma—you are quite a pale blue, and I certainly feel as I never did before;" and Miss St. Clair pulled up the windows, and wrapped her roquelaure still closer. The French valet and abigail, who sat on the dicky, looked round with pitiful faces, as though to ask, " Qu'est-ce que cela ? " Even the postillion seemed affected in the same manner; for, stopping his horses, he drew forth a ponderous many-eaped great coat, and buttoning it up to his nose, with a look that bade defiance to the weather, he pursued his route. The air grew colder and colder — the mist became thicker and thicker—the shrieks of the sea-fowl louder and louder — till a tremendous hail shower burst forth, and dashed with threatening violence against the windows of the carriage, and the undaunted driver was compelled to bend his purple face beneath its pitiless pelting, while he urged his horses as if to escape from its influence.

" This is Scotland, and this is the month of May !" exclaimed Mrs. St. Clair with a groan, as she looked on the whitened fields, and her thoughts recurred to the smiling skies and balmy vernal airs of Languedoc.

" Scotland has given us rather a rude welcome, I must confess," said her daughter ; " but, happily, I am not superstitious ; and, see, it is beginning to smile upon us already."

In a few minutes the clouds rolled away—the sun burst forth in all his warmth and brilliancy — the tender wheat glittered in the moisture — the lark flew exulting aloft — the sea-fowl spread their white wings, and skimmed over the blue waters — the postillion slackened his pace, and put off his great coat: such is Scotland's varying clime — such its varying scenery '.

CHAPTER III.

My father's house ! Send me not thence
Dishonour'd, but to wealth, to greatness raised. Sophocles.

It was on a lovely evening that the travellers reached their destination near the western coast of Scotland. The air was soft, and the setting sun shed his purple light on the mountains which formed the back-ground of the Rossville domains. The approach wound along the side of a river, which possessed ail the characteristic variety of a Scottish stream — now gliding silently along, or seeming to stand motionless in the crystal depth of some shaded pool—now chafing and gurgling, with lulling sound, over its pebbly bed—while its steep banks presented no less changing features. In some places they were covered with wood, now in the first tints of spring— the formal poplar's pale hue and the fringed larch's tender green mingling with the red seared leaf of the oak and the brown opening bud of the sycamore. In others, grey rocks peeped from amidst the lichens and creeping plants which covered them as with a garment of many colours, and the wild rose decked them with

its transient blossoms.

S 4

Farther on the banks became less precipitous, and gradually sunk into a gentle slope, covered -with smooth green turf, and sprinkled with trees of noble size. The only sounds that mingled with the rush of the stream were the rich full song of the blackbird, the plaintive murmur of the wood pigeon, and the abrupt but not unmusical note of the cuckoo. Gertrude gazed with ecstasy on all around, and her heart swelled with delight as she thought this fair scene she was destined to inherit; and a vague poetical feeling of love and gratitude to Heaven caused her to raise her eyes, swimming in tearful rapture, to the Giver of all good. But it was merely the overflowing of a young, enraptured, and enthusiastic mind; no deeper principle was felt or understood — no trembling mingled with her joy—no dark future cast its shadow on the mirror imagination presented to her ; but visions of pomp and power, and wealth and grandeur—visions of earthly bliss—swam before those eyes which yet were raised from earth to heaven. ' She was roused from her reverie by a deep sigh, or rather groan, from her mother, who leant back in the carriage, seemingly overcome by some painful sensation either of mind or body. Miss St. Clair was accustomed to hear her mother sigh, and even groan, upon very slight occasions, sometimes upon no occasion at all; but, at present, there was something that betokened an intensity of suffering too sincere for feigning.

" You are ill, mamma !" exclaimed she in terror, as she looked on her mother's pale and agitated countenance.

It was some moments ere Mrs. St. Clair could find voice to answer — but at length, in much emotion, she said,

" Is it surprising that I should feel, at approaching that house from which my husband and myself were exiled — nay, were even denied an entrance ? Can you imagine that I should be unmoved at the thoughts of beholding that family by whom we were rendered outcasts, and whom I have only known as my bitterest enemies ? "

Mrs. St. Clair's voice and her colour both rose as she enumerated her injuries.

" Oh ! mamma, do not at such a time suffer your mind to dwell upon those painful recollections; it is natural that melancholy

thoughts should suggest themselves ; but ah • there is the

castle," cried the young heiress, forgetting all her mother's wrongs as the stately mansion now burst upon their view ; and again her heai't exulted as she looked on its lofty turrets and long range of arched windows glittering in the golden rays of the setting sun. In another moment they found themselves at the entrance ; a train of richly liveried servants were stationed to receive them. Mrs. St. Clair's agitation increased—she stopped and leant upon her daughter, who feared she would have fainted; but making an effort, she recovered her self-possession; and following the servant, who led the way to the presence of

his lord, she gracefully presented her daughter to him, saying, " To your lordship's generous protection I commit my fatherless child."

Lord Rossville was a "bulky, portentous-looking person, with nothing marked in his physiognomy except a pair of very black elevated eyebrows, which gave an unvarying expression of solemn astonishment to his countenance. He had a husky voice, and a very tedious elocution. He was some little time in preparing an answer to this address, hut at last he replied, —

" I shall, rest assured, madam, make a point of fulfilling, to the utmost of my power and abilities, the highly important duties of the parental office."

He then saluted his sister-in-law and niece ; and, taking a hand of each, led them to a tall thin grey old woman, with a long inquisitive-looking nose, whom he named as Lady Betty St. Clair.

Lady Betty rose from her seat with that sort of deliberate hustle which generally attends the rising up and the sitting down of old ladies, and may be intended to show that it is not an everyday affair with them to practise such condescension. Having taken off her spectacles, Lady Betty carefully deposited them within a large work-basket, out of which protruded a tiger's head in worsted work, and a volume of a novel. She next lifted a cambric handkerchief from off a fat sleepy lapdog which lay upon her knees, and deposited it on a cushion at her feet. She then put aside a small fly table, which stood before her as a sort of outwork; and thus freed from all impediments, welcomed her guests ; and after regarding them with looks only expressive of stupid curiosity, she motioned to them to be seated, and replaced herself with even greater commotion than she had risen up. Such a reception was not calculated to call forth feelings of the most pleasurable kind; and Gertrude felt chilled at manners so different from the bland courtesy to which she had been accustomed, and her heart sunk at the thoughts of being domesticated with people who appeared so dull and unpleasing. The very apartment seemed to partake of the character of its inmates; it had neither the solid magnificence of ancient times, nor the elegant luxury of the present age; neither the grotesque ornaments of antiquity, nor the amusing litter of fashionable baubles for the eye to have recourse to. Lady Betty's huge work-basket was the only indication that the apartment was inhabited — an air of stiff propriety, of splendid discomfort, reigned throughout.

The usual, and more than the usual questions, were put by the Earl and his sister, as to time and distance, and roads and drivers, and inns and beds, and weather and dust; and all were answered by Mrs. St. Clair in the manner most calculated to conciliate those with whom she conversed — till, in the course of half an hour, Lord Rossville was of opinion that she was one of the best-bred, best-informed, most sensible, ladylike women he

had ever conversed -with — and his lordship -was not a person who was apt to form hasty opinions upon any subject.

Lord Rossville's character was one of those whose traits, though minute, are as strongly marked as though they had been cast in a large mould. But as not even the powers of the microscope can impart strength and beauty to the object it magnifies, so no biographer could have exaggerated into virtues the petty foibles of his mind. Yet the predominating qualities were such as often cast a false glory around their possessor — for the love of power and the desire of human applause were the engrossing principles of his soul. In strong capacious minds, and in great situations, these incentives often produce brilliant results; but in a weak contracted mind, moving in the narrow sphere of domestic life, they could only circulate through the thousand little channels that tend to increase or impair domestic happiness. As he was not addicted to any particular vice, he considered himself as a model of perfect virtue ; and having been, in some rsspects, very prosperous in his fortune, he was thoroughly satisfied that he was a person of the most consummate wisdom. With these ideas of himself, it is not surprising that he should have deemed it his bounden duty to direct and manage every man, woman, child, or animal, who came within his sphere, and that, too, in the most tedious and tormenting manner. Perhaps the most teazing point in his character was his ambition — the fatal ambition of thousands — to be thought an eloquent and impressive speaker, even on the commonest affairs of domestic life : for this purpose, he always used ten times as many words as were necessaiy to express his meaning, and those too of the longest and strongest description. Another of his tormenting peculiarities was his desire of explaining every thing, by which he always perplexed and mystified the simplest subject. Yet he had his good points; for he wished to see those ai'ound him happy, provided he was the dispenser of their happiness, and that they were happy precisely in the manner and degree he thought proper. He was a sort of petty benevolent tyrant; and any attempt to enlarge his soul, or open his understanding, would have been in vain. His mind was already full, as full as it could hold, of little thoughts, little plans, little notions, little prejudices, little whims, and nothing short of regeneration could have made him otherwise. He had a code of laws, a code of proprieties, a code of delicacies, all his own, and he had long languished for subjects to execute them upon. Mrs. St. Clair and her daughter were therefore no small acquisitions to his family — he looked upon them as two very fine pieces of wax, ready to receive whatever impression he chose to give them; and the humble confiding manner in which his niece had been committed to him had at once secured both to mother and daughter his favour and protection. Lady Betty's character does not possess materials to furnish so long a commentary. She was chiefly remark-

able for the quantity of -worsted work she executed, -which, for a person of her time of life, was considered no less extraordinary than meritorious. She was now employed on her fifth rug — the colours were orange and blue — the pattern an orange tiger couchant picked out with scarlet upon an azure ground. She also read all the novels and romances which it is presumed are published for the exclusive benefit of superannuated old women, and silly young ones; such as " The Enchanted Head" — "The Invisible Hand " — " The Miraculous Nuptials," &c. &c. She was now in the midst of " Bewildered Affections, or All is not Lost," which she was reading, unconsciously, for the third time, with unbroached delight. Lastly, she carefully watched over a fat, pampered, ill-natured lapdog, and asked a great many useless questions which few people thought of answering.

These were the only members of the family who appeared; but Lord Rossville mentioned that two of his nephews were on a visit in the neighbourhood, and might be expected the following

day.

" Since you are now, madam," said he, addressing Mrs. St. Clair, " become as it were incorporated in the Rossville family, it is proper and expedient that you should be made acquainted with all its members. I do not mean that acquaintance which a personal introduction conveys, but that knowledge which we acquire by a preconceived opinion, founded upon the experience of those on whose judgment and accuracy we can rely. I shall therefore give you such information regarding the junior members of this family as observation and opportunity have afforded me, and which, I flatter myself, may not prove altogether unacceptable or unavailing." The Earl paused, hemmed, and proceeded. " The senior of the two juvenile members to whom you will, in all probability, be introduced in the course of a very short period, is Lieutenant-Colonel Frederick Delmour, youngest son of the late Lord George Delmour, who was second son of James Duke of Burlington, by the Marchioness of Effen-ford, widow of the deceased Charles Chaloner, Marquis of Effenford, who died at an early period, leaving one son, the present Augustus Marquis of Effenford, married to the Lady Isabella Cadrington, daughter of the Duke of Litchfield, and one daughter, the present much-admired Countess of Lyming-ton ; — on the other hand, William Henry, the present Duke of Burlington, espoused the only daughter of that illustrious statesman John Earl of Harleigh, by whom he has issue one son, the Marquis of Haslingden, now abroad on account of the delicate and precarious state of his health. Thus it happens, and I hope I have made it sufficiently clear, that certain members of this family are at the same time united either by consanguinity, or by collateral connection of no remote degree, with many — I might say with most — of the illustrious families in the sister kingdom.

" My sister, the Lady Augusta Delmour, -widow of the late Lord George Delmour, at present resides in the metropolis with her three daughters — one of whom is, I understand, on the eve of forming a highly honourahle and advantageous alliance with the eldest son of a certain Baronet of large fortune and extensive property in the southern extremity of the island — hut of this it might not he altogether delicate to say more at present. Colonel Frederick Delmour, then— the subject of our more immediate consideration — is in himself a gentleman of figure, fashion, accomplishments, and of very distinguished bravery in his highly honourable profession. He has already had the honour of being twice slightly wounded in the field of battle, and in being made very honourable mention of in the despatches from the Earl of Marsham to his Royal Highness the Commander-in-chief. In these respects, the dignity and untarnished honour of the noble families to which he belongs have suffered no diminution in his person ; but it is to his elder brother " (and he now turned towards Miss St. Clair) " that we — that is, the Duke of Burlington and myself—look as to one who is to add still greater lustre to the coronets with which he is so intimately connected. To all the natural advantages, accomplishments, and acquirements of his brother, he unites address and abilities of the highest order, by means of which he has already acted a most distinguished part in the senate, and bids fair to become one of the first, if not the first, statesman of this, or, indeed, of any age." The Earl paused, as if overcome with the prophetic visions which crowded on his mind.

" What time of night is it?" asked Lady Betty. The Earl, recalled from his high anticipations, and reminded of the lapse of time, resumed his discourse, but in a less lofty tone. " The junior member of this family, whom I have now to present to you, is Edward Lyndsay, esquire, of Lynnwood, in this county, only child of the late Edward Lyndsay of Lynn-wood, esquire, and my youngest sister, the deceased Lady Jane St. Clair. The late Mr. Lyndsay was descended from an ancient and highly respectable family, but, by certain ancestral imprudences, was considerably involved and embarrassed during his life, insomuch that he was under the necessity of accepting a situation in one of our colonial settlements, whither he was accompanied by Lady Jane. Both, I lament to say, fell victims, in a short period, to the pestilential effects of the climate, leaving this young man, then an infant of three years and a half old, to my sole protection and guardianship. How these duties were discharged it is not for me to say; only, in justice to myself, I deem it right and proper to state, that at the expiry of the minority the estate then was (I say nothing of the means or management — let these speak for themselves — I simply deem it due to myself to state that the estate was then) free! If it is so no longer " And the Earl bowed, and waved his hands in

that significant manner -which says, " I wash my hands of it." But his lordship took a long time even to wash his hands; for he still went on — " Had Mr. Lyndsay followed the path which, with infinite consideration, I had marked out for him, he might now, hy means of those great and noble family connections he possesses, have been on the high road to honour, wealth, distinction, and self-approbation. As it is, he has chosen, contrary to my recommendation, to decline the highly advantageous situation offered to him in our Asiatic dominions, assigning as his sole reason that he was satisfied with what he already had, and meant to devote himself to the management and improvement of his own estate. A young man in his situation in life, scarcely yet twenty-six years of age, highly educated, as I made it a point he should be, and possessed of an ancient family estate, by no means great, and, I much fear, not wholly unincumbered, to refuse a situation of such honour, emolument, and patronage !— Mr. Lyndsay may be a good man; but it was my most anxious wish and endeavour to have made him more — I would have made him had he submitted to my guidance and control — I would have made him a great man! "

The solemn and dignified silence which followed this was happily broken by the announcement of supper. The evening wore slowly away, for each minute seemed like a drop of lead to Miss St. Clair, who was more of an age and temperament to enjoy than to endure. At length it ended, and she retired to her apartment with mingled feelings of pleasure and disappointment.

CHAPTER IV.

O life ! how pleasant in thy morning, Young Fancy's rays thy hills adorning! Cold-pausing Caution's lessons scorning,

We frisk away, Like schoolboys at th' expected warning,

To joy and play. Burns.

The following morning Gertrude rose early, impatient to take an unmolested survey of what she already looked upon as her own. The suite of public rooms engaged but little of her attention ; she had already settled, in her own mind, that these must be completely new-furnished, and with this sweeping resolution she passed quickly through them, merely stopping to examine the few pictures they contained. An open door, an almost dark passage, and a turnpike stair, at length presented themselves as stimulants to her curiosity, and tempted her to diverge from the straight line she had hitherto followed. It was the original part of the building, to which a modern Gothic front had been affixed,

and she soon found herself in all the inextricable maze of long narrovr passages, leading only to disappointment,— steps which seemed to have been placed as if on purpose to make people stumble — and little useless rooms, which looked as if they had been contrived solely for the pastime of hide and seek. At length she entered one she guessed to be Lord Rossville's study, and was hastily retreating, when her eye was caught by an old-fashioned glass door opening upon a shrubbery. She tried to open it, but it was locked ; the prospect from without was alluring, and she felt unwilling to turn away from it; the windows were but a little distance from the ground, and, having opened one, and smelt the perfume of the violets that grew beneath, her next impulse was to spring lightly through it into the garden. As she inhaled the fresh morning air, fraught with the sweets of early summer, where " the scent comes and goes like the warbling of music," and looked on the lovely landscape as it shone in the deep calm radiance of the morning sun, her heart, glowing with all the joyousness of youth and health, exulted in the brightness of creation. She wandered to a considerable distance, till, having gained the top of an eminence, she stood to admire the effect of some cottages situated on the green shelving bank which overhung the river. " What a pretty picturesque thing a cottage is," thought she to herself; " how gracefully its smoke rises from among the trees, and contrasts with the clear atmosphere around. When this is mine, I will certainly have some pretty cottages built in sight of the castle, and have the good people to dance on the green sward before their doors in an evening when their work is done. O, how easy it must be to be good, when one has the power of doing good !"

Ignorant of herself and of the nature of the human heart, Gertrude believed that to will and to do were one and the same ; as yet untaught that all vague baseless schemes of virtue, all vain romantic dreams of benevolence, are as much the cobwebs of imagination as the air-built castles of human happiness, whether of love, glory, riches, or ambition.

The beauty of the morning — the interest each object excited—the song of the birds — the smell of the opening flowers— the sound of the waters— all combined to lull her visionary mind into an Elysium of her own creating; and as she walked along, in all the ideal enjoyment of her Utopian schemes, she found herself at the door of one of those cottages whose picturesque appearance had charmed her so much at a distance. A nearer survey, however, soon satisfied her that the view owed all its charms to distance. Some coarse, lint-haired, mahogany-faced, half naked urchins, with brown legs and black feet, were dabbling in a gutter before the door; while some bigger ones were pursuing a pig and her litter, seemingly for the sole purpose of amusement.

" What a pity those children are all so ugly! " thought Miss
St. Clair; " it would have been so delightful to have had them all nicely dressed, and have taught them myself; but they are so frightful, I could have no pleasure in seeing them." However, she overcame her repugnance so far as to accost them. " Should not you like to be made nice and clean, and have pretty new clothes ? "

" Ay !" answered one of them with a broard stare, and still broader accent.

" And to go to school, and be taught to read, and write, and work ? "

" Naw ! " answered the whole troop with one voice, as they renewed their splashing with fresh vigour. Miss St. Clair made no farther attempts in that quarter; but she entered the cottage, carefully picking her steps, and wrapping her garments close round her, to prevent their contracting any impurities. The smoke, which had figured so gracefully out of doors, had a very different effect within, and she stood a few minutes on the threshold before she could summon courage to penetrate farther. At length, as her eyes got accustomed to the palpable obscure, she discovered the figure of a man, seated in a wooden chair by the fire in a ragged coat and striped woollen nightcap. " He is ill, poor creature," thought she ; and quickly advancing, she wished him good morning. Her salutation was respectfully returned ; and the man, making an effort to rise, invited her to be seated with considerable courtesy.

" I am afraid you are ill," said Gertrude, declining the invitation, and looking with compassion on his lean sallow visage.

" Oo, 'deed he's very ill, my leddy," cried a voice from behind; and presently advanced a stout, blooming, broad-faced dame, clad in a scanty blue flannel petticoat and short gown. She was encompassed by a girr or hoop supporting two stoups *, a piece of machinery altogether peculiar to Scotland. Having disengaged herself from this involvement or convolvement, she dropped a courtesy to her guest; and then wiping down a chair, pressed her to be seated.

" The gudeman's really extraordinar ill, my leddy," continued she in a high key. " I'm sure I ken na what to do wi' him; it was at first a sutten doon cauld, an' noo he's fa'n in till a sort o' a dwinin like, an' atweel I dinna think he'll e'er get the better o't."

" Have you any doctor to see him ? " inquired Miss St. Clair. " Oo, 'tweel he's had doctors eneugh, an' naething's been spared on him. I'm sure he's pitten as muckle doctor's stuff o' ae kind an' anither in till himsel' as might hae pushened him twenty times ower; but weel a wat, I think the mair he taks the waur he grows."

* A stoup is neither a bucket, nor a pitcher, nor a jar, nor an anv thing but e stoup.

" Perhaps he takes too much medicine." " 'Deed I'll no say but he may ; but ye ken, my leddy, what can be do? — he maun tak what the doctor sends him — the things canna be lost; but 'tweel he's very sweered to tak them whiles, tho' I'm sure muckle money they cost, an', as I tell him, they're dear morsels."

" Perhaps if he were to leave off the medicines, and try the effect of fresh air and good milk, and soup, which I shall endeavour to procure for him "

" I'm sure we're muckle obliged to you, my leddy; but he need nae want for fresh air, he can get eneugh o' that ony day by gawen to the door; but there's nae gettin him to stir frae the chimley lug; and, 'deed, I canna say he wants for milk or broth either, for ane o' tbe young gentlemen up by spoke to my lord for us, and he's really no to mean for his meat if he wad tak it; as I tell him whiles, my certy! mony a ane wad be glad to hae't for the takin."

" Is there any thing else, then, in which I can be of use to you ? " inquired Gertrude, now addressing the invalid,—" is there any thing you particularly wish for?"

The man heid up a ragged elbow — "Gin your leddyship has an auld coat to spare," said he, in a hesitating voice.

" An auld coat!" interposed his dame; " oo, what could pit an auld coat in your head, Tarn? I'm sure there's a hantel things mair needfu' than an auld coat — no that he wad be the waur o' a coat neither, for he has naething atween that puir dud on his back and his marriage ane, and his Sabbath-day suit in the kist there."

" Pray let me know what things are most wanted for your husband's comfort," said Miss St. Clair, " and I shall make a point of sending them—a bit of carpet, for instance," looking upon the damp clay floor.

" Wud ye like a bit carpet, Tam, the leddy asks?" roared his wife to him; then, without waiting for an answer,

" Oo, 'deed he disna ken what he wud like; an' he's ne'er been used till a carpet, and I daur say it wud just be a discon-venience to him, noo that he canna be fashed wi' ony thing — no but what he might pit up wi' a bit carpet, I'se warran', if he had ither things that are a hantel mair needfu'."

" A more comfortable chair, then, I may surely send," said Gertrude, still persisting in her benevolent attempts.

" The leddy's for sendin' ye anither chyre, Tam," again shouted his tender helpmate — the husband nodded his assent: " but, 'tweel, he's sutten sae lang in that ane, I doot it's no worth his while to chynge 't noo ; and I dinna think he could be fashed wi' anither chyre — no but what we micht pit up wi' anither chyre or twa, if we had aw thing else wise-like."

" I am sorry there is nothing I can think of that would be acceptable to you "

" Oo, I'll no say that, my leddy," briskly interrupted the hostess; " there's a hantel things, weel a wat, we hae muckle need o'— for ae thing — hut I maist think shame to tell't — an' it's really nae faut o' mine neither, my leddy ; hut it's just sae happent, wi' ae thing an' anither, I hae ne'er gotten a steek o' the gudeman's dead claise ready — and noo to think that he's drawin' near his end, I'm sure I canna tell the -vexation it's cost me." Here the dame drew a deep sigh, and wiped her eyes with the corner of her apron ; then proceeded — " Siena a discreditable like thing to hae said, an' sic a comfort as, nae doot, it wad be to him to see aw thing ready and wise-like afore he gaed out o' the world. — A suit o' gude bein comfortable dead claise, Tammes," appealing to her husband, " wad set ye better than aw the braw chyres an' carpets i' the toon. No but what if ance ye had the tane, we micht pit up wi' the tither; but wad nae't be a bonny-like thing to see you set up wi' a braw carpet, and a saft chyre, an' to think ye had nae sa muckle as a wiselike windin' sheet to row ye in ? "

A great deal of the pathos of this harangue was, of course, unintelligible to Miss St. Clair ; but she comprehended the main scope of it, and, somewhat shocked at this Scotch mode of evincing conjugal affection, she put down some money and withdrew, rather surprised to find what different ideas of comfort and respectability prevailed in different countries, and a good deal disappointed in the failure of her benevolent intentions.

CHAPTER V.

What kind of catechizing call you this ? Much Ado about Nothing.

Time had passed unheeded, and chance, rather than design, led Gertrude to retrace her steps, when, as she drew near the castle, she was met by one of the servants, who informed her that he and several others had been sent in search of her, as it was long past the breakfast hour, and the family had been some time assembled. Ashamed of her own thoughtlessness, she quickened her steps ; and desiring the servant to show the way to the breakfast room, without waiting to adjust her dress, she hastily entered, eager to apologise for her transgression. But the dread solemnity that sat on Lord Rossville's brow made her falter in her purpose. With the teapot in one hand, with the other he made an awful wave for her to be seated. Lady Betty was busy mixing a mess of hot rolls, cream and sugar, for uev epileptic lapdog. An impending storm sat on Mrs. St. Clair's face, but veiled under an appearance of calm dignified displea-s ire, Gertrude felt as if denounced by the whole party — she

c

knew not for what, unless for having heen twenty minutes too late for breakfast, and, in some trepidation, she began to apologise for her absence. Lord Rossville gave several deep sepulchral hems ; then, as if he had been passing sentence upon a . criminal, said, —

" I am not averse to postpone the discussion of this delicate and painful investigation, Miss St. Clair, until you shall have had the benefit of refreshment."

Gertrude was confounded. " My lord!" exclaimed she, in amazement, " I am very sorry if any thing has occurred," — and she looked round for an explanation.

Lord Rossville hemmed — looked still more appalling, and then spoke as follows: —

" You are doubtless aware, Miss St. Clair, that in all countries where civilisation and refinement have made any considerable progress, female delicacy and propriety are — are ever held in the highest estimation and esteem."

His lordship paused; and as no contradiction was offered to this his proem, he proceeded, —

" But you must, or certainly ought to be likewise aware, that it is not merely these virtues themselves which must be carefully implanted, and vigilantly watched over, in the young and tender female—for even the possession of the virtues themselves are not a sufficient shield for the female character. It was a maxim of Julius Caesar's (unquestionably the greatest conqueror that ever lived), that his wife must not only be spotless in herself, but that she must not even be suspected by otheTs : a maxim that, in my opinion, deserves to be engraven in letters of gold, and certainly cannot be too early, or too deeply, imprinted on the young and tender female breast."

His lordship had gained a climax, and he stopped, overpowered with his own eloquence. Mrs. St. Clair made a movement expressive of the deepest attention and most profound admiration.

" Such being my sentiments — sentiments in which I am borne out by the testimony of one of the greatest men who ever lived — it is not surprising that I should feel, and feel deeply too, the glaring indiscretion you have, I grieve to say, already committed, since your entrance within these walls."

Then, after another solemn pause, during which Miss St. Clair sat in speechless amazement, he resumed with more than senatorial dignity.

" I wish to be correctly informed at what hour you quitted your apartment this morning, Miss St. Clair?"

" Indeed, my lord, I cannot tell," answered Gertrude, with perfect naivete. " I had forgot to wind up my watch, and I did not hear any clock strike ; but, from the appearance of the morning, I am sure it was early."

" And what, may I ask, was the mode or manner, Miss St-

Clair, by which you thought proper to quit my house at so untimely and unusual an hour ?" demanded the Earl in a voice of repressed emotion.

Gertrude blushed. —" I am afraid I was guilty of a transgression, my lord, for which I ask your pardon ; but, allured by the fineness of the morning, and the beauty of the scenery, I was desirous of getting out to enjoy them, and having in vain tried to make my way through a door, I was tempted to step out by a window."

Miss St. Clair spoke with so much simplicity and gentleness, and there was so much sweetness and even melody in her voice and accent, that any other than Lord Rossville would have wished her offence had been greater, that her apology might have been longer. Not so his lordship, who possessed neither taste nor ear, and was alive to no charm but what he called propriety. At the conclusion of his niece's acknowledgment, the Earl struck his forehead, and took two or three turns up and down the room ; then suddenly stopping, —

" Are you at all aware, Miss St. Clair, of the glaring—the — I must say — gross impropriety of such a step in itself— of the still more gross construction that will be put upon it by the world ? The simple fact has only to be told, and one inference, and but one, will be drawn. You have quitted the apartment assigned to you under my roof at an — an untimely, consequently unbefitting hour ; and you — you — most imprudently and improperly precipitate yourself from a window—and what window? why, the window of my private sitting room! A young female is seen issuing from the window of my study at a nameless hour in the morning—the tale circulates — and where, I ask,— where am I?"

" Where was you?" inquired Lady Betty.

Mrs. St. Clair put her handkerchief to her face.

"lam very sorry, my lord, that I should have done any thing to displease you—if I have done wrong "

" If you have done wrong! Good heavens! is it thus you view the matter, Miss St. Clair? What/think wrong! Who that has proper feelings of delicacy and propriety—who that has a due regard for character and reputation, but must view the matter precisely as I do ? Such a step — and at such an hour!"

And his lordship resumed his troubled walk.

Unacquainted with her uncle's character, and ignorant of the manners and customs of the country, Gertrude was led to believe she had committed a much more serious offence than she had been aware of, and she was at length wrought up to that degree of distress which the Earl deemed necessary to mark her contrition. Softened at witnessing the effect of his power, which he imputed to the fine style of his language, he now took his niece's hand with an air of tender pomposity, and addressed her in what he intended for a more consolatory strain.

"I have considered it my duty—a painful one, doubtless, but, nevertheless, my duty—to point out to you the impropriety you have—I hope and believe inadvertently—committed. As a member of my family, and one for whose actions the world will naturally consider me responsible, it is necessary that you should henceforth look up to me as the guide of your future steps, and that I should henceforth take upon myself the entire regulation of your manners and conduct in life."

Miss St. Clair's blood ran cold at the thoughts of being subjected to such thraldom.

" But before dismissing this subject — I trust for ever — let me here state to you my sentiments with regard to young ladies walking before breakfast — a practice of which, I must confess, I have always disapproved. I am aware it is a practice that has the sanction of many highly respectable authorities who have written on the subject of female ethics; but, I own, I cannot approve of young ladies of rank and family leaving their apartments at the same hour with chamber-maids and dairymaids, and walking out unattended at an hour when only the lower orders of the people are abroad. Walking before breakfast, then, I must consider as a most rude masculine habit—as the Right Honourable Edmund Burke observes, ' an air of robustness and strength is highly prejudicial to beauty' (that is, as I apprehend, female beauty), ' while an appearance of fragility is no less essential to it;'—and certainly nothing, in my opinion, can be more unbecoming, more unfeminine, than to behold a young lady seat herself at the breakfast table with the complexion of a dairy-maid, and the appetite of a ploughman. At the same time, I am an advocate for early rising, as there are, doubtless, many ways in which young ladies may spend their mornings without rambling abroad; and you will find, by looking in your dressing-room, that I have made ample provision for your instruction, and amusement, and delight. Let morning walks, therefore, from henceforth have an end." And he pressed his niece's hand with that air of pompous forgiveness so revolting from one human being to another. Luckily, his lordship was here summoned away; but ere he left the room, he signified his intention of returning in an hour to show the ladies what was most worthy of observation in the castle and demesnes.

Absurd as this scene may appear, few will deny the undue importance which many people attach to the trifles of life, and how often mole-hills are magnified into mountains by those with whom trifles are indeed " the sum of human things."

CHAPTER VI.

By'r lakin, I can go no farther, sir, My old bones ache : here's a maze trod, indeed, Through forth-rights and meanders ! By your patience, I needs must rest me. The Tempest.

True as the dial to the sun,
Even though it be not shined upon,

Lord Rossvtlle returned at the hour appointed, to do the honours of his castle. But, as most of my readers have doubtless experienced the misery of being shown a house where there was nothing to be seen, and can tell " how hard it is to climb" from the lowest sunk story to the uppermost garrets, I shall not be so unmerciful as to drag them " up stairs and down stairs to my lady's chamber," and into all the chambers except his lordship's own, which he was too decorous to exhibit. Neither shall I insist upon their hearing every thing explained and set forth even to the Dutch tiles of the dairy, the hot and cold pipes of the washing-house, the new-invented ovens, the admirably constructed larder, the inimitable baths, with all the wonderworking steam-going apparatus of the kitchen. Here Mrs. St. Clair acquitted herself to admiration ; for to see judiciously requires no small skill in the seer, and there are few who see things precisely as they ought to be seen. Many see too much — many too little. Some see only to find fault — some only to admire; some are, or pretend to be, already acquainted with every thing they are shown — some are profoundly ignorant, consequently cannot properly appreciate the inventions or improvements exhibited. Some are too inquisitive—some too indifferent ; but it is as impossible to describe the vast variety of seers as of mosses, neither is it easy to point out the innumerable rocks on which a seer may strike. A treatise, illustrated by a few memorable examples or awful warnings, might possibly be of some use to the unskilful beholder. But, as in most other arts and sciences, much must depend upon natural genius. Mrs. St. Clair was so happily endowed, that she was enabled to see every thing as it was intended to be seen, and to bestow her admiration in the exact proportion in which she perceived it was required, through all the intermediate degrees, from ecstatic rapture down to emphatic approval. With Gertrude it was far otherwise; she had no taste for poking into pantries, and chimneys, and cellars, or of hearing any of the inelegant minutiae of life detailed. It seemed like breaking all the enchantments of existence to be thus made to view the complicated machinery by which life, artificial life, was sustained; and she rejoiced when the survey was ended, and it was proposed, after luncheon,

c 3

to take a drive through the grounds. Gertrude flattered herself that here she -would, at least, enjoy the repose of inactivity, and be suffered to see as much as could be seen from a carriage window of the beauties of nature. But Lord Rossville's mind -was never in a quiescent state in any situation; there was always something to be done or to be seen — the windows were to be either let down or drawn up — the blinds to be.drawn up or pulled down — there was something that ought to be seen, but could not be seen — or there was something seen that ought not to have been seen; thus his mind was not only its own plague, but the plague of all who had the misfortune to bear him company.

In vain were creation's charms spread before his eyes. There is a mental blindness, darker than that which shrouds the visual orb; and Nature's works were to Lord Rossville an universal blank, or rather they were a sort of account-book, in which were registered all his own petty doings. It was here he had drained, there he had embanked—here he had planted, there he had cut down—here he had built a bridge, there he had made a road—here he had levelled, there he had raised, &c. &c. &c. To all that his own head had planned he was feelingly alive; but, for the " dread magnificence of heaven," he had neither eye, ear, nor soul, and must therefore be forgiven if insensible to its influence. Mrs. St. Clair was not much more highly gifted in that respect, but she could speak, if she could not feel; and she expatiated and admired, till Lord Rossville thought her, without exception, the cleverest woman he had ever met with.

" Since you are so great an enthusiast in the beauties of nature, my dear madam," said he, addressing his sister-in-law, " we shall extend our drive a little farther than I had purposed, that I may have the pleasure of showing you, at a single coup aVceil, the whole extent of the Rossville possessions in this country, while, at the same time, you will embrace some other objects in which I am not wholly unconcerned. —Benjamin," (to the servant,) " to Pinnacle Hill;" and to

Pinnacle Hill the horses' heads were turned. " Pinnacle Hill," continued the Earl, " is a very celebrated spot: it is a purchase I made from Lord Fairacre some years ago; and is much resorted to by strangers, as commanding, with few if any exceptions, one of the finest views in Scotland."

Mrs. St. Clair hated fine views, and she tried to get off by pretending scruples about encroaching so much on his lordship's time, goodness, and so forth — but all in vain ; to Pinnacle Hill they were driven; and, after being dragged up as far as horses could go, they were (as, indeed, the name implied) obliged to alight and ascend on foot. With considerable toil they reached the top; and scarcely were they there, when the wind, having changed to the east, its never-failing accompaniment, a raw mist, began to gather all round. But Lord Rossville was insen-

sible even to an east-wind—his bodily sensations being quite as obtuse as his mental ones ; and having got to the top of the Pinnacle, he faced him round, and, in the very teeth of the enemy, began to point out what was and what was not to be seen.

" Here you have a very commanding view, or would have had, if the atmosphere had been somewhat clearer; as it is, I can enable you distinctly to trace out the boundary line of the Rossville estate. Observe the course of the river in the direction of my cane — you see it plainly here — there it disappears amongst the Millbank woods—now it takes a turn, and you have it again to your left — you follow me ? "

" Perfectly, my lord," replied Mrs. St. Clair, although she saw nothing but a wreath of mist.

" Undoubtedly that must be the river we see," said his lordship doubtingly ; " but, at the same time, we never can rely, with perfect security, upon the watery element; it has many resemblances, which are not easily detected at a distance — a bleachfield, for instance, has not unfrequently been mistaken for a piece of water; and we read of a very singular deception produced upon sand in the eastern countries, and termed the mirage."

" Water is, indeed, a deceitful element," said Mrs. St. Clair, hoping, by this affirmative, to get to the lee-side of the discussion.

" On the ether hand, it is a most useful and invaluable element ; without water, where would be our navigation — our commerce — our knowledge — our arts ? — in one word, water may be termed the bulwark of Britain."

" It may indeed," said Mrs. St. Clair, her teeth chattering as she spoke ; u to water we owe our existence as a nation, — our libei'ties, civil and religious;" and she retreated a few steps on the faith of having settled the matter.

" Pardon me there, my dear madam," said the Earl, retaining his original footing; " that is, perhaps, going a little too far. Strictly speaking, we cannot, with propriety, be said to owe our existence to water, since, had we not been an island, a highly favoured island! we should certainly have formed part of the vast continent of Europe — and with regard to our liberties, the Magna Charta, that boast of Britain, was unquestionably procured, and, I trust, will ever be maintained, on terra firma."

Mrs. St. Clair could almost have given up the game at this point — to stand on the very pinnacle of a pinnacle, in the face of an east wind, and be talked to about bulwarks and Magna Chartas — it was too much!

" How very cold you look, mamma," said Miss St. Clair, compassionating her mother's feelings.

" Cold !" repeated Lord Rossville, in a tone of surpribe and displeasure ; " impossible — cold in the month of May! The daj would be too hot, were it not for this cooling breeze."

This was worse and worse — Mrs. St. Clair groaned internally, as she thought " how will it be possible to drag out existence with a man who calls a piercing east wind a cooling breeze !"

Lord Rossville raised his cane, and resumed his observations at great length upon the ravages committed by the river on his friend and neighbour Boghall's property. Mrs. St. Clair wished the Boghall acres in the bottom of the Red Sea, though even from thence Lord Rossville might, perhaps, have fished them up ; as a thorough-bred tormentor, like a first-rate magician, can call spirits, even from the vasty deep, to torment his victims.

" Here," continued the Earl, taking his sister-in-law by the hand, and leading her to the utmost verge of all she hated — a bleak exposed promontory; " here we command a no less charming prospect in a different style:—observe that range of hills."

" Superb !" exclaimed Mrs. St. Clair, with an aguish shudder.

" Why, yes—the hills themselves are very well; but do you observe nothing, my dear madam, that relieves the eye from what a friend of mine justly calls ' a boundless continuity of shade?'"

Mrs. St. Clair almost cracked her eyeballs straining in the direction pointed out; but, like sister Anne, could see nothing to the purpose.

" I suspect you are looking rather too high; nearer the base, and allow your eye to run along by the point of my cane— there, you must have got it now."

There are, perhaps, few every-day situations more tormenting to a scrupulous mind than that of being called upon to see what you cannot see —you must either disappoint the views of the view-pointer, or you must sacrifice your conscience (as it is much to be feared too many do), and, sinking under the torture, pretend that you have at last hit the mark, whether it be a puff of smoke indicative of a town, a white cloud of the ocean, or a black speck of an island.

" Ah! I think I discover something now," cried Mrs. St. Clair, quite at a loss to guess whether the white mote in question was a church steeple, or a ship's mast, or any other wonderful object of the same nature, which generous long-sighted people will always make a point of sharing with their less gifted friends.

" And you think the effect good ? "

" Admirable — inimitable!"

" Why, the situation was my own choice ; there was a committee appointed to make choice of the most favourable site, and they fortunately fell in with my views on the subject, and, indeed, paid me the compliment of consulting my feelings on the occasion : — a public monument, I conceive, ought, undoubtedly, to be placed in a conspicuous and elevated situation ; but more especially when that situation happens to be in the very grounds of not only the original proposer and principal heritor in the

county, but likewise the personal friend of the illustrious dead to whom this tribute is decreed — for, I am proud to say, our renowned patriot, the great Lord Pensionwell, was (with the excellent Lord Dunderhead) the associate of my youthful years — the friend of my maturer age."

" Happy the country," said Mrs. St. Clair, now driven almost to frenzy, " whose nobles are thus gifted with the power of reflecting kindred excellence, and perpetuating national virtue, on the broad basis of private friendship."

Mrs. St. Clair knew she was talking nonsense; but she also knew who she was talking to, and was sure it would pass. Lord Rossville, to be sure, was a little puzzled; but he saw it was meant as a compliment, and contained a fine-sounding sentiment, and it was therefore well received. Fortunately, the rain now began to fall; and every object being completely shrouded in mist, his lordship was obliged to give in; but he comforted himself, and thought he comforted his companions, by promising to return, when the weather was more propitious, to repeat and complete their enjoyment.

CHAPTER VII.

Most musical, most melancholy ! Milton.

The dinner hour was an early one, for Lord Rossville liked to secure his victims for a long evening. The meal was prolonged to its utmost extent, and passed heavily; for, although its arrangements were faultless, there was a want of that ease which is the essence of good cheer. The evening entertainment was still worse; for Lord Rossville piqued himself upon his musical talents, and Miss St. Clair, whose taste and execution were both of a superior order, was doomed to the tortures of his lordship's accompaniment. His false chords — his overstrained cadences — his palsied shakes—his tones half and whole, grated upon her ear, and she felt that music and melody were sometimes very different things. He affected to despise all music, except that of the great composers, and chose for the subject of his execution Beethoven's " Synfonia Pastorale."— "Here," said he, as he placed it before his niece and himself, " observe, the great point is to have your mind duly impressed with the ideas these grand and characteristic movements are designed to express. Here we have, in the first place, ' The Prospect;' — we must, of course, infer that it is a fine or pleasing prospect, such, fi r example, as we viewed to-day, that the great composer intended to represent — let your movements therefore be graceful and aerial — light and shade; — then follows ' The Rivulet,' — that,

I need scarcely inform you, must be expressed by a gentle, murmuring measure. Next we have the ' Village Dance,'—gay and exhilarating — rustic, but not vulgar. As a powerful contrast to these simple scenes, now bursts upon us ' The Storm,'—awful, sublime, overpowering as the conflict of the elements, — howling winds, descending torrents, thunder and lightning, all must be conveyed here, or the mighty master's aim is rendered abortive. To soothe the mind after this awful explosion of genius, we wind up the whole with the ' Shepherd's Song,' breathing the soft accents of peace and pastoral innocence — and now da capo."

Miss St. Clair might well shudder at the prospect before her, and her tortures were exquisite, when she found her ear, taste, feeling, science, all placed under the despotic sway of his lordship's bow and foot; but, at length, her sufferings were ended by the announcement of supper. This was another of Lord Rossville's inflictions — he had a heavy hot supper regularly served, round which all his victims (i. e. his family and guests) were compelled to be seated, while he did the honours in his most elaborate and massive style till the hour of midnight. " Ha!" exclaimed he, starting up, " it seems we take no note of time here." This was a favourite jeu de mot of the Earl's, and, indeed, it was suspected that he sometimes allowed himself to be surprised for the pleasure of repeating it.

Supper was nearly over, when the trampling of horses, barking of dogs, ringing of bells, and all the usual clamour which attends the arrival of a person of distinction, caused a sensation in the company. Lady Betty asked what that was, while she took her favourite on her lap, and covered it with her pocket-handkerchief; from beneath which, however, issued, ever and anon, a low asthmatic growl.

" It is Colonel Delmour, my lady," answered the pompous maitre d'hotel, who had despatched a messenger to inquire. " It is an extraordinary and somewhat improper time of night, I think "

But his lordship's remarks were stopped by the entrance of the party in question. Merely touching his uncle's hand as he passed him, and scarcely noticing Lady Betty, Colonel Delmour advanced to Mrs. and Miss St. Clair, and paid his compliments to them with all the graceful high-bred ease of a man of fashion; then calling for a chair, he seated himself by his cousin, seemingly regardless of one having been placed by Lord Rossville's orders on the other side of the table. Colonel Delmour was strikingly handsome, both in face and form; and he possessed that high hereditary air of fashion and freedom which bore the impress of nobility and distinction. There might, perhaps, be something of hauteur in his lofty bearing; but it was so qualified by the sportive gaiety of his manners, that it seemed nothing more than that elegant and graceful sense of his own superiority, to which, even without arrogance, he could not be insensible.

He talked much, and well, and in that general way which allowed every one to take a part in the conversation without suffering any one, not even the Earl, to monopolise it. Altogether, his presence was like sunshine upon frost-work, and an air of ease and gaiety succeeded to the dulness and constraint which had hitherto prevailed. Lady Betty had three times asked, " What brought you here at this time of night?" before Colonel Delmour answered; at last he said, —

" Two very powerful motives, though scarcely fit to be named together — the first was my eagerness to do homage here," bowing gracefully to Miss St. Clair; " the other was to avoid the honour of driving Miss Pratt."

" I thought Mr. Lyndsay was to have returned with you," said the Earl.

" I offered him a seat in my curricle, which he wanted to transfer to Miss Pratt, but I could not possibly agree to that arrangement ; so he remains like a preux chevalier to escort her in a hackney-chaise, and also, I believe, to attend a Bible meeting, or a charity sermon, or something of that sort. It is more, I suspect, as a paymaster than a protector, that his services are required, as she discovered it would cost her I can't tell how many shillings and sixpences ; and though I would willingly have paid her expenses, yet really to endure her company for a nine-mile tete-a-tete was more than my philosophy dreamt of."

Much depends on the manner in which things are said as to the impression they convey to the unreflecting mind. Colonel Delmour's voice and accent were uncommonly pleasing ; and he had an air of gay good humour, that gave to his words rather the semblance of airy levity, than of selfishness or ill nature. Even when he carelessly sketched on the tablecloth a caricature of Mr. Lyndsay, with a large Bible under his arm, handing Miss Pratt, with a huge bandbox in hers, into a hackney-chaise, Gertrude could not resist a smile at their expense.

" Miss Pratt coming here to-morrow!" exclaimed the Earl in a tone expressive of any thing but pleasure ; " that is somewhat an unexpected " and his lordship made an effort as

if to bolt some word too hard for utterance. Then addressing Mrs. St. Clare, though with a very disturbed look, " As, in all probability, madam, that lady's visit is designed out of compliment to you and your daughter, it is necessary, previous to her arrival, that you should be aware of the degree of relationship subsisting between Miss Pratt and the members of this family."

Lord RossYille's air, looks, manner, hems, all portended a story ; it was but too evident that breath was collecting and reminiscences arranging for the purpose, and the pause that ensued was prophetic — not, alas ! of its end, but of its beginning. But Colonel Dehnour seemed quite aware of the danger that was im-

pending; and just as his uncle had opened his mouth with "Miss Pratt's great-grandfather

" he interposed.

" I beg pardon, but I cannot think of devolving the task of being Miss Pratt's chronicler upon you ; as I was guilty of introducing her to the company, mine be the punishment of becoming her biographer." Then, with a rapidity which left the Earl with his mouth open, and Miss Pratt's great-grandfather still vibrating on his tongue, he went on —

" Miss Pratt, then, by means of great-grandfathers and great-grandmothers (who, par parenthese, may commonly be classed under the head of great bores), is, somehow or other, cousin to all families of distinction, in general, throughout Scotland, but to this one, from its local advantages, in particular. I cannot pretend to show forth the various modifications of which cousin-ship is susceptible,—first, second, and third degrees, as far as numbers and degrees can go. And, indeed, I have already committed a great error in my outset, by having introduced Miss Pratt by herself Miss Pratt, when I ought to have presented her as Miss Pratt and Anthony Whyte. In fact, as Whittington without his cat would be nobody in the nursery, so neither would Miss Pratt be recognised in the world without Anthony Whyte. Not that there exists the same reciprocal attachment, or unity of fortune, between the aunt and the nephew which distinguished the master and his cat; for Anthony Whyte is rich, and Miss Pratt is poor — Anthony Whyte lives in a castle, Miss Pratt in a cottage — Anthony Whyte has hoi'ses and hounds, Miss Pratt has clogs and pattens. There is something so uninteresting, if not unpromising, in the name, that"—addressing himself to Miss St. Clair — "you, at present, will scarcely care whether it belongs to a man or a cat, and will be ready to exclaim, ' What's in a name ?' But do not expect long to enjoy this happy state of indifference—by dint of hearing it repeated day after day, hour after hour, minute after minute, upon every possible and impossible occasion; it will at length take such hold of your imagination that you will see the mystic letters which compose the name of Anthony Whyte wherever you turn your eyes — you will be ready to ' holla out his name to the reverberate rocks, and teach the babbling gossips of the air to cry out'— Anthony Whyte ! "

" What's all that nonsense ? " asked Lady Betty.

"Ihave been rather prosy upon Miss Pratt and her adjunct — that's all," answered Colonel Delmour slightly ; " and must have something to put away the sound of Anthony Whyte"— and he hummed a few notes. " Do, Miss St. Clair, join me in expelling those hideous names I have invoked for your gratification — you sing, I am sure."

But Gertrude was afraid to comply, for no one seconded the request. Lord Rossville, indeed, looked evidently much displeased; but it was no less manifest that his nephew neither

thought nor cared for any body's feelings hut such as he was solicitous to please ; and, before the party broke up, he had contrived to make a very favourable impression on the only person present whose favour he was anxious to obtain.

CHAPTER VIII.

Her tongue runs round like a wheel, one spoke after another ; there is no end of it. You would wonder at her matter to hear her talk, and would admire her talk when you hear her matter. All the wonder is, whilst she speaks only thrums, how she makes so many different ends hang together. — Richard Fleckno, 1658.

Many visitors arrived the two following days from various quarters, though all from similar motives,— viz. to see the young heiress and her plebeian mother. But amongst all the varieties of life, how few can even serve " to point a moral or adorn a tale."

The most distinguished of those individuals were Lady Millbank and her daughters, who drove up in the usual eclat of an equipage which at once denotes wealth and consequence. The ladies were in the same style with their outward bearings, — tall, showy, dashing personages, with scornful looks and supercilious manners. They surveyed Miss St. Clair from head to foot with a bold stare ; and, after making some trifling remarks to her, turned their whole artillery against Colonel Delmour, who received their addresses with a sort of careless familiarity, very different from the refined attentions he displayed towards his cousin.

" Good heavens! " exclaimed one of the ladies, who had stationed herself at a window, " do look at this, Colonel Delmour ! "

And at the piercing exclamation, the whole party hastened to ascertain the cause. The phenomenon appeared to be a hackney-chaise of the meanest description, which was displacing the splendid barouche, to the manifest mirth of the insolent menials who stood lounging at the door.

" Who can that be, I wonder ?" asked Lady Betty.

Mrs. St. Clair turned pale with terror lest it should be any of her bourgeois relations forcing their way.

" I conclude it must be our cousin Miss Pratt," said the Earl, in some agitation, to Lady Millbank; and, while he spoke, a female head and hand were to be seen shaking and waving to the driver with eager gesticulation.

" And Mr. Lyndsay, I vow!" exclaimed Miss Jemima Mill-bank, throwing herself into a theatrical attitude of astonishment.

The hack-chaise, with its stiff resty horses, had now got close to the door; and the broken jingling steps being lowered, out stepped a young man, who was immediately saluted with shouts of laughter from the party at the window. He looked up and smiled, but seemed nowise disconcerted, as he stood patiently waiting for his companion to emerge.

" I hope they are to perform quarantine," said Colonel Del-mour.

"I vote for their being sent to Coventry," said Miss Augusta.

" I prepare to stand upon the defensive," said Miss Maria, as she seized a smelling-bottle from off the table.

At length Miss Pratt appeared, shaking the straw from her feet; and having alighted, it was expected that her next movement would be to enter the house ; but they knew little of Miss Pratt who thought all was done when she had reached her destination. Much yet remained to be done, which she would not trust either to her companion or the servants. She had, in the first place, to speak in a very sharp manner to the driver, on the condition of his chaise and horses, and to throw out hints of having him severely punished, inasmuch as one of his windows would not let down, and she had almost sprained her wrist in attempting it — and another would not pull up, though the wind was going through her head like a spear ; besides having taken two hours and a quarter to bring them nine miles, and her watch was held up in a triumphant manner in proof of her assertion. She next made it a point to see with her own eyes every article pertaining to her (and they were not a few) taken out of the chaise, and to give with her own voice innumerable directions as to the carrying, stowing, and placing of her bags, boxes, and bundles. All these matters being settled, Miss Pratt then accepted the arm of her companion, and was now fairly on her way to the drawing-room. But people who make use of their eyes have often much to see even between two doors, and in her progress from the hall door to the drawing-room door Miss Pratt met with much to attract her attention. True, all the objects were perfectly familiar to her; but a real looker, like a great genius, is never at a loss for a subject — things are either better or worse since they saw them last — or if the things themselves should happen to be the same, they have seen other things either better or worse, and can, therefore, either improve or disprove them. Miss Pratt's head then turned from side to side a thousand times as she went along, and a thousand observations and criticisms about stair carpets, patent lamps, hall chairs, slab tables, &c. &c. &c. passed through her crowded brain. At length Miss Pratt and Mr. Lyndsay were announced, and thereupon entered Miss Pratt in a quick paddling manner, as if in all haste to greet her friends.

" How do you do, my lord ? No bilious attacks I hope of late.

— Lady Betty as stout as ever I see, and my old friend Flora as fat as a collared eel. — Lady Millbank, I'm perfectly ashamed to see you in any house but your own; but every thing must give way to the first visit, you know, especially amongst kinsfolk," taking Mrs. St. Clair by the hand, without waiting for the ceremony of an introduction.

While this and much more in the same strain was passing with Miss Pratt at one end of the room, Mr. Lyndsay had joined the younger part of the company at the other, and been introduced by Colonel Delmour to Miss St. Clair. There was nothing so striking in his appearance as to arrest the careless eye, or call forth instant admiration ; yet his figure, though not much above the middle size, was elegant, his head and features were finely formed, and altogether he had that sort of classical tournure which, although not conspicuous, is uncommon, and that air of calm repose which indicates a mind of an elevated cast. Still, seen beside Colonel Delmour, Mr. Lyndsay might have been overlooked. He had nothing of that brilliancy of address which distinguished his cousin; but he had what is still more rare, that perfect simplicity of manner which borrows nothing from imitation ; and, as some one has well remarked, few peculiarities are more striking than a total absence of all affectation. Scarcely allowing time for the introduction, Miss Millbank began in a tone intended to be very sympathetic.

" How dreadfully you must have been bored to-day with la pauvre Pratt! Good heavens! how could you inflict such a penance upon yourself? Did you not find her most shockingly annoying, and dreadfully tiresome ?"

" Annoying and tiresome to a certain degree, as every body must be who asks idle questions," answered Mr. Lyndsay, with a smile, which, though very sweet, was not without a meaning.

The rebuff, if it was intended for such, was, however, lost upon his fair assailant.

" Then, how could you bore yourself with her ?"

" She was my mother's friend and relation," replied he calmly.

" Of all descriptions of entail, that of friends would be the most severe," said Colonel Delmour.

" O heavens ! what a shocking idea! " exclaimed the three Miss Millbanks in a breath.

" What's the shocking idea, my dears ?" demanded Miss Pratt, as she pattered into the midst of the group. " I'm sure there's no shocking realities here, for I never saw a prettier circle," darting her eyes all round, while she familiarly patted Miss St. Clair, and drawing her arm within hers, as she stood by the window, seemed resolved to appropriate her entirely to herself. Gertrude's attention was no less excited by Miss Pratt, who had to her all the charms of novelty; for though there are many Miss Pratts in the world, it had never been her fortune to meet with one till now.

Miss Pratt then appeared to her to be a person from whom nothing could be hid. Her eyes were not by any means fine eyes — they were not reflecting eyes — they were not soft eyes — they were not sparkling eyes — they were not melting eyes — they were not penetrating eyes ; — neither were they restless eyes, nor rolling eyes, nor squinting eyes, nor prominent eyes

— but they were active, brisk, busy, vigilant, immoveable eyes, that looked as if they could not be surprised by any thing — not even by sleep. They never looked angry, or joyous, or perturbed, or melancholy, or heavy ; but morning, noon, and night, they shone the same, and conveyed the same impression to the beholder, viz. that they were eyes that had a look — not like the look of Sterne's monk, beyond this world — but a look into all things on the face of this world. Her other features had nothing remarkable in them ; but the ears might evidently be classed under the same head with the eyes — they were something resembling rabbits' — long, prominent, restless, vibrating ears, — for ever listening, and never shut by the powers of thought. Her voice had the tone and inflexions of one accustomed to make frequent sharp interrogatories. She had rather a neat compact figure, and the tout ensemble of her person and dress was that of smartness. Such, though not quite so strongly defined, was the sort of impression Miss Pratt generally made upon the beholder. Having darted two or three of her sharpest glances at Miss St. Clair, —

" Do you know I'm really puzzled, my dear, to make out who it is you are so like — for you're neither a Rossville nor a Black

— and, by the by, have you seen your uncle, Mr. Alexander Black, yet ? What a fine family he has got. I heard you was quite smitten with Miss Lilly Black at the circuit ball t'other night, Colonel Delamour ; but you're not so ill to please as Anthony Whyte. That was really a good thing Lord Punme-down said to him that night. Looking at the two Miss Blacks, says he to Anthony, with a shake of his head — ' Ah, Anthony,' says he, ' I'm afraid two Blacks will never make a White! ' ha ! ha! ha! — Lord Rossville, did you hear that ? At the circuit ball Lord Punmedown said to Anthony Whyte, pointing to the two Miss Blacks — 'I fear,' says he, ' two Blacks will never make a White.' — ' No, my Lord,' says Anthony, ' for you know there's no turning a Blackamoor white !' ha! ha! ha! ' A very fair answer,' says my lord. Lady Millbank, did you hear of Lord Punmedown's attack upon Mr. Whyte at the ball — the two Miss Blacks "

" I black-ball a repetition of that bon mot," said Colonel Delmour.

" You will really be taken for a magpie if you are so black and white," said Miss Millbank.

" 'Pon my word, that's not at all amiss — I must let Anthony Whyte hear that. — But bless me, Lady Millbank, you're not

going away already?—won't you stay and take some luncheon? — I can answer for the soups here — I really think, my lord, you rival the Why te Hall soups ; " but, disregarding Miss Pratt's pressing invitation, Lady Millbank and her train took leave, and scarcely were they gone when luncheon was announced.

" Come, my dear," resumed the tormentor, holding Gertrude's arm within hers, " let you and I keep together—I want" to get better acquainted with you; but I wish I could find a likeness for you"—looking round upon the family portraits as they entered the eating-room.

" They must look higher who would find a similitude for Miss St. Clair," said Colonel Delmour.

Miss Pratt glanced at the painted ceiling, representing a band of very fat full-blown rosy Hours. " Ah ha! do you hear that, my lord ? — Colonel Delmour says there's nothing on earth to compare to Miss St. Clair, and that we must look for her likeness in the regions above. Well, goddess or not, let me recommend a bit of this nice cold lamb to you — very sweet and tender it is; and I assure you I'm one of those who think a leg of lamb looks as well on a table as in a meadow :"—then dropping her knife and fork with a start of joy —" Bless me, what was I thinking of?—that was really very well said of you, Colonel—but I've got it now —a most wonderful resemblance I See who'll be the next to find it out ?"

All present looked at each other, and then at the pictures. Lord Rossville, who had been vainly watching for an opening, now took advantage of it; and with one of his long-suppressed sonorous hems, bespoke him as follows: —

"Although I have not given much of my time or attention to the study of physiognomy, as I do not conceive it is one likely to be productive of beneficial results to society; yet I do not hesitate to admit the reality of those analogies of feature which may be, and undoubtedly are, distinctly traced through successive generations—the family mouth, for example," pointing to a long-chinned, pinky-eyed lady, with a pursed-up mouth, hanging aloft, " as pourtrayed in that most exemplary woma::. the Lady Janet St. Clair, has its prototype in that of my niece," turning to Gertrude; " while, in the more manly formed nose of Robert first Earl of Rossville, an accurate physiognomist

might discern the root, as it were "

" My dear Lord Rossville!" exclaimed Miss Pratt, throwing herself back in her chair, " I hope you're not going to say Miss St. Clair has the nose of Red Robby, as he was called. Root, indeed ! — a pretty compliment! If it was a root, it must have been a beet root — as Anthony Whyte says, it's a nose like the handle of a pump-well; and as for Lady Janet's mouth, he s^ys it's neither more nor less than a slit in a poor's-box."

" Mr. Anthony Whyte takes most improper liberties with the family of St. Clair, if he presumes to make use of such unwar-

D

rantable, such unjustifiable—I may add, such ungentlemanly expressions, towards any of its members," said Lord Rossville, speaking faster in the heat of his indignation ; " and it is mortifying to reflect, that any one allied to this family should ever have so far forgot what was due to it as to form such coarse, and vulgar, and derogatory comparisons."

" One of them is rather a flattering comparison," said Mr. Lyndsay ; " I'm afraid there are few mouths can be represented as emblems of Charity."

" Very well said, Mr. Edward," said Miss Pratt, nowise disconcerted at the doivnset she had received ; " shall I send you this nice rib in return ? — Lord Rossville, let me recommend the rhubarb tart to you.—Miss Diana, my dear—I beg your pardon, Miss St. Clair, but I'll really never be able to call you any thing but Diana—for such a likeness!—What have you all been thinking of, not to have found out that Miss St. Clair is the very picture of the Diana in the Yellow Turret!"

Lord Rossville, in a tone of surprise and displeasure, repeated,—

" The Diana in the Yellow Turret! impossible! "

" Impossible or not, I can assure you it's the fact. — Mrs. St. Clair, have you seen the Diana?—come with me, and I'll show it you—come, my dear, and see yourself as a goddess—come away — seeing's believing, my lord." And she jumped up, almost choking in her eagerness to display the discovery she had made.

"Miss Pratt!" cried the Earl, in a tone enough to have settled quicksilver itself, —" Miss Pratt, this behaviour of yours is — is — what I cannot possibly permit—the Yellow Turret is my private dressing-room, and it is surely a most improper and unwarrantable liberty "

" I beg you ten thousand pardons, my dear Lord Rossville! — I really had quite forgot the change you have made in your dressing-room; but, at any rate, I should have figured every creek and corner of yours fit to be seen at all times. — There's Mr. Whyte—his dressing-room is a perfect show, so neat and nick-nacky,—his silver shoe-horn would be an ornament to any drawing-room."

"Miss Pratt, this is really—I" And his lordship hemmed in a manner which showed the greatest discomposure.

As we cannot be gratified with a sight of Mr. Whyte's shoehorn," said Colonel Delmour, " it would certainly be some solace to be allowed to behold your lordship's goddess; — I had forgot that picture, it is so long since I have seen it — but I should certainly wish to prostrate myself at her shrine now." And he looked to Miss St. Clair as he spoke, in a manner to give more meaning to his words than met the ear.

The Earl was much embarrassed. He was provoked at the irreverent and indecorous manner in which Miss Pratt had been going to rush into his dressing-room; and he was piqued at the insinuation she had thrown out of its not being fit to be seen. He therefore wavered between his desire of punishing her presumption by exclusion—or vindicating his own character by instant and unpremeditated admission. After maturely weighing the matter, he decided upon the latter mode of proceeding, and said,—

" Although I have certainly no idea of permitting my private apartments to be thrown open whenever idle or impertinent, or, it may be, ill-disposed curiosity, might prompt the wish; yet I do not object to gratify either my own family and friends, or even the public in general, with a view of them, when the request is properly conveyed, and at a proper and reasonable hour; for, if there is a time for every thing, it should likewise be remembered there is a manner for every thing; and although I do not consider a gentleman's dressing-room as the most elegant and delicate exhibition for ladies, yet, upon this occasion, if they are so inclined,"—bowing all round—" I shall be happy to conduct them to my private apartments."

The sooner the better," cried Miss Pratt, while the very ribbons on her bonnet seemed to vibrate with impatience. " Come my dear, and see yourself as a goddess;" and again seizing Miss St. Clair, away she pattered full speed.

" There's a broom where a broom should'nt be," darting her eyes into the dark corner of a passage as she whisked through it; then peeping into a closet, " and for all the work he makes, I don't think his maids are a bit better than other people's."

CHAPTER IX.

What doth he get who e'er prefers The scutcheon of his ancestors? This chimney-piece of gold or brass; That coat of arms blazon'd in glass; "When these with time and age have end, Thy prowess must thyself commend: True nobleness doth those alone engage Who can add virtues to their parentage.

Mildmay Fane, Earl of Westmorland.

Upon entering the turret, the first thing that caught Miss Pratt's eye was a shaving-glass, which she asserted was by no means the proper size and shape for that purpose, being quite different from the one used by Anthony Whyte, which was broader than it was long, while Lord Rossville's was longer than it was broad. A dispute, of course, ensued, for the Earl would not be bearded upon such a subject by any woman — when, suddenly giving him the slip in the argument, she exclaimed, " But bless me,

we're forgetting the Diana — and -what a bad light you've put her in! There's a great art in hanging pictures: Mr. Whyte brought a man all the way from London to hang his; and I'll never forget my fright when he told me the hangman was coming. — Now I see her where I stand — Mrs. St. Clair, come a little more this way — there now — was there ever such a likeness?"

" Astonishing!" exclaimed Mrs. St. Clair in amazement.

" Diana never had such incense offered to her before," said Colonel Delmour.

" The resemblance, if, indeed, there is a resemblance," said the Earl, in manifest displeasure, " is extremely imperfect; the portrait represents a considerably larger and more robust-looking person thau Miss St. Clair; it has also something of a bold and masculine air, which, I own, I should be sorry to perceive in any young lady in whom I take any interest; since nothing, in my opinion, derogates so much from female loveliness as a forward or presuming carriage."

" My dear Lord Rossville! how any body who has eyes in their head can dispute that resemblance —just turn round, my dear, and show yourself,"—to Miss St. Clair, who, ashamed of the scrutiny, had turned away, and was conversing with Colonel Delmour a little apart. Mr. Lyndsay contemplated the picture with a thoughtful air, and occasionally stole a glance at Gertrude, but said nothing.

" How do you account for such an extraordinary likeness ? " inquired Lady Betty of Mrs. St. Clair, as she stood, with her fat Flora under her arm, staring at the picture.

" I am quite at a loss — if this picture is an ideal creation of the painter's imagination "

" It's not that, 1 can assure you," interrupted Miss Pratt — " the original was a real flesh and blood living person, or I've been misinformed," —with a look of interrogation to Lord Rossville.

" If one of the family, however remote, the resemblance, as Lord Rossville justly remarked, does sometimes revive, even at

distant periods, in the person of ;" but Mrs. St. Clair did

not get leave to finish her sentence.

" O if Diana had been a St. Clair, there would have been no wonder in the matter, you know!" again dashed in the intolerable Pratt; " but the truth of the matter is, she was neither more nor less than bonny Lizzie Lundie, the huntsman's daughter. Much I've heard about Lizzie Lundie, and many a fine song was made upon her, for she was the greatest beauty in the country, high or low. There's one of the songs that's all the fashion now, that I remember singing when I was young, but they've changed the name from Lundie to Lyndsay;" and Miss Pratt, in a cracked and unmusical voice, struck up, Will ve go to the Ilielands, Leezy Lyndsay, &fc.

Lord Rossville seemed somewhat disconcerted at this abrupt disclosure of his Diana's humble pedigree; and, anxious to account for Lizzie Lundie, the huntsman's daughter, being permitted a place amongst the nobles of the land, and that too in his private apartment, he therefore made all possible haste to atone for this solecism in dignity; and having hemmed three times, began—

" Since this picture has attracted so much attention, and called forth so much animadversion, it is proper, and, indeed, necessary, that some elucidation should be thrown on the circumstances to which it owes its birth."

And again the Earl paused, hemmed, and looked round, like a peacock spreading its plumage, and straining its neck in all directions, before it can even lift the crumb that has been thrown to it — while Miss Pratt, like a pert active sparrow, taking advantage of its attitudes, darts down and bears off the prize.

" O the story's soon told, for there's no great mystery about it. The late lord there," (pointing to a picture of a fat chubby gentleman in a green coat, hunting-horn, and bag-wig,) " was a second Nimrod in his young days, and had a perfect craze for dogs and horses; and he brought a famous painter here from some place abroad, I foi'get the name of it now, to take the beasts' likenesses — as old Lady Christian used to say, it was a scandal to think of dogs sitting for their pictures — ha! ha! ha! — In particular, there was a famous pack of hounds to sit, and the painter chancing to see Lizzie one day with them about her, was struck with the fancy of doing her as a Diana; and it was really a good idea, for I think she's the outset of the picture — Anthony Whyte says he would give a hundred guineas merely for her head and shoulders."

Mrs. St. Clair had changed colour repeatedly during this piece of biography,. and seemed not a little mortified at discovering that her daughter's beauty claimed no higher original than the huntsman's daughter. Upon a more close inspection, she therefore declared, that although there might be something in the tout ensemble to catch the eye at first sight, yet, upon examination, it would be found the features and expression were totally different.

But Lord Rossville, resolved not to be baulked of his story, now commenced a more diffuse narrative of the circumstances to which Lizzie Lundie owed her posthumous fame, concluding with his most unqualified dissent as to the possibility of there being the slightest resemblance except in the colour of the hair. But, to do Miss Pratt justice, the resemblance was \e v j remarkable. The Diana's features were on a larger scale, and her countenance had a less soft and intellectual cast than Miss St. Clair's; her figure was also more robust than elegant, her complexion rather vivid than transparent, and her air rather V than dignified; but there was the same long-shaped, soft, daik-

blue eyes ; the same Grecian nose and mouth; the same silky, waving, dark ringlets, curling naturally around the open ivory forehead, — forming altogether that rare and peculiar style of beauty where the utmost delicacy of feature is yet marked and expressive, and the strongest contrasts of colour are blended into one harmonious whole.

" Pray, what became of this divinity ?" inquired Colonel Delmour.

" I'm sure I can't tell you ; I think the story was, that she had been crossed in love with some gentleman, and that she married a Highland drover, or tacksman, I can't tell which, and they went all to sticks and staves."

" How provoking," said Colonel Delmour, as he still stood contemplating the picture, " that so much beauty should have been created in vain."

" How do you know that it was created in vain ?" said Mr. Lyndsay.

" Considering how very rare a thing beauty, perfect beauty is, there certainly seems to have been rather a lavish expenditure of it on the huntsman's daughter and drover's wife."

" Colonel Delmour, don't you remember what the poet says on that? —

There's many a flower that's born to grow unseen, And waste its beauty on the senseless air."

" However rare beauty may be," said Mr. Lyndsay, passing over Miss Pratt's misquotation, " your desire of confining it to the higher orders is rather too arbitrary."

" They certainly can better appreciate it," returned Colonel Delmour : " there is a refinement of taste requisite to admire such beauty as that;" and he glanced from Diana to Miss St. Clair. " How could one of the canaille possibly comprehend the fine antique cast of those features, the classic contour of the head, the swan-like throat, the inimitable moulding of the cheek ? Would not a pair of round white eyes, and blowzy red cheeks, with a snub nose, and a mouth from ear to ear, have been quite as well bestowed on the drover ?"

" I dare say he could not talk so scientifically on the subject as you do," said Mr. Lyndsay ; " but, for all that, he might have been as fond of his wife, and as proud of her too, as either you or I could have been."

" Impossible—that is, supposing she had been of my own rank and station — not Venus herself could have won me to a mesalliance."

" Suppose the huntsman's daughter had been as perfect in mind and manner as in person "

" The idea is absurd — the thing is impossible," interrupted Colonel Delmour, impatiently.

" It is certainly difficult to conceive refinement of manners in a person of low birth ; but why may not a noble mind be conferred on a peasant as well as on a prince ?"

" "What!" cried Colonel Delmour, indignantly, "do you really pretend to say that the offspring of a clown or a mechanic animals who have walked the world iu hob-nailed shoes, or sat all their lives cross-legged with their noses at a grinding-wheel, can possibly possess the same lofty spirit as the descendants of heroes and statesmen ? The very thought of being so descended must elevate the mind, and give it a conscious superiority over the low-born drudges of the earth."

" Then you must feel yourself greatly superior in mind to Virgil, Horace, Shakespeare, Milton, Spenser, and a long et cetera of illustrious names down to the present day, who, if not absolutely low-born, have yet no pretensions to high birth. For my own part, I think it is rather humbling than elevating to reflect on the titled insignificance of this very family, who, though possessed of honours, wealth, and power for centuries, has never produced one man eminent for his virtues or his talents — nor, if we may trust to painters, one female celebrated for such beauty as this poor huntsman's daughter."

" You see her as a goddess, remember," said Colonel Delmour, ironically; "perhaps in her blue flannel jupon, unsandalled feet, ' and kercheft, in a comely' cotton gown, carrying a mess to the dogs, she would have had fewer attractions, even for your noble nature."

" There is a taste in moral as well as in corporeal beauty," said Mr. Lyndsay, " and I can love and admire both for their own intrinsic merits, without the aid of ornament. You, Delmour, must have them in court dress, with stars and coronets — but with beauty such as that," (and his eye unconsciously rested on Gertrude,) " had the mind, principles, and manners corresponded to it, I could have loved even Lizzie Lundie—perhaps too well."

" Had the huntsman's daughter been an angel and a goddess in one," replied Colonel Delmour warmly, " I could never have thought of her as my wife—there is degradation in the very idea."

All this while Miss Pratt had, as usual, been gabbling to the rest of the party, in a manner which prevented their hearing or joining in this argument. Miss St. Clair, indeed, had contrived to pick up a little of it, and warmly adopted Colonel Delmour's sentiments on the subject.

" I wonder what became of Lizzie's family, for I think always I heard she had a daughter as great a beauty as herself, — I've a notion it was a daughter of hers Mrs. St. Clair, are you w r ell enough ? — Bless my heart, she's going to faint!"

All crowded round Mrs. St. Clair, who seemed, indeed, on the point of fainting—the windows were thrown open—water was brought — smelling-bottles applied —till at length she revived, and, with a faint smile, avowed that she had been indisposed for

D 4

some days, and was subject to spasms of that nature. Lord Rossville bent over his sister-in-law, as she sat at the open window, with the utmost solicitude — he felt really interested in her; for she had listened to him with the most unceasing attention, and without once interrupting him — a degree of deference he was little accustomed to in his own family. At length she declared herself perfectly recovered, and, supported by his lordship and her daughter, she retired to her own apartment.

" That was an unlucky remark of yours, Colonel, about low marriages," whispered Miss Pratt; " I really think it was that overset her—though I suspect Lizzie Lundie had something to do with it too; very likely some relationship there, for you know the Blacks are not just at the top of the tree," — with a knowing wink: " that, and the smell of Lord Rossviile's boots and shoes together, was really enough to overset her;" but Miss Pratt was now left to gabble to herself, for the rest of the party had dispersed.

CHAPTER X.

I cannot blame thee, Who am myself attached with weariness To the dulling of my spirits. Tempest.

" How weary, stale, flat, and unprofitable, seem to me all the uses of this world," is a feeling that must be more or less experienced by every one who has feeling enough to distinguish one sensation from another, and leisure enough for ennui. There are people, it is well known, who have no feelings, and there are others who have not time to feel; but, alas ! there are many whose misfortune it is to have feeling and leisure, and who have time to be nervous — have time to be discontented — have time to be unhappy — have time to feel ill used by the world—have time to weary of pleasure in every shape—to weary of men, women, and children — to weary of books, grave and witty — to weary of authors, and even of authoresses — and who would have wearied as much of the wit of a Madame de Stael as of the babbles of Miss Pratt.

In this disposition, perhaps, the only solace is to find some tangible and lawful object of which to weary — some legitimate source of ennui; and then " sweet are the uses of adversity," when they come, even in the questionable shape of a Miss Pratt. In the humdrum society of a dull county, what a relief to the weary soul to have some person to weary of! To have a sort of bag-fox to turn out, when fresh game cannot be had, is an enjoyment which many cf my readers have doubtless experienced.

Such was Miss Pratt. Every body wearied of her, or said they wearied of her, and every body abused her; while yet she was more sought after and asked about, than she would have been had she possessed the wisdom of a More or the benevolence of a Fry. She was, in fact, the very heart of the shire, and gave life and energy to all the pulses in the parish. She supplied it with streams of gossip and chit-chat in others, and subject of ridicule and abuse in herself. Even the dullest laird had something good to tell of Miss Pratt, and something bad to say of her — for nothing can convey a more opposite meaning than these apparent synonymes.

But there was no one to whom Miss Pratt was so unequivocal a pest as to Lord Rossville, for his lordship was a stranger to ennui — perhaps cause and effect are rarely combined in one person, and those who can weary others possess a never-failing source of amusement in themselves. Besides, the Earl was independent of Miss Pratt, as he possessed a wide range for his unwearying wearying powers in his own family; for he could weary his steward — and his housekeeper — and his gamekeeper— and his coachman — and his groom — and his gardener, all the hours of the day, by perpetual fault-finding and directing. Perhaps, after all, the only uncloying pleasure in life is that of finding fault. The gamester may weary of his dice — the lover of his charmer — the bon-vivant of his bottle — the virtuoso of his virtu ; but while this round world remains, with all its imperfections on its head, the real fault-finder will never weary of finding fault. The provoking part of Miss Pratt was, that there was no possibility of finding fault with her. As well might Lord Rossville have attempted to admonish the brook that babbled past him, or have read lectures to the fly which buzzed round his head. For forty years Lord Rossville had been trying to break her in, but in vain. Much may be done, as we every day see to alter and overcome nature: ponies are made to waltz — horses to hand tea-kettles — dogs to read — birds to cast accounts — fleas to walk in harness; but to restrain the volubility of a female tongue is a task that has hitherto defied the power of man. With so much of what may be styled dissonance in similarity, it may easily be imagined that Lord Rossville and Miss Pratt, even when most in unison, produced any thing but harmony. Yet they only jarred — they never actually quarrelled, for they had been accustomed to each other all their lives; and while she laid all the rebuffs and reproofs she received to the score of bile, he tolerated her impertinence on account of blood.

The softness and suavity of Mrs. St. Clair's manners formed so striking a contrast to the sharp gnat-like attacks of ML J Pratt, that Lord Rossville became every day more attached to his sister-in-law's company; and she soon found herself so firmly fixed in his good graces, that she ventured to request permission

that she and her daughter might he allowed to visit her relations, with whom she had hitherto only communicated hy letter.

" Certainly, my dear madam," replied the Earl; " nothing can he more proper and reasonable than that you should recognize and visit the different members of your own family, who, I am happy to think, are all persons of unblemished reputation, and respectable stations in life, which respectability is in a fair way of being increased by votes which, I understand, an uncle and brother of yours have lately acquired in the county; and as there is every appearance of our having a warmly contested election shortly, their political influence, if properly directed, cannot fail of proving highly beneficial to them. I therefore give my unqualified assent as to the propriety of your visiting your own family, as soon as we can arrange" the proper time, mode, and manner of doing so; but, with regard to the daughter of the Honourable Thomas St. Clair, I must candidly acknowledge to you, my dear madam, I have not yet brought my mind to any fixed determination on that point. Your own good sense will naturally point out to you the very peculiar situation in which she stands. Miss St. Clair is at present to be viewed as the heiress presumptive to the titles, honours, and estates of this family; but, observe, although presumptive, she is by no means heiress apparent — for there is a wide and important distinction betwixt these apparent synonyms."— Here his lordship entered into a most elaborate explanation of these differences of distinction. — " And now, my dear madam, I am sure you will agree with me, that, in a situation of such peculiar delicacy, every step which Miss St. Clair takes ought to be weighed with the utmost nicety and deliberation; since what might be befitting the heiress presumptive might be deemed derogatory to the heiress apparent — and what dignity demands of the heiress apparent the world might censure as an undue assumption of consequence in the heiress presumptive."

Mrs. St. Clair, though choking with indignation at this roundabout insinuation that her family was scarcely fit to be associated w T ith by her own daughter, yet repressed her indignation.; and, as she did not consider it of much consequence that she should accompany her on her first visit, she readily yielded the matter with a good grace. But no sooner had she done so, than the Earl, as was often his custom, immediately tacked about, and took the opposite side of the argument. The result was, that Mrs. and Miss St. Clair should immediately proceed to visit the respective members of the Black family, and the Earl's travelling chariot-and-four, with all appliances to boot, was ordered out for the occasion. It was with a thrill of delight Mrs. St. Clair took her place in it, and drove off in all the eclat of rank and state.

CHAPTER XI.

Pictures like these, dear madam, to design,
Ask no firm hand, and no unerring line.
Some wandering touches, some reflected light,
Some flying stroke alone can hit 'em right. Pope.

Fearful anticipations mingled with Mrs. St. Clair's natural affection, as she thought of the meeting with her own family. Its only members consisted of a brother, who, partly by industry, partly by good fortune, had become the proprietor of a large tract of unimproved land in the neighbourhood — two unmarried sisters residing in the county town, — and an old uncle from the East Indies, a half-brother of her mother's, reported to be enormously rich. When she had left home her brother was a mere raw unformed lad ; but he was now an elderly man, the husband of a woman she had never seen, and the father of a numerous family. After quitting the noble domain of Rossville, the country gradually assumed a less picturesque appearance — rocks, woods, and rivers, now gave way to arable land, well-fenced fields, and well-filled barn-yards ; while these, in turn, yielded to vast tracts of improveable land, thriving belts of young plantation, ring-stone dikes, and drains in all directions.

It was in the midst of this scenery that Bellevue stood preeminent. It was a showy, white-washed, winged-house, situated on the top of the hill, commanding an extensive view of " muirs and mosses many, O," with traces of cultivation interspersed, and which by many was considered as a very fine, and by all was styled a very commanding prospect. A dazzling white gate, with spruce canister lodge, opened upon a well-gravelled avenue, which led to the mansion, surrounded by a little smiling lawn, with a tuft of evergreens in the centre. On one hand appeared a promising garden wall; on the other, a set of commodious-looking farm offices. Every thing was in the highest order — all bespoke the flourishing gentleman farmer. The door was opened by a stout florid footboy, in flaunting livery, whose yellow locks seemed to stiffen at sight of the splendid equipage that met his view. The interrogatories, however, at length recalled him to a sense of duty; and upon the question being put, for the third time, whether his master or mistress were at home — he returned that cautious answer which marks the wary, well-tutored, though perplexed menial, — i. e. that he was not sure, but he would see. After an interval of about five minutes, during which much opening and shutting of doors was heard, and many a head was seen peeping over blinds and from behind shutters, the prudent Will returned with an invitation to the ladies to alight; and, leading the way, he conducted them to a well-furnished, but evidently uninhabited drawing-room, where he left them, with an assurance that his mistress would be there in a

minute. Many minutes, however, elapsed, during which the visitors were left to find amusement for themselves, which was no easy task where the materials were wanting. In such circumstances, a fire is a never-failing resource — if bad, we can stir it; if good, we can enjoy it; but here was no fire, and the high-polished stove was only to be admired for itself, and the profusion of white paper which filled it. The carpet was covered, the chairs were in their wrappers, the screens were in bags — even the chimneypiece, that refuge of the weary, showed only two handsome girandoles. There were two portraits, indeed, large as life, hanging on each side of the fireplace, in all the rawness of bad painting, glaring in tints which Time himself could never mellow. The one, it might be presumed, was Mr. Black in a bright blue coat, pure white waistcoat, and drooping Fall-of-Foyers-looking neckcloth, holding a glove, and looking very sensible. The other, it might be inferred, was Mrs. Black, sitting under a tree, in a yellow gown and ill-put-on turban, smiling with all her might; and both evidently bent upon putting all the expression they possibly could into their faces, by way of getting a good pennyworth for their money.

At length the door opened, and Mrs. Black, in propria persona, entered, followed by a train of daughters. She was rather embonpoint, with a fine healthy colour, clear blue eyes, and an open good-humoured expression of countenance—forming, altogether, what is expressively termed a comely woman, which, if it mean something less than beauty, is often more attractive. She had evidently been dressing for the occasion, as her gown seemed scarcely yet out of the fold, but looked like a thing apart from her, and had that inexpressible air of constraint which gowns will have when gowns are made things of primary importance.

Mrs. Black welcomed her guests in a manner which, if it had nothing of the elegance of ton, was yet free from affectation or pretension. She expressed her regret that Mr. Black should be from home ; but she had sent in search of him, and hoped he would soon cast up. Mrs. St. Clair, resolving to be delightful, sat with her sister-in-law's hand in hers, and, with a face of the most affectionate interest, was presently deep in inquiries as to the state of her family, the number of her children, their ages, sexes, names, pursuits, and so forth. The amount of the information she received was this : — Mrs. Black was the mother of eleven children living, and two dead ; — her eldest daughter (who had just gone to take a walk) was going to be married, and her youngest to be weaned. It was thought a very good marriage for Bell, as Major Waddell had made a handsome fortune in the Company's service, and was very well connected in the county, being cousin-german to Sir William Waddell of Waddell Mains, and very likely to succeed to him, if he was spared. He was also related to the Bogs of Boghall; and the present Boghall had married a daughter of Lord Fairacre's, and

their son was going to stand for the county. Major "Waddell, to be sure, was a good deal older than Bell; but he had kept his health well in India, and, though not a beauty, was very well — at least he pleased Bell, and that was every thing. Due congratulations were here offered by Mrs. St. Clair, with the customary remarks, of its beiDg a pleasant and desirable thing for the first of a family to form a respectable connection; that any disparity of years was on the right side, &c. &c. &c.; concluding with a request to be favoured with a sight of the young people. Mrs. Black's eyes beamed delight as she pulled the bell, and gave orders for the children to be brought, observing at the same time that they were sad romps, and seldom fit to be seen. Miss St. Clair, meanwhile, was engaged with her cousins, pretty goodnatured-looking girls, one of whom talked much of balls, and officers, and poetry ; but as the children entered she sighed, and said there was an end of all rational conversation. The young Masters and Misses Black had all evidently been preparing for exhibition. They were fine, stout, blooming, awkward creatures, with shining faces, and straight-combed though rebellious-looking hair—while a smart cap, red eyes, and sour face bespoke the sufferings of the baby. Altogether they formed what is politely called " an uncommon fine family "— they all made bows and courtesies—walked with their toes in—stood with their fingers in their mouths—and, in short, were a very fine family. Of course, they were much commended and caressed bv their new relations, till the entrance of Mr. Black turned the attention into another channel. Mr. Black was the only one of the family on whom the phenomenon of a carriage-and-four had produced no visible effect; — he entered ill-dressed, over-heated, and with a common, even vulgar air — though, in reality, he was rather a good-looking man. Mrs, St. Clair had expected something of a scene at meeting with her brother ; but he seemed to have no thoughts of any thing of the kind, for he received his sister with that look and manner of plain, hearty welcome, which showed that any thing of fine feeling would be completely thrown away. Yet his greeting was sufficiently affectionate in its own blunt, homely kind.

" It is a long time since you and I have met, Sally," said he, as he seated himself beside his sister, with a child on each knee; "but you have kept your looks well — to be sure you haven't had so large a share of the evils of life as I have had," — looking round with evident pride and exultation on his offspring, and affecting to sigh at the same time. Mrs. St. Clair shook her head, and sighed too; but her sigh was a much better-got-up sigh than her brother's — it said, or was intended to say, " Heaven only knows what I have suffered for that one !"

Mrs. Black seemed to understand it; for she said, with a look of sympathy,—

" I'm sure an only child must be a great misfortune; and we have great reason to be thankful, Mr. Black, that so many of ours have been spared." Then, beckoning one of her daughters, she whispered some instructions to her, accompanied with a key. The young lady left the room, and in a few minutes the yellow-haired laddie entered, bearing a massive silver tray, conveying the richest of cakes, and the strongest and sweetest of wines. As Miss St. Clair threw back her bonnet to partake of the hospitalities, her uncle regarded her with more earnestness than good-breeding, then glanced all round on his own offspring.

" I'm trying if I can make out a likeness betwixt your daughter and my brats," said he to his sister; " but I don't think she has much of a Black face."

" She is thought to resemble her father's family more than mine," replied Mrs. St. Clair, — colouring deeply, and looking rather displeased.

" None of them that I have ever seen," returned Mr. Black;

— " her father, if I remember right, had light hair and a flat face, and "

" There is no end to arguing upon resemblances," interrupted Mrs. St. Clair, rising hastily; " the general expression is sometimes very strong, when every feature is different;"—and she was preparing to depart, when one of the children, who was looking out at a window, exclaimed, " Here's Bell and the Major!"—and to depart in the face of Bell and the Major was declared to be impossible; so Mrs. St. Clair, though fretting at the delay, was obliged to await the entrance of the lovers.

Fortunately Miss Bell had no toilette duties to perform; for she was dressed for the Major in a fashionable gOwn made by Miss Skrimpskirt of Tattleton, from a pattern of Miss Gorewell's in Edinburgh, who had got it from Miss Fleecewell of London, who had had hers direct from Madame Chefdceuvre of Paris. Miss Bell, therefore, felt no disheartening doubts as to her appearance ; but firmly relying on the justness of her proportions, and the orthodox length of her waist, and breadth of her shoulders, and strong in the consciousness of being flounced and hemmed up to the knees, she boldly entered, followed by her betrothed. Miss Isabella Black was really a very pretty girl — she had a pretty figure, pretty features, pretty hair, a pretty complexion, a pretty bonnet, a pretty shawl, pretty boots, and a pretty watch. But over all this prettiness was diffused an intolerable air of folly, affectation, and conceit, which completely marred the effect of her charms.

Major Waddell was a very passable sort of person for a nabob;

— he had a dingy bronze complexion; tawny eyes; tolerable teeth; and a long, wrinkled, smirking, baboonish physiognomy.

" Why, Bell, we were afraid you had run away with the Major," said Mr. Black, facetiously, addressing his daughter on her entrance.

" That is a very odd speech, I think, papa, to one in my situation," said Miss Bell, affecting to look much disconcerted.

" Come, come, here are no strangers, so there need be no secrets: — it is pretty well known that if you don't run away with the Major, the Major will run away with you some of these days."

Here Mr. Black laughed, and Mrs. Black laughed, and all the Masters and Misses Black laughed loud and long,—while in the general laugh the fair bride, as if overwhelmed with confusion, took her cousin aside and whispered —

" This is a very awkward scrape I am brought into by papa's bluntness. It certainly -was my intention to have announced the matter to my aunt and you at a proper time, but not just at present; so I must request, as a particular favour, that you will say nothing about it at Rossville — it is so very unpleasant to be the talk of the whole county upon an affair of this kind, that the Major and I had resolved to have it kept as quiet as possible. It was only yesterday he communicated it to Sir William Wad-dell, and he has not yet mentioned it to Lord Fairacre, or any of his other relations."

Mrs. St. Clair was too impatient to be gone to allow any farther latitude for the lovers to show off, but was again in the midst of leave-taking. Much was said about having a longer visit — of taking a family dinner — of spending a few days — of leaving Miss St. Clair to spend a little time and get acquainted with her cousins; and Mrs. St. Clair could only disengage herself from this well-meant hospitality by promising to take the earliest opportunity of repeating her visit. " I trust I may be excused from returning this visit," said Miss Bell, with a look of modest importance, " as in my situation I go no where at present."

Escorted by Mr. Black and the Major, and followed by the whole family, Mrs. and Miss St. Clair resumed their places in the carriage, and were soon driven beyond the precincts of Bellevue. Their next destination was to the house of the Miss Blacks, in the county town, and there they were accordingly driven.

CHAPTER XII.

Lulled in the countless chambers of the brain,
Our thoughts are link'd by many a hidden chain.
Awake but one, and lo ! what myriads rise !
Each stamps its image as the other flies !
Each, as the various avenues of sense
Delight or sorrow to the soul dispense,
Brightens or fades ; yet all, with magic art.
Control the latent fibres of the heart. Pleasures of Memory.

There are few minds so callous as to revisit the scenes of their childhood without experiencing some emotion. And whether
these scenes lie in the crowded city, amidst all the coarse and ordinary objects of vulgar life, or in the lonely valley, with its green hills and its gliding stream — the same feelings swell the heart as the thoughts of the past rush over it; for they speak to us of the careless days of our childhood, of the gay dreams of our youth, of the transient pleasures of our prime, of the faded joys of our old age. They speak to us of parents now sleeping in the dust, of playfellows in a far-distaut land, of companions altered or alienated, of friends become as strangers, of love changed into indifference. They speak to us — it may be — of time misspent, of talents misapplied, of warnings neglected, of blessings despised, of peace departed. They may speak to us, perchance, of God's holy law slighted, of his precepts contemned, of himself forsaken — of hearts, alas ! not purified and renewed by that grace whose aid they never sought, but, like the wasted volcano,

parched and blasted in their own unholy fires. Fairer scenes all may have viewed than those on which their eyes first opened; but in them we behold only the inanimate objects of nature, which, however they may charm the senses or fill the imagination, yet want that deep and powerful interest which seems entwined with our existence, and which gives " a local habitation and a name" so powerful a mastery over us.

Something too there is of solemn thought in returning to a father's house — whether that father's arms are open to receive his long-absent child, or whether the eye that would have welcomed, and the tongue that would have blessed us, are now mouldering in the grave. Ah! many are the wild tumultuous waves that roll over the human mind, and obliterate many of its fairest characters — its fondest recollections. But still the indelible impression of a parent's love remains impressed upon the heart. Even when steeped in guilt or seared in crime, one spot — one little spot — will still be found consecrated to the purest, the holiest of earthly affections.

It was with these mingled emotions Mrs. St. Clair found herself at the door of that mansion she had quitted thirty-three years before. It was the house in which she had first seen the light — where her parents had dwelt — and where she had left them surrounded by a numerous family ; but all were gone save the brother she had just seen, and two sisters, now its sole tenants. Even the most artificial characters still retain some natural feelings; and as Mrs. St. Clair crossed the threshold of her once happy home, and the thoughts of the past rushed over her* she exclaimed with a burst of anguish,—

" Would to God I had never left it!" and, throwing herself upon a seat, she wept without control.

There is something in real emotion that always carries conviction along with it. Although well accustomed to the ebullitions of her mother's character, Miss St. Clair saw and felt the depth of her present feelings, and sought by her tender and

affectionate sympathy to soften her sense of sorrow. But, with a look and gesture expressive only of abhorrence, her mother repelled her from her. At that moment a lady approached, and, throwing herself into her arms, Mrs. St. Clair sobbed in bitterness of spirit, while her sister mingled her tears with hers. Miss Black was the first to regain her composure ; and she said, in a voice which, though still tremulous with emotion, was yet soft and sweet, —

" I love those feelings, my dear Sarah! they are so natural. You miss all those you left behind, and you are thinking what a happier meeting this might have been, had it pleased God to have spared them to us — but I trust there is a happy meeting yet in store for us."

" Oh, no, no!" sobbed Mrs. St. Clair almost convulsively, as she leant her head on her sister's shoulder.

" My dear Sarah!" said Miss Black, in a tone of tender reproach, accompanied by an affectionate embrace ; " but come, let me take you to our poor Mary, who cannot go to you."

Mrs. St. Clair raised her head, and made an effort to subdue her emotion, as she suffered herself to be led to the apartment where her youngest and favourite sister was. When she had quitted home, she had left her a lovely romping child of five years old, with laughing blue eyes and curling flaxen hair; and this image of infant beauty she had ever treasured in her memory, though reason had told her the reality had long since fled. But, alas! reason can but imperfectly picture to us the slow and silent ravages of time—and at sight of her sister Mrs. St. Clair felt as much shocked as though the change had been the metamorphose of an instant, instead of the gradual progress of years of suffering and decay. Imagination, indeed, could not have pictured to itself aught so affecting as the contrast thus presented by a glance of the mind. Mrs. St. Clair thought only of the gay, rosy, frolicksome creature, whose fairy form seemed even yet to bound before her eyes, or hang round her neck in infantine fondness; and on that selfsame spot where last she had parted from her, she now beheld her a monument of premature decay— pale, motionless, and paralytic. For a moment she shrunk from the half-living, half-beatified-looking being, with that instinctive horror with which the worldly mind recoils from all that reminds it of perishable nature. A faint streak of red tinged her sister's pale cheek, and a tear glistened in her soft blue eye, and her heart seemed to swell—perhaps -with some almost forgotten feelings of humiliation at her own infirmities. But when Mrs. St. Clair again looked, the slight hectic had fled, the tear was dried, and the sigh was checked.

" God's will be done, my sister! " said she, with a look and accent of meek and holy resignation. Mrs. St. Clair could not speak, but she threw herself on her sisters neck and wept. Gertrude, meanwhile, had stood aloof—her heart oppressed

E

with sorrow, and her eyes filled with tears, as she contrasted her mother's feelings towards her sisters with those she had testified towards her; and the painful conviction that she was not heloved, forced itself upon her in all the bitterness such a discovery was calculated to excite. At length the agitation of the meeting between the sisters began to subside, and Miss Black, approaching her niece, tenderly embraced her, and led her to her sister. " Here is a stranger who has been too long overlooked," said she; " but once seen she will not be soon forgotten ;" and she gently untied her bonnet, and looked on her with eyes of delighted affection. Her aunt Mary sweetly welcomed her, and also regarded her with an expression of love and tenderness, such as Gertrude felt she never had read even in her mother's eye. There was, indeed, little resemblance between Mrs. St. Clair and her sisters, either in miud or appearance. Elizabeth, the eldest, belonged to that class who can neither be called handsome nor ugly, but are yet sometimes thought both. She had regular features, and a mild sensible countenance; but she was pale and thin, and, to casual observers, had altogether an air of mediocrity, which, in fact, was rather indicative of the consistency and uniformity of her character. She was a Christian in all things ; and its simple, unostentatious spirit pervaded all her looks, words, and actions, and gave to them a charm, which, in her station, no worldly acquirements could have imparted. Her sister was many years younger, and, in spite of sickness and suffering, still retained traces of great beauty. Every feature was perfect—but the dim eye, the pale cheek, and the colourless lip, could now only claim pity, where once they had challenged admiration. Yet neither pain nor sickness had been able to chase the seraphic expression which beamed on her countenance like sunshine amid ruins. It was the look of one already purified from all earthly passions, but who still looked with tenderness on the frailties of her fellow-mortals.

Mrs. St. Clair seemed little gratified by the fondness her sisters testified for her daughter. She remained silent and abstracted, with her eyes fixed on the memorials of former days; for every thing remained in the same primitive order as when she had left them, and every thing told some long-forgotton tale, or roused some sad though slumbering recollection. She fixed her eyes on some foreign shells which decorated the old-fashioned chimney piece,— and what a train of associations did these mute and insiguificant objects conjure up ! They were the gift of one who had loved hcr in early youth, and who had brought them to her (all that he had to bring) from afar — and dearly had she prized them, for then she had loved the giver. But he was a poor and friendless orphan boy and she became the wife of an earl's son!

All may choose their own path in life ; but who can tell where that path may lead ? " The lot," indeed, " is cast into the lap, but the whole disposing thereof is of the Lord." Mrs. St. Clair had chosen that of ambition, and for thirty years she had dragged out life in exile, poverty, and obscurity — while the one she had forsaken, that of faithful and disinterested affection, would have led her to the summit of fame, wealth, and honour. The poor despised sailor boy had distinguished himself for his skill and bravery, and, in the honourable career of his profession, had won for himself a noble fortune, and a name that would descend to posterity. This Mrs. St. Clair knew, for she had heard of his heroic exploits with feelings of the bitterest regret and self-reproach ; and it was those feelings which spread their gloom over her countenance, as she looked on the tokens of his youthful love, and thought of the valiant high-minded being she had bartered for a shadow of greatness. She withdrew her eyes, and they fell upon a venerable family Bible, from whence she had been accustomed to hear her mother read a chapter morning and evening to her family. She recalled, as though it had been yesterday, the last evening she had passed in her father's house. The figure of her mother was before her — her voice sounded in her ears — the words recurred to her then as they had often done since. It was the last chapter of Ecclesiastes, beginning with that touching exhortation— " Remember now thy Creator in the days of thy youth, while the evil days come not, nor the years draw nigh when thou shalt say I have no pleasure in them;" and ending with that awful assurance —" For God shall bring every work into judgment, with every secret thing, whether it be good or whether it be evil." Mrs. St. Clair uttered an involuntary groan, and closed her eyes.

" You see much to remind you of the days that are gone, my dear sister," said Miss Black tenderly; " but when the first impression is over, you will love to look upon those relics, as we do for the sake of those who loved us."

" Never ! ah, never!" exclaimed Mrs. St. Clair, starting up, and going to the window ; " every thing here is torture to me — the very air suffocates me."

She threw open the window and leant out, but it was only to behold other mementos of days past and gone. She looked upon the little garden, the scene of many a childish gambol—it lay in the full blaze of a meridian sun, and all was fair and calm. An old laburnum tree still hung its golden blossoms over a rustic seat at one corner of the garden, and the time since she had sat there and decked herself in its fantastic garlands seemed as nothing. She remembered, too, when, after a long childish illness, her father had carried her in his arms to the garden, with what ecstasy she had breathed the fresh air, and looked on the blue sky, and plucked the gaudiest flowers. " It was on such a day as this," thought she ; " the air is as fresh now as it was then —the sky is as fair — the flowers as sweet; — but my father —

ah! were he still alive, would he thank Heaven now, as he did then, for having preserved his child! "

And again the bitter drops fell from her eyes as she turned sickening from the view. The chord of feeling had been stretched too high to regain its ordinary pitch without an effort; — it is sometimes easier to break the chain than to loosen it. Mrs. St. Clair felt her mind untuned for ordinary communing, and she therefore took an abrupt leave of her sisters, with a promise of returning soon when her nerves should be stronger. Hurrying through the crowd collected around the gay equipage, she threw herself into it as if afraid of being recognized, and called impatiently to her daughter to follow. The postillions cracked their whips—the crowd fell back, and the proud pageant rattled and glittered along till lost to the gaze of the envying and admiring throng.

CHAPTER XIII.

Nothing is lost on him who sees
With an eye that feeling gave; For him there's a story in every breeze,

And a picture in every wave. Song.

Mrs. St. Clair and her daughter proceeded for some time in profound silence. The former seemed plunged in painful meditation, the latter felt grieved and mortified at her mother's caprice and unkindness to her. The first thing which roused Mrs. St. Clair was the view of Rossville Castle, rising proudly above the woods which embosomed it — and, as she looked, gradually her brow cleared, her eye brightened, and her countenance regained its usual expression.

" Gertrude, my love," said she, taking her daughter's hand, " I have almost forgot you to-day. But your own heart will enable you to conceive what mine must have suffered;" and she sighed deeply.

" Yes," answered Miss St. Clair, in some agitation, " I can conceive that you have felt much; but I cannot conceive why — oh! mamma, what had I done that you should have shook me from you like a venemous reptile ? "

" My dear Gertrude! what an idea! that is the mere coinage of your brain—how can you allow yourself to be so carried away by your imagination ? Come, my dear, let us have have no more such foolish fancies. Strange, indeed, it would be "— continued she, as the park gate was thrown open to receive them — " in any one to cast off like a reptile the fair heiress of this princely domain."

But, however strange, her daughter felt it was so, and she remained silent. Mrs. St. Clair resumed —

"Apropos, Gertrude, when you are lady of Rossville, you must build me a little tiny cottage on yon lovely green bank, where I may live quietly as a humble cottager, while you play the great lady : — come, promise me, Gertrude, that I shall have a croft from you — a butt and a ben — a cow's grass and a kail-yard."

There was something so forced and unnatural in her mother's sudden gaiety, that Miss St. Clair, accustomed as she was to all the inequalities of her temper, felt almost frightened at it, and she was at a loss how to reply.

" So you won't promise me, Gertrude, even a humble independence for my old age?—Perhaps you are right to be cautious —Lear's daughters spoke him fair, and after all turned him out of doors, and why should I expect more from you?"

Oh mamma! " exclaimed Miss St. Clair, bursting into tears, " do not kill me with such cruel words."

" Is it so cruel, then, in a mother to crave a pittance from the bounty of her child ? "

" It is cruel to doubt that I would give you all—yes, were all this mine to-morrow, I could not be more mistress of it than you should be."

" So you think at present, Gertrude •, but you know not as I do the mutability of the human mind. You will form other ties

— other connections—you will marry, and your mother will be forgotten—perhaps forsaken. You will marry," cried she with increased violence,—"you will marry, and I shall be left to starve

— you will fall a prey to the artifices of a Colonel Delmour — a needy, desperate spendthrift. I see already he is paying court to the future heiress ; and, once the wife of that designing extravagant man, you will have nothing to bestow."

Shocked and amazed at her mother's violence, Miss St. Clair sought to tranquillize her by assurances that she was mistaken in supposing Colonel Delmour-had any such views, when Mrs. St.Clair interrupted her—"Promise me, then, that you will never become his wife."

There is always something revolting to an open ingenuous mind in being fettered by promises; but there was something more than even that natural repugnance to make Gertrude shrink from thus binding herself to her mother's will, and she remained silent; but the deep blush that burned on her cheek spoke more eloquently than words. Mrs. St. Clair regarded her with a piercing look—then exclaimed, in a transport of anger, "And is it even so — and all that I have done and suffered is " Then, suddenly stopping, she added, in a milder

tone, —" Gertrude, my wish is to save you from the dangers with which you are already surrounded — promise me, at least, that you will not marry until you have attained the age of

E 3

twenty-one—that you will never marry without my consent, and until you have provided for my old age."

" Mamma," said Miss St. Clair, with a calmness and self-possession which bespoke her determination, " I here promise that I will not marry, without your consent, before the age of twenty-one, and until I have provided for you as becomes my mother — more I cannot —I dare not— I will not promise."

" Then with that I must be satisfied," said Mrs. St. Clair, as the carriage stopped at the castle door; and having alighted, she entered the house, while her daughter stood some minutes on the lawn, inhaling the mild freshness of a west wind laden with the balmy sweets of opening buds and blossoms. Insensibly she strolled on ; and gradually the impression of the unpleasant scene she had just had with her mother wore away beneath the calming influence of nature's charms — the clear cloudless sky —the lulling flow of the river—the bright green woods in all the luxriance of early summer.

Miss St. Clair wandered on till she reached a little secluded spot she had not yet seen. On the top of a green knoll that rose gradually from the river stood part of an ancient building of an irregular and picturesque form, but now almost covered with ivy. Some wild cherry, or what, in the language of the country, are called geen trees, grew almost close to it; •— they were now white with blossoms, and formed a fanciful contrast to the emblems of age and decay with which they were combined. The ground between the river and the ruin appeared to have been originally a garden or orchard; and some old apple trees still remained, whose mossy trunks and shrivelled branches bore evidence of their antiquity, while here and there a cluster of rich pink blossoms showed that

Life was in the leaf, for still between The fits of falling snow appear'd the streaky green.

Some aged weeping willows dipt their silvery foliage in the dark waters, as they glided slowly and silently along. It was a scene where the contemplative mind might have mused over the mournful record of time, and things, and people, past and gone, with their joys and their sorrows,—where the youthful imagination might have pictured to itself some ideal paradise yet to be realized.

" Ah! " thought Gertrude, " how willingly would I renounce all the pomp of greatness, to dwell here in lowly affection with one who would love me, and whom I could love in return! How strange that I, who could cherish the very worm that crawls beneath my foot, have no one being to whom I can utter the thoughts of my heart—no one on whom I can bestow its best affections!" She raised her eyes, swimming in tears, to heaven; but it was in the poetical enthusiasm of feeling, not in the calm spirit of devotion. She was suddenly roused by hearing some one approach; and presently Colonel Delmour, forcing his way through some wild tangled hushes, hastened towards her with an appearance of the greatest delight. At sight of him the thoughts of her mother's warning rushed to her recollection, — the dislike she had expressed—the suspicions she harboured — the promise she would have exacted — all seemed to give him a sort of inexplicable interest in her eyes. She coloured deeply, and the consciousness she had done so added to her confusion.

' s I have to apologize to you," said Colonel Delmour, " for thus literally forcing my way to you. Lyndsay and I were practising archery when I descried you: to see you, and not to fly to you, was impossible, had Briareus himself opposed my passage ; so, leaving Edward master of the field, I winged my way to you like one of my own arrows—but I fear I startled you?" *

Miss St. Clair felt as though she were acting in direct disobedience to her mother, in thus meeting, even accidentally, with the man she had just heard denounced by her. In great embarrassment she begged he would resume his exercise •, and she was moving away, when Colonel Delmour caught her hand, and in a low tone said,—

" Do not stir from hence, unless you wish to encounter Miss Pratt's observations ; she is beating about here; I saw her as I came along, but I trust she will lose scent: do remain till that danger is past."

Almost equally averse to encounter Miss Pratt at any time, but more particularly at present, she suffered Colonel Delmour to seat her on a little mossy knoll; and throwing himself on the grass at her feet —

" Be this your throne, and behold your subject," said he, in a half-serious, half-sportive tone ; then raising his eyes to hers, he repeated,—

" Le premier jour qu'on aime on se plait en secret A mettre au rang des rois l'objet que

Ton adore ; Et s'il etoit un rang plus eclatant encore Ce seroit la celui que le coeur choiseroit."

Miss St. Clair tried to reply in a strain of badinage; but the words died on her lips, and, colouring still more deeply, she remained silent. At that moment Mr. Lyndsay appeared; but ere he had time to address her, the shrill voice of Miss Pratt was heard, and presently she broke in.

" Ah, ha! so you're all here! — Upon my word, here's a meeting of friends. It puts me in mind of a scene in a play, where all the lovers meet to run away with pretty Mistress Anne Page, and the one cries mum, and the other cries budget."

" Two excellent words," said Colonel Delmour, looking uuch. provoked ; " of course you understand their meaning— be silent and begone."

e 4

" Two very impertinent words, in my opinion," said Miss Pratt, seating herself beside Gertrude; " and, to tell you the truth, I've no great notion of your mums. — There's a family in this country all so tongue-tied, that Anthony Whyte calls their house the mummery; and by the bye, Mr. Edward, I really think you may cry mum any day, — you're grown very silent of late."

" A proof I am growing wiser, I suppose," answered he, laughingly, " according to some great authority, who, I think, says most men speak from not knowing how to be silent."

" The saying of some dull blockhead, I suspect," said Colonel Delmour, still evidently out of humour.

" Indeed, I think so too, Colonel," cried Miss Pratt; " any body can hold their tongue, but it's not every body that can speak."

" Not every body that ought to speak, or, at least, ought to be listened to," said Colonel Delmour, contemptuously turning from her, and addressing some words in French in a low tone to Gertrude; while Miss Pratt gabbled on —

" Bless me ! what a tear I've got in my gown ! There's really an ill luck attends this gown.— I never have it on without its meeting with some accident — that's all I've got by hunting after you youngsters ;" and in the twinkling of an eye her huswife was out — her thimble on her finger, and her needle flying through all the intricacies of " a very bad cross tear."

" What's this we were talking about ? O! about people holding their tongues — I really wish these birds would hold theirs, for I'm perfectly dieved with their chattering—sh, sh," shaking her parasol at a goldfinch. " I really think young people should be made to hold their tongues, and only speak when they're spoken to. — Was that a fish that leapt in the water just now ? What a pity but one of you had had a fishing-rod in your hands instead of these senseless bows and arrows — it would have been some diversion to have seen you hook a nice three-pound weight caller trout: — and really old people should be cautious of speaking — they're sometimes rather slow, you know — not but what I can listen to any body. — Bless me! how the wind's blowing these blossoms about— I'm like to be blinded with them."

" Come, you shall listen to me then," said Mr. Lyndsay, as he caught some of the falling blossoms, " while I apostrophize them in some pretty lines of Herrick's.

TO BLOSSOMS.

Fair pledges of a fruitful tree, Why do you fall so fast ? Your date is not so past; But you may stay here yet awhile, To blush and gently smile ; And go at last.

What! were ye born to be An hour or half's delight, And so to bid good night ? 'T was pity nature brought ye forth, Merely to show your worth, And lose you quite.

But you are lovely leaves, where we May read how soon things have Their end, though ne'er so brave ; And after they have shown their pride Like you a while, they glide Into the grave.

Miss Pratt testified great impatience while the verses were repeating ; but the purpose was answered — the time was passed while the fracture was repairing — and afraid of more poetry, for which she had a mortal antipathy, she readily assented to Miss St. Clair's proposal of returning home.

" I can tell you one thing, my dear," whispered she to Gertrude, " that mum should be the watch-word here to-day; — a certain person," with a wink at Colonel Delmour, " is but a younger brother, and not the thing. He can be very pleasant when he pleases ; but take my word for it he's not to ride the ford upon : — but, bless me, I had no notion it was so late, and I've a bit of lace to run upon my gown before dinner! " — and away ran Miss Pratt to her toilette, while Gertrude retired to her chamber to ruminate on the events of the day.

CHAPTER XIV.

Keep, therefore, a true woman's eye, And love me still, but know not why ; So hast thou the same reason still

To doat upon me ever. Old Madrigal.

That " she who deliberates is lost," is a remark that has been so often verified, that although there are innumerable instances of women deliberating to be saved, yet when a lover suspects the object of his wishes to be debating the question of—to love or not to love, he feels pretty secure that it will be decided in his favour. At least so felt Colonel Delmour, as he marked the thoughtful cast of Miss St. Clair's countenance when she entered the drawing-room before dinner. She had, indeed, that day deliberated more than she had ever done in the whole course of her life before, though her deliberations had not yet assumed any distinct form. By nature tender and affectionate in her disposition, she was likewise high-spirited and impatient of unjuft control; and the situation in which she was now placed was calculated to call forth all the latent energies of her character. " Il y a quelquefois dans le cours de la vie, de si chers plaisirs ti do

si tendres engagements que Von nous defend, qu'il est naturel de de-sir er, du moins, qu'ils fussent per mis."

Miss St. Clair certainly could not help wishing that she had not been forbidden to love her cousin ; for, although he had not absolutely declared himself her lover, he had said more than enough to convince her that he was deeply in love, and that the happiness of his life hung upon her decision. When she thought of her mother's prejudice against him, so unjust, so unaccountable, it seemed next to impossible for her to remain in a state of indecision. She must either adopt her mother's sentiments, and hate, fly, abjure him ; or she must yield to her own inclinations, and listen to him — look on him, and love him. In this state of mental embarrassment, it was impossible for any one so ingenuous to conceal what was passing in her mind. But those who were most interested in observing her construed her behaviour each according to their own wishes. In her constrained manner and averted eyes whenever Colonel Delmour addressed her, Mrs. St. Clair flattered herself she saw symptoms of that distrust and dislike she had endeavoured to inculcate ; while he, for the present, felt satisfied in the consciousness that he was, at least, not an object of indifference.

But it was impossible for any ruminations to be carried on long-in the presence of Miss Pratt, whose own ruminations never lasted longer than till she had made herself mistress of the dresses of the company or the dishes on the table. Having finished her scrutiny of the former, she addressed Mrs. St. Clair —

" You were very soon home to-day, I think ; you must really have paid fashionable visits to your friends — to be sure, your sister's is not a house to stay long in. — Poor Miss Mary, what a pretty creature she was once, and as merry as a grig; but she has taken taken rather a religious turn now — to be sure, when people have not the use of their legs, what can they do ? I'm sure we should be thankful that have all our faculties."

" Except the faculty of being religious," said Mr. Lyndsay with a smile.

" A certain degree of religion I think extremely proper," said Miss Pratt in a by-way-of, serious manner; — " but I'm just afraid it's rather overdone — not that I mean to say any thing against the Miss Blacks, for I assure you I have a very high respect for them; — and old Mr. Ramsay! how did you find him ? — in a tolerable tune I hope ? "

" I was afraid of trespassing too far on Lord Rossville's goodness by detaining his carriage and servants, and therefore delayed visiting my uncle till another opportunity."

" That was being extremely considerate, indeed," began his lordship ; but, as usual, was cut short by Miss Pratt.

" Bless me! what's the use of carriages and servants but to wait ? If yon had played your cards well, you would have gone urs>i to your uncle — an old man in a nightcap, worth good seventy thousand pound, and as cross as two sticks, is not to be sneezed at, as Anthony Whyte says ; but there's the gong. — O Lord Rossville, I -wish you would really get a bell, for I declare there's no hearing one's self speak for that gong—or Avhat would you think of a trumpet ? Bells and gongs are grown so common, that Anthony Whyte's going to get a trumpet."

" Being already provided with a trumpeter, it is quite proper that Mr. Whyte should have a trumpet," said Colonel Delmour.

" Considering with what deadly intentions we assemble at the dinner-table," said Mr. Lyndsay, " I really think a warlike instrument a much more appropriate symbol than a peaceful, fasting, matin-sounding bell — indeed, the organ of destructiveness is always so strong with me at this hour, and I feel so much of the fee fa fum about me, that I can scarcely ask you to trust yourself with me ; " and he good-humouredly gave his arm to Miss Pratt, as she was pattering away to the dining-room, with rather a discomfited look, by herself: " and now for the pride, pomp, and circumstance of glorious war," — as the party seated themselves at the splendid board. But Miss Pratt's mortification never could be made by any possible means to endure much longer than the shock of a shower-bath — and by the time the dishes were uncovered, " Richard was himself again."

" Colonel Delmour, what's that before you?—I think it looks like fricasseed chicken — I'll thank you for some of it;" and Colonel Delmour with the most indifferent air as to Miss Pratt's wants, and talking all the while to Miss St. Clair, sent her a part which did not suit her taste.

" Just take that back," said she to the servant;" with my compliments to Colonel Delmour, and I'll be obliged to him for a wing. Colonel, don't you know it's the fashion now, when you help game or poultry, to ask, ' Pray do you run or fly?' meaning do you choose leg or wing. There was a good scene at Anthony Whyte's one day fat Lady Puffendorf was there — you know she's so asthmatic she can hardly walk ; so when she chose chicken, ' Pray, ma'am,' says Anthony, ' do you run or fly ?' Of course a fine titter ran round the company. Lord Rossville, did you hear that ? — Colonel Delmour, remember I fly."

" I shall have great pleasure in assisting your flight," said he with an ironical smile; " pray, when may we expect to see Miss Pratt take wing ? "

" Is that that you may have a shot at me with your bow and arrow ? I thought, indeed, you looked as if you were rather bent upon wounding hearts than harts to-day — you understand the difference, don't you, Miss St. Clair?" who only coloured a reply, and even Colonel Delmour seemed disconcerted. " Well, never mind, mum's the word, you know," with a provoking wink; " only I advise all young ladies who value their hearts to cry budget to gentlemen with bows and arrows." Lord Rosville's ideas, fortunately, never could keep pace with Miss Pratt's tongue : he had now only overtaken her at the " run and fly," and was busy preparing, with all the powers of his mind, a caveat against the use of cant terms—to begin with a quotation from Lord Chesterfield, and to be followed up by a full declaration of his own sentiments on the subject. In short, his mode of proceeding was something like bringing out a field-piece to knock down a fly, which, in the meantime, had perched itself on the very mouth of the cannon, and, unconscious of the formidable artillery that was preparing against it, buzzed away.

" Let me help you to some asparagus, my lord ?" helping herself largely in the meantime ; " very fine it is, though rather out of season now — it has been long over at Whyte Hall. But who can help asparagus with asparagus tongs ? Anthony Whyte says, if ever he's prevailed upon to go into parliament, it will be for the sole purpose of bringing in three bills for the relief of the rich. One of them is to be an act for the suppression of asparagus tongs ; another is to make it felony for -a cook to twist the legs of game, or force a turkey to carry its head under its wing; and a third is "

But here Lord Rossville's indignation got the better of his good-breeding, and even overcame the more tardy operations of his mind; and before Anthony Whyte's third bill could be brought forward, he exclaimed, " Mr. Anthony Whyte bring bills into parliament! — Pray, Miss Pratt, have you any authority for supposing, or insinuating, that Mr. Whyte has the most distant shadow of an idea of attempting to procure a seat in parliament? If he has, I can only say I have been most grossly misinformed — if he has not, it is highly improper in you, or in any of his relations or friends, who the world will naturally conclude are in his confidence, to start such a supposition ; — it is a serious, a very serious matter, to tamper with a gentleman's name in politics, more particularly in the troublesome and factious times in which we live." Even Miss Pratt was for an instant discomfited by the solemn indignation of this address ; but she quickly rallied, and whispering to Mr. Lyndsay, " He's very bilious to-day,—his eyes are like boiled gooseberries, honest man !"—she resumed, — " Bless me, Lord Rossville, one would think I had spoken high treason, but I was only joking; Mr. Whyte, I can assure you, has too much good sense to think of going into parliament; if he had had a mind that way, he might have been in long ago: I'm told, from pretty good authority, he might carry the county any day he liked."

Here the Earl absolutely gasped in the attempt to bring up words long and strong enough to immolate the presumption of Miss Pratt and Anthony Whyte. " I can assure you, both Lord Punmedown and Sir Thomas Turnabout spoke seriously to Mr. Whyte about it some time ago —' Anthony,' says my lord, ' if you wish to sit, you've only to stand.' Nothing could be stronger than that, you know. ' Faith, my lord,' says he, ' I believe I

would have to lie in the first place.' Very good, wasn't it? Anthony's always ready with his answer; I assure you, if he was in parliament he would keep his own."

" Is there any hody talked of in opposition to Robert?" asked Colonel Dehnour, as if he had not even deigned to hear Miss Pratt — " apropos, I had a letter from him this morning."

" Indeed!" exclaimed the Earl with great earnestness. " I am rather surprised that such a piece of information should have been only communicated to me in this accidental manner — I have been anxiously looking for letters from Mr. Delmour for some days—what does he say with regard to the sitting of parliament, and does he point at any probable time for coming north?"

" I merely glanced at his letter," answered Colonel Delmour, with an air of indifference; " it seemed filled as usual with politics, and I am no politician."

" I am not so sure about that," said Miss Pratt, in an under tone, and with a most provoking significant look.

" But you shall hear what he says. — Smith," turning to his servant, " you will find some letters upon the writing-table in my dressing-room; bring them here."

" I hope you don't leave your love-letters lying about that way, Colonel?" cried the incorrigible Pratt. " I assure you, if I was a young lady, I would take Care how I corresponded with you — you're not like Anthony Whyte, who keeps up all his letters like grim death."

The letters were brought; and Colonel Delmour, taking his brother's from amongst them, glanced his eye over it, and read in a skimming manner—" Animated and protracted debate — admirable speech—legs two hours and a quarter — immense applause — 197 of majority — glorious result — opposition fairly discomfited," &c. &c.; he then read aloud —

" Pray inform the Earl there is no longer a doubt as to the dissolution of parliament next session, — we must therefore prepare to take the field immediately. Lord P. and Sir J. T. intend to oppose us, I understand, and to bring forward some tool of their own; but I have little fear as to the result. I now only wait the passing of the road bill, and the discussion on the resumption of cash payments, to be off for Scotland; my uncle may, therefore, expect me in the course of a few days, when I trust we shall be able to make a tolerable muster. — P. S. I see a Major Waddell has lodged claim for enrolment,—do you know any thing of him ? "

" Major Waddell!" repeated the Earl, putting his hand to his forehead in a musing attitude, as if endeavouring to recollect him.

" Major Waddell," said Mrs. St. Clair, in her softest manner, ■' is a gentleman of large fortune, lately returned from India — heir, I understand, to Sir William Waddell, and upon the point

of marriage with a niece of mine—his vote, I am sure "

Luckily, before Mrs. St. Clair could commit herself and Major Wadde'll's vote, Miss Pratt dashed in. —"Aye ! Miss Bell Black going to be married to Major Waddell! Ton my word she has fallen upon her feet—that will be a disappointment to many a one ; for I assure you the Major's a prize, and I know three ladies he was supposed to be looking after—he even went so far as to present one of them with a very handsome Paradise plume — that I know to be a fact, for I was staying in the house at the time, and there was a great debate whether she should have accepted it before he had made his proposals.—Aye! I was told that Miss Bell had lately said, in company, that she never would marry any man who couldn't give her silver tureens and corners.—He's very well connected too.—Let me see; his mother was a Bog, and his father a Waddell of the Waddell Mains family— so he has good blood both ways."

All this was very agreeable to Mrs. St. Clair — it was giving consequence to her family, which was an advantage to herself. Miss Pratt's pribble prabble was therefore music to her ear ; and while she gave her whole attention to that, Colonel Delmour contrived to render his conversation no less interesting to her daughter, whose deliberations, like Othello's doubts, were gradually assuming a more decided form. For in 4ove, as in jealousy, it will commonly be found that " to be once in doubt is once to be resolved."

As the ladies rose from table, Lord Rossville, who had evidently been struggling for some time to give utterance to some exquisite idea, called Miss Pratt, just as she had reached the door : — they all stopped.

" Miss Pratt," said his lordship, making an effort to subdue any appearance of risibility, — " Miss Pratt, I think your friend who received the present of a plume from Major Waddell will have no great cause to plume herself upon that — as, from your account, it can no longer be a feather in her cap."

The Earl was too much elated with this sally to think of Lord Chesterfield, and he indulged himself in a laugh tolerably loud and intolerably long.

" Ha! ha! ha! very good indeed !" cried Miss Pratt. " I must let Anthony Whyte and Lord Punmedown hear that — very well indeed! — Poor Miss Kitty Fansyflame, as you say, it will be no great feather in her cap now, poor soul! — ha ! ha ! ha! Lady Betty, did you hear that ?" Then pinching Gertrude's arm, she whispered, " As Anthony Whyte says, it's a serious matter when Lord Rossville makes a joke —honest man — ha ! ha! ha! — very fair indeed." And Miss Pratt kept up a running laugh all "the way to the drawing-room.

CHAPTER XV.

The pilot best of winds does talk,
The peasant of his cattle ;
The shepherd of his fleecy flock,
The soldier of his battle. Aiuosto.

The expected dissolution of parliament was all in favour of the growing attachment of the cousins. Gertrude, indeed, tried, or thought she tried, to avoid receiving the attentions of Colonel Delmour ; hut in the thousand minute, and almost imperceptible opportunities, which are for ever occurring where people dwell under the same roof, he found many occasions of insinuating the ardour and sincerity of his passion, yet in a manner so refined and unobtrusive, that it would have seemed downright prudery to have disclaimed his attentions.

Lord Rossville was, or, what was the same thing, fancied he was, so overwhelmed with business, that, contrary to his usual practice, he now always retired immediately after tea to his study, — there to con over the map and count over the roll of the county, and to frame the model of a circular letter, which was to surpass all the circular letters that ever had issued from a circular head.

Mrs. St. Clair was busy too — she had begun to canvass with her brother and her uncle, to bespeak their votes, and had written to offer a visit to the latter the following day, by the Earl's desire. Lady Betty sat, as usual, at her little table, with her rug, her novel, and her fat favourite. Miss Pratt gabbled and knotted. Mr. Lyndsay read. Colonel Delmour and Gertrude alone seemed unoccupied; but " how various their employments whom the world deems idle." —" You are in an uncommon quiescent state to-night, Delmour," said Mr. Lyndsay, closing his book and rising — " neither music, nor billiards, nor ennui • — most wonderful! "

" Etre avec les gens qxCon aime, cela snffit; rever, leur parler, ne leur parler point, aupres oVeux tout est egal," replied he, casting a look towards Gertrude, but affecting to address Miss Pratt. — " Is it not so, Miss Pratt ?"

" To tell you the truth, Colonel," answered she with some asperity, " when people speak French to me, I always lay it down as a rule that they're speaking nonsense — I'm sure there are words enough in plain English to say all that any body has to say."

" Ah ! but they are too plain — that is precisely my objection to them ; for you, I am sure, are aware," — and again he stole a glance at Miss St. Clair,— iii combien dechoses qu'on n'apercoit que par sentiment, et dont il est impossible de rendre raison! ' Now, the

French is the language of sentiment — the English of reason — consequently it is most unreasonable in you, my dear Miss Pratt, to insist upon my expressing my sentiments in a plain reasonable manner; but come, since*you profess to be insensible to sentiment, try whether you cannot prevail upon Miss St. Clair to give us some music."

" Music!" reiterated Miss Pratt; " fiddlesticks! For any sake, let us have one night of peace and rest—for I declare Lord Rossville makes a perfect toil of music ; but, indeed, it's the same every where now — there's not a house you go into but some of the family are musical. I know one family where there's five grown-up daughters that all play upon the harp; and such a tuning, and stringing, and thrumming goes on, that I declare I get perfectly stupid. Not only that, but, as Anthony Whyte says, you used to be aware of your danger when you saw a piano or a fiddle in a house ; but now you have music in all shapes, and such contrivances ! — there's musical glasses, and musical clocks, and musical snuff-boxes, and now they've got musical work-boxes. The t'other day, when I was at Lady Restall's, I happened to want a thread in a hurry, and was flying to her work-box for it.—' Stop, stop,' says she,' and I'll give you something better than a thread;' so she locks up her box and sets it a-going, and, to be sure, I thought it never would have done — tune after tune. ' And isn't that a lovely waltz,' says she, ' and isn't that a sweet quadrille !'— Thinks I, my friend, if you was mine, I would soon stop your mouth, and make you mind your own business."

" But I hope you got your thread ? " inquired Lady Betty.

" Yes, yes, I got my thread at last; but isn't it a hard case that one can't get a black silk thread, if it was to save their life, without getting half a dozen tunes into the bargain ? But that's not the most ridiculous part ; for, says she, ' I've commissioned a walking-cane for my lord from Paris (you know Lord Restall can't walk the length of his toe without a stick), and it is to play three waltzes, two quadrilles, a hornpipe, and the Grand Turk^s March — it will be such an amusement,' says she, 'when he's walking with his friends, to set his stick a-going.' — Thinks I, he'll be clever if ever he sets it a-going about my ears. Miss St. Clair, my dear, have you no nice nacky little handy work, that you could be doing at while we sit and chat ?"

" That is a proper reproof for my idleness," said Gertrude, rising to fetch her work.

" How I detest the stupid vulgar industry of working ladies!" said Colonel Delmour; " come, let me lead you to the music-room," and he took her hand.

" What are you going to play ? " inquired Lady Betty.

"Tibbie Fowler," answered Miss Pratt —"Miss St. Clair, my dear, did you ever hear Tibbie Fowler?" and, in her cracked voice, she struck up that celebrated ditty. Colonel Delmour,

with an expression of disgust, immediately hurried Miss St. Clair to the adjoining room, leaving Miss Pratt to carol away to Lady Betty and fat Flora.

Much has been said of the power of music ; and all who have ears and souls will admit that its influence has not been exaggerated even by its most enthusiastic votaries. In every heart of sensibility nature has implanted a chord which, if rightly touched, will yield fine issue, whether to the loftier or the gentler passions of the mind — whether that chord vibrates responsive to the pealing organ, the spirit-stirring drum, or the nightingale's soft lay. Some there are, indeed, to whom music is merely a science, an assemblage of fine concords and discords ; and who, possessed of all that skill and knowledge can impart, are yet strangers to those " mystic transports," whose movements are in the soul, and which constitute tbe true charm of melody. But Colonel Delmour could not be said to belong to either of those classes, or, rather, he partook somewhat of both : he was passionately fond of music, and sang with much taste and expression ; but it might be doubted whether his was

Le chant qui se sent dans Fame.

Be that as it may, he had hitherto, in the various flirtations in which he had been engaged, found music a most useful auxiliary, and by much the safest, as well as the most elegant, medium for communicating his passion. It was, therefore, an invariable rule with Colonel Delmour to use other men's verse, as well as other men's prose, instead of his own. For similar reasons, he also preferred declaring his passion either in French or Italian ; and having read all the lighter works in these languages, and being gifted with a good memory and a ready wit, he was seldom at a loss for expressions suited to each particular case. The words he selected for the present occasion were those beautiful ones, —

 Felice chi vi mira,
 Ma piu felice chi per voi sospira, &c.

When suddenly Miss Pratt burst in with " Wisht, wisht — there's somebody coming that will make us all change our note, I'm thinking;" and while she spoke, a spattered chaise-and-four, with horses in a foam, drove up, which was recognized by its bearings to be that of Mr. Delmour. All was bustle and sensation ; and the family, with the exception of Lord Rossville, had dropped in one by one to the music-room, where Mr. Delmour was ushered in. He was what many would have called a very fine-looking man — tall and straight, with handsome regular features, although somewhat resembling Lord Rossville, both in person and manners. He paid his compliments rather with the well-bred formality of the old school, than with the easy disengaged air of a man of fashion, and totally devoid of that air of empressement towards Miss St. Clair, which had marked the

attentions of his brother from their first meeting. In fact, Mr. Delmour seemed little engrossed with any of the party, but looked round as if in search of a far more intei'esting object, and then anxiously inquired where Lord Rossville was. But ere an answer could be returned the Earl himself entered, and mutual pleasure was testified by the uncle and nephew at sight of each other.

" Although, upon ordinary occasions, I confess I am no friend to what are termed unexpected pleasures," said his lordship; " yet, in the present instance, my dear Robert, I own I do not feel my pleasure at your arrival at all diminished by the unexpectedness of your appearance. At the same time, it would not have been amiss, perhaps, to have apprised me of your intention at this important time."

" Impossible !" replied Mr. Delmour eagerly ; " quite impossible ! In fact, I set off the instant the house rose, which was on Friday morning at half past five, after a most interesting debate on the paper currency, which, I am happy to tell you, we carried by a majority of eighty-five."

" Bravo! " exclaimed the Earl. — " And our road bill ? "

" Is passed. But how stands the county ? — Have you felt its pulse at all ? — I understand a brisk canvass has commenced in a certain quarter. I got a hint of that from Lord Wishton, which, in fact, induced me to set off without a moment's delay."

" You acted wisely and well," said the Eai'l , " delays are always dangerous — more especially upon occasions such as the present."

" It's high time you had begun to canvass, if you expect to succeed in your election, I can tell you," interposed Miss Pratt, with one of her sharp pithy glances at Colonel Delmour and Gertrude, who kept a little apart; and to j udge by the blush and the smile which occasionally flitted over her beautiful features, as she sometimes bent her head to his whispers, the conversation was of rather a more interesting nature than what was carrying on between the uncle and nephew.

Miss Pratt's remark did not hit either of them, and the latter resumed — "I am told the opposite party give out they can already reckon upon twenty-nine votes—that, I suspect, is a ruse de guerre; but still it shows the necessity of our taking the field immediately."

" Precisely my own sentiments ! " exclaimed Lord Rossville, with delight; " as you justly observe, there is not a moment to lose."

" Something might yet be done to-night," said Mr. Delmour, looking at his watch.

" Something has been done already," replied his lordship, with an air of conscious importance; " but it is now almost supper time, and you must be much ftttigued with your long and rapid journey ; I must, therefore, vote for an adjournment."

As the servant at that moment announced supper, this was a very bright sally for the Earl, though it did not produce all the effect he had expected.

" Mr. Delmour, you -will conduct Miss St. Clair to the supper room; " and Colonel Delmour, with infinite reluctance, "was obliged to relinquish her hand to his brother. With no less unwillingness did she bestow it; and her chagrin was not lessened at finding herself placed between the uncle and nephew at supper, and condemned to hear, without being able to listen to their conversation, which now, in spite of Miss Pratt's desultory gabble, continued to flow in the same political channel. Gertrude heard, with weariness, the whole preliminaries of an active canvass fully discussed across her; and while her imagination yet dwelt with delight on the melodious accents and impassioned sentiments which had so lately been poured into her ear, and found entrance to her heart, she mentally exclaimed — " How impossible would it be ever to love a man who can only talk of votes, seats, rolls, and qualifications ! "

CHAPTER XVI.

Certainly it is heaven upon earth to have a man's mind move in charity, rest in Providence, and turn upon the poles of truth. — Lord Bacon.

" "Well, what do you think of our member ?" was Miss Pratt's first salutation to Gertrude, as they met next morning in their way to breakfast — then, without waiting a reply, " I thought you looked very wearied last night, and no wonder, for I declare my back was like to break with their politics. — I've a notion vou don't think he's likelv to be anv great acquisition as a member of the family, whatever he may be to the county — he! he! he! — I must tell Anthony Whyte that — he will be so diverted; — but come, my dear," taking her arm. "we're too soon for breakfast yet. so we may just scent the morning air, as what do you call the man's ghost says in the play — but you should have something on your head, you must not get that pretty white skin of yours sunburnt; but we'll not go farther than the portico. — I looked into the room as I passed, and there was nobody there but Lord Rossville, sitting, as usual, watching the teapot, like a clocking hen. It's a great pity that he will make the tea himself. I declare I'm like to choke sometimes before I can get a drop, and. after all, it's really just water bewitched. — It's a thousand pities, hui. ?st man ! that he will think he can do every thing better than any body else. — But here comes Edward Lyndsay from his walk. — I dare say he has been at some srood turn already. — Good morning, Mr. Edward; where have vou been strolling to this

F 2

fine morning ? Miss St. Clair and I are just taking a little chat here, in the sun, till the breakfast's ready ; for, as Anthony Whyte says, I don't like to descend to vacuity. — What do you think Miss St. Clair says of our member? that she does not think him any great acquisition as a member of the family, whatever he may be as a member of the county : isn't that very good?"

Gertrude was about to disclaim the witticism, when Mr. Lyndsay saved her the trouble.

" So good," replied he, " that I am surprised you should give the credit of it to any body else. — Miss St. Clair, I am sure, is incapable of making such a remark."

" Is that meant as a compliment to you or me, my dear? " addressing Gertrude. —" But I wish you would explain, Mr. Edward, what makes you think Miss St. Clair incapable of saying that?"

" Because, as a physiognomist, I pronounce .Miss St. Clair incapable of making so ill-natured a remark upon one of whom she has as yet had no opportunity of forming an opinion."

" And what do you call that remark of your own, pray, Mr. Edward?" interrupted Miss Pratt with considerable pique; ; 'for my part, I think it as ill-natured a one as ever I heard."

" You wished to hear the truth," said he, with a smile; " it is not my fault if it is not agreeable."

" To tell you the truth, Mr. Lyndsay, it's not by speaking what you call the truth upon every occasion, that people will ever make friends to themselves in this world. I never knew any of your plain-spoken people that didn't make twenty enemies for one friend. I know nobody that likes to have what you call the truth told them ; do you, my dear?"—to Gertrude. " Yes," answered Gertrude; " I think I should like to hear the truth from an amiable person; but the reason it is so disagreeable, I suppose, is, because people are always so cross when they speak what they call the truth, that it seems as if they only used it as a cloak for their own ill-humour and caprice, and a thousand other deadly sins."

" Well, I'm sure, if you've a mind to hear the truth, you could not be in better hands, my dear, than your cousin's for it. — But there's that abominable gong again — we must really fly, for Lord Rossville will be out of all patience;" and off pattered Miss Pratt, leaving her companions to follow her nimble steps. Nobody had yet appeared at the breakfast-table but Lord Rossville and Mr. Delmour, who had resumed the subject of the election with renewed vigour. Miss Pratt, seeing his lordship so engrossed, had seized upon the teapot, and w r as enjoying the luxury of filling her cup by stealth. Mr. Lyndsay seated himself by Gertrude ; it was the place Colonel Delmour usually occupied, and she looked a little disappointed at seeing it filled by another — he did not appear to notice it, but continued the conversation.

" I perfectly agree with you in what you were saying of the use or abuse of truth," said he ; " but even that is not so dangerous as the delusions of falsehood and flattery, commonly called politeness and admiration."

" These are hard words to give to very agreeable things," answered Gertrude.

" My quarrel is not with the things themselves," said he, "but with their counterfeits."

" Yet, if every one were to tell another exactly what they thought of them, I dare say we should be all scratching each other's eves out."

" Not if ours was the charity that thinketh no evil."

" Oh ! that is to say, if we were all angels."

" No; it is to say, if we were all Christians." — Gertrude stared with some surprise ; for her idea of a Christian, like that of many other people's, was, that all were Christians who were bcrn in Christendom, had been baptized, learnt their creeds, and went now and then to church.

" I flatter myself I am a Christian," said she; " and yet I cannot help thinking there are people in the world who are very tiresome, very impertinent, and very disagreeable; yet, I don't think it would be a very Christian act were I to tell them so."

" Certainly not," answered Mr. Lyndsay with a smile ; " you may think them all those things; but if you think of them, at the same time, in the spirit of kindness and Christian benevolence, you will pity their infirmities, and you will have no inclination to hurt their feelings by telling them of faults which you cannot mend."

" But if I were asked — or suppose I were to ask you to tell me my faults ?"

" I should certainly endeavour to do it to the best of my ability."

" Well, pray, begin, I should like to have my character drawn in a Christianlike manner," said she, laughing.

" Yes; but I must have many sittings before I can attempt it. — I am not one of those nimble artists who can take striking likenesses in five minutes."

" So much the better; for they are always hideous performances ; but how long will you take to make a good full-length portrait of me, for I really long to see myself in my true colours — as a mere mortal, not as a goddess ?"

" You run no such risk with me, I assure you," said he; "but as to the time, that must depend upon circumstances and opportunities — perhaps in a year."

" A year ! " exclaimed Gertrude, — " O heavens! I shall die of impatience in a month — to be a whole year before I h^ar of a single fault!"

" I did not say so," replied Mr. Lyndsay; " as errors, like straws, you know, always float on the surface, I shall be able to pick up plenty of them, I have no doubt, very soon (if I have

F 3

not got hold of one or two already); but you would not have me pronounce upon your character from them ? — many pearls of great price may lie hid below."

" Which, I'm afraid, you will never discover," said Gertrude, laughing; " so, if my picture is not to be drawn till then, I fear I shall be wrinkled, and old, and ugly, before you have found a single gem to deck me with."

" I hope not," answered he : " you say you love truth and sincerity; these are jewels in themselves, and their light may lead even my darkened eyes (as you seem to think them) to discover more. But to drop metaphor, and speak in plain terms, — why, since we both profess to like truth, should we not agree to speak it to each other ? "

" With all my heart," answered Gertrude ; " but we must settle the preliminaries, draw up the code of laws, and swear to observe them:—in the first place, then, we must make a solemn vow on all occasions to speak the truth, and nothing but the truth, coute qu'il coute —in the second place, that nothing so said is to give mortal offence to the one party or the other — in the third, that however disagreeable we may think each other, we are to make a point of declaring it in the civilest and most Christianlike manner imaginable — in the fourth place "

" Beware," said Mr. Lyndsay, interrupting her, " of coming under any engagements, since Lord Bacon says, ' It asketh a strong wit and a strong heart to know when to tell the truth,' and you know not what a savage man you have to deal with; — no, let it be a discretionary compact, with mutual confidence its only guarantee ; " and he held out his hand. Gertrude gave him hers; and as she did so she was struck, for the first time, with the bland and beautiful expression of his countenance. " I never can fear you," said she, with a smile ; — but the conversation was broken off by the entrance of the rest of the family, and the consequent matin greetings that ensued. Colonel Delmour was the last who entered, and a shade of displeasure darkened his brow at finding the seat he considered as exclusively his own occupied by another. Gertrude observed his chagrin, and felt secretly flattered by it. The only vacant seat was one by Miss Pratt, who had hitherto restrained her tongue for the benefit of her ears, both of which had been on the full stretch,—the one to pick up certain little pieces of information, which it had reason to suppose were not intended for it; the other to make itself master of what was going on at the opposite side of the table between Miss St. Clair and Mr. Lyndsay.

It was wonderful how well these two members contrived to execute their respective ofiices, though certainly the chief merit was due to their mistress, who had trained these, her faithful servants, to such perfection in their calling that each of them, singly, could perform the work, and more than the work, of any ordinary pair of ears in the kingdom. What the industrious ear

had collected the active brain was not long of concocting, nor the nimble tongue of circulating. " You look very grave this morning, Colonel," said she, addressing her neighbour ; " I wish you had been here a little sooner, — it would have done your heart good to have seen and heard the fine flirtation that's been carrying on over the way," — with a significant nod to the opposite side of the table. " I can tell you Mr. Edward and a certain fair lady have been looking very sweet upon each other — it's not often he takes a flirting fit; but I'm really glad to see your godly people can be just like their neighours sometimes, and come as good speed, too, when they set about it. What do you think ? " — lowering her voice — " she's going to sit to him for her picture — a full-length, with pearls in her hair; and what do you think?"—still lower — " he's to make her a present of the pearls — there's for you! I've a notion they were his mother's, for I know she had a very fine set. — He did not seem inclined (to tell the truth) to part with them so soon, for I heard him say something about a year ; but, says she, with her pretty winning smile, what's the good of keeping things till one's old, and bald, and toothless, and can't enjoy them ? So much for French ease — who would expect that, to look at her? — But, my gracious! Colonel, do you see what you've done ? spilt your whole cup of coffee upon my good new gown — I wonder how you contrived it — and you're going to pour the cream upon me next," — pushing her chair from him with the greatest velocity.—"'Pon my word, one would think you did it on purpose."

Colonel Delmour made no attempt to vindicate himself from so foul an insinuation ; but, with his shoulder turned to the offended fair, lounged over the " Morning Post," as if quite unconscious of her presence. But, although he despised her too much to deign to express his disbelief of her communication, he was secretly provoked at the good understanding that seemed to exist between the cousins. He had too high an opinion of himself to have any fear of Lyndsay as a rival; but he had his own private reasons for wishing to have him kept at a distance, at least till he had secured, beyond a doubt, the affections of Miss St. Clair. Besides, he was one of those who disliked all interference with whatever object he chose to appropriate to himself, be it horse, hound, or heart. He, therefore, determined to put a stop to this growing intimacy, and to seize the first opportunity of bringing matters to an issue.

In the presence of Colonel Delmour and Miss Pratt, it was seldom Mr. Lyndsay had an opportunity of being duly appreciated, for in their company he was generally silent. Not that he had such a respect for their conversation as induced him to play the part of a mere listener; on the contrary, he gave little attention to either of them; but he was not a person to interrupt, or watch for a pause, or in any way seek to attract the

F 4

notice of the company. The unobtrusive qualities of his mind, therefore, did not strike upon the fancy v/ith the same glare as the more dazzling characteristics of Colonel Delmour; and where, as in the minute occurrences of domestic life, there are few or no opportunities of displaying the loftier and nobler attributes of mind, it can only be by slow and imperceptible degrees such a character gains upon the affections. A single sentence might have summed up his, in the brief but comprehensive words of an elegant writer — for of Lyndsay it might truly be said, that " he set an example of all the moral virtues without pride, and dared to be conspicuous for all the Christian graces without false shame." *

But Gertrude saw nothing of all this — she saw only that a gloom hung upon Colonel Delmour's brow, which she would fain have dispelled ; and for that purpose she would have lingered beyond the rest of the party, to have given him an opportunity of expressing his disquiet; but she was called away by her mother, to prepare for a visit to her uncle, Mr. Adam Ramsay.

CHAPTER XVII.

He 's a terrible man, John Tod, John Tod ;
He's a terrible man, John Tod ;
He scolds in the house,
He scolds at the door,
He scolds on the very high road, John Tod,
He scolds on the very high road, John Tod.
He's weel respeckit, John Tod, John Tod ;
He's weel respeckit, John Tod ;
Wi' your auld strippit coul,
You look maist like a fule ;
But there 's nouse in the lining, John Tod, John Tod,
But there's nouse in the lining, John Tod. Old Song.

The day was hot even to sultriness, and neither Mrs. St. Clair nor her daughter were inclined to converse, beyond a passing remark now and then on the heat, dust, road, sun, &c. Both, indeed, were too agreeably occupied with their own meditations for any interchange of thought. The former was busy revolving how she was to carry uncle Adam and his seventy thousand pounds by a coup de main; and, as a preliminary step, had provided herself with a French musical snuff-box, and a dozen of embroidered cambric pocket-handkerchiefs. But Mrs. St. Clair little knew the person she had to deal with, when she thought to propitiate him by any such sacrifices. Mr. Adam Ramsay was a man of a fair character and strong understanding, but particular temper and unpleasing manners — with a good deal

* Tour to Met, &c.

of penetration, which (as is too often the case) served no other purpose than to disgust him with his own species. He had left home pennyless, at an early period of life, to push his fortune in the world; and after having toiled and broiled for fifty years, he had returned to what was now become a stranger land, laden with wealth, which he had no longer even the wish to enjoy. He felt that he had lived in vain. He had no one to love — no one to share in his possessions ; and that only cordial which can give a relish even to the dregs of life, was not his — the treasures he had laid up were all of this world ; and to a childless cynical old man, perhaps great wealth is even more galling than great poverty. Yet there were good points in his character; and perhaps, had he been a husband and father, and had his heart been kept alive to the tender charities of life, he might have proved an amiable man, and an agreeable member of society. He possessed strong natural affections, which, though they had lain long dormant, were not yet extinct. • It was said that in early youth he had loved and been beloved by one as poor and as friendless, and somewhat lower in degree than himself; and that it was in the hope of gaining affluence for her he had crossed the seas, and sought his fortunes in a foreign land. But many are the disappointments that precede the fulfilment of our hopes, and many a year rolled on, and found Mr. Ramsay as poor as at the first; till, despairing of ever being able to return and claim his bride, he wrote to release her from her promise of awaiting his return. The fortune at length was made, but too late — the gay dreams of youth were fled for ever! —His mistress had married, and was dead ; and the sanguine adventurous stripling was grown into the soured misanthropic old man. Such was the outline of uncle Adam's story, and little more remains to be said of him.

He lived much alone, had all the habits of a recluse, and all the little peculiarities which are supposed to belong to single gentlemen of a certain age. In particular, he had an extreme dislike to receiving those delicate attentions which are sometimes so assiduously rendered to the rich and the childless. Not Timon himself was more tenacious in this respect than uncle Adam, or more disposed to buffet all whom he suspected of a design to prey upon his hoards. The house he now inhabited was one he had taken as a temporary residence on his first arrival; and although he had bought a fine estate with a suitable mansion in the immediate vicinity, and every day had purposed taking possession of it, yet each revolving term found him sitting in the selfsame parlour, in the selfsame chair, and in the selfsame frame of mind. It was at this suburban villa that the handsome equipage of the Earl of Rossville nov stopped. It was a small, vulgar, staring red house, with a plot of long bottle-green grass in front, and a narrow border of the coarsest of flowers (or rather flowering weeds, interspersed

with nettles), growing thin and straggling from a green slimy-looking soil, and covered with dust from the road—from which it was only separated by a railing. Mrs. St. Clair reddened with shame, as she marked the contemptuous air with which the consequential footman rapped on the humble door—for bell or knocker there was none. The door was speedily flung open to its farthest extent by a fat, rosy, stamping damsel, in a flaming gown and top-knots, who testified the greatest alacrity in doing the honours of the entrance.

" What a habitation for a man with seventy thousand pounds ! " exclaimed Mrs. St. Clair, as she entei'ed; but there was no time for pursuing her observations, for she was the next minute in the little parlour of uncle Adam. It was a small close room, with a meridian sun streaming full into it, and calling forth to view myriads of " dancing motes that people the sunbeams," while innumerable hosts of huge flies buzzed and revelled in all the luxury of its heat; and an expiring fire, with its usual concomitants of dust and ashes, seemed fast sinking beneath the influence of the god of day. A small dining-table, and a few hair-cloth chairs stuck against the walls, comprised the whole furniture of the room. A framed table of weights and measures, an old newspaper, and a parcel of dusty parchments tied with a red tape, formed its resources and decorations. Altogether it wore the comfortless aspect of a bad inn's w r orst parlour — a sort of place where one might pass five minutes while changing horses, but w r here there was no inducement even for the weary traveller to tarry.

Mr. Ramsay sat by the side of the expiring fire, seemingly contemplating the gaists and cinders which lay scattered over the hearth ; but he had somewhat the air of a man prepared (rather unwillingly) to receive company. He was above the middle size ; of a meagre form ; with high stooping shoulders ; sharp cross-looking elbows, projecting far beyond his back; a somewhat stormy, thin, blue face ; and little pale eyes, surmounted by shaggy white eyebrows. His ordinary head-piece, a striped woollen nightcap, had been laid aside for a capacious powdered peruke, with side curls and a long queue. To complete the whole, he was left-handed, which gave a peculiar awkwardness to his naturally ungainly deportment. He welcomed Mrs. St. Clair with a mixture of cordiality and awkwardness, as if he wished to be kind, but did not know very well how to set about it. She had too much manner, however, to allow him to remain under any embarrassment on that score ; and was squeezing uncle Adam's somewhat reluctant hand, and smiling on his rugged visage, and uttering a thousand soft and civil things to his rather averted ear, when suddenly she stopped, for she felt that all was thrown away : her uncle had fixed his eyes on Gertrude, and regarding her with visible emotion, seemed unconscious of every other object.

" Who is that ? " at lengh demanded he, in an agitated voice.

" Pardon me, my dear uncle," replied Mrs. St. Clair ; " but, in my happiness at seeing you, I forgot that my daughter was likewise a stranger to you."

" Your daughter !" exclaimed Mr. Ramsay,— " it's not possible !"

" Why so, my dear uncle ?" asked Mrs. St. Clair with a smile, and in full expectation of a gallant compliment on her own youthful appearance.

" She's the very picture of ; but you'll no mind Lizzie Lundie — bonny Lizzie Lundie ! " He gave a sort of growling sigh, and a pause followed. Visions of former days seemed to crowd into the old man's mind, and he went on as if communing with himself. " I little thought when I parted frae her, fifty year come Martinmas, that I had ta'en my last look o' Lizzie; and as little did I think, when I heard she was gane, that I should ever live to see her like in this warld — no that she just matches Lizzie neither;" and something like a tear gleamed, in his eye as he continued to gaze on the image of his youthful fancy. Gertrude's style of dress was such as helped to heighten the illusion: owing to the heat of the day, she had thrown off her bonnet, and the band that confined her hair wore almost the appearance of the snood which had been the prevailing fashion for damsels of Lizzie's degree in her day; her throat also was uncovered, and the whole contour of the head was thus displayed at once in all the simplicity of nature, and one more strikingly beautiful could scarcely be conceived.

Confused by the blunt admiration thus expressed for her, Gertrude looked to her mother, and, struck with the deadly paleness of her countenance, she hastily exclaimed, " Mamma, you are ill;" and Mrs. St. Clair, gasping for breath, sunk almost lifeless in her daughter's arms. — " Air, air," was all she could articulate ; and that certainly was the one thing needful in uncle Adam's apartment, for the atmosphere was indeed suffocating. The door and window were instantly thrown open; Gertrude held a glass of water to her mother's pallid lips; and Mr. Ramsay stuffed a bunch of southernwood into her powerless hand. At length these restoratives appeared to produce their effects, and Mrs. St. Clair slowly revived. Due apologies were of course made and accepted ; the uncommon heat of the day was much commented on, aod the closeness of the room delicately hinted at. Some refreshments, not of the choicest description, were now brought in by the great awkward heavy-footed maid-servant ; and Mr. Ramsay, taking a glass of wine, drank a welcome to his niece on her return to Scotland, " and to the bonny creature you've brought with you," added he, again fixing his eyes on Gertrude. " After all," continued he, " the thing's not impossible ; Lizzie was a relation of ours — a distant one to be sure ; let me see— Lizzie's father and my father were cousin-germans' bairns; but that'll no do, for it's by the other side o' the hoos —. it "was by my father."

Mrs. St. Clair's colour rose to the deepest crimson, and she seemed struggling to subdue her feelings. At length, making an effort at self-controul, she said with affected pleasantry — "I have no doubt my daughter has great reason to be flattered at the resemblance you have discovered for her; but, my dear uncle, you know there are certain prejudices — certain notions that some people entertain. In short, the thing to be talked of amongst ourselves is very -well, and it is very flattering to me that my daughter's looks should afford you pleasure; but I own I — I should be sorry — I would rather that a report of such a resemblance were not to reach the Rossville family ; they now consider my daughter as one of themselves; and their pride might be hurt, you know, and a prejudice created, that might prove highly detrimental to Gertrude's best interests."

" Set them up with their pride !" cried Mr. Ramsay — all softer emotions giving way to indignation; " their pride hurt, indeed, at being compared to Lizzie Lundie! — There's no a Rossville or a St. Clair among them that e'er I saw was fit to tie Lizzie Lundie's shoe — the queen upon the throne might have thought it an honour to be compared to Lizzie ;" — and the little chamber seemed as though it would not contain him in his wrath as he paced up and down its narrow bounds, with his hands crossed behind his back : all shyness and embarrassment had vanished in this burst of passion, and uncle Adam stood revealed in his own character. Then suddenly stopping — " And what would ha'e come o' ye if Lizzie Lundie had been what I ance thought she would ha'e been — my wedded wife ? — What would your Rossvilles ha'e done then ? — Would you ha'e thought it a disgrace then that your daughter should ha'e been likened to your uncle's wife ?"

" Oh ! this is too much !" exclaimed Mrs. St. Clair, bursting into tears.

" What's too much ? " cried he, continuing to walk up and down in great discomposure. Then suddenly stopping, and softening at sight of his niece's distress — " Come, Come — What's a' this for ? — waes me, ye ha'e suffered little in the warld if the hasty word o' an auld man can set ye off this way — ye'll ken me better by and bye than to mind a' that I say;" — then patting Gertrude on the shoulder, as she hung over her mother —" It's you that has made us cast out, and it's you that maun make us 'gree."

Gertrude took her mother's hand, and put it in her uncle's -he took it kindly; and Mrs. St. Clair, as soon as she found voice, said — " Excuse me, my dear uncle, I am ashamed of my weakness — but my nerves are now so shattered, and my spirits are not what they once were — I have a difficult part to play, and it is not surprising if In short, dependent as I am on the relations of my child — and that dear child's interest so much at stake too — you cannot wonder if I am sometimes driven — if I sometimes stoop — if I should sometimes tremble "

Mrs. St. Clair seemed at a loss to finish — hut her uncle saved her the trouble. — " Aye, aye, you have a proud thrawn pack to deal wi', I believe."

" Then you understand, my dear uncle, the reason of my wishing that "

" Aye, aye — ye needna be feared for me — but I maun aye think the likeness maist wonderful — maist wonderful — maist wonderful"— repeated he two or three times as he contemplated, and severally enumerated every feature, summing up the whole with, " Since I saw Lizzie Lundie, I've never seen the woman that I thought worth the looking at till now." At that moment a smart female figure, feathered and furbelowed, entered the little yard, and approached the house. — " There's ane o' the fule tribe," cried he; "my bonny niece, Miss Bell Black.— I ne'er see that craatur that I dinna wish myself blind, and deaf, and doited." And thereupon entered Miss Bell.

CHAPTER XVIII.

He had a sowre behaviour, and a tongue immoderately free and full of taunting. — Livy.

" What's brought you here, Miss Bell ?" was his salutation on entering; but nowise daunted with what, indeed, she was well accustomed to, she boldly shook hands with all around, and then showing a small basket—" I have brought you some very fine strawberries, uncle: they are the first we have had in our garden ; and I assure you I have had much ado to keep them from the children for you;" — and, with a consequential air, she disclosed some dozen or two of very so-so-looking strawberries.

" You had very little to do then," said Mr. Ramsay — "I wad na gi'e a bawbee for a' the berries in your garden — so ye may just tak them back to whar ye brought them frae; or stay, since ye ha'e robbed your brithers and sisters o' them, puir things, there's a barber's bairn twa doors aff that wad maybe be glad o' them — it's lying in the mizzles."

" Ton my word, uncle," said Miss Bell, in great indignation, " I have something else to do than to pick strawberries for barber's brats, indeed." — But uncle Adam, going to the door, called the maid; and giving her the strawberries, directed her to " carry the berries to Rob

Rattray's bairn, and to ask how he was." Miss Bell prudently turned a deaf ear to the message, and was apologizing, with all her powers of eloquence, to Mrs. St. Clair and her daughter for not having been to visit them. — " But the truth is," said she, with a well-got-up air of modesty, " that, in my situation, visiting is out of the question. If I were to go to one place, I should have to go everywhere; and the Major has so many connections in.the country, who, of course, would expect me to come to them, that it would be extremely unpleasant in my situation, where the thing is so well known. This, I assure you, is the only place I ever go to, as I think it a positive duty — (lowering her voice) — to pay attention to my uncle, poor man, and I am the only one of the family who understands his ways and can manage him." Mr. Ramsay, having for the moment appeased the antipathy he bore his niece by the insult he had offered her, was now restored to something like good humour. " Weel, Miss Bell," said he, " what have you made of your nawbob — your swain — your loveyer— your what-do-ye-call-him ? "

" If you mean the Major," said Miss Bell, with dignity, " he walked into town with me, and is gone to look at a pair of carriage-horses that are for sale at the White Bear; I suppose he will be here in a little ;"—then drawing back from the window with a face of alarm, as a carriage passed—

" I really wish, uncle, if you mean to remain here, you would get a blind for your window, for every body is seen in this room ; and in my situation it is not very pleasant, I assure you, to be exposed to everybody that passes ; — that was the Bog-hall carriage that passed just now, and they must think it very odd to have seen me sitting here when I declined an invitation to dinner there for to-morrow, upon the plea that I went nowhere at present."

" Then what brings you here, if you're no fit to be seen ?" demanded uncle Adam in a most wrathful accent.

" I must confess, my dear uncle," said Mrs. St. Clair, glad of an opening for expressing her sentiments, and, at the same time, softening the tone of the conversation, " this house does not seem quite suitable for you."

" What ails the house ? " asked he sharply.

" I beg pardon, I understood (perhaps I was misinformed) that you were the proprietor of a charming place in this neighbourhood."

" Weel?" This was put in so startling a manner that Mrs. St. Clair's courage failed her, and she feared to reply; —not so Miss Bell.

" Well! to think of any body in their senses living in this' little, vulgar, shabby hole, when they have such a house as Broom Park standing empty—I assure you, uncle, it has a very odd appearance in the eyes of the world."

"Miss Bell Black, you that's such a wise, sensible, weel-informed woman, that kens aw thing, will you just ha'e the good-ness to tell me what are the eyes of the warld, and wbar do they stand ? For muckle I ha'e heard of the eyes o' the warld, but I ha'e never been able to see them yet;" and Mr. Ramsay fixed his upon her, while he advanced his face almost close to her, and put his hands on his knees, in a manner that seemed to say, " Answer me this before you stir."

Miss Bell hesitated a little. —" Why, I can only tell you, uncle, that Lord Fairacre was quite confounded when the Major told him you had never taken possession of Broom Park yet, and said it was most extraordinary that you should continue to live in a house that was hardly good enough for a dog-kennel; and Boghall, who was present, said, he did not believe the whole house was the size of his kitchen, and the Major himself I know thinks "

" And so these are the eyes of the warld!" cried Mr. Ramsay, with a sort of growling sardonic laugh; " pretty eyes they are, to be sure, to drive a man out of his ain hoose ! — The ane a poor silly spendthrift, the t'ither a great gormandizing swash, and the third — but how comes the world to have but three eyes ? — can you no mak out a fourth ? — I beg your pardon, I suppose your ain was to be the fourth, and that makes aw right, for then ye can gi'e the world twa faces — Fairacre's and Bog-hall on the ae face, Major Waddell and Miss Bell Black on the t'ither ;" — then in a lower key, and muttering to himself, " Spendthrifts and ne'er-do-weels on the ae side, fules and taw-pies on the t'ither,—a true picture o' the warld!"

Any other than Miss Bell would certainly have given in here ; but Miss Bell was one of those gifted mortals who are quite invulnerable to the shafts of envy, hatred, or malice, when it is their interest to be so; and though she did look a little hot and disconcerted for a few minutes, she quickly rallied, and resumed—

" I assure you, uncle, whatever you may think, the opinion of the world is not to be despised."

" Miss Bell Black, I have lived rather longer in the warld than you have done, and I've seen rather mair o't than you're ever likely to see — and I would nae gi'e that," snapping his fingers, " for either its gude word or its ill •, it canna say that ever I oppressed them that were beneath me, or cringed to them that were aboon me,— or that I ever wranged ony creature o' a boddle,—or that I ever said the thing I didna think; and if either 3*011 or your warld think I'm to be dictated to in my ain hoose, you're much mistaken."

" Well, uncle, I can only say I think it is a great pity that so fine a place as Broom Park should be standing empty ; and since you seem resolved not to live at it yourself, there's many a one, I assure you, would be glad to take it off your hands. The Major has been looking at Elm Grove — but I think there is no comparison between Broom Park and it."

" What then?" demanded Mr. Ramsay.

" O, nothing. Only if you had any thoughts of letting it, it is such a Paradise, that "

" I could be at nae loss for an Adam and Eve to put in it," interrupted her uncle; your nawbob and you, for instance," with a growling grin ;—" but I can tell you, ye'll no play your gambols there if I can help it."

Miss Bell looked very indignant as she replied, " As to that, the Major cares very little about the matter ; if I am pleased, that is all he is anxious about, and the rent is no object, but I find it very difficult to get a place to suit us in every respect — but here is the Major himself," — and the Major was presently ushered in. Mr. Ramsay received him with tolerable civility; and Mrs. St. Clair, desirous of receiving his vote at the approaching election, was preparing the way by a soft speech about nothing. But Miss Bell never permitted the Major to speak to, or look at, or listen to any body else when she was present, and she therefore called him off, with — "Well, Major, did you see the carriage-horses, and what do you think ofthem?"

" They seem good serviceable horses—not particularly handsome," replied he.

" What colour ? — I'll thank you for a glass of water, Major."

" Pray — allow me to put a little wine in it.

" The least drop — and you think they will do ?— Oh ! not so much."

" That is not for me to decide," replied the Major, with a bow — which was graciously acknowledged with a smile. " Perhaps you will take a look ofthem yourself?"

" Why in my situation,"—in a modest key—"I hardly think I should like to go to the White Bear. — Major, will you take this glass ? "

" But I shall desire the ostler to bring them up here ; 'tis but a step from the stables

" I'm for none of your horses brought to my door," cried Mr. Ramsay ; "it will be through the town I'm setting up my chaise next, and a bonny hullybaloo there'll be," and he paced the room in great perturbation at the bare supposition of such a thing.

" My dear sir," — began the Major, but he was cut short ■with —

" Now I'm for none of your horses at my do^r."

" Bless me, uncle !" cried Miss Bell, " I think you may be very well pleased to get the credit of a carriage at such an easy rate."

" Great credit to be sure ! — to get the credit of being an auld ostentatious fule."

" Such nonsense, uncle !—at any rate, I thought you did not care what the world said of you."

" You thought! " repeated uncle Adam, with the most sovereign contempt; "and what entitles you to think?—but ye

need say nae mair aboot it — there's to be nae horses brought to my door. If ye maun ha'e horses, ye maun gang to the horse-market for them, like other folk — I'm no to ha'e my house turned into a White Bear."

" My dear sir " said the Major.

" In my situation "— interrupted Miss Bell — " it would have

a very odd appearance in the eyes of the world " But here

Mrs. St. Clair interposed, by offering to chaperon her niece to the White Bear in Lord Rossville's carriage, hoping to be repaid for this civility by securing the Major's vote. The offer, after a little affected demur, was accepted, and the Major was despatched to have the horses in readiness.

" I really think, uncle, you might dispense with a fire now," remarked Miss Bell, as she rose to depart.

" Do ye ken naething else I could dispense wi'?" demanded Mr. Ramsay, with a look and emphasis that might have made a tortoise fly : — not so Miss Bell, who still lingered in the desperate hope of showing her consequence, and proving her influence over uncle Adam and his seventy thousand pounds.

" Well, uncle, when are we to see you at Bellevue ? "

" I would prefer my claim for a visit," said Mrs. St. Clair, with her most winning smile ; " but Lord Rossville intends nimself to have the pleasure of calling upon you, and "

" In hopes of getting my vote," interrupted Mr. Ramsay, impatiently; " but he may just save himself the trouble—I'm no gaun to be hunted out o' my senses by your election hounds. — I'll gi'e my vote to wha I like, or may be I'll keep it to mysel—but there's ae thing I can tell you, it's no to be had for the asking."

Mrs. St. Clair prudently received this rebuff in silence ; but Miss Bell plucked up fresh spirit at witnessing another's discomfiture, and taking her uncle by the breast of the coat, and drawing him back, she began in an under tone of voice, as if desirous of not being overheard,—

" By-the-by, uncle, talking of votes, there's one thing that I

feel very anxious about; and that is, that the Major and you

should concert something together as to your votes—it would

. be extremely awkward, I think, if you were to take different

sides, and have a very odd appearance in the eyes of the world."

Whatever uncle Adam's thoughts might be, his looks portended a storm ready to burst forth; but as Gertrude turned towards him, to wish him good morning, his features relaxed, and his frown gradually softened into something like a smile.

" The eyes of the world!" repeated he ^ "I would na gi'e a glisk o' thae bonny een of yours for aw the eyes o' the weld put thegither, — and dinna you, my dear, let the eyes o' the world scare you, as they ha'e done mony a ane, frae your ain happiness. Now, fare ye week my dawtie," patting her shoulder; " an' I'll say to you what I wad na say to mony — I'll aye be glad to see you, come when you like — fare ye weel. — Gude morning to you, Miss Bell; and ye may tak the eyes o' the world on your back, and muckle gude may they do ye ;" — and, with a laugh of derision, uncle Adam saw his visitors drive off, and returned to his little dusty sunny parlour, elate with the triumph of having defied the world and its eyes.

But before parting with Mr. Ramsay, we must here observe, that he is not the only one who has attempted to walk as if uncontrolled by the scan of that dread power, commonly called the eyes of the world. Few, if any, however, have ever arrived at entire emancipation from its influence, which extends more or less over all mankind. Uncle Adam flattered himself that he was one of the happy few who had escaped from its thraldom — but, alas ! poor man, its yoke was still upon him, and, unconscious of its chains, he hugged himself in his freedom. He cared not, indeed, that the world should call him a miser — he cared not that the world should call him a churl—he cared not that the world should call him odd—he cared not that the world should say he lived in a mean house, or wore a shabby hat, or an old-fashioned wig ; but he cared lest the world should think he cared for the world — or lest the world should say that he was vain, or proud, or ostentatious, or expensive; and it was this which made him often deny himself many a little comfort, many a harmless gratification, many an innocent desire he had in common with that world he so much despised. To be free from the eyes of the world has been the aim of many, but the attainment of few. Man is not born to be free ; and when all restraint is laid aside, the wickedness of the human heart displays itself in the most hideous forms. 'Tis to the Christian alone that such freedom belongs ; and he only can say, " J'e crains Dieu et rCai point d'autre crainter

CHAPTER XIX.

A merry going out often bringeth a mournful return ; and a joyful morning a sad evening. — Thomas a Kempis.

During their progress to the White Bear, Miss Bell indemnified herself for the mortifications she had received from her uncle by expressing herself in terms of the greatest pity and contempt for him.

" Poor man !" said she, " I really feel for him, — for you must know it is alleged I am his great favourite ; and when that is the case, of course one will put up with a great deal. Indeed, for my part, I know his temper so well, I never should think of being affronted at any thing he could say; but I own I am sometimes afraid of the Major — a man of his rank is not to be tampered with; and he has such a high spirit, there is no saying how he might resent any thing the least like disrespect to me, though I know my poor uncle is far from meaning any thing of the kind. It is entirely his manner, for I have been told he speaks very handsomely of me behind my back; and when that is the case, one should not mind what is said to their face. However, in my situation, it is certainly not pleasant; and when I am a married woman, the thing must be put a stop to."

Here Mrs. St. Clair put a stop to that subject by introducing the one uppermost in her thoughts, that of the election, and requesting her niece to use her influence with her lover on the occasion. But Miss Bell, like all fools, had her share of cunning, as well as of consequence ; and she was aware that the more doubts and difficulties she could attach to the Major's vote, the more the Major's importance and her own importance would be increased ; and she therefore made answer,—

"Why, really aunt, to tell you the truth, the Major has a very difficult part to act; and it will require no small management, I assure you, both in him and me, to avoid giving offence to one side or the other. Connected as he is with the Fairacre and Boghall families, it will be a strong step in him to give his vote to the opposite party. At the same time, I know I have only to say the word to secure him for my friends ;— but, as I said to him, the world might reflect upon me, were I to make use of my influence in so important a matter. Besides, you know, aunt, I can say nothing till the Major has been waited upon by Lord Rossville, and has been paid proper attention to •by the family ; and it would also be right, I think, if some of the ladies were to be introduced to his sister, Mrs. Fairbaira, a very sweet woman, who lives a little way from this."

But here the carriage drove up to the "White Bear, where neither the Major nor the horses were to be seen ; but they were told both would be forthcoming presently. There was nothing for it, therefore, but to wait patiently in the midst of the usual assemblage that is to be seen lounging at an inn door—hostlers, drivers, stable-boys, beggars, waiters, travellers, &c. &c. &c.

"This is very unpleasant," said Miss Bell. "I wonder how the Major could think of exposing a person in my situation in this manner. I am sure I would rather have gone without carriage-horses than have had all these people's eyes upon me. There is one man, I declare he stares in such a manner I don't know where to look. I wonder what he means — I really wish he would bestow his attention on somebody else ; — but, perhaps, cousin, he's one of your French beaux ? "

Mrs. St. Clair and Gertrude both looked in the direction pointed out by Miss Bell, and both were struck by the appearance of the person in question, or rather by the earnest scrutinizing look with which he regarded the party; for, although

handsome, there was nothing very striking either in his dress or figure—nothing that was even indicative of the station to which he might he supposed to belong. He was a man seemingly-turned of thirty, but might be more ; with a sunburnt complexion — long ill-cut hair — handsome, though rather hawk nose, and keen bright black eyes. Taken singly, his features had no peculiarity in them; but there was something in the general expression of the countenance of a marked and unpleasing character.

"I have surely seen that face before," said Mrs. St. Clair, endeavouring to recollect when and where.

"I'm sure he won't forget some of ours," said Miss Bell; |* for I really never saw any thing so impudent as the manner in which he stares ; and such a shabby-looking creature, all covered with dust! I dare say he is just off the top of some coach—I'm sure if the Major catches him staring so impudently at me — but here comes the Major and the carnage-horses — don't they look very well?"—and then ensued a colloquy between the lovers.

"How do you like your steeds, Isabella ?"

"Not mine, Major—you know I have nothing to do with them ; but what do you think of them yourself? "

"My thoughts must be guided entirely by your taste."

"Very gallant indeed!"—and so forth in the usual style of some such silly pair.

The stranger all the while kept his station, after asking a question of one of the servants ; but his looks, which at first had wandered from one or other of the party, finally rested on Gertrude, with an expression which it was impossible to comprehend or define. It was neither admiration, nor curiosity, nor pleasure, nor any of the common emotions which a stranger might be supposed to entertain; but his countenance assumed a sort of smile of exultation, no less strange than offensive. In some displeasure at so rude and persevering a gaze, Gertrude raised her hand to pull down the blind, when, suddenly springing forward, he laid his hand on the door of the cai'riage.

" What insolence!" exclaimed Mrs. St. Clair. The stranger looked at her for a moment with a bitter, contemptuous smile ; then said—

" I would speak with you."

" Speak, then—say what is your business?" answered she, somewhat impatiently.

" You wouldn't choose me to speak out before the ladies, I guess," replied the man, with a still more familiar look and manner. Miss Bell's body and soul were both half out of the opposite side of the carriage, as she leaned over communing with the Major. Mrs. St. Clair, therefore, answered haughtily—

" You can have nothing to say to me that my daughter may not hear."

" Possible !" exclaimed the stranger in an ironical tone. " So then " Mrs. St. Clair involuntarily bent her head towards him, and the rest of the sentence was whispered in her ear, when, uttering a half-stifled shriek, she sunk back pale, trembling, and convulsed.

" What's the matter?" ci'ied Miss Bell, turning round.

" Mamma has been frightened by that strange-looking man," answered Gertrude, in a low voice.

" Bless me!" cried Miss Bell, " such nonsense to be frightened for any man when the Major is here."—Then in a loud key—> " Major, I wish you would ask that person what he wants?"

" Not for the world!" exclaimed Mrs. St. Clair, suddenly starting up in the most extreme agitation — "I know him—I have seen him before — I—I must speak to him myself," gasped she, as she motioned to have the carriage door opened.

" Oh, mamma!" cried Gertrude, taking her mother's trembling hand to detain her—"you are unable — allow me;" but her mother seemed not to hear her, as, with the assistance of the servants, she alighted, and, with an unsteady step, drew near the stranger, who had withdrawn a few paces from the carriage, apart from the bystanders.

" Good gracious!" exclaimed Miss Bell, in a whisper to Gertrude — "I see my aunt is terrified at the thoughts of involving the Major with that man ; and, to be sure, if he had only seen how he stared at me, I dare say he would have knocked him down, so it's better she should speak to him herself, as I am under her protection at present, you know."

Gertrude made no reply ; and Miss Bell, too much interested in her carriage-horses to bestow her attention on any mere human concerns, quickly returned to the discussion of hoofs, tails, manes, &c. Mrs. St. Clair, meanwhile, having exchanged a few words with the stranger, returned to the carriage, still bearing visible signs of great mental disquiet.

" So, aunt, you have very soon disposed of your beau," began Miss Bell, no less deficient in common observation than in delicacy. " Dear me! are we driving away, and nothing settled about the carriage-horses yet! — and where's the Major ? — Major —Major—stop, driver, for theMajor;" and presently the Major's willow-green visage presented itself, panting with the exertion of running after the carriage.

" I can make nothing of that fellow," said he, addressing Mrs. St. Clair; " he seems a most confounded insolent dog. If I had been a justice of the peace, I should certainly have committed him."

"I think you would have done quite right," said Miss Bell; "and I really think, aunt, you were a great deal too soft with him. What did he say to you, Major?"

"O, he was confoundedly impertinent: and if I had had my bamboo, I should certainly have laid it across his shoulders."

"Well, I dare say it was better that you got out to speak to him yourself than that the Major should have taken him in hand; but he would have deserved it," said Miss Bell, "if it had only been for his impudence in staring at me in the manner he did— but, by-the-by, did not you say you knew him, aunt?"

Mrs. St. Clair's colour had undergone many variations during this conversation, and Gertrude thought she read torture in every feature and lineament of her countenance. But in a voice which she vainly tried to render firm and composed, she replied, "I have seen him before only once, and that under circumstances of distress in my husband's." Here her emotion choked her utterance; and Miss Bell and the Major, who were no nice observers, ascribed her agitation to the only legitimate source of a widow's tears, the remembrance of her departed lord; and not being at all in a mood to sympathise in any such sorrowful feelings, Miss Bell proposed to alight and walk home with her lover, which was readily acceded to by her aunt. "I trust I shall soon have the pleasure of presenting Mrs. Waddell to you," said the Major in a half whisper to Mrs. St. Clair.

"Upon my word, Major, you are too bad," said his fair, affecting to turn away in displeasure.

"Have you bespoke your cousin's good offices on the occasion, my love?" asked the inamorato, in still softer accents.

"No — I really, Major — you know there is no hurry"

"I beg your pardon, I know just the reverse," replied the gallant Major; but Mrs. St. Clair, sick of their vulgar airs, here wished the happy pair good morning; and making a sign to the servant, the carriage bounded away, leaving them far behind. Gertrude naturally expected that her mother would now give some explanation of the strange mysterious scene that had taken place, though she had too much delicacy to express any curiosity on the subject; but Mrs. St. Clair remained silent and abstracted during the whole drive, and was only roused from her musings by the sudden stopping of the carriage as it drew up at the castle.

"Home already!" exclaimed she, looking round as if awakened from a dream — then in a languid oppressed voice, "Gertrude, I am ill — but I want no attentions," waving her off; they can do me no good." Colonel Delmour, who had been lounging on the lawn with his dogs, was now hastening towards them. "Gertrude," continued she, grasping her daughter's hand, — "be silent on the events of this day, as you value my life" Gertrude shuddered; but the next moment her hand was pressed in that of Colonel Delmour, as he assisted her to alight, and her mother's fearful words were almost driven from her thoughts by the raptures he expressed at her return. His words were too delightful not to be listened to, and she loitered a few minutes on the steps. "Is it possible," thought she, as she looked on her lover, "that this elegant graceful being can belong to the same species with an uncle Adam or a Major Waddell!" Colonel Delmour saw that he had lost nothing by her absence; and as her mother turned to call her, he ventured to whisper somewhat of a more serious import than he had yet done: — Gertrude blushed, smiled, and was gone.

CHAPTER XX.

What silence hides, that knowest thou. Gaky's Dante.

On joining her mother in her apartment, Gertrude found her walking to and fro in that manner which plainly indicates great mental disquiet. She continued to pace backwards and forwards for some time, as if lost in thought; then suddenly stopping, she said, somewhat abruptly — " Gertrude, do you remember your nurse ?"

" Ah, mamma! can I ever forget her ?" replied her daughter, tears springing to her eyes at the remembrance of all the care and teDderness she had experienced for years from the faithful creature.

" Yes, I know you were very fond of her, and she of you. Well, the stranger who caused me so great an alarm to-day was her husband."

" Her husband, mamma!" repeated Gertrude. " He looks very young! And I thought her husband had been dead many years ago ?"

" I thought so too; but unfortunately it is not so — I say unfortunately, for he is likely to prove a troublesome appendage to us—those sort of people are always unreasonable; and he seems to think his wife's care and attention to you, and her long services in the family, give him a claim upon our gratitude, which I fear I shall not find easy to answer. In short, he seems a needy rapacious man, urgent for money, which I have not to give, and yet am loth to refuse."

" It is certainly my duty to do something for him, mamma," answered her daughter; " but you know I have nothing in my own power—all I can do is to speak to my uncle for him "

" No, no," cried Mrs. St. Clair, impatiently, " that will never do ;" and she resumed her pacing up and down.

" Why may I not ask Lord Rossville to assist him, mamma?" inquired Gertrude, in some surprise. " Surely the husband of my nurse, of one whom I loved so dearly, has a right to expect something from us ? " .

" Something — yes, something — but what is that something to be?—How much money have you got at present, Gertrude?"

Her daughter named the sum, which was a very trifling one. " What shall I do ? " exclaimed her mother with the look and

g 4

accent of despair; " how shall I ever be able to raise a sufficient sum "

" Dear mamma! why should you distress yourself so much about it ? — only suffer me to speak to my uncle "

" Gertrude, you will drive me mad—have I not told you that it would be destruction to me to breathe a syllable of this matter to any human being!"

" Destruction, mamma ! " repeated her daughter in astonishment, not unmixed with terror at her mother's vehemence.

" Bring me what money you have — every sous, and no questions — you will perhaps know all soon enough," murmured she, throwing herself into a chair, as if exhausted with the violence of contending emotions; then rousing herself as her daughter was leaving the room to obey her, — " And fetch me your ornaments, Gertrude — all of them — quick, no more words ; " — and she waved her hand impatiently for her to begone. Gertrude was too well acquainted with her mother's imperious manner to attempt any remonstrance, but she could not conceal the astonishment and reluctance with which she set about obeying her. Having collected all the money and the few jewels she possessed, she brought them to her mother.

" Surely, mamma," said she, " it cannot be necessary for me to give my ear-rings and bracelets to my nurse's husband ? The money he is welcome to ; but really I am churlish enough to grudge him my trinkets."

" Keep them, then," said Mrs. St. Clair, pushing them from her with contempt — " keep the paltry baubles, since it is too great a sacrifice to part with them even to a parent."

" O, mamma, what cruel words! — I spoke in jest — take them — take all — every thing that I have ;" and she drew the rings off her fingers, and unclasped those in her ears.

" No, no," said her mother, in the same cold bitter tone, "keep your precious gewgaws — you surely would not give your pearl necklace to save me from ruin ? — that would be too much, indeed!"

Mrs. St. Clair well knew how to turn to her own purposes the quick generous temper of her daughter.

Stung to the soul by her mother's reproaches, Gertrude burst into tears ; she besought her forgiveness — she implored her to take the baubles, till at length she prevailed; and what Gertrude would, in other circumstances, have considered a sacrifice, she now looked upon as a privilege ; — so differently do things appear, according to the state of our minds.

To show that I do not exact more from you than I do from myself," said Mrs. St. Clair, going to her jewel-case, " I too must part with all I possess;" and she took out all her own ornaments, and began putting them up along with those of her daughter. Gertrude assisted with a good grace, for she was still in a state of excitement. She saw all her elegant and fashionable bijouterie — all the cherished tokens of rememhrance — all the little gifts she had received from far-distant friends and companions, one hy one folded up, and she still felt only joy in the thought that she had parted -with them for her mother; but she could not suppress a sigh when she came to an old-fashioned hair-brooch, in the form of a heart, set round with garnets — " That was the gift of my dear nurse," said she timidly, " and she made me promise that I never "

" Would part with it," subjoined Mrs. St. Clair. " Well, keep your promise and your locket, Gertrude, it is of little value — it can make no difference — surely he would not grudge vou that."

" He !" repeated Gertrude indignantly— "it is not for him, it is for you — but why ? "— she stopped, and looked inquiringly in her mother's face.

" Gertrude, it is natural that your curiosity should be excited by what you have seen and heard, and the time may come — perhaps too soon—when it will be amply gratified; but when it is, I tell you that it will — it must be at the expense of my life.

— Now speak — ask what you will, and I will answer you; but it must be on these terms."

" Oh, mamma! what a wretch you must think me!" said Gertrude, again giving way to her tears. — " Headstrong — perverse

— disobedient — you may have found me, but surely I do not deserve such killing words. Would that I could share in your distresses, whatever they are, if by sharing I could lessen them!"

Mrs. St. Clair shook her head, and sighed deeply. " I believe you, Gertrude — I know you are superior to the meanness of mere curiosity, and I think I may rely on your affection — may I not ?"

Her daughter answered by throwing herself into her mother's arms, and Mrs. St. Clair pressed her to her bosom with emotions of tenderness and affection, such as she had never before displayed. When she regained her composure, she said, —

"Now, my love, we understand each other; you are aware that my reserve proceeds from no distrust of you. I feel that your forbearance is the result of your affection for me — henceforth all that you have to do is to prove your sincerity by your silence. You bave only to promise that you will never disclose what you have witnessed, or what you may yet witness in my conduct, that may seem strange and mysterious, and that you will never reveal what I have now told you about that man — neither his name, nor his connection with us, must you ever breathe, as you value my life."

Gertrude promised—solemnly promised; and her mother again tenderly embraced her, declaring herself satisfied.

"You know not what a load it takes from my mind to find you thus prudent, tractable, and confiding — with feeling enough to participate in my vexations — with delicacy to repress all idle curiosity —with affection to assist me in my difficulties.— May Heaven reward you, Gertrude, for all you have done and will do for me ! And now," continued she, as she finished the packet she had been making up, " I am going to give you a yet stronger proof of the trust I place in you. This packet must be delivered to-night to the person for whom it is destined. I have promised to meet him at the temple, near the end of the lime avenue, next the deer-park, at eleven o'clock, and you must accompany me — the family will then be at supper — I shall plead a headach — alas! no vain pretext I"— and she pressed her daughter's hand to her throbbing temples — " as an excuse for retiring to my room — you will of course attend me, and we shall then find no difficulty in stealing out unperceived. I know all you would say, Gertrude," continued she, in a quick impatient tone, as she read her daughter's disapprobation in the glow that mantled on her cheek ; " but there is no alternative — it must be so — yet if you repent your promise, I am ready to release you from it, though my ruin should ensue. — Speak, do you wish to be free ? "

Gertrude could not speak, but she gave her mother her hand in token of her submission, then turned shuddering away. Her mother again caressed her.

"Be composed, my love — all will yet go well — let us dress for dinner," continued she, as her maid entered for the purpose of preparing her toilette. Then whispering, " Try to look cheerful, my love — remember looks may betray a secret as well as words: put some flowers in your hair, and make yourself at least look gay for my sake — do, my sweetest!"

Gertrude sighed, and they separated.

CHAPTER XXI.

Plus sonat quam valet.

More sound than sense. Seneca.

It would have argued ill for Gertrude if she could have obeyed her mother's injunctions, and looked the thing she was not. Time and suffering may teach us to repress our feelings; but the young and untried heart can with difficulty learn to conceal them. The most ingenuous and upright mind may practise self-controul; but it is only the artful and the mean who will ever stoop to dissimulation. Agitated and perplexed, in vain she strove to appear tranquil and disengaged — the very attempt sei'ved only to defeat the purpose. The more she thought of her mother's strange mysterious behaviour—and of what else could she think ? — the more bewildered she became in the maze of her own fancy; till at length, despairing of regaining self-possession from her own secret communings, she hastened to seek it in company, and, quickly dressing herself, she descended to the drawing-i'oom.

It required no great share of penetration to discover that something more than common was passing in her mind. Her varying colour— her clouded brow — her thoughtful yet wandering eye, so different from the usual open, bland expression of her countenance, plainly indicated the state of her feelings.

Lord Rossville, Mr. Delmour, and Mrs. St. Clair were at the farther end of the room in earnest conversation. She was giving such an account of her visit to Mr. Ramsay, and her meeting with Major Waddell, as suited her own purposes; and she dilated so much upon the difficulties and importance of their votes, and the management that would be requisite to secure them, that she at last succeeded (no very difficult matter) in completely mystifying at least one of her auditors. In short, she convinced Lord Rossville, and almost persuaded his nephew, that the whole issue of the election depended upon her and her family.

" I have a strange headstrong set of beings to deal with," said she ; " but I think, with a little address and a good deal of attention, we shall prevail at last."

" On such an occasion," said his lordship, " neither ought to be wanting, my dear madam. I natter myself we are none of us deficient in the the former qualification, and the latter depends entirely upon ourselves. To-morrow Mr. Delmour and I shall make a point of waiting upon such of your relatives and connections as " Mr. Delmour here took out his memorandum-book, and began to write down the names of Major Waddell, Mr. Ramsay, and Mr. Black, in his list for the following day. " I wish we could secure your uncle," said he to Mrs. St. Clair; — then turning to Lord Rossville, — " I find he is the purchaser of the superiorities of Deafknows, which, with Tonglands and Kilspindie, might, with ease, be split certainly into four, but I think, probably, into five qualifications ; these on our side would make it quite a hollow business — don't you think so ? "

" Why, in all human probability, it would," replied his lordship ; — " at the same time, we must be cautious how we admit or mistake mere probabilities for absolute certainties — in all such cases there must ever be contingencies, which it is impossible, or at least extremely difficult, to foresee or guard against. It is a matter of doubt with me whether Mr. Ramsay has yet been infeft in these lands of Kindyford and Caulfauld, and whether there is not a wadset on the lands of Ogilface and Haggiescape. In all likelihood, our opponents are using every means to bring some such corps de reserve into the field. Also, I understand, there were two new claims preferred for enrolment on the lands of Stonykirk and Kilnettles at the last meeting of freeholders ;

and we may reasonably conclude that the roll will be still farther augmented by the adverse party — that is, if it is possible for them to do so."

While this colloquy, and much more of the same kind, was carrying on at one end of the room, the other presented Lady Betty, spread out in full dress on a sofa, with Flora by her side, and Colonel Delmour and Mr. Lyndsay at a little distance engaged in some debate. Gertrude, on entering, almost unconsciously seated herself at one of the windows, apart from every body ; but she was immediately joined by her cousins. Colonel Delmour remarked, with secret satisfaction, the agitation of her look and manner. He imputed it entirely to the declaration he had ventured to make, which he thought had probably given rise to some discussion betwixt her mother and her, and which he had no doubt would end, as all such discussions between mother and daughter generally do, in favour of the lover. But this was not precisely the time when he wished his pretensions to be publicly known—and he was rather desirous that Miss St. Clair's emotion should pass unobserved.

Colonel Delmour's manner, however, although guarded and respectful, nevertheless carried with it that nameless something which made even the object of his professed idolatry feel he had gained an ascendency over her, and that the worshipped was also the worshipper. While he leant on the back of her chair Mr. Lyndsay once or twice addressed some remark to her, but, absent and occupied, she scarcely seemed to hear him.

" Is it to-day that you would have me begin to sketch your portrait ? " said he, with a smile.

" No—not to-day," replied she, in some confusion.

" And why not ? To paint from nature, one must take nature in all her various moods and aspects."

" But I don't love stormy cloudy pictures," said Gertrude, with a sigh.

Colonel Delmour looked reproachfully at her as he whispered, " Strange that this day, which has been the brightest in my life, should seem cloudy to you.—Ah, Gertrude! why do we not view it with the same eves ?"

at

Gertrude blushed deeply, but remained silent,

" What o'clock is it ? " inquired Lady Betty.

" Seven minutes to six," said Miss Pratt, as she entered, and, tripping past Lady Betty, joined the group in the window. " Any thing new going on here ? — It's changed days with you, Colonel, to be in the drawing-room before dinner — we seldom used to see you till the first course was going away." Surveying Gertrude from head to foot, " What's come over you to-day, my dear? You're not looking like yourself. — I think you've got too many of these passion-flowers in your head. — Mr. Edward, you must not take your cousin's picture to-day, or else she must part with some of these passion-flowers—I really don't think

they're becoming—just let me take out that one " and she

was preparing to lay her hands upon it, when hers were seized by Colonel Delmour.

" Bless me, Colonel! don't be so violent; I'm sure I wasn't going to take off Miss St. Clair's head;—they may well be called passion-flowers, for they really seem to have put you in a fine passion — and you've crumpled all my ruff, and squeezed one of my fingers to the bone."

Colonel Delmour, colouring a little at the transport of indignation he had given way to, affected to laugh it off, and, releasing Miss Pratt's hands from his grasp, said in a loud whisper,—

" I beg pardon if, in the ardour of my passion, I did press your hands too—too tenderly — impute the blame "

" I don't know what you mean, Colonel Delmour," cried Miss Pratt aloud, as she stroked down her ruff and caressed her injured finger with every appearance of ill-humour; " but I know you've left your marks upon me in a pretty manner. I didn't know Miss St. Clair's head had been your property, or, I assure you, I would'nt have offered to touch it — but I know if she's wise, she'll take care how she trusts you with her hand, after seeing how you've used mine," and she held up a red angry-looking finger, and shook her ruff— " and only look at my ruff!

" What's the matter with your ruff ? " asked Lady Betty; " it looks very neat, I think."

" Neat! it was more than neat; but Colonel Delmour has spoiled the seat of it, and I'll have to get it all goffered over again."

" By-the-by, Miss Pratt," said Colonel Delmour, " since you denounce me as the destroyer of your ruff—it is a deed for which I think I merit the thanks of all pious, well-disposed persons in general, and of the kirk- session in particular. I read a history of ruffs t'other day, which harrowed up my soul, and made my young blood to freeze. I assure you, ever since I have been initiated into the shocking mysteries of ruff-making, Hamlet's horror at sight of his father's ghost has been nothing compared to mine, when I behold a stiff well-appointed ruff, so completely is it associated, in my mind's eye, with hoofs and horns, blackness and brimstone ; " — then, going to the library, he presently returned with an ancient folio in his hand; and turning over the leaves, he read as follows, with an air of ludicrous horror and dismay : — " The Anatomie of Abuses, containing a Discoverie or brief Summarie of such Notable Vices and Imperfections as now raigne in many Counteries of the World, &c. &c. By Phillip Stubbes, 1583."

" They have greate and monsterous ruffes, mad %

either of cambricke, lawne, or els of some other of the finest cloth that can be got for monie, whereof some be a quarter of a yarde deepe, yea, some more, very fewe lesse: so that they stande a fulle quarter of a yarde (and more) from their neckes.

hanging over their shoulder pointes insteade of a vaile. Eut wot ye what ? the deivill, as he, in the fullnesse of his malice, first invented these greate ruffes, so hath he now found out also two greate pillars to heare up and maintaine this his kingdome of pride withal. The one arche or pillar, wherebj-e his kingdom of greate ruffes is underpropped, is a certain kinde of liquide matter which they call starch, wherein the deivill hath willed them to washe and to drie their ruffes well, which being drie, will then stand stiffe and inflexible aboute their neckes. The other pillar is a certaine device made of wiers crested for the purpose, whipped either over with golde thred, silver, or silke, and this he calleth a underpropper. Beyond all this, theye have a farther fetche, nothynge inferior to the reste, as, namely, three or four decrees of minor ruffes placed in gradatim, one beneathe another, and all under the Mayster Deivill Ruffe. Sometimes they are "

" Such nonsense! " exclaimed Miss Pratt. " I really never heard the like of it. I wonder how you have patience to listen to it, Lady Betty. I really think Miss St. Clair might show more sense than to laugh at such ridiculous stuff. There's the gong, that's better worth attending to; " and away walked Miss Pratt and her ruff.

The politicians were also roused at the sound; and as they broke up, Mrs. St. Clair said to Lord Rossville,—

" Rest assured, my lord, nothing shall be wanting on my part to gain the suffrages of my family ; and I have little doubt of accomplishing it, since your lordship has thus kindly and considerately given me a carte blanche, as it were, for my actions upon the occasion. I feel most deeply the value of the confidence you have thus reposed in me."

Lord Rossville had done no such thing as give, or dream of giving, Mrs. St. Clair a carte blanche for her actions; — but he loved to hear himself commended, whether for what he had done, or for what he had not done ; and he therefore allowed it to pass, in the belief that he was indeed all that was kind, wise, and considerate. Gertrude, as a matter of course, was again placed between Lord Rossville and Mr. Delmour, and condemned, during a tedious dinner, to hear the same political jargon carried on. Mr. Delmour now and then changed the conversation, indeed, out of compliment to her, and talked of the views, the weather, the races, and such subjects as he seemed to think suited to a female capacity; but it was evidently an effort to descend to such things, and Gertrude felt only provoked that he should even attempt to be agreeable.

When they rose from table, her mother made a sign for her to follow her to her own room.

CHAPTER XXII.
Never in my breast
Did ignorance so struggle with desire

Of knowledge,
As in that moment; nor — dared I
To question, nor myself could aught discern. Cary's Dante.

" You are a poor dissembler, Gertrude," said Mrs. St. Clair, after having shut the door of her chamber, and carefully examined each lurking recess —" your looks have already betrayed to the family that something is wrong — even stupid Lady Betty asked me at dinner whether you were well enough. It is, therefore, obvious you are suffering either from mental disquiet or bodily indisposition, and it must be your part to play the invalid this evening." Then seeing her daughter about to express her dislike of the deception, " It is easily done — you have only to remain here, and leave it to me to account for your absence in the drawing-room ; " — then with a profound sigh, " The headach and the heartach are both mine, God knows! but if you will only affect to bear the one for me, you will assuredly alleviate the other."

Gertrude felt that she was become a mere tool in her mother's hands, and that it was in vain to contend. She therefore yielded a passive assent to remaining a prisoner for the rest of the evening.

Various were the conjectures, and numberless the remedies, called forth by Mrs. St. Clair's communication of her daughter's indisposition. The heat of the day — the drive — the roads — the dust — the dinner — Uncle Adam and his airless room; all these, and many more, were each assigned as a sufficient cause for headach, and eau de Cologne, aromatic vinegar, and all the thousand perfumed specifics, down to Lady Betty's home-made double-distilled lavender crater, were recommended and accepted. As for Lord Rossville, he made it quite a matter of life and death.— A fever commonly began with a headach—was there any disposition to shivering on the part of the patient ? — any thirst — any fever — any bile ? — how were the eyes — how was + he tongue — how was the pulse ? — A little blood taken in time was perhaps the most effectual antidote. — He possessed some knowledge of medicine himself—and, in short, Mrs. St. Clair only prevented him from going to prescribe for his niece in person by assuring him that she felt a great disposition to sleep, and had requested that she might not be disturbed. It was therefore finally settled, that if Miss St. Clair was no better by to-morrow morning, she was then to be given up to his lordship's direction.

Colonel Delmour suspected there was some deception in the case, and was at no loss, as he thought, to fathom the mystery. He helieved their mutual attachment had been discovered by Mrs. St. Clair, and that Gertrude was suffering persecution on his account; but he felt little apprehension as to the result; he knew enough of human nature to be aware that, to a romantic ardent nature such as hers, a little opposition would have rather a good effect, and that there is sometimes no surer way of creating an interest in one party than by exciting a prejudice in another.

Meanwhile the object of all this solicitude sat at her window, watching " the coming on of grateful evening mild." It was at that lovely season when day and night are so imperceptibly blended into each other, that a night seems only a softer, sweeter day. There were none of those magnificent masses of clouds which, in this climate, generally form the pomp and circumstance of a fine sunset. The sky was cloudless and serene, and a soft silvery moon shone in one quarter of the heavens, while the mellow golden lustre of the sun gradually melted away in the other.

When the last sunshine, with expiring ray, In summer twilight weeps the close of day,
Who hath not felt the softness of that hour Steal o'er his heart like dew-drops on the flower ?

Then came the deeper blue of the silent night, with her " solemn bird and glittering stars."

But Gertrude was withdrawn from the contemplation of these consecrated things by the entrance of her mother. She threw herself on a chair, and sighed heavily ; — then starting up —

" Prepare yourself, Gertrude ; in a few minutes we must set forth ; — fetch your green travelling-cloak, — it will completely cover your dress, and conceal your figure, should we unfortunately meet any one, which Heaven forbid !"

Gertrude brought her cloak, and did as she was directed, while her mother wrapt herself in a similar disguise, and both awaited in trembling expectation the signal for sallying forth. At length the gong sounded—voices were heard as the family passed through the hall to the supper-room — the doors were shut, and all was silent.

" Now is the time," said Mrs. St. Clair, in a voice almost inarticulate from agitation. " Yet stay — should it by any unforeseen mischance ever reach Lord Rossville's ears that we were seen leaving the house together at such an hour — no, that will never do— Gertrude, you must go first, and I will follow."

" O no, no !" cried her daughter, turning pale with terror; " why should that be—surely that can make no difference? "

" No difference in reality, but much in appearance," said Mrs. St. Clair, impatiently. " Your stealing out to take a ramble by

moonlight, however silly, would not sound very improbable, and my following you would be perfectly natural; but both going out together is quite unaccountable, and must not be — go — make haste."

" Oh, mamma! — do not — I beseech you do not ask me to go alone. I cannot — indeed I cannot;" and she sank upon a chair.

" Ridiculous ! " exclaimed her mother, in a tone of suppressed anger ; " of what are you afraid ? "

" I know not— I cannot tell. I am going 1 know not where — to meet I know not whom — and at midnight. No, I cannot— I will not go,-" and she threw back her cloak, and shook off her hat, with gestures of impatience and indignation.

" Obstinate—unfeeling—ungrateful wretch!" exclaimed Mrs. St. Clair, giving way to her passion; " is it for you that I suffer— that I — why do I not give you up to your fate at once — why — but I will be obeyed. I command you on your peril to obey me."

Gertrude threw herself on the floor at her mother's feet. " Kill me — trample on me," cried she, in an accent of despair ; " but my soul revolts from these mysteries. Oh ! my mother! " continued she in broken accents, " is it you who command me thus to steal from my uncle's house at midnight — disguised and alone — to meet a low-born, needy, desperate man?"

Mrs. St. Clair remained silent for a few moments, as if struggling with her feelings ; she then spoke in a voice of unnatural calmness —

" Be it so. — My entreaties—my prayers—my commands are in vain—the die is cast by your hand, and my doom is fixed. I told you that my life depended upon your unreserved obedience — and — the forfeit shall be paid."

Gertrude looked on her mother's face—every feature was convulsed with powerful and fearful emotion — then every idea vanished but that of her mother dying — dead — and she the cause. All personal fear — all lofty feeling fled : the right chord was touched, and her whole frame vibrated with emotion. She clung to her mother's knees — she sued for pardon — she vowed the most implicit obedience, the most devoted submission to her will — she called Heaven to witness that henceforth she would do all that was required of her—she prayed that she might be tried once, only once more. She spoke with all the ardour and sincerity of powerful emotion; but it is not with a throbbing heart and a burning brow the mastery is obtained — if vows made in pain are void, those formed under the influence of excited feeling are no less vain and fleeting. Mrs. St. Clair's features gradually relaxed, and, in a more natural voice, she said —

" I forgive you, Gertrude—I forgive your doubts, your fears, however injurious to me. — Go, then—but, ere you go, reflect on what you have undertaken — remember you have vowed zm-

qualified obedience—there is now no middle course — you are either my preserver or my destroyer:" — she poured out a glass of water, and held it to her daughter's trembling lips. — " Now, listen to my instructions : — Glide quickly and softly along till you reach the south turret stair—be cautious in descending it, and making your way along the old passage to the west door, which is seldom locked — when there, you have only to cross the lawn — keep by the river side, and wait me at the ivy bridge — fear nothing — I will follow you immediately."

Gertrude again muffled herself in her cloak, and, with a beating heart, went on her way as fast as terror and agitation would permit. She groped her way down the little turnpike-stair, and along a dark passage, in an old part of the house, to a door which opened upon the lawn. But there all things stood disclosed in the light of a full moon, and calm, cloudless sky, and her heart almost failed her as she marked her own dark shapeless shadow stealing along on the silvery path. She soon gained the bank of the river; and there, in the deep shade of the rocks and trees, she felt secure, at least from discovery, if not from danger. A few steps more and she reached the bridge, where she was to await her mother.

At another time she would have been charmed with the romantic loveliness and grandeur of the scene. — Rocks, trees, and waterfall, all gleamed in the pale pellucid light—not a leaf was stirring ; and the solemn stillness was only broken by the rushing of the river, and the whooping of the owls. But to enjoy the tranquillity of nature requires that there should be some sympathy between the mind and the scene; and Gertrude's feelings were but little in unison with the calm, the holy majesty of moonlight. Scarcely daring to breathe, every instant seemed an age, till she beheld her mother advance with a quick but agitated step.

" We are late," said she in a low tone ; " let us make haste ;" and taking her daughter's arm, they proceeded together in silence for a considerable distance till they came within sight of a temple situated on the summit of the bank.

" It was there I appointed to meet him," said Mrs. St. Clair ; and as she spoke the figure of a man was seen approaching towards them. — " Wait here, Gertrude," cried she, waving her daughter back, as she would have clung to her. " I shall be within sight and call of you. Do not stir from hence, and re-remember your promise."

And disengaging herself from her, she hastily advanced to meet the stranger. It was not in human nature not to have felt the most intense curiosity at this moment; and Gertrude certainly experienced it in no common degree, when she beheld her mother's meeting with this mysterious man. Although beyond the reach of hearing what passed, their gestures told a tale of no common import. After remaining a few minutes in deep

and earnest conversation, she saw Mrs. St. Clair offer him a packet, which she guessed was the one containing the money and jewels. She then saw the person reject it, as if with scorn, and even turn away from it, as Mrs. St. Clair seemed to press it upon him. This dumh show lasted some minutes, till at length he snatched it from the hand she held out to him, and threw it upon the ground, and made some steps towards the place where Gertrude stood. Mrs. St. Clair caught him hy the arm ; she seemed to be arguing, imploring, supplicating. Now she clasped her hands, as if in an agony; then she raised them, as if in solemn appeal to Heaven, and Gertrude caught the sound of her voice in tones of the deepest anguish. At length she seemed to prevail. Having herself lifted up the packet he had so contemptuously cast away, she again offered it to him, and it was accepted. They now advanced together till within a few paces of Gertrude, when Mrs. St. Clair quitted her companion and approached her daughter. The shade of the trees covered her face, but her voice was expressive of the utmost agitation.

" Gertrude, my love," said she in a low tone, " Lewiston wishes to see you, to talk with you — as the husband of your nurse, and a sort of confidential person in the family, he thinks he has a right to address you in his own way. I dare not refuse, Gertrude — he will converse with you alone."

Mrs. St. Clair placed her hand on her daughter's lips, as she saw an indignant refusal ready to burst forth.

" Oh, Gertrude! dearest Gertrude! as you value my life, as you value your own happiness, do not refuse—do not provoke him. — I am in his power — one hasty word, one contemptuous look, may undo me. Oh, Gertrude! for the love you bear to me—for the love you bore your nurse—for the love of Heaven — be calm and patient. Speak — tell me I may trust you ? "

And she led her a few steps towards the stranger. Gertrude started with terror, as the moonbeams now fell on her mother's face, and showed it wild, and even ghastly, from excessive emotion.

" Compose yourself, mamma," said she ; " I will do — I will be all you desire."

There was no time for more ; for the stranger, as if impatient of delay, had now joined them. He held out his hand to Gertrude with an air of familiarity, which at once roused her indignation, and had almost thrown her off her guard, when a look from her mother subdued her. With ablush of wounded pride, she suffered him to take it, and Mrs. St. Clair walked apart. He surveyed her for some minutes without speaking, while her cheek burned and her heart swelled at the indignity to which she was thus subjected. At length he said abruptly —

" Do you remember your nurse, young lady ?"

" Perfectly."

" How old might ye be when she died ?"

H 2

" I was nine years old."

" You were pretty considerably fond of her, were you not ? "

" I loved her as my mother!" answered Gertrude in a voice of deep emotion.

" That was well — you know that I was her husband, so I may put in for a hould of your amotions. Do you think you will be able to bestow any of thim upon me ? "

Gertrude's spirit was ready to burst forth at the insolent freedom of this address ; but she repressed it, and answered coldly—

" As the husband of my nurse I am willing to assist you as far as I am able, but I have little in my power at present."

" That's a pity, for I'm plaguy poor, — but the time will come when you will have a nice thing of it — that's a fact, and no mistake."

" When I have," answered Gertrude, wishing to end the conference, " the claims of my nurse's husband shall not be forgotten ;" and she was moving away.

" Stop," cried he, " not so cliver—the claims of your nurse's husband are not so easily sattled as you seem to calculate. I wish to put a few more questions to you, young lady, before we part:— How am I to avoid bein' deceived?"

"All that I can say is — if ever it is in my power to befriend you, for the sake of your wife, I shall be ready to do it," said Gertrude.

"Only for the sake of my wife!" repeated he with a smile.— "We shall see how that is when the time comes, whether I shall not have a somethhr to say with you for my own sake."

In silent displeasure Gertrude turned proudly away, when he caught her cloak to detain her.

"Well, we shall settle that afterwards; but if you play your cards well, you will one day have a splendid location here, or the deuce is in it. The worst of it is, that day may be a while of comin', and your friends may starve in the meantime; but your uncle is a pretty old boy, and you are sure of steppin' into his shoes, that's a fact."

Gertrude was choking with indignation; but she remembered her promise, and remained silent.

"What are you aplannin' for the futur'?" demanded he abruptly.

"I am not in the habit of communicating my plans to strangers," answered she haughtily.

"But I have a right to know your plans," said he fiercely; "I insist upon an answer to my question. — What are you aplannin' for the futur'?"

Gertrude was terrified. — "I am ignorant of your meaning," said she faintly.

"I mean, in the case of your uncle's death, what would you do?—would you be agoin' marry, or remain single? — and has your mother been asettin' you on any how in favour of any body? — answer me that — does she wish you to marry or not? — say away."

"It is impossible for me to answer — I do not know — I cannot tell," answered Gertrude, almost overcome with the contending emotions of terror and indignation.

"Are you mortal sure of that? — is there no Colonel Del-mour jist aready to chouse the heiress out of her estates? — But that won't do — you must have a care how you entangle yourself there —you must have a care how you commit yourself— or, by Jupiter! Come, you must make me your father confessor— I must know how the land lies — I must know how you stand affected to those fortin'-hunters, who are looking after you, for I must tell ye which way to drive in the matter;" and he would have taken her hand with an air of familiarity, which now completely threw her off her guard. Uttering a cry, which echoed through the woods, she flew wildly past him, and cast herself into her mother's arms.

CHAPTER XXIII.

Since in the toils of fate
Thou art enclosed, submit, if thou canst brook Submission. JEschylus.

"When Gertrude awoke the following morning from a feverish and disturbed sleep (the effect of a narcotic), her mind, like the broken fragments of a mirror, presented only disjointed and distorted images, which she vainly endeavoured to arrange and combine into one connected whole. Hideous di'eams were mingled with no less hideous realities, and confusion only became worse confounded in the attempt to separate them. At length she opened her eyes, and beheld her mother sitting by her.

"Oh, mamma!" cried she, " speak to me — tell me what has happened last night — was it — Oh! was it all a dream?"

"Compose yourself, Gertrude," answered Mrs. St. Clair; — " whatever it was it is now past — think of it no more."

"Impossible — I can think of nothing else! — I must know — I implore you to tell me at least this much — last night — Mr. Lyndsay—Oh! tell me, did he not rescue me from the grasp "

" Gertrude! " interrupted her mother in great agitation, " of what use is it to talk or think of what is past ? — it is distressing to yourself—to me."

" It was then even so ! — I now remember it all — their high words — their threatening language — and that man "

" Hush, Gertrude, hush !" again interposed her mother ; — " you know not what you say."

" Yes — I know it all — he dared to assert that he had a right over me — he, the husband of my nurse, to dare to claim a right over me! " and her voice was almost choked at the thoughts of having been subjected to such an indignity.

"But, mamma, surely this was — this must have been a dream—I know it was," and she gasped as she spoke. " When he appealed to you — you — Oh! — you said it was so — I know I must have dreamt that;" and she looked wildly and eagerly in her mother's face, but Mrs. St. Clair remained silent.

" Oh! you did not — you could not speak of engagements — of entanglements — of—I know not what — yet strange and dreadful words of that import still ring in my ears — tell me— only tell me it is all a dream."

"Gertrude, this is agonizing to yourself—to me — repress — in mercy repress those feelings."

" I will—I will," cried her daughter, in increasing agitation ; " only say you did not so traduce me as to sanction the horrible belief that I could be so base — so vile — Oh! how it degrades me even to utter it — as to have plighted myself to a menial."

" Compose yourself, Gertrude ; I cannot talk to you while you are in this state."

" "Well, I will — I am composed," making a violent effort to appear calm, while her frame trembled with the violence of her emotion. — " Now, only say that you, my mother, did not so calumniate me — but no, you cannot," cried she, again giving way to the impetuosity of her feelings. — " It is no dream — I heard it all—I heard you—you, my mother, assert that man had a claim to me, and — I believe I was mad at the moment. — Did I not throw myself at my cousin's feet, and implore him to save me?—did I not cling to him in agony, while that man would have torn me from him ? "

" Gertrude, I would have spared you the repetition of your folly, your madness — I would have spared you the painful recollection of your broken promise, your injurious distrust of me. — I warned you of the consequences of disregarding my injunctions—my entreaties—my commands ; but all were disregarded. What right have you, then, to upbraid me for having told you the truth ? "

" No, you did not tell me the truth — you did not tell me you were leading me to insult — to degradation."

" Say not that I led you — but for your own pride and folly all would have been well. Had you remembered my warning, and not provoked the person it was your interest as well as mine to have conciliated, nothing of all this would have happened ; but your absurd outcry reached Mr. Lyndsay, who unfortunately had been enticed by the beauty of the night to take a moonlight ramble, and who hastened to the spot, unhappily at the same moment "when the other advanced —but the worst is over. Mr. Lyndsay is a noble-minded honourable man, and we have nothing to fear from him — he has promised to be for ever silent on the subject."

" But what — Oh! what must he think of me !" exclaimed Gertrude, in an accent of the deepest dejection. " Be assured he thinks nothing injurious of you." " Yet that man dared to assert that my father had given him a right to me — he, the husband of my nurse !— No, 1 will not — I cannot for an instant live under such a sense of degradation — I must seek Mr. Lyndsay — I must tell him it is false ! " And she attempted to rise, but sank back on her pillow, overwhelmed with the force of her emotions.

" For Heaven's sake, Gertrude, do not give way to these transports ! " cried her mother. " Every thing is now settled — the object of your alarm is already many miles distant — never more, I trust, to return — why then dwell upon what is past, when it can be productive of no good ? Come, my love, for my sake try to forget it all."

" Forget it!" repeated Gertrude ; " forget that I have been exposed to insult — to degradation, and by my mother ! — that I never can forget!"

" No, do not forget it," cried Mrs. St. Clair, bursting into tears; " treasure it in your heart's core — let all my love, and care, and tenderness be forgotten — let your duty — your obedience — your promises be forgotten ; but do not forget this one unfortunate action — record it — proclaim it, and then let me end a miserable existence. — Shall I summon Lord Rossville and the family," said she with affected calmness, putting her hand to the bell, " to hear you denounce your mother ? "

Time had been when this appeal would have produced its intended effect upon Gertrude ; but her feelings had been already excited to their utmost, and she felt too wretched herself to have much sympathy to bestow on the author of her wretchedness ; she therefore remained silent. Mrs. St. Clair repeated the question.

" I have not deserved this," replied Gertrude coldly ; " but I am still willing to obey you—what would you have me do? "

Mrs. St. Clair embraced her, and would have coaxed and soothed her, —but she shrunk from these demonstrations of affection, and again coldly asked what remained for her to do.

" I would have you appear, if possible, at breakfast, my love ; if you do not, Lord Rossville will insist upon sending for medical advice, and will make a talk and a bustle about you, which may excite speculation and surmise, and any thing of that sort had better be avoided at present; you will, therefore, oblige me, my dearest, if you will endeavour to look and be as much yourself as possible. And now I shall leave you to make your toilet, while I change my dress, for I have not been in bed all

h 4

night. I have watched by you, Gertrude, and that not for the first time."

Gertrude was touched by this proof of her mother's solicitude, and all the recollected proofs of her maternal anxieties for her in her childish days rushed to her heart, and with the returning tide brought back something of tenderer, kindlier feelings. Yielding, as she always did, to the impulse of the moment, she received her mother's embrace, and the scene ended in a reconciliation.

CHAPTER XXIV.

There is no resource where there is no understanding. St. Therese.

Mrs. St. Clair and her daughter descended together to the breakfast-room; but at the thoughts of meeting her cousin after what had so recently occur^d, Gertrude's agitation almost overcame her, and she seated herself at the table without daring to lift her eyes. Many were the inquiries with which she was of course assailed; but Miss Pratt's observations, as usual, predominated.

"I'm afraid, my dear, there's more than a common headach the matter with you; you put me very much in mind of Anthony Whyte when he was taking the influenza; he had just such a little pink spot on the top of one cheek, and all the rest of his face as white as the tablecloth; and your eyes, too, seem very heavy, just like his—he never looked up for two days." The little pink spot had gradually increased with Miss Pratt's remarks; but, making an effort to look up, Miss St. Clair raised her eyes, and encountered, not Mr. Lyndsay's dreaded gaze, but that of Colonel Delmour, fixed upon her with anxious scrutiny. Lyndsay was not present, nor was there even a place reserved for him. Miss Pratt seemed to read what was passing in her thoughts.

"So you have lost one of your beaux, you see? Mr. Edward went off this morning, it seems. It must have been a sudden thought, for he said nothing of it yesterday; and, by-the-by, what became of him at supper last night? I wonder if he had a headach too? — They say there's a sympathy in bodies as well as in minds sometimes; Colonel Delmour, do you believe that?"

"I have heard ' there is in souls a sympathy with sounds,'" replied Colonel Delmour, with an ironical contemptuous air; "but my soul is, I grieve to say, so lost to all that is edifying and delightful, it can rarely boast any sympathy with the sound of Miss Pratt's voice,—by which means, unhappily, one half of her dulcet notes fall powerless on my dull spirit. May I beg to know what I am called upon to believe?"

"There's an old saying, Colonel, that there's none so deaf as those that won't hear; and I suspect that's your case sometimes," retorted Miss Pratt, in a very toothy manner, though affecting to turn the laugh against her opponent.

The entrance of the post-bag here attracted Miss Pratt's attention. It was Lord Rossville's enviable prerogative to open it himself, and to dole out the letters in the most cautious and deliberate manner to their respective destinations — a measure which very ill accorded with the mercurial powers of Miss Pratt, who, in spite of his lordship's precautions in holding the mouth of the bag as close as he possibly could, always contrived to dart her eyes down to the very bottom of it, and to anticipate its contents long ere the moment of delivery arrived. Like all weak important people, Lord Rossville loved power in any form or substance in which it presented itself, even in that of a leather bag, which he grasped with the air of a Jupiter holding his thunderbolt, and lingered over it as though it had been another Pandora's box. Although his lordship, for upwards of forty years, had been in the daily, nay hourly practice, of declaring that he would not be hurried — that he would take his own time, &c. &c, nevertheless, in the very teeth of this assurance, Miss Pratt did still persist in her attempts to accelerate the Earl's movements, which, of course, had invariably the effect of protracting them. On the present occasion, it seemed doubtful whether the letters were ever to see the light; as upon Miss Pratt remarking that it would be much better if there was no bag at all, for then people would get their letters at once without being kept on the tenter-hooks this way, his lordship closed its mouth, and, opening his own, commenced a very elaborate harangue on the impropriety, irregularity, and inconvenience of such a mode of proceeding. Meanwhile Gertrude gradually regained her composure, and was even able to receive Colonel Delmour's assiduities with something like pleasure. At length, Miss Pratt having knocked under, — for, as she observed, in an underhand way, there was no disputing with a man who held the key of the post-bag,—the contents were duly distributed, and she received her portion, which kept her silent for a few minutes. • Gertrude trembled as a letter was handed to her; but her alarm subsided when she saw it was directed in a feeble affected-looking female hand, and sealed with a fat bouncing heart, skewered with an arrow, — motto, " La peine est douce." The contents corresponded with these exterior symbols, and were as follows : —

" Bellevue, July .

" Ma chere Cousine,

" From what passed in your presence, you will, I suspect, not be very much surprised to hear that a certain person, who shall be nameless, has carried his point; and that I have at length been prevailed upon to name Thursday next as the day when I am to enter a new state of existence ! Eh bien! my dear coz — I hope your time is coming; and -when it does, most fervently do I pray you may prove as fortunate in your choice as I have done in mine. The Major is indeed all that I could wish—far, very far heyond my poor deserts ; — and I should consider myself as the most ungrateful of women, if I did not look upon myself as the most fortunate of my sex ! That being the case, I certainly feel less than I should otherwise do at taking this most important and solemn step ; but the certainty that I am bestowing myself upon one who is in every respect worthy of my warmest admiration, esteem, and affection, supports me; and be assured, my dear cousin, it is the only thing that can support the spirits at such a time. How much, alas ! are they to be pitied, who do not possess that certainty, without which, believe me, all the advantages of birth and fortune are nothing — for without that, I assure you, the Major's rank, fortune, connections, manners, &c. &c. &c. never would have influenced me. Such being the state of affairs here at present, I am very desirous that you, ma chere cousine, should participate in my feelings, and also take a lesson for what, rest assured, will one day be your own fate. I therefore request, as & particular favour, that you will give us the pleasure of your company to pass the intervening days with me, and to officiate as bride's-maid upon a certain occasion. The Major unites with me in this request; so it will be a double disappointment if any thing should prevent you. Papa and mamma also join in the wish that my nuptials should be graced with your presence. The Major offered to drive down for you any day in the gig — (apropos, I must tell you he admires you very much — but I am not jealous') — but I own, at present, I think that would be making the thing rather public; and besides, shall I confess my weakness ? — I feel particularly timid at the thoughts of the Major risking himself in a gig at present — only conceive my situation, if any thing should happen to him ! ! ! I trust you will be at no loss for an opportunity, and that I shall soon have the pleasure of seeing you here, and of making you better acquainted with my lord and master to be. Adio mia cara,

" Isabella.

" Pray have you heard any more of your beau? The Major thinks he must be a spy. " I. C. B.

" Excuse haste; but the Major is sitting by, and says he is ready to quarrel with you, for engrossing so much of my time.

" I. C. B."

In great distress at the vulgar, affected familiarity of this performance, Gertrude handed it to her mother in silence, resolved in her own mind to return a brief denial to Miss Bell's invitation. Not so Mrs. St. Clair, who thought nothing could be

more apropos than this proposal. She was desirous of removing her daughter from the observation of the family until her mind should have regained its usual tone, and she knew nothing would be so likely to effect that as change of scene and necessity of exertion. It would require a little management, perhaps, to obtain Lord Rossville's consent; but, in the present state of affairs, that would be easily obtained ; and having settled all this, she put the letter in her reticule with an air that said, this requires consideration.

Miss Pratt now made known the contents of her despatch, which was a pressing invitation to spend a few days at old Lady M'Caw's, to meet Mrs. Chatwell and the Miss Knowalls—just a nice little female party. It was a pleasant thing for old friends to meet, and talk over old stories now and then, &c. &c. &c.

" So, Miss Pratt, we are going to lose you then, it seems ?" said the Earl, in an accent of agreeable surprise, and a visage beaming with delight.

" Indeed, it's not very wellbred, my lord, to run away in this manner; but it's an old promise of mine to Lady M'Caw, honest woman, and I would not like to disappoint her, especially as she is so good as say she'll send the carriage for me to-morrow morning. However, I shall make out my visit to you yet ; and if I can get hold of Anthony Whyte, will bring him with me."

Lord Rossville's countenance fell at this assurance. He had been anxiously waiting the termination of Miss Pratt's visit, that he might give a dinner to some of the stateliest of the neighbouring grandees; a thing which could not be got up with good effect while that lady was his guest. Her light frothy babbles disconcerted his heavy sonorous speeches; her brisk familiarity detracted from the dignity of his manner;—it was as impossible for him to be the dignified nobleman, with Miss Pratt at his elbow, as it would have been with an ape on his shoulder. However, it was a great point gained to have got her fairly off the field; and he flattered himself, with a little management, he might contrive to exclude her till it suited his time to receive her again. Contrary to his usual practice, but in conformity with the vulgar proverb, he therefore resolved to make hay while the sun shone, and straightway set about issuing his cards immediately. In this complacent mood, Mrs. St. Clair found little difficulty in obtaining his consent to Gertrude's visit to Bellevue, which she took care to insinuate would prove highly advantageous in a political point of view ; — a bait which the Earl instantly caught at. He even declared his intention, and that of Mr. Delmour, to pay their respects to the worthy family at Bellevue the following day ; and, finally, it was settled that they should accompany Mrs. and Miss St. Clair there, leaving the latter to officiate at her cousin's nuptials ; — an office which, in the present state of the political contest, was not deemed derogatory, even for the heiress presumptive of Rossville.

Colonel Delmour seemed somewhat chagrined at first hearing of this arrangement; hat, upon reflection, he hegan to discover that it might rather advance his purpose to have the ohject of his pursuit withdrawn for a while from the watchful eyes of her guardians; and he secretly resolved to be a daily visitor at Belle-vue while she remained. As for Gertrude, whatever repugnance she felt at first to the proposal, she soon yielded to her mother's solicitations, for she was a stranger to that selfishness which is obstinate in trifles.

Miss Pratt's departure was hailed as a joyful release hy the whole party, with the exception, indeed, of Lady Betty and Mr. Delmour. The one was too stupid, and the other too much engrossed, to have any discrimination in their choice of company; — with the one words were words, and Miss Pratt's words were as good, if not better, than other people's words ; — with the other Miss Pratt was Miss Pratt, and one Miss was very much like another during a contested election.

CHAPTER XXV.

They who love you for political service, love you less than their dinner; and they who hate you, hate you worse than the devil— Wesley.

The whole Black family were evidently prepared for the reception of their visitors; and as they w r ere all good-looking, and well dressed, the tout ensemble was highly prepossessing. Indeed, had it been otherwise, they would still have found favour in the eyes of Lord Rossville and his nephew, who, in each and all of the human beings now assembled, even to the baby, beheld simply a vote, or the article or particle of a vote. The Earl, therefore, parsed and prosed away to good Mrs. Black, who sat listening to him with the most perfect reverence and admiration. Had the speaker been their neighbour old Mr. Longlungs, she might perhaps have thought him rather long-winded ; but it was still the golden age of innocence with Mrs. Black, for it never once occurred to her that it was possible for an earl to be as tiresome as a commoner. She, therefore, hung enamoured on his lordship's accents ; but when he condescended so far as to take one of the children on his knee, and to drink the healths of the whole family in what he declared to be the very best Malmsey Madeira he had ever tasted, the conquest of Mrs. Black was completed ; and she secretly vowed in her heart that she would never rest night or day till, by hook or by crook, she had secured Mr. Black's vote for him. And then, as he seemed so taken with them all, there was no saying but he

might get a company for Bob, and give his business to Davy. And with these splendid visions, Mrs. Black's comely good-humoured face beamed upon the Earl with an expression he was little accustomed to on the countenances of his auditors.

Mr. Delmour, on his part, was not idle, having talked very sensibly with Mr. Black on Russet lawns and fallows gray, Where the nibbling flocks do stray ;

that is, in plain prose, on the rearing and feeding of cattle, succession of crops, &c. &c. He next addressed himself to a very pretty particle of a vote in the person of Miss Lilly Black, who had made some faint and inefficient attempts to discover whether he wrote poetry — till, growing bolder as she advanced, she at length popped the question, whether he would not write something in her album. Mr. Delmour protested, with the most perfect truth, that he never had written a verse in his life ; but, to soften the disappointment, added, with a bow and most expressive look, that if ever he was to be so inspired, it must be on the present occasion. Miss Lilly blushed, and had no doubt that Mr. Delmour was over head and ears in love with ber already ; and having read every novel in tbe circulating library at Barn-ford, Miss Lilly was ready to be fallen in love with at a moment's warning.

Mrs. Major Waddell (to be) was the only one of the family then at home who did not appear. She said that, in her situation, it was extremely unpleasant to be stared at by strangers; and as Lord Rossville and Mr. Delmour must know perfectly well how she was situated, they would easily understand her reasons for declining all introductions in her present situation. Miss Bell, however, secretly flattered herself that her absence would be too striking to be passed over in silence, and that Lord Rossville would make a point of seeing her; great was her mortification, therefore, when the whole party drove off, with the exception of Gertrude, who was left behind. The bride-elect descended to the drawing-room, in hopes of hearing tbat the Major and she had formed the principal subject of conversation ; but there she found Mrs. Black trying to remember all that Lord Rossville had said about the line of the New Canal, and Mr. Black already anticipating the arrival of a couple of pure Merinos, which Mr. Delmour was to procure for him from his uncle the Duke of Bui'lington ; Miss Lilly was expressing her wonder to Miss St. Clair whether it was really true that Mr. Delmour did not write poetry ; and the children were squabbling over the remains of the cake.

" I hope there was no particular allusion to the Major and me," said Miss Bell, seeing it in vain to wait for any voluntary communication ; " in my situation such things are not very pleasant."

" There was no mention made of you whatever, Bell," was the reply.

" I assure you I am very happy to hear it," said Miss Bell, in evident displeasure ; to which she could only give vent hy turning the children out of the room for making a noise, which they, of course, redoubled outside the door, till dragged shrieking away hy their maid.

Miss St. Clair already felt the discomforts of her situation — seated in a dressed drawing-room for the day, with Mrs. Black and her daughters, who seemed to have renounced all occupation for that of being company to their guest — and " labour dire it is, and weary woe," in such cases, whether to the entertainer or the entertained.

Gertrude felt too strange — too much out of her own element, to give free scope to her mind ; she felt she was amongst those who did not understand her, nor she them ; the tone of their minds was pitched in a totally different key ; and their ideas, tastes, and habits, she was convinced, never could assimilate with hers. At length Miss Lilly produced her album for the amusement or admiration of her cousin, and turned over page after page, emblazoned with miserable drawings of dropsical Cupids with blue aprons — doves that might have passed for ptarmigans—stout calico roses—heart's-ease that was eyesore, and forget-me-nots that ought to have been washed in the waters of Lethe. All these had, of course, appropriate lines, or lines that were intended as such. Beneath a rose, which bore evident traces of having been washed with a sponge, was written in a small die-away hand, scarcely visible to the naked eye, Cowper's pretty verses, —

A rose had been washed, just washed in a shower, &c.

A bunch of heart's-ease, which might have served for a signpost, was emblematic of a sonnet to a violet, beginning —

Sweet modest flower that lurk'st unseen, &c.

But the forget-me-nots had called forth an original effusion addressed to Miss Lilly B., as follows: —

Forget thee, sweet maid ? — ah ! how vain the request,— Thy image fond memory has stamped on my heart;

And, while life's warm pulses beat high in my breast, Thy image shall ne'er from that bosom depart!

The moon she is up, and the sun he is down ;

The wind too is hush'd, and silent's the rill ; The birds to their little nests long since have flown;

But when will forget my sad bosom to thrill!

Forget thee ! — ah ! who that has ever beheld

Thy eye of sky-blue, and thy locks of pure gold, Thy cheek

" Oh! you really mustn't read that," cried Miss Lilly, putting her hand affectedly on the place ; " it is only some nonsense of Lieutenant O'Brien's."

" Pray allow me to proceed," said Gertrude, a little amused at the wretchedness of the rhymes.

" O, indeed I can't," said Miss Lilly, affecting to he ashamed.

" I assure you, I am in great pain for your cheek," said Gertrude ; " I'm afraid it must have swelled in order to rhyme to ' heheld.'"

" Oh no ! I assure you it wasn't my cheek, hut his heart, that swelled," said Miss Lilly, in perfect simplicity.

" The Captain has a great genius for poetry," said Mrs. Black.

" Very great," said Miss Lilly, with a gentle sigh. " I am certain that address to the moon we saw in the newspaper was his writing."

" It's very well for people to write poetry who can't afford to buy it," said Miss Bell, with a disdainful toss; " the Major has bought a most beautiful copy of Lord Byron's works, bound in red morocco — rather too fine for reading, I think ; but he said he meant it to lie upon my sofa-table, so I couldn't find fault."

" To be sure, Bell, as you say, it's a better business to buy poetry than to write it," said Mrs. Black.

" There is nothing more worth reading," said Miss Lilly, as her cousin continued to turn over the leaves of the book ; " that is only some dull stupid stuff aunt Mary copied for me ; I've a good mind to tear it out, it is just like a sermon ; " and she was preparing to execute her threat when Gertrude begged leave to read the offending lines before they were committed to the flames.

When I look back, and in myself behold The wandering ways that youth could not descry ; And mark the tearful course that youth did hold, And melt in mind each step youth stray'd awry j My knees I bow, and from my heart I call,

0 Lord ! forget these faults and follies all.

For now I see how void youth is of skill,

1 see also his prime time and his end; I do confess my faults and all my ill, And sorrow sore for that I did offend ; And with a mind repentant of all crimes, Pardon I ask for youth ten thousand times.

Thou that by power to life didst raise the dead;
Thou that of grace restor'dst the blind to sight;
Thou that for love thy life and love outbled ;
Thou that of favour madest the lame go right;
Thou that canst heal and help in ail essays,
Forgive the guilt that grew in youth's vain ways. Lord Vaux.

" I like the verses," said Gertrude ; " and should be glad to have them ; something tells me," added she with a sigh, as she read them over again, " that they may some day be applicable to myself."

" God forbid, my dear! " said Mrs. Black, with a look of

horror — " God forbid that any of us should ever he brought to such straits as that, aud I see no good in putting such dismal thoughts into young folk's heads ;—but if you would like to put off your bonnet before dinner, it's time you were thinking of it."

" For there comes the Major," cried Miss Bell.

CHAPTER XXVI.

Une froideur ou une incivilite qui vient de ceux qui sont audessus de uous, nous les fait hair, mais un salut ou uu sourire nous les reconcilie.— La Bruyere.

The following day brought Colonel Delmour ; and Gertrude watched, with some solicitude, the effect her relations would produce upon him. But he was upon his guard, and none but a nice observer could have detected supercilious contempt in the lofty ease of his manner. But there is an ease which causes only constraint in the minds of others, and such was Colonel Delmour's. He was much too elegant and highbred to have any thing of the familiar ease so often a concomitant of the vulgar — but he had as little of that open simplicity of manner which is the characteristic of a noble ingenuous mind. It was that sort of ease which implies conscious superiority in its possessor, and consequently produces the opposite feeling in those less gifted mortals with whom it comes in contact. Such was the sort of undefinable sensation it created in the Black familv, from the eldest to the youngest.

Simple Mrs. Black's profound and earnest inquiries after Lord Rossville — her hopes that he had not been the worse of his ride —that he had got home before the hearty shower, &c. &c, were all answered in a general way, and with an air of indifference, which, as Mrs. Black afterwards declared, said very little for his natural affection. Even Miss Bell had an instinctive feeling that her airs would be all thrown away upon him: and though she did drop her carbuncle brooch (a present from Hyder Ally to the Major) upon the carpet, Colonel Delmour never so much as moved his chair or assisted in looking for it; while Miss Lilly turned over her album in vain, and in answer to her usual question of whether he was fond of poetry, he returned so brief and decided a negative as put a complete stop to all proceedings on that subject. The only one who made no attempts at display was the third daughter, Anne, a sensible, mild-looking girl, who, from her quiet unobtrusive manners, was generally overlooked, and who now pursued her work in her usual calm way, careless alike of notice or neglect.

Colonel Delmour certainly was at no pains to gain the good graces of the family. He saw at once they were not the sort of people likely to acquire any influence over Miss St. Clair ; consequently, he had no motive to make him wish to ingratiate himself with them. And to have been at the trouble of making the agreeable to such a set of plebeians, would have required some very strong stimulus for one whose ruling principle was selfishness, and who never cared to please, unless to serve his own purpose. He staid long, in hopes Mrs. Black and her daughters would have had the tact to discover that they were great bores in their own house ; but no such discovery was made ; — on the contrary, Mrs. Black redoubled her efforts to entertain her visitor — she made many apologies for Mr. Black being from home, and asked Bell what had come over the Major — just as the Major entered. The case was now desperate — scarcely able to conceal his ill-humour, he merely noticed the introduction of Major Waddell by a slight and somewhat haughty bow, and took his leave.

" Well, cousin," cried Miss Bell, as he drove off, " I really cannot say a great deal for your Colonel; I think I never saw so ill-bred a man."

" I can't just say that, Bell," said her mother. " I 'm sure he was nowise indiscreet; and we must make allowance for him, for you know we were all strangers to him, and I dare say he was just a little shy and strange at first—but that '11 wear off."

"It's the oddest thing that he should not like poetry," said Miss Lilly ; " for he is so handsome."

"I don't think much of his looks," said Miss Bell; " he is a great deal too tall," eyeing the Major, who was the Apollo Belvidere in her opinion, and who was, at least, a head shorter.

"I think our Bob must be as tall by this time," said Mrs. Black; " but I wish he may have taken the breadth with him, poor fellow!"

"I don't think he has the manners of a man who has seen much of the world," resumed Miss Bell again, looking at her lover ; " no general conversation—has he ever been abroad, I wonder?"

"Come, now," said the Major, turning up his bronzed visage, gilded with a strong yellow beam of delight, " are you not rather too severe? Colonel Delmour is surely a fine-looking man, and much admired, I understand, by the ladies."

"I beg you will make some exceptions, Major — but perhaps I have a very bad taste," with a conscious smile.

"I am afraid you have, indeed," returned the Major, with a laugh of perfect ecstasy. — "I'm very much afraid of it, indeed. —What do you say to that, Mrs. Black ? — Miss St. Clair, don't you think your cousin discovers a very bad taste in her choice of some things ? "

Gertrude felt too much disgusted with the vulgarity and ill-

I

breeding of her relations to be able to reply ;—indeed, the only one she could, with truth, have made must have been a cordial assent, and she recoiled from their familiarity with a hauteur foreign to her nature. Mrs. Black observed her displeasure, but mistook the cause.

" You must excuse our freedom, my dear," said she ; " but you see we make no stranger of you—we just look upon you as one of ourselves, and forget sometimes that your friends and relations are not ours. But there's one thing I can tell you," continued she, with a significant smile and a half whisper, " that, though the Colonel's not just so taking as his brother, we all think a great deal of him, and are all much pleased to think that

— you know"—and Mrs. Black smiled still more significantly.

— "I assure you, Mr. Black thinks a great deal of him — he says he's really a pleasant, sensible, gentlemanly, well-informed young man."

Still Gertrude's countenance did not clear up, to Mrs. Black's great surprise ; for, like many other excellent wives, she thought her husband's opinion carried the greatest possible weight with it, and that Miss St. Clair must needs be much flattered to hear that her intended was so much approved of by Mr. Black. For the Earl, to advance his favourite political schemes, had dropped some ambiguous mysterious hints of the projected alliance between his nephew and niece, which Mrs. Black had easily manufactured into an approaching marriage. Rather at a loss what to make of Miss St. Clair, and the coolness with which she listened to the praises of her supposed lover, Mrs. Black now proposed that the young people should take a walk, and show their cousin something of Bellevue — there was the burn, and the Hawkhill, and the new plantation; and there was the poultry-yard—if Miss Gertrude was fond of poultry, the Bellevue poultry were reckoned the finest in the country side ; and, loaded with Mrs. Black's directions and suggestions, the party set forth.

No party, perhaps, ever set out upon a walk without some difference of opinion as to the road to be taken; but, on the present occasion, the matter was soon settled by Miss Bell, who remarked to the Major, that it was so long since she had seen his sister, Mrs. Fairbairn, that, if her cousin had no objections, she should like much to walk as far as the Holm.

"I have not seen your sweet little namesake, Major, since he has had the measles, and I quite long to see him, dear little fellow! And although it is an understood thing "— addressing Gertrude — " that, in my situation, I go nowhere, yet the Major's sister, you know, is an exception ; and she is such a sweet domestic woman, she scarcely ever stirs from home —it is quite a treat to see Mr. and Mrs. Fairbairn in their own family — it is really a beautiful sight!"

The Major was, of course, all joy and gratitude for this proposal, and highly flattered by the interest expressed for his little

name-son in particular, and the eulogy bestowed on the family in general. As for Gertrude, she cared little where she went. When people are uncomfortable, they flatter themselves any change must be for the better, and there is relief even in variety of wretchedness. Forward, then, they set for the Holm.

The road was not of the most picturesque description ; but, indeed, it would not have been easy to have found any such in the environs of Bellevue. But at length, after skirting many a well-dressed field, covered with flourishing crops of oats, pease, beans, potatoes, &c. &c. &c, they entered upon the sheep farm, which, although it had nothing of the romantic or beautiful to charm the eye, yet, like all spots of unsophisticated nature, was not without attractions to those who love nature even in her simplest scenes.

The ground was hilly, covered with a carpet of close, shorti sweet herbage ; except here and there, where still remained patches of heath and broom, or a whin bush and a wild rose scented the breeze, their prickly stems decked with "small woolly tufts, spoils of the vagrant lamb."

The air was pure and fresh, " nimble and sweet;" and Gertrude stood inhaling it with delight, as she felt her spirits rise under its exhilarating influence. The Major and Miss Bell had walked on before ; Miss Lilly had left the party for higher ground, which commanded a view of the county town where Lieutenant O'Brien was quartered; and Gertrude, to her great relief, was left alone with her cousin Anne.

" If there were but deer bounding instead of sheep bleating here," said she, " I courd fancy myself upon the very ' Braes o' Balquither,' which you were singing about last night;" and she hummed the air. — " No, I can't make it out—pray sing it to me again;" — and Anne sung some verses of that sweet simple ditty.

Will ye go, lassie, go,
To the Braes o' Balquither, Where the blaeberries grow
'Mang the bonnie bloomin' heather.
Where the deer and the roe,
Lightly boundin' thegither, Sport the lang simmer day
'Mang the Braes o' Balquither.
I will twine thee a bow'r
By the clear silver fountain, And I '11 cover it owre
Wi' the flowers o' the mountain.
I will range through the wilds,
And the deep glens sae dreary, And return wi' their spoils
To the bower o' my deary.
Now the simmer is in prime,
Wi' the flowers richly blooming, And the wild mountain thyme A' the m airlands perfuming. Will ye go, &c. &c. I 2

" Who would not be a hunter's love," said Gertrude, " to realize so sweet a picture! "

" Ah ! " said her companion in a mournful tone, " if poverty were there represented as it is in reality, this world would be a paradise, and we might all be happy."

" So, then, you think poverty the only evil in life ? " asked Miss St. Clair.

" No, I spoke idly; — not the only one;—but " — she blushed, and the tears stood in her eyes, as in a low voice she added, " but the only one I have ever known ;"— then, as if ashamed of having said so much, she turned away her head.

For a moment Gertrude was at a loss to understand her cousin's meaning; but it presently struck her that she must have formed some attachment where poverty was the obstacle; and she would have continued the conversation in hopes of gaining her confidence, but at that moment the Major and Miss Bell, having retraced their steps in search of their companions, interposed.

" We thought we had lost you! " exclaimed the lady. — " Major, will you give my cousin your other arm ? — the descent is very steep now."

Gertrude declined the proffered aid, which she thought more likely to encumber than accelerate her movements ; and, besides,

she wished to renew the conversation with Anne, but in vain

The lovers having exhausted their silly talk for the present, were now glad of a little variety, and they kept all close together till they reached the Holm.

CHAPTER XXVII.

The great use of delineating absurdities is, that we may know how far human folly can go ; the account, therefore, ought, of absolute necessity, to be faithful. — Johnson.

The first appearance of the Holm was highly prepossessing. It was a large, handsome-looking house, situated in a well-wooded park, by the side of a broad placid river ; and an air of seclusion and stillness reigned all round, which impressed the mind with images of peace and repose. The interior of the house was no less promising — there was a spacious hall and a handsome staircase, with all appliances to boot; but as they approached the drawing-room, all the luxurious indolence of thought inspired by the tranquillity of the scenery was quickly dispelled by the discordant sounds which issued from thence, and, when the door was thrown open, the footman in vain attempted to announce the visitors. In the middle of the room all the chairs were collected

to form a coach and horses for the Masters and Misses Fairhairn. — One unruly-lookiDg urchin sat in front, cracking a long whip ■with all his might — another acted as guard behind, and blew a shrill trumpet with all his strength — while a third, in a nightcap and a flannel lappet, who had somewhat the air of having quarrelled with the rest of the party, paraded up and down in solitary majesty, beating a drum. On a sofa sat Mrs. Fairbairn, a soft, fair, genteel-looking woman, with a crying child of about three years old at her side, tearing paper into shreds, seemingly for the delight of littering the carpet, which was already strewed with headless dolls, tailless horses, wheelless carts, &c. As she rose to receive her visitors it began to scream.

" I'm not going away, Charlotte, love — don't be frightened," said the fond mother, with a look of ineffable pleasure.

"You no get up — you shan't get up," screamed Charlotte, seizing her mother's gown fiercely to dctain hcr.

" My darling, you'll surely let me go to speak to uncle — good uncle, who brings you pretty things, you know,"—but, during this colloquy, uncle and ladies had made their way to the enthralled mother, and the bustle of a meeting and introduction was got over. Chairs were obtained by the footman with some difficulty, and placed as close to the mistress of the house as possible, aware that, otherwise, it would not be easy to carry on even question and answer amid the tumult that reigned.

"You find us rather noisy, I am afraid," said Mrs. Fairbairn with a smile, and in a manner which evidently meant the reverse; "but this is Saturday, and the children are all in such spirits, and they won't stay away from me. Henry, my dear, don't crack your whip quite so loud, there's a good boy — that's a new whip his papa brought him from London; and he's so proud of it! — William, my darling, don't you think your drum must be tired now? If I were you, I would give it a rest. — Alexander, your trumpet makes rather too much noise — one of these ladies has got a headach — wait till you go out, there's my good boy, and then you'll blow it at the cows and the sheep, you know, and frighten them — Oh! how you'll frighten them with it!"

"No, I'll not blow it at the cows; I'll blow it at the horses, because then they'll think it's the mail-coach." And he was running off, when Henry jumped down from the coach-box.

"No, but you shan't frighten them with your trumpet, for I shall frighten them with my whip. Mamma, aren't horses best frightened with a whip?" — and a struggle ensued.

"Well, don't fight, my dears, and you shall both frighten them," cried their mamma.

"No, I'm determined he shan't frighten them; I shall do it," cried both together, as they rushed out of the room, ana the drummer was preparing to follow.

"William Pitt, my darling, don't you go after these naughty boys; you know they're always very bad to you. You know they wouldn't let you into their coach -with your drum." Here William Pitt began to cry. — "Well, never mind, you shall have a coach of your own — a much finer coach than theirs; I wouldn't go into their ugly dirty coach; and you shall have" Here something of a consolatory nature was whispered; William was comforted, and even prevailed upon to relinquish his drum for his mamma's ivory workbox, the contents of which were soon scattered on the floor.

"These boys are gone without their hats," cried Mrs. Fair-bairn in a tone of distress. "Eliza, my dear, pull the bell for Sally to get the boys' hats." — Sally being despatched with the hats, something like a calm ensued, in the absence of he of the whip and the trumpet; but as it will be of short duration, it is necessary to take advantage of it in improving the introduction into an acquaintance with the Fairbairn family.

Mrs. Fairbairn was one of those ladies who, from the time she became a mother, ceased to be any thing else. All the duties, pleasures, charities, and decencies of life, were henceforth concentrated in that one grand characteristic; every object in life was henceforth viewed through that single medium. Her own mother -was no longer her mother, she was the grandmamma of her dear infants; her brothers and sisters were mere uncles and aunts, and even her husband ceased to be thought of as her husband from the time he became a father. He was no longer the being who had claims on her time, her thoughts, her talents, her affections; he was simply Mr. Fairbairn, the noun masculine of Mrs. Fairbairn, and the father of her children. Happily for Mr. Fairbairn, he was not a person " of very nice feelings, or refined taste; and although, at first, he did feel a little unpleasant when he saw how much his children were preferred to himself, yet, in time, he became accustomed to it, — then came to look upon Mrs. Fairbairn as the most exemplary of mothers,—and finally resolved himself into the father of a very fine family, of which Mrs. Fairbairn was the mother. In all this there was more of selfish egotism and animal instinct, than of rational affection or Christian principle ; but both parents piqued themselves upon their fondness for their offspring, as if it were a feeling peculiar to themselves, and not one they shared in common with the lowest and weakest of their species. Like them, too, it was upon the bodies of their children that they lavished their chief care and tenderness ; for as to the immortal interests of their souls, or the cultivation of their minds, or the improvement of their tempers, these were but little attended to, at least in comparison of their health and personal appearance.

Alas! if there " be not a gem so precious as the human soul," how often do these gems seem as pearls cast before swine; for how seldom is it that a parent's greatest care is for the immortal happiness of that being whose precarious, and at best transient

existence, engrosses their every thought and desire! But, perhaps, Mrs. Fairbairn, like many a foolish ignorant mother, did her best; and had she been satisfied with spoiling her children herself for her own private amusement, and not have drawn in her visitors and acquaintances to share in it, the evil might have passed uncensured. But Mrs. Fairbairn, instead of shutting herself up in her nursery, chose to bring her nursery down to her drawing-room ; and instead of modestly denying her friends an entrance into her purgatory, she had a foolish pride in showing herself in the midst of her angels. In short, as the best things, when corrupted, always become the worst; so the purest and tenderest of human affections, when thus debased by selfishness and egotism, turn to the most tiresome and ridiculous of human weaknesses, — a truth but too well exemplified by Mrs. Fairbairn.

"I have been much to blame," said she, addressing Miss Bell, in a soft, whining, sick-child sort of voice, " for not having been at Bellevue long ago; but dear little Charlotte has been so plagued with her teeth, I could not think of leaving her — for she is so fond of me, she will go to nobody else — she screams when her maid offers to take her — and she won't even go to her papa."

" Is that possible ? " said the Major.

" I assure you it's very true — she's a very naughty girl sometimes," bestowing a long and rapturous kiss on the child. " Who was it that beat poor papa for taking her from mamma last night ? Well, don't cry — no, no, it wasn't my Charlotte. She knows every word that's said to her, and did from the time she was only a year old."

" That is wonderful! " said Miss Bell; " but how is my little favourite, Andrew ? "

" He is not very stout yet, poor little fellow, and we must be very careful of him." Then, turning to Miss St. Clair, " Our little Andrew has had the measles, and you know the dregs of the measles are a serious thing — much worse than the measles themselves. Andrew—Andrew Waddell, my love, come here and speak to the ladies." And thereupon Andrew Waddell, in a nightcap, riding on a stick, drew near. Being the Major's namesake, Miss Bell, in the ardour of her attachment, thought proper to coax Andrew Waddell on her knee, and even to open her watch for his entertainment.

" Ah! I see who spoils Andrew Waddell," cried the delighted mother.

The Major chuckled — Miss Bell disclaimed, and for the time Andrew Waddell became the hero of the piece ; the blains of the measles were carefully pointed out, and all his sufferings and sayings duly recapitulated. At length Miss Charlotte, indignant at finding herself eclipsed, began to scream and cry with all her strength.

I 4

" It's her teeth, darling little thing," said her mother, caressing her.

" I'm sure it's her teeth, sweet little dear," said Miss Bell.

"It undoubtedly must be her teeth, poor little girl," said the Major.

"If you will feel her gum," said Mrs. Fairbairn, putting her own finger into the child's mouth, "you will feel how hot it is."

This was addressed in a sort of general way to the company, none of whom seemed eager to avail themselves of the privilege, till the Major stepped forward, and having with his forefinger made the circuit of Miss Charlotte's mouth, gave it as his decided opinion that there was a tooth actually cutting the skin. Miss Bell followed the same course, and confirmed the interesting fact — adding, that it appeared to her to be "an uncommon large tooth."

At that moment Mr. Fairbairn entered, bearing in his arms another of the family,—a fat, sour, new-waked-looking creature, sucking its finger. Scarcely was the introduction over — "There's a pair of legs!" exclaimed he, holding out a pair of thick purple stumps with red worsted shoes at the end of them. "I don't suppose Miss St. Clair ever saw legs like these in France; these are porridge-and-milk legs, — are they not, Bobby?"

But Bobby continued to chew the cud of his own thumb in solemn silence.

"Will you speak to me, Bobby?" said Miss Bell, bent upon being amiable and agreeable; but still Bobby was mute.

"We think this little fellow rather long of speaking," said Mr. Fairbairn; "we allege that his legs have ran away with his tongue."

"How old is he?" asked the Major.

"He is only nineteen months and ten days," answered his mother, "so he has not lost much time; but I would rather see a child fat and thriving, than have it very forward."

"No comparison!" was here uttered in a breath by the Major and Miss Bell.

"There's a great difference in children in their time of speaking," said the mamma. "Alexander didn't speak till he was two and a quarter; and Henry, again, had a great many little words before he was seventeen months; and Eliza and Charlotte both said mamma as plain as I do at a year — but girls always speak sooner than boys; as for William Pitt and Andrew Waddell, the twins, they both suffered so much from their teething, that they were longer of speaking than they would otherwise have been — indeed, I never saw an infant suffer so much as Andrew Waddell did — he had greatly the heels of William Pitt at one time, till the measles pulled him down."

A movement was here made by the visitors to depart.

"O! you mustn't go without seeing the baby," cried Mrs.

Fairbairn — "Mr. Fairbairn, will you pull the bell twice for baby?"

The bell was twice rung, but no baby answered the summons.

"She must be asleep," said Mrs. Fairbairn; "but I will take you up to the nursery, and you wi!l see her in her cradle." And Mrs. Fairbairn led the way to the nursery, and opened the shutter, and uncovered the cradle, and displayed the baby.

"Just five months — uncommon fine child — the image of Mr. Faii-bairn — fat little thing — neat little hands — sweet little mouth — pretty little nose — lovely little toes," &c. &c. &c. were as usual whispered over it.

Miss St. Clair flattered herself the exhibition was now over, and was again taking leave, when, to her dismay, the squires of the whip and the trumpet rushed in, proclaiming that it was pouring of rain! To leave the house was impossible; and, as it was getting late, there was nothing for it but staying dinner.

The children of this happy family always dined at table, and their food and manner of eating were the only subjects of conversation. Alexander did not like mashed potatoes — and

Andrew Waddell could not eat broth — and Eliza could live upon fish — and William Pitt took too much small beer — and Henry ate as much meat as his papa — and all these peculiarities had descended to them from some one or other of their ancestors. The dinner was simple on account of the children; and there was no dessert, as Bobby did not agree with fruit. But to make amends Eliza's sampler was shown; and Henry and Alexander's copy-books were handed round the table ; and Andrew Waddell stood up and repeated "My name is Norval" from beginning to end; and William Pitt was prevailed upon to sing the whole of " God save the King," in a little squeaking mealy voice, and was bravoed and applauded as though he had been Braham himself.

To paint a scene in itself so tiresome is doubtless but a poor amusement to my reader, who must often have endured similar persecution. For who has not suffered from the obtrusive fondness of parents for their offspring ? — and who has not felt what it was to be called upon, in the course of a morning visit, to enter into all the joys and the sorrows of the nursery, and to take a lively interest in all the feats and peculiarities of the family ? Shakespeare's anathema against those who hated music is scarcely too strong to be applied to those who dislike children. There is much enjoyment sometimes in making acquaintance with the little beings — much delight in hearing their artless untutored prattle, and something not unpleasing even in witnessing their little freaks and wayward humours; — but when a tiresome mother, instead of allowing the company to notice her child, torments every one by forcing or coaxing her child to notice the company, the charm is gone, and we experience only disgust or ennui.

Mr. and Mrs. Fairbairn had split on this fatal rock, on which so many parents make shipwreck of their senses ; and so satisfied wei'e they with themselves and their children, so impressed with the idea of the delights of their family scenes, that vain would have been any attempt to open the eyes of their understanding. Perhaps the only remedy would have been found in that blessed spirit which "vaunteth not itself, and seeketh not its own."

The evening proved fine ; and Gertrude rejoiced to return even to Bellevue.

CHAPTER XXVIII.

Il y en a peu qui gagnent a etre approfondies. La Bruyere

" What a sweet woman your sister is!" said Miss Bell, who at present beheld every object connected with the Major tinged with " love's proper hue."

" I am very glad you like her," replied the delighted lover; " and I flatter myself the longer you know her the more you will be pleased with her."

" O, I have no doubt of that," said the lady.

" You will find her always the same," continued the Major.

" That is delightful!" said Miss Bell; " and what a charming family she has, — it is really quite a treat to see them — I assure you, I don't know when I have passed so pleasant a day."

" I trust you will pass many such," returned the Major, brightening still more. " I flatter myself my sister and you will be sisters indeed."

While this colloquy was carrying on betwixt the lovers, Miss St. Clair tried to bring her cousin Anne back to the subject of their morning's conversation ; but Anne seemed either afraid or ashamed of having said so much, and rather shunned any renewal of the subject. Gertrude did not think the worse of her upon that account, but rather gave her credit for that delicacy of mind which made her shrink from making a confidant of one who, though a relation, was, in fact, almost a stranger to her.

" It would be folly in me, my dear cousin," said she, " to make a parade of offering to assist you at present in any way. I am neither old nor wise enough to advise, and I am quite as poor and as powerless as you can possibly be; but if ever the time should come when I have either wisdom or power — both I can never hope to have together," said she, with a smile,—" promise that you will then riddle me right, and tell me why poverty is the greatest misfortune in the world."

They were here interrupted by a band of young Blacks, who, having descried them from the window, had rushed out to meet them — all breathless with haste to hear where they had been, and to proclaim that Bob and Davy were arrived; and upon advancing a little farther, Bob and Davy presented themselves in propriis personis.

Bob and Davy were two tall good-looking youths, dressed in all the extremes of the reigning fashions — small waists — brush-heads — stiff collars — iron heels and switches. Like many other youths, they were decidedly of opinion that dress " makes the man, and want of it the fellow," and that the rest was " mere leather and prunella." Perhaps, after all, that is a species of humility rather to be admired in those who, feeling themselves destitute of mental qualifications, trust to the abilities of their tailor and hairdresser for gaining them the goodwill of the world ; and who can tell whether there may not be more true lowliness of mind in a mop-head and high-heeled boots, than has been lodged in many a pilgrim's scalloped hat and sandalled shoon ? Be that as it may, it was evident that Bob and Davy rested their claims to distinction solely on the outward man, and that the sentiment of Henry the Fifth was by no means theirs, —

It yearns me not that men my garments wear, Such outward things dwell not in my desire, &c.

Introduced to their cousin, and the first ceremonials over, Bob and Davy each began to play his part. Bob, being a military man, talked of parades, reviews, mess-dinners, and regulation epaulettes — while Davy, the writer's apprentice, was loud upon Edinburgh belles, playhouse rows, assembly rooms, and new quadrilles.

" We are to be reviewed on the 27th," said Bob, addressing his cousin. " Gunstown is only about thirty miles from this. I hope you will do us the honour to come and look at us — we shall give a ball and supper after it — my mother and the girls will, of course, be there. — Bell, you will be at our turn-out, won't you?"

" I wonder how you can ask such a question, Bob, of a person in my situation," said Miss Bell, with dignity.

" What a famous deal of fun we had in Edinburgh last winter," said Davy ; " I was very often at three balls in a night. You dance queydrills of course : country-dances are quite exploded now in Edinburgh—they call them kitchen-dances there—there's nothing goes down now but walltsays and queydrills. By-the-by,

I dare say we could make out a que) drill here. Bell, do you dance queydrills?"

" I never heard of a person in my situation dancing," replied Miss Bell, with an air of contempt.

" Aye, that's always the way whenever you misses get hus-hands, you grow so confoundedly stupid ; — hut I shall not suffer my wife to give herself such airs, I can tell you. I shall make a point of her dancing every night."

The brothers had come on purpose to he present at the celebration of the nuptials, which they merely thought of as Bell's going off— a consummation to he devoutly wished for in a family of eleven, and an event indissolubly united in their minds with new coats, white gloves, wedding favours, bride's maids, capital dinners, jovial suppers, dances, flirtations, and famous fun. Such being Bob and Davy, it may be inferred they were no great acquisitions to the family party, though they certainly were additions to it. Under the mistaken idea of being too genteel to do any thing for themselves, there was a constant ringing of bells, and calling for this, that, and t'other; and if the hapless footboy could have cut himself into a thousand pieces, and endowed each particular piece with locomotive powers, all would scarcely have sufficed to answer the demands made upon him. Then, without any bad temper, there was a constant jangling and jarring from mere vacancy of mind and want of proper pursuit. They were all warmly attached to each other in a disagreeable way; and, upon the strength of that attachment, thought they might dispense with all the ordinary rules of politeness, and contradict and dispute with each other upon the most trifling occasion. In short, it was not a pleasant dwelling-place ; there was neither the peace and tranquillity which the true spirit of Christianity diffuses amongst its votaries, nor the refined courtesies which spring from cultivated minds and elegant habits. Anne, indeed, was an exception; but she was so quiet and pensive, that she was completely sunk in the commotion that prevailed.

Miss St. Clair suffered particularly from the assiduities of the two beaux, being both bent on engaging her in a flirtation ; but their attentions were received with so much coldness at times, even amounting to hauteur, that at length they discovered that their old flames Cecy Swan and Clemmy Dow were much prettier girls, and to Cecy Swan and Clemmy Dow they accordingly betook themselves.

Heartily tired of Bellevue and its inhabitants, Gertrude longed impatiently for the rnarriage-day, that she might return to Ross-ville. She felt anxious, too, about her mother; and the thoughts of the mystery in which she was involved disquieted her, and rendered her situation doubly irksome. Unconsciously she cherished the desire of penetrating that dread secret, although, with the natural thoughtlessness and gaiety of youth, her mind was often diverted from the contemplation of it; yet there were times

■when it gained an almost overwhelming ascendency over her, and she thought she could easier have submitted to any known evil than have endured this unknown fear.

In Colonel Deimour's company, indeed, every painful idea was suspended, and she gave herself up to the charms of his brilliant conversation, and varied powers of pleasing, with a complete forgetfulness of every thing, save the consciousness of loving and being beloved; while, at the same time, with all the delusion of passion, she yet closed ber eyes against the light of conviction. His visits became so frequent and so long, that they might have called forth some animadversion in the family, who had been led by Lord Rossville to look upon her as the affianced bride of the elder brother, but all were too busy with the substantials of marriage to have much time to bestow on the empty speculations of love. Mr. Black had settlements to read over and sign, &c. Mrs. Black had the innumerable departments of mother and housekeeper to fill—duties which are always trebled tenfold upon such momentous occasions. All the powers of Bob and Davy's minds were exerted to the decoration of their persons — but all the emanations of their genius had proved insufficient to enlighten the understanding of the Barnford tailor. Bob's coat was sent home when too late for alterations at least half an inch too long, while Davy's waistcoat was as much too short. The young ladies' gowns pleased better, and the children were charmed with their respective suits and sashes.

As for Miss Bell, she was like some bright planet, the centre of its own system, round which all inferior orbs revolve. She it was to whom all must look for bride-cake, and gloves, and favours, and all such minor consolations as fall to the lot of the single on such occasions. But no one's cup, however it may froth and mantle, is ever full, even to the overflowing. Miss Bell's certainly seemed to foam to the very top, but it could still have held a little more. Many were the wedding presents she had received from kindred and friends, according to their various means, till her chamber might have vied with the shrine of some patron saint. But amidst all the votive offerings, there was none from uncle Adam, although she had settled in her own mind that uncle Adam could not possibly avoid presenting her with something very handsome, whether in plate, jewels, or specie, and her only doubt was which of the three she would prefer. However, time wore on, and uncle Adam was only to be seen in his usual attitude, with his hands in his pockets, as if strictly guarding his money, and with a face of the most hopeless sourness. Miss Bell, notwithstanding, still kept up under the expectation that uncle Adam would surprise her in his ovn i rough queer way some day when she was not thinking of it. When that day would be it would have been difficult to say, as there was no day in which she was not fully prepared for the surprise.

CHAPTER XXIX.

Bid them cover the table, serve in the meat, and we will come in to dinner. — Shakspeare.

The day previous to the marriage, the hustle that reigned in and around Bellevue was increased to that intense degree which attends all great events as they approach towards their consummation. Uncle Adam, Miss Black, and Mr. and Mrs. Fairbairn were expected at dinner; and, during the whole day, the steam of the soups, pies, pasties, &c. &c. which issued from Mrs. Black's kitchen, and penetrated to the very interior of the drawing-room, might (as some one has parodied it) have created a stomach beneath the ribs of death. To Gertrude the commotion caused by what is called giving a dinner was something new ; the total bouleversement of all orders of the community, where much was to be done without the proper means — where a sumptuous banquet was to be prepared by the common drudges of the kitchen, and where every servant had double their usual portion of work to perform, besides being thrown out of their own natural sphere of action. Then there was the running backwards and forwards — the flying up stairs and the rushing down stairs — the opening and shutting of doors, or rather I should say the opening of doors, as the shutting was an evil not to be complained of, unless, indeed, when the call of " shut the door" was answered with a slam which shook the house to its foundation. Added to all this, was the losing of Mrs. Black's keys, with the customary suspicions attached to every individual of having somehow or other got them about them — suspicions only to be removed by repeated raisings and shakings of the party suspected, and even then not completely effaced, till the keys were found as usual in some place where somebody must surely have put them, and where nobody would ever have thought of looking for them.

Then the nursery maid was transformed into the cook's assistant, and the children were committed to a girl who could not manage them; and they broke loose, and overran the house, and resisted all authority. But doubtless many of my readers must have witnessed similar scenes, and endured similar persecutions, pending the preparations for a dinner, which, like worthy Mrs. Black's, was to be about three times as large and as elaborate as was necessai-y. But many are the paths to the temple of Fame, and hard it is to climb by any of them ! Mrs. Black was chiefly emulous of a character for her dinners, and probably laboured infinitely harder to stuff a dozen dull bodies than the Author of Waverley does to amuse the whole world. It was for this she thought by night and toiled by day; but, strange to

say, she had an enjoyment in it too, though, when that was, it would have heen difficult to determine ; for the anticipation was care and fatigue — the reality was ceremony and anxiety— the retrospect was disappointment and provocation.

Uncle Adam was the first of the guests who arrived, and Miss St. Clair was the only one of the family ready to receive him. She was in the drawing-room when he entered, and the habitual vinegar expression of his long triangular visage relaxed into something like a smile at sight of her—he even seated himself by her side, and entered into conversation with a degree of complacency very unusual with him.

Emboldened by his good humour, Gertrude ventured to admire a very fine camellia japonica, which, together with a piece of his favourite southernwood, decorated the breast of his coat.

" I ken naething aboot the things mysel'," said he, hastily tearing it out of the button-hole, as if ashamed of wearing any thing to be admired—then, stuffing it into her hand, " Ha'e, tak it, my dear— it cam' frae that place up bye " — pointing in the direction of Broom Park. — " I'm sure they need nae ha'e sent it to me.—What ca' ye it ?"

Gertrude repeated the name.

" It's a senseless-like thing, without ony smell," — applying the southernwood to bis nose as he spoke; —" but I daresay there's plenty o' them, and I've nae use for them; so you may gang up bye when you like, and tak what you like."

Gertrude thanked him : and as she adjusted the japonica in her dress, the old garnet brooch, now her only ornament, fell out, and in his gallantry the old man stooped to pick it up. But no sooner had he taken it in his hand than he uttered an exclamation of astonishment, and, turning it over and over, examined it with the deepest interest.

" Wha's aught this ? " inquired he.

" It is mine," replied Gertrude, in some surprise.

" Yours!" repeated he ; " yours ! And whar did ye get it ? tell me the truth, whar did ye get it ? "

" I got it from my nurse; she gave it to me when she was dying, and I have kept it for her sake."

" And did she no tell you whar she had got it ? "

" I think she said she had got it from her mother."

" From her mother ! It was ance my mother's,— it was mine, and I gi'ed it to Lizzie wi' my ain hands whan last we parted, and she promised to keep it till her dying day — there's our initials " — pointing to the back —" and the very year we parted." — Then, after a long pause, " What was the name o' your nurse, and whar did she come frae ? "

" Her own name was Marianne Lamotte — her husband's Jacob Lewiston, and she came from America; her father was French; but, I believe, her mother was Scotch, for she used to sing me many an old Scotch song, which she said she had learned from her."

" I canna mak it oot," said Mr. Eamsay thoughtfully—" hut it disna signify ; though I could, it wadna hring back life and time ;■" and with a sigh he tendered the brooch.

" Pray keep it," said Gertrude ; " it seems you have a better right to it than I have. I valued it merely for the sake of my nurse ; but it is a still dearer memorial to you, and therefore I willingly part with it."

" No, no," said he, rejecting the hand that offered it; " what wad I do wi't ? At your age, you may please yoursel' wi' thae kind o' dead toys, but I'm ow'r auld noo to ha'e ony enjoyment in sic thinks ; the young may tak pleasure in thae romantic gewgaws ; ye like to look back when ye ha'e nae far to cast your eye — but at threescore and ten it's a dreigh sight to see the lang and weary road we ha'e wandered.—No, no, there's nae pleasure to the aged in sic mementos; they canna bring back youthfu' days and youthfu' hearts, and they are the only jewels o' life."

Gertrude could not urge it; but, from a feeling of delicacy towards her uncle's painful reminiscences, she put aside the trinket, and resolved never again to wear it in his presence.

It is rarely that feelings raised above the ordinary pitch can be long indulged in this strange world, where the most opposite emotions are constantly coming in contact, and where the mind is for ever in a state of ebb and flow. Mr. Ramsay's nature had been softened, and all its best ingredients called forth, at the sight of the love-token of his early days, and the mournful associations which followed in its train ; but the gentler current of his soul was speedily checked by the entrance of various members of the family, as they came severally dropping in fresh from their toilettes ; and last, if not least, uncle Adam's antipathy, Miss Bell.

Squeezing herself on the little sofa between Miss St. Clair and him, she exclaimed, " What a beautiful flower that is, cousin ! — -where did you get it?"

" Mr. Ramsay was so good as to give it to me," answered she.

" Indeed! I suppose then it is from Broom Park, uncle? You have charming greenhouses there, I understand—that is what I regret so much at Thornbank. You know the Major has taken that in the meantime ; but I don't think it will answer, as there are no hothouses, and the Major has been accustomed to such charming fruits in India, that I'm afraid he will miss his pines sadly."

" I suppose there will be plenty o' gude neeps," said Mr. Ramsay ; "neeps like succur — he can take ane o' them when he's dry."

Miss Bell reddened; but, affecting not to hear, returned to the charge.

" Thornbank is no great distance from Broom Park, uncle; quite an easy walk, I should think."

" I never measured it," was the laconic reply.

Finding it was not by way of Broom Park she was likely to arrive at uncle Adam's pocket, Miss Bell now went more directly to the point.

" Do you know, uncle, I could be almost jealous of my cousin for having got that beautiful japonica from you, while poor I have not so much as a single leaf from you by way of keepsake."

Mr. Ramsay, with a bow and a sardonic smile, here presented her with the piece of southernwood he held in his hand.

" Well, uncle, I assure you, I shall value this very much, and lay it up with the rest of my wedding presents — and, by-the-by, I have never showed you all the fine things my kind friends have presented to me. Good old Mrs. Waddell of Waddell Mains has presented me with a most beautiful antique silver cup, which, it seems, was the Major's christening bowl."

" It will be ancient enough then, nae doot," observed uncle Adam.

" My excellent aunts have sent me a very handsome teapot, and "

" A fool and his money's soon parted; they had very little to do to send ony such thing."

" Why surely, uncle, you know it is the custom, all the world over, for persons in my situation to receive presents, and "

" Miss Bell Black, I've seen something mair o' the world than you've done ; and I can tell ye some o' its customs that ye maybe dinna ken yet — in Russia, for instance, the present to persons in your situation is "

"O! for Heaven's sake!"—interrupted Miss Bell, with an instinctive dread of the knout—"don't set up these bears as models for us — the customs of our own country ought surely to guide us on these occasions."

"It's a very senseless custom, in my opinion," said Mr. Ramsay. " It's like casting pearls before swine to be lavishing presents on a woman that's at the very pinnacle o' human happiness and grandeur—it's you that should mak presents to puir single folk that ha'e nae Major Waddells to set them up wi' Ingee shawls, and carbuncles, and fans — and —oo, I can compare ye to naething but a goddess the noo — let me see, which o' them is't ? A Juno ? na, — I'm thinkin' it'll rather be a Vaiytass."

Here uncle Adam was so tickled with his own jeu de mot, that he laughed till the tears ran down his cheeks. The insult was too broad, even for Miss Bell, who walked away in silent indignation ; then, recovering himself, he pointed after her to Gertrude, and said—

K

...

That creature's folly's just like dust — drive it out o' ae thing, and it just flees to anither."

Miss Black was the next of the party -who arrived; and Gertrude, attracted by her mildness and good sense, would fain have exchanged the gall and vinegar of uncle Adam for her more pleasing converse. But the obstreperous mirth of the children, and the noisy tattle of Bob and Davy, effectually precluded any interchange of speech beyond the ordinary salutations of meeting.

The Fairbairn family (including the Major) were now waited for with outward impatience by Mr. Black, with inward anxiety by Mrs. Black ; — Mr. Black openly avowed his hunger — Mrs. Black vainly endeavoured to disguise her apprehensions that the beef would be roasted to a cinder (a thing Mr. Black could not endure) — and that the rice (which the Major was so particular about) would be all in a lump, instead of being — as well-boiled rice ought to be — each and every particular grain separate by itself. All this, and much more, poor Mrs. Black revolved in her own mind, as she sat, like a second Mrs. Blue Beard, ever and anon calling to the children to look out, and see if they saw any body coming.

At length the Fairbairn coach was descried, and loudly proclaimed. The bell was rung — the dinner was ordered. Bob and Davy were ordered out of two arm-chairs they had taken possession of. Mrs. Black smoothed her gown, and put on a ceremonious face; while Mr. Black hastened to the door to be ready to receive Mrs. Fairbairn with due respect. But no Mrs. Fairbairn was there — in her stead, however, was Miss Becky Duguid, her cousin ; and the cause of Mrs. Fairbairn's absence was accounted for by reason of poor little Charlotte having been very cross all day, and her mamma thinking there was a tooth coming ; and she would not leave her mamma, and her mamma could not leave her, &c. &c. &c. All this was duly set forth by Mr. Fairbairn on one hand, while Miss Becky was making her own personal apologies on the other. She was really such a figure, she was quite ashamed to appear; but she had no idea of coming, for it had been all settled that she was to stay with Charlotte while Mrs. Fairbairn was away ; and at one time Charlotte had agreed to let her mamma go, and her mamma had dressed herself, and was all ready to set out; and then she took a crying fit when the carriage was at the door, and so her mamma was obliged to give up the point, and stay at home ; and then Mr. Fairbairn had insisted on her coming in Mrs. Fairbairn's place just as she was. Miss Becky's apologies were of course met with protestations that there was no occasion for any—that she was perfectly well-dressed — that it was merely a family dinner—an easy party—none but friends, and so forth. But, to tell the truth, Miss Becky's dress did require an apology ; for the marks of children's fingers were

upon her gown — her cap looked as if it had heen sat upon, and her shawl even bore symptoms of having served to play at bo-peep ! In short, Miss Becky had the tout ensemble of a poor elderly maiden aunt; and such, indeed, was her history and character, as it is, alas! of many others ; but a slight sketch may serve to describe the genus, and give a tolerably faithful picture of Auntimony.

CHAPTER XXX.

How happy is the blameless vestal's lot! Pope.

Miss Betty Duguid, as a single woman, had vainly expected to escape the cares and anxieties of the married state. She had heard and seen much of the indifference or the ill humour of husbands — of the troubles and vexations of children — and she thought from these evils I am at least free ; — I can go where I like, do what I like, and live as I like. But poor Miss Becky soon found her mistake. Brothers and sisters married; — nephews and nieces sprung up on all hands, each and all expecting to be distinguished by aunt Becky's bounty, while every parent levied the most unconscionable taxes upon her time and capabilities.

" Aunt Becky will give me this," said one ; " you know she has no use for money."

" Aunt Becky will do that," said another; " for she has always plenty of time."

" Aunt Becky will go there," cried a third; " she likes a long walk."

But even the labours imposed upon her by her own relations were nothing compared to the constant demands made upon her by the world in general, — i. e. by the whole circle of her acquaintances; — all under the idea that, as a single woman, she could have nothing to do but oblige her friends. When in town, her life was devoted to executing commissions from the country — inquiring the character of servants — hiring governesses and grooms — finding situations for wet nurses — getting patterns of pelisse cloths from every shop in town — trying to get old silks matched with new — gowns made — gauzes dyed — feathers cleaned — fans mended, parcels booked, &c. &c. The letters always beginning, " As I know you do not grudge your trouble, and will be walking about at any rate, I must beg the favour, when you are quite at leisure," and so and so ; and ending with, " As I find I am really in want of the things, and the carrier leaves town on Thursday, I trust you will contrive to have every thing ready by that time." But one of the let-

ters, dropped by Miss Becky in the course of her perambulations, will best illustrate this part of her personal narrative.

" My dear Miss Becky,

"I take this opportunity of letting you know we are all tolerably well at present, and trust you continue to enjoy your usual good health. I return the tea you sent last, as we all think it very inferior to that you sent formerly; and as there has been rather a fall upon the price of teas, there can be no reason for such a falling off in the quality ; and unless Candytuft can give something very superior at the same price, I would just return it, and try some other shop, and have nothing more to do with Candytuft. Eliza and Jane, with their best love, take this opportunity of sending in their old black velvet pelisses, which they wish you to consult Yellowlys the dyer about; they have been told that black velvet can be dyed either grass green or bright crimson ; and if Yellowlys can warrant their standing, they would prefer having them done a good rich crimson ; but if not, they must just put up with a full green, as much on the grass and off the bottle as possible.

" I am sorry to tell you your protege, Jenny Snodgrass, has turned out very ill. I find her lazy and idle, dirty, disobliging, and insolent, and not at all the person I was led to expect from your character of her. I must, therefore, trouble you to be on the look-out for another. You know it is not much I require of my servants ; but there are some things it is impossible to dispense with, and which I must make a point of. Of course, she must be perfectly sober, honest, conscientious, and trustworthy, and, in every respect, unexceptionable in her morals. She must be stout, active, cleanly, civil, obliging, quiet, orderly, good-tempered, neat-handed, and particularly tidy in her person. All that I. require of her is to be an excellent worker at her needle, a thorough washer and ironer, and a generally useful and accommodating servant. For such a servant I shall not grudge fifty shillings for the first half year (tea included) ; and, if she gives perfect satisfaction in every respect, I shall not stand with her for ten shillings more for the next term. Margaret sends her affectionate remembrance, and, when you are at leisure, requests you will order a pair of stays for her from Brisbane's as soon as possible, as she is in great want. She sends a pair of old ones for a pattern, but they don't fit; you must tell him they are both too tight and too short, and the shoulder-straps too narrow by a. full straw-breadth. The old busk, she thinks, may do; or, if it should be too short, perhaps you may be able to get it exchanged for one longer. As Flint the gun-smith's is no great distance from Brisbane's, John would be much obliged to you when you are there, if you would step to him, and tell him that he is going to send his gun to have the lock mended, and to be sure to have it done in the most complete manner, and as soon

as he possibly can, as the shooting season is coming on. When done, he may send it to you, with a couple of pounds of gunpowder, and a bag of small shot, No. 5. As the holiday time is coming on, we may look for the boys some of these days ; and (if it is not putting you to any inconvenience), as the coach stops, you know, at the Blue Boar, perhaps you will have the goodness to have your Nanny waiting at the office for them; and if you can manage to keep them till Monday, it will be adding to the favour ; but they will require constant watching, as you know what romps they are, and, for any sake, contrive to keep them out of the way of the gunpowder. I do not expect to be confined before the 29th at soonest; so if you can manage to come to us betwixt and the 20th, it will be very agreeable to us all, I assure you. I was in hopes I should not have had any more to trouble you with at present; but upon hearing that I was writing to you, Tom begs me to say that he wishes very much to get some good fly-hooks for trout-fishing, four red cock's hackle-body, four black green plover's tuft, with a light starling's wing body, and four brown woodcock's wing, and hare's-foot body. I hope you will be able to read this, as I assure you it has cost me some labour to write it from Tom's diction. He desires me to add, you will get them best at Phin's, fishing-rod maker, at the east end of the High Street, fifth door up the second stair on the left hand; you will easily find it, as there is a large pasteboard trout hanging from the end of a fishing-rod for a sign. He also wants a pirn of fishing-line, and a few good stout long-shanked bait-hooks. If you happen to see your friend Miss Aiken, you may tell her the turban you ordered for me is the very same of one she made for me two years ago, and which I never liked. I have only worn it once, or twice at most; so, perhaps, she will have no objections to take it back, and make me a neat fashionable cap instead. I am afraid you will think us very troublesome, but I know you do not grudge a little trouble to oblige your friends. Mr. Goodwilly and the young people unite with me in best wishes; and I remain, my dear Miss Duguid,

" Yours most sincerely,
" Grace Goodwilly.
" P. S. — Eliza and Jane beg you will send them some patterns of summer silks, neither too light nor too dark, both figured and plain, with the different widths and prices; and also that you would inquire what is the lowest price of the handsomest ostrich feathers that can be had; and if you happen to see any very pretty wreaths, you might price them at the same time, as they are divided between feathers and flowers: those you sent from Trashbag's were quite soiled, and looked as if they had been worn. Mr. Goodwilly takes this opportunity of sending in a couple of razors, which he begs you will send to Steele the cut-

ler's, at the back of the Old Kirk Stile, to be sharpened immediately, as these are things he cannot want. Margaret bids me tell you to desire Brisbane not to put magic laces to her stays, and to be sure that the stitching is stout and firm. Any day that you happen to be passing Seaton the saddler's, Mr. Goodwilly begs you will have the goodness to inquire what would be the lowest price of new-stuffing the side-saddles, and new-lackering the carriage harness. I think it as well to send in my turban, that you may try Miss Aiken ; and I shall think her extremely disobliging if she refuses to take it back, as it will be money thrown into the fire if she does not, for it shall never go upon my head.

" Yours with much Regard,
" G. G.
" P. S. — I find it will be necessary to send Jemima in to Bain the dentist, to get some of her teeth taken out, as her mouth is getting very crowded. I would take her myself, but cannot stand these things; so must beg the favour of you to go with her, and see it done. I fear it will be a sad business, poor soul! as there are at least three that must come out, and great tusks they are ! Of course, it is not every one I would trust her with for such an operation; but I know I can rely upon your doing every thing that can be done. If Miss Aiken agrees to exchange the turban for a cap (as I have no doubt she will), be so good as tell her to keep it rather more on the forehead, and not quite so much off the ears, as the last one she made for me — which I never liked. Will you ask that good-for-nothing creature, Heelpiece, if the children's shoes are ever to be sent home ?
" Yours, in haste."

Sometimes Miss Becky betook herself to the country; but though she often found retirement, there was seldom rest. Whenever a gay husband was leaving home, Miss Becky was in requisition to keep his dull sickly wife company in his absence — or, vice versa, when a young wife wished to amuse herself abroad, " that good creature, Becky Duguid," was sent for, to play backgammon with her old ill-natured husband; and when both man and wife were leaving home, then Becky Duguid was called upon to nurse the children and manage the servants in their absence. Invitations abounded, but all to disagreeable scenes or dull parties. She was expected to attend all accouchements, christenings, deaths, chestings, and burials ; but she was seldom asked to a marriage, and never to any party of pleasure. " O, Miss Becky doesn't care for these things; she would like better to come to us when we're in a quiet way by ourselves," was always the come off. " I don't know what the cares of the married life are," Miss Becky would sometimes say, and oftener think ; " but I'm sure I know what the troubles of the single state are to a stout, healthy, easy-tempered woman like me. — What is it to

be the -wife of one crabbed old man, to having to divert all the crabbed old men in the country ? And what is it to be the mother of one family of children, to having to look after the children of all my relations and acquaintances ? "

But Miss Becky's reflections (like most people's reflections) came too late to benefit herself. She was completely involved in the toils of celibacy before she was at all aware of her danger, and vain now would have been the attempt to extricate herself. Such was Miss Becky Duguid, — walking in the vain show of liberty, but, in reality, fettered hand and foot by all the tender charities of life. As such, it may be guessed, she formed no very brilliant addition to the Bellevue party. Indeed, such is the force of habit, she now felt quite out of her element when seated at her ease, without any immediate call on her time and attention ; for even her little doings carried their sense of importance along with them ; and, perhaps, Mrs. Fry never felt more inward satisfaction at the turning of a soul from darkness to light, than did poor Miss Becky when she had triumphantly despatched a box full of well-executed commissions.

Dinner passed off uncommonly well — every thing was excellent. Uncle Adam behaved with tolerable civility—the Major's black servant did wonders — the room was hot — the party was large — the dishes were savoury — the atmosphere was one ambrosial cloud of mingled steams — the ladies' complexions got high;—but, at length, toasts having gone round, the signal was made, and all was over!

CHAPTER XXXI.

Busk ye, busk ye, my bonny bride, Busk ye, busk ye, my winsome marrow; Busk ye, busk ye, my bonny bride, And let us to the Braes of Yarrow.

There will we sport and gather dew,
Dancing while lav'rocks sing in the morning;
There learn frae turtles to prove true;
O ! Bell, ne'er vex me with thy scorning ! Allan Ramsay.

Bright shone the morning of Miss Bell's nuptials, and all things looked auspicious. The collation stood ready ; for Mrs. Black, like Lady Capulet on a similar though less happy occasion, had been astir from the second crowing of the cock.

The guests were assembled — the clergyman had arrived — the family were all in full dress, — the Major, in his cat's eye "Drooch and London coat (the envy of Bob and Davy), looked the gay bridegroom from top to toe. Nothing was wanting but the beauteous bride ; and, at the proper moment, decked in India

K 4

muslin—a full-dressed head, done up with a profusion of heads, and hraids, and bands, and hows — a pocket-handkerchief at her face, — Miss Bell was led in.

The solemnity deepened — the clergyman cleared his voice— the children were admonished by a reproving look that it was time to put on their grave faces — the clatter of Bob and Davy was hushed, and all the little disjointed groups were broken up ; till at length the whole company was regularly formed into one large, formal, silent, solemn circle Miss Bell was now on the verge of becoming Mrs. Major Waddell — a metamorphosis which could not be expected to take place without some commotion.

Persons of fine feelings naturally shed tears upon these momentous occasions, and persons of ordinary feelings think they ought to do so too. In short, the thing is always done, or appears to be done, and not to be outdone — Miss Bell sobbed aloud, and had even the vulgarity to blow her nose — although, as Bob and Davy afterwards declared, that was all in the eye.

Dr. Johnson has remarked of the Episcopal marriage service, that it is too refined — that it is calculated only for the best kind of marriages — whereas there ought to be a form for matches of an inferior description, probably such as that which now took place between Major Andrew Waddell and Miss Isabella Black. That objection certainly does not apply to the Presb\'7d T terian form, which depends entirely upon the officiating clergyman ; and, accordingly, is susceptible of all the varieties of which the mind and manners of man are capable—from the holy meekness and simplicity of the evangelical pastor, to the humdrum slipshod exhortations of the lukewarm minister, or the dull dogmas of the worldly-wise doctor. It was a person of the latter description who now performed the ceremony in a manner which even Dr. Johnson would scarcely have deemed too good for the pai*ties.

Mrs. Major Waddell having received the congratulations of the company, withdrew, according to etiquette, to change her nuptial robe for a travelling habit, and speedily re-entered, arrayed in a navy-blue riding habit (the Major's favourite colour), allowed to sit uncommonly well — a black beaver hat and feathers — yellow boots — gold watch, and brooch containing the Major's hair set round with pearls. Altogether, Mrs. Major Waddell looked remarkably well, and bore her new honours with a happy mixture of dignity and affability.

The company were now conducted to the banquet, which, though neither breakfast, dinner, or supper, was a happy combination of all. There was, of course, much cutting, and carving, and helping, and asking, and refusing, and even some pressing, and Will the footboy broke a decanter, and Black Caesar spilt a very elaborate trifle ; but, upon the whole, every thing went on prosperously. Mrs. St. Clair took care to seat

herself by the Major; and, aware that when people are -very-happy, they are commonly very weak, she seized her opportunity, and easily cajoled him out of his -vote.

And now the trampling of steeds and crush of wheels announced the bridal equipage; and the Major, his lady, and Miss Lilly, who was to accompany them, prepared to depart. The lady, according to custom, was hurried, or appeared to be hurried, into the smart carriage-and-four that awaited her. Miss Lilly followed; but as she took leave of Miss St. Clair, she whispered, " I should like very much to correspond with you,

if " but here Lilly was dragged away by her father, with a

reproof for keeping the young people waiting. The happy party were now seated — the door was shut — the smiles, and bows, and kissing of hands were renewed—the Major's black servant skipped on the dicky—"Go on" was pronounced — the drivers cracked their whips — the carriage set off with a bound, and was soon rattling through the streets of Barnford, where many a gazing eye and outstretched neck hailed it as it passed.

A great philosopher has asserted, that, " upon all such joyous occasions, our satisfaction, though not so durable, is often as lively as that of the persons principally concerned ;" but, upon the present occasion, there certainly was little sympathy in Mrs. Major Waddell's feelings and those of her friends and acquaintances. While she rolled on, supremely blest, they solaced themselves with commiserating her hapless fate. " Quite a mercenary marriage — poor thing — a sad sacrifice — a man old enough to be her grandfather — has met with seventeen refusals—fortune come in of the telling — liver like a plum-pudding—false teeth—dreadful temper," &c. &c, were buzzed from one end of the town to the other; but, happily, none of their stings penetrated the ear of the bride, who sat in all the bliss of pompous ignorance.

Though births, marriages, and deaths occur every day, still they continue to excite an interest beyond the ordinary events of life. The former and the latter, indeed, though apparently more important occurrences, certainly do not engage the attention or occupy the minds of the great mass of mankind (or, at least, of womankind) so much as the less solemn act of marriage. Whether these being performed without our own consent asked or obtained afford less scope for animadversion, or that marriage is a state in which all are inclined to sympathize — the married from fellow-feeling — the single from feelings which the moralist or the metaphysician may declare, but which it is no part of my business to investigate, — I shall, therefore, leave the point to be discussed by those who are more compeient, and return to the company.

It is no easy matter for a party in full dress to pass away the morning when the business for which they assembled is over 3

and where there is nothing to gratify any one of the five senses, it is then people feel, in their fullest extent, the pains and penalties of idleness. As soon as their respective carriages drew up, the guests, therefore, droptoff; and, as the last of them wheeled out of sight, Mrs. Black thanked her stars she had seen all their backs.

CHAPTER XXXII.

Thou wilt be like a lover presently, And tire the hearer with a book of words.

Much Ado about Nothing.

It was with pleasure Gertrude hailed the stately turrets of Rossville, as she beheld them rising above the rich masses of wood which surrounded them — and again her heart bounded with delight as she thought " All this will one day be mine— mine to bestow "

She did not finish the sentence even to herself, but the image of Colonel Delmour rose to her view; and she felt that even the brilliant destiny that awaited her would be poor and joyless, unless he were to partake of it. On alighting, Mrs. St. Clair hastened to Lord Rossville to report to him the success of her canvass; and Gertrude soon found herself, she knew not how, strolling by the banks of the river with Colonel Delmour by her side.

It is universally allowed that though nothing can be more interesting in itself than the conversation of two lovers, yet nothing can be more insipid in detail — just as the heavenly fragrance of the rose becomes vapid and sickly under all the attempts made to retain and embody its exquisite odour. Colonel Delmour certainly was in love — as much so as it was in his nature to be ; but, as has been truly said, how many noxious ingredients enter into the composition of what is sometimes called love ! Pride — vanity — ambition — self-interest, all these had their share in the admiration which Colonel Delmour accorded to the beauties and the graces of Miss St. Clair. In any situation of life, his taste would have led him to admire her— but it was only as the heiress of Rossville his pride would have permitted him to have loved her. But he was aware of the obstacles that stood in the way of his wishes, and deemed it most prudent not to oppose himself openly to them at present.

He was conscious of the odium he would incur, were he to enter the lists as the rival of his brother; knowing, as he had all along done, that that brother was the destined husband of the heiress of Rossville. His aim, therefore, was to secure her affections in a clandestine manner — leaving it to his brother to make his proposals openly ; and when they had been rejected,

he would then come forward and prefer his suit. This manoeuvre would, to be sure, expose Gertrude to the whole weight of her uncle's displeasure, and, probably, bring much persecution upon her; but with a character such as hers, that would only tend to strengthen her attachment, and Colonel Delmour was too selfish to prize the happiness, even of the woman he loved, beyond his own ; or, rather, like many others of the same nature, he wished that her happiness should be of a reflected nature, emanating solely from himself. Having bewailed the necessity he was under of leaving Rossville the following day, he then gave way to the most vehement expressions of despair at the thoughts of leaving one a thousand times dearer to him than life ; and that, too, without the only solace that could soften the anguish of separation,—the belief that his feelings were understood — the hope that they might one day be mutual.

Gertrude remained silent—but there was a deep struggle in her breast: her mother's prejudice—her uncle's plans — made her feel the dangers and difficulties of their attachment, while they, at the same time, served to heighten it. Colonel Delmour saw what was passing in her mind, and that he must now bring the matter to a decision.

With all the impassioned sophistry of which he was master, he contrived to draw from Gertrude an indirect acknowledgment that he was not indifferent to her, and he then urged the necessity there was for carefully concealing their attachment for the present.

" Can this be right ?" thought Gertrude — and her conscience told her — no ; but, averse as she was to every species of dissimulation and deceit, she was equally a stranger to the meanness of suspicion, and to suspect the man she loved was not in her nature — love and suspicion were the very antipodes of her mind. She therefore quickly banished the slight doubt that had arisen, though she could not so easily reconcile to herself the idea that she was acting a clandestine part in thus deceiving by not disclosing to her mother what had passed. But Colonel Delmour besought her with so much earnestness to withhold the communication for the present, and she dreaded so much to en-counter her mother's violence and prejudice, that perhaps, on the whole, she was not sorry for an excuse to indulge undisturbed yet awhile in " Love's young dream." Had Mrs. St. Clair ever been the friend of her daughter, Gertrude would not have acted thus; for her nature was open and ingenuous, and she would have disdained every species of concealment and duplicity. But the whirlwind and the tempest are not more baleful in their effects on the material world, than tyranny and violence are destructive of all the finer qualities of the mind with which they come in contact. They must either irritate or deaden all those freeborn affections of the soul, which, like the first vernal

shoots, possess a charm in their freshness alone which art and culture would in vain seek to impart.

When the lovers reached the castle, it was within a few minutes of the dinner hour; and Gertrude flew to her room, where she found her mother waiting for her.

" Where have you been, child ?" cried she, in no very complacent tone. " Lord Rossville has been asking for you at least a dozen times, and no one could give any account of you."

" I have been walking by the river, mamma," replied her daughter, in some confusion.

" I wish you would leave off these idle rambles of yours. — I am quite of the Earl's opinion, that the less young ladies indulge in solitary rambles the better."

" Mamma, I was not — alone," Gertrude would have added, though in some little trepidation, but Mrs. St. Clair interrupted her.

" Come — come, there is no time to waste in excuses — you will be late as it is, so make haste — you ought to have remembered there was to be company here to-day, to whom Lord Rossville wished to present you in due pomp—perhaps to serve some little political purpose; but no matter—he is a generous noble-minded man, in spite of his little peculiarities. He was anxious to have seen you to-day for two purposes, which I am commissioned to fulfil; the first is, that you are to bestow your attention exclusively upon Mr. Delmour; the next is, to decorate you with a splendid gift for the occasion — luckily you are in looks to do credit to my work — see, here is what your kind generous uncle presents you with ;" and opening a jewel-case, she displayed a set of costly pearls. A pang shot through Gertrude's heart, as she thought, " Would he have bestowed these upon me, if he had known that I am acting in opposition to his wishes ? — Oh! why am I compelled thus to play the hypocrite?" And she sighed, and shrunk back, as her mother would have decked her in oriental magnificence. Mrs. St. Clair looked at her with astonishment.

" What is the matter, Gertrude ? — this is a strange time to sigh, when adorning with jewels which even the future Countess of Rossville might be proud to wear."

Gertrude passively extended her arm to have the costly bracelets clasped on it; but Mrs. St. Clair knew not that to those who had just been plighting hearts even Golconda's mines would have seemed poor and dim— at that moment Gertrude felt that wealth and honours were but as " painted clay."

CHAPTER XXXIII.

Is there place to write above one lover's name, With honour in her heart ? Old Play.

Meanwhile the carriages were beginning to draw up in rapid succession; and Lord Rossville, though fretting inwardly at his niece's delay, yet received the company with much outward serenity. He felt that he was master of his own person and manners, and all the dignity and urbanity for which he flattered himself he was so celebrated had now full scope in the absence of Miss Pratt. His step was firmer — his chest was broader — his nose was higher — his language was finer — his sentences were longer — his periods were rounder — in short, " Richard was himself again."

Already he had uttered many sensible, and even some witty sayings, to such of his guests as had arrived; while his mind was busy concocting a pun to be applied to Sir Peter Wellwood, when he should appear. But, alas! for the insecurity of the best-laid schemes of human wisdom ! Sir Peter and Lady Well-wood were announced ; and — horror of horrors! who should enter with them but Miss Pratt! Who can paint the Earl as he stood, " pierced with severe amazement ?" Not Celadon, when he beheld his Amelia struck a blackened corse, gazed with more marble aspect than did his lordship at sight of the breathing form of Miss Pratt. The half-formed pun died on his lips — a faint and indistinct notion of it floated through his bewildered brain; it was to have been something about a well and a wood, or a wood and a well; but the Earl's wits were in a wood, and he could certainly have wished Miss Pratt in a well. In vain did he even attempt to say something of welcome ; — the words clove to the roof of his mouth, and his looks did not make up for the deficiencies of his tongue. But Miss Pratt had not been looked at for fifty years to be disconcerted, at that time of life, by the looks of any man living, and she therefore accosted him in her usual manner.

" Well, my lord, you see I've been better than my word ; I dare say you didn't think of seeing me to-day, and, to tell you the truth, I didn't think of it myself; but Sir Peter and Lady Wellwood happened to call, en passant, at Lady M'Caw's, and as they were so good as offer me a seat in their carriage, I thought I couldn't do better than just come and make out the rest of my visit to you. — How goes it, Lady Betty? — I'm delighted to see you, Lady Millbank,— LadyRestall, I'm enchanted!" &c. &c. &c.; aod in a moment Miss Pratt was buzzing all round the room.

At sound of the gong, Mrs. St. Clair had hastily put the last
finish to her daughter's dress, ana hurried her to the drawing-room. As they entered all eyes were turned towards them. Lord Rossville was struck with the surpassing beauty of his niece ; and attributing it entirely to the effect of his pearls, he advanced from the circle in which he was standing, and taking her hand with an air of gratified pride, led her towards the company. He was in the act of presenting her to a dowager-marchioness, for whom he entertained a high veneration, when, at that moment, Mr. Lyndsay entered from the opposite side of the room. Their eyes met for the first time since that eventful midnight scene in the wood — a slight suffusion crossed his face ; but in an instant the colour mounted to her very temples, and in answer to the Marchioness's introductory remarks, she stammered out she knew not what. The consciousness of her confusion only served to increase it — she was aware that the eyes of the company were upon her, but she felt only the influence of Colonel Delmour's.

Lord Rossville, attributing his niece's embarrassment solely to awe and respect for himself and his guests, was beginning to reassure and encourage her in a manner to increase her confusion tenfold, when fortunately dinner was announced. Amid the usual bustle of fixing the order of procession, with all the accompanying cei'emonies necessary to be observed in walking from one room to another, Gertrude was recovering her presence of mind, when, as Miss Pratt passed, leaning on the arm of her ally, Sir Peter, she whispered, " Aye ! these are pearls of great price, indeed! So, so — somebody has come good speed. Love, like light, will not hide, — ah, ha!" and with an intolerable tap of her fan, and a significant chuckle, on she pattered, while again

Gertrude's cheeks were dyed with blushes. At that moment Colonel Delmour, who had heard Miss Pratt's remarks, accidentally trod upon her gown in such a manner as almost to tear away the skirt from the body.

" Was there ever the like of this?" cried she, reddening with anger. " My good Plowman's gauze ! Colonel Delmour, do you see what you've done?" But Colonel Delmour, without deigning to take the least notice of the injury he had inflicted, passed on to offer his arm to one of the Miss Millbanks.

Miss Pratt's only solace, therefore, was the sympathy of Sir Peter, to whom she detailed all the mischief Colonel Delmour had done her, first and last, concluding with a remark, which, though in an affected whisper, was intended to reach his ear — that, indeed, it was no wonder he came such bad speed at the courting— she had need to be both a bold woman and a rich one who would choose such a rough wooer. This disaster, however, had the effect of a quietus upon Miss Pratt for some time ; and Lord Rossville got leave to expand to his utmost dimensions, unchecked by any interruptions from her.

None of the company, now assembled, seemed to have any

particular part to play in the great drama of life ; they were all commonplace, well-bred, eating-and-drinking elderly lords and ladies, or well-dressed, talking, smiling, flirting masters and misses. Gertrude was, as usual, appropriated by Mr. Delmour, who paid her much attention, and some very pretty compliments, in a gentlemanly but somewhat business-like manner. Colonel Delmour sat, on the other hand, silent, thoughtful, and displeased, neglecting even the common attentions which politeness required.

Mr. Lyndsay was on the opposite side of the table; and upon his asking Miss St. Clair to drink wine with him, Colonel Delmour turned his eye quickly upon her, and again a deep blush mantled her cheeks, — something, perhaps, of wounded pride at the suspicion implied in his glance, or it may be of that shame natural to the ingenuous mind at the sense of mystery and concealment. Whatever its cause, its effect was sufficiently visible on Colonel Delmour; he turned pale with suppressed anger — bit his lip—nor addressed a single word to her during the whole of dinner.

There is only this difference between a summer and a winter pai'ty, that in winter the company form into one large cluster round the fire, and in summer they fall into little detached groups, and are scattered all over the apartment. Upon entering the drawing-room, Gertrude had unconsciously seated herself apart from every body at an open window, where she thought she was contemplating the beams of the setting sun as they glowed upon the hills, and glittered through the rich green foliage of some intervening elms. But, in fact, she was ruminating on the various occurrences of the day, and the awkward predicament in which she found herself placed with Mr. Lyndsay.

She was roused from her reverie by some one putting their hands before her eyes; and presently the dreaded accents of Pratt smote her ear, as she struck up, " As pensive I thought of my love, eh ? " Then, drawing in a chair, she seated herself close by Miss St. Clair; and taking her hand with an air of friendly sympathy and perfect security, she began —

" I'm sure it must be a relief to you to have got away from the dinner-table to-day. I really felt for you, for I know by experience what my gentleman is, when he is in his tantrams ; did 3'ou see how he was like to tear me in pieces to-day for nothing but because I happened to see how the land lay between a certain person and you? Just look at my good Plowman's gauze," turning round. " I assure you, my dear, I was very much afraid, at one time, that you would have been taken in by him; for I saw that he made a dead set at you from the first, and he can be very agreeable when he chooses; but, take my word for it, he's a very impertinent, ill-bred, ill-tempered man, for all that."

Colouring with confusion and indignation, Gertrude had sat silently enduring the obloquy lavished on her lover, from utter

...

inability to interrupt her ; but at this climax she made a movement to extricate herself, which, however, was in vain.

Miss Pratt again seized the hand which had been withdrawn, and with a significant squeeze, resumed — " You needn't be afraid of me, my dear, — your secret's safe with me; and to tell you the truth, I've suspected the thing for some time. I only wish you had looked about you a little ; there's Anthony Whyte has never so much as seen you yet; if he would but make up his mind to marry, what a husband he would make ! Very different from our friend the Colonel, to be sure; many's the sore heart his wife will have, and many a sore heart he has given already with his flirtations, for he's never happy but when he's making love to somebody or other, married or single, it's all the same to him."

" Miss Pratt," cried Gertrude, in great emotion, as she again tried to disengage herself from her, " I cannot listen to "

" Well, my dear, it's very good of you to stand up for him," with a pat on the shoulder ; " for it's seldom ladies take such a lift of their cast lovers: but it's as well you should know all you've escaped." — Then lowering her voice to a mysterious whisper, " Just to give you one single trait of him, which I know to be a fact — what do you think of his owing Edward Lyndsay seven thousand pound for his game debts ? — That I can pledge myself for — I was staying in the house with them both at the time. I was upon a visit to Lady Augusta in London, and I had good access to see what went on; and I saw rather more too than what they thought of. — Edward Lyndsay was just of age then; and he was invited there to be presented and introduced by the Delmours, — I suspect there was a scheme for getting Edward to one of the misses — but it wouldn't do. Well, the Colonel was by way of introducing him into the fashionable circles, and he soon handed him to the gaming-table, where he lost some money ; but what do ye think of his having to pay seven thousand pound and upwards for the Colonel ? — seven thousand pound gambled away in one night, and not a shilling to pay it! The consequence was, he must have sold out, and been ruined for ever, if Edward Lyndsay had not advanced the money ; and, to this day, I'll be bound for it, he has never touched one halfpenny of principal or interest. Where was it to come from ? He lives far beyond his income — anybody may see that, — with his curricle and his fine horses, and his groom and his valet; while there's the person that he owes all that money to keeps no carriage, and rides all over the country without so much as a servant after him; and my gentleman can't go to a neighbour's house without carrying a retinue like a prince along with him. But the provoking thing is, there's Lord Rossville and many other people crying out upon Edward for his extravagance and folly in having muddled away his money, and not living as he should do, and making no figure

in the world — when I know that he's just pinching and saving to make up the money and clear his estate from the debt he contracted upon it for his pretty cousin there ! I once gave Lord Rossville a hint of how matters stood; but he's so infatuated with these Delmours, I thought he would have worried me — not that he's very fond of the Colonel, or likes his company — but he's proud of him, because he's the fashion, and has made a figure — and so he goes on telling every body what great characters the Delmours are. I assure you, it's all I can do to keep my tongue within my teeth sometimes ; — but Colonel Delmour's a man I wouldn't like to provoke. — What do you think of his having the impertinence to tell me, that, if he found me meddling in his affairs, he would pull Anthony Whyte's nose for him! I should like to see him offer to lay a finger on Anthony Whyte! But that's just a specimen of him — O ! he's an insolent, extravagant, selfish puppy! — But, are you well enough, my dear ? "

Gertrude had made many ineffectual attempts to stop the torrent of Miss Pratt's invective ; but that lady was no more to be stopped in her career than a ship in full speed, or a racer on the course. At length, uttering an exclamation, she abruptly extricated herself from her grasp, and quitted the room.

There was commonly a mixture of truth and falsehood in all Miss Pratt's narrations ; but it must be owned the present formed an exception—perhaps a solitary one — to her ordinary practice. She had for once told a round unvarnished tale, with merely a little exaggeration as to the sum; and for once she had spoken from actual knowledge, not from mere conjecture. Miss Pratt had, by some means or other, best known to herself, contrived to lay her hands upon a letter of Colonel Delmour's, which had led her into the secret of the money transaction — a transaction which, from honour and delicacy on the one side, pride and shame on the other, would otherwise have been for ever confined to the parties themselves.

In vain did Gertrude strive to still the tumult of her mind in the silence of her own chamber — in vain did she repeat a thousand times to herself— " Why should I for an instant give ear to the paltry gossip of a person I despise ? — How is it that I can be guilty of injuring the man I love by yielding the shadow of belief to the calumnies of a Miss Pratt ? — No, no, I do not — I will not believe them. — Shame to me for even listening to them! — False — fickle — mercenary — a gamester — impossible!"

Alas! Gertrude believed it was impossible, because she loved — because all the affections of a warm, generous, confiding heart, were lavished on this idol of her imagination, which she had decked in all the attributes of perfection. And yet, such is the delusion of passion, that, could she even have beheld him bereft of all those virtues and graces with which her young romantic heart had so liberally invested him — even then she would not have

L

ceased to love. Ah ! what will not the heart endure, ere it will voluntarily surrender the hoarded treasure of its love to the cold dictates of reason, or the stern voice of duty!

CHAPTER XXXIV.

O ! how hast thou with jealousy infected
The sweetness of affiance ! Shakspeare.

It was so long ere Gertrude could compose herself sufficiently to return to the drawing-room that, when she did, she found the gentlemen had already joined the party. In some confusion she took the first seat that offered, which happened to be part of a sofa on which one of the Miss Millbanks was lounging, and on the back of which Mr. Lyndsay was leaning. But it was not till she had seated herself that she was aware of his vicinity. To add to her embarrassment, Miss Pratt crossed from the opposite side of the room, and took her seat alongside of her.

" I was just going to look for you, my dear," said she, in one of her loud, all-pervading whispers ; " I was afraid you wasn't very well; but upon saying that to Mrs. St. Clair, she said she daresay'd you were just taking an evening ramble, for that you're a great moonlight stroller, like some other people," with a significant smile at Mr. Lyndsay; and again Gertrude felt the colour mount to her cheeks. She raised her eyes, but met his fixed on her with such an expression of deep and thoughtful inquiry as redoubled her confusion ; and, scarcely knowing what she said, she uttered an exclamation at the heat of the room.

" Are you too hot, my dear?" asked her tormentor, taking a fan out of her pocket, and rising as she spoke; " then here's work for you, Mr. Edward; sit you down there and fan Miss St. Clair—not that I want to make a coolness between ye," added she, in a half whisper, loud enough to reach Colonel Delmour, who stood by the fire sipping his coffee ; " but I really don't think the room's hot; it must just be coming in from the cold air that makes you feel the room warm. — You would do well, Mr. Edward, to give this fair lady a lecture on her moonlight rambles. I "

" It is insupportable! " cried Gertrude, starting up, unable longer to endure Miss Pratt's observations.

" It is very hot," said Lyndsay, scarcely less embarrassed than herself. " Shall we seek a little fresh air at the window ? " And offering his arm, he led her towards one, and threw it open. Gertrude's agitation rather increased than diminished.

" Oh!—what must you think of me!" at length she exclaimed, in a low voice of repressed anguish.

" Were I to tell you," replied Mr. Lyndsay, in some emotion, " I fear you would think me very presumptuous."

" Impossible!" said Gertrude, with increasing agitation as she advanced on this perilous subject — "I feel that I must

ever " She stopped — her mother's caution, her own

promises, recurred to her, and she felt that her impetuosity was hurrying her beyond the bounds prescribed. Both remained silent; but Lyndsay still held her hand, and looked upon her with an expression of no common interest. He was, however, recalled to other considerations by the approach of Mr. Delmour ; when, relinquishing her hand, he made some remark on the heat of the room having been too much for Miss St. Clair.

" It is only in the sphere of my fair cousin herself," said Mr. Delmour, with a bow and a smile; " the fire of her eyes seldom fails to kindle a flame wherever their influence is felt."

Gertrude scarcely heard this flat, hackneyed compliment; but she felt the taunt implied, when Colonel Delmour, who was always hovering near her, said with asperity —

" Such fires, however, are sometimes mere ignesfatui, which shine only to deceive."

" A cruel aspersion upon glow-worms and ladies' eyes," said Mr. Lyndsay—" since both may, aod certainly do, sometimes shine without any such wicked intention."

" Were it not that the thing must be," said Mr. Delmour, with a bow to Miss St. Clair — " I should imagine it would be difficult to overheat this room ; it is large, not less, I take it, than forty by thirty, — lofty, prodigious walls, and a north-west exposure. If it were well lighted, indeed, that might have some effect, but at present it is rather deficient; tbere ought to be, at least, a dozen lamps instead of those pale ineffectual wax candles ; but, in fact, it is not every one who knows how to light a room ; — in a well-lit room there ought not to be a vestige of shade, Avhile here, for instance, where we are standing, it is absolute darkness visible."

" Yes, it is a sort of Pandemonium light," said Colonel Delmour, scornfully.

" The mind is its own place, you know, Delmour," said Lyndsay ; " ' and in itself ' " he stopped, and smiled.

" Go on," cried Colonel Delmour, in a voice of suppressed anger; " pray don't be afraid to finish your quotation."

Mr. Lyndsay repeated — " ' Can make a heaven of hell, a hell of heaven.' "

Colonel Delmour seemed on the point of giving way to his passion ; but he checked himself, and affected to laugh, while he said —" A flattering compliment implied, no doubt; but if I am the Lucifer you insinuate, I can boast of possessing his best attributes also ; for I too bear a mind not to be changed by place or time, and in my creed truth and constancy still rank as virtues." He looked at Gertrude as he pronounced these words in an emphatic manner.

" What are you all doing in this dark corner ? " asked Lady Betty, as she advanced with Flora under her arm.

" We came here to be cool," answered Mr. Lyndsay, " and we are all getting very warm."

" That is most extraordinary," said her ladyship — " but did any of you lift the third volume of ' The Midnight Wanderer ? ' "

" We'll thank you to pull down that window," cried Miss Pratt. " I wonder what you're all made of, for we are perfectly starving here — sit a little more this way, Sir Peter — your moonlight days and mine are both over. — Indeed, as Anthony Whyte says, J never see any thing but a swelled face and a flannel lappet in the moon." Then going to Mr. Lyndsay, she touched his elbow, and beckoned him a little apart.

"So — I wish you joy —the cat's out of the bag — but take care what you're about, for a certain person," pointing to Colonel Delmour, "will be ready to bite your nose off—'Pon my word, you quiet people always play your cards best after all;" — and with a friendly pat on the back, Miss Pratt whisked away, and the next minute was bustling about a whist party with Lord Rossville and Sir Peter.

The arrangement of their table was always a work of delicacy and difficulty—the Earl was fond of whist, and so was Miss Pratt; — and for upwards of thirty years they had been in the occasional habit of playing together in the most discordant manner imaginable. Miss Pratt played like lightning — the Earl pondered every card, as though life depended on the cast. Every card — every spot of a card, out or in, was registered in Pratt's memory, ready at a call. The Earl was a little confused, and sometimes committed blunders, which were invariably pointed out, and animadverted upon by Miss Pratt, whether as his antagonist or his partner. Then she had the impertinence to shake her head, and hem, sigh, and even groan at times ; and, to sum up the whole, when they played together she had the assurance to insist upon taking the tricks, which was an usurpation of power beyond all endurance.

While the seniors of the company were arranging themselves at their several card parties, the younger part repaired to the music-room, where Gertrude was urged to sing by all present, except Colonel Delmour, who preserved a moody silence. Teazed into compliance, she at length seated herself at the harp, and began to prelude.

"You accompany Miss St. Clair, Frederick?" said Mr. Delmour to his brother, in a tone of inquiry.

" Miss St. Clair has found out that I am a bad accompaniment," answered he in a manner which only Gertrude could understand. " To one who sings so true, so perfectly free from all falsetto, it must be a severe penance to find herself clogged with me, who am a perfect novice in that art, as in every other."

"I prefer singing alone," said Gertrude, vainly trying to conceal her agitation at this insulting speech.

"It is extremely mortifying," said Mr. Lyndsay, instantly attracting the attention to himself, " that I am seldom or never asked to sing. It is difficult to account for this insensibility on the part of my friends in particular — of the world in general; but I am resolved to remain no longer silent under such contumely. Miss St. Clair will take me under her patronage—my wrongs shall be heard in full bravura this very night — where shall I find words vast enough to express my feelings ? " And he turned over the music, while he hummed Guarini's " Bring me a hundred reeds of decent growth to form a pipe," &c. — Then selecting the beautiful arietta—

Io t'amerd, fin che saprS di Flora, Coi baci i fiori accarezzar el monte E sul mattin la rugia rosa Aurora, Vedi molte stille, fecondar le piante, Io t'araerb, io t'amerd, io t'amerd !

he placed it before Miss St. Clair, saying, " Will the mistress allow her protege to choose for herself and him ? "

Gertrude, though in some degree restored to self-possession, could only bow her acquiescence ; but the state of her feelings was such as prevented her doing justice either to herself or her accompaniment. She was scarcely sensible of the beauty of his style of singing. Neither was it then she was struck with the singularity of having lived so long under the same roof without being aware that he possessed a knowledge of music which, with most people, would have formed a prominent feature in their character, and which they would long ere then have found an opportunity of displaying. But Lyndsay did nothing for display, and now his talents were merely brought out when they could be of service to another. Gertrude, however, saw nothing of all this — she saw nothing but that Colonel Delmour had disappeared upon Mr. Lyndsay taking his station by her. The song ended, she hastily relinquished her seat to another lady, and it was occupied in rotation till carriages were announced, and the party broke up. Gertrude availed herself of the bustle of departures to make her escape to her own chamber; but as she passed through the suite of apartments, she found Colonel Delmour in one of the most remote, pacing up and down with every mark of disquiet. She would have retreated, but, quickly advancing, he seized her hand; then, in the same cold ironical manner he had hitherto practised, he requested that Miss. St. Clair would honour him so far as to endure his presence for a few moments.

" I know nothing Colonel Delmour can have to say to me,"

L 3

answered Gertrude, roused to something like indignation; — " unless, indeed, to apologize for his behaviour."

" Apologize!" repeated he, with vehemence. " No, that certainly is not my purpose — unless Miss St. Clair will first deign to account for hers ; but the thing is impossible; however I might distrust others, I cannot disbelieve the evidence of my own senses "

" I am ignorant of your meaning; — I cannot listen to such

frantic expressions " and she sought to withdraw her hand

from him.

" Frantic I Yes, I am frantic to seek that explanation from you which I have a right to demand — and will demand from another quarter."

" For mercy's sake! tell me what is the meaning of this ?" eried Gertrude, in great emotion. " Why am I subjected to hear such violent, such insulting language — and from you!" And the tears burst from her eyes.

Colonel Delmour gazed upon her for a few minutes in silence ; then in a somewhat calmer tone, and heaving a deep sigh, he proceeded —

"But a few hours ago, and tears from your eyes would have been as blood from my own heart—and even yet, deceived and

injured as I am " he stopped in much agitation ; then again

giving way to his passion — " But you ask me why you are subjected to such language?—your own heart might have spared you that question."

" I have not deserved this — I will not endure it;" and Miss St. Clair again sought to leave the room.

" Then why have *I* deserved — why must *I* endure to be mocked and deluded with hopes you never meant to realize ? — Yes — that cold-blooded systematic puritan Lyndsay dares to love you — and you but he shall answer for this to me."

For a moment Gertrude regarded him with a look of the most unfeigned astonishment, which only gave way to the deep blush that dyed her cheeks ; but it was not the blush of shame or confusion, but the glow of indignation, and, with an air of offended dignity, she said —

" Since you believe me capable, after what passed to-day, of loving another, you might well treat me as you have done; but what am I to think of one who could, for a single instant, suspect me of such base — such monstrous duplicity ? "

"Gertrude," cried Colonel Delmour, in great agitation—"Gertrude, I am a wretch if you — but why those blushes — that confusion at sight of him ? — Why that air of intelligence that attends your intercourse ? and — did I not hear you myself, when you withdrew with him to the window, ask, with all the solicitude of the most heartfelt interest, what he must think of you ? — he ! — "What would his thoughts signify to you if your affections -were mine ?"

Gertrude felt almost despair as she thought of the impossibility of clearing herself from suspicions, which she was aware there was but too much reason to attach to her — and she remained silent, while Colonel Delmour's eyes were fixed upon her with an expression of the most intense anxiety. At length, with a deep sigh, she said —

" That there exists a mutual cause of embarrassment between Mr. Lyndsay and me, I do not deny; but it is one which involves the interest of a third person, and I dare not divulge it even to you — that, and that only, is the cause of the confusion you witnessed, aud of the words you overheard. — More I cannot — dare not say — I am pledged to silence."

" By him ? " demanded Colonel Delmour impetuously.

" No — by another — but that other I may not name."

Colonel Delmour still looked doubtingly.

" And how long is this mysterious connection to continue ? "

" Heaven only knows ! — but do not — do not ask me farther."

And as she bent her head dejectedly forward, the string of pearls which hung from her neck attracted her lover's eye, and again his wavering suspicions were roused, as he remembered the conversation repeated by Miss Pratt.

" And these precious baubles !" cried he, pointing contemptuously to them — " do they form part of the mysterious chain which links your fate so indissolubly with that of Mr. Lyndsay ? "

" I see I am doubted — disbelieved — it is degrading to be thus interrogated ! " and with an air of displeasure foreign to her natural character, she rose to quit the room.

" Gertrude," cried Colonel Delmour, detaining her, " you know not — you cannot conceive how my heart is racked and tortured. — I will — I must have my doubts ended one way or other ere we part — perhaps for ever : — tell me then — are not these the gift of that — of

Edward Lyndsay ?"

"The gift of Edward Lyndsay!" repeated Gertrude, in the utmost amazement. "What an idea!" and she almost smiled in scorn. "The pearls are a present I received not many hours since from Lord Rossville — I thought little .of them," added she, "with a simple tenderness, which carried conviction even to Colonel Delmour, " for I had just then parted from you."

"Gertrude, dearest Gertrude, can you forgive me?" and he poured forth the most vehement reproaches on himself, mingled with such expressions of love towards her as failed not to obtain pardon. He related to her what had passed with Miss Pratt relative to the pearls, and in so doing he served a double purpose, by clearing himself from the charges that had been brought against him by that lady. This trait of her served to show

L 4

THE INHERITANCE.

Gertrude how little dependence ought to he placed on her report, and she felt as though she too had heen guilty of injustice towards her lover, in even listening to her malicious insinuations.

Though somewhat pained, yet, on the whole, she was not displeased at what had passed. Like many others, she cherished that fatal mistake — that jealousy is the offspring of love, rather than the infirmity of temper, and, as such, its excesses were easily forgiven. In short, this was a lovers' quarrel — a first quarrel too, and, consequently, served rather to heighten than diminish the mutual attachment. ~\

Delmour was to set off early the following morning; and Gertrude, too much agitated to return to the company, took leave of him, and hastened to her own apartment, to hide her parting tears.

END OF THE FIRST VOLUME.

SECOND VOLUME.

CHAPTER I.

Quoique ces personnes n'aient point d'interet a ce qui'ls disent, il ne faut pas conclure de la absolumently qu'ils ne mentent point. — Pascal.

Mr. Lyndsay was neither a weak nor a vain man, and he was too well acquainted with the nature of Miss Pratt to attach much credit to any thing she said. He was aware that, without absolutely speaking falsehood, she very rarely spoke truth — that, like many other people, she failed in repeating precisely what she heard, not so much from design as from confusion of brain, redundancy of fancy, imperfect organic construction, or, in short, some one or all of the causes which seem to render simple repetition infinitely more difficult than the most compound multiplication or addition. Much might be said upon this subject, but few readers are fond of digressions, especially when of a moral or didactic nature; the cause of Miss Pratt's observations must, therefore, be left to the construction of the world, which is seldom disposed to be over charitable in its conclusions.

Mr. Lyndsay, indeed, was little in the habit of attending to her words, being possessed of that enviable power of mental transmigration which placed him, when even within her grasp, quite beyond the influence of her power. He had, however, been struck with the mystical fragments of speech she had bestowed on him the preceding evening — he was aware how little dependence was to be placed on them; but, like the spider, her webs, even though wove out of her own intellectual resources, must still have something to cling to, and he resolved to lose no time in demolishing those cobwebs of her imagination. He therefore accosted her the following morning, as, according to custom, she stood airing herself at the hall-door ; and, without allowing her time to spread her wings and fly off in any of her discursive flights, he gravely begged to know the meaning of the words she had addressed to him the evening before.

" My words!" exclaimed she, in some astonishment at being, for the first time in her life, asked for words — " My words! what are you going to make of my words, my dear? "

" Not much; but I confess I am rather curious to know in what way I am thought to have played my cards so well, as "

" O! I know where you are now — but if you want to take me in, Mr. Edward, that won't do — they say, ' Daylight peeps through a small hole,' and ' Love, like smoke, will not hide ;' so you needn't trouble yourself to go about the bush with me — but you needn't be afraid — mum's the word — mum and budget, ha, ha, ha! — do you remember that ? It's mum with you, it seems, and budget with a certain gay colonel, for he's off the field — aye! you've really been very sly — but what will my lord and his member say to it, think you ? "

" It would be affectation in me to pretend that I do not understand your allusions, groundless and absurd as they are," said Lyndsay; " but I do assure you, upon my word of honour "

" Bow wow! my dear, don't tell me of your words of honour in love affairs; I'll rather trust to my own eyes and ears than to any of your words of honour. I declare you're as bad as Anthony Whyte. I thought he would have raised the country at the report of his marriage with Lady Sophia Bellendean. — He certainly did pay her some attentions, but he never went the lengths that people said, though it wasn't for want of good encouragement."

" Well, but as I have never presumed to pay attentions, and cannot boast of having received any encouragement, any report of that kind must have originated in some mistake, and would place both parties in an awkward predicament."

" Fiddle faddle! Really, my dear, when the lady doesn't deny it, I don't think it sets you very well to be so discomposed about it — aye, you may look, but I assure you it's the case, that she as much as confessed it to me last night — now !"

" Confessed what ?" asked Mr. Lyndsay in amazement.

" Just that the Colonel had got his offset— Oh! how I enjoy that! — and that a certain person," with a bow, " was her humble servant."

" Impossible! your ears have deceived you."

" My ears deceive me, indeed ! what would they do that for ? — you surely don't think I'm deaf? and if I am, I'm sure I'm not blind. You lovers seem always to think other people have lost their senses as well as yourselves; but it's only love that's blind, my dear."

" Miss Pratt, I beg you will listen to me seriously, while I assure you, in the most solemn manner, that you are under a complete delusion. For myself, I can only be honoured by such a supposition —but it is injurious, it is insulting to Miss St. Clair, to have it imagined that she has already bestowed her regards upon me, who am, in fact, still almost a stranger to her."

Mr. Lyndsay spoke with an air of truth and sincerity that would have carried conviction to any other mind.

" As to that, it doesn't take a lifetime to fall in love, and your
sudden love is always the strongest — many a one has been over head and ears before you could say Jack Robinson. I really don't see why you should take it so much to heart, when the lady puts up with it so quietly; but more than that, I happened to hear something last night — I may as well tell you what it was, if it was only to save you telling any more fibs to me about it. I happened to be takiug a turn through the rooms last night, just to cool myself a little after losing

seven points, all owing to your good uncle's obstinacy—when 1 came to the — what-do-ye-call-it-room there —the door was open, and there I heard the Colonel say, in a voice like any lion," raising hers in imitation, "' You love that — that —' (no matter what) — ' that Edward Lyndsay,' says he, ' and you've deceived and bamboozled me — I know that you've given your affections to him; but he shall answer for it' — and so he went on like any madman. I didn't hear so well what she said, — for, you know, she doesn't speak very loud; but I heard her say that she couldn't and wouldn't endure such insolence, and that he had no right to speak to her in that way. But just then Lord Rossville was calling me to go and play the game over again with him — and, at any rate, you know, I wouldn't have staid to listen."

" All that is nothing to the purpose," cried Mr. Lyndsay, in some little emotion ; " at least the only purpose is to show how little dependence you ought to place on any of your senses, since they must all have beguiled you in this matter. You will, therefore, act a prudent part for yourself, and a more delicate one towards Miss St. Clair, if you refrain from making any such comments in future — be assured you will only render yourself highly ridiculous "

" O! you needn't be afraid; I'm not going to trouble my head about the matter," returned Miss Pratt, reddening with anger; " but you'll not easily persuade me that I've lost my senses, because I happen to have a little more penetration than my neighbours." And away pattered the offended fair, rather confirmed than shaken in her preconceived notions on the subject.

Disbelieving, as he certainly did, the greater part of Miss Pratt's communications, still it was not in nature that Mr. Lyndsay should have felt altogether indifferent to them. Although not a person to yield his affections lightly, he certainly had been charmed with Miss St. Clair's beauty and grace — with the mingled vivacity and softness of her manners, and with the open naif cast of her character. There was all to captivate a mind and taste such as his ; but there was still something wanting to render the charm complete. Firm in his own religious principles, he vainly sought in Gertrude for any corresponding sentiments. Gertrude was religious —what mind of any excellence is not ? But hers was the religion of poetry — of taste — of feeling — of impulse — of any and every thing but Chris-

tianity. He saw much of fine natural feeling — but in vain sought for any guiding principle of duty. Her mind seemed as a lovely, flowery, pathless waste, whose sweets exhaled in vain

— all was graceful luxuriance—hut all was transient and perishable in its loveliness. No plant of immortal growth grew there — no " flowers worthy of Paradise."

Mr. Lyndsay had discernment to trace the leading features of his cousin's mind, even through the veil which was cast over it by Lord Rossville's tyranny and Mrs. St. Clair's artifice. He saw her ardent, enthusiastic, and susceptible ; but rash, visionary, and unregulated—he feared she was in bad hands, even in her mother's ; but he dreaded still more lest Colonel Delmour should succeed in gaining her affections. He suspected his design ; and, from his previous knowledge of his habits and principles, was convinced that such an union would be the wreck of Gertrude's peace and happiness.

Since that strange and mysterious adventure in the wood, he had felt a still deeper interest in her; and he wished, if possible, to gain her friendship and confidence, that he might endeavour to save her from the snares with which she was beset. In short, Lyndsay's feelings towards her were compounded into one which could not have been easily defined — it was neither love nor friendship, yet partook of the nature of both ; for it had somewhat of the excitement of the one, with the disinterestedness of the other.

The mutual embarrassment of the cousins was not lessened when they next met, and they seemed, by a sort of tacit agreement, to avoid each other, which Miss Pratt set down as a proof positive that there was a perfect understanding between them ; but she was highly provoked that, with all her watching and spying, she never could detect stolen glances, or soft whispers, or tete-a-tete walks, or private meetings, or any of those various symptoms which so often enable single ladies to anticipate and settle a marriage before it has been even thought of by the parries themselves.

Not daring, however, to give utterance to her thoughts where she was, and unable any longer to keep her discovery pent up within her own bosom, she availed herself of the opportunity of a, free cast, as she called it, to make out her visit to Lady Mill-bank ; and there she accordingly betook herself with her budget

— containing, in strict confidence, all the particulars of Colonel Delmour's refusal — his impertinent perseverance — his frightening Miss St. Clair into hysterics by his violence, &c. &c. &c. Then came the history of Mr. Lyndsay's acceptance — her own bright discoveries — a full and minute description of the pearls, well garnished with conjectures as to how it would all end, when Mr. Member came to poll, and found another elected and returned. Some of these dark sayings she had even dared to throw out to Lord Rossville; but his lordship's thoughts were

so engrossed by the realities of electioneering, that he had none to throw away upon it metaphorically.

Miss Pratt's departure was, as usual, a relief to the whole party; but to none so much as to Miss St. Clair and Mr. Lynd-sav, who soon found themselves conversing together, if not with their former ease — with more than their former interest in each other. She could not be insensible to the quiet elegance of his manners, and the superiority of his conversation, but yet she failed to do him justice; for, solely occupied with one engrossing object, she merely sought in every other wherewithal to lighten the tedium of his absence. Two different pictures had been presented to her in the characters of the cousins—the one rich, varied, and brilliant in its colouring — the other correct and beautiful in its outline. The one attracting instant admiration — the other appreciated only by the careful and discriminating. Had perfection itself now been placed before her, it had failed to captivate the heart over which a dazzled imagination had cast its deceitful hues. The idol of that heart had gained an absolute ascendency over her affections; and on it she looked — not with the steady eye of sober truth, but with the fascinated gaze of spellbound illusion.

CHAPTER II.

Many, like myself, are sick of this disease: that when they know not how to write, yet cannot refrain from writing. — Erasmus.

The following letters were put into Gertrude's hand one morning. The first she opened was sealed with an evergreen leaf— motto, Je ne change qu'en mourant.

" I am inexpressibly pained to think what an opinion my dearest cousin must have formed of me, from having allowed so much time to elapse, ere I commenced a correspondence, from which, believe me, I expect to derive the most unfeigned and heartfelt delight. But you, my dear friend, whose fate it has been to roam, ' and other realms to view,' will, I am sure, make allowance for the apparent neglect and unkindness I have been guilty of, which, be assured, was very far from designed on my part. Indeed, scarce a day has elapsed since we parted that I have not planned taking up my pen to address you, and to attempt to convey to you some idea, however faint, of all I have seen and felt since bidding adieu to Caledonia. But, alas! so many of the vulgar cares of fife obtrude themselves even here, in ' wilds unknown to public view,' as have left me little leisure for the interchange of thought.

" Were it not for these annoyances, and the want of a congenial soul to pour forth my feelings to, I could almost imagine myself in Paradise. Apropos, is a certain regiment still at B. ? and have you got acquainted with any of the officers yet ? You will, perhaps, be tempted to smile at that question ; but, I assure you, there is nothing at all in it. The Major and Bell (or Mrs. Major Waddell, as she wishes to be called in future, as she thinks Bell too familiar an appellation for a married woman) are, I think, an uncommon happy, attached pair — the only drawback to their happiness is the Major's having been particularly bilious of late, which he ascribes to the heat of the weather, but expects to derive the greatest benefit from the waters of Harrowgate. For my part, I am sure many a ' longing lingering look ' I shall cast behind when we bid adieu to the sylvan shores of Winander. I have attempted some views of it, which may serve to convey to you some idea of its beauties. One on a watch paper, I think my most successful effort. The Major has rallied me a good deal as to who that is intended for — but positively that is all a joke, I do assure you. But it is time that I should now attempt to give you some account of my travels, though, as I promise myself the delight of showing you my journal when we meet, I shall omit the detail of our journey, and at once waft you to what I call Lake Land. But where shall I find language to express my admiration!

" One thing I must not omit to mention, in order that you may be able to conceive some idea of the delight we experienced, and for which we were indebted to the Major's politeness and gallantry. In order to surprise us, he proposed our taking a little quiet sail, as he termed it, on the lake. All was silence; — when, upon a signal made, figure to yourself the astonishment and delight of Mrs. Major and myself, when a grand flourish of French horns burst upon our ears, waking the echoes all around, while the delightful harmony was repeated from every recess which echo haunted on the borders of the lake ! At first, indeed, the surprise was almost too much for Mrs. Major, and she became a little hysterical; but she was soon recovered by the Major's tenderness and assurances of safety. Indeed, he is, without exception, the most exemplary and devoted husband I ever beheld ; — still I confess (but that is entre nous) that, to me, the little taste he displays for the tuneful nine would be a great drawback to my matrimonial felicity.

" After having enjoyed this delightful concert, we bade a long adieu to the sylvan shores of Ulls Water, and proceeded to Keswick, or, as it is properly denominated, Derwent Water, which is about three miles long; its pure transparent bosom, studded with numberless wooded islands, and its sides beautifully variegated with elegant mansions, snow-white cottages, taper spires, pleasant fields adorned by the hand of cultivation, and towering groves that seem as if impervious to the light of day. The celebrated fall of Lodore I shall not attempt to depict; but figure, if you can, a stupendous cataract, rushing headlong over enormous rocks and crags, which vainly seem to oppose themselves to its progress.

" With regret we tore ourselves from the cultivated beauties of Derwent, and taking a look, en passant, of the more secluded Grassmere and Rydall, we at length found ourselves on the shores of the magnificent Winander.

" Picture to yourself, if it be possible, stupendous mountains rearing their cloud-capped heads in all the sublimity of horror, while an immense sheet of azure reflected the crimson and yellow rays of the setting sun as they floated o'er its motionless green bosom, on which was impressed the bright image of the surrounding woods and meadows, speckled with snowy cottages and elegant villas ! I really felt as if inspired, so much was my enthusiasm kindled; and yet I fear my description will fail in conveying to you any idea of this never-to-be-forgotten scene. But I must now bid you adieu, which I do with the greatest reluctance. How thought flows upon me when I take up my pen ; — how inconceivable to me the distaste which some people express for letter-writing!

" Scribbling, as they contemptuously term it! — How I pity such vulgar souls ! You, my dear cousin, I am sure, are not one of them. I have scarcely left room for Mrs. Major to add a P. S. Adieu! your affectionate

"Lilly."

Mrs. Waddell's postcript was as follows: —

" Ma chere Cousine, " Of course, you cannot expect that I, a married woman, can possibly have much leisure to devote to my female friends, with an adoring husband, who never stirs from my side, and to whom my every thought is due. But this much, in justice to myself, I think it proper to say, that I am the happiest of my sex, and that I find my Waddell every thing generous, kind, and brave !

" Isabella Waddell."

The perusal of this letter was a severe tax upon Gertrude's patience, as it has doubtless been upon all who have read it — though tempted to laugh at it, she was, however, too generous to expose it to ridicule, and therefore hastened to commit the fair Lilly's lucubrations to the flames.

Poor Miss Lilly, like many other misses, had long aimed at the character of an elegant letter-writer, and this epistle she looked upon as one of her happiest efforts ; she had studied it— she had meditated upon it — she had written a scrawl of it— she had consulted her journal upon it — in short, she had composed it. One may compose a sermon, or an essay, or an any thing, save a letter; but when a letter is composed, all persons

of taste must feel it is an odious composition. To speak with the pen is the art of letter-writing ; and even a confused vulgar natural letter, flowing direct from the brain, or it may be from the heart, of one of uncultivated intellect, is more pleasing than the most studied and elaborate performance from the same source. But in letter-writing, as in conversation, many seem to study to make themselves tiresome, who, had they allowed their pens and their tongues to take their natural course, might have remained at least inoffensive. Yet many have lived to write good plain matter-of-fact letters who have spent the early years of their life composing sentences, and rounding periods, and writing descriptions, from the false ideas they entertained on this subject. But enough of condemnation on this, after all, venial transgression.

The other letter was in a different strain, as follows: —

" My dear Cousin, " I feel encouraged to the liberty I am going to take by the kindness you showed me when at Bellevue. Your good-will may now be the means of rendering me an essential service, and I should feel myself to blame if false diffidence were to hinder me from unbosoming myself to you. I was several times on the point of explaining myself to you, but thought I could more easily do it in writing ; and now that I take up my pen, I wish I had rather spoken to you when I had so many favourable opportunities. But why am I so wavering and foolish, when I ought with confidence to look to Him who has promised to direct the Christian's path, and who has promised that He will never leave nor forsake those who put their trust in Him, and acknowledge Him in all their ways ? I must now trust to your patience, while I tell my tale. A mutual attachment has subsisted between William Leslie and myself from our earliest years ; but he is poor, and on that account, and that only, it is not sanctioned by my parents — of course, you will believe that I never would enter into so sacred a connection without their consent. I love and reverence them too much, and, above all, I fear God; but fain would I hope that, had he a competency, their prejudices (for prejudices I must call them) would be overcome.

William's choice was early pointed to the church, and his clerical education has for some time been completely finished ,• but hitherto all his efforts to procure a living have proved ineffectual. My father might assist him ; but he is very lukewarm in the cause, as both my mother and he declare they cannot bear the idea of seeing me the wife of a poor minister. But I have learnt that poverty is a comparative thing, and that a competence to some is riches, while to others wealth seems little better than splendid want. It is true riches will be denied me ; but the greater blessings of peace and mutual affection may, by the blessing of God, be my happy lot. Even when called upon to endure hardship and privations, our souls will not be cast down; for with one heart and one faith -we will cheerfully bear the crosses of this life, looking forward to the inseparable and everlasting happiness of that which is to come.

"' Better is a dinner of herbs where love is,' than to sit in the joyless ease of indifference amidst heartless grandeur, or to drink the bitter cup of variance. Ah, my dear cousin! God only can put gladness in the heart, and 'tis not by the world or the things of the world. — If, as I believe, religion be indeed the soul of happiness, then may I reasonably hope for that peace which the world cannot give, with one whom I have known and loved from my earliest years, and whose faith and practice are those of a follower of Jesus Christ.

" This attachment is no phantom of a heated imagination. Our mutual love is now a principle — it cannot be extinguished, but it may be sacrificed to a still more sacred claim. I again repeat, I never will marry without the consent and blessing of my parents ; but were my dear William provided for, I think their pride would yield to their stronger feeling of affection for me. Yet I almost blush to trouble you with my selfish concerns, though I know you will befriend me if you can. The church of Clearburn is in Lord Rossville's gift — the present incumbent is old and infirm, and an assistant and successor is to be immediately appointed. I do not ask you to recommend William Leslie, because you ought not to recommend one to fill so sacred an office who is utterly unknown to you; but if you would name him to Lord Rossville — if you would request of him to inquire into his character and qualifications of those who can judge of them, and then if you will support him with your influence, you will confer a heartfelt obligation on your faithful and affectionate cousin,

"Anne Black."

CHAPTER III.

With a great understanding as a round orb that tumbles hither and thither, able to guess at the depth of the great sea. — Hindoos' Description of their God.

To feel and to act were with Gertrude commonly one and the same thing — reflection seldom was allowed to interpose its cooling influence; and scarcely had she finished reading the letter w r ben she flew to Lord Rossville to ask (and she had no doubt to obtain) the boon solicited. She found the Earl alone in his study, surrounded with papers and parchments, and looking, if possible, even more than usually portentous.

" I am come, my lord, to ask — to beg a favour,"— she began, almost breathless from haste and emotion.

M

" Miss St. Clair, this is rather an interruption ; but be seated— be seated — and be composed. You, and indeed all who have any claims upon my time, influence, or assistance, will ever find my ear open to the voice of proper solicitation — therefore, I again repeat, be composed, and allow this flow of spirits to subside ere you commence."

There is nothing less likely to promote its end than a recommendation to be cool and composed when one is all ardour and and eagerness ; but this was one of Lord Rossville's methods of tormenting his victims. He was always composed himself, even when in anger — that is, he was always heavy, dull, and formal — and no subject could warm him so as to make him neglect the slow and pompous formation of his sentences. His body was heavy — his nerves were tough — his blood was thick — he was a dull man —but, like many other men, he deceived himself; for he thought his dulness was self-command, and that he had the same merit in being composed as one whose perceptions are lively, whose blood flows rapidly, and whose ready imagination comprehends whole sentences such as his lordship composed ere they were half pronounced — one, in short, who thinks and speaks with natural feeling and animation. Different, indeed, was Lord Rossville's composure from that of one who " hath learned to rule his own spirit;" for he had a temper to rule, but no spirit. He had a sluggish, obstinate, thick-headed, pragmatical temper; incapable of hurrying him into the ebullitions of passion, 'tis true, but not the less troublesome and tormenting to those who opposed it. But this desideratum (for it was mere absence of animal heat, that kept his lordship cool) was more than compensated by what he deemed the masculine tone and nervous energy of his language, heightened as it was by gesticulation suited to the subject.

" Be composed," repeated he again, after a pause — his own composure becoming more and more heavy.

" O, it is nothing — I only feel a little afraid, lest you should think me too presuming when I ask — but I believe the petition itself will plead its own cause better than I can do;"— and she put her cousin's letter into his lordship's hands, with very sanguine anticipations as to the result.

Lord Rossville perused it in silence; but his looks became darker at every line, and his head shook, or rather trembled, from beginning to end.

" A most wild, dangerous, and improper letter," said he, when he finished it, vainly endeavouring to speak quicker — "I am pained to think that such a letter should have been addressed to you — that such a letter should have been presented by you to me," — and his lordship walked up and down the room in composed discomposure, while Gertrude remained aghast and motionless, at seeing her church in the air thus vanish like the baseless fabric of a vision. " Is it possible, Miss St. Clair,"—

asked he, his hand slowly rising — " is it possible that you had perused this letter ?" pointing with his obstinate-looking fingers to the paper in question — " and is it possible that, having read, you can also sanction, and approve, and assist a young female in setting up her own judgment in opposition to the known will and intention of her parents, and to the opinion and approval of the world in general ? "

" Although my cousin is so unfortunate as to differ from her parents on that subject," said Gertrude, timidly — "shedeclares that she will not disobey them."

" Not disobey them ! — Good Heavens ! Miss St. Clair, what do you term disobedience ?" The dignity of this appeal was interrupted by a cough. " / have lived longer in the world, and have seen rather more of mankind than you have done; and I do not hesitate to say, that the principles contained in this letter, if acted upon by the bulk of mankind (and it is only by generalizing principles that we can fairly bring them to the test), must eventually prove highly destructive to the present order of things, inasmuch as they are totally subversive of all filial obedience and parental authority."

Gertrude was much at a loss to answer this tirade, which confounded, without in the smallest degree convincing her. Again, however, she tried to urge something in extenuation; but it was, as Jeremy Taylor expresses it, treading on the corns of his lordship's mind to attack any of his opinions or prejudices; and it was resented accordingly.

" I own I am distressed—mortified — Miss St. Clair, that a letter containing such sentiments should be advocated by you—sentiments fraught with so much mischief—principles destructive of the mutual relationship of parent and child — wild, fantastical, new-fangled notions, setting at defiance all proper doctrines of religion, and only calculated to disturb, and finally abolish all orders of society; and yet it is such—such— I say I should consider myself as acting a most highly culpable part, were I to lend the smallest countenance or sanction to such measures;"—and he walked up and down the room, his shoes creaking at every step. — " Mr. Black is a sensible, well-principled man, and obviously views the matter in the same light as I do, and as, indeed, all persons of a right way of thinking should do. A young female to presume to judge for herself, in opposition to the wishes of her parents — to the opinion of the world — to the general voice of mankind ; and to seek to — to assume the mask of religion, in order to — to stifle the voice of duty — it is lamentable — it is deplorable — it is monstrous! — "What was it but by such steps as these the established order of things in a neighbouring country was gradually undermined, and at length finally overthrown ? — It was by such steps as these (knocking the letter slowly with his knuckles) that the altar and the throne—religion and—and — and loyalty — and —

and sound morality — all that were formerly held sacred, fell sacrifices to these very levelling principles ;" — and he threw the letter from him with all the energy of virtuous indignation.

Gertrude could scarcely refrain from smiling at the idea of Anne Black's marriage endangering church and state ; and something of that sort she ventured to express.

" I beg pardon, my lord," said she ; " but even supposing my cousin's marriage were to take place, I cannot perceive any bad consequences that would result from it, unless to herself."

" You do not perceive — you do not perceive the pernicious effects of such an example operating on young females in the same sphere ? — operating, too, under my sanction and countenance — and — and — and 1 to become the patron of rebellious undutiful children! — the conniver at low and improper and clandestine connections! Were such a precedent once established, where is it to end ? You yourself, I shall suppose, for the sake of illustrating my argument — you, presuming upon my licence in this instance, deem yourself authorized to select — choose — and — and — and declare that you will select and choose — nay, that you have selected and chosen, a— a partner for yourself, not only without my concurrence, but in direct opposition and contradiction to my will and authority! 1 ask, would not such behaviour on your part be—I do not scruple to say — monstrous ?"

Gertrude was not prepared for this digression; but she saw by his lordship's bend that, an answer was expected, and in some trepidation she replied—

" I hope it never will be my misfortune to differ from your lordship on this subject. But if it should " she stopped in much agitation.

" You hope it will never be your misfortune to differ from me !" — repeated his lordship, with a very dissatisfied look— " that is a style of language, Miss St. Clair, I own, which does not satisfy me. On that subject I can allow no differences. No young lady, of a right way of thinking, ought or can have a different opinion on so important a point from those whom it is her duty to reverence and obey."

His lordship paused, and seemed to be revolving some mighty matter in his mind ; and Gertrude, trembling at what this might lead to, rose, and taking up her cousin's letter was preparing to leave the room, when her uncle motioned with his hand for her to resume her seat; then in a slow, solemn tone, spoke as follows: —

" It certainly formed no part of my original plan, with regard to you, that, at this early period, you should have been made acquainted with the plans I had formed for your final disposal; but, from what has passed, I am inclined to think that, in deviating from my former purpose, I shall do wisely and well."— He then proceeded in the same prolix manner to unfold to Gertrude the future web of her life, as spun and wove by his lordship's own haud — or rather head.

Gertrude heard, without surprise, but not without emotion, that she was the destined wife of Mr. Delmour, and in that light was considered by him, and by all the members of the family, and by all the freeholders in the county ; and her heart glowed with resentment at the thoughts of any one having thus dared to appropriate her without her own consent. Scarcely could she listen with patience, while Lord Rossville detailed, in the most minute yet guarded manner, his plans with regard to her future establishment, as if afraid of making her too happy, or raising her expectations too high. Thus, after having settled every thing regarding her marriage with more than a lawyer's precision, he hastened to undo his own work in the same breath, by adding, that it was not his intention that the marriage should take place until she had attained the age of twenty-one, at soonest; — perhaps not even then, as he was no advocate for early alliances — that is, too early. " There was a time for all things, and that time must be regulated by circumstances ; but in the meantime "

" In the meantime, my lord," cried Gertrude, with great emotion, " I must be allowed to disclaim any engagement with Mr. Delmour."

The Earl regarded her for some moments with the greatest astonishment, and seemed as if wholly bereft of the power of expressing the indignation which swelled in his bosom almost to suffocation at this overt act of rebellion. At length he found words, though ideas were still wanting.

" What am I to understand from this most extraordinary speech, Miss St. Clair ? " interrogated he, with some difficulty.

Gertrude, in much emotion, but with the utmost gentleness of manner, repeated her words.

" Allowed to disclaim any engagement with Mr. Delmour ! A most extraordinary proposal at such a time ! — at a time when so much is at stake — a most improper, nay, a most indelicate proposal, in the present posture of affairs."

His lordship cleared his voice, hemmed, coughed, and proceeded : — " You cannot be ignorant, Miss St. Clair, of the very important contest at present carrying on in this county — a contest which is of vital importance to the power and consequence of this family — and, I may add, of some interest to the country at large ; as, in these times of anarchy and rebellion, when the throne and the government are assailed on all sides by factious and turbulent demagogues, it is of the utmost importance that our representation in parliament be sound, loyal, and patriotic, if we expect that our religion and laws should be preserved, and handed down unimpaired to our posterity."

M 3

Her assent seemed to be expected to this opening speech; but Gertrude could make none. The Earl went on —

" You are probably not aware of the motives which have actuated me in thus developing my schemes and intentions to you, and to the world in general, at this period ; and, in doing so, I certainly have deviated from my original plan. But we must all occasionally be regulated by circumstances ; and, I think, 1 have only to state to you, that the success of this most important political contest depends very considerably upon the understanding that Mr. Delmour will eventually, and in all probability, one day become, through your instrumentality, the lawful possessor of the family estates in this county: in one word, I could not with propriety offer Mr. Delmour as the representative of this county (he having little more than a nominal interest in it at present) — unless — as the — as the, in all likelihood — the intended husband of the presumptive (observe I say presumptive, not apparent) heiress of Rossville."

His lordship was so much pleased with the eloquence and brilliancy of his harangue that, as he went on, he gradually spoke himself into good humour ; and by the time it was ended he had almost forgot the origin of his elocution. Gertrude remained silent, struggling with contending feelings. On the one hand, was the fear of betraying her secret predilection for Colonel Delmour ; — on the other, her scorn and detestation of every thing resembling duplicity and deceit. At length her natural love of truth and candour prevailed; and, mustering courage, she said —

" Much as it pains me to oppose you, my dear uncle, yet I should be still more unworthy of your affection were I to leave you in an error. — Forgive me"—she paused—her heart throbbed, and her colour rose — " forgive me, —I will not deceive you. I cannot sanction the engagement you have formed for me — I never can be the wife of Mr. Delmour."

This was something so far beyond what Lord Rossville could have anticipated, that it was some time ere the fact could find admittance to his brain, choked up as it always was with his own notions. While the process of conviction was carrying on, he therefore sat as if petrified. At length the light began to penetrate the dim opaque of his understanding; but his lordship had, as usual, recourse to other people's words till he could muster his own forces.

" Never can be the wife of Mr. Delmour!" repeated he, in the tone of one who was not quite sure whether he were asleep or awake — " not sanction the engagement I have formed for you! "What — what, in the name of Heaven, am I to undertand from such language, Miss St. Clair ? "

The understanding seemed so perfectly obvious, that Gertrude
felt much at a loss how to make it clearer. The question was again repeated.

" Excuse me, my lord; hut Mr. Delmour is not the person I — hut, indeed, I do not know how to express myself in a manner less likely to offend. I would say that I wish to he left free, that I might he allowed to choose in so important "

" You wish to he left free! — You wish to he allowed to choose in so important! — hem ! — Really, Miss St. Clair, I am too much astonished at the — the — the — the — the — the — what shall I call it ? the unwarrantable levity of such a proposal, to answer it as it ought. You wish to he left free to choose! and that in a point of such vast — such vital importance ! — Are you aware in what capacity it is that a suitable alliance is formed for you ? — That it is not as Miss St. Clair, daughter of the Honourable Thomas St. Clair — hut as niece to the Earl of Rossville, and presumptive heiress to the title and estates thereof; with the exception of the Barony of Larchdale, which, by deed of entail of Alexander, first Earl of Rossville, devolves upon the heirs-male of the family; and, therefore, it is to consolidate these properties, that they may be again reunited in the persons of your mutual heir or heirs, — an arrangement which has Mr. Delmour's entire approbation ? I say that, under these circumstances, there is not — there cannot — there must not be a choice in the matter ; — but, indeed, I am very much at a loss to know what to understand by such an expression. / certainly have not been accustomed to hear of young ladies of family, and fortune, and distinction, choosing for themselves in their matrimonial course. / can only say, for my own part, I — I — had no choice !" Gertrude could, scarcely restrain a smile at hearing Lord Rossville quote himself as a pattern to be followed, instead of a rock to be shunned ; — but, such is the blindness of human nature, we are all but too apt to hold ourselves up as guides, when we ought to be satisfied to serve as beacons.

" Allowed to choose! — I—I—and pray, Miss St. Clair, supposing, for one moment, it was so—where, I ask—where would you—where could you find such another gentleman as Mr. Delmour— a gentleman of birth and fashion — of fine address — of appearance — of accomplishments — possessing a first-rate understanding, of which he has already given undoubted proofs to the world, by having been appointed one of the Financial Committee, which, for so young a man, I consider as a very distinguished mark of pre-eminence, — but who, notwithstanding all those advantages, submits himself, in this case, solely to my guidance and management? — I ask again, where could you find such another perfect gentleman ? "

"I acknowledge Mr. Delmour's good qualities, my lo. d — so far as I can pretend to judge of them upon so slight an acquaintance," answered Gertrude, hesitatingly; " but — pray

M 4

forgive me if I still repeat that I must be allowed to consider myself as perfectly disengaged."

" Miss St. Clair," cried the Earl, now absolutely gasping — " I can only say that — that if you persist — if you presume to report yourself throughout the county as — as — as disengaged

— I " The pulse of life seemed to stand still, and " nature

made a pause, an awful pause, prophetic of its end." — The clenched hand was slowly uplifted—then descended with a weight that shook the table "I cannot answer for the consequences !" This is a threat which always forms a happy climax to an argument, from its vagueness, and consequently its sublimity.

At that moment the party in question entered — his hands full of open letters, and with an air of bustle and business not at all calculated to fascinate a romantic imagination such as Gertrude's. He was beginning some rather formal and complimentary apology for his interruption, when she rose, and in some confusion stammered out a few words in reply; then, bowing to the Earl, was retiring, when Mr. Delmour begged to know whether she had any friends in the western extremity of the county, as he was afraid he should be under the necessity of setting off for that quarter immediately, and should be much honoured by being the bearer of Miss St. Clair's commands.

Gertrude disclaimed all interest in that part of tbe county; and, scarcely able to express the common civilities of parting, hastily withdrew.

CHAPTER IV.

My love's so true,
That I can neither hide it where it is,
Nor show it where it is not. Dryden's All for Love.

In every generous mind there is a spring, which, if touched rightly, yields fine issues; but if struck by an unskilful hand, produces only discord. So it was with Gertrude: affection would have led her — reason might have guided — but mere authority could never controul her. To one of an independent spirit nothing, therefore, could be more irksome than the situation in which she was placed. She felt that, to be approved of, she must cease to act, cease to think, cease to feel, cease to love, but as directed by the will of her mother and uncle. A spirit such as hers could not at once be thus subdued; and no one who has any thing noble in their nature can be subdued but by their own will — their understanding acknowledging the fitness of their submission. The

Christian, indeed, has his spirit subdued to yield obedience, contrary to his own inclination, to those who are placed over him by nature. But Gertrude's principles were not derived from this high and unerring standard ; and though she gave a general assent to the doctrine that children owed obedience to their parents, yet it was with so many limitations that the principle only wanted sufficient temptation to be set aside.

With regard to her uncle, his right to controul her seemed very doubtful; and, indeed, the authority of uncles commonly comes in a very questionable shape, and is, perhaps, only to be considered as binding, when the uncle has received authority from a living parent, or has early and long supplied the place of a departed one. As for aunts, they are always accustomed to dictate, but are seldom so unreasonable as to expect to be obeyed. Yet love and tenderness, almost maternal, have sometimes given them a power over a young and affectionate heart, which all the violence of improper authority never could have obtained. These would have subdued a mind such as Gertrude's ; but those gentle weapons were unknown and unused either by Lord Rossville or Mrs. St. Clair. Authority with the one—artifice with the other, were the means used to gain their different purposes with one whom opposite methods would have rendered submissive as a child, and open as noonday.

Gertrude's first impulse was to hasten to her mother, and relate to her all that had passed between Lord Rossville and her. She expected to encounter reproaches; but Mrs. St. Clair seemed almost frantic at her daughter's disclosure, and absolutely shook with terror while she listened to Gertrude's account of what had passed. But ere she had time to express her sentiments on the subject, a message was brought from the Earl, requesting her presence for half an hour in the study. It was easy to guess at the subject in hand; and Mrs. St. Clair, though in great agitation, instantly obeyed the summons. Gertrude waited with impatience for nearly an hour and a half, ere the conference was ended and her mother appeared. When she did, she read vexation and discomfiture in her countenance. She was, however, too prudent to express her feelings; but contented herself with saying that she had found Lord Rossville in great displeasure against his niece, and had left him quite immoveable as to the proposed alliance and declared engagement; and this was all Gertrude could draw from her mother. She therefore sat down to answer the unfortunate letter that had been the innocent cause of this premature eclaircissement, which she did by lamenting her present inability to aid her cousin in any shape; but concluding with the warmest assurances of regard and. promises of assistance, should it ever be in her power to befriend her. She was then preparing to dress for dinner, when the following note was presented to her: —

" The Earl of Rossville presents compliments to Miss St. Clair; and "while matters remain in their present unpleasant position, and until some arrangement of an amicable nature has taken place, it is his wish and expectation that Miss St. Clair should confine herself to her own apartment — it may be presumed from indisposition. " Rossville Castle, 29th Aug., 18—"

His lordship, when he perused this masterpiece of a billet, had fondly imagined it would speak daggers to the soul of his niece; and he piqued himself not a little at the finesse of punishing her in this exemplary manner, and at the same time keeping her transgression a secret from the rest of the family, whom he wished to remain in ignorance of this defiance of his power. Gertrude, of course, submitted to this embargo, and left it to her mother to give what name she pleased to her disorder.

A week elapsed, and Gertrude still remained in durance; but she bore her imprisonment with great heroism, and its languid hours were enlivened by a packet received through some unknown channel from Colonel Delmour. It affected to be merely a parcel of music; but it contained a letter full of all that love-letters are usually full of—hopes—fears—lamentations—vows — reproaches — raptures — despair. It may be supposed this did not tend to render Gertrude more compliant to her uncle's wishes; and his lordship was beginning to feel much at a loss how to proceed, when all the combustible particles of his composition were roused into action, and he hastened to array himself in all his honours and take the field in full force. The report of his niece's engagement with Mr. Lyndsay had, by the ingenuity of Miss Pratt, quickly circulated throughout the county, and had resounded and reverberated from all the corners of it before the last echo reached the dull ear of Lord Rossville; — but when it did, it produced all the effect of a thunderbolt upon his senses. Not that he could all at once give credit to such a monstrous supposition; but it was quite bad enough that the thing should be said, or for one instant believed. As soon as he recovered so far as to be able to ruminate, he therefore resolved upon his plan of proceeding; and, as the first step, summoned his niece to his presence. For some minutes he regarded her with a look which he vainly expected would cause her to sink to the ground; for the Earl thought of expression as Glendower did of spirits, — that he had only to call them, and they would come. After waiting in vain for the effects he had anticipated, his lordship found he must have recourse to his voice—not that he was averse to using that, but having witnessed the magic influence of a Siddons and a Kean, he had no doubt but that he too could look unutterable things ; and he had intended first to kill with the lightning of his eye, and then to revive with the gracious sound of his voice. All this he had intended; but how often are the best intentions frustrated!

Gertrude was quite ignorant of these intentions; and in her uncle's persevering stare saw nothing but a stare, which, being always a disagreeable thing, she sought to avoid by casting down her eyes. Still having somewhere read that women can see even with their eyes shut, Lord Rossville flattered himself that his piercing gaze would penetrate through the eyelids of his niece ; and he waited a little longer in hopes of seeing her at his feet.

At length she raised her eyes, but it was to exclaim at seeing a hawk dart past the window in pursuit of a dove. The Earl now spoke.

" Miss St. Clair, look at me."

Gertrude obeyed, and did look; but with an expression which seemed to say, and what then ?

" Look at me, Miss St. Clair, if, indeed, it is possible for you to meet my eye, after what has recently come to my knowledge. — Miss St. Clair, this is neither a subject nor a time for trifling, and I will have neither equivocation nor prevarication. — I ask you again — and I warn you to be cautious how and in what manner you frame your reply — I ask you again, are you willing to be restored to my favour and protection, upon the terms I proposed, namely, that you consider yourself as engaged, and as having been for some time past engaged, to Robert Burlington Delmour, Esquire, Member of Parliament, the heir-male of this family ? and do you consent that the nuptials be solemnized at such a time as I shall deem proper ?"

" My lord, I grieve that I cannot obey you; but I will not deceive you. Mr. Delmour has my good wishes — my affections " she stopped and coloured deeply ; then added, in a low voice, " are not mine to bestow ! "

Lord Rossville was struck dumb at this daring avowal, which seemed to mock the thunderbolt he held in his hand ready to hurl when the proper moment came.

" Miss St. Clair," gasped he at length, " are you aware of the construction that may be put upon such language ? — that it amounts, in the ordinary language of the world, to an avowal or confession of a very particular, I may add improper nature ? Miss St. Clair, what am I to understand from such a declaration ; — a declaration which, in the eyes of the world, would be considered as tantamount to an express and explicit declaration of a prior and illegal attachment, unsanctioned by me ?"

Gertrude bowed her head, either to hide her blushes, or to testify her assent. The Earl resumed —

" Miss St. Clair, my delicacy would have spared you this — to you humiliating, to me distressing avowal; but you have thrown aside the disguise which — which — which — but I must now inform you, that I am no stranger to this most improper, unaccountable, and unjustifiable transaction; and that, as the preliminary step towards gaining my forgiveness for this, I must

say, unpardonable offence, I must insist upon a complete and total renunciation of all farther intercourse with the party implicated."

" My lord," said Gertrude, frying to repress her tears, " I can only repeat what I have already said — I am sensible of your goodness — I grieve that I should have offended you; but I never will renounce the right of choosing for myself—that choice is made — would it were one more pleasing to your lordship !"

" Miss St. Clair, I will not hear another syllable," — cried the Earl, with an energy unparalleled in the annals of his life and conversation — "I here lay my positive injunctions upon you to refrain from speaking, thinking, or acting any farther in this most faulty and improper transaction; and I shall, at the same time, signify to the other party concerned that, from this time, he likewise must cease to consider you in any other light than that which the present relationship by blood warrants. I here positively annul any engagements, or contract, by which this clandestine, and, consequently unlawful and improper correspondence, has been "

" No, my lord," cried Gertrude, in her turn roused by such opprobrious epithets ■— " you cannot annul the affections of the heart. I am not a slave, to be thus bought and sold ! " exclaimed she, giving way to her long-suppressed tears.

" Miss St. Clair, such language — such sentiments — are no less unbecoming for you to utter, than they are improper for me to hear. I will listen to nothing more of the kind; but it is proper you should be made acquainted with what you have to expect from me should you persist in this obstinate, and infatuated, and destructive course, in which you have begun. You are then to learn that, in the event of your persisting in your headstrong and unaccountable refusal to fulfil the engagement I have contracted for you with the heir-male of this family, it is my firm resolution, and final determination, instantly to withdraw from you my countenance — alienate from you and your heirs every sixpence of property, heritable and personal, which it is in my power to dispose of; and farther, there is good reason to believe that it will bear a question whether I am not at liberty, under the deed of Simon, second Earl of Rossville, to dispone and bequeath the whole of the lands and estates according to my will and pleasure. At all events, the right of tying them up for an indefinite term of years is undoubted, and shall most unquestionably be put in force. You have, therefore, to choose between an annual income of 20,000Z., to which you are at present presumptive heiress (that is, eventually), or to sink at once into comparative poverty, and insignificance, and obscurity."

" My choice is made, my lord," said Gertrude, instantly calmed into the most perfect composure.

"Then, Miss St. Clair, you know and are fully aware of the consequences."

Gertrude only bent her head in silent acquiescence; and, rising to leave the room, the Earl rang the bell with rather more of energy than was his custom, and as she retired she heard him desire that Mr. Lyndsay might attend him immediately.

CHAPTER V.

The man scarce lives who is not more credulous than he ought to be, and who does not upon many occasions give credit to tales which not only turn out to be perfectly false, but which a very moderate degree of reflection and attention might have taught him could not well be true. — Adam Smith.

There is nothing tends so much to brace the nerves, and keep up the tone of the spirits, as the sense of having been treated with injustice. For some time, therefore, Gertrude felt as though she had gained a triumph by the sacrifice she had made to her lover; she exulted in the thought of thus proving to him the sincerity and the devotedness of her affection, and delighted her fond and simple fancy by imagining how much dearer she would be to him as the (for his sake) poor Gertrude St. Clair, than she ever could have been as the heiress of Rossville. But the first glow of enthusiasm over, she sighed as she thought, " Yet how sweet would have been the pleasure of bestowing upon him all that I now see—these noble woods, this far-spreading domain, I had hoped to have made him master of! They tell me he is expensive,—that is, he has a magnificent taste, and loves show and splendour, and pictures, and fine horses, and every thing that is beautiful. Ah! how happy I should have been in the means of gratifying him, and of making him so happy— oh! so happy, that he should have had nothing to wish for—yet all these he will sacrifice for me, for he has often declared my affection was all the world to him.—What signifies then the loss of wealth to those who can be rich in mutual love?" Thus communed Gertrude with herself; and, at nineteen, who would not have done the same?

Meanwhile the Earl was somewhat at a loss what course to pursue with the other supposed offender, Mr. Lyndsay. His lordship, unknown to himself, had that sort of intuitive respect for his nephew which weak minds (however against their grain) must always feel towards strong ones; but he still trusted to his powers of expression, and therefore arranged his aspect, as nearly as he could, into that cast with which he imagined Brutus had passed sentence on his sons. But looks were as much thrown away upon Mr. Lyndsay as they had been

•upon Gertrude; — that gentleman testified no sort of emotion ▪whatever at heholding his lordship's hrows hent full upon him, and the Earl again found himself reduced to the vulgar method of explaining himself in words. He then entered upon a speech, ▪which, for intricacy of design and uselessness of purpose, might have vied with the far-famed labyrinth of Crete. Poor Mr. Lyndsay toiled after him in vain, quite unable even to conjecture where his lordship was driving, and what was to be the issue of his tortuous harangue. At length the Earl emerged from the dim eclipse in which, shorn of his beams, he had so long shed disastrous twilight, if not upon nations, at least upon individuals, and the truth burst upon Lyndsay's almost benighted senses. For a moment a strange glow of delight came over his heart at hearing himself called upon to renounce all claim to the hand and affections of Miss St. Clair; but it as quickly faded as he thought of the difference of their views and sentiments, and he smiled in scorn at his own credulity for having, for an instant, given ear to such a delusion. "It is impossible for me to relinquish what I never possessed," said he, in answer to the Earl's appeal, " nor can even flatter myself it is in my power to obtain. This is some of Miss Pratt's idle rumours, which have found their way to your lordship's ear;—believe me, they are quite unworthy of a moment's consideration."

But it was in vain to hold this language to Lord Rossville ; it was seldom an idea found entrance into his head, and when once there it was no easy matter to dislodge it— it became, not the mere furniture of the head, to be turned or changed at will, but seemed actually to become a part of the head itself, which it required a sort of mental scalping or trepanning to remove. In vain, therefore, was Mr. Lyndsay's denial — the Earl remained steadfast in his belief, and rejected the idea of Miss Pratt with the greatest contempt. — He " was perfectly informed of the whole, from authority it was impossible to question." He then went over the same ground he had taken with Gertrude — the loss of his countenance— the breaking of the entail — the tying up of the property, &c. &c. " Were I, as you imagine, honoured with Miss St. Clair's partiality," said Lyndsay, " I must frankly tell you, that all you have now said would not have the slightest influence upon me — I hope it never will have upon the man who is so fortunate as to gain her affections. Much as he may value your lordship's favour, and the Rossville estates, I trust he will never put either of them in competition with Miss St. Clair."

This was past answering. Lord Rossville took two or three turns through the room before he could trust himself to reply, then spoke —

" Mr. Lyndsay, I can only impute this tergiversation of yours (to call it by no harsher name) to a very mistaken and destructive sense of honour; but what will you say, sir, when I inform you, that not many minutes have elapsed since, in this very apartment, and on this very spot, I received from the lips of the young lady herself the open and avowed acknowledgment of her — her — her—what shall I call it?—her highly improper attachment to and engagement with yourself? "

" Impossible! " exclaimed Lyndsay, his face flushing with a variety of contending emotions ; — " she did not — she could not say so."

Mr. Lyndsay knew his uncle to be a weak, tiresome, conceited man ; but he also knew him to be a man of perfect veracity — one who, at least, always intended to speak the truth. Such an unqualified assertion, therefore, as that he had just made, could not fail to be heard by him with some emotion, however mingled with incredulity.

Lord Rossville, in great displeasure that his word should be doubted, repeated his nephew's last words with more than usual pompous indignation ; then added — "I should deem it derogatory to myself to insist farther upon this subject. I can only repeat, and that upon the honour of a peer, that I have received from Miss St. Clair the avowal of her clandestine attachment to you; and, farther, heard her assert and maintain her right to make such a choice."

" Enough, my lord," cried Lyndsay ; " 'tis in vain to attempt to answer such assertions at present—but I shall endeavour to furnish you with some explanation of this mystery ere long." And he hastily withdrew, despairing of any elucidation from Lord Rossville. Yet how or where to find it he knew not, still less could he form any plausible conjecture as to the truth; there was none to whom he could apply, for there was no one on whose judgment or principles he could place any reliance. At one time he thought was it possible Gertrude could be playing false, and using his name as a cover to some clandestine engagement — the stranger? — Colonel Delmour? — but the next minute he checked the idea as unworthy of her, of himself. Whatever her faults might be, duplicity certainly was not of the number —there was an air and expression of candour and openness in her countenance, manners, words, which placed her above the meanness of suspicion. At length he resolved to seek her himself, and try whether he could not penetrate this mystery.

Gertrude had remained standing at the window of one of the public rooms she had to pass through in leaving Lord Rossville's apartment—she had been gazing with a vague mingled feeling of pride and regret at the lovely scene that lay before her in all the glowing tints of autumn, when she was roused from her reverie by the entrance of Mr. Lyndsay. He accosted her with an inquiry after her health, and then one of those awkward silences which every body has felt ensued. At length, as she turned to quit the room, he spoke —

" Once, my dear cousin," said he, " you conferred upon me the privilege of a friend — that of speaking the truth to you."

<' It is one you have hitherto made little use of," replied she ; then deeply colouring as the thoughts of the midnight rencontre rushed to her mind, she added, " I have, perhaps, no right to expect that Mr. Lyndsay should do what circumstances must have rendered so disagreeable a task for him."

" You wrong yourself and me by such a supposition," said he. " However inexplicable some things may appear, a few words of truth, I am very sure, will set all to rights."

" No!" exclaimed Gertrude, in much agitation: " inexplicable I must still remain to you—ask me nothing—I cannot, indeed I cannot answer any questions."

" Gertrude," said Lyndsay, with great emotion, " it is essential to my happiness — perhaps to yours—that we should understand each other." He paused; then, by a strong effort, proceeded, — " You will call it folly, presumption, madness, when I tell you that Lord Rossville, under the influence of some unaccountable delusion, has called upon me to resign all pretensions to your favour—to your hand ." He stopped, and

Gertrude, overwhelmed with surprise and confusion, remained silent.

" Had I dared to aspire to it," continued he, in increasing agitation, " I know no earthly motive that would have induced me to relinquish my claims, Gertrude,"—and he would have taken her hand; but Gertrude stood aghast, and for a few moments remained overwhelmed with confusion ; at length roused to self-possession, she saw there was only one course she could now pursue—she must throw herself upon the generosity of her cousin—she must confide to him the secret of her attachment to Colonel Delmour. Noble and disinterested as he was, she knew him to be incapable of abusing her confidence; and, with a mixture of embarrassment and simplicity, she disclosed to him the situation in which she stood.

Mr. Lyndsay heard her with the deepest interest, while she lamented the misunderstanding that had occurred with her uncle, and avowed that her affections were no longer her own to bestow; but when, with faltering tongue and downcast eyes, she named Colonel Delmour as the object of her choice, a shade of anguish overcast his face.

"'Tis then as I feai'ed!" exclaimed he. "Ah, Gertrude! would I could have saved you from this!"

" Saved me!" repeated Gertrude, colouring deeply with shame and displeasure as she turned away.

" Forgive me, my dear cousin," cried he—"I did not mean to offend you—I spoke too abruptly ; but I cannot retract what I have uttered. Did not you promise to hear, and to bear the truth from me ? "

" I was ignorant then that, under the name of truth, I was to
be called upon to give ear to detraction, and detraction against the absent."

Lyndsay looked upon her more in sorrow than in anger, while he answered—" Yet, if you saw one in whom you were interested on the brink of a precipice, would any consideration withhold you from giving them warning of their danger, — from saving them, if you possibly could? But do not injure me so far—do not suppose me so base as to have said to you what I have not said—what I will not again repeat to Colonel Dclmour himself. I have warned him, that I would do all in my power to save you from ever becoming his, if that is detraction "

" Be it what it may," cried Gertrude, " I will hear no more .— already I have heard too much ;" and her voice quivered with emotion —" I will go to Lord Rossville—I will clear up this error—be the consequences to myself what they may;" and, rejecting Lyndsay's effort to detain her, she flew to Lord Rossville, and, in all the excitement of wounded feeling, acknowledged Colonel Delmour as the object of her preference.

It was some time ere the Earl could open his eyes to this flood of new light; but when he did, long and tiresome was the scene that ensued. This was worse and worse—to have chosen the wrong brother;—'twas strange — 'twas passing strange; and a parallel was drawn between the two brothers that, in his lordship's estimation at least, might have rivalled that of Hamlet. In vain was her lover denounced ; even had she credited the aspersions cast upon him, they would have now come too late : they might grieve, but they could not change her heart. At length the whole concluded with her being discarded from her uncle's presence and protection. Mrs. St. Clair was next summoned, and a long consultation ensued. Her anger and dismay were at least equal to the Earl's, though caused by different views of the same subject. How to dispose of the offender was the next question. To permit her to bask in the light of his lordship's countenance, after her sentence of excommunication, would never do — yet to confine her to her apartment, or discard her utterly, would be making the matter public. And as he expected he should ultimately prevail, he was anxious, he said, that the flame of rebellion should not blaze forth, as he had no doubt of speedily extinguishing it. In this emergency, the only course Mrs. St. Clair could suggest was, that her daughter and she should pay a visit to her sisters. To this his lordship at first objected; but, upon hearing that they lived in the most retired melancholy manner, and that it would be a perfect act of penance for Gertrude to reside there, he consented. Under pretence of change of air, therefore, for Miss St. Clair's cold, it was settled that they should immediately depart ; and the necessary arrangements having been made, for the sake of appearances, and, as he expressed it, to stifle any unpleasant surmises to which this hasty removal might give birth, they were escorted to the carriage by the Earl himself; — he handed in Mrs. St. Clair, but only appeared to assist Gertrude — thus preserving the beautiful unity of his design to the last.

CHAPTER VI.

Il ne faut pas croire que la vie des Chretiens soit une vie de tristesse, on ne quitte les plaisirs que pour d'autres plus grands. — Pascal.

To the worldly mind there is always something depressing in the transition from grandeur to mediocrity. This Mrs. St. Clair and her daughter experienced upon entering the simple dwelling of the Miss Blacks. The one loved the pomps and the luxuries of high life, the other its elegancies and refinements; and both had lost their relish for the humbler sphere which they were now entering. They were received by the sisters with an affection and tenderness which seemed to flow from a better source than mere worldly politeness. There was an openness of character, — a calm, sweet gentleness of manner, which could not fail to please; but there was, at the same time, a difference of tastes, principles, and pursuits, between them and their visitors, which no courtesy of manner, or cordiality of reception, could entirely do away. The Miss Blacks were no vain professors of that religion which all pretend to honour with their lips, while with many their heart is far from it — their time, their talents, their fortune, their hearts were devoted to its service ; and in devoting the heart to God, how various and comprehensive are the duties which it embraces! Different portions, indeed, had been assigned them, but both were labourers in the same vineyard.

    Thousands at His bidding speed,
And post o'er land and ocean without rest:
They also serve who only stand and wait. Milton.

    The word of God was the rule of their faith am practice — they believed, and they obeyed. Yet, impressed as they were themselves with the importance of those divine truths, they were aware that it is not. by the mind, but with the heart, that man believeth unto salvation ; and they sought rather to make Christianity loved and desired, than to prove its divine origin by reasoning and disputation. As the glories of the firmament are reflected in the placid bosom of some deep unruffled stream of the valley, so did Divine truth shine in them with a clear yet subdued light; while the charity which " vaunteth not itself, is not easily provoked, thinketh no evil," was visible in that deportment of its votaries, and shed an indescribable charm over the tone of their conversation. Without neglecting their own avo-actions, or sacrificing their own pursuits, they nevertheless en-

deavoured, by every means in their power, to render their house agreeable to their visitors, and to promote, if not mirth and revelry, at least cheerfulness and amusement. Still there was something in her sisters with which Mrs. St. Clair could not assimilate — she felt their faith and their practice a reproach to herself; and she turned with aversion from their excellence, as Lucifer did from the sunbeams, only because of their brightness. Thus it is with true Christian piety, which seldom fails to be an offence to some part of the world, which denounces, as zealots and fanatics, all who rise above its own low standard. It was otherwise with Gertrude : though not sufficiently enlightened to be above imbibing prejudices, she was too liberal-minded and candid to retain them; and she had not lived many days with her aunts ere she arrived at the conviction that all religious people are not necessarily fools, hypocrites, or bigots. The unvarying mildness and gentleness of her aunts, their charity to all, their indulgence towards young people, could not fail to gain her affections ; and though their sentiments were totally different from hers, and what she deemed very out of the way, still the fruits were so fair that she could not but apply to them Pope's often misapplied maxim, —

    They can't be wrong whose life is in the right.

    But it was a species of virtue Gertrude felt no inclination to imitate; all her ideas of virtue were those of imagination ; she loved to expatiate in thought on deeds of romantic, sentimental excellence : her money, and her tears, and her emotion were always ready to bestow ; but when she herself was brought into contact with real genuine human wretchedness, she shrunk with horror and disgust from the encounter. The dirtiness of the houses, the coarseness of the people, the ugliness of the children, were all revolting to her fine-spun notions of the beauty of benevolence ; and she longed to discover some fair specimens of elegant woe, some interesting vestiges of human calamity, on whom to lavish the ardent sensibility of her warm and generous but unrenewt heart; — in short, her religion was the religion of impulse and feeling; and, as has been finely said, "Virtue requires habit and resolution of mind as well as delicacy of sentiment; and, unfortunately, the former qualities are sometimes wanting, where the latter is in the greatest perfection." Alas! it is not in this world that charity assumes the fair and graceful form with which painting and sculpture, in all the riches of their imagination, have so often decked it!

Although the Miss Blacks lived, according to the worldly phrase, out of the world, they, nevertheless, had a society,"« hich even Mrs. St. Clair and her daughter felt it no degradation to mix in. Their doors were open to all; for they practised hospitality towards all, though their chosen friends were those whose faith and practice most closely assimilated with their own.

William Leslie, the innocent origin of Gertrude's present disgrace, was a frequent visitor, and could not fail to make a favourable impression on her from his interesting appearance, and the modesty and propriety of his manners. From the delicacy of his features, he looked even younger than he was; and may he represented in the words of an ancient and somewhat quaint description, as " seeming much about twenty years of age, brown-haired, tall, of a sweet face, and of a most neat composure." She felt as much interest in the success of that attachment as the engrossing influence of her own would admit of her taking in any subject foreign to it. But to the disquiets of absence was now added a sort of restless anxiety to receive renewed assurances of affection from her lover; not that she doubted his fidelity, or for a moment believed it could be shaken by any vicissitude of fortune that might befall her ; but still, as she knew Lord Rossville had communicated to him what had passed, it would have been gratifying to have been assured that his faith was unshaken. She saw by the papers that his regiment was still in England; perhaps, then, he meant, to come himself, and bear her through the storm to which her attachment to him had exposed her; and day after day—hour after hour, Gertrude waited, till waiting degenerated into watching, and watching turned into the sickness of hope deferred.

Mrs. St. Clair read what was passing in her daughter's mind, and tried to take advantage of it, by prevailing on her to renounce the man who, at such a crisis, could leave her in doubt for a single moment as to the nature of his sentiments ; but 'tis long ere the the young and generous heart can believe in any thing so monstrous as the deceit of the object beloved: and Gertrude, even •while she felt the anxieties of doubt, yet rejected, almost with horror, the idea of his unworthiness. In vain did her aunts endeavour to lead her thoughts to better things, or even to direct her mind to other sources of occupation. Gertrude, under the influence of a wayward and domineering passion, could listen only to its voice ; and the voice of the charmer, charm it ever so wisely, fell unheeded on her ear: she felt almost provoked at their calmness and placidity, and secretly sighed at the insipid monotony of her life.

CHAPTER VII.

In hope a king doth go to war,
In hope a lover lives full long,
In hope a merchant sails full far,
In hope just men do suffer wrong,
In hope the ploughman sows his seed ;
Thus hope helps thousands at their need;
Then faint not, heart, among the rest,
Whatever chance, hope thou the best. Richard Alison.

Hitherto the weather had been fine ; and though fine weather in any town, hut more especially in a little, dull, dirty, provincial one, never appears to less advantage, still it was a relief to Gertrude to saunter alone in her aunt's little garden, and sometimes to extend her rambles to the neighbouring fields ; but two days of incessant rain deprived her even of this resource, and she found herself shut up in the same apartment with her mother and her aunts, unable to take any interest either in their occupations or conversation. Where people's hearts are in unison, a very small space indeed suffices for their bodies; but where there is no blending of tastes and pursuits, social intercourse necessarily becomes irksome and oppressive, and we sigh for even the joyless freedom of solitude. In the narrow dull streets of Barnford there was little to amuse or attract; but Gertrude sat at the window most part of the morning, gazing she knew not at what. Perhaps there are few stronger proofs of aberration of intellect than that of a person looking out of a window, where there is nothing to be seen ; and at another time she would have smiled in scorn at the idea of ever being reduced to so pitiful a resource. Certainly the objects upon which she looked with vacant eye were not of the most attractive order. At the opposite house, an old gentlewoman sat knitting—her hands at one side of her body, her head at the other, in the manner usually practised by expert knitters. This old gentlewoman then sat knitting a large thick-shaped white lamb's-wool stocking, with wires and quills, like those " upon the fretful porcupine," stuck in her girdle, and which her well-trained fingers ever and anon exchanged and adjusted in a manner which none but a knitter could comprehend or explain. It is a galling thing to those whose hands will not move a finger without the superintendence of the head thus to behold other hands performing all the intricacies of heel and toe, apparently by their own free will and accord. There are few servants who do not require to be occasionally looked after; but these trusty and vigilant members never appeared to relax in their labours, though the eyes of their mistress never were once directed towards them, but seemed to be in active observance of all that was to be seen beyond the sphere of her own dwelling. Much might be said upon this

subject; but, doubtless, my readers love a well-knit story as much as a well-knit stocking, and it would be like letting down a stitch, to enter upon a long digression at present.

At the next house a great washing was going on—maidservants, with pinned-up sleeves, crimson arms, and loose caps, came occasionally to the door to discharge tubs full of soap-suds; while a roaring infant was dandled at the window by a little dirty dog-eared-looking minx, with her hair en papillote. On the other side of the knitting lady nothing was visible to the naked eye ; but the sound of an old cracked jingling spinnet was heard unceasingly practising Barbadoes Bells and Nancy Dawson. Below was a shop, and over the half-door leant the shop-master, with a long sharp raw nose, looking as anxiously as ever did Sister Anne to see if there was anybody coming. Now and then the street was enlivened with the clank of a pair of pattens (probably Miss Becky Duguid's) ; — at another time, a spattered cow was driven reluctantly along, lowing most plaintively. There was also an occasional cart shaking the houses in its progress as it rumbled over the rugged pavement. A hoarse shrieking balladsinger, with a wooden leg, made an attempt to collect an audience by vociferating—

Bright Chanticleer proclaims the dawn,
And spangles deck the thorn ; The lowing herds now quit the lawn ;
The lark springs from the corn. Dogs, huntsmen, round the window throng,
Fleet Towler leads the cry; Arise, the burden of my song, This day a stag must die. With "a hey, ho, chevy ! Hark forward, hark forward, tantivy! Hark, hark, tantivy! This day a stag must die. This day, &c.

But his only listeners were a boy going to school, and a servant girl bound on a message which required despatch. These were sounds of hopeless misery, — but the blowing of a horn, with what is it not fraught to the watching heart and listening ear ? Gertrude strained her eyes; but a long coach, covered with red cloaks and umbrellas, was just setting off—there were not even the hopes and fears of an arrival to agitate.

The day was beginning to close in—dinner had been ordered; and Gertrude, with a deep sigh, was turning from the window, when again the sound of wheels was heard — she turned —a carriage was in sight — it approached in the dubious straggling manner of one uncertain of its destination—the glasses were up, and dimmed with rair.—but, oh! agitation unspeakable ! as it stopped for a moment opposite the window, Gertrude recognized the well-known Delmour crest! For some moments she saw— heard nothing—all was silent tumult in her mind, as she thought " He is come !—even now he seeks me !"—She looked up—the carriage had moved on a few doors, but there it stood—she saw

the hind wheels; but she could see no more, save that it seemed to be causing a little bustle — heads were put out from the opposite windows, and two or three people came out of their dwellings, and crossed the street to it. Every instant seemed an age to Gertrude, and some minutes elapsed, when again it was set in motion. It turned — she saw the horses' heads—they were almost at the door — there was no longer doubt — it was soon reality—the carriage drew up — a loud knock at the door startled even the Miss Blacks—the bustle of an arrival was heard below — what was said Gertrude heard not — a mist was before her eyes — a rushing sound in her ears. The door was thrown open, and in an instant the whole illusion vanished, as if by the touch of some fell enchanter; for in pattered—Miss Pratt.

CHAPTER VIII.

How convenient it proves to be a rational animal, who knows how to find, or to invent, a plausible pretext for whatever it has an inclination to do ! — Franklin.

" My dear Miss Black, this is really too much ! — Now, don't let me disturb you. But what do you think ? — I've got into a fine scrape, thanks to my pretty madam of a maid. — Miss Mary, I hope you feel yourself getting stouter — this is sad weather for rheumatism, Mrs. St. Clair. Miss Gertrude, my dear, are you well enough ? — But, as I was saying, I really never was in such a situation in my life before. — I've been staying for the last week at old General Crabtree's; poor man! the gout really does not improve his temper—and the house is small; and altogether, to tell you the truth, I was glad of an excuse to get away — so when our friend Mr. Delmour, who's there for a day or two on his political purposes, proposed sending in his carriage to get something done to the lamps, I thought I would just take the opportunity of coming in, having a little business of my own at this time — but what do you think ? Upon coming to my own house, lo and behold it's hard and fast locked up; and that light-headed tawpee is off to a sick mother, or a brother from the sea, or some such sham, and I'm left to shift for myself—without a hole to put my head in. If she had had but the sense to have left my key, I could have made a shift "

At that instant Miss Black's servant entered with a large key, bearing to be the key of Miss Pratt's house, which, she said, had been sent by Mrs. Dunsmure, the grocer, with whom Babby Braidfoot had deposited it at her departure.

" That's my key, is it ? " asked the owner, regarding it with a very bitter look ; " and much the better I'll be of that, to be

sure," taking it with great reluctance. " I'll find cold quarters there, I think, for any body just come off a journey."

Miss Black was too sincere to make speeches, or express pleasure she did not feel; but she took advantage of the first pause afforded by Miss Pratt to express her wish that she would remain with them, and to assure her of a hearty welcome to such accommodation as they had.

" My dear Miss Black, this is really kind! — a friend in need is a friend indeed. Well I may say that! — But are you sure it's not putting you to any inconvenience ? I know I may depend upon your telling me honestly. To be sure nobody need mind me, for, I thank my stars, I am easily put up ; I'm not one of those who can't sleep out of their own house ; I can lie in any bed, if it's not too hard, and is well made, and has plenty of

pillows, and enough of nice light blankets, and just a touch of a warming-pan through it, and a bit clear spunk of fire in my room. Well, since you insist upon it, I'll just take the liberty of having my bits of things brought out here ; they can easily be moved afterwards. Then, my dear,"—to the servant girl — " will you just tell the coachman to take out my luggage? He must get somebody to help him with the largest trunk ; and tell him to keep the small one with the right end upmost. And do you hear, my dear, will you take care in carrying up the bandboxes ?—and there's a large green bag, see that it's well fastened at the mouth ;—and there's a pair of stout walking-shoes in one of the pockets, and my work-bag, and a little brown-paper parcel in the other—and there's a little basket in the corner, and that's all. — Well, this is really comfortable," drawing in her chair, " for a person just come off a journey," taking off her shoes, and holding up her feet to the kindly influence of a blazing fire ; —" and what's more, it is really kind," seizing Miss Mary's hands, and giving them a most emphatic squeeze ; as much as to say, "And there is your reward." The servant now entered, to say every thing had been taken out; and the coachman begged to know " if there was any word ?" This Miss Pratt well knew was, in other words, craving a douceur; and she looked a little blank as she answered, " No word—he is just to take the carriage, as his master desired him, to Springwell, the coach-maker's, in the High Causeway, and show him what's to be done to the carriage ; and he's just to leave it there, and make the best of his way home, with my compliments."— Then, as if communing with herself, " If I had been at home, I would have given him something this wet day—not that he's come so far as to need it, for it's but scrimp six miles — but to be sure the day's bad."

Miss Black here resolved these doubts by giving orders for the coachman to have some refreshment.

" Well, that is really very humane of you, my dear Miss Black ; — but I've my doubts whether it's right to give other

people's servants any thing. Indeed it's a principle with me never to give them money" — with a look as much as to say, "Am I not right ?"

" When people give trouble," said Mrs. St. Clair, who was rather in a bad humour, and consequently very sensible in her remarks, " they ought to give something besides."

" I beg your pardon, Mrs. St. Clair — I know many people who set their faces against allowing their servants to take money

— many —they think it makes them greedy and rapacious, and I think so too. Indeed, I'm satisfied it's a wrong thing to give other people's servants money ; but I think I ought to give my pretty light-headed Mrs. Babby a month of the Tolbooth as a reward for her behaviour."

Dinner, which had been retarded by Miss Pratt's arrival, was now announced. " Bless me ! is it that time of day ? "—looking at her watch—" I declare it's twenty minutes past five ;"—then forcing on her shoes — " You must excuse my sitting down in my pelisse — for, I assure you, I little thought of dining in anybody's house but my own to day." Then, having taken her station at the table — " Barley-broth,"— peeping into the tureen

— " and a very good thing it is, when well made — and this is very nice — clear and strong — it's a great favourite of mine.— Miss Mary, let me recommend the broth to you. Miss St. Clair, my dear, you don't look as if you were hungry—that's with not being out to-day. — I wish Anthony Whyte could see you just now ; for he says an elegant female at dinner ought always to look as if she did not care whether she were eating or not — I really think you would please him there."

"I am sure I seldom care whether I sit down to dinner or not," said Mrs. St. Clair, with a sigh ; though, by-the-by, she generally contrived to pick up the best of what was going.

"My dear Mrs. St. Clair, did you ever try to go without your dinner ? "

"I dare say I have frequently."

"I beg your pardon, but really I think you must be mistaken there—take my word for it, nobody that has tried it once will ever try it again—I speak from experience. — I once fried to go without my dinner; but I can tell you it was any thing but agreeable ; in short, it will not do, let people say as they will.— What nice-looking whitings—that's one of Mr. Whyte's favourite dishes, nicely crisped with bread crumbs—and this is a Bellevue chuckie, I'm sure, fat and fair. — I declare it's a treat to me to sit down to such a dinner; for I'm perfectly sick of the sight of turtle soup and great fat venison. — I was really wearying to get to my own house for a little, if it was only to refresh myself with a drop plain barley-broth, and a bk boiled mutton ; and what a pleasant thing for a few friends to meet this way, instead of these great hubbleshows of people one sits down with now, where there's no carrying on any thing like rational conversation. —

Mrs. St. Clair, allow me to help you—Miss Mary, you're doing very little — Miss St. Clair, my dear, take a little wine with me to cheer you this bad day. —Is this elder-flower wine, Miss Black? —Upon my word, it's very little inferior to Anthony Whyte's Frontiniac. —' Here's a health to them that's awa,'"— with a significant look, and an attempt at the tune. "By-the-by, what did you think when you saw Mr. Delmour's carriage stop ? — I doubt you were a little disappointed, eh ? "

Gertrude felt too miserable even to be moved by Miss Pratt's ill-timed jests; and she remained pale, cold, and silent. To attempt to carry on any thing resembling conversation in Miss Pratt's company was impossible; yet to endure her idle tattle for a whole evening was a sacrifice, too great even for Miss Black's patience and good breeding. It was in vain to have recourse to music, as she then fastened herself upon some one of the company, and carried on her colloquy in loud whispers, even more annoying to a nice-toned ear than open declamation. The only effectual mode of silencing her, then, was by reading aloud ; and although she highly disapproved of that manner of passing the time, and indeed remarked what a wearing-out thing it was for the reader, and how much easier it was for all parties just to sit and chat, yet her objections were politely waived : and Miss Mary, taking up a volume of Mackenzie, read the exquisitely beautiful story of La Roche, which served as a prelude to the solemn acts of devotion with which the evening closed.

CHAPTER IX.

1 play the torturer by small and small,
To lengthen out the worst that must be spoken.

SHAKSPEAREc

The sacred emotions which had been raised in Gertrude's soul had, while they lasted, shed their soothing influences on her heart; but -when these ceased she felt gladness only that the day was done, and that she should now be alone. Hurrying to her chamber, she took out the often-perused letter of her lover — the only one she had ever received from him ; but that one, did it not stand for a thousand ? There was all that the warmest, tenderest passion could dictate — there was every assurance of devoted, unchanging, everlasting attachment — and again and again she repeated that to doubt was base — was dishonourable ; but even while she repeated it a vague secret doubt lurked in her mind, unknown to herself. She was roused from her contemplation by a knock at her door ; and ere she had time to reply to the summons. Miss

Pratt's head, in a nightcap, presented itself, "with " May I come in ? " — And taking it for granted (as people generally do on those occasions), she immediately entered. — " So, I guessed you would not be in a hurry to go to your bed — young people all like to sit up late — and, indeed, I'm not over fond of very early hours myself; so we'll just have a little chat," carefully extinguishing her candle. — " This is a nice snug little room, and I dare say you'll sleep as sound here as in your fine silk bed at Rossville — and, by-the-by, how long is it since you left the castle, and how came your uncle to part with you ? "

Contrary to Miss Pratt's usual manner, she waited for an answer; and Gertrude replied, that they had left Rossville almost three weeks since, and there she stopped.

" And your uncle made no objections to your coming here? Of course, you could not have come, indeed, if he had opposed it; and I suppose you're to make some stay in that case ? "

Gertrude replied, that there was no time fixed for their departure, and Miss Pratt for a moment looked as if a little baffled; but, quickly recovering, she seized Gertrude's hand, and trying to look tender —

" My only reason for asking, my dear, is, that I really don't think you agree with this town—you don't look so well as when I saw you at Rossville — I wish all may be quite right," patting the hand which was withdrawn from her with something of a look of displeasure. But the ice was now broke, and she plunged boldly in. — " My only reason, indeed, for supposing there was any thing wrong is, that I've received a most extraordinary letter since I saw you from Lord Rossville — really a most impertinent letter,"— rummaging her pockets, and dragging out from each receptacle a vast collection of letters, notes, memoranda, &c. &c, amongst which she picked for some time, but to no purpose, for the missive in question; then, with a look of alarm — " Bless my heart! I wish I mayn't have lost it" — shaking herself most vehemently. — " It would really be an awkward thing; for, 'pon my word, it's a letter not fit to be seen by anybody — what he could mean by writing such a letter to me of all people! In short, the substance of it was this, that Lord Rossville had heard, with inexpressible astonishment and pain (or some such round-about phrase), that Miss Pratt had presumed to circulate certain reports of a clandestine, and consequently improper nature, regarding certain juvenile members of his family, which reports — and so he went-on, you know his style — but the short and the long of it was this, that I was not to say black or white about any of his juvenile members, and that I was to contradict every thing I had said, or might have said, or had heard, or might have inferred, previous to this period — but I can give you no idea of the way it was worded. But what do you think he can mean ?"

Gertrude well knew what he meant; but, shocked at her uncle's absurdity, and at the publicity he was thus giving to her attachment, she remained silent.

" Such a fancy to take into his head, that I, of all people in the world, should have set any such reports agoing ! — So far from that, I'm the very person that has put a stop to them, for I can't tell you all the nonsensical stories that were going about.

— One said you were positively engaged to the Colonel—another had it that you were to be married the 27th of next month to the Member ; and that cards for a grand ball to the county, on the 31st, were making out already in Mrs. Delmour's name — a third had it that the brothers were on the point of fighting a duel for you, when Lord Rossville got word of it, and threatened to disinherit them, and send you to a French nunnery ; and, in the meantime, he has sent you here, as the next thing to it; — but, in short, I can't tell you half the nonsense that was going, and everybody came to me for the truth — but they made little of me ; for my uniform answer was, that, to my certain knowledge, neither the one brother nor the other would ever be the husband of Miss St. Clair—that it was quite a different person from either of them that would be her choice — so I leave you to judge if that was spreading reports! But I see how it is. Lord Rossville, honest man, has seen over his nose at last, and he's mad at my having had more penetration than himself; and, to be sure, it was a most extraordinary piece of blindness in him not to have seen how the land lay long ago.

— But, bless my heart! there's twelve o'clock — I'm afraid you're sitting up too late, my lamb—you're looking very white; go to your bed as fast as you can. — Good night, good night, my dear!" — And lighting her candle, she was hastening off, when Gertrude, roused into displeasure, said —

" Ere you go, suffer me, once for all, Miss Pratt, to assure you that you are in an error in every thing relating to me, and that Mr. Lyndsay never "

" Never can be any thing to you," interposed the incorrigible Miss Pratt, with an incredulous smile. " Very well, that's enough. — I'm quite convinced, from what I saw, that Mr. Lyndsay's nothing to you, no, no!" — in the tone and manner used by false nurses to wayward children when assuring them of some monstrous falsehood.

Gertrude turned from her in silent indignation, as she repeated her good nights, and was softly closing the door, when, popping in her head again —

" O! by-the-by, I wish you joy of being quit of a certain disappointed lover — he's fairly off, his brother tells me, at last

— a fair wind and a good voyage to him, and I wish him better luck another time. — Now go to sleep, my dear."

" Gone!" repeated Gertrude to herself, in an agony, as the door at length closed on her tormentor. " Gone ! and without one word! For him I am driven from my uncle's house — for him I have renounced all; and he neglects — abandons me! " And she gave way to the long-suppressed anguish of her heart, and for a while experienced all that agony of spirit of which her ardent and enthusiastic nature was susceptible. But hers was not a mind long to suffer despair to have dominion over her — it is not the first stroke of grief, however heavy it may fall, that can at once crush the native buoyancy of youthful spirits — it is the continuance of misery which renders its weight insupportable ; and where there is even the possibility, there is generally the wish to escape from its pressure. So it was with Gertrude — the first burst of grief over, the dreadful surmise which she had at first hugged to her bosom with frantic eagerness she now cast from her with scorn and indignation. That there was deceit somewhere she could not doubt — but that deceit was not with Colonel Delmour — it was impossible that he should have quitted England without writing to her; — but, surrounded as she was by his enemies, how could she suppose his letters would now be permitted to reach her ? Lord Ross-ville and her mother both so violently opposed to him, both acting in concert, and carrying on a constant correspondence with each other, though the contents of the letters were kept a profound secret from her : all these circumstances she revolved in her mind, till, from the first faint suspicions, they gradually grew into proofs strong as holy writ. Her heart felt lightened by the supposed discovery ; and in the morning she took her place at the breakfast-table, with her nerves braced, and her eyes kept from tears, by the determination of rising superior to all the petty artifices that might be practised against her. Breakfast was but just over, when the return of the renegade Babby Braidfoot was formally announced to Miss Pratt, who immediately left the room for the purpose, as she said, of giving her a good hearing.*

CHAPTER X.

On met tout en ceuvre pour assortir les fortunes, on ne se met point en peine d'assortir les cceurs. — Massillon.

Our morals are corrupted and vitiated by our admiration of wealth. — Cicero.

While this was carrying on, Mrs. Black was announced, and presently entered, her blooming good-humoured face expressive of even more than usual satisfaction; which, after the ordinary greetings had been exchanged, she hastened to commu-

* A good hearing in Scotland signifies the very reverse of what it expresses, and means neither more nor less than a downright scold.

nicate. The sum and substance of Mrs. Black's intelligence was this, that her daughter Lilly, having gone with the Major and Mrs. Waddell to Harrowgate, had there made a conquest of a wealthy young London merchaDt, who had made his proposals; and that the whole party were now on their way down, and were to be at Bellevue the following day to dinner. Due congratulation, of course, ensued; but Gertrude was too much surprised at this sudden revolution in the fair Lilly's affections to be able to express hers in proper form. Mrs. Black, however, was so well satisfied herself, that she took it for granted everybody else was the same; and she proceeded to enlarge upon the merits of this most excellent match, as she termed it. Mr. Larkins was in good business (it was an old-established house, — Larkins, Barlow, and Company), of a most respectable family, and himself an uncommon clever, genteel, handsome young man ; indeed, had it been otherwise, the Major and Bell never would have countenanced any thing of the kind: she only wished (with a deep sigh) that some other folks were in the way of making as prudent and creditable a connection. This was evidently in allusion to her daughter Anne ; and Miss Black mildly replied, that it was indeed agreeable when parents and children were agreed upon so important a point, but that it was not surprising they should often view it in very different lights. " Parents," said she, " complain that children are apt to be led away by romantic notions, which can lead only to disappointment ; while children lament that parents look only to wealth and worldly aggrandizement in their estimate of happiness; and I fear there is often but too much justice in the reproaches of both parties."

" I think it is the duty of all parents to prevent their children from marrying only to become beggars," said Mrs. Black.

" I think so too," answered her sister; " but I fear worldly-minded parents too often confound what they consider poverty with beggary."

" There is not much to draw between them, I think," said Mrs. Black.

" Undoubtedly, beggary implies poverty ; but what by many is called poverty does not necessarily include beggary," replied Miss Black. " Wealth itself may, and often has, proved insufficient to save the vain, the selfish, and the extravagant from beggary; but Christian principles, virtuous habits, and an independent mind will ever preserve even the poor from becoming burdensome to others."

" It's very easy speaking," said Mrs. Black, with some pique; " but everybody knows that in these times it's not little that supports a family; what with taxes and servants' wages, and children's schooling and outfit in the world—it's a very serious matter."

" All these things are, or ought to be, proportioned to the

means afforded," replied Miss Black. " If the poor will live like the rich, and educate their children in the same style, beg-gary, or at least its sister, dependance, must ensue; but if they would live according to what they have, and not according to what they think they ought to have, poverty would not he the hideous bugbear it is so often represented."

" In my opinion," said Mrs. St. Clair, who thought she had an interest in the question — " in my opinion, poverty is Xhf most intolerable evil in life, and has, I am convinced, the mo*i. demoralizing influence upon society."

" Poverty, like beauty, is, perhaps, not easily defined," said Miss Black; " and I believe the ideas people entertain on the subject are even more various than the discrepancy of taste that prevails as to personal charms : some would call it poverty not to be able to keep two or three carriages and a score of idle horses and servants."

" You know that's nonsense," said Mrs. Black.

" That's an extreme case," said Mrs. St. Clair.

" Then where is the boundary that separates wealth and poverty?" asked Miss Black. "What is the precise meaning of a poor marriage ?"

Both ladies hesitated, but Mrs. Black took the lead. —" I certainly would think any daughter of mine had made a poor hand of herself who could not afford to go as well dressed, and give as good and full dinners, as she had been accustomed to in her father's house."

Mrs. St. Clair could not repress a smile in scorn at the vulgar simplicity of her sister-in-law's notions.

" But suppose," said Miss Black, " as we cannot have every thing, that she is willing to wear a less costly gown, and have fewer dishes on her table than you, my dear sister, in your liberality, bestow upon your hospitable board—if, as an equivalent, she is rich in the virtuous principles, intellectual endowments, and rational affection of him she has chosen as the companion of her earthly pilgrimage?"

" All that," said Mrs. St. Clair, " sounds very fine, my dear Elizabeth, and very logical to those who have not seen so much of the world as I have done; but be assured a young woman of any refinement must be completely wretched under the cares, and drudgery, and privations attendant upon a poor marriage. For example, there are certain luxuries, as you call them in this country, though in France they are mere necessaries, matters of course, — such as a carriage, wax-lights, French wines, a suitable establishment, handsome mirrors, society that is not company,—these things, and many more of the same sort, I certainly consider as absolute parts of that exquisitely combined essence we call happiness, at least to a person of delicate taste and refined habits."

" Such airs!" thought Mrs. Black to herself. " French wines
and wax candles every day, indeed! Set her up! I -wonder what entitles her to such extravagance!"

" Poverty has really heen gently handled hy hoth of you," said Miss Black, laughing—"I don't suppose there ever was so fair a picture drawn of the squalid phantom before. You, my dear sister," to Mrs. Black, " merely represent him as not having his cheeks stuffed out like a plump Dutch burgomaster ; and you, Sarah, quarrel with him for not having all the airs and graces of an epicurean petit-maitre. Now, although I am too old to fancy that love — wedded love, at least — can live upon smiles and flowers, yet I do believe there is a species of attachment which can exist without being stall-fed on the one hand, or tricked out in foreign luxuries on the other, and which could be happy even in mediocrity."

" I never mentioned such a word as stall-fed," said Mrs. Black, a little ruffled — " but I'm astonished, Elizabeth, that anybody come to your time of life, and who has kept a house so long, can think that people can live upon deaf-nuts now-a-days."

" The rich are, at least, free from the vulgar sordid cares of life," said Mrs. St. Clair, bitterly, —" which, I repeat, to a mind of any refinement, must be wretchedness."

" I wonder what she calls the vulgar sordid cares of life ?" thought Mrs. Black.

" To a mind of any feeling and refinement," said Miss Black, " I believe it would be far greater wretchedness to be linked to a vulgar sordid spirit, even had its master all tha: rank and riches can bestow, than it would be to endure privations with a mind congenial to its own — to such a mind there are cares which love only can sweeten."

" There can be little peace where there's not plenty," said Mrs. Black; — "but it's lucky everybody's not of your way of thinking, or the country would soon be swarming with beggars, and we would be perfectly ate up."

Gertrude could not quite repress a smile, as she looked at Mrs. Black's jolly person, and thought how groundless such an apprehension was on her part.

; ' There is little cause for alarm on that account," said her sister-in-law —" as your sentiments are much more popular than mine; besides, I am not so unreasonable as to insist upon everybody's marrying for love, whether they will or not. Many people, I believe, are quite incapable of forming a disinterested attachment, or having even a preference for one person more than another, except according to worldly motives — a fine house — fine clothes — a carriage — precedence; in short, some one of the thousand paltry baits which catch the vulgar mind, To talk to such of the superiority of virtue and talent would be as absurd as to insist upon the blind seeing, or the deaf hearing: on the other hand, there are those who, with taste, feeling, and refinement, have neither pride, vanity, nor ambition to gratify. It is surely, therefore, the height of tyranny to insist upon their placing their happiness in the indulgence of those things—upon their sacrificing all their purer, better feelings, to gratify the pride and prejudices of others."

" I really -wonder to hear a woman of your sense speak such nonsense," said Mrs. Black, affecting to look cool in the face of a very high complexion.

" Such sentiments can only tend to the subversion of all proper principle," said Mrs. St. Clair, with solemnity — " to the encouragement of low r and degrading alliances, contracted under the high-sounding names of disinterested attachment, congenial souls, intellectual superiority, and such fulsome phrases as can only lead to the annihilation of all ranks and degrees of society. A weak romantic girl has only to find a congenial soul in her dancing-master, or to prove her disinterested attachment to her father's footman, and, according to your doctrine, she has done nobly — she has proved herself superior to the vulgar allurements of pride, ambition, and what not— O! it is an admirable, a beautiful theory !" and Mrs. St. Clair trembled -with virtuous indignation.

" Pardon me, Sarah, you cannot disapprove of such connections more than I do; but a poor marriage, and a low one, I consider as very different things, although I suspect many people are but too apt to confound them. Undoubtedly a gentlewoman, -who has the feelings and ideas of one, will only unite herself •with a gentleman, — -with one who has had the education, and who has the manners and habits of one, who exercises the profession and is accustomed to the society of such. That may be a poor marriage, but it cannot be called a low one. Indeed I am convinced there can be no solid happiness in a union where all the advantages of birth and education are renounced on one side ; and I am so far from upholding those who violate the established orders of society, and sacrifice all that is valuable in feeling to the indulgence of their own selfish passion, that, on the contrary, I will venture to affirm such connections (like those formed without the consent of parents), so far from being productive of domestic happiness, are generally marked with disappointment, misfortune, and sorrow."

" There's really no knowing what you would be at," said Mrs. Black, with an air of perplexity ; for Mrs. Black, like many other people, carried her prejudices all on one side, and nothing puzzled her so much as when she met in argument with a person of an unbiassed judgment and a liberal mind; and so in-dissolubly united in her imagination were the ideas of a poor marriage being a low marriage on the one hand, and a rich one being an elevated one on the other, that to separate them was utterly impracticable. The dullest wight or coarsest booby, with ten thousand a-year and a title, would have struck Mrs.

o

Black with awe, or at least respect; while the finest mind or most distinguished talents, destitute of the glare of wealth or the insignia of grandeur, would have been wholly overlooked.

The entrance of Miss Pratt soon turned the tide of the conversation ; for she had learned from her " pretty Miss Babby" that there was not a morsel of coal or a crumb of meat in the house; and the coals you bought on the street were always bad, and there was no getting meat — everybody knew that—unless on a market day ;—and, in short, it ended in Miss Pratt consenting to remain Miss Black's guest for another day, until her mansion should be duly prepared and stocked for her reception. In the mean time she set forth, as she pretended, on her business, which, in fact, was that of interfering in that of every other person.

Mrs. Black also departed; but as she was really good-natured in the main, she consented that her daughter Anne should spend the evening with her aunts, even at the risk of meeting William Leslie, who, along with some others of their friends, was expected.

CHAPTER XI.

Even as some sick men will take no medicine, unless some pleasant thing be put amongst their potions, although perhaps it be somewhat hurtful — yet the physician suffereth them to have it. So, because many will not hearken to serious and grave documents, except they be mingled with some fable or jest, therefore reason willeth us to do the like. — Sir Thomas Moke.

Speak nobly of religion, but let it be well timed; for people avoid those who are perpetually preaching— Ganganelli's Letters.

Miss Pratt's visit would have been reckoned rather ill-timed by most people, as the Miss Blacks had invited some of their own friends to spend the evening with them; and the pleasure, if not the harmony, of the party bid fair to be deranged by her audacious tattle. But they were too tolerant and enduring to allow any considerations of that kind to stand in the way of their hospitalit\'7d-, though well aware of Miss Pratt's enmity towards all whose creed and practice in matters of religion differed from her own; for Miss Pratt, like too many people, deemed her own the only proper standard of religious and moral excellence. She had her bed of iron for the soul, as Procrustes had for the body; with this difference, that she was far more lenient towards those who fell short of her measure than to such as went beyond it.

Not that Miss Pratt carried her hostility so far as to decline having any intercouse with or receiving any favours from these wild people, as she called them. On the contrary, she was always happy at an opportunity of meeting with such of

them as she thought she could turn to any account by taking her beggars off her hands; and she was always ready to make use of their time, money, and old clothes, to save her own. However, she took every occasion of letting it be known that she had met with great want of charity amongst those very people who make such a phrase about it, as they had refused to recommend to the Destitute Society, Anthony Whyte's nurse, a decent, respectable woman, and Anthony Whyte a subscriber too! But Miss Pratt was not bitter in her resentment; and upon hearing of the party that was expected, she expressed much satisfaction, and resolved to be uncommonly pleasant, and at the same time serious in her conversation, out of compliment to the

Miss Blacks. Mrs. St. Clair liked company of any kind better than none; and to Gertrude, in the present state of her mind, all company and all scenes were alike. Hers was a state of passive endurance, not of actual enjoyment. She was roused, however, by a visit from Mr. Delmour and Mr. Lyndsay. The latter held out his hand to her, with a look which seemed to say, " Have you forgiven me?" but, colouring deeply, she turned away, and bestowed her whole attention upon his companion. Mr. Delmour was secretly nattered by the air of profound attention with which (for the first time) she listened to to every word he uttered, in the hope that something would lead to the subject uppermost in her thoughts, but farthest from her tongue; but nothing was said which had the slightest reference to Colonel Delmour, and her countenance betrayed her extreme vexation when the gentlemen rose to take leave. Upon hearing that they were both to be in attendance at a county meeting in town, which, of course, was to conclude with a dinner, Miss Black invited them to return in the evening, which they promised to do, and departed. It was evident, from Mr. Delmour's manner, he knew nothing of what had passed; but Gertrude had paid no attention to his manner, nor once thought of the very flattering construction he might put upon hers. As for Lyndsay, she scarcely observed him at all — it only struck her after he was gone that he was more than usually silent, and that his features wore a more pensive cast than common—but what was Mr. Lyndsay to her ? And she listened with weariness and chagrin to the eulogium her aunts pronounced upon him.

Evening came; and Miss Pratt, in a grave gown, bottle-green gloves, a severe turban, and a determined look of strong good sense, seemed to say, " I'll show you what a rational, respectable, wise-like character I am—I'll confound you all, or I'm mistaken!" And she took her ground as usual, as though she had been mistress of the mansion, and prepared to do all its honours accordingly.

Even in the Christian world there are great varieties —there are narrow minds as well as great minds — there are those who

o 2

pin their faith upon the sleeve of some favourite preacher — others who seem to think salvation confined within the four walls of the particular church in which they happen to sit! But, as has been well said by the liberal-minded Wesley, " how little does God regard men's opinions ! What a multitude of wrong opinions are embraced by all the members of the Church of Rome; yet how highly favoured have many of them been !" *

And who has not their imperfections ? — who has not their besetting sin—their thorn in the flesh? Even the best of Christians; but piety to God, and the desire to benefit their fellow-creatures, is, and must be, the universal characteristic of the Christian of every church. The few friends assembled were certainly favourable specimens of what is termed the religious world—they were persons of agreeable manners, enlarged minds, and cultivated tastes ; the conversation was animated and interesting, in spite of Miss Pratt's attempts to turn it into her own low channel by relating the bits of gossip she had picked up in her morning perambulations, and which she thought to set oif with some trite moral reflection. There was occasionally music from both gentlemen and ladies, which even Gertrude's fastidious ear acknowledged to be fine in its way — for all knew what they were saying or doing ; and there were no mawkish attempts at singing in an unknown tongue — there was no " poetry strangled by music,"— but " airs married to immortal verse,"

Untwisting all the chains that tie The hidden soul of harmony.

Ah! who can hear the divine strains of a Handel, or the dear familiar songs of their native land, without feeling their souls elevated, or their hearts melted into love and tenderness ! Both were sung by different members of the company with much taste and feeling — but by none so much as by Mary Black, who, with seraphic sweetness, sang the inspired strain,

Kow beautiful are the feet of those
Who bring the glad tidings of faith to man !

" Every thing that Miss Black sings must be charming," said Mr. Delmour, with his fade gallantry; " but if I may be permitted to offer an opinion, I should say there is perhaps something rather too sectarian in sacred music, unless upon solemn occasions; and I should be apprehensive that, were a taste for it to become general, it would prove destructive to every other species of composition — I may add, even to the fine arts in general." Mr. Delmour had a genteel horror at every thing he deemed approaching to what he thought Methodism — though a most zealous supporter of the church in so far, but no farther, than as it was connected with the state.

" Pardon me," said Miss Mary Black ; " but it appears to me

* Wesley's Journal.

that such apprehensions are groundless. The "blessing of God, and the applause of posterity, seem to have perpetuated the fame of genius devoted to religious subjects more than the fame of those men who ahused their noble gifts by dedicating them solely to the service of their fellow-creatures."

" For instance ? " asked Mr. Delmour, with an incredulous smile.

" True," said Mr. Lyndsay — "it certainly has heen so in many instances. Milton is undoubtedly the first poet of our country, and what was his theme ? He sang in noble strain of Him

Unspeakable, who sitt'st above these heavens, To us invisible, or dimly seen In these thy lowest works.

The greatest poet of Germany was Klopstock, and his subject the Great Messiah ; and of his deathless work it has been well observed, that ' when music shall attain among us the highest powers of her art, whose words will she select to utter but those of Klopstock ?' The noblest bards of Italy were Dante and Tasso — Metastasio has had recourse to sacred subjects for his operas— Racine for his Athalie — Young, in his Night Thoughts, sung to Him who

From solid darkness struck that spark, the sun,

invoking Him to ' strike wisdom from his soul.' The amiable and elegant Cowper cast all his laurels at the feet of his Saviour :

I cast them at thy feet — my only plea Is, what it was, — dependence upon thee.

" You are really eloquent, Lyndsay," said Mr. Delmour, with an ironical smile ; — " but, in the fervour of your zeal, you have entirely overlooked those immortal, though profane authors, whose works are still more popular than any of those you have quoted, — Shakespeare, for instance."

" Shakespeare is, perhaps, the most favourable exception," replied Mr. Lyndsay; " he is, indeed, a poet of Nature's own creating ; but the dross of his compositions is daily draining off in improved editions, and even in theatrical representation, while the pure parts of his morality are not thought unworthy of being quoted from evangelical pulpits, and one day, I doubt not, it will be with him as with some of the poets I have just mentioned. They have written some things unworthy of their pens; but their fame is perpetuated only as the authors of what is pure and good. The profane and licentious works of Lord B. will live only in the minds of the profane and impure, and will soon be classed amongst other worthless dross; while all that is fine in his writings will be culled by the lovers of virtue, as the bee gathers honey from even the noxious plant, and leaves the poison to perish with the stalk, — so shall it be with Burns — so shall it be with Moore. The same argument applies to music. Handel derives his fame from his oratorios, and the Creation of Haydn will immortalize his name — a performance in which the genius of the composer has struck a chord which calls forth any genius which happens to be in the breast of the audience. To mention the great painters who have dedicated a portion of their time and talents to sacred subjects, would be to enumerate the whole catalogue ; and I have already to apologize for having so long monopolized this subject," said, he, turning to a clergyman who stood near him, and whose looks testified the interest he took in the debate — " when there are those present who could have done much more justice to the cause." Beneath the simple, meek, unpretending exterior of Mr. Z , few would, indeed, have guessed at the profundity of his learning, the extent and variety of his acquirements, and the ardour of his zeal in the cause of Christianity. Firm in his principles, yet soft in his manners — warm in feeling, yet mild and gentle in temper — able to speak, yet willing to listen — his mind was full of information, while his manners were those of one seeking instruction.

Thus appealed to, Mr. Z was about to reply, when Miss Pratt interposed with — " What do you say to these two great writers, Fielding and Smollett ? I suspect there's none of these you have mentioned will ever be half so popular as Tom Jones and Humphry Clinker."

" The works of Fielding and Smollett, even the more highly gifted ones of Voltaire and Rousseau, are passing away, like noxious exhalations," said Mr. Z , mildly. " If the principles of the age in which we live are equally defective with the former, at least a better taste prevails; and grossness, profanity, and licentiousness are no longer the standards to which the young look with admiration. Impure writers are now chiefly known to impure readers — but where virtue and genius unite, their powers are known to all. O! what injury to the human mind is derived from the perusal of the works of writers whose corrupt imaginations have given the impulse to their licentious pens ! Of such it may truly be said, though highly esteemed amongst men, yet are they abominations in the sight of God. Yet alas! how few look to that guiding principle, which alone ought to direct the pen! — how few consider that, to do good, ' a work is not to be raised from the heat of youth, or the vapour of wine — nor to be attained by the invocation of Memory and her siren daughters — but by devout prayer to that Eternal Spirit who can enrich with all utterance and knowledge, and sends out his Seraphim with the hallowed fire of his altar, to touch and purify the lips of whom he pleases.'" *

There was so much Christian meekness, even in Mr. Z 's fervour, that it was impossible not to be touched with his manner, even where the matter failed to carry conviction along with it.

* Milton.

Mr. Delmour affected to bow with deference to the opinions of a clergyman — the conversation took another turn — music succeeded, till at last the party broke up. — Gertrude had been interested in the discussion; but soon it passed from her mind, as " a lovely song of one who hath a pleasant voice."

CHAPTER XII.

Let us proceed from celestial things to terrestrial Cicero.

Jests are, as it were, sawce, wherebye we are recreated, that we may eat with more appetite ; but as that were an absurd banquet in which there were few dishes of meat and much variety of sawces, and that an uupleasant one where there were no sawce at all, even so that life were spent idly where nothing were but mirth and jollity, and, again, that tedious and uncomfortable where no pleasure or mirth were to be expected. — Sir Thomas More.

Again Gertrude felt the bitterness of disappointment. She had watched and hung upon every syllable that Mr. Delmour had uttered ; but he made no mention of his brother, and, with all the timidity of love, she felt it impossible to breathe the name on which her destiny was suspended.

The following morning saw Miss Pratt depart with all her packages, and many reiterated professions and promises ; and scarcely had she left the house when Mr. Adam Ramsay arrived. As uncle Adam's visits, like those of angels, were few and far between, his nieces welcomed him according to the rarity of the occurrence ; and as he appeared to be in unusual good humour, he received their attentions with tolerable civility. But even his civility was always of a rough nature — something akin to the embrace of a man-trap, or the gentle influence of a shower-bath ; while his kindness commonly showed itself in some such untoward shape as was more grievous to be borne than aught that malice could invent.

" What's this come ower ye, my dear?" said he, addressing Gertrude, with as much affection as it was in his nature to testify. " You're white, and you're dull, and you're no like the same creature you was ;" and he gazed upon her with more of interest than of good breeding. His remarks, of course, called the colour into Gertrude's cheeks; and Miss Black, seeing her at a loss to reply, hastened to relieve her, by throwing the blame, where, in this climate, it is always thrown — upon the weather. But uncle Adam spurned the idea of the weather having the slightest influence on the health and spirits of any thing but potatoes and leeches.

" The weather! " repeated he, contemptuously. " You'll no tell me that a shower o' rain can bleach a young creature's cheeks white, or put the life out o' her een; — but I'll tell you

o 4

what it is — it's the synagogin' — the tabernaclin'— the psalmin' that goes on in this hoose, that's enough to break the spirits o' ony young creature."

" My dear uncle " said Miss Black, with a smile.

" Now I'm no gawin' to enter into ony o' your religious controversies," cried Mr. Ramsay, holding up his hand, and turning away his head ; " but I'll tell you what I'll do, my dear," patting Gertrude on the shoulder, " I shall tak' you to see a sight that'S divert you, and drive away thae wild notions you've been getting your head stuffed wi' — to gang an' mak a bairn like that miserable wi' your nonsense ! " with a fresh burst of indignation at his nieces. Then again softening down — " Put on

your bonnet, my dear, an' come wi' me As I came up the

street the noo, I saw ane o' thae caravan things standing in the market-place, wi' a picktur o' a giant an' a dwarf hingin' on the outside ; and though I wadna cross the floor to see aw the giants and dwarfs that e'er were born, yet I ken young folk like ploys o' that kind — so put on your things, and I shall treat you to the show ; " and he put his hand into his pocket, and tumbled his money to and fro, as much as to say, " I have plenty of shillings and sixpences, and therefore you need have no scruples of delicacy as to taking advantage of my offer."

The cold drops stood upon Mrs. St. Clair's brow, at the thoughts of her elegant distinguished daughter, the future Countess of Rossville, mingling with the canaille of a country town, in a caravan, to gaze upon a giant and a dwarf! What would Lord Rossville say ? There was distraction in the thought — yet she dreaded to offend uncle Adam by a hasty rejection of his plan. " We are all, I am sure, sensible of the kindness that prompts your offer, my dear uncle," said she, in her most conciliating manner; " but I am afraid the remedy you propose would only tend to aggravate the evil.—My daughter's complaint is headach, occasioned solely by the confinement to which she has been subjected for some days, and the close air of a caravan would be extremely prejudicial. — If I could have given her an airing —but having no carriage of my own !"

and the sentence died away in a sort of indistinct ejaculation about the misery of being dependant upon others for those accommodations.

" You might let her speak for hersel'," said Mr. Ramsay, with some asperity; " say what you would like best, my dear? " and Gertrude, gladly availing herself of the excuse suggested, declared that fresh air would be her best restorative.

Mr. Ramsay pondered a while, still turning his money, like his thoughts, to and fro. At length after an apparently severe struggle he spoke —

" Weel, since that's the case, instead o' takin you to the show, I've no objections to hire a cbaise and treat you to a ride— I shall step to the Blue Boar mysel' and order ane up, so you may be puttin' on your mantle; an' there will be room for three, so you can settle among yoursels which o' you is to gang."

Mrs. St. Clair had been caught in a snare of her own setting — she had thrown out a hint about a carriage, in hopes that her uncle's partiality for her daughter would have made him grasp at it at once, and that he would have been induced to keep one for her sole use and accommodation. This would have been a very convenient arrangement for her mother, who could not get the command of Lord Rossville's quite so often as she wished. Her blood almost froze at the idea of a ride in a hackney-chaise — but it required more courage than she could muster to oppose this second project, and, in silent despair, she saw uncle Adam snatch up his little old rusty hat and set off. Her only hope was that the Blue Boar equipages would be all engaged, but that was soon at an end ; for, in a short time, uncle Adam was descried returning on foot, followed by a high-crowned, jangling, tottering chaise, with a lame brown horse and a blind grey one, urged along by a ragamuffin driver, seated on a wooden bar almost touching the windows. Such was uncle Adam's triumphal car, — and not Boadicea, when dragged captive at the wheels of her conqueror, experienced bitterer feelings than did Mrs. St. Clair, when she found herself compelled to take her place in this vehicle. True, she might have refused, but at the certainty of affronting uncle Adam, who could stand any thing but airs; and to affront seventy thousand pounds was a serious matter, especially in the present posture of affairs. The iron steps were thrown down with a mighty clang, as far as they could reach; and having, with some difficulty, contrived to mount, she seated herself with great disgust and ill-humour, vainly attempting to disengage herself from the straw with which it was carpeted, and which at once seized upon her silk stockings and lace flounces.

" So much for the beauties of poverty," whispered she, in no very sweet accent, to her daughter, as she took her place beside her. " For Heaven's sake, pull your bonnet more over your face, that you may not be recognized,"—and she carefully adjusted her own veil in triple folds over every feature. Mr. Ramsay followed, and the driver waited for orders.

" Whar wad ye like to gang to, my dear ?" asked he of Gertrude; "but it's aw the same, ae road's just like anither—tak' the best and the driest," to the driver.

But Gertrude, who bad got her cue from her mother, interposed, saying—

" If it is not disagreeable to you, my dear uncle, I should like to see your own Broom Park."

" Broom Park!" repeated Mr. Ramsay, in evident discomposure ; " what wud tak' ye to

Broom Park ? —What's put that in your head? — I'm sure there's naething to be seen there."

" Pardon me," said Mrs. St. Clair, seeing her daughter would not urge the matter; " but that beautiful specimen you gave Gertrude of your greenhouse has made her absolutely pine to visit your flowers."

Mr. Ramsay's brow looked rather thundery ; but, after demurring a little with himself, he desired the driver, in a voice of repressed anger, to take them to Broom Park. The patched cracked windows were drawn up — the driver mounted his seat — the horses were with some difficulty set in motion ; and off they went, the chaise rocking and jingling as though it would never reach its destination. To speak, or at least to hear, was out of the question; so the party proceeded on their pleasure excursion in profound silence, till, at the end of an hour, and a half of incessant jolting and clattering, they found themselves at the gate of Broom Park. It was a fine, showy, modern place, with a large handsome house standing in the middle of an extensive, but somewhat new-looking park, sprinkled with a few large old trees, and many young ones still in their cages. There was nothing picturesque or beautiful in the scenery ; but there was much comfort, even luxury, denoted in the appearance of the gay, airy, spacious mansion, with its French windows, verandas, porticos, and conservatory — in the smooth gravel walks, diverging in all directions—in the well-stocked fish-pond—in the stupendous brick garden-walls, with flues and chimney tops—in the extensive range of hothouses, and, in short, all the appliances of affluence and enjoyment. Nothing could look more unlike the place than the owner. That Mr. Adam Ramsay should have become the proprietor of such a place was the wonder of some, and the ridicule of others ;— but the simple fact was, that upon this very estate the race (if not the family) of Ramsays had been born, and bred, and lived, certainly time immemorial, for it was in the humble rank of cottars. Here also Lizzie Lundie had first seen the light; and here it was that uncle Adam's youngest and happiest days had been spent— for here they had " run about the braes, and pu'ed the gowans fine;" and " though seas between them braid had rolled" for many an intervening day, and the grave had long closed over the object of his early affection, he still cherished the fond remembrance of " auld lang syne." Before his return from India, he had heard that the estate of Broomyknows—now changed into Broom Park — was in the market; he became the purchaser, partly as a means of investing money which he was rather at a loss how to dispose of, and partly from a secret penchant towards it, which, however, he would have scorned to acknowledge, and, perhaps, of which he was scarcely aware. Great was his surprise and indignation, however, when he did visit it, at beholding the ravages refinement and luxury had committed upon the primitive charms of Broomyknows—for, pilgrims as we are in a stranger land, how do our hearts cling with fond tenacity to the simple memorials of transient, childish, perished joys!—But not a trace of his old haunts remained. The banks, and braes, and knowes, had all been levelled with the dust—the little wimpling burn, o'erhung with saughs and hazels, where many a summer's day Lizzie and he used to " paiddle " for minnows, was gone to swell some mighty stream. The Mavis-hill, a rude unenclosed eminence, covered with wild roses, and brambles, and blue bells, and sloes, where many a mavis and lintie's nest had been found, was now a potatoe field — not a whin scented the air—and how often beneath India's burning sun had uncle Adam sighed for a breeze from the whinny braes of his native land ! But, worst, of all, on the very spot where once stood his grandfather's and his father's old green slimy cabins, with their fungous roofs, and their kailyards and their middens, now rose an elegantly ornamented dog-kennel. That he instantly ordered to be demolished — indeed, it was said, he had remained upon the ground to see it done—and from that time he had never looked near the place till now, that he had come in compliance with Gertrude's wish, but very contrary to his own inclination.

Mrs. St. Clair was in ecstasies with all she saw — the interior of the mansion was perfection—the suite of apartments elegant —the furniture superb—in short, there was not a superlative she did not exhaust in attempts to express her admiration. But the thought that was uppermost in her mind she would not have ventured to utter so readily, viz. that if the worst should happen, and Lord Rossville should discard his niece, there was another string to her bow at Broom Park ; and she could almost have been satisfied to have renounced the ambitious prospects of the one for the luxurious certainty of the other. But Mrs. St. Clair's raptures were completely thrown away upon uncle Adam, who cared not a rush what she or any one else thought of his property ; and he followed rather than led the way through his own house, with a kind of dogged impatience, as if his only wish were to be out of it. This was not lessened when, the news of his appearance having spread, he found himself beset by a host of retainers, indigenous to an extensive and neglected property. Greeves, gardeners, gamekeepers, tenants at will, and tenants on lease, all came thronging with wants to be supplied, and grievances to be redressed, and all looking with evil eyes on the visitors, in the fear of their becoming residents, and so ending their respective reigns; while the housekeeper, as she went swimming on before in all the conscious dignity of undisturbed power, detailed at great length all her own doings and sayings, with the various means used by her for the preservation of the furniture, and the annihilation of mice, moths, "clocks (beetles), and beasts of every description."

" Things are no just in the order I could wish," said the old curmudgeon of a gardener, as he unwillingly led the way to the kitchen-garden; " and there's an awfu' heat here; you'd better no come in for fear of cauld, leddies," as he produced the key of the extensive range of hothouses, and, with a sour face, found himself compelled to fill a large basket with the choicest of fruits, which he had more profitable ways of disposing of.

At length Mr. Ramsay's patience was exhausted, and they set off loaded with the most exquisite fruits and flowers, which, as he possessed not the organs of either taste or smell for aught beyond haggis and southernwood, he looked upon merely as sort of artificial excrescences which grew about large houses.

" Noo," said he, addressing Gertrude, as he seated himself in the chaise, " I dinna begrudge this, if it's to do you ony gude — and, as I tell't you before, gang when you like, and tak what you like —but dinna ask me to gangwi'you ; for I'm ower auld noo to be plagued and deeved about drains, and fences, and young plantations, out o' doors ; and pipes, and plaster, and aw the rest o't, within—and the gardener he canna get the apples keepit — and the gamekeeper, he canna keep the pheesants preserved — an' I'm sure I dinna care though there was nae an apple or a pheesant in the kingdom, if they wud only let me alane."

" It unquestionably would be a great advantage to the place as well as a relief to you, to have the house occupied with some

one who could take a judicious management " began Mrs.

St.Clair; but a bitter look from her uncle made her perceive she was treading on dangerous ground, and she allowed the noise of the carriage to drown the rest of the sentence.

CHAPTER XIII.

Lord of love ! what law is this, That me thou makest thus tormented be ? Spenser.

They were returning by a different road from that which they had taken in going, and had not proceeded far when they were suddenly hailed by a pedestrian from the side of the road, and Major Waddell was immediately recognized. The chaise was stopped, and, mutual salutations having been exchanged, was again about to proceed, when the Major entered so vehement a remonstrance against their passing his door, without inquiring in person after his dear Isabella, that, as they were within a few yards of the gate, it was scarcely possible for even uncle Adam to hold out; and accordingly, preceded by the Major, the chaise turned up the romantic winding approach which conducted to the mansion. Black Caesar, bowing and grinning, hastened to receive them, and usher them into the presence of massa's lady, who, in all her bridal finery, sat in the attitude of being prepared to receive her marriage guests. Having welcomed Mrs.

and Miss St. Clair with a tone and manner of encouraging familiarity—"And my uncle, too ! — this is really kind. — I assure you I'm quite flattered, as I know how seldom you pay visits to anybody."

Mr. Ramsay had entered with the heroic determination of not opening his lips during his stay — he therefore allowed that to pass with a sort of scornful growl; but Mrs. St. Clair, in her softest manner, took care to let her know that the visit was neither a premeditated nor a complimentary one, and that she owed it entirely to their accidental rencontre with the Major.

" Bless me, Major! " exclaimed the lady in a tone of alarm, " is it possible that you have been walking ? — And the roads are quite wet!—Why did you not tell me you were going out, and I would have ordered the carriage for you, and have gone with you, although I believe it is the etiquette for a married lady to be at home for some time;"— then observing a spot of mud on his boot, " And you have got your feet quite wet; — for Heaven's sake, Major, do go and change your boots directly ! — I see they are quite wet!"

The Major looked delighted at this proof of conjugal tenderness, but protested that his feet were quite dry, holding up a foot in appeal to the company.

" Now, how can you say so, Major, when I see they are quite damp?—Do, I entreat you, put them off—it makes me perfectly wretched to think of your sitting with wet feet — you know you have plenty of boots. —I made him get a dozen pairs when we were at York, that I might be quite sure of his always having dry feet. —Do, my love, let Caesar help you off with these for any sake ! — for my sake, Major, — I ask it as a personal favour."

This was irresistible —the Major prepared to take the suspected feet out of company with a sort of vague mixed feeling floating in his brain, which, if it had been put into words, would have been thus rendered: —

" What a happy dog am I, to be so tenderly beloved by such a charming girl! and yet what a deal of trouble it is to be obliged to change one's boots every time one's wife sees a spot of mud on them!"

" Now, you won't be long, Major?" — cried the lady, as the Major went off, attended by Csesar. " The Major is so imprudent, and takes so little care of himself, he really makes me quite wretched — but how do you think he looks ? "

This was a general question, and rather a puzzling one.

" As ugly as possible," thought Gertrude, who wouhl have been much at a loss to combine truth and politeness in her reply. Luckily there are people who always answer their own questions, when no one else seems disposed to do it, and Mrs. Waddeli went on —

" He certainly was much the better of Harrowgate — he was
really looking so ill when he went there, that, I assure you, I ■was very uneasy."

" Whan did he ever look weel ? " was ready to hurst from uncle Adam's lips ; but by a magnanimous effort he drew them in, and remained silent.

" Have you been lately at Broom Park, uncle ; for I understand there are pretty doings going on there ? "

Mr. Ramsay's only reply was a deep sonorous hem, and a bow, something in the style of a bull preparing to toss.

" We are just come from thence," replied Mrs. St. Clair, immediately launching forth into raptures at all she had seen and tasted.

" Indeed! " exclaimed Mrs. Waddell; " you have been either more fortunate or more favoured than I have been — for the Major and I went there yesterday, and could get no admittance, which, I must say, I thought very odd : — the people at the lodge had the impertinence to refuse to let us in, which, to be sure, to a man of the Major's rank in life, and me a married woman, was a piece of insolence I never met with any thing to equal; but I told them I would let you know of their behaviour."

" I'm obliged to you," was the laconic reply.

" I really think they deserve to be turned off for their insolence."

" Turned off for doing their duty ! " demanded uncle Adam, preparing to cast off his armour.

" A strange kind of duty, I think," retorted the lady, in equal indignation, " to exclude your nearest relations from your house, — and me a married woman, and a man of the Major's rank!"

" I never excluded you frae my house, Miss Bell," quoth uncle Adam, now divested of all restraint, and disdaining to recognize her by her married appellation; " but if you mean that I'll no mak you mistress of my property, you are perfectly right. —What's your business at my hoose when I'm not there mysell ? — What taks you there ?" in a key of interrogation at least equal to a squeeze of the thumb-screw.

" I think it was a very natural curiosity "

" Naatral curiosity! " interrupted uncle Adam, now brimming high ; " a bonny excuse, or else no, for breakin' into other folk's hooses—I wonder what your naatral curiosity will lead you to next!"

" I think you are much obliged to anybody that will take the trouble of looking a little after your affairs in that quarter— for I must tell you, uncle, that you are making yourself quite ridiculous by submitting to be plundered and cheated on all hands, and "

" And what if it's my pleesure to be plundered and cheated, Miss, by the poor, instead o' the rich ? "

" I really "wish, uncle, you would recollect you are speaking to a married woman," said Mrs. Waddell, with much dignity j " and that a man of the Major's "

At that moment the Major entered, with a very red face, and a pair of new boots, evidently too tight.

" You see what it is to be under orders," said he, pointing to his toes, and trying to smile in the midst of his anguish.

" It's lucky for you, Major, I'm sure, that you are — for I don't believe there ever was anybody on earth so careless of themselves as you are.—What do you think of his handing Lady Fairacre to her carriage yesterday in the midst of the rain, and without his hat too ? But I hope you changed your stockings as well as your boots, Major?"

" I assure you, upon my honour, my dear, neither of them were the least wet."

" O ! now, Major, you know if you haven't changed your stockings, I shall be completely wretched," cried the lady, all panting with emotion.— " Good gracious ! to think of your keeping on your wet stockings—I never knew any thing like it!"

" I assure you, my dear Bell " began the Major.

" Oh! now, my dearest Major, if you have the least regard for me, I beseech you put off your stockings this instant.— Oh! I am certain you've got cold already—how hot you are!" taking his hand; " and don't you think his colour very high ? — now I'm quite wretched about you."

In vain did the poor Major vow and protest as to the state of his stockings—it was all in vain—the lady's apprehensions were not to be allayed — and again he had to limp away to pull off boots which the united exertions of himself and Caesar had with difficulty got on.

" I really think my wife will be for keeping me in a bandbox," said he, with a sort of sardonic smile, the offspring of flattered vanity and personal suffering.

As he was quitting the room his aid-de-camp, Csesar, entered, with a mien of much importance, and, in his jargon, contrived to make it known that something had happened to springs of . Massa Ramsay's chaise — that postboy had. gone to smith's to mend it, and that smith said chaise no be mend for soonest two hours.

" Then I shall find my way hame mysel'," cried uncle Adam, starting up; " for I'll no wait twa hours upon ony chaise that ever was driven."

In vain were all attempts to detain him — he spurned the Waddell carriage — the Waddell dinner — refused even to wit till the Major had changed his stockings; in short, would do nothing but take his own way, which was to walk home, leaving Mrs. and Miss St. Clair to stay dinner and return in the evening.

No sooner was uncle Adam s back turned, than Mrs. Wad-
dell gave free scope to her indignation against him. — Turning to Gertrude —

" I really think he is much worse than he was—I don't think you have any credit in your management of him, cousin — unless he alters his behaviour, I don't think it will be possible for the Major to keep company with him. — Did you hear how he Miss'd me to-day ? — me, a married woman ! If the Major had been present he must have resented it." Having, at last, exhausted her invectives, she next began to play off her airs, by showing her house and furniture — boasting of her fine clothes — fine pearls — fine plate — fine connections — and, in short, taking all possible pains to excite the envy of her guests, by showing what a thrice-happy married woman Mrs. Major Wad-dell was. But Mrs. St. Clair had seen too much to be astonished at Mrs. Waddell's finery, and Gertrude's more refined taste felt only pity and contempt for the vulgar, sordid mind, that could attach ideas of happiness to such things. Provoked at the indifference with which her cousin saw and heard all this, she said —

" I suppose, cousin, you are above regarding terrestrial objects now, since you have been living so long with our good aunts — I suppose you have learnt to despise the things of this world as beneath your notice ?"

" I have certainly learnt to admire goodness more than ever I did before," said Gertrude, quite unconscious of the offence she had given by her indifference.

" Oh! then I suppose you are half converted by this time — we shall have you one of the godly ladies next."

" If you mean by godly those who resemble my aunts, I fear it will be long before I merit such an appellation ; but although, in comparison with them, I feel myself little better than a heathen, yet that does not hinder me from seeing and admiring their excellence — to deny excellence to others, merely because I do not possess it myself, is a sin, from which I shall ever pray, * Good Lord, deliver me!'"

" O, I see you are bit," cried Mrs. Waddell, with a toss of her head ; " I know that sort of thing is very infectious, so I hope you won't bite me, cousin ; for, however it may do with misses, I assure you it would never answer in a married woman — and the Major has no notion of your very good ladies — he seems quite satisfied with me, bad as I am. — Are you not, Major?" to the poor Major, who once more made his appearance rebooted, and trying to look easy under the pressure of his extreme distress.

" Now, are you quite sure you changed your stockings, Major? Are you not cheating me ? — Caesar, did the Major change his stockings ? "

Ca?sar, with a low bow, confirmed the important fact, and that interesting question was, at length, set at rest. Mrs. St. Clair

was too politic to betray the disgust she felt; but Gertrude, alarmed at the prospect of sitting audience for the day to the Major and his lady, expressed her wish to take a -walk.

" Dear me, cousin ! are you so vulgar as to like walking ?" exclaimed Mrs. Waddell; " I thought you would have been more of a fine lady by this time—for my part, I really believe I have almost forgot how to walk — when one has a carriage of their own, you know, they have no occasion to walk, and I suppose few people do it from choice—you have quite spoilt me for a pedestrian, Major."

Gertrude could not wait for the complimentary reply she saw about to issue from the Major's lips, but said —

" As I am still so vulgar as to like walking, though not so unreasonable as to insist upon others doing it, you will, perhaps, allow me to take a peep at the beauties of Thornbank by myself;" and she rose to leave the room, when the Major interposed, and, making a lame attempt to be agile —

" O, impossible ! — you must allow me to have the honour of escorting you."

" Now, Major," cried his lady, " I must lay my commands upon you not to stir out to-day again — it is a very damp raw day — I am sure my cousin will excuse you," turning to Gertrude ; " he had a most dreadful cold in his head last week,— I assure you I was quite frightened at it."

" Phoo! nonsense, my dear," said the Major, still hovering between delight and vexation; " nobody would have thought any thing of it but yourself."

" How can you say so, Major, when I counted that you sneezed seventeen times in the course of an hour and a half— and that's what he calls nonsense !"

Leaving the loving pair to settle this tender dispute, Gertrude contrived to steal away from them. — " Oh ! the luxury of solitude after the company of fools!" thought she, when she found herself outside the house, and alone.

CHAPTER XIV.

Now rest thee, reader ! on thy bench, and muse

Anticipative of the feast to come ;

So shall delight not make thee feel thy toil.

Lo ! I have set before thee; for thyself

Feed now. Cary's Dante.

Thornbank was situated on the side of a rapid gurgling river, abounding in picturesque rocky scenery. It was a meek, grey, autumnal day, when earth borrows no tint from sky, but, rich in its own natural hues, presents a matchless variety of colour,

P

from the wan declining green to the gorgeous crimson and orange

— nature's richest, saddest panoply ! The sweet mournful song of the rohin was the only sound that mingled with the murmur of the stream. It was a day for musing and tender melancholy

— a day that came o'er the heart " like a melody that's sweetly played in tune."

Trite as the reflections are which have "been drawn from this solemn season, and obvious as is the moral which points to the heart at witnessing the decay of the beauties and the graces of the material world, still the same train of thought will naturally arise in every mind of sensibility, and the same sober hue insensibly steal over the soul, — "hues which have words, and speak to ye of heaven."

Relieved from every tormenting object, Gertrude sat down on a rustic seat, hung round with many a drooping scentless flower; and resigning herself to the soothing influence of the day and the scene, she gradually sunk into those enchanting day-dreams —those beautiful chimeras, which a young romantic imagination can so readily create. The pleasures of imagination certainly were hers, but as if only to render her more susceptible to the annoyances of real life.

She was recalled from the illusions in which she had been indulging by sounds little in unison with the harmonious stillness that surrounded her: a weak giggling laugh falling at intervals upon the ear, its pauses filled by a sharp loud English tongue, louder and louder, still drew near; and presently Miss Lilly Black, leaning on the arm of a little, spruce, high-dressed young man, appeared. Much surprise, and joy, and affection was testified by Miss Lillias at this meeting with her cousin; and Mr. Augustus Larkins was introduced with an air of triumph and delight. Mr. Augustus Larkins was what many would have called a pretty young man — he had regular features — very pink cheeks — very black eyebrows — and what was intended for a very smart expression. He was studiously dressed in the reigning fashion, but did not look, fashionable for all that. He had a sharp, high-pitched voice; and a very strong, but not a pure, English accent. Such was the future cousin to whom Miss St. Clair was now introduced ; and with many flourishing bows, and with much mouthing about honour, pleasure, and so forth, on his part, the ceremony was happily got over.

" Dear me, cousin, have you been sitting here by yourself?" said Miss Lilly, in a soft pitying tone ; — " what a pity we did not know, and we could have come sooner, you must have been so dull!"

" I did not find it so," replied Gertrude.

" Ah, you Scotch ladies are all fond of solitude," cried Mr. Larkins. — " Witness that noble apostrophe of my Lady Randolph's in your celebrated tragedy of Douglas, ' Ye woods and wilds, whose melancholy gloom accords with my soul's sadness,

and draws forth the tear of sorrow from my bursting heart!' — How uncommonly well that was got up last season at Drury Lane : you have, of course, "been in town, mem ? "

Gertrude replied in the affirmative.

" And which of the houses did you give the preference to ? "

She had not visited the theatres.

" No, sure! — is it possible, mem, to have been in town without seeing either of the houses ? how prodigiously unfortunate! But," — with a significant smile to Miss Lilly — " I hope we shall have the pleasure of showing your cousin the lions by and by; in town, we call it showing the lions to show the sights and shows to our country cousins."

" O! that will be delightful, won't it, cousin ?" asked the simple Lilly, — but her cousin only coloured with contempt at the idea.

" The theatre is a favourite amusement of mine," continued Mr. Larkins.

" And of mine too, I am so fond of the playhouse," said Miss Lilly—bent upon all occasions to prove the congeniality of their souls.

" Did you ever see Young in Romeo ? "

" No, I don't think I ever saw Mr. Young act it; but I once saw a Mr. Something else — I forget his name — do it."

"La! I have seen Young at least a dozen times in Romeo,— it is a favourite character of mine; indeed, I have the whole part by heart."

"Is that possible?" exclaimed Miss Lilly, in tenfold admiration of her lover's perfections;—"do let us hear you repeat, some of it — I'm sure my cousin would like it so much."

"You must learn Juliet, and then I shall be your Romeo -vou would make a capital Juliet — your hair is exactly the colour of Miss O'Neil's."

"Is it really? how I should like if I could act Juliet!"

"When 1 have you in Liquorpond Street," whispered Mr. Larkins, "we shall have some famous scenes."

"That will be charming! I am so fond of deep tragedies!"

"You don't dislike comedy, I hope?"

"O, no, I delight in comedies and farces — I like farces very much too."

"Some of the after-pieces we have in town are famously good — what a prodigious run Midas had, for instance; ' Pray, Goody,' was sung for a whole season."

"O, ' Pray, Goody,' is, without exception, the most beautiful thing I ever heard!" exclaimed Miss Lilly, turning up her eyes in rapture.

"How amazingly you will be pleased with some of our pantomimes in town! What a famous good thing we had last winter at Covent Garden, called ' The Oyster in Love!'"— Here Miss Lilly giggled.

P 2

"Ton my soul, the Oyster in Love was the title; and, to let you into a little of a secret, it was composed, music and all, by

a friend of mine "

"O, goodness! was it really?—do tell us all about it." "Why, the piece opens with a splendid marine view—waves

— waves as high, mem, as these trees, and as white — as white as your gown — roaring in the most natural manner imaginable. Two of the ladies of my party, who had just returned from Margate, became, in short, perfectly sea-sick — 'pon my soul, I thought they'd have fainted. However, it was the first night, and I was a friend of the author; so I wouldn't have stirred to have handed the finest woman in the house."

"O! you cruel creature!" cried Miss Lilly with a giggle — " And what became of them?"

"O! they recovered, with the assistance of smelling-bottles and oranges — but, 'pon my souh I felt a little queer myself. Well, after the waves — these curly-headed monsters, as Shakspeare calls 'em — had rolled backwards and forwards, till, 'pon my honour, I thought they'd have been into the pit, — at last they retired in the most graceful manner possible, leaving behind 'em an enormous large oyster at the foot of a rock; but the beautiful thing, mem, was to see the stage, which, you know, represented the beach, all covered with shells, and spar, and sea-weed. You can have no conception of any thing so natural."

"O! how I should like to have seen it!" sighed Miss Lilly.

"Well, then, there was this oyster, which you'd have sworn was a real oyster but for the size, lying at the bottom of the rock — then enters the divine Miss Foote, dressed as a princess, with the most splendid crown upon her head, all over with precious stones, but looking very melancholy, with her pocket-handkerchief in her hand. She is attended by a troop of young damsels, all very beautiful, and most beautifully dressed

— they sing and dance a most elegant new quadrille ; and while they are dancing the oyster begins to move, and heaves a deep sigh, upon which they all take to their heels, and dance off in all directions, shrieking most musically in parts. The princess, however, remains — draws near the oyster — contemplates it for some time — clasps her hands — falls upon her knees beside it, while it rolls and heaves and sighs — 'pon my honour, it was quite affecting — I saw several handkerchiefs out."

" How terrified I should have been!" exclaimed Miss Lilly. " Well, then, the princess sings that charming song, which, of course, you know, —

This oyster is my world, And I with love will open it.

She then takes a diamond bodkin from her hair, and tries to open the shell. No sooner has she touched it than it opens a little bit, and the point of a beautiful long black beard comes

out — the princess, in the greatest rapture, drops her hodkin — seizes the beard in both hands — kisses it — bedews it with her tears — presses it to her heart — and, in short, is in the greatest transports of joy at recognizing her lover's beard."

" Good gracious! was the oyster her lover ?" cried Miss Lilly.

" Wait and you shall hear. Well, while she is indulging in all these graceful demonstrations of the fondest affection, suddenly a sort of dragon or sea-horse starts up, seizes the bodkin, and disappears. At the same moment the sky, that is the stage, becomes almost quite dark — thunder and lightning ensue — the sea rises with the most tremendous noise, and threatens to engulf, in its raging bosom, the princess and the oyster "

" How interesting!" exclaimed Miss Lilly; — "I never heard any thing like it!"

" The sea gains upon them every moment. — Now they are completely surrounded — she raises her eyes — sees the rock

— a sudden thought strikes her — she merely stops to sing that sweet little air, ' By that beard whose soft expression ' (by-the-by, that was twice encored); then, in the most graceful distress, she begins to climb the rock."

" How high was the rock ?" asked Miss Lilly.

" Why, I take it, not less than thirty feet high, and almost quite perpendicular. Soft music is heard all the time she is ascending. She stops when about half way up quite exhausted — then comes forward to the point of rock where she is standing, which, upon my soul, I don't think was larger than my hand ;

— and, while she stops to recover her breath, sings one of your beautiful Scotch songs —

Low down, in the broom, He's waiting for me ; Waiting for me, my love, &c.

looking down upon the oyster all the while. — There was a great row then : — one half of the house called ' Encore,' the other ' Go on.' At length she was allowed to proceed, and she gains the top of the rock just as an enormous wave is on the point of overwhelming her oyster."

" O! how dreadful!" wailed the sympathising Lilly.

" What should you have done there ?"

"O! I'm sure, I don't know."

"Well, she advances close to the edge of the rock — 'pon my soul, it made me a little giddy to see her! — takes off her crown — unbinds her hair — lies down with her head hanging over the rock, and her hair falls down to the very bottom of the rock where the oyster is lying."

"Goodness! and her own hair?"

"Of course, you know, a lady's wig becomes her own hair." "O, you are so droll!" with a giggle.

"Well — the hair sticks to the oyster, or the oyster to the

P 3

hair, I can't tell -which, and, slowly rising, she hoists him up — an(j U p— a nd up— you might have heard a pin drop in the house while that "was going on — till at last she has him on the very top of the rock! — then the house gave vent to its feelings, and a perfect tumult of applause and admiration ensued."

"No wonder — I can't conceive how she could do it. How "big was the oyster?"

"Why as large, I suppose, as a washing-tub." "And to pull that up with her hair! Did you ever hear any thing like it, cousin?" "Never!" said Gertrude. "Now, tell us what at as acted next?"

"Then there's a fight between the dragon and a whale — and the whale throws up a fine diamond oyster-knife at the feet of the princess — she seizes it — rat-tat-tats upon the shell, which instantly flies open with a prodigious noise, and out rushes a warrior, all clad in a complete suit of mother-of-pearl, with a fine long hlack pointed beard, the same he had shook out of his shell — he slays the dragon — the sea hecomes as smooth as glass — Venus rises out of it in a car drawn by two doves harnessed with roses, and guided hy two young Cupids."

"How delightful! And then I suppose they are married?" "Ah! their happiness would have been very incomplete without that termination," said Mr. Larkins, tenderly.

"It must be late," said Miss St. Clair, rising; "almost dinner time, I should suppose."

"Alas! that Love, whose view is muffled still, Should, without eyes, see pathways to his will. Where shall we dine?"

cried Mr. Larkins, in a theatrical manner. "You know, of course, that is out of Romeo."

"O, is it? — I had forgot that; hut it is heautiful," said the complaisant Lilly.

Mr. Larkins continued to talk and spout all the way home, and his fair to giggle and admire.

"Well, cousin," said she, seizing upon Gertrude, as they entered the house, "what do you think of him? Is he not charming? So genteel, and so droll, and, at the same time, he has so much sensibility — he never travels without poetry — and he plays the flute too most beautifully — and he is so fond of the country; he says he is to drive me out of town every Sunday in his .tilbury. — O, I wonder how Bell could ever fall in love with the Major! — He hasn't the least taste for poetry — and Andrew is such an ugly name : don't you think I have^ been most fortunate in a name, for it is so uncommon to meet with an Augustus? — and I think Larkins very pretty too — don't you?"

But they were now at the drawing-room door, which put a stop to Miss Lilly's raptures, and soon after dinner ended all tete-a-tetes.

Mrs. Major "Waddell played the nabob's lady as though she had been born a nabobess — she talked much and well of curry and rice — and old Madeira — and the liver — and the Company, which did not mean the present company, but the India Company. Her silver corners were very handsome, and she had to take off some of her rings before she could carve the grouse. In short, nothing could be better of its kind. Nevertheless, Mrs. Major had her own petty chagrins, as every petty mind must have — nobody seemed sufficiently dazzled with the splendour which surrounded them; and Mr. Larkins had the ill-breeding to talk much of Birch's turtle, and Thames salmon, and town. At tea it was still worse — like all under-bred people, he mistook familiarity for fashionable ease, and either lounged upon her fine sofa, or stood with his back to the fire.

At length the chaise was announced -, and as Mrs. and Miss St. Clair took leave, the gallant Major presented his arm. " Oh! now, Major, I hope you're not going to the door without your hat, and at this time of night! Now, it will make me perfectly wretched. — Pray now, Major — aunt — cousin — Mr. Larkins — for Heaven's sake "

Mrs. Waddell was getting hysterical; and the poor Major, withdrawing his offered aid, Mr. Larkins advanced.

" And, oh! put on your hat!" sighed Miss Lilly, in imitation, as he boldly presented his brush head to the evening air.

" How sweet the moonlight sleeps upon this bank ! Here will we sit, and let the sounds of music Creep in our ears "

spouted Mr. Augustus, as he handed the ladies into the carriage. They bowed, and drove off.

CHAPTER XV.

On s'ennuie tres bien ici. Voltaire.

But the present order of things could not long endure. Mrs. St. Clair grew impatient under the secret sense of her sisters' superiority, and weary of their simple uniform style of living. Her habits were luxurious — her mind was joyless. Gertrude, too, in all the restlessness of suspense, longed to return to Rossville. She would there hear her lover's name mentioned — she would be amidst the scenes with -which his image was associated — and there would be enjoyment even in these shadowy fantastic pleasures. While such were the feelings of the mother and daughter, Lord Rossville felt no less impatient for the return of his niece — not for the charms and graces of her society, but because

P 4

she was a being subject to his management and controul. True, this act of rebellion might have staggered his faith as to the extent of his dominion; but he flattered himself that was a sort of thunder-cloud, which, by the wise and vigorous measures he had adopted, must already have passed away. Besides, Gertrude's prolonged absence would have an appearance in the eyes of the world — suspicions might arise — things might be said. Even in the bustle of electioneering, Mr. Delmour had remarked upon the impropriety of Miss St. Clair being allowed to reside so long in a paltry provincial town, and associating with people who might be very good in their way, but were not quite suited to her station, or such as he would wish his wife to be intimate with. On the other hand, Mrs. St Clair, in the course of her correspondence with the Earl, had taken care to insinuate that such was Mr. Adam Ramsay's partiality for her daughter, it was more than probable he would make a point of her residing entirely with him, unless she were speedily recalled to his lordship's protection. The visit to Broom Park strengthened this insinuation, and decided him as to the necessity of immediately recalling his

niece.

A most laborious and long-winded letter was therefore penned to Miss St. Clair, in which, while he deprecated the idea of ever taking her into his favour, until she had renounced the error of her ways, he, at the same time, announced his intention of receiving her again under his roof, in the confident hope that she would ere long perceive the absolute necessity, and imperious duty, she was under of acceding to his long-projected, thoroughly digested, and firmly-determined-upon plan for her ultimate disposal. His lordship next proceeded to state, that he had consulted the most eminent counsel as to the deeds of entail; and that three of them were of opinion, that the whole of the property could and might be most effectually alienated, disponed, and otherwise disposed of, to the utter exclusion of Miss St. Clair, as heiress at law. — Such being the case, it was his firm intention, and absolute purpose, to act upon this opinion, by executing a new deed of entail within three months from the present date, unless, before the expiry of that period. Miss St. Clair should think proper to accede to his plan, and pursue the course he had pointed out to her. — Such was the substance of a letter filling nearly seven pages of closely-written paper.

" I am sorry — very sorry," said Gertrude, with a sigh, as she finished reading it, " for the trouble and vexation I am causing Lord Rossville; and perhaps it were better that I should never return to Rossville again, than that I should go there only to make him cherish hopes which can never be realized. —I never can act as he would have me — I never can change my sentiments."

" You can at least keep your sentiments to yourself, considering how much is at stake on their account," said her mother,

with asperity; " and, indeed, setting every thing else out of the question, I think delicacy alone demands that much of you; — at least, I should be cautious how I expressed an attachment, which, to all appearance, is no longer — if indeed it ever was— reciprocal."

" Even were it so," replied her daughter, making an effort to repress her emotion, while her faltering voice betrayed the anguish of such a supposition — " deceived I may be myself, but I never will deceive others. Let, then, Lord Rossville know that, if I return to his house, I return unchanged—unchangeable."

" Beware how you provoke me, Gertrude ; for I too am unchanged — unchangeable in my determination, never to see you the prey of that man — I have pledged my word it shall not be."

" Pledged your word !" repeated her daughter, indignantly; — " who had a right to demand such a pledge ?"

" One who has the right, and will exercise it," said Mrs. St. Clair, in some agitation ; " but this is wandering from the point. You have promised you will not enter into any engagement until you have attained the age of twenty-one —on that promise I rely ; meanwhile, all I require of you is only what is due to yourself—leave me, therefore, to manage matters with the Earl, and do you remain passive for the present."

" I am sick of management—of mystery," exclaimed Gertrude, dejectedly— "already," cried she, giving way to tears, " I am almost weary of the world — I feel myself a puppet — a slave — nay, the slave of a slave—subject, it seems, to the control of a very menial; but I will not endure this mockery of greatness,—mingled, too, with such degradation !"

There was a height and a depth in Gertrude's feelings, which, when once roused, her mother could not always contend with. She sometimes felt that her only chance of victory was in appearing to yield; and upon this occasion, as upon many others, she contrived to work upon her daughter's affections, and prevailed upon her to acquiesce in her wishes, provided she were not considered as a party in Lord Rossville's plans.

The following day the Earl's equipage and attendants arrived ; and again Mrs. St. Clair's worldly mind exulted as she looked on the proud pageant at which the whole town of Barn-ford had turned out to gaze. It was not without emotion Gertrude bade adieu to her aunts, who were not less affected at parting with her; they saw she was not happy, but were too delicate to intrude upon her confidence.

"Farewell, my love!" said her aunt Mary, as she pressed her in her arms — " and ever bear in mind that in this world, not to be grieved — not to be afflicted—not to be in danger, is impossible : — yet, dearest Gertrude! even in this world, there is a rest of heart — ah! would you but seek it where only it is to be found!"

But to the young unchastened spirit nothing seems less desirable than that rest of heart, - which, in their minds, is associated with the utter extinction of all that is noble, and graceful, and enthusiastic; and Gertrude shrank from the wish breathed for her by her aunt.

"No," thought she — " wretched as I am, yet I would not exchange my feelings, tortured as they are, for that joyless peace -which is to me as the slumber of the dead !"

And where is the youthful, ardent spirit, untaught by heavenly lore, which has not, at some period of its life, perilled its all on some baseless fabric, and preferred even the shattered wreck of its happiness to the waveless calm of indifference ?

Gertrude's melancholy was not diminished by her return to Rossville. But a few weeks had passed since she had left it in all the pride and magnificence of early autumn — while nature seemed scarcely past its prime — while life was in the leaf, and spirit in the air, and the bright-toned woods glowed in all their variegated splendour beneath a clear blue sky and cloudless sun.

And now the cold autumnal dews are seen
To cobweb every green ; And by the low-shorn rowans doth appear
The fast declining year ; The sapless branches"doff their summer suits,
And wane their winter fruits ; And stormy blasts have forced the quaking trees To wrap their trembling limbs in suits of mossy frieze.

In plain prose, it was a bleak, raw, chill November day, when nature seems a universal blank even to her most ardent admirers ; and, to use an artist phrase, nothing could be more in keeping with the day than the reception Miss St. Clair met with from her uncle. It was cold, formal, and unkindly, and every word fell like a drop of petrifying water on her heart.

Lord Rossville never had been upon easy terms with his niece — indeed, it was not in his nature to be upon easy terms with anybody; but the additional stiffness, and solemnity, and verbosity he thought proper to assume, were truly appalling, and caused her to feel something of that sensation sensitive beings are said to experience while under the influence of a thunder-cloud.

The Earl's aspect was, indeed, enough to blight hope itself. There was positive determination itself in every line and lineament— his eyes had grown rounder — his eyebrows higher — his lips more rigid — his hands longer — his steps were more ponderous—his head was immoveable—there was no speculation in his eye—his very wig looked as hard as marble. In short, over the whole man was diffused an indescribable air of hopeless inflexibility.

There was no company — nothing to relieve the hard outline of the piece—not even the usual members of the family:

nobody but Lady Betty, and her eternal rug, and her fat lap-dog, and her silly novel; and the dulness and tedium -which reigned may have been felt, but cannot be described.

CHAPTER XVI.

If thou hast dipt thy foot in the river, yet pass not over Rubicon. — Sir Thomas Brown.

Several days passed in this state of cheerless monotony, when one morning, as the ladies pursued their different avocations in unsocial companionship, a letter was brought to Mrs. St. Clair, which she had no sooner opened than Gertrude observed her change colour, and betray visible signs of agitation. The servant said that the bearer waited an answer; and in manifest confusion, she rose and left the room. Although superior to the meanness of curiosity, Miss St. Clair could not help feeling a natural desire to know the contents of a letter which had produced so visible a change on her mother, and she sat a considerable time, vainly looking for her return. At length, unable to repress her anxiety, she put aside her drawing materials, and hastened to her mother's dressing-room. Upon entering, she found Mrs. St. Clair seated at a table, with writing implements before ber, and her head resting on her hand, seemingly buried in profound meditation.

" I was afraid something was the matter, mamma," said her daughter, gently advancing towards her.

" Leave me," cried her mother, in an angry impatient tone ; " leave me, I say — I can't be disturbed."

" Mamma, can I do nothing for you ? " asked her daughter, as she reluctantly prepared to obey.

" Much, much," — murmured Mrs. St. Clair, with a deep sigh — " but, at present, I desire you will leave me," raising her voice in an authoritative tone; and Gertrude, however unwillingly, found herself compelled to obey. Uneasy and restless, she could not compose her mind to any of her ordinary occupations. She saw something had occurred to agitate her mother, and she longed to participate, and, if possible, to aid her in her distress. After a while she again returned to her, and was again repulsed with anger. Seeing that her presence only caused irritation she desisted from farther attempts; and, taking advantage of a watery gleam of sunshine, which streamed fr^m a pale sickly sky, she set out on a solitary ramble, to which fresh air and exercise only could give a zest. She slowly pursued her way through leafless woods, where the only sounds she heard were those of her own footsteps amongst the fallen leaves, and the monotonous rush of the swollen stream. But each step

was fraught with sad yet soothing recollections — for rocks, woods, and waters seemed all as the registers of her lover's vows; and in each silent memorial she felt as though she looked on the living witness of his faith. Thus nursing her fond contemplations, she had wandered a considerable length of way, when she was roused to observation by the sudden darkness of the sky ; but whether caused by the lateness of the hour, or the approach of a storm, she was not sufficiently mistress of signs and times to ascertain. Whichever it might be, it had the effect of dispelling all romance, and making her wish herself once more safe at home. She was, however, more than two miles from it by the way she had come; but, if she could get across the river, there was a short cut, which would take her home in ten minutes; and she walked a little farther on, in search of some stepping-stones, which had been placed there instead of a bridge which had been swept away by what, in the language of the country, is called a speat.

A great deal of rain had fallen the preceding night, and the river was so much swollen she could hardly recognize the huge blocks by which she had frequently crossed the clear pebbly stream when it scarcely laved their sides. Now they merely held their broad heads above the brown sullen waters— but still they were above it — and, trusting to her own steady head and firm step, she, with some little palpitation, placed her foot on the first stone. " C'est ne que le premier pas qui coute," said she to herself; but, notwithstanding this comfortable assurance, there she stood for some minutes, ere she had courage to venture on a second step. But the sky was getting blacker, and some large straggling drops of rain began to fall. Ashamed of her irresolution, she was about to proceed, when she heard some one calling loudly to her to stop ; and immediately she beheld, on the opposite bank, Mr. Lyndsay, approaching at full speed on horseback. In an instant he urged his horse into the river; but the current was so strong it was with the utmost difficulty the animal was enabled to gain the shore.

"Is it possible," cried Lyndsay, as he threw himself off, " that you were going to attempt to cross the river in its present state ?"

"I not only mean to attempt, but to succeed," answered she, as she felt her courage rise to its utmost pitch, since she had now an opportunity of displaying it; and she was about to proceed, when he seized her hand.

"You are not aware of the danger: — the river, you may see, is far above its usual height, and is rising every moment. A great deal of rain has fallen, and a fresh flood will be down directly."

"Well, it seems merely a choice of evils, as I seem destined to be drowned one way or another," said Gertrude, as the rain now began to fall in earnest.

"I assure you, then, you will find it much the least evil to he drowned on dry land — so, pray, take my advice for once."

But Gertrude felt as though it were due to Colonel Delmour to accord nothing to Mr. Lyndsay, against whom she laboured to keep up what she deemed a due resentment, and she therefore persisted in her intention.

"I am far from desiring Mr. Lyndsay's attendance," said she, somewhat disdainfully. " I beg he will take his way, and allow me to take mine."

Lyndsay made no reply but by hastily snatching her from the place where she stood; and, at the same instant, a sound, as of many waters, was heard — a sea of foam was tearing its course along— and, in the twinkling of an eye, the stones were buried in the waves For some moments Gertrude remained motionless, gazing on the mass of discoloured waters as they roared along, till she was aroused by the cry and the struggle of some living thing, which was swept past with the speed of lightning and ingulfed in the raging flood. She turned shuddering away ; and Lyndsay, taking her arm in his, would have led her from the spot — but, smote with the sense of her own injustice towards him, she exclaimed, " Not till I have here acknowledged my rashness, — my folly; you risked your life to save mine, while I — unjust — ungrateful that I was "

"Not to me, my dear cousin, is any such acknowledgment due," said Lyndsay, mildly ; — " give your thanks to God— only let us be friends."

Gertrude gave him her hand. — " When can I cease to look upon you as my friend! — you who have saved me from destruction ! "

Lyndsay sighed, but made no reply ; and they walked on in silence, till the rain, which had hitherto fallen at intervals in an undecided manner now burst forth in what in Scotland is emphatically called an even-down pour. Neither rocks nor trees afforded any shelter; but they were now in sight of a summer-house, and thither they hastened. "While Lyndsay stopped on the outside to fasten his horse, intending to leave him until he could send his servant to fetch him home, Gertrude rushed in, and, almost blinded by the rain, did not, at first, perceive that some one had already taken possession of it, and was pacing up and down with visible signs of impatience. But, at her entrance, the person turned quickly round, and she encountered the sharp baleful glance of Lewiston.

"My ! this is more of a trate than I expected," cried he, in an accent of pleasure and surprise; then taking her passive hand, " This is well — this is as it should be—come, my pretty messenger, sit down, don't be afraid."

But this caution, though uttered in a soft conciliating manner, was in vain. At first amazement had rendered Gertrude mute and motionless; but as he attempted to seat her, and place him-self beside her, she instantly regained her faculties, and, struggling to release herself from his hold, she called loudly—

" Mr. Lyndsay, save me ! oh ! save me ! "

But Lyndsay had withdrawn a few yards to place his horse under the shelter of a projecting rock, and the roar of the river drowned all other sounds.

" What a plaguy fool ye are after all!" exclaimed Lewiston, as he held both her hands, and squeezed them with almost painful violence. " Be quiet, I tell you, can't ye, and you have nothing fear ; but if ye're aprovokin'me, ye'll repint, I tell ye, as sure as I'm a gintleman! " and he compelled her to be seated.

Gertrude would have spoken, but the words died on her lips ; and she sat pale and trembling, unable to articulate.

" Why, this is being narvous," cried he; but, in a gentler tone

— " Have I not told you that you have nothing to be afeard of

— that I love you too well ? " Gertrude again called wildly on Mr. Lyndsay. — " Why did you come here only to squall ? — Why did she not come herself, and where is the money ? — answer me, I say.—A squire too!" exclaimed he, as Lyndsay now entered. — " Well, sir, what may your business be here ?"

Mr. Lyndsay started with surprise, as he beheld Miss St. Clair seated by the side of this man, whom he instantly recognized as the same from whom he had foi'merly rescued her; but her extreme paleness, and the terror depicted on her countenance, showed what her endurance cost her. The insolent question was repeated in a still higher key. Even Lyndsay's usual calmness was almost overcome; but he repelled the rising of his wrath, and answered —

" My business here is to protect this lady from insult or intrusion,"— and, advancing to her, he placed himself by her side.

" O let us begone ! " cried Gertrude, as she rose and took hold of his arm ; but she trembled so much she could scarcely stand.

" You cannot go yet," said Lyndsay; then turning to Lewiston

— " but as your presence seems to agitate Miss St. Clair, I must request of you to withdraw."

" By what right do you interfere between this lady and me ?" demanded he fiercely.

" I know of no right you have to ask me such a question," said Mr. Lyndsay coolly.

" You know of no right I have ! — and what may you know of me or my rights ? "

Lyndsay's blood rose at this continued insolence ; but, making an effort to master his spirit, he replied —

" You say true, — I know nothing of you; but I know you can have no right to alarm Miss St. Clair — if you have any claim upon her notice, this is neither a place nor a time for it."

" Her notice ! " repeated Lewiston, with a scornful smile. — " Well, and I have claims upon her notice then ; and you will do well to look arter ye'r own consarns, and leave us to settle our own affairs."

" Oh, no — no ! " cried Gertrude, as she clung to her cousin's arm — " do not leave me — I have nothing to say!" — But as she thought of her mother's mysterious connection with him, she trembled while she disclaimed him.

" Do not be afraid," said Lyndsay, trying to reassure her — " there is nothing to fear, except insolence ; and that I shall spare you, if this gentleman will walk out with me for a few minutes."

" I have already told you, that I have no business with you," said Lewiston — " and it is yours is the insolence, who breaks in upon my appointments.—Come, my dear, rid yourself of your spark quietly ; for I don't wish to harm the young man — tell him the fact, and bid him begone."

Never in his life had Lyndsay's self-controul been so severely tried, but he still had firmness to keep himself in check.

" I know of no appointment," said Gertrude faintly, as she thought of the letter her mother had that morning received, — " accident alone brought me here."

Lewiston looked steadfastly at her.

" Sure! then she's a holler one, and that's a fact; but you had best take care how you attempt to draw the wool over my eyes — your hand upon it."

Gertrude involuntarily recoiled.

" Audacious !" exclaimed Lyndsay, provoked beyond farther forbearance, and, seizing him by the collar, shook him with a force that made him stagger. " This lady's presence alone prevents me from punishing you as you deserve."

Gertrude shrieked, as Lewiston instantly drew a small dagger-sword from his walking-cane.

" Do you see that ? " cried he, with a scornful laugh. " How would ye like to take ye'r change out of that? — But I don't think the worse of you for this touss, and only give you this handsome piece of advice gratis,— before you talk of punishing, to be sure you have the means in your own hands, or you'll have the worst of it by a long chalk."

" I thank you," said Lyndsay, as he led Gertrude to the door; then, turning back, he added, in a low voice, "and I shall return to repeat my acknowledgments — only wait me here."

The rain had not ceased, but its violence had abated, and they walked on for some time in silence, till they both at the same moment descried Mrs. St.Clair approaching, muffled in a large cloak; but she, too, seemed to have perceived them, for she instantly turned back, and in another moment disappeared by one of the many paths which traversed the wood.

" Oh!" exclaimed Gertrude, with a burst of bitter feeling at this confirmation of her mother's clandestine intercourse, — " Ob ! that the flood from which you saved me had swept me away, rather than that I should live to endure this degradation "

" My dear cousin," said Mr. Lyndsay, gently, " do not give way to such dreadful thoughts — were you steeped in crime, you could not do more than despair— even then you ought not to do that."

" Crime there must be somewhere, cried Gertrude in the same tone of excitement; " else why all this mystery — and why am I subjected to the insults of that man, unless "

" Do you know who and what he really is ?" said Mr. Lyndsay.

" O, ask me no questions !" cried she, again giving way to tears.

" Pardon me, I have done wrong—it is not from you I ought to seek information."

" Seek it not at all—leave me to my fate—abject and degraded I already am in your eyes."

" How little you know me, if you think that circumstances, over which you evidently have no control, could ever lessen you in my eyes! — It is not the misdeeds of others that can touch your soul—and they ought not to influence your character. There is not—there cannot be degradation but in personal sin."

"Yet I owe it entirely to your generous confidence that I am not suspected—despised"

"Suspicion itself scarcely could suspect you; and for despising you—do not think so falsely, so meanly of yourself, as to imagine that any one would dare to despise you. I fear something is wrong, and that you are not in good hands ; but put your trust in God, my dear cousin—preserve your own natural integrity, and all will one day be right;—meantime, if I can be of service to you, look upon me as a friend—as a brother— will you promise me this ?"

Gertrude, in somewhat calmer accents, promised she would. Lyndsay continued to talk to her in the same soothing yet strengthening strain till they reached the castle, when they separated with sentiments of reciprocal interest and regard.

CHAPTER XVII.

What man so wise, so earthly witt, so ware
As to descry the crafty cunning traine,
By which deceit doth maske in visour faire,
And cast her colours died deep in graine,
To seem like truth, whose shape she well can feigne.
Faery Queen.

No sooner had Mr. Lyndsay seen Miss St. Clair safe within the castle walls, than he instantly retraced his steps, with the intention of returning to the summer-house, for the purpose of extricating her, if possible, from the mysterious thraldom in which she seemed to be held by this person. At the midnight rencontre in the wood lie had asserted a right over her, which although she herself had disclaimed with almost frantic wildness, her mother had tacitly acknowledged by not directly denying. In the short conversation he had held with Mrs. St. Clair, subsequent to that meeting, she had with tears implored his silence—his secrecy—his forbearance—and, in broken and indirect terms, had given him to understand that this person had been engaged with her husband in certain money transactions, which, out of regard to his memory, she was desirous of keeping concealed ; and it was upon this ground he had asserted a claim upon Miss St. Clair's fortune, which he had unwarrantably extended to her hand. This mangled and absurd account could not impose upon Lyndsay; but, at that time, he was almost a stranger to Mrs. St. Clair, and did not conceive himself authorized to interfere in her concerns. He, therefore, contented himself with mildly admonishing her on the impropriety of such clandestine meetings, and recommending to her to lay this person's claims before Lord Rossville, as the proper protector of his brother's memory and his niece's interest. In the meantime, he yielded to Mrs. St. Clair's entreaties, and gave her his promise not to divulge what had passed, upon her solemn assurance that the affair was in the way of being amicably adjusted, and that she had taken effectual means of ridding herself for ever of this person's importunity. This promise, it now appeared, had not been kept; again Miss St. Clair had been exposed to fresh insult in his presence, and he now thought himself entitled to interpose. "With this purpose he walked quickly back, and had almost reached the summer-house, when he was met by Mrs. St. Clair; her countenance was agitated, and traces of tears were visible in her eyes. She did not, however, now seem to shun him ; for she stopped and extended her hand to him, saying— "You are the very person I most wish to see—give me your arm, and let us return together — I have much to say to you."

"But there is a person there to whom I also have much to say ; and I cannot attend you till I have first spoken with him." And he was passing on, when Mrs. St. Clair caught his arm, —

"I know whom you seek; but spare yourself the trouble — he is gone."

"Where? — which way?" eagerly demanded he; "but I must ascertain that myself," and he ran with all his speed to the summer-house. But it was deserted; and, though he looked long and keenly in all directions, not a trace of any one was to be seen. He was therefore obliged to retrace his steps, and soon overtook Mrs. St. Clair.

" You would not give credit to me, then ? " said she, in a tone of reproach.

" I.shall give credit to you now," answered he, " if you will tell me where I am likely to find the person I left here half an hour ago."

" I cannot tell — and, if I could, perhaps I would not. No good could possibly result from your meeting. — Your -wish, I know, is to befriend my daughter and myself; and, be assured, I am far from insensible of the value of such a friend. — But, come with me, — I have much to say to you, much to confide to you of my dearest Gertrude."

Mrs. St. Clair's hyperbolical jargon was always offensive to Mr. Lyndsay's good taste and right feeling; but there was something absolutely revolting in it at this time—there was something so strained and unnatural in it—such a flimsy attempt at thus seeming to court explanation, that he felt armed against the duplicity he was aware would be practised upon him.

" At another time I shall be ready to listen to any thing which concerns Miss St. Clair," said he, coldly; " but, at present, I wish to put a few questions to the person "

" Pardon me ; but I know all you would say, my dear Mr. Lyndsay, and you must allow me to anticipate those questions by the confidential communication I am now about to make to you. On your honour — on your secrecy, I know I may place the most unbounded reliance — I therefore require no assurances to satisfy me."

" I certainly can give none until I know how far secrecy may be compatible with honour."

Mrs. St. Clair affected not to hear this implied doubt, but went on —

" You have now had opportunities of becoming acquainted with my daughter — of forming your own opinion of her character— of—pardon a mother's vanity — of appreciating her charms and her graces; — but you know not — none but a mother can know, the treasures of her heart and mind."

Mrs. St. Clair paused and sighed, and Mr. Lyndsay was too much surprised at such an opening to make any reply.

" Judge, then, at my grief and anguish at finding this gifted being, this idol of my affections, ensnared by the artifices of one every way unworthy of her, has been led to bestow her regards "

" Pardon me," cried Lyndsay ; " but I can have no possible right to be made the depository of Miss St. Clair's sentiments by any but herself. I must be excused from listening to any thing more on that subject — I simply wish to know where I am likely to find the person who has, twice in my presence, dared to insult her."

" Yet it is only by hearing me patiently, and suffering me to take my own way in divulging the circumstances of the case as I think best, that I can possibly make you acquainted with them — either my lips must be sealed as to the whole, or you must listen to the whole without interruption. — I am mistaken if I tell you any thing new when I allude to my daughter's misplaced partiality; still more mistaken, if her future happiness is a matter of indifference to you."

Lyndsay made no answer; he felt that Mrs. St. Clair was weaving a web around him, but he could not bring himself to burst from its folds, and he suffered her to proceed.

" I will not attempt to paint to you the anguish of my heart at discovering that the innocent affections of my unsuspecting child had been thus artfully and insidiously worked upon by Colonel Delmour. I know him, and you know him, to be a selfish, mercenary, unprincipled man, as incapable of appreciating such a being as Gertrude, as she would have been of bestowing her affections on a character such as his, had not her imagination been dazzled and misled. But, alas ! at nineteen, where is our judgment and discrimination ? Yet at nine-and-twenty they will come too late — then, long before then, if she becomes the wife of Colonel Delmour, she will be the most wretched of women. Formed to find her happiness solely in the being she loves — noble, generous, upright, sincere herself, what will be her feelings when the mask drops, as drop it will, from this idol of her fancy, and she beholds him in his native deformity! — No,—sooner than see her the wife of Colonel Delmour, I take Heaven to witness, I would rather look upon her in her coffin."

Inflated as all this was, still there was some truth and right feeling in it; and he insensibly forgot his suspicions, and listened with profound attention.

" Yet I dare not express to Lord Rossville all that I feel, for neither can I accede to his views for the disposal of my daughter. Gertrude has too much taste and feeling — too much heart and soul, to be sacrificed to family pride and political influence ; in fact, as far as regards her happiness, there is but a choice of evils in these brothers; but there is one " she stopped and hesitated— " there is one to whom I would, with pride and pleasure, have confided my dearest treasure, in the certainty that, as her judgment matured, so her love and esteem would increase towards that one. — Why should I conceal from you my wish?"

Mrs. St. Clair made a full stop, and looked at Mr. Lyndsay in a manner he could not misunderstand.

This was something he had not anticipated — it went far beyond what he had calculated upon, and he was thrown off his guard. His features betrayed his emotion, although he remained silent. There was a long pause. At length Mrs. St. Clair resumed —

" The time will come when the veil will fall from my daughter's eyes — as her judgment ripens, her imagination will decline — already I can perceive the work is begun, and time is all that is wanting to finish it; — but if, as may happen, she is hurried into a clandestine engagement, my hopes — her happiness—will be for ever blasted ! — On the other hand, if, by any sacrifice, any stratagem, I can save her, can you blame me for the attempt, however wild or desperate it may appear ?"

" I certainly could not blame a sacrifice, however vain it might prove," said Lyndsay; " but I must always disapprove of stratagems, even when successful — both together seem to me incompatible."

For a moment Mrs. St. Clair was thrown into confusion by this remark ; but, quickly rallying, she replied —

" Yet the one may prove the consequence of the other — in my case I fear it has ; and that in using what I conceived an allowable stratagem to save my daughter, I have sacrificed what I value next — the good opinion and esteem of Mr. Lyndsay."

" It rests with yourself to remove any unfavourable impression I may have received — a few words will suffice."

" I feel that you will blame me—that you will condemn the step I have taken," said Mrs. St. Clair, in evident embarrassment; — it must appear to you strange — unworthy — unnatural; but you know not the difficulties of my situation. — Gertrude rash and ungovernable — Lord

Rossville inflexible and exacting. If she marries Colonel Delmour, her fortune and her happiness are both alike blasted. To save her from that — at least to gain time, can you altogether condemn me if I have taken advantage of this person's unwarranted claim upon her fortune, to induce a belief in her mind that that claim does in reality extend to her hand, and that But, oh Heavens!" exclaimed she, as they suddenly came in sight of the castle, " it must be very late—lights in the drawing-room, and company assembled — if I am missed To morrow we shall resume this subject; meantime I must fly;" — and she would have withdrawn her arm from Mr. Lyndsay's, but he detained her.

" No," said he, " before we part, promise me solemnly that you will lay open to me the whole of this dark transaction — strange thoughts have taken possession of my mind — I will no longer connive at this mystery."

It was too dark to see the working of Mrs. St. Clair's features; but he felt the hand he held tremble in his grasp.

" To-morrow, then — to-morrow, dear Mr. Lyndsay, I promise to satisfy you more fully," said she in a voice faint from agitation— " till then be silent, I conjure you — for Gertrude's sake be silent. — Oh ! do not detain me — there is the warning bell."

And she darted forwards, and ran till she reached the door; then, turning round, she pressed Lyndsay's hand, and in breathless accents whispered, " For Gertrude's sake, then, you will be silent till to-morrow — you promise me this."

" Till to-morrow, then, be it," said he.

Mrs. St. Clair again pressed his hand in token of gratitude, then entered softly, and stole up stairs to change her dress; while Lyndsay, as he walked openly and deliberately to his apartment, thought " She has got the better of me, I fear, after all — but to-morrow will show."

CHAPTER XVIII.

Such deep despondence rends her trembling heart,
Conscious of deeds which honour cannot own. Euripides.

Although Mr. Lyndsay had made all despatch in dressing, yet, upon entering the drawing-room, he found Mrs. St. Clair had got the start of him.

No appearance of hurry or agitation was now visible, unless in her more than usually brilliant colour. Her dress was handsome, and well arranged — her air, to common observers, easy and unembarrassed ; and altogether she formed a striking contrast to her daughter, who sat by her, pale, thoughtful, and dejected, with the look of one who had almost unconsciously suffered herself to be dressed.

As Lyndsay entered he heard Mrs. St. Clair say to Lord Rossville, in answer to some remark of his —

" I was, indeed, caught to-day — I foolishly took alarm at Gertrude's absence during that prodigious shower, and set out in search of her myself; but we missed each other, and have now only met by the side of your lordship's charming fire."

Lord Rossville loved to be complimented upon his fires, "which were always' constructed after a model of his own, and were, of course, notoriously bad ; but Mrs. St. Clair knew how to throw out a tub for a whale —her well-timed compliment led to a discussion upon fires, stoves, and coals, which ended in the whole company being speedily involved in the intricacies of one of the Earl's own coal-pits, from which they were only rescued by a summons to dinner.

Mr. Delmour had returned, bringing a band of his second-rate political allies along with him; and the conversation consequently took its cast from them, and was as dull as political discussions always are, unless when worse than dull — violent. Mrs. St. Clair entered into all that was^ said con amore, and was consequently thought, by the greater part of the company, to be an uncommonly charming, well-informed, and very fine woman. Lady Betty asked some questions as efficient as usual, and passed for a very worthy, sensible, affable old lady. Miss St. Clair sat silent and absent, and indifferent to what was going on, and was pronounced a cold, haughty, insipid automaton. Such are the judgments daily passed upon as slight a knowledge of that within which passeth show — and so superficial a thing is popularity.

On quitting the dining-room, Mrs. St. Clair whispered "her daughter to follow her to her own apartment; and no sooner were they there than, shutting the door with violence, she seemed as if eager to indemnify herself for the constraint she had been under.

" Gertrude !" cried she, all at once giving way to her agitation —" again you see me in your hands — again my fate hangs on your decision — again it is yours to save or to destroy me!"

Gertrude could not speak — her heart sickened at the evil she anticipated.

" But I will not go over the same ground I have done: — I tell you, I am at your mercy; hut I will neither supplicate nor command — I leave you free — pronounce my doom, and do not fear even my reproaches."

Gertrude's senses almost forsook her, as the dreadful idea flashed upon her that she was to be required to save her mother's life at the expense of becoming the wife of the dreaded Lewiston ; and, sinking at her feet, in wild broken accents she besought her to spare her.

" Compose yourself, Gertrude," cried Mrs. St. Clair, suddenly calmed herself at sight of her daughter's still stronger emotion — "I tell you you have nothing to fear from me — I have promised that I will not even seek to influence you; all I require of you is to hear the alternative."

" Oh, no — no — spare me that dreadful alternative—kill me —but save me from him!" and she clung to her mother's knees with convulsive energy.

" Gertrude, this is madness — it rests with yourself to rid me of that man, I trust for ever. — Come, sit down by me, and listen ;" and she seated herself at a writing-table, and placed her daughter beside her. After a pause, during which she seemed to be struggling with her feelings, she spoke —

" Gertrude, I cannot conceal from you that we are both in the power of a villain — I have told you, and I again repeat it — the circumstances which have placed me there I will only disclose with my dying breath, if even then ; — how soon that may be, depends upon your decision. I cannot conceal from you that he does possess a claim over you — nay, be still, and hear me — which he is ready to relinquish, if, within twenty-four hours, I can raise five hundred pounds — this I must accomplish, or my ruin — your wretchedness for life, is inevitable."

Gertrude began to breathe at this unexpected relief.

" If he obtains this sum, he has pledged himself to quit the kingdom ; and with worlds, if I had them, would I purchase his absence."

" But what are those mysterious claims which this man has upon me ? why not bring them forward openly? —let them be urged in the face of the world : — in this land of freedom — in my uncle's house— what have I to fear ? "

"As you value your father's memory, as you value my peace
— my life — let this transaction be for ever buried in silence. — If there were a way to escape — if it were possible to release ourselves from him, can you suppose that I would have suffered what I have done—that I would have submitted thus to humble myself to my own child ? "

And Mrs. St. Clair dropt a few tears.

" But where is such a sum to be procured ?" asked her daughter, as she thought how she had already been stripped of every thing she could call her own. " I have nothing in my power!"

" I know you have nothing to give; but you have only to ask and you will obtain. — My uncle can refuse you nothing; and it is no such mighty matter in the future Countess of Ross-ville to borrow a few hundred pounds from a man to whom wealth is an absolute drug. — Here," said she, placing some paper before her, and putting a pen into her hand, " you have only to write, and I will dictate."

But the pen dropt from Gertrude's fingers.

" No—I cannot—indeed I cannot be guilty of such meanness
— it is too degrading."

Mrs. St. Clair made no attempt to argue or remonstrate ; but, waving her hand with a sort of desperate calmness, she merely said—

" I am answered—leave me."

" Oh, mamma!—give me the paper—you shall be obeyed— tell me what I must say."

Mrs. St. Clair testified neither joy nor gratitude at this concession ; but immediately began to dictate the form of a letter to Mr. Adam Ramsay, which her daughter implicitly followed
— scarcely conscious of what she wrote. In a calmer mood, she would have revolted from the duplicity and servility with which every line was fraught; but, in her present excitement of mind, her powers of thinking were suspended, and she was the mere passive instrument of her mother's will. At length it was finished; and, as Mrs. St. Clair sealed it, she looked at her watch —

" It will be just in time for the letter-box and no more; we must return to the drawing-room, and we can put it into the box as we pass through the hall."

" I cannot return to the company," said her daughter. " I am unfit for society after such a scene as this — I cannot dissemble."

" You can at least, it is to be hoped, exercise some self-control, and not suffer yourself to be read and commented up^n by every curious eye which chooses to look in your face. Happily 'tis one that even crying cannot spoil; you have only to wipe away your tears," and she applied her own handkerchief; " and

Q 4

see, not a trace of them remains. — Come, I insist upon it." And Gertrude suffered herself to be led to the drawing-room.

The only person with whom she now felt any companionship was Mr. Lyndsay. There was a sort of protection in his presence which made her like to be near him: some unknown evil hung over her, from which it seemed as if he only could deliver her; and when he entered the room and approached her, she welcomed him with the only look of gladness that had brightened her face that day.

Although Lyndsay was pretty well aware of Mrs. St. Clair's real character, and saw, moreover, that she had some strong motive for wishing to mislead him, still her words had made some little impression upon him. He gave her full credit for her anxiety to detach her daughter from Colonel Delmour ; but he was somewhat sceptical as to her sincerity in wishing to bestow her upon him. He saw that Gertrude loved with all the delusion of romance, and, like many a young enthusiast, had mistaken her imagination for her mind. To have saved her from the fatal consequences of such infatuation he would have made any sacrifice, but his nature was too noble to join in a stratagem. With these feelings he drew near Gertrude; but Mrs. St. Clair had contrived to get herself and her daughter so built in by Lady Betty, her little table, her large basket, and her fat dog, that it was impossible to engage in a separate conversation. He could only talk to her, therefore, as he leant on the back of her chair, on common topics; but that he did in a manner to render even these amusing and instructive, without beino- either satirical or pedantic—for he possessed an accurate knowledge of most subjects of science and literature, and, like all really well-informed people, he threw out ideas and information without the slightest design of instructing others, or displaying his own acquirements. Insensibly Gertrude became interested in his conversation, and did not observe the entrance of the rest of the gentlemen till she heard Mr. Delmour say, in answer to a question from one of the voters —

" Certainly we may rely upon Frederick — indeed, he will probably return to Britain in the course of a very few months. It was quite unexpected, I believe, his having to accompany the regiment, as it was at one time settled that Colonel Brookes was to°take the command, and I have never heard it explained why he devolved it upon my brother; but I understand he is to follow immediately, and then unquestionably Frederick will obtain leave—so we may reckon upon him confidently."

At the first mention of Colonel Delmour's name, Gertrude had ceased to be conscious of any thing else; and, as his brother went on, she scarcely dared to breathe, lest she should lose a syllable of a subject so interesting — her very soul seemed to hang upon his words, insignificant as they were, and when he ended a deep flush of joy overspread her countenance, and lighted up her eyes.

" He will come then to clear himself from all unjust suspicions !" thought she; and as the transporting thought rushed upon her mind, she raised her eyes beaming -with delight to Lyndsay. But they met his fixed upon her with an expression so grave, so uncongenial with her own, as instantly to make her feel how little his sentiments were in unison with her own, and a slight shade of displeasure crossed her face as she turned it away. He said nothing, hut left his station, which was soon taken by Mr. Delmour, to whose insipid verbiage she listened with sustained interest, in hopes of hearing the subject renewed. But nothing more was said. Mr. Lyndsay had disappeared, and the evening wore away in a dull tedious manner.

CHAPTER XIX.

I am not a man of law that has my tongue to sell for silver or favour of the world. — John Knox.

The following day Mrs. St. Clair was confined to bed with a severe cold and rheumatism, the consequences of her walk the preceding day. All was anxious expectation, on her part and Gertrude's, for the answer from Mr. Ramsay; but the post arrived, and brought only a note from the joyful Lilly, announcing the day of her nuptials, and inviting her aunt and cousin to be present at the celebration. As Mr. Larkins had no vote, a civil refusal was immediately returned. This disappointment was only a passing knell, as the thought suggested itself that uncle Adam might not think proper to trust a bill for five hundred pounds to the post, and would most probably send it by a special messenger.

By her mother's desire, Gertrude therefore stationed herself at the window, to watch the arrival of any one likely to be the bearer of the important despatch. Not sister Anne herself looked with more wistful eyes, or was oftener called upon to declare what she saw; and when, at length, she descried the identical old red hack-chaise belonging to the White Bear rocking up the avenue—not Blue Beard himself, sword in hand, could have caused greater consternation. This was an evil Mrs. St. Clair had never contemplated — a personal inquiry set on foot by the awful uncle Adam, was an idea too dreadful to have entered into her imagination; and when it was announced that Mr. Ramsay wished to see Miss St. Clair alone, her agitation was almost too much for her. Although trembling herself, Gertrude yet tried to soothe her mother into calmness ; and

having again and again assured her that she would not betray her—that she would take the whole responsibility upon herself, she left her to obey the summons. But her heart failed her when she reached the door of the apartment where he was, and she stood some minutes with her hand on the lock ere she had courage to turn it. At length she entered, but dared not lift her eyes to the cold sour visage whose influence she felt even without seeing. She tried to say something about trouble and kindness; but, in the agitation of her mind, she could not put a sentence together — she could only invite him to sit down, and that she did with trepidation. But, instead of complying, Mr. Ramsay drew from his pocket an old black leather pocket-book, from which he took Gertrude's letter, and, showing her the superscription, asked—

" Is that your writing ? "

" It is," answered Gertrude, in a voice scarcely articulate.

" And wi' your ain free will and knowledge ?"

She could not reply; but, in silent confusion, bent her head.

" And you're in want o' five hundred pound ? "

Gertrude's colour rose to the deepest carnation, while she faintly answered— " I am."

Mr. Ramsay gave something between a hem and a groan as he drew a paper from the very inmost pocket of his venerable repository, and held it out to her ; then suddenly drawing back, and looking sternly upon her, he asked— ,

" You're no gawn to flee the country ? •— speak the truth."

Gertrude felt her very temples glow at this ignominious question; and, without speaking, there was something in her look and gesture which dispelled the old man's hasty suspicion.

" There's the money, then," said he, in a cold bitter tone.

Gertrude involuntarily shrunk from the ungracious-looking hand that was scarcely extended to her.

" Tak' it," cried he, in a still more angry voice — " tak' it; but you maun tak' this alang wi't — I would rather hae parted wi' five thousand — ay, five times five thousand, than that such a letter should hae come frae you;" and, tearing it in pieces, he threw it into the fire.

" Oh! do not say so," cried Gertrude, in great emotion, and catching his hand as he was about to leave the room.

" I maun say what I think — I'm no ane o' the folk that can say ae thing and think anither — I'm disappointed in you."

" Yet if you knew — if the circumstances "

Mr. Ramsay shook his head.

"Ay, ay,—circumstances — that's aye the cry — but they maun be ill circumstances that need aw this concealment — even frae your ain mother."

" The time may perhaps come," cried Miss St. Clair, in increasing agitation, " when I shall be able to convince you that I am not to blame — in the meantime, if you will trust me "

" Dinna think it's the money I care for," interrupted Mr. Ramsay ; " I value that five hundred pound nae mair than if it were five hundred chucky-stanes; hut I'll tell you what I valued, I valued you — and I valued your truth — and your openness — and your downrightness — and I'm disappointed in you!"

" Oh! do not judge so hardly of me," cried Gertrude ; " the time will come when you will think better of me."

" The time o' a man o' threescore and ten will no be very lang in this world — we'll maybe meet nae mair — but, before we part, there's ae thing I maun tell you — Trust me, ye'll ne'er buy true friends — nor true love — nor true happiness, o' ony kind, wi' money — so beg, and borrow, and spend, as you will, but mind my words."

" Do not — oh! do not leave me in displeasure," cried Gertrude, bursting into tears, as he was again moving away.

" I feel nae displeeshure against you— I am only vexed, and mortified, and disappointed — I had ta'en a liking to you; but, as the auld sang says,

Whene'er you meet a mutual heart,
Gold comes between and makes them part.

It was gold that parted me frae her that was aw the world to me, and it was a pleeshure to me to like you for being like her — but gold — gold — gold — has parted us next."

Gertrude had been prepared to stand the burst of uncle Adam's anger; but there was something in his querulous sorrow that went to her heart. There is, indeed, a feeling inexpressibly painful in adding to the afflictions of the aged, and heaping fresh sorrows upon the hoary head — many a bitter drop must even the most prosperous have drunk in the course of their long and weary pilgrimage, and woe be to the hand which would willingly pour fresh gall into the very dregs of their cup!

Some thought such as this filled Gertrude's heart, even to overflowing.

" My dear kind uncle!" cried she, as she again seized his hand, and even pressed it to her lips with reverence, while her tears dropped upon it—"Oh! that you could read my heart!"

Mr. Ramsay, like all caustic people, thought it necessary to be more severe as he felt himself getting soft.

" It might soon be better worth reading than your letter — but there need be nae mair said about it — let byganes be by-ganes."

" But can you — will you forgive me?"

" I hae naething to forgi'e — I tell you I value the money nae mair than the dirt beneath my feet — but I'm vexed — I'm mortified, that you should hae brought yoursel' to such straits already."

" At least, in mercy, suspend your judgment."

"That's impossible. Suspend my judgment! that's ane o' your fashionable phrases — you seem to think a man can suspend his judgment as he would hang up his hat! — I canna help judging o' what comes to my ain knowledge ; and I judge that, for a bairn like you to want five hunder pound, without the knowledge o' your ain mother, or ony relation ye hae, canna be right — it's no possible — I maun be a born ideot if I'm no fit to judge o' that; and your letter! — I wad rather hae scrap it the mool for my bread, as I wad hae blacket paper to beg for siller!"

And taking up his little old bare shapeless beaver, he was moving away. Gertrude saw with grief it was in vain to attempt to clear herself in Mr. Ramsay's eyes; he was evidently no less displeased at the demand than disgusted by the manner in which it had been made. Indeed, in proportion as he despised money himself, so he seemed to despise those who set any value upon it; and while he literally looked upon his purse as trash, nothing enraged him so much as a direct attack upon it.

" I am very unhappy at having lost your good opinion," said Gertrude, in a tone of deep dejection — "but nothing shall ever make me forget your kindness, my dear — dear uncle — may God bless you!"

Mr. Ramsay made no reply — his heart yearned to the image of his beloved Lizzie, and he was on the point — not of taking her to his breast, for that was a weakness he would have blushed at even in thought, — but of holding out his cold blue jointless hand, and of according his forgiveness. He, however, checked himself as he thought of the magnitude of the offence, and the encouragement it would be giving to that, in his estimation, the most heinous of all offences — extravagance. With a sort of repressed " Weel — weel!" and a small wave of his hand, he therefore moved on without betraying his emotion, and seated himself in his old chaise, satisfied that he had done his duty in discountenancing vice by being as disagreeable as possible.

How rarely can we judge of people's hearts by their manners I and how seldom do we see " the manner suited to the action," except in skilful actors or untaught children! How many a soft smile covers an unkind deed! — while it sometimes happens that we meet with acts of friendship from those who would be ready to " bandy words with us as a dog." But how much is it to be regretted when charity and good-will thus assume the garb of enmity, and when kind-hearted people convey their admonitions in a manner calculated to make us dislike the reprover, even while we admit the justice of the reproof!

On the present occasion Mr. Ramsay's roughness and asperity produced no corresponding emotions in Gertrude's gentle heart. She felt only regret and sorrow at having been the

means of embittering the scanty measure of the old man's enjoyment, and of having, she feared, for ever forfeited his good opinion and affection.

CHAPTER XX.

Qu'un ami veritable est une douce chose ! La Fontaine.

But Mrs. St. Clair was in no mood to sympathize in the nature of her daughter's distress, as her own joy at receiving the money seemed to absorb every other consideration.

" There is still something for you to do, Gertrude, love," said she. " I had promised to have some conversation with Mr. Lyndsay to-day; but you see my situation, and how unfit I am for such an exertion. You will, therefore, represent it to him, and, at the same time, convey to him my determination to meet him to-morrow, coute qu'il coute ;" then, reading surprise in her daughter's countenance, she added, in a solemn tone, " Gertrude, whatever has appeared strange and mysterious in my conduct towards you, I am now going to confide to him — will that satisfy you ? "

" Is it possible!" exclaimed Miss St. Clair, in an accent of astonishment and pleasure ; " then, I am sure, all will be right."

" Mr. Lyndsay appears to have made very rapid strides in your good graces," said her mother, with a look of displeasure. " Yesterday you seemed to me to be scarcely upon speaking terms. — Well, although I am no great admirer, scarcely a believer, in Platonics in general — yet there may be exceptions, when there is Methodism in the case;—you may, therefore, indulge in a sentimental religious flirtation if you will, though I must always think a daughter's best friend must be her mother; at any rate, she will be cautious how she talks of her mother, and suffers others to do it — you have simply to deliver my message, and beware of all comments. Now give me my writing materials—light that taper, and leave me."

Accustomed as she was to her mother's crooked policy even in the merest trifles, Gertrude's mind misgave her that something very false lay at the bottom of this pretended confidence ; and she could not repress the painful suspicion that it was all a scheme to dupe him and deceive her. She, however, sought her cousin for the purpose of delivering her message ; but it was not without embarrassment she repeated it, and she thought she read doubt and distrust in the manner in which he received it. Without expressing their mutual thoughts, both felt that sort of intuitive knowledge of what was passing in each other's minds, which needed not the aid of words to impart. Nothing could be said, indeed, to serve any purpose, beyond that of mere speculation and conjecture; and although to many a mind there is nothing more delightful than that sort of guess-gossip, yet Mr. Lyndsay's rose superior to any such petty enjoyment, and he rather sought to divert Gertrude's from dwelling on so disagreeable a subject.

To-morrow came as to-morrow hitherto has done ; but, as is equally common, to-morrow fulfilled not the hopes of yesterday. Mrs. St. Clair's malady had assumed a more serious aspect. A physician was called in, who pronounced her disorder to be an acute rheumatic and nervous fever, which, though not of a malignant nature, was likely to prove severe and tedious in its operation. Here could be no deception; and as Gertrude was almost wholly confined to her mother's apartment, Mr. Lyndsay felt his presence was useless, and therefore resolved on returning home. But, before he went, he sought an interview with Miss St. Clair.

" I flattered myself," said he, " that before I lost sight of you again, I should at least have had the satisfaction of knowing the nature of the evils you are exposed to — but Mrs. St. Clair's situation puts an end to that hope for the present. I trust I leave you in safety, and I shall not stay long away; but if, in my absence, any thing should occur to alarm you, promise that you will write to me instantly." Seeing her hesitate, he quickly added, " I am not seeking to engage you in any clandestine correspondence. I abhor all concealment as much as you can do, but — must I say it? — you require a protector."

" I have my mother—my uncle," said she, faintly; for she felt that her lips belied her when she named her mother, and she shrunk from the idea of appealing to her uncle ; " and, besides," added she, " I have mamma's solemn assurance that this person has left Scotland, probably for ever;" but the manner in which she said this showed how little reliance she placed on this assurance.

" I cannot, to you, say what I think," said Mr. Lyndsay ; " but will you then promise, if ever you have the slightest reason to

suppose you are again to encounter the insolence of that man "

and Lyndsay's soft mild eyes flashed fire as he spoke, " promise me, then, that you will instantly claim Lord Rossville's protection."

But Gertrude dared not promise, and she remained silent.

" As it is," continued he, " I scarcely know whether I am justified in withholding from him what I have witnessed "

" Oh! do not—my dear cousin, do not, I beseech you, breathe a syllable of what has passed to Lord Rossville, or any one else — for my sake do not "

" For your sake I would do much — well, then, you give me your word "

" Do not urge me—why should you involve yourself in trouble— perhaps in danger — forme? — already you have risked

your life to save mine.—No, leave me to my fate, whatever it is."

" I hate the word fate," said Lyndsay ; " like chance, it is ' a word easily pronounced, but nothing more ;' so I shall not leave you to any thing so vague and mystical. As for me, I am no duellist; and, besides, this person scarcely appears to be of that rank in society which would what is called entitle him to such satisfaction. Be assured, therefore, you will find me a bloodless champion; but without some assurance from you, I will not leave you unprotected."

Gertrude gave him her hand.

" My dear, generous cousin!" said she, much affected by the interest he showed for her, " I promise that if ever I am again in difficulty, and can have recourse to your assistance, I will — more I cannot, I dare not promise."

" Then, with that I must be satisfied—look upon me as your friend, my dear cousin, and let us leave the rest to Heaven.— Farewell!"

Lyndsay's absence caused a blank to Gertrude, which she in vain tried to fill up; for, to an affectionate heart and refined taste, what can supply the want of that social intercourse which is the very aliment of the soul ? Nothing could be more triste than this state of existence. The only varieties she experienced were in the querulous complaints of her mother — the verbose harangues of Lord Rossville — the senseless questions of Lady Betty—and the twice-told compliments of Mr. Delmour.

" Is this life ? " sighed she — " Ah! how different from what I had pictured it to myself! —' And thus I am absorbed, and this is life!'"

" But Gertrude only felt what all persons of acute sensibility have felt in similar situations, that " to be no part of any body is to be as nothing."

CHAPTER XXI.

Avaunt! and quit my sight! — let the earth hide thee ! Macbeth.

The dreary monotony of a snow-storm now reigned in all its morbid solemnity. All nature was shrouded in one common covering — neither heavens nor earth offered any variety to the wearied sight — any sound to the listening ear. All was sameness and stillness — 'twas as the pulse of life stood still — of time congealed; or if a sound perchance broke the dreary silence that reigned, it fell with that dull muffled tone which only denoted tUe still burdened atmosphere.

Nothing can be more desolate and depressing than this exterior of nature to those who, assembled under one roof, are yet

strangers to those fireside enjoyments, that home-horn happiness which springs from social intercourse. Here were no intimate delights — no play of fancy — no pleasures to deceive the hours and embellish existence. Here was nothing to palliate dullness —nothing to give time a zest — nothing to fill the void of an unfurnished brain. There was stupor of mind, without tranquillity of soul — restlessness of body, without animation of spirit. Gertrude felt her heart drop beneath the oppressive gloom which surrounded her, and thought even actual suffering must be preferable to this total stagnation of all enjoyment. But,

. . . . All human things a day

In darkness sinks — a day to light restores.

It was drawing towards the close of a day when the snow had fallen without intermission, but was now beginning to abate. Lord Rossville stood at his drawing-room window speculating on the aspect of the clouds, and predicting a change of weather, when he suddenly uttered an exclamation which attracted the whole of the family to where he stood.

A huge black object was dimly discernible entering the avenue, and dragging its ponderous length towards the castle; but -what was its precise nature the still falling snow prevented their ascertaining. But suddenly the snow ceased — the clouds rolled away — and a red brassy glare of the setting sun fell abruptly on this moving phenomenon, and disclosed to view a stately full-plumed hearse. There was something so terrific, yet so picturesque in its appearance, as it ploughed its way through waves of snow — its sable plumes, and gilded skulls, nodding and grinning in the now livid glimmering of the fast-sinking sun — that all stood transfixed with alarm and amazement. At length the prodigy drew near, followed by two attendants on horseback; it drew up at the grand entrance — the servants gathered round — one of the men began to remove the end board, that threshold of death

" This is — is " gasped the Earl, as he tried to throw open

the window and call to his servants ; but the window was frozen, and, ere his lordship could adopt another expedient, his fury was turned from the dead to the living; for there was lifted out — not " a slovenly unhandsome corpse, betwixt the wind and his nobility," but the warm, sentient, though somewhat discomfited, figure of Miss Pratt. All uttered some characteristic exclamation ; but Lord Rossville's tongue clove to the very roof of his mouth, and he in vain laboured to find words suited to the occasion.

Whether the contents of the hearse should be permitted to enter his castle walls from such a conveyance, was a doubt in itself so weighty as for the moment to overpower every faculty of mind and body. True, to refuse admission to one of the blood of Rossville — a cousin to himself—the cousin of many noble families — the aunt of Mr. Whyte of Whyte Hall — would be a

strong measure. Yet to sanction such a violation of all propriety ! —to suffer such an example of disrespect to the living— of decorum to the dead ! — to receive into his presence a person just issued from a hearse!—Who could tell what distempers she might not bring in her train ? That thought decided the matter. — His lordship turned round to ring the bell, and, in doing so, found both hands locked in those of Miss Pratt! The shock of a man-trap is pi*obably faint compared to that which he experienced at finding himself in the grasp of the fair, and all powers of resistance failed under the energy of her hearty shake.

" Well, my lord, what do you think of my travelling equipage?— my Jerusalem dilly, as Anthony Whyte calls it?—Ton my word, you must make much of me — for a pretty business I've had to get here; I may well say I've come through thick and thin to get to you ; at one time, I assure you, I thought you would never have seen me but in my coffin — and a great mercy it is, it's only in a hearse. I fancy I'm the first that ever thought themselves in luck to get into one ; but, however, I think I'm still luckier in having got well out of it — ha ! ha! ha!"

" Miss Pratt!" heaved the Earl as with a lever.

" Well, you shall hear all about it by and by. In the meantime, I must beg the favour of you to let the men put up their hearse and horses for the night —for it's perfectly impossible for them to go a step farther — and, indeed, I promised, that if they would but bring me safe here, you would make them all welcome to a night's lodging, poor creatures.!"

This was a pitch of assurance so far beyond any thing Lord Rossville had ever contemplated, that his words felt like stones in his throat, and he strove, but strove in vain, to get them up, and hurl them at Pratt's audacious jaws. Indeed, all ordinary words and known language would have been inadequate for his purpose. Only some mighty terror-compelling compound, or some magical anathema—something which would have caused her to sink into the ground — or have made her quit the form of a woman, and take that of an insect, would have spoke the feelings of his breast. While his lordship Mas thus gasping (like one under the influence of the nightmare) for utterance, Miss Pratt called to one of the servants, who just then entered —

" Jackson, you'll be so good as see these men well taken care of—and I hope Bishop will allow a good feed to the horses, poor beasts ! and "

" Miss Pratt!" at length bolted the Earl—" Miss Pratt, this conduct of yours is of so extraordinary—so altogether unparalleled a nature, that "

" You may well say that, my lord — unparalleled indeed, if you knew all."

" There's eight horses and four men," said Lady Betty, who had been pleasing her fancy by counting them. " Who's burial is it ? "

" It's Mr. M'Vitae's, the great distiller.—I'm sure, I'm much obliged to him—for if it hadn't been for him, poor man ! I might have been stiff and stark by this time." And Miss Pratt busied herself in taking off her snow-shoes, and turning and chafing herself before the fire.

" Miss Pratt," again began the Earl, mustering all his energies —" Miss Pratt, it is altogether inconceivable and inexplicable to me how you, or any one else, could possibly so far forget what was due to themselves and me as to come to my bouse in a manner so wholly unprecedented, so altogether unwarrantable, so—so—so perfectly unjustifiable — I say, how any person or persons could thus presume "

A burst of laughter from Miss Pratt here broke in upon the Earl's harangue.

" My dear Lord Rossville, I beg your pardon ; but really the notion of my presuming to come in a hearse is too good—'pon my word, it's a piece of presumption few people would be guilty of, if they could help it. I assure you I felt humble enough when I was glad to creep into it."

" I repeat presume, Miss Pratt," cried his lordship, now fairly kindled into eloquence, " to presume to bring to my house an equipage and attendants of—of—of the most hideous description —and farther, to presume to expect that I am to permit the hearse of Mr. M'Vitae, the distiller—the—the democratic distiller, with eight horses and four men, to—to—to—to—to transform Rossville Castle into an inn—a—a caravansera of the very lowest description—a—a—a charnel-house—a—a—a receptacle for vehicles employed for the foulest—the vilest—the—the most unseemly of all purposes !—Jackson, desire those people, with their carriage and horses, to quit my grounds without one moment's delay."

" My dear Lord Rossville ! — (stop, Jackson)—Bless my heart! you're not going to turn away the people at this time of night! — Only look how it's snowing, and the sky as black as pitch —there's neither man nor beast fit to travel a foot this night.— Jackson, I'm sure you must be sensible that it's perfectly impossible for them to find their way now."

Jackson, who had, like his betters, felt considerable ennui during the storm, and rather rejoiced at the thoughts of any visitors, however inferior to himself in rank and station, confirmed the assertion with all due respect—but to little purpose.

" At all events, whatever may be the consequence," said his master, " they certainly can, and indeed positively must, return by the road which they have recently traversed."

" They may just as well attempt to fly as to go back the way they came — a pretty fight they had to get through ! I only wish you had seen it—the horses up to their shoulders more than once in the snow even then, and it's now snowing ten times worse than ever—so I leave you to judge how they are to drag a hearse back nine miles at this time of night."

Here Jackson re-entered with a manifesto from the hearse-drivers and company, stating that they had been brought two miles and a half out of their way, under promise of being provided in quarters for the night, and that it was now impossible for them to proceed.

" It will be a pretty story if I'm landed in a lawsuit," cried Miss Pratt, in great alarm, as the Earl was about to reiterate his orders ; " and it will make a fine noise in the county, I can tell you."

Mr. Delmour, who had been out investigating matters, here struck in; and having remarked that it might be an unpopular measure, recommended that Mr. M'Vitae's suite should be accommodated for the night, with strict charges to depart by dawn the following morning; and the Earl, though with great reluctance, was prevailed upon to agree to this arrangement.

CHAPTER XXII.

Our life is but a pilgrimage of blasts ;
And every blast brings forth a fear,
And every fear a death. Quarles.

Miss Pratt having carried her point, and dried, warmed, fed, and cherished her person in all possible ways, now commenced the narrative of what she called her unparalleled adventures. But, as has been truly said, there are always two ways of telling a story, and Miss Pratt's biographer and herself are by no means at one as to the motives which led to this extraordinary expedition. Miss Pratt set forth that she had been living most comfortably at Skinflint Cottage, where she had been most kindly-treated, and much pressed to prolong her visit; but she had taken an anxious fit about her good friends at Rossville,—she had had a great dreaming about them the night before last, and she could not rest till she had seen them all. She had, therefore, borrowed the Skinflint carriage, and set out at the risk of her life—but the horses had stuck in the snow, &c. &c. &c.

Miss Pratt's biographer, on the other hand, asserts that Miss Pratt, in the course of circulation, had landed at Skinflint Cottage, which she sometimes used as a stepping-stone, but never as a resting-place; here, however, she had been taken prisoner by the snow-storm, and confined for a week in a small house full of children — some in measles — some in scarlet fevers — some in hooping-coughs — the only healthy individuals two strong unruly boys, just broke loose from school for the holidays. The fare was bad — her bed was hard — her blankets heavy — her pillows few—her curtains thin—and her room, ^vhich was

R 2

next to the nursery, to use her own expression, " smoked like a killogie."*

To sum up the whole, it was a retreat of Miss Becky Duguid's, and at this very time Miss Becky was in such requisition that it was resolved to send the carriage for her — in the double hope that, as Rossville Castle was in the way, their guest would avail herself of the opportunity of taking her departure. Accordingly, a pair of old, stiff, starved, superannuated horses, were yoked to a large heavy family coach, to which Miss Pratt joyfully betook herself, even in the very teeth of the storm. But the case was a desperate one; for she had received several broad hints about one of the children in the hooping-cough, Charles Fox by name, having taken a fancy to sleep with her, in consequence of her having, in an unwary fit of generosity, presented it with a peppermint drop. All these minute particulars, however, Miss Pratt passed over, which occasioned some little discrepancy betwixt herself and her faithful biographer; but from this point they can now proceed hand in hand.

The old horses tugged their way through the snow most manfully till they came to Cocklestonetop Muir, and there it lay so deep as to baffle their utmost exertions. After every other alternative had been tried in vain, there remained no other than to leave the carriage; and for Miss Pratt, her green bag,, and the coachman to mount the horses, and proceed to the nearest habitation. But the snow fell thick and fast — Miss Pratt could not keep her seat on the bare back of a huge stiff plough-horse, whose every movement threatened dislocation, if not dissolution;

and even her dauntless spirit was sinking beneath the horrors of her situation, when, as she expressed it, by mere dint of good luck, up came Mr. M'Vitae's hearse, drawn by six stout horses, who had been living for the last two days at heck and manger in Mr. M'Vitae's well-filled stables. After a little parley, and many promises, they were induced, nothing loth indeed, to turn out of the way and deposit Miss Pratt and her bag at Rossville Castle.

But even this account failed to still the tumult in the Earl's breast—there was something in having a hearse, and the hearse of Mr. M'Vitae, the radical distiller, thus forced within his walls, he could not away with. Death, even in its most dignified attitude, with all its proudest trophies, would still have been an appalling spectacle to Lord Rossville; but, in its present vulgar and almost burlesque form, it was altogether insupportable. Death is indeed an awful thing, whatever aspect it assumes. The King of Terrors gives to other attributes their power of terrifying: the thunder's bolt — the lightning's flash — the billow's roar—the earthquake's shock—all derive their dread sublimity from Death — all are but the instruments of his resistless sway.

* Kiln.

From these, and even from his more ordinary emissaries, Lord Rossville felt secure; but still a lurking fear had taken possession of his mind, and he could not divest himself of the train of ideas which had been excited by beholding, in horrid array, Death's cavalcade approach his dwelling. He passed a restless night — he thought of what the county would say, and what he should say to the county — he thought of whether he would not be justified in banishing Miss Pratt for ever from his presence. When the first faint grey streak of light appeared, he rang his bell to inquire whether the funeral procession had departed; but a fresh fall of snow during the night had placed the castle and hearse in a complete state of blockade. He rose and opened the window to ascertain the fact, but nothing was to be seen but a fast-falling blinding snow — he next went to the door, but there the snow lay six feet deep — he returned to bed, but not to sleep — and when his servant entered in the morning, he found his master a lifeless corse.

Whence it came, who can tell ? Whether from cold, apoplexy, mental disquiet, or irreversible decree ?

" When houre of death is come, let none aske whence nor why!"

CHAPTER XXIII.

And feel I, Death, no joy from thought of thee ? Young.

Gertrude was now Countess of Rossville, and how often had her heart bounded at the anticipation! How slight a thing seems the life or death of an individual to whom we are united by no ties of affection, when merely thought of as " to be or not to be," and Death and his awful attributes are not made manifest to our senses! But how sad and solemn when we come to witness, even in those most alien to us, the last struggle—the dread change—the total extinction of mortality!

As the youthful Countess looked on her uncle's cold remains, she forgot all her dreams of vanity, and wept in real sadness, as she thought how many a painful emotion of anger and disappointment she had excited in that now still unconscious form. Oh! how bitter are the upbraidings which come to us from the lips of the dead! Would that the living could lay the too tardy reflection to heart!

Gertrude could not blame herself; but she sorrowed in the sorrow of a warm ingenuous heart that she should ever have offended the pale and peaceful image now stretched before her. But tears, though shed in earnest, are, alas! often shed in vain.

As from the wing no scar the sky retains. The parted wave no furrow from the keel; So dies in human hearts the thought of death,
>   when that thought is not embalmed by affection.

The funeral obsequies were celebrated with a pomp of heraldry — a display of solemn state, which would, if aught on earth could, have brightened the dull cold eye of the dead to have witnessed.

The Earl had left no settlements — he had destroyed his original ones, and been planning others of a totally different nature, which, had he lived, would certainly have been put in execution, to the utter exclusion of Lady Rossville, unless as the wife of Mr. Delmour.

Gertrude wished for nothing more ardently than for an opportunity of coming to an explanation with that gentleman, and at once putting an end to the delusion under which he evidently laboured. But there was so much formal politeness — so little of the energy of passion, in his addresses, that she felt it would be like anticipating, were she to appear to look upon him in the light of a lover.

She was, therefore, obliged to endure tne annoyance of his little punctilious assiduities, which, though for ever claiming her notice, were yet too vapid and insignificant either to please or offend—they were merely flat, stale, and unprofitable. From these she was soon, however, unexpectedly released. A few days after the Earl's funeral an express arrived with the intelligence of the death of his cousin, the Marquis of Haslingden — he had died of the breaking of a blood-vessel, and, in so doing, had rendered Mr. Delmour presumptive heir to the dukedom. As his presence was now required in the south, he immediately set about preparations for his departure; but, previous to setting off, he sought an interview with Lady Rossville, for the purpose of expressing his regret at being under the necessity of leaving her at such a time, and his assurances of returning as speedily as the nature of the mournful circumstances under which he was called away would permit — concluding with the hope that, whenever propriety sanctioned the fulfilling of his late lamented uncle's intentions, his fair cousin would at once testify her respect for the wishes of the dead, and complete the happiness of the living. However much Gertrude had longed for this opportunity, she now felt, as every delicate mind must feel in a similar situation, that 'tis a nervous and a painful thing to tell a person face to face,

> I don't like you, Dr. Fell, The reason why, 1 cannot tell; But I don't like you Dr. Fell;

for, however it may be expressed, that is generally the substance of a refusal. The words must be uttered, however, in some shape or other; and, collecting herself, she, with that self-possession which, in such cases, speaks even plainer than words,

> expressed her regret at the misunderstanding that had so long been allowed to exist — assured him that the Earl had been perfectly aware of her sentiments — they were such as made it impossible she ever could do honour to her uncle's intentions.

— Politician as he was, Mr. Delmour could not conceal the surprise and pique with which he received this communication. He had all along been led to consider his union with the heiress of Rossville as a settled point — he had, therefore, looked upon her as his destined bride — fortunately a very beautiful, charming, elegant girl, to whom it was his part to be more than usually polite and attentive — and now, at the very moment when he had extended his hand to seize the prize, like a second Ixion, he found he had grasped a cloud. But whatever were his feelings on the occasion, he had too much pride to express any thing beyond mere surprise at the very awkward and unaccountable misapprehension which had thus involved both parties in so unpleasant a dilemma. He certainly could not accuse Gertrude of having varied with the circumstances of her fortune, since his own was now, to all appearance, much more brilliant than at the commencement of their acquaintance; but it was evident he thought himself extremely ill used by her, and therefore took a very distant and stately farewell.

When informed of Mr. Delmour's dismissal, Mrs. St. Clair's indignation against her daughter was no less violent than unaccountable.

" You were born to be my ruin!" was her first exclamation. — " To refuse, situated as you are, an alliance that would have secured you against the possibility of You know not what you have done — infatuated that you are!"—And she paced the chamber with a disordered mien; while Gertrude, too much accustomed to her mother's wayward moods to attach any peculiar meaning to her words, in silence allowed the storm to take its course. But, as is commonly the case with unjust displeasure, it took such a wide range, and branched out into so many ramifications of anger and invective, that " labour dire and weary woe" it would be to attempt to follow her through all the labyrinths of her ill-humour. Mrs. St. Clair was, indeed, a riddle hard to solve. Although not quite so hypocritical as to pretend to be inconsolable at the death of the Earl, yet certain it was that event had agitated her in no common manner or degree. And her daughter's exaltation, which, for so many years, had been the sole object of her ambition, seemed, noAV that it was obtained, to have lost all its value in her eyes — the only visible effect it had yet produced had been to render her more than ever violent, irritable, and capricious. She still kept her own apartment — refused to see anybody on the plea of her health—was restless and dissatisfied—and, in short, showed all the symptoms of a mind ill at ease.

R 4

CHAPTER XXIV.

Love!
There is no spirit under heaven that works
With such delusion. Ben Jonson.

The want of a will is a desideratum which invariably causes disappointment to many an expectant. Perhaps, on the late occasion, no one felt more chagrined at this failure of the Earl's than Miss Pratt. Although there was little difference in their ages, yet from being of a lighter and more active nature, she had always looked upon herself as at least twenty years younger, and had all along settled in her own mind that he was to die long before her; and from having at first contemplated the possibility of his leaving her a small legacy, she had next considered it as highly probable that he would leave her something very handsome, and, at length, all her doubts had resolved themselves into the absolute certainty of his doing something highly to his own credit. Not, to do her justice, that she looked to it merely for her own aggrandizement, but as something to bequeath to Anthony Whyte in his necessities; as she declared that, in these times, Anthony found he was pinched enough with his three thousand a-year.

Mi^s Pratt could not, therefore, reconcile herself to this desideratum ; but spent her days in rummaging the house, and expressing her amazement (which, far from lessening, seemed daily to increase) that the will—for a will there must be — should be missing, and her nights in dreaming that the will had been found. The will, she was certain, would cast up yet — nobody knew poor Lord Rossville better than she did — she might say they had been like brother and sister all their lives ; and nobody that knew him — worthy, well-meaning man that he was ! — could ever believe that he would go out of the world, and leave things all at sixes and sevens. Not so much as ten guineas even for a mourning ring to his oldest friends and nearest relations — the thing was quite impossible. She only wished she had access to his repositories, she was sure she would soon bring something to light — some bit paper, or letter, or jotting, or something or another, just to show what his intentions were; and she was sure Lady Rossville would willingly act up to it, whatever it was—for he was a just, upright, friendly, liberal, well-pincipled, well-meaning, kind-hearted man—an honourable-minded man, with a great deal of strong natural affection — a man that had always, and upon all occasions, shown himself her steady friend and well-wisher, &c. &c. &c. There was one drawer in particular, the right-hand drawer of his writing-table, the end next the window —she had several

times, when she had occasion to speak to him in his study, found him busy there. — Poor man! the very last time she saw him there, he was working amongst some papers in that very drawer—she wondered if it had been well searched, and so on.

Gertrude had no doubt but that due search had been made there as in other places by the constituted authorities — and she had too much respect for the late Earl's feelings when living to suffer Miss Pratt to invade his repositories now that he was dead ; but, weary of hearing the same changes rung upon this drawer, she one day suddenly resolved to examine it and some other of her uncle's private repositories. For that purpose she repaired to his apartment, and began her scrutiny. It was with a feeling of solemnity she displayed the relics of the departed, and sought in vain for any indication of his will or intentions — nothing of the kind was to be seen, for nothing of the kind was in existence—only bundles of bills and packets of letters were contained in the drawer, which Miss Pratt had vainly flattered herself held her future fortunes. The Countess was about to close it, when her eye was arrested by one of those packets—it was titled, " Correspondence with Colonel F. Del-mour—Private—No. 1."

" Can this be the correspondence," thought she, " on which the happiness of my life depends ?" and her colour ebbed and flowed as the contending emotions of hope and fear rushed over her heart. " And am I justified in thus stealing on the secrets of the dead?—is it right—is it honourable?" she paused— " Yet my all of happiness is at stake—why should I hesitate?" And with a trembling hand she unfolded the copy of a letter from Lord Rossville, written, it seemed, on his first discovering the attachment that existed. It was very angry and very wordy; and the substance of it was calling upon his nephew instantly to resign all pretensions to Miss St. Clair's hand, and to authorize him to annul any engagement subsisting between them, upon pain of his most serious displeasure. Gertrude's heart throbbed violently as she turned to the answer to this, in the well-known, careless, elegant hand of her lover. It was short —expressed the deepest regret at having incurred his uncle's displeasure — pleaded the excess of his passion as the only excuse, and declared, in the most unequivocal terms, the utter impossibility there was in his ever complying with his lordship's commands by relinquishing that which was dearer to him than life.

Tears of delight burst from Gertrude's eyes as she read this decided avowal of unalterable attachment.

" How could I be so base as ever to doubt — ungenerous that I am ! " was her first exclamation ; and, in the exultation of the moment, she felt as though worlds could never again for a moment shake her faith. But there were more letters to peruse. The next in order was another from Lord Rossville. It was in

part a repetition of what her uncle had said to herself, when he declared his intention of disinheriting her and settling the estates upon Mr. Delmour; but his resolutions were still more strongly expressed and fully detailed in the letter ; and he concluded by an offer of instantly paying his nephew's debts, and settling ten thousand pounds upon him, provided he would come under an engagement never to marry Miss St. Clair.

" This, then, is the test!" thought Gertrude ; and, with a beating heart, she opened another letter in Colonel Delmour's hand-writing, and read as follows: —

" My dear Uncle, " It was only on my return here late last night that I found your letter ; and I have passed a sleepless night ruminating on the heartrending alternative you offer to me. Were my own interests solely at stake, I should not hesitate a single moment; —but the thought of reducing the adored object of my affections to poverty — of being the means of bereaving her of the possessions of her ancestors, and depriving her of your favour, is so overwhelming, that I find myself quite unable to come to any conclusion at present. Heaven knows how much I could endure for her sake ! but it is torture to me to think of her sacrificing so much for mine. Yet, to resign her for ever, is distraction. I repeat, it is impossible for me all at once to resolve upon a point on which the happiness of my life is at issue. Pray, allow me a few days to form my resolution, and believe it is my most earnest wish to gratify you in all possible ways. The regiment is on the point of embarking for Gibraltar; but I expect Brookes to take the command, and that I shall obtain leave to remain at home for the present. You shall hear from me again whenever I can summon resolution to cast the die. Meantime, you will, of course, suspend all farther proceedings. Believe me,

" My dear Uncle, " Yours, with the sincerest esteem and affection,

" F. M. H. Delmour.

" P. S.—You may rely upon my secrecy; and I agree with you that it is better Robert should not be made acquainted with what has passed — at present."

Here was " confirmation strong as proofs of holy writ," to the generous, confiding heart of Gertrude.

Yes! it was upon her account that he hesitated — it was for her nappiness that he was tempted to sacrifice his own! — Ah ! how little did he know her, if he deemed that wealth and grandeur could ever stand in competition with his affection — that, the peculiar treasure of her soul — that, the pearl of great price — the rest, was it not all mere eaithly dross ? . Without that, what were rank and fortune to her ? But to share them — to bestow

them upon the chosen of her heart, was indeed a blissful privilege ! And the whole tenor of her mind became bright as

The first blush of the sun-gilded air.

Impatient to vindicate the honour of her lover, she hastened to her mother's apartment. She found Mrs. St. Clair in the same posture in which she had so frequently observed her since the Earl's death — seated at a writing-table—her head resting on one hand—a pen in the other, as if meditating how to begin a letter, which after all this preparation, did not appear yet to have been commenced.

With cheeks glowing, and eyes sparkling with triumph and delight, Gertrude placed the packet in her hands.

" Read these, mamma," said she, in a tone of exultation — " and if ever you had a doubt, surely these must satisfy you."

Mrs. St. Clair took the letters, and read them in silence; then, as she folded up the last, she said, with a sarcastic smile —

" My doubts are indeed ended — I am now confirmed in what I have all along suspected: Colonel Delmour loved you from the first as the heiress of Rossville — as the Countess of Rossville I have no doubt he will adore you."

Gertrude was struck dumb : her mother went on —

" It is evident to me — it would be to any one in their senses — that the only struggle here is caused by self-interest. He, like many other people, doubted whether Lord Rossville really possessed the power of disinheriting you; and he, therefore, prudently evades the question, until he has ascertained that point. It would have been selling his right, indeed, for a mess of pottage, to have resigned the heiress to twenty thousand a-year for a paltry ten thousand pounds, and the payment of his tailor's bill; but, on the other hand "

" It is enough," said Lady Rossville, as, with a burning cheek, and in a tone of wounded feeling, she collected the letters, and was turning to leave the room.

" No, Gertrude, it is not enough," cried her mother, pointing to her to be seated; " sit down, and listen to me, at least with calmness, if not with respect — I will not be interrupted — I will be heard."

Her daughter seated herself in silence, but evidently struggling with her feelings.

" I cannot see you as I do, the dupe of an artful unprincipled man, without making an effort to open your eyes to the dangers of your situation — yet I own I almost despair when I behold you thus wilfully closing them against the light, which wc old carry conviction to any mind that was not the slave of its own delusions — yes, I repeat, it is clear as noonday that it is solely as the heiress of Rossville you are the object of Colonel Del-mour's attachment. He hesitate about reducing the adored object of his affections to poverty! he distracted at the thoughts of

bereaving her of the possessions of her ancestors! — stuff! — who that knows any thing of the character of the man would, for an instant, believe that he would hesitate about sacrificing the whole world, were it to promote his own interest? Gertrude, I would not unnecessarily pain you, but I consider it my duty to save you from the snares I see set for you.—Why should you distrust me ? —What interest can I have in deceiving you, my child?"

" I know not — I cannot tell," said the Countess, with a sigh; " If I am distrustful "

She stopped, but Mrs. St. Clair felt the reproach implied in her look and accent.

"'Tis I who have made you so, you would say — you can distrust me, your guide — your companion — your friend — your mother!" Mrs. St. Clair's voice here faltered with emotion — " although you cannot even doubt the faith of one who, but a few months since, was an utter stranger to you."

"But in those few months, what have I not learnt?" said Lady Rossville, in much agitation ; " enough to make me sometimes doubt the evidence of my own senses — certainly enough to teach me to distrust even my own mother."

Mrs. St. Clair's face crimsoned.

" Beware how you provoke me, Gertrude!" cried she, with much vehemence ; " I will endure no taunts or reproaches from you. Although, as Countess of Rossville, you may wish to forget what is due to me as your mother, I will not relinquish my claims to you as my daughter — I will be obeyed!" continued she, with increasing violence, " and I command you from henceforth to think of that man no more."

" Then you command me to do what is impossible," said the Countess, giving way to tears. " Oh, mamma! why will you force me to this alternative ? Why must I be accounted rebellious — undutiful — because I cannot see as you see, and think as you think ? I call Heaven to witness, I would ever render to you the respect — the reverence of a child; but I cannot — no, I cannot — yield you the submission of a slave."

" And where is the child who owes to a parent what you owe to me ?" demanded Mrs. St. Clair, warmly; " where is the child possessed of such an inheritance — of rank — of power — of riches — of beauty — of talents ? — and where is the mother who would not feel as I do, at seeing them all sacrificed to the cupidity of an artful unprincipled man ? "

"And is it because I possess all these advantages that I am to be denied the privilege of the poorest and the humblest?" asked Lady Rossville, her voice faltering with emotion. "Of what value to me are all those gifts, if I may not share them with those I love? — ah! how much rather would I forego them all"

"Than not indulge your own weak, wayward, childish fancy," cried her mother, with indignation: "this is not to be borne! How shall I tear that bandage from your eyes! — If you doubt me, will you credit the testimony of your friend — your counsellor — your Platonic admirer, Mr. Lyndsay?"

"I respect and esteem Mr. Lyndsay," said the Countess; "but I will not adopt his prejudices."

"Will you believe the voice of tbe world, then?"

"I already know all that the world caD say. It will tell me he is thoughtless — extravagant — imprudent—erring, it may be, in many things; but all that he has told me himself— such he once was — till — till he loved."

Mrs. St. Clair groaned. "Then whose testimony will you admit, since you reject mine?—You reject Mr. Lyndsay's —you reject that of the whole world."

"I will receive none," said Lady Rossville, mildly, but firmly. — "Erring, perhaps faulty, he may have been; but to doubt that he loves me there I will receive no one's testimony but his .own."

"Then you are lost!" exclaimed Mrs. St. Clair, in violent agitation. — "But it must not — shall not be. You dare not marry without my consent — without the consent of" she stopped — "I tell you"

"If I am to be ruled by any authority, it must be solely by my mother's," said Gertrude, proudly; "no other being has, or ever can have, the right to control me in this point. Once before I promised that I would form no engagement without your consent until I had attained the age of twenty-one — I am now willing to repeat it — but, in the meantime, my preference must be left free. And now, mamma, let us end this strife — it may be my misfortune to differ from you — do not — oh! do not let that difference divide us! — I will be always yours in affection, if not in sentiment." — And she would have embraced her, but her mother repelled her.

"Such a compromise is a mere mockery," said she, with bitterness; "but I too am sick of altercation — such as it is, then, for the present your promise must suffice — let me trust in Heaven that your delusion may be dispelled ere it be too late!"

"If it is a delusion, I too join in the prayer," said the Countess, but more in the tone of lofty assurance than of lowly supplication.

This contest with her mother only served to strengthen Gertrude — as violence invariably does — in her own opinions. There was something too in the very suspense calculated to give a play to her imagination, and fascinate the youthful heart ftur more than any sober certainty of waking bliss could have done. She would have shrunk from acknowledging even to herself that she harboured a doubt; but how many a stranger feeling mingles unknown to ourselves with the home-born sentiments of our hearts!

CHAPTER XXV.

With an old bachelor, how things miscarry!
What shall I do? Go hang myself—or marry? Horace.

There was a duty which Gertrude was particularly anxious to discharge, and that was the debt she had incurred to Mr. Adam Ramsay. Having procured a bill for the money, she therefore ordered her carriage one day; and having contrived to elude the curiosity of Lady Betty and the vigilance of Miss Pratt, she set out alone in hopes of making her peace—at any rate of relieving her mind from the weight of pecuniary obligation. A thaw had begun — but just begun; consequently, both earth and atmosphere were in that raw, chill, dubious state, which combines all the discomforts of foul and frosty weather, and even in the narrow precincts of uncle Adam's parterre both were displayed in perfection. The snow, though soft, lay deep betwixt his house and the little gate which separated him from the road; no attempt had been made to clear it away or open a passage; and an avalanche, which had fallen from the roof of the house, lay undisturbed upon the steps, and effectually blocked up the door. Altogether it had a desolate, uninhabited look, different from the neatly scraped paths and sanded steps belonging to the houses on either side ; and Gertrude began to fear, she knew not what, from this desolate exterior. Meanwhile the footman having, with some difficulty, contrived to wade up to the door, knocked loud and long in all the energy of insolence and ill humour — but no answer was returned. Again and again the summons was repeated, in a manner enough to have raised even the drowsy porter in Macbeth — but with no better success. At length the servant turned away in despair.

" There is nobody within, my lady."—But at that moment his lady's eye was caught by a view of the back of uncle Adam's wig, as its queue hung in expressive silence over a chair in the parlour. It retained its posture, however, so immovably, that it seemed as though it would have required a touch of galvanism to ascertain whether it was suspended from a dead or a living skull. Alarmed at the immobility of this appendage of uncle Adam's brain, Lady Rossville hastily called to have the carriage door opened ; and, without exactly knowing what she would or could do, she stepped out, and made the best of her way through the snow towards the house. Scarcely had she touched the door, when, to her surprise, it flew open, as if impelled by the invisible hands of the White Cat herself. No invisible hands were there, however ; for there stood uncle Adam in propria persona, with his pigtail, and his cold blue radish-looking fingers.

" Come in — come in," cried he, in no very inviting tone, as

Gertrude stood for a moment transfixed with astonishment at this sudden resuscitation ; " I'm sure this is no weather to be stannin' at open doors,"— and violently shutting it, he led the way to his little parlour. A dead fire — a dirty hearth — and the remains of a wretched breakfast, were the only traces of civilization to be descried.

" I was afraid something was the mattei'," said Gertrude, as she entered. " My servant knocked repeatedly, but could get no answer; but I am happy to find it was a false alarm, and that I have the pleasure of seeing you well, my dear uncle."

Mr. Ramsay hemmed.

" You may see something's the matter, or the things wadnae be stannin' there till this time o' day — there's naebody in the hoose but mysel'; and I wasna gawn to play the flunky to thae idle puppies o' yours," pointing to the Countess's dashing lacquey, as he strutted before the window; " and I never wish to see onybody at my door that cannot chap at it themsels ;" then, muttering between his teeth, " fules shouldnae hae chap-pin-sticks," he seemed to recover a little, at having thus vented his venom in ignominious epithets, applied to his niece and her spruce serving-man.

Lady Rossville was much at a loss how to proceed. At no time did she perfectly comprehend the breadth of uncle Adam's dialect; but, on the present occasion, he was more than usually unintelligible ; and, as she could neither divine what was meant by fules nor chappinsticks, she prudently passed them over, and proceeded to business.

" I am come to repay my debt to you," said she, in her sweetest manner ; " that is, the pecuniary part of it; but your generous trust and confidence in me I never can repay. My dear uncle, will you accept of my warmest — my most grateful thanks for your kindness? " And she put the money enclosed in a pocket-book of her own embroidering, into his hands, and affectionately pressed them as she did so.

" An' what has that to do wi't ? " demanded Mr. Ramsay, eyeing the souvenir with no gracious aspect.

" That is a pocket-book I have worked on purpose for you ; and I hope you will keep it for my sake."

" Weel, I may do sae ; though it's nonsense to gie me the like o' thae foolish things ;" and, taking out the bill, he carefully wrapt the pocket-book in a piece of paper, and opening an old bureau that stood in the corner of the room, deposited it in a little drawer, then, cautiously locking it, returned to his seat. " Next to no borrowin', the best thing's ready payin', and I'm glad to ^ 'e you hae that muckle discretion ;" and his features gradually relaxed into a more benign expression, as he slowly took out his spectacles to peruse the bill ; when, suddenly resuming their usual stormy cast — " What's this?" cried he; " whars the interest for my money ? "

In great confusion at this unthought-of demand, Gertrude apologized by saying she had been so little accustomed to money transactions, that she had entirely forgot that part of the claim.

" I think it's time you "was learnin' something o' the vaala o' money, noo that ye've learnt hoo to spend and to borrow sae readily. —I dinna care ae bodle aboot it for my ain part, but I like to see folk ken what they're aboot, and gie aw body their due ; " and taking up an old blackened stump of a pen, he began to cast up his account on the back of the bill; then showing it to Lady Rossville, " There's what I was inteetled to frae you ; but I tell you I dinna want it—I only want to mak you sensible o' what vou're aboot."

Gertrude acknowledged the justice of his admonition ; and having thanked him for it, she was again taken into favour, but it was of short duration.

" Haenae you got your feet wat wi' that snaw ?" said he, in a complacent tone — then glancing at her little silk slippers, all his wrath revived. " Bonny-like feet, to be sure, to be wadin' through the snaw ! I thought you had mair sense than till hae come oot wi' such daft-like things in such weather — they're liker dancin'-schule pumps than sensible walkin' shoes."

And uncle Adam walked up and down in great discomposure, his own huge leathern buckets creaking at every step.

" I did not know all I had to encounter, else I certainly should have provided better for it," said Gertrude, smiling ; — " but I am not at all subject to colds, so don't be alarmed on that account ; and when your servant comes in, she will dry my shoes at your kitchen fire."

" You'll sit a while before you see ony servant o' mine — I hae nae servant— and the kitchen fire's black oot."

" No servant, and no fire ! " exclaimed Lady Rossville, horror-struck at such an avowal. — " Good Heavens! what a situation ! How—what has occasioned this ? "

" Just the occasion is, that that impudent thief that's been wi' me these twa year, thought proper to own a marriage wi' a scoondrell o' a dragoon that she ne'er saw till within this month ; — and what do you think o' her assurance ? —she had the impudence to tell me last night that she would leave my service immediately, unless I wad buy her husband's discharge, tak' him into my service, and settle an annuity on her for life — I daursay there ne'er was the like o't! "

"That was certainly very audacious," said Gertrude—" and she ought, at least, to have remained until you had procured another servant."

"Her remain ! do you think I wad left mysel at the discraa-tion o' such a slut as that? I just took her by the shoothers, and gi'ed her the outside o' the door for her answer. — Settle an annuity upon her! I've settled her wi' a vengeance. — Tak' a dragoon into my service! I wad just as soon tak' the hangman into my service !"

"What a picture of lonely old age!" thought Gertrude — " left at the mercy of a mercenary unprincipled servant — destitute even of the necessaries of life — how dismal! "

Even the unfortunate peculiarity of his temper, which kept him aloof from all fellowship with others, she viewed — as, indeed, it was — an additional misfortune, and she felt anxious to alleviate the wretchedness of his state by every means in her power. But to have insinuated to uncle Adam that his comfort at all depended either upon a servant or a fire, would have been an insult he would have resented accordingly.

"You must come to Rossville with me, my dear uncle," said the Countess, taking his hand, with her sweetest look and accent of entreaty.

"Me gang to Rossville!" exclaimed Mr. Ramsay, with a sudden start of horror; " I'll do nae such thing — what wad tak' me to Rossville ?"

"To pay me a visit—to give me the pleasure of seeing you in my own house. You know you must visit me some time ; and this is so good an opportunity, that indeed I will not excuse you."

"I suppose you think I canna contrive to live four-and-twenty hours by mysel'—but you're much mista'en, if you think I depend for my comfort either on man or woman ; at ony rate, there's a tyelor and his wife, down bye there, very discreet folk, that wad be ready to do ony thing I wanted, so you neednae fash your head aboot me."

"I have no doubt you could have abundance of service," said Lady Rossville, still persisting in her benevolent intentions —" to say nothing of your own domestics at Broom Park—my aunts too — I am sure, if they knew of your situation "

"My situation !" interrupted Mr. Ramsay, sharply.—" What's my situation? — a great situation, to be sure, to hae got rid o' a gude-for-nothing impudent thief that wanted to pick my pocket — I'm only thankful I'm quit o' her—and that's what you ca' my situation — what else could you say if I was lyin' wi' my throat cut ? "

"I beg your pardon — but you must make allowance for my blunders — you know my tongue is not so Scotch as my heart, and that is another reason why you must come to Rossville to give me some lessons in my dear native accents—I must now learn to speak Scotch to my poor people." And Gertrude hung coaxingly round him, till even uncle Adam's flinty nature began to melt.

"What, wad ye mak o' me at your braw castell, amang aw your fine folk? — I'm no used to your grandees, and I'm no gawn to begin to learn fashionable mainners noo — so dinna ask me — I'm no gawn to mak a fule o' mysel' at this time o' day."

s

"I assure you, we have no fine people at Rossville, my dear uncle — not one ; and, indeed, I do not like what are called fine people any more than you do. We are a very plain, quiet, old-fashioned family—quite clock-work in our ways and hours; and besides, if you don't like them or us, you shall take your own way in every thing — you shall breakfast, dine, sup, if you please, in your own apartment, and be quite at home,—now don't—pray, don't refuse me."

"An' be made a sang o' to aw the hoos, high and low? I suppose it'll be through the toon next that I couldnae mak a shift for a day without that impudent thief, Chirsty Carstairs.— No, no, I'm no gawn to be dragooned out o' my ain hoose by her.'"

Gertrude was certainly not a persevering character; and, despairing of success, she had risen to depart, when her heart smote her at the thoughts of abandoning the desolate old man to his cheerless solitary state—at his advanced age, and in such inclement weather, to be left in a house alone ! — the idea was frightful. Again she returned to the charge, and at length she prevailed; for she held out an inducement uncle Adam was not proof against. She told him of the picture he would see at Rossville" of her he had so truly loved, and the right string was touched. A silken thread might have led uncle Adam over half the globe when Lizzie Lundie was paramount. His little preparations were soon made ; the tailor's wife was summoned, and invested with the charge of the mansion ; and Mr. Ramsay, covered with shame and confusion at his own folly in being thus led by a child, sneaked into the carriage with his head on his breast, and his ears hanging down to his shoulders. Lady Rossville tried to animate him; but he still retained his humbled discomfited air, till the carriage stopped at the castle gate, when the old man burst forth —

" I've a gude mind just to gang back the way I cam —auld idiot that I am, to be rinnin' after pickters like a bairn !"

But it was now too late—the movements of the great are commonly conducted with a celerity that baffles ail calculation ; and uncle Adam was scarcely aware that he had reached his destination ere he found himself in the hall, surrounded by a train of servants. All that was left for him, therefore, was to scowl upon them as he passed along; but they were too well-bred to testify either mirth or surprise at sight of such a phenomenon, and, in spite of himself, he was ushered to the saloon with all the customary demonstrations of respect. It was vacant — and Lady Rossville, having safely deposited him by the side of a blazing fire, and vainly tried to persuade him to partake with her of some refreshment, left him, for a little, to solace himself with the newspapers of the day, while she went to announce his arrival to her mother.

CHAPTER XXVI.

Listen to me ; and if you speak me fair,

I'll tell you news. Shakespeare.

When Gertrude had left her mother in the morning she had left her as usual fretful and gloomy — but, on returning, she was struck with the change which, in the course of a few hours, had taken place. Her countenance was lightened—her air was almost joyous ; and though some slight traces of agitation were visible, yet it was evidently of no painful kind, for the tout ensemble was that of a person who had thrown off a load of cares and of fears. She was seated at her toilette, which, ever since the Earl's death, had been much neglected; but upon her daughter's entrance she dismissed her maid.

" Come away, my love," cried she, holding out her arms, and affectionately embracing her ; " I have been tiring to death for you. — Where have you been, my sweetest ?"

Gertrude, but not without wondering at this sudden overflow of love and tenderness, related to her the particulars of her visit to Mr. Ramsay, and its consequences.

" Ah! nothing could be better managed," said Mrs. St. Clair; " and his arrival to-day is quite apropos, as I mean to make my appearance at dinner, and it may very well pass for a compliment to my good uncle ;" then, changing her tone to one of deep solemnity —" Since I saw you in the morning, love, I have been a good deal shocked with a piece of news I accidentally stumbled upon in a provincial paper I happened to take up — my nerves, to be sure, have been sadly shattered of late," and she sighed, and took up her smelling-bottle. " But 'tis impossible not to be struck with such an event.— Gertrude, you have no longer any thing to fear from that unfoi'tunate man — he — he has perished !" added she, in strong but transient emotion.

Gertrude involuntarily shuddered. There is always something revolting in the gaiety that springs from the death of a felloM r -being; and, for a moment, she turned away her head from the wild unnatural pleasure that gleamed in her mother's eye.

" What was this man's life or death to me!" exclaimed she, suddenly. " Surely now the time is' come when you will tell me all!"

" Not now, my love — do not urge me — the time may com ! when I shall have no secret with you; but, at present, it can serve no purpose but that of agitating and distressing me. Perhaps I should not have mentioned this disagreeable occurrence to you at all, but for the fear that it might have come upon you unawares, and so have betrayed you into some symptom of recognition that had better be avoided; for, I think, you could scarcely

fail to be struck as I was at reading the account. — As yet, it has got no farther than the Barnford Chronicle ; but it will, of course, appear in the London papers, and you will probably hear it read and commented on at all hands, so 'tis better you should receive it from mine— forewarned is forearmed;" and taking up a newspaper, she pointed out a paragraph under the head of " Melancholy Shipwreck." It set forth, in the usual terms, a most elaborate and high-drawn narrative of the wreck of the Dauntless Packet, bound for America, on the coast of Ireland, when every soul on board had perished. Several pieces of the wreck, and some of the bodies of the unhappy sufferers, had been cast on shore, and were all minutely described ; amongst others, that of a " gentleman, seemingly turned of thirty years of age—tall—fair complexion—brown hair—black eyes—high nose — linen marked J. L. On his person were found a watch, a small sum of money, and a pocket-book; the latter containing papers and bills, but so much damaged by the water that the writing was wholly obliterated — only on one of the bills the letters ' S lair' could be traced, and those were the only marks which could throw any light on the unfortunate gentleman's identity," &c. &c. &c.

" It is very sad to be called upon to rejoice over an event fraught with so much misery," said the Countess, with a sigh, as she finished it.

" I do not call upon you to rejoice, Gertrude," said Mrs. St. Clair, solemnly. " God forbid that I should! I merely wished you to see that you have nothing more to fear in that quarter."

" But, after all, mamma, how can you be quite sure that this ill-fated sufferer is the very person you suppose — Lewiston?"

" Because I have it under his own hand that he had actually engaged his passage in that very vessel; and it is surely very improbable that there should have been two men on board a small packet answering so completely to the same description in every particular ; and, even if there were, both must have shared the same fate.—And now let us drop the subject, and every thing relating to it. Should it pass without any observation from those two tiresome fools, Lady Betty and Miss Pratt, 'tis well; if it is noticed and commented upon, you will, of course, be prepared to talk about it as any one else would do."

" But Mr. Lyndsay ? " said Gertrude — " surely you will explain every thing to him ?"

" I have already explained enough to Mr. Lyndsay," said Mrs. St. Clair, angrily. — " I know not what more he would require."

" Yet you said you had promised to lay open the whole "

" But the whole is now at an end; and I do not feel myself called upon to revive old and disagreeable stories, merely to gratify his curiosity."

"In justice to yourself — to me," said Gertrude, urgently,
" you ought not to lose a moment in clearing up, if possible, every thing that appears wrong in your conduct and in mine."

" In justice to myself," said Mrs. St. Clair, colouring with anger, " I will not harrow up my feelings, and endanger my health, by recurring to any thing of a painful or agitating nature at present. Mr. Lyndsay, I repeat, knows all that it is necessary for him to know : if he would know more, let him know that the Countess of Rossville, in her own house, and under the protection of her mother, stands in no need either of his advice or assistance."

" No! that he shall never hear from me," said Gertrude, warmly. Mr. Lyndsay may have been duped — he shall never be insulted under my roof, if I can prevent it."

" Is this the language I am now to hear ? " cried Mrs. St. Clair, passionately. " Am I so degraded by your exaltation that I must submit to be stigmatized—and by you? But, beware!—Lewis-ton is gone, but his power remains." Lady Rossville remained silent, but tears fell from her eyes ; at length she said, " I am no longer a child to be frightened by a bugbear — either tell me who this person really was, and what power he possessed over me, or, if you refuse to gratify me in this, at least let his name be no more mentioned between us. Already," cried she, giving scope to her emotion, and speaking under its excitement—" already my feelings have been sacrificed — my reputation endangered— certainly sullied in the eyes of one person ; and yet to him you refuse that explanation which is due both to him and to me."

While her daughter spoke, Mrs. St. Clair seemed to be struggling with her passions — at length, by a violent effort, she obtained the mastery over them, and, in a feeble languid tone, said —

" I am unable to contend with you, Gertrude ; you are mistress here, and may command, it seems, even your mother to obey you ; — but, exhausted as I am by a long and dangerous illness,—my nerves shattered—my mind unstrung,—you might have spared me yet a little But why should you weep, Lady Rossville,—you who have all that this world can bestow ? Me-thinks you might, at least, have left tears for your mother — poor dependant—humble as she is ! Gertrude, I am in no situation to oppose your will — with a worn-out frame — broken spirits — depending on your bounty for my daily bread "

Accustomed as she had all her life been to her mother's acting, still Gertrude never could hear a reproach from her lips without the bitterest sorrow and compunction ; and, on the present occasion, every word went as a dagger to her heart. Her attention had artfully been led away from the point at issue, and now she only beheld herself as the oppressor of a mother, feeble, old, and poor.

With her usual impetuosity, she at once flung herself into her mother's power—sued for forgiveness; and the scene ended, as such scenes always did end, in Mrs. St. Clair's victory. Still she felt it was hut a temporary one, as a mere triumph over the feelings always is. There might be silence,—but there was no submission at heart, for there could be no conviction of mind. Such as it was, however, it served for the present—a hasty reconciliation was patched up, on a sort of mutual understanding that all relating to the unfortunate Lewiston was to be consigned to oblivion. Mrs. St. Clair was not to be urged to any explanation till she should see fit to make it — and Lady Rossville was never more to be offended with the mention of a name connected, as it was, in her ideas, with so much degradation. Mrs. St. Clair then rung for her maid to resume her office, and the Countess returned to the saloon to her guest.

CHAPTER XXVII.

Mes yeux sont trop blesses, et la cour et la ville
Ne m'offrent rien qu' o'ojets a m'echauffer la bile;
J'entre en une humeur noire, en un chagrin profond,
Quand je vois vivre entre eux les hommes comme ils font;
Je n'y puis plus tenir, j'enrage; et mon dessein
Est de rompre en visiere a tout le genre humain. Moliere.

Upon entering the apartment, Gertrude's surprise was great at finding Mr. Ramsay and Miss Pratt seated together, seemingly in a most harmonious tete-a-tete. She had anticipated almost with dread a meeting between two such opposite natures, and had expected something to result from it little less discordant than the union of a bagpipe and fiddle; instead of which, she found their tastes and sentiments completely blended into one beauteous whole, and the current of their conversation gliding on so smoothly that it did not seem even to require Cowper's animated

No —

To brush the surface, and to make it flow.

But the extraordinary conjunction of two such distant planets is easily accounted for. It was not brought about by any heavenly influences, for such were not the tests for their spirits — but simply by means of a sufficient quantity of well-expressed, well-applied abuse, which is perhaps the strongest of all cements for worldly minds.

Uncle Adam, it is already known, had been left like one of the fortunate adventurers in the Arabian Tales, in a luxurious apartment, surrounded — not with singing damsels, and silver tissue, and sherbet, 'tis true — but with what to him were far greater enjoyments—silence, and freedom, and a newspaper. Perhaps another in his place would have taken a survey of the room, or have pondered a little over his comforts ; but he was none of these — he was quite unconscious of the finery that surrounded him, and not at all aware of the difference between the crimson and gold damask fauteuil in which he was seated and his own little strait-backed hair-cloth one — neither was he at all struck with the contrast between the profusion of lamps which diffused their brilliant light and his long-wicked, dim, streaming tallow candles. The bright blooming fire, indeed, was too powerful an object to be overlooked; but that only drew forth a peevish exclamation as he pushed back from its overpowering influence, and sought for his spectacles to see how stood the stocks. But no spectacles were to be found ! Every pocket (and they were not a few) was searched, and its depths profound explored — but in vain ; the case — the shagreen case was there, as if only to mock his hopes, for it was empty ; and uncle Adam at length recollected, with infinite vexation, that he had left its precious contents on the little table in his own parlour. How tormenting to behold with the mind's eye the very object we are in search of, lying on a particular spot, where our own hands have placed it!—to see it, as it were, within our grasp, and yet to be in torments for the want of it! Such as have experienced this will sympathise in the sufferings of uncle Adam, as he saw his spectacles lying afar off upon their broad end — their arms extended as if to grasp his temples — while yet the spectacles saw not him !

" I deserve this for my folly in comin' to such a place! " was his mental ejaculation, as he shuffled away to a window to see whether it was not yet too dark for him to find his way home to his own house and his spectacles. But, at that critical moment, the door opened; and Miss Pratt, like another Fairy Paribanon, entered. She had discovered his arrival; and having had the advantage of hearing his character and peculiarities thoroughly discussed upon various occasions, she was prepared to meet him accordingly.

Miss Pratt, like many other people, had a sort of instinctive reverence for riches, even where she had not the slightest prospect of profiting by them. She, therefore, accosted Mr. Ramsay with the greatest respect and courtesy—expressed the pleasure it gave her to see him at Rossville — hoped he had taken something since he came — it wanted a long while to dinner yet — and, in short, did the honours as though she had been mistress of the mansion.

Uncle Adam, who knew not who he had to deal with, was not displeased at the empressement testified in his behalf by a stranger, and he declined the proffered civility in his politest manner—adding, that he never took any thing between breakfast and dinner.

" And an excellent rule it is," said Miss Pratt, in her most emphatic tone, " for them who can keep it; for I really think there's a great deal too much eating and drinking goes on in the present day, especially amongst young people. The consequence is, you hear of nothing but bile — bile — bile, from the oldest to the youngest. I really think poor Lord Rossville hurt himself very much by his manner of eating—not but what he was a moderate man in the main — but, to tell the truth, I never can help thinking he dealt too deep in a fine fat venison pasty that was at dinner, the very last day he sat at his own table ; and such a supper as he ate that night, poor man ! "

" I dinna doot it," said Mr. Ramsay, secure that he never would come to an untimely end by any excesses of the kind.

" I've given our young Countess a hint about that," resumed Miss Pratt; " for I really think there's need for a little reform in the kitchen here. It was just yesterday I was saying to her, that, for all the cooks she had, and for all the grand things they send up, I didn't believe she had one that could make a drop good plain barley-broth, or knew how to manage a sheep's head and trotters. — She laughed, and desired Phillips, the maitre de hotel, to be sure to have one Scotch dish on the table every day ; but I've no great brew of any Scotch dish that'll ever come out of the hands of a French cook."

" There'll be nae want o' a fire to cook the dinner, I'm sure," said uncle Adam, pointing to the well-filled chimney; " there's a fire might roast an ox. There's no possibility o' going near it."

" I'm sure that's true; for I'm quite o' your opinion, Mr. Ramsay, as the old byeword says, 'better a wee ingle to warm ye, than a muckle fire to burn you.' It's really a sin to see such fires; and it's all the same way, every room in the house blazing with fires and lamps, till, I declare, my eyes are like to be put out o' my head ; but Lady Rossville's so fond of light, she never can get enough of it— and her eyes are young and strong ; but she'll maybe feel the frost of it yet, when she comes to know the value of them like you and me, sir."

Miss Pratt was quite conscious that her stout, active, indefatigable eyes wei'e not to be mentioned in the same breath with Mr. Ramsay's little, weak, pale, bleared ones ; but when people are resolved to please, they must sometimes make great sacrifices. The compliment was not wholly thrown away, though it was not returned in kind, for ; with one of his vinegar smiles, uncle Adam replied —

" I set mair value upon my spectacles than my een noo, for I find the ane o' very little use to me wanting the ither; but I've forgotten my glasses in my ain hoose, and I canna read ae word o' thae papers that she put into my hands !"

" That is really a hai'd case !" exclaimed Miss Pratt, with the most ardent expression of sympathy ; " but I'll tell you what, Mr. Ramsay, you need be at no loss for spectacles in this house, for poor Lord Rossville, I'm sure, if he left one pair, he left a score — always changing his glasses! I really think he hurt his sight very much by it — I would get you a pair in an instant, but Lady Rossville has the keys of all his places, and she's with her mother just now, so perhaps you'll wait till she comes out; but if you'll give me leave, I'll read the papers to you, for I haven't seen them myself yet—somebody or other whipt them out of the room this morning, before I had time to look at them — I suspect some of the servants, for they are really getting out their horns at no allowance. Lady Rossville stands much in need of some experienced judicious friend to take some management, for they're really going off at the nail. I do not know what servants are to come to, for my part; the'll be no living with them by and by. I have but one; and what do you think, sir, of the trick she played me the t'other day ? It's but seldom I leave my own house, for I'm one of those who think there's no place like home, but you know one must give up their own way sometimes; and I had been away upon a visit, and came home one dreadful night very wearied and far from well — had been just comforting myself all the way with the thoughts of a cup of warm tea and getting into my own bed, when, instead of that, lo and behold! I found my house shut up—my key nobody knew where — and my fine madam off on some junketting match! The consequence was, I must have lain in the street, if your worthy nieces, the Miss Blacks, hadn't accidentally heard of the situation I was in, and made a point of my coming to them —and after all this, I'm obliged to keep her for six months, or pay her wages and board wages!"

All this was oil and honey to uncle Adam's wounds; and Chirsty Carstairs' enormities, great as they were, looked somewhat smaller beside the still more monstrous offence of Babby Broadfoot. He had had the satisfaction of turning the delinquent out of his doors, instead of having endured the humiliation of being locked out by her; consequently, whatever similarity there might be in their injuries, still he stood upon higher ground, and he gave a faint chuckle of delight at finding his new friend's misfortune so much worse than his own.

Miss Pratt now turned to the newspaper. — " I'm just taking a glance of the stocks; for though it's but little I have to do with them, still, you know,' we all bow to the bush we get bield frae.' — Ay! there's another tumble, I see, down to 80 and a fraction — rose to 80| — some done so high as 81^—left off, at the close, at 80i."

" That's the 3 per cents. — and what are India bonds?" a c ked Mr. Ramsay.

" India bonds, 61 to 63 premium — long annuities shut, short ditto," &c. &c. &c. And Miss Pratt, in the twinkling of an eye, ran through the whole range of the money-market, displaying, in her career, the most complete knowledge of each and every branch, as though she had been born and bred a stock-jobber.

Uncle Adam was astonished! He had read of women ascending to the skies in balloons, and descending to the depths of the sea in bells ; but for a woman to have entered the sanctum sanctorum of the Stock Exchange, and to know, to a fraction, the difference between 3 per cents, red. and 3 per cents, ace. — and to be mistress of all the dread mysteries of scrip and omnium!

— it was what uncle Adam in all his philosophy never had dreamed of, and Miss Pratt rose at least 5 per cent, in his estimation.

Having discussed the stocks in all their bearings, she proceeded with the varied contents of the paper; but the fall of the 3 per cents, had not sweetened her tempei', and she was very bitter in her indignation at " Proposals for publishing, by subscription, a Print of the Reverend Peter Pirie, proofs 2/. 2s." &c.; and at the announcement that the lady of a " Lieutenant Duncan Dow, late of his Majesty's 119th Regiment," bad presented him with a son and heir. But the whole measure of her wrath was reserved for the obituary record, which, as usual, contained the apotheosis of some, it may be, very worthy, but certainly very insignificant individual, as in the present instance.

" Died, at the house of his father, No. 2, East Cotton Row, where he had gone for the recovery of his health, on the 13th ult., aged 45, Nathaniel Lamb, Esq., hosier and glover, after a long and lingering illness, which he bore with the most heroic patience and Christian resignation. To the purest benevolence, the most enlightened piety, and the most devoted patriotism, Mr. Lamb, junior, united the firmest principles, the most perfect integrity, and the most affable address "

Here uncle Adam broke out with — " Affable address! the affability o' a hosier! I never could bear that word aw my days, and far less noo — dinna read ony mair, ma'am. — Affable ! affable ! I wonder wha wad tak affability aff the hands o' a glover!

— but it's just o' a piece wi' awthing else in this world now. Half-pay lieutenants maun hae leddies and heirs — and bodies o' schule-maisters and ministers maun sit for their pickters, and hae their faces printed as though they war' kings and conquerors. The newspapers are filled wi' the lives o' folk that naebody ever heard o' till they war' dead—I dinna ken what things are to come to!"

" Indeed, sir, that's my wonder, for I really think the world has been turned fairly topsy-turvy since our days; but I assure you it would be well if people were satisfied with putting their deaths in the papers. What do you think, sir, of having to pay, as I had the t'other day, thirteen-pence halfpenny for a notification of the death of a woman that wasn't a drop's blood to me — just thirteen-pence halfpenny out of my hand, and that for a person that, to tell the truth, I thought had been dead twenty years ago."'

This was another nut for uncle Adam, who had long brooded
over the mortification of having had to pay a penny for a similar compliment, and even thought how he should obtain redress, or at least revenge. Miss Pratt went on —

" As Anthony Whyte (my nephew, Mr. Whyte of Wbyte Hall) says, ' I've given orders to take in no letters from the post-office now with black seals — they're either disagreeable or expensive, and sometimes both.'"

" It's a very sensible regulation," said uncle Adam, warmly.

" And as for burial letters — what do you think, sir, of Anthony Whyte being asked to three burials in one week — and two of them people he had never broke bread with ? "

" I think a man had better be a saullie* at once," said Mr. Ramsay, vehemently.

But here the colloquy of these two congenial souls was interrupted by the entrance of Lady Rossville.

" That's an ooncommon sensible woman," said uncle Adam, as his friend and ally pattered away to the other end of the room for a fire-screen for the Countess.

" I really am agreeably surprised with your uncle," whispered Miss Pratt, as she drew Lady Rossville a little aside; " a fine shrewd old man — I assure you, he knows odds from ends; it's not every body that will do with him — he puts you to your trumps in a hurry."

CHAPTER XXVIII.

If a man be gracious and courteous to strangers, it shows he is a citizen of the world, and that his heart is no island cut off from other lands, but a continent that joins to them. — Lord Bacon.

Gertrude watched with some solicitude the meeting between her mother and Mr. Lyndsay, as she entered the drawing-room before dinner, leaning on her arm in all the parade of convalescence. When he came up to offer his congratulations, her cheek was slightly suffused, and for a moment her eye fell beneath the mild yet searching expression of his. But quickly regaining her self-possession, she replied to his salutation in that distant ceremonious manner which plainly indicated the sort of footing they were henceforth to be upon. Mr. Lyndsay had too much tact not to feel what was implied; and the inference he drew was, that he must now cease to expect any explanation from her as to the past. The Earl's death had deprived him of the only hold he had over her, for there was no one now who had a right to interpose their authority. Averse as he was to interference in general, yet upon this occasion he considered

* A hired mourner.

himself called upon to act a decided part, and he resolved to take the first opportunity of coming to an understanding with Mrs. St. Clair on the subject of the mysterious interviews.

Lady Rossville felt that some apology was due to her cousin for the introduction of so uncouth a companion as uncle Adam; and she hastened to explain to him the cause of his becoming her guest, and to request that he might not consider him as any tax upon his politeness, or think it incumbent upon him to entertain a person who, she assured him, despised entertainment in every shape.

But Lyndsay was not one of those fastidious beings who can only tolerate the chosen few, whose endowments place them at least on a level with themselves. Although the gulf was wide which separated Mr. Ramsay and him in mind and manners, yet he did not disdain all fellowship with him, but welcomed the old man with that politeness which, when it springs from benevolence, can never fail to please ; and, at the same time, with that' ease and simplicity, which, of all modes of expression, are, without doubt, the most attractive. Although quite alive to the peculiarities of his new associate, and not a little amused with many of them, yet his better feelings always prevailed over his sense of ridicule; and instead of " giving play" to uncle Adam's foibles, he led the conversation to such objects as were best calculated to show him to advantage.

It is only well-informed people who are capable of extracting information from others. We require to know something of a subject ourselves before we can even question others to any purpose upon it; and, perhaps, it often happens that our own ignorance is in fault, when we throw the blame upon other people's stupidity. Such was not Edward Lyndsay's case ; and while he unconsciously displayed his own knowledge even in seeking information, he drew forth the hidden stores of Mr. Ramsay, and rendered him almost an instructive and an entertaining companion.

Uncle Adam was no Othello; but still, in the course of his long life, he had met with his " disastrous chances," his " moving accidents," his " hair-breadth 'scapes," and had traversed many an " antre vast and desert idle;" and though he would have disdained any thing like a regular detail of aught he had ever seen or met with, yet, by judicious management, a great deal could be extracted from him in his own homely manner.

Meanwhile Miss Pratt's cloven foot began to display itself to his piercing ken. Vague notions at first floated through his brain about her, but they were such as only wanted a little more time and opportunity to body forth into real shapes. He had a notion that she spoke too much—that she took too much upon her—that she tasted of too many different dishes, instead of dining upon one thing, which was one of his cardinal virtues — then, it was not her business to press him to eat in his own

niece's house, -where he felt he had a hetter right to eat and to speak than she had. But the head and front of her offending -was her asking him to drink a glass of Madeira -with her during dinner—that -was a piece of assurance he could not away with. In his time, it used to be a serious and solemn thing for a gentleman to invite a lady to drink wine with him; but here was a total bouleversement of the natural order of things, and uncle Adam actually blushed an acceptance as he wondered what was to come next. To counterbalance these improprieties, she had, in the twinkling of an eye, suited him in a pair of spectacles, which seemed as though they had been made for him, or he for them— she had bespoke a haggis for dinner the following day, and undertaken to direct Monsieur Morelle in the art of stuffing it— then she lost seven games at backgammon, for which she paid down three and sixpence, with very evident reluctance too, which always serves to enhance the value of the winnings tenfold ; so that, upon the whole, uncle Adam was rather inclined for once to suspend his judgment, and, instead of decidedly condemning her, he merely began to look upon her as a sort of doubtful character.

Lady Rossville had ordered an apartment for her uncle, communicating with the yellow turret, which contained the goddess of his idolatry, and which she intended should henceforth be his sanctum sanctorum. She, therefore, introduced him to it the following day; but that he might feel more at liberty to indulge his soft emotions, she was retiring, when looking round, he called to her —

" But whar's the pickter you promised me ? "

" There," said Gertrude, pointing to the Diana.

" That!" exclaimed he, in a tone of surprise and indignation. " That Lizzie Lundie ! they're no blate that evens her to it!" And he walked round and round the turret, something in the manner of an obstreperous horse in a mill.

" This is very strange," said Gertrude —" both Lord Rossville and Miss Pratt seemed to know the history of this picture so perfectly, that I never imagined there could be a doubt about it; I am really sorry that you have been so disappointed."

" Disappointed!" repeated uncle Adam, stopping short, and looking almost black with wrath,— "I'm mair than disappointed —I'm perfectly disgusted!" Then taking another look— "Lizzie Lundie was a daacent, wise-like, sensible craater, as ever lived—and to compare her to that brazen-faced tawpie, wi' a moon upon her head, and a great bow and arrow in her hand!"

And again he turned away in increasing animosity against the Diana.

" But, my dear uncle, these are merely adventitious embellishments— you see she is represented in the character of Diana "

" And -what business had they to represent her as ony such thing?"

This was a question Lady Rossville was aware she could not answer to his satisfaction, therefore prudently waived it by asking another.

" So, then, you don't discover any resemblance?"

" Resemblance ! — Hoo is't possible there can be ony resemblance ? Wha ever saw her in that mad-like unnatural condition, mair like a stage actress than an honest man's dochter! — you might just as well set me up for a—a—an Apollo !"

The idea of uncle Adam, with his long cross blue face and pyramidical peruke, personating the God of Day, diverted Lady Rossville so much, that she laughed outright; but he retained his inflexible severity of countenance, and seemed quite unconscious of the ridicule of such a supposition.

" Well, since you don't like the picture, you shall not be offended by it again," said the Countess, laying her hand gently on his arm to lead him from the place ; " you shall have another dressing-room to your apartment, and you have only to forget the way to this one."

But uncle Adam now fixed himself opposite to the huntress queen, and, having carefully wiped and adjusted his spectacles, he contemplated her for some time without speaking ; at length, with a groan, he said, —

" I'll no say but what there may be something o' a likeness in the face, when you come to consider it — there's the brow,

the bonny brent brow " Then, kindling anew — " Rut wha

e'er saw her brow wi' that scnseless-like thing on the tap o't ? They could nae pent her een, to be sure, for they might as weel hae tried to pent twa diamonds — the bit mouth's no entirely unlike, but it has nae her bonny smile." And uncle Adam gazed and commented, till he gradually lost sight of the moon and the bow, and all the offensive peculiarities of the sylvan goddess, and at length saw only the image of his long-loved Lizzie.

From that time the turret became his favourite haunt; and as he was there perfectly unmolested, and was left at liberty to follow his own devices, secure from even the interruptions of Miss Pratt, he remained tolerably quiescent. Every day, indeed, he made an attempt to break off, and return to his own comfortless abode; but every day he was overruled by Lady Rossville, whose influence over him was daily increasing, although he was perfectly unconscious of it, and would have spurned the idea of being influenced by any thing but his own free will. But there was also another inducement for him to prolong his stay, which he would have been still more ashamed to have acknowledged.

In a paroxysm of ennui one bad day he had tal<en up the first volume of Guy Mannering, with little expectation of deriving

either amusement or instruction from it; but, once fairly entered upon it, he found himself compelled, nolens volens, to proceed ; which he did, however, in the most secret and stealthy manner. Uncle Adam had been no novel-reader even in his younger days ; and with him, as with many other excellent, but we must suppose mistaken people, novels and mental imbecility were ideas inseparably united in his brain. Novel-writers he had always conceived to be born idiots, and novel-readers he considered a something still lower in the scale of intellect. It was, therefore, with feelings of the deepest humiliation he found himself thus irresistibly carried along on a sort of King 's-cushion, as it were, by Meg Merrilies and Dominie Sampson. Not that he traversed the pages with the swiftness of a modern reader — or that he read them probably with half the rapidity with which they were written — for he was one of those solid, substantial readers who make what they read their own — he read and reread, and paused and pondered — and often turned back, but never looked forward, even while experiencing the most intense anxiety as to the result — in short, uncle Adam's whole being was completely absorbed in this (to him) new creation ; while, at the same time, he blushed even in private at his own weakness in filling his head with such idle havers, and, indeed, never could have held it up again if he had been detected with a volume in his hand.

CHAPTER XXIX.

Oh ! scene of fortune, which dost fair appear
Only to men that stand not near ! Cowley.
O why should Fate sic pleasure take

Life's dearest bands untwining? Or why sae sweet a flower as Love
Depend on Fortune shining ? Burns.

And now visions of earthly bliss — of pomp — of power — of pleasure, — began to float before those eyes scarce dried from natural tears. But Gertrude had not now so much time as formerly to indulge in the idle day-dreams of romance. With her change of situation, the penalties of greatness came thronging upon her. Unthought-of claims upon her time — her talents — her attention, followed in rapid and never-ceasing succession; and she found, with surprise and disappointment, that the boundless freedom she had so fondly anticipated as the attribute of power was farther from her than ever. To will, indeed, was hers ; but how many obstacles intervene to the accomplishing of the will, even of the most absolute! — obstacles which conscience itself raises as barriers against the encroachments of self-indul-

gence and natural inclination ; and which, though as thin air to some, are as rocks of adamant to others. But Lady Rossville possessed a more powerful monitor than even conscience would have proved in the person of Edward Lyndsay. " Unefemme est aisee a gouverner," says a French satirist, " pourvu que ce soit un homme qui s'en donne la peine ;" — and the truth of the assertion Gertrude seemed in a fair way to realize. Ardent and enthusiastic in her nature, and as such always prone to fall into extremes, the sense of dependence she felt towards her cousin, as the only person on whose judgment and rectitude she could safely rely, would gradually have assumed the habit of implicit deference to most of his views and opinions ; not from conviction — for on many subjects they widely differed — but simply because, like many other people, she loved to be directed in matters where her affections were not concerned, and was always ready to sacrifice her judgment, provided it did not interfere with her inclination. There is, indeed, much of luxury to an indolent, or a fanciful mind, in thus casting its cares upon another, while it floats calmly along in undisturbed serenity, or abandons itself to the thick-coming fancies of its own imagination. In every situation of life this disposition, alas! has its dangers; but how much more in those gifted ones whom God has set on the high places of the earth! But Mr. Lyndsay was not a person to take advantage of this flexible form of mind. He had too much delicacy to assume any authority, or interfere in any department openly — too much honour to use his influence in an indirect or underhand manner. He aimed to guide her principles, not to direct her actions — to strengthen her mind, not to govern it; but, above all, he strove to impress upon her the responsibility of the duties assigned her — the account which would one day be required of the talents committed to her. But such doctrine, even though uttered in the mildest and most persuasive accents, still sounded harsh to ears just opening to the blandishments of the world. Imagination had stretched a broad and flowery path in endless perspective before her, and she recoiled from that strait and narrow way which the Christian pilgrim has been commanded to tread. Life — young life's enchanting scenes were now bursting on the sight in all their exquisite, but transient, delusive beauty ; and at that joyous season, when " the common air, the earth, the skies," seem to the exulting heart to breathe of " opening Paradise," how does it turn from the holy precepts — the solemn admonitions of Divine truth — as from that which would annihilate all that is delightful in existence!

So felt the child of prosperity, as she looked on all the pride of life, and, with the fallen cherub, was ready to exclaim —

O Earth, how like to Heaven, if not preferr'd !

But with all her faults — and they were many — Gertrude

was not one of those selfish, sordid spirits, whose enjoyments centre solely in their own gratification. Her nature was lofty, and her disposition generous ; but her virtue was impulse —

her generosity profusion. She wished to diffuse happiness around her; and she imagined she had only to scatter money with a lavish hand, and it would necessarily spring up, hearing the fruits of peace, and love, and virtue, and joy. Like all enthusiastic novices, her schemes of philanthropy — if schemes they might he called which plan had none — were upon the most magnificent scale; and it was with mortification she he-held her baseless fabrics melt away beneath the plain practical results of Mr. Lyndsay's rational benevolence. Schools were the only establishments for which she could obtain his concurrence, and even there she thought his ideas much too humble. A plain school-house was an odious, frightful thing — she must positively have it elegant, if not expensive; and the children must be all prettily dressed; — and she drew a design for the building, and invented a uniform for the children, both so classical and so unique, that she was all impatience to behold these models of her taste and fancy realized.

There was another object which Gertrude was still more anxious to accomplish, and that was to make the happiness of William Leslie and Anne Black, by providing him with a church. But the one for which her cousin had applied had been given away by Lord Rossville, and there was no immediate prospect of another vacancy occurring. Even Mr. Lyndsay could not assist her here, for his interest was already deeply engaged; but he was little less desirous than herself of befriending a young man, whose amiable character, evangelical doctrine, mild attractive manners, and exemplary conduct, were more powerful recommendations than aught that rank and beauty could have urged.

Matters were in this state, when Anne accompanied her father and mother one day on a visit of condolence to Rossville. While Miss Pratt, as usual, did the honours of the mansion to the seniors of the party, Lady Rossville took her cousin apart to converse with her on the subject; for, although too modest and diffident to make a direct application, there was an anxious appeal in her pensive countenance that could not be misunderstood. She at once frankly owned that the cause of her dejection proceeded from the apparent hopelessness of her prospects.

" But is the want of a church really the only obstacle to your union ? " inquired Gertrude.

" Alas, no! " said her cousin mournfully ; " my father and mother, and indeed my whole family, oppose it now more than ever, because of the superior establishments my sisters have got; and they talk of the degradation I am bringing upon them all by such a poor connection, till I am sometimes ready to give it up in despair— and so I would, were it only my own happiness that

T

is at stake— that I would willingly sacrifice to theirs — but William loves me so truly, and has loved me so long—ever since we were children — and to give him up now, I am sure would break both our hearts." Here Anne " dropt some natural tears, but wiped them soon," and, in a firmer tone, added — " But I am wrong—very wrong, to give way to such desponding thoughts — if it is God's will, we shall yet be happy in his good time — and if He sees good to disappoint us, I trust we shall both be able from our hearts to say, His will be done! "

Gertrude was for an instant smote with the difference of her cousin's sentiments from her own — her meek submission, her humble acquiescence, seemed as a reproach to the wayward feelings of her own rebellious heart; but quickly she dispelled the gathering conviction — " She cannot love as I do," thought she, " or she could not reason thus — hers may be virtue, but it is not love."

CHAPTER XXX.

Thy house and pleasing wife ! Horace.

The snow had now disappeared — the waters had subsided — the air was soft for the season — the cloudy welkin had cleared up into a fleecy dappled sky, and sanguine spirits deemed that winter was past and gone. For, in the quaint words of Cuddy, in the Shepherd's Calendar,

When the shining sun laugheth once, You deemen the spring is come at once.

Even the faintest breath of spring brings pleasure to all whose hearts are not seared, and whose bodies are not iron. We feel as if we were about to renew our existence — the opening skies seem to smile upon us as they did in the days of our youth, and again their bland influence steals upon our senses. Again we cast away the cares and the griefs of the world, with its clouds and its storms; and again spring up in our numbed hearts,

Hopes that are angels in their birth, But perish young, like things of earth!

But it is not every one who owns such influences. Amongst the inmates of Rossville Castle a fine day produced its pleasures, but they were of a different nature. Mrs. St. Clair liked it, that she might take an airing in state; and, accordingly, set forth in all the pomp of a stately equipage. Lady Betty liked the sun, because it would shine upon fat Flora, who was sent out to profit by it. Miss Pratt, having rummaged every creek and cranny in the interior of the house, took advantage of it to look about her a little without doors, to see what abuses she could detect. Uncle Adam, having seen Dandie Dinmont and Dumple safe home, closed his book, and crept away with his hands behind his back to take a saunter. Lady Rossville, taking Mr. Lynd-say's arm, set out, as she had done on many a worse day, to mark the progress of the improvements she had begun—to accelerate, if possible, by her impatience, the building of her school-house, and to visit some of the cottages of her poor, with whose ways and wants she was now beginning to make herself acquainted.

Her romantic expectation of finding elegant distress in mud cabins was now gradually dwindling away; for wherever she went, she met only the homeliness of matter-of-fact poverty

Gratitude, and respect, and blessings, indeed, were hers; for how easy is it for the great to make themselves beloved by the poor—how cheap the purchase of the best feelings of humanity! Gertrude was new to the luxury of doing good; and her heart would swell, and her eyes fill with tears, as the trembling hand of age was raised to Heaven to call down its blessings on her head— and she could look, almost with pleasure, on the children her bounty had clothed, even though their features were coarse, and their dialect uncouth.

In the course of her domiciliary visits, she found herself at the door of the cottage she had visited the memorable morning after her arrival at Rossville; and, somewhat curious to know the state of affairs there, she was about to enter, when, at that moment, uncle Adam was descried approaching. They waited till he came up, and then invited him to join in the visit, which, after a little humming and hawing, he agreed to do.

The door was hard and fast shut; but, upon knocking, it was banged open by our ci-devant friend, the dame of the stoups, who immediately recognised and most cordially welcomed her former visitor.

" Eh! my leddy, is this you? — I ax your pardon, my leddy, but I really didna ken weel wha you was the first time you was here — just come foret, my leddy —just stap in ower, sir, — dinna be feared, my leddy, just gang in bye," &c. &c. &c.; and carefully closing the door against the breath of heaven, she ushered her guests into the dark precincts of her foul-aired smoky cabin. A press-bed, with a bit of blue checked stuff hanging down, denoted that the poor sufferer had now exchanged his seat by the fire for his bed; and the chair which he had formerly occupied stood with its back to the fire, covered with linens, apparently drying.

" How does your husband do? " inquired Lady Rossville.

"Oo, 'deed, my leddy, he's just quite silly-wise," responded the dame, in a whining melancholy key; " he just lies there snottering awa'," pointing to the bed.

" Is he confined to bed ?" asked Mr. Lyndsay.

"No — no, sir, he's no confined ony ways — he gets up v/hiles, but 'deed it's no aye convenient for me to hae him up ; for, as I tell him, what can he do when he is up ? — for he's no fit to put his hand to ony thing — and he's mair out o' the way there than he wad be ony place else."

" More out of the way of regaining health certainly," said Mr. Lyndsay.

" Health, sir!" interrupted the hostess; " 'deed he '11 ne'er hae health as langas he lives — he's just been draggle dragglen on these twunty month by Martimas — I'm sure I've had a weary time o't wi' him, and noo I canna get a hand's turn maist done for him — the hoose an'aw things just gawin' to destruction; and, I'm sure, I really think shame o' mysel'," surveying two large dirty arms from top to toe; " and there's the weans, puir things, gawin' in perfect rags, for I ne'er can get a steek put in either to their duds or my ain."

Here the voice of the sick man was heard in a faint accent, calling the gudewife.

" That's just the way he gangs on, my leddy—he just lies there and yelps — yelps — yelps even on for me.—What is't noo ? " in her loudest sharpest key, as she banged up to the bed. " A drink ? I wonder ye hae nae mair sense, Tarn, than to ask for a drink the noo, when her leddyship's here, an' Maister Lyndsay an' aw, speerin' for you."

Lyndsay here took up a jug of water, which was standing on the top of a chest by the bed-side, and held it to the sick man's lips; but the reproof was thrown away, or rather misconstrued, by his soothing helpmate.

" Oh, sir! I think shame o' your takin' sae muckle trouble — for he's just like a bairn— he's aye wantin' something or anither, and he's just lost aw discretion thegither— I wonder you dinna think shame o' yoursel'" (to her husband) " when you see the fashery you mak'."

Mr. Lyndsay, meanwhile, having felt the invalid's pulse, began to put a few queries to him touching his complaint.

" Have you much thirst ? " asked he.

" O, sir, he wad drink the very ocean, an let him."

" Pray, let him speak for himself," said Lyndsay, again putting the question to the patient, who seemed so unused to the privilege that he was evidently at a loss how to make use of it.

" Have you any pain in your head ? "

" 'Deed, sir, I dinna think he has muckle pain in his head, though he compleens o't whiles; but, as I often tell him, I wiss he had my back. I'm sure I've a pain whiles atween my shouthers, sir " rolling a huge, fat, strong-looking back, as she spoke.

" I shall attend to your pains some other time, if you will be so good as keep them quiet for the present," said Lyndsay; .then, once more turning to the sick man, he asked whether he had pain or weakness in his limbs that prevented him from rising.

" I'm sure I dinna ken what it is," again interposed the incorrigible matron. " He canna be sair, I'm positive o' that; he's very silly *, to be sure, but that canna be helpit, ye ken."

" Do you never allow your husband to answer for himself?" asked Mr. Lyndsay, at a loss whether to laugh or be provoked at this intolerable woman.

" Oo, sir, I'm sure he's walcome to speak for me ; but 'tweel I dinna think he kens very weel what till say, or what it is that ails him. — Tam," — shouting into his ear—" the leddy wants to hear an you can speak ony. Canna you thank her for the braw claise and siller she gied you?"

" Should not you like to be up— out of bed?" asked Gertrude, now trying her skill to extract an answer ; but before he had time to reply, his mouth-piece again took up the word.

" Up, my leddy! 'Deed he just craik craiks to be up, and then whan he's up he craik craiks to be doun ; an' it wad be very disconvenient for to hae him up the day, for you see,"—pointing to the linens that were spread over the chairs, — " the fire's aw ta'en up wi' his dead-claise, that I was gi'en an air to; for they had got unco dampish-wise wi' the wat wather ; an' I'm thinkin' he'll no be lang o' wantin' them noo ; and this is siccan a bonny-day, I thought what atween the fire and the sun they wad be sure to get a gude toast." f

Uncle Adam had hitherto practised a degree o. forbearance which had scarcely a parallel in his whole life and conversation; but, indeed, from the moment the dame had first opened her lips, he had felt that words would be weak weapons to have recourse to, and that nothing less than smiting could at all satisfy his outraged feelings. Luckily, at this moment, she was not within reach of his arm, otherwise it is to be feared his wrath would have vented itself, not in thin air, but in solid blows. As it was, he at last burst forth, like a volcano, with —

" Airing the honest man's dead-claise, when the breath's in his body yet! Ye're bauld to treat a living man as ye wad a sweel'd corpse, and turn his very hoose into a kirk-yard! How dare ye set up your face to keep him frae his ain fireside for ony o' your dead duds ?"

And snatching up the paraphernalia so ostentatiously displayed, he thrust the whole into the fire. — " There —that'll gie them a gude toast for you!" said he ; and as they broke into a blaze he quitted the cabin.

" Eh, sirs! the bonny claise, that cost sae muckle siller!" sobbed the mistress, in an hysterical tone, as she made an ineffectual effort to save them ; — " the ill-faur'd carle that he is, to tak upon him for to set low to ony honest man's windin'-sheet!"

* Silly — in England meant to express mental imbecility; in Scotland, signifies bodily weakness, t From real life.

T 3

Lady Rossville was confounded; for, as she but imperfectly-comprehended the pith of the parley that had taken place, the action appeared to her, as indeed it was, perfectly outrageous, and her purse was instantly opened to repair this breach of law and justice. But Lyndsay could scarcely keep from laughing at the tragi-comic scene that had just taken place. From his knowledge of the character and modes of thinking of the Scottish peasantry, he was not at all surprised at the gudewife's preparations ; — but while she was engrossed with her attempts to redeem some bits of the linen from the flames, he took the opportunity of carrying on his colloquy with the husband.

" So I see your wife does not attempt to conceal from you the danger you are in," said he.

" Na, na," said the invalid, perking up; " what for wad she do that ? — they wadna be a true freend that wad hide a man's danger frae him—we're aw ready enough to hide it frae oursells, and forget the care o' our ain immortal sowls."

" You have seen your minister, then, I suppose?"

" Oo aye, honest man ! he ca's in nows and thans, and muckle edification I get frae him ; " — then, calling to his dame, he began to comfort her for the loss she had sustained, as though it had been her own holiday suit.

" What a shocking woman!" exclaimed Gertrude, as they quitted the cottage ; " how worse than unfeeling to have prepared her husband's dead-clothes, and have them even displayed before his eyes in that manner !"

" She certainly is not a favourable specimen of a Scotch gude-wife," answered Mr. Lyndsay; " but I have seen the most affectionate wife talk of the death of her husband, even while administering to his wants with the greatest solicitude ; but they are much less sophisticated in their ideas upon these subjects than we are—they would think it highly wrong to use any deception at such a time."

" But how shocking to hear one's death talked of as inevitable "

" But they do not talk of it in that manner—they believe that all things are possible with God—they send for the doctor as they do for the minister, and pray for a blessing on the means used—they leave all in the hand of God. I have seen many on their death-beds in various circumstances, and I have always found that they who were in the habit of hearing of death and eternity — of conversing with their ministers and religious people — have, generally speaking, looked forward to death with resignation and composure."

" I can, indeed, easily imagine," said Lady Rossville, " that the poor man we have just left must look forward to heaven with great complacency, were it only to be rid of that tormenting creature, and out of that vile smoky cabin."

"A smoky house and a scoldingwife have, indeed, always been

looked upon as the ne plus ultra of human misery ; but this is only amongst the rich—when you have seen more of the poor, you will be satisfied there are still greater evils—you are still a novice in the miseries of life, Gertrude."

" Perhaps so, and yet " she stopped, and sighed, and
they proceeded homewards in silence.

CHAPTER XXXI.

She hath forgott how many a woeful stowre
For him she late endured ; she speaks no more
Of past; true is it that true love hath no powre
To looken backe. Spenser.

All must have felt what it is in this ungenial clime to part with a fine day. It seems as though we were bidding farewell to some long-lost friend; and we love to watch even with pensive regret the last rays of the softly sinking sun, as we would trace the lingering steps of some loved one whom it may be long ere we behold again.

" Fatigued as I am, still I must enjoy this lovely day to the last," said Lady Rossville, as they approached the castle, and she threw herself on a garden chair that stood upon the lawn ; "it is one that sends such a ' summer feeling to the heart,' that I feel as though I were a better being while sitting here listening to the faint notes of that sweet thrush, than I should be shut up in the drawing-room with Lady Betty and Miss Pratt."

" It is much more agreeable at least," said Lyndsay, also seating himself—" as to its being more amiable and virtuous, I fear I may scarcely lay that flattering unction to my soul. I am apt to distrust myself since "

" Since when ?" asked the Countess.

" Since I knew you, Gertrude "

This seemed rather to have burst from his lips involuntarily than to have been uttered deliberately; and there was something in the tone which made Gertrude start, as a vague suspicion darted across her mind that Lyndsay loved her. But she had scarcely time to admit the idea ere it was as quickly dispelled ; for, when she turned to look on him, the earnest expression with which he was regarding her fled ; and in a gay manner, he added—

"I flattered myself I had been an infinitely wiser, better, and more respectable person than I find I am —for I begin to feel myself, under your influence, gradually sinking into a soft, simple, neat-handed, somewhat melancholy sort of a souffre douleur; and, if I stay much longer with you, I must provide myself with a flute and a silk dressing-gown — and then "

"What then?" asked Lady Rossville, laughingly.

" Why, then you must promise to look upon me as a very interesting creature ; and I will stand, or sit, half the night at my open window, playing lovelorn ditties, that will cause, as Gray says, the very cat to wring its hands."

" Well, I shall provide the silk dressing-gown and the flute — hut for the lady and the cat, you must find these for yourself."

" But these will he only a small part of the stock in hand necessary for me to commence business with. I must he able to write sonnets upon every occasion—often upon no occasion at all. I must be able to take the most correct and striking likenesses without a single sitting "

" 'Tis time you had begun to practise that part of your profession, certainly," said Gertrude. " Do you remember how long ago it is since you promised to draw my picture ? — Pray, begin now — I have nothing else to do; and this lovely setting sun will invest me with a little of his radiance, and soften down all my uglinesses : — see how beautiful every thing looks in its light!"

" But, you know, I warned you I never flattered in my portraits—mine profess to be ' truth severe'—cold, dry, hard facsimiles, without a single Claud Lorraine tint."

" No matter, let me see myself such as I am, or at least appear to my friends."

" Well, not to shock you at the very outset, I must say you appear to me to love truth, and to be sincere in the search of it — but you have some pride and a little obstinacy to prevent your arriving at it; then, your fancy is too lively to permit you to take the right way, and while you are under its fantastic dominion you will never judge correctly."

" Not very flattering, certainly," said the Countess, affecting to laugh—" ' is just not ugly, and is just not mad,' seems to be the amount of your panegyric — but pray go on."

" You do not want penetration, but you form your opinions too hastily; you will be accused of inconsistency and caprice, but unjustly; you will only be undeceived "

" I seem to have got into the hands of a fortune-teller rather than a portrait-painter," said Lady Rossville, somewhat pettishly; " and as I never listen to predictions that bode me no good, I'll none of yours—'tis an idle art, and no coming events shall cast their shadows upon me Come, this is enough for one sitting; you shall have another to-morrow, when, perhaps, you will do me such as I am, not as I may be."

" To-morrow I must leave you," said Lyndsay.

" No, pray do not talk of leaving me," cried Gertrude quickly. " What will become of me when you are gone ? I shall have no one being with whom I can have any companionship—no one to talk with—no one to read with—no one to sing with—no one to walk -with—no one to teach me any good thing—my dear cousin, say you will not leave me."

But Lyndsay shook his head.

" Come, Zoe," to a little Italian greyhound that lay at her feet, " do you join your pretty little entreaties to mine," and she made it assume a begging attitude. The dog was a gift from Delmour, and Lyndsay turned away his eyes.

"I must begone," said he.

"Nay, rather say shall, or will begone," cried the Countess, pettishly; "I do not believe there is any must in the matter— you are your own master, free to go or stay, as you yourself incline."

"Even were it so, do not be so much of a spoiled child, Gertrude, as to quarrel with your friend, merely because he has, what it is said all men have, and some women too, a will of his own."

"But I have more than once, of late, sacrificed mine to Mr. Lyndsay's," said Gertrude, coldly.

"But were I to sacrifice my will, I must, at the same time, sacrifice my conscience along with it," said Lyndsay; "or rather, to confess the truth, they are somewhat at variance upon this occasion: the one urges me to stay—the other warns me to begone."

"The conscience may be mistaken as well as the will sometimes," said Gertrude; —"in this matter I suspect yours is, otherwise it would have told you how much good you may do by remaining here."

"No — it never tells me such flattering tales; that is the province of hope or fancy, and sometimes, perhaps, I may have been weak enough to listen to their idle tales" He stopped in some emotion, and for an instant fixed his eyes on Gertrude's face; but if his words had any particular meaning, it was not caught by her, for not the slightest change was perceptible on her speaking countenance. "If I thought I could be of any real service to you, I would remain here even at the sacrifice of my own" happiness was on his lips, but he checked himself, and substituted time; "but I have no right to interfere in the only way where I might be of use, and I cannot linger on for an indefinite time as a sort of spy upon the actions of others. You require protection, I know, and are now in a situation to claim it; choose, then, guardians for yourself, or allow the law to appoint them for you."

To think and to speak were commonly one and the same thing with Gertrude, and she instantly exclaimed —

"Then I shall choose you for one of my guardians."

"Choose me!" exclaimed Lyndsay, in astonishment. "No, that cannot be."

"Why not? I know nobody I should like so much to have for my guardian. — I am sure you would never scold me, or lecture me, however naughty I might be Now, don't—pray don't propose to me any of your old cross things, with round wigs, and square buckles, and long pockets, who would preach me a sermon upon every five-pound note I squandered."

"Such guardians are scarcely to be met with now, except upon the stage," said Lyndsay, smiling.

"Perhaps the wigs and pockets—but the long faces and long lectures, I fear, prevail every where. I must know the person before I can put myself in such jeopardy."

"You may be in greater jeopardy, Gertrude," said her cousin gravely.

Lady Rossville blushed—she saw to what he alluded; and after a pause, she said, in some emotion—

"The danger which you seem to apprehend no longer exists — the person whose audacious conduct to me you twice resented is no more—he has perished at sea." And she recapitulated the account of the shipwreck, and her mother's testimony, confirming the fate of Lewiston.

" So far, then, I shall leave you with a lightened mind," said Lyndsay; " there seems no more to apprehend from that quarter at least.— If there are other dangers "

But at that moment a post-chaise and four, the horses in a foam, came driving up the avenue full speed.

" Who can this be ? " exclaimed Lady Rossville; — then, as the thought flashed upon her that it might be Colonel Del-mour, she started up—her heart beat violently—her colour went and came—she would have moved towards the house, but her agitation was so great she sunk upon the seat, while her eyes remained fixed upon the carriage. It drew up at the castle gate ; and scarcely had it stopped when the person from within burst open the door, and Colonel Delmour himself sprung out with such impetuosity that it was but a single glance could be caught of him as he rushed into the house — but that was enough. Again Gertrude rose ; but, ashamed of her emotion, she could not lift her eyes to Lyndsay's, or she would have seen that he was little less agitated than herself—she could only accept of the arm he offered her, and in silence they proceeded together towards the house.

As they entered the hall the voice of one of the servants was heard, as in reply to an interrogatory, " Her ladyship has been out for some hours with Mr. Lyndsay;" and at that instant Colonel Delmour, with a hurried step and agitated air, rushed from the saloon. Joy, fear, doubt, displeasure, love, a thousand mingled emotions, were all struggling in Gertrude's breast—she tried to withdraw her arm from Lyndsay's, but she only clung the more helplessly to him ; while he felt her increasing weight, and feared she would have fallen to the ground.

" Lady Rossville is fatigued -with her walk," said he, addressing Colonel Delmour, and mastering his own agitation at sight of hers; " a glass of water here quickly," to the half-dozen of servants who stood idly lounging in the hall, and the whole instantly vanished in all the bustle and importance of their bearing. But, mortified and ashamed at this display of her weakness, the Countess instantly regained, in some degree, her self-possession. Even while her heart beat high, and her whole frame trembled with excessive emotion, she said, with a lofty air,—

" I have to apologize to Colonel Delmour for this uncourteous reception on his return to "

At that moment Lyndsay, taking the water from the servant, presented it to her himself, in the manner of one privileged to render those little attentions.

" Desire my carriage to wait," cried Delmour, in a loud and passionate voice, as it was driving away.

Lady Rossville was now nerved to perfect self-command, and, with a blush of offended dignity, she passed on to the saloon, where sat only Lady Betty, still lost in wonder at her nephew's sudden appearance and no less sudden flight. Lyndsay's indignation had been excited by the rudeness and violence of Colonel Delmour's address ; but anger with him was at most but a transient feeling, and a moment after they had entered the saloon, he held out his hand to him in a friendly manner. But the other turned hastily on his heel, and paced the room with disordered step, utterly regardless of the questions Lady Betty continued to pour out upon him. At length, approaching Gertrude, he said, "I would speak with Lady Rossville alone."

For a moment the Countess hesitated at the abruptness of the demand, and her pride revolted at the manner in which it was made ; but she rose, and with an inclination of the head led the way to another apartment. Colonel Delmour followed, when having shut the door—

"Gertrude," cried he, as he seized her hands, while his own shook with the violence of his emotion, " now speak my doom —from your own lips only will I hear it—say but the word — tell me I have been deceived—forgotten—forsaken ?"

" O, no — no — never !" exclaimed Gertrude, giving way to tears, as her resentment began to subside at sight of her lover's anguish.

" Call it what you will then—but do not rack me by equivocating. Already I have endured tortures for your sake that worlds would not have bribed me to undergo — despair itself would have been a blessing, compared to these distracting doubts."

*" 'Tis I who have had cause to doubt," said the Countess, as she seated herself at a table, and shaded her eyes with her hand,

ashamed of the tenderness her tears betrayed for one whose constancy she had such cause to question.

" You who have had cause to doubt!" cried Delmour, impetuously ; " could you then doubt me, Gertrude ?"

" Had I not cause ? — Why was I left at such a time, when a single word from you "

" Would have consigned you for ever to poverty and obscurity. — Is it not so ? You would have been mine, had I been base and selfish enough to have plunged you in ruin—to have sacrificed your happiness to my own."

" Ah ! by what a degrading standard did you measure my happiness, if you thought pomp and wealth could ever compensate for broken vows—for a deceived heart!—you would have renounced me !"

" No, by Heavens, I would not— I will not! — But, yes—you are right, I would—I will renounce you, Gertrude—if, by doing so, I can insure your happiness, it matters not though mine be a wreck."

Lady Rossville spoke not — her heart heaved with emotion — and Colonel Delmour, leaning against the chimneypiece, contemplated her for some moments without speaking : at length, taking her passive hand, he seated himself on the sofa by her; then, in a voice for a moment calmed into tenderness, he said—

" Gertrude, there was a time when, had an angel spoken it, I would not have believed that aught on earth could ever have induced me to resign this hand—and even now worlds should not wrest it from me but, fickle—faithless as you are, why should I seek to retain it ?"

" Release me, Colonel Delmour," cried the Countess, in a voice choking with emotion — " I have not deserved — I will not endure such language," and she struggled to withdraw her hand.

" Yet hear me one moment — my fate is on your lips — tell me that our vows are cancelled, and, in doing so, seal my doom at once and for ever !"

But Gertrude spoke not.

" Gertrude—in spite of all—dearest—most beloved—I cannot resign you but with my dying breath—why do you impose upon me so cruel a sacrifice ? " He unclasped the hand in which he had held hers locked—" Why suffer your hand to remain for an instant in mine ? — Gertrude, you are free ! "

Lady Rossville slowly withdrew it, then, raising her head, she shook off the tears which gemmed her eyes, and cast on him a look which spoke all the confiding tenderness of her soul, — then, replacing her hand within his, she turned away her head, to hide the blush that mantled her cheek.

CHAPTER XXXII.

O Jove ! why hast thoa given us certain proof
To know adulterate gold ; but stamp'd no mark
Where it is needed most — on man's base metal ? Euripides.

Lyndsay passed the intervening time in a state of feverish agitation very foreign to his natural equanimity of mind. That he loved Gertrude he could no longer conceal from himself; but his love was not of that violent yet contracted nature which seeks to engross and appropriate the affections exclusively to itself. He had proposed a nobler aim—a purer gratification; as his love was without idolatry, so was it free from selfishness. He had not sought to undermine her affections — he had aimed at elevating and ennobling them by extending their sphere beyond the narrow, perishable limits of human attachment; and he had hoped that a mind so pure, so lofty, so generous as hers, might yet become enamoured of virtue — might yet be saved from uniting itself with a nature unworthy of its love. And now was the test; on this interview her fate seemed suspended. Her emotion at sight of Colonel Delmour had, indeed, evinced the power he still retained over her ; but that power might be urged too far. Though Gertrude was soft and feminine in her feelings, yet her spirit was high, and ever ready to rise against violence and injustice ; and thus the tie, which a tenderer hand could not have unloosed, might, by his own impetuosity, be broken. Such were the hopes and fears that alternately rushed over Lyndsay's heart, as he waited, in an agony of impatience, the result of the conference, his eyes fixed immovably upon the door which led to the adjoining apartment. Their usually soft benign expression had given way to dark and troubled melancholy, and Lady Betty's questions fell unheeded on his ear. At length the door opened, and the first glance sufficed to show Lyndsay that his doom and hers were sealed. Gertrude's eyes were still moist with tears, 'tis true; but there was a smile on her lip—a flush of joy on her cheek—a lightness in her step— an aerial grace diffused over her whole face and figure, that told a tale of reconciled love, and seemed as though Happiness itself were embodied in a mortal form. All had been explained, and explanations were received as proofs of holy writ—for what imperfect evidence suffices where the heart is willing to believe! Colonel Delmour told a tale of suffering — he told of the agonizing alternative that had been offered to him to make her his, and in doing so to make her, at the same time, an outcast from the home of her fathers — to reduce her to obscurity and want: — he told her of the struggles of his mind — of the menacing fears — the half-formed resolutions — the desperate thoughts

-which had harassed his fancy, and destroyed his peace "by day;— the horrid dreams— the agonizing forms -which had haunted his couch by night — till at length nature sunk under the conflict, and a violent fever ensued. No sooner was he sufficiently recovered to encounter the voyage, than, unable longer to endure this state of suspense, and yet still more unable to come to any decision until he had seen her, he formed the resolution of returning to Britain, he the consequences what they might — of sounding the depths of her affection, and of receiving his sentence from her own lips. The voyage proved tedious and hazardous, and, on landing, he proceeded direct to London. He had there heard, for the first time, of the death of Lord Ross-ville ; and his hrother, at the same time, made known to him his rejection hy the Countess, and the fact, that her marriage with Edward Lyndsay was a settled point, and was to take place as soon as propriety admitted. Almost maddened at this intelligence, he had thrown himself into a post-chaise, and travelled night and day till he had arrived there, when his worst fears were confirmed by the answer he received to his inquiry for her, as well as from the footing she appeared to he upon with Lyndsayl

This was Colonel Delmour's way of telling his own story, and it was correct in every thing save the motives. " What's done we fairly may compute," but who can trace actions to their source ? who can fathom the depths of the human heart, or discern those secret springs, which, although they send forth waters alike pure to the eye, are yet as the issues of life and death ? Colonel Delmour had told a tale which in every circumstance was true, and yet the colouring was false. He had ascribed to disinterested affection what, in reality, proceeded from self-interest ; for although he assuredly did love, it was love compounded of such base materials as adversity, like the touch of Ithuriel's spear, would soon have shivered to atoms. But she saw nothing of all this, and she gave her tears—her faith—her love to him, whom she thought more than worthy of them all. His looks too seemed to confirm his words, for he looked thin, and pale, and hai'assed ; but as the cloud cleared away from his hrow, and the traces of passion which had disfigured his fine features disappeared, that gave him an interest in her eyes which more than atoned for the want of more dazzling attributes.

On her part, Gertrude could also have told much ; hut 'tis woman's part to suffer, man's privilege to speak on those occasions ; and while Colonel Delmour poured forth the history of his feelings in all the eloquence of excitement, it was plain to see that he touched an answering chord in her heart, and that she too had endured all that he expressed. But, now that the storm was past, the sunshine of the soul was theirs, only varied ac-cording to the different natures from which it emanated ; and as Lyndsay beheld the April-like joy that beamed in Gertrude's

face, and met the haughty exulting glance of Delmour, he, for a moment, closed his eyes, as though he could also have closed his heart against the conviction that Gertrude vras lost to him —lost to the higher, happier destiny, that he had fondly traced out for her.

" What's taking you away in such a hurry, Frederick ? " asked Lady Betty, laying down her book and her spectacles on their entrance.

" I only came in haste, and have no intention of returning the same way," answered he, with a smile of meaning to the Countess ; then ringing the bell, he gave orders to discharge his carriage.

"Where did you come from to-day?" was Lady Betty's second interrogatory.

" That I really cannot tell; having travelled day and night since I landed at Falmouth, their boundaries are not very accurately defined in my mind or my mind's eye either."

" What was the need of that ? " demanded her ladyship. " Had you heard of your good uncle's death ?"

." In London, where I only stopped half an hour."

" Did you see your brother ? Did he tell you that he had given up the election ? Did your mother and sisters tell you that ? "

" I did—he did—they did—let us have done."

" And what was the nonsense of your posting down, then ? "

" To put a stop to absurd pretensions," answered Colonel Delmour, with a sort of insolent nonchalance, as he looked at Mr. Lyndsay.

" But do you think you'll succeed ? "

Colonel Delmour smiled a smile of haughty disdain; Lady Rossville coloured; and Lyndsay, looking steadily at him, said calmly—

" I have heard of no absurd pretensions—none who had not, at least, an equal right to try their merits if they had thought proper."

Ere Colonel Delmour could utter the scornful retort which had risen to his lips, the door opened, and uncle Adam walked in, with his antique peruke, and blue boot hose ; for he had now got so tame, that he had learnt to walk the house at all hours of the day. He was not aware of the arrival of a strangei", otherwise he would certainly have skulked to the last moment — if, indeed, he would not actually have fled the country to his own city of refuge in Barnford.

Colonel Delmour surveyed him for a moment from head to foot with unfeigned astonishment, when Lady Rossville introduced him as her uncle, Mr. Ramsay. He then, quickly recovering himself, saluted him with a bow, twice repeated, so condescendingly profound, and with such an air of high breeding, as formed a ludicrous contrast to uncle Adam's awkward repulsive gait, and dry uncouth manner. The latter possessed too

much tact not to feel what was implied, and that such lofty courtesy only betokened one " proud enough to be humble," and a new stock of wrath began to ferment within him—that on hand having previously been disposed of at the expense of Dame Lowrie's dead-clothes. For the first time Lady Rossville blushed for her relation; but, ashamed to show that she was ashamed, she hastened to make some remark to him on the scene they had witnessed in the cottage; then, as if afraid to hear him answer, she went on—" But I must tell the story, and my cousin Lyndsay will help me in my Scotch ;" and with her musical voice, and refined accents, she attempted to take off the barbarous dialect of the cottars ; but when she came to the denouement, uncle Adam burst out with " The impudent thief! She deserved to hae been sent the same gate as her duds !"

Colonel Delmour absolutely stared, and that -was a great deal for a man like Colonel Delmour to do. Lady Rossville, covered with confusion, tried to laugh ; but the thought that Colonel Delmour was shocked with her uncle made it rather a difficult matter. Luckily at that moment her servant entered to say that Mrs. St. Clair had returned from her airing, and begged to see her ladyship immediately. The Countess rose to obey the summons. Colonel Delmour attended her to the door, pressed her hand; whispered some soft nothing in her ear, to which she replied with a blush and a smile; then, calling his servant, said he should go to dress, while she repaired to her mother's apartment.

CHAPTER XXXIII.

O ! how this spring of life resemhleth
Th' uncertain glory of an April day ;
Which now shows all the beauty of the sun,
And by and by a cloud takes all away. Shakespeare.

What is this I hear ? " was the exclamation that greeted Gertrude on her entrance. " Is it possible that Colonel Delmour has had the effrontery to come to this house ? Is it credible that you have had the weakness to receive him under your roof after what has passed?"

" I know nothing that ought to render Colonel Delmour an unsuitable or an unwelcome guest in my house," answered the Countess, endeavouring to speak calmly and decidedly.

"•Then you do not know that as the poor, dependent Gertrude St. Clair, he slighted, disowned, and in a manner rejected you ; and that now, as Countess of Rossville, he flies to you, worships you, would marry you ? Is it not so? and did I not foretell how it would be ? "

" While we view Colonel Delmour's conduct in such different

lights, 'tis impossible we should agree. Mamma, I beseech you, say no more. I am satisfied — completely — perfectly satisfied, that he has acted all along from the noblest and most disinterested motives."

" How has he proved that? Who is there credulous enough to believe his averments of disinterested affection? — Why should they be believed ? What right has he to expect such monstrous credulity ? "

" The right which every generous mind feels it has upon the faith and confidence of another."

"Gertrude, your words are those of a child — I may say of a fool. Who else could be weak enough to credit assertions contradicted by the whole tenor of the man's conduct ?"

"Be it so then!" cried Lady Rossville, vainly struggling to retain her composure ; "I am a child — a fool — for I believe in Colonel Delmour's truth and honour. The prejudices of the whole world would not shake my conviction."

"And what is to be the consequences of your madness ? Will you dare to brave my authority, and marry him against my consent ?" cried Mrs. St. Clair, giving way to one of her transports of passion. Lady Rossville remained silent. "Speak, I desire you," continued she, with increasing impetuosity ; "I repeat, will you dare to marry him against my consent ? "

"Mamma, I have twice solemnly passed my word to you that I will not marry until I have attained the age of twenty-one."

"If you would have me trust to that, then till that period arrives dismiss your lover—this very day let Colonel Delmour leave your house, and leave you free: — consent to that, and I will believe you sincere."

"Impossible !" exclaimed the Countess, in agitation.— "How can you require of me to act in such a manner ?"

"Then leave it to me. I am the fittest person to act for you in this matter. I will see Colonel Delmour myself;" and she was moving towards the door, when Gertrude laid her hand upon her arm, and, with a cheek coloured with resentment, exclaimed — "If my friends are to be turned from nnder my roof, then is iny own house no longer a habitation for me. — I will seek another home — other protection."

Mrs. St. Clair turned pale with passion, and, in a voice almost suffocated, she said — "In the meantime, I command you, by the duty you owe me, to confine yourself to your own apartment for the present. — Do not think to brave my power — I still possess it, and will use it."

There are bounds beyond which passion cannot go without counteracting its own purpose ; and Mrs. St. Clair had scarcely uttered the words, when she was sensible she had gone too far to be obeyed. Lady Rossville instantly became calm; but it was not the calm of fear or of submission, but that of settled deter-

u

mination, as she bent her head in silent acquiescence, and, without uttering a syllable, was about to withdraw.

"Stay — where — what do you mean ?" cried her mother, interrupting her in her progress to the door.

"To obey," answered Lady Rossville, calmly.

"Gertrude, why — why do you drive me to such extremities?"

"'Tis I who am driven to extremities, God help me !" exclaimed her daughter, bursting into tears.

"Gertrude, what is your meaning — what is your purpose ?" cried her mother, in violent agitation.

Lady Rossville was silent for a few moments. The question was repeated, when, after a struggle to regain her composure, she said — "This house, and all that I call mine, is yours to command ; but my affections, my liberty, will brook no control. For this day I submit to be a prisoner in my own house — tomorrow I will place myself under the protection of the laws of my country — from these I shall surely meet with justice — let these appoint guardians for me "

Mrs. St. Clair was struck with consternation. She felt the error she had committed in goading to the utmost a spirit such as her daughter's ; and there remained but one way to extricate herself from the dilemma she had brought herself into by her violence: true, that was the old way, but it had hitherto succeeded, and might still answer the purpose better than any other.

" No, Gertrude," cried she, " since it is your wish that we should part, it is for me to seek another home. Suffer me to remain here for this night, and to-morrow you shall get rid of me for ever. I feel / can neither contribute to your greatness nor your happiness \ but all that I would lay claim to — peace of mind and respectability — are in your hands. Spare me, at least, the misery and disgrace of being denounced to the world by one for whom I have done and suffered so much ! " and Mrs. St. Clair wept real genuine tears.

But at that moment Mrs. St. Clair's maid tapped at the door, to inform her lady that dinner was upon the table ; and, at the same moment, the gong sounded, in confirmation of the intelligence. In an instant all high-wrought feeling was put to flight by this vulgar every-day occurrence.

" Good Heavens ! " exclaimed she, aware that her elaborate toilette required at least an hour to arrange— " What is to be done ? — How came we to miss the dressing-bell ? — It is impossible for me to appear ; and both to be absent would have a strange appearance. Gertrude, you must join the company ; do make haste." Then, as her daughter stood irresolute — " As you love me, obey me now. Let there be mutual forgiveness — mutual confidence. Away, my love ;" and she kissed her forehead. To avoid farther contention, Gertrude hastened to her apartment to dress, and recover her composure as she best could.

CHAPTER XXXIV.

My soul, sit thou a patient looker-on ;
Judge not the play before the play is done ;
Her plot has many changes ; every day
Speaks a new scene : the last act crowns the play. Quarles.

But there was no fairy awaiting her there to dry her tears and deck her from head to foot by a touch of her wand, hut a mere human, though very expert waiting-maid, lost in a maze of conjecture at her lady's non-appearance at this, the most important crisis of the day, in her estimation.

" I have put out your black crape robe with bugles, my lady," began the important Miss Masham ; " and your black satin and your pearls, my lady, and your "

" Pray, don't teaze me, Masham," interrupted her lady, in a fretful manner, very foreign to her natural one.

" My lady ! " exclaimed the bewildered maid.

"Desire Jourdain to say, that I beg the company may not wait for me — I will join them at the second course — and give me — no matter what; no, not that odious velvet — never let me see it again."

" Crape, to be sure, my lady, is much more suitable now; though satin, you know, my lady, is the most properest demme schuchong." *

The Countess sighed as she threw herself upon a seat, and allowed herself, for the first time, to be dressed according to Miss Masham's taste.

" What a frightful head ! " was the reward of Masham's toils, as her lady looked at herself in the glass; then, smote with the mortification she had inflicted, she added, " But I believe 'tis because I look so cross — don't I, Masham ? "

" Cross! dear, my lady, that is such an idear ! As if your ladyship could ever be cross ! —

and your head, my lady, looks charmingly becoming." But her lady demolished part of Miss Masham's work before she descended to the dining-room.

Notwithstanding that Miss Pratt had instantly voted that Lady Rossville's message should be acted upon, and loudly protested that it would be very ill-bred were they not to eat their dinner, the same as if she were present when she had desired it, yet Colonel Delmour as promptly decided otherwise, and ordered the dinner to be taken down stairs again. Then, quitting the room, he repaired to the gallery through which he knew the Countess must pass from her own apartment, there to wait her appearance, and lead her to dinner.

* Demi-saison. U 2

The old feud between Pratt and him had lost nothing by absence, and they had met with the same feelings of hostility as they had parted. She had expressed in the loudest manner her astonishment at sight of him — he was the very last person she had dreamt of seeing at Rossville — had figured him still at Gibraltar with his regiment — it was so long since he had been heard of, and sometimes it was " out of sight out of mind," &c. &c. &c.

On Colonel Delmour's part, he, in a contemptuous manner, had congratulated Miss Pratt on having accepted an official situation in Lady Rossville's household, which insured her friends the enjoyment of her company at all times, and at all seasons, however unseasonable.

No sooner was his back turned than Miss Pratt and uncle Adam began to lay their heads together, for he had already become a new bond of union between them.

" What do you think of this new-comer, Mr. Ramsay ? " whispered she, as she made up to him in the out-of-tbe-way corner where he usually sat. Uncle Adam, who scorned to whisper, and, indeed, would not have whispered to have saved the Capitol, only replied by an expressive grunt, which was, however, sufficiently encouraging for his friend to proceed.

" What do you think of his taking it upon him to order the dinner down again, after Lady Rossville had sent to desire us to begin ? I'm sure I didn't care a pin-head, for my part, about the matter, but I really thought it vastly impertinent in him of all people to say black or white in this house; for, between ourselves, I can tell you he is no favourite in a certain quarter."

"I dinna wonder at it, for he's a proud, upsetting-like puppy."

" Proud! I only wish, sir, you had seen as much of his pride and impertinence as I've done."

" I've just seen enough o't. — Didna I see him boo to me as if he were the Prince o' Wales ? "

" That's exactly Anthony Whyte! — my nephew, Mr. Whyte of Whyte Hall! He says he can stand any thing but Colonel Delmour's bow, for that he bows to him as if he was his shoemaker — a man that cauld buy and sell him, and all his generation ! As for me, I assure you, I am thankful he gives me none of his civilities."

" What's brought him here ? " demanded uncle Adam, gradually winding up to the sticking-point.

" Indeed, sir, that's more than I can tell you, unless it's to try whether he can come better speed with the Countess than he did with the heiress. But there's little chance of that, or I'm mistaken."

" She has mair sense, I hope."

" That she has! — Not but that I will always think she might have waited and looked about her a little; for, you know, to use an old saying, ' There's as gude fish i' the sea as ever came out o't,' and she needn't have been in any hurry."

" I see nae gude that comes o' waiting," said uncle Adam, with a sigh, as he thought how he had waited in vain ; — " but I am at a loss to understand wha ye ca' the fish, for I dinna think she's ta'en up wi' onybody that I've seen."

" My dear Mr. Ramsay ! Is that possible! I really would have given you credit for greater penetration! Ay! not to have found out what's been going on all this time,"—and her eyes took the direction where Lyndsay sat reading, or at least appearing to read, for his thoughts were otherwise employed.

Uncle Adam shook his head.

" No, Mr. Ramsay — you know, if you doubt that, you may doubt any thing. Even Lady Betty, honest woman, who seldom sees over her nose, asked me t'other day if I did not think we were like to have a wedding soon ? In fact, every thing, I believe, was pretty much settled before poor Lord Rossville's death — though, whether he would have given his consent, I can't pretend to say — I only speak of what I know for a certainty."

Mr. Ramsay still looked incredulous.

" But what makes you doubt it, sir?—there's nothing very unlikely in it. To be sure, as I said before, Edward Lyndsay's no match for her in point of fortune, you know ; but she has plenty for both. And he's a genteel, elegant-looking creature ; and though I think his notions, on some things, a great deal too strict, yet I know him to be an honourable fine creature as ever lived, and she'll change him, depend upon it — she'll bring him round to her way of thinking before it's long.

" "VVeel, weel; we shall see—time will show," said Mr. Ramsay, still in that unconvinced manner which is infinitely more provoking than flat contradiction.

" The old ram-horned goose, that he is," thought she, " what can he know about these things ? " Then aloud, " See! —'pon my word, Mr. Ramsay, I think we've seen enough to satisfy anybody — and heard too, some of us ; for instance, what would you say, if it had so happened that I was so situated as to be actually obliged to hear (without the slightest intention of listening, but this between you and me) her give our friend, the Colonel there, his conge, and, at the same time, acknowledge herself engaged to Edward Lyndsay?—and that I heard with my own ears."

Miss Pratt had told this story so often that it had gradually grown upon her hands, and was so firmly impressed upon her own mind that she now told it with all the force of truth.

Uncle Adam was vanquished. " Ye ken, if ye did that, there need be na mair said about it. But I woudna hae said that she was in love wi' him, though I'll no say but I've sometimes thought there might be something on his side for her. Weel, if it is sae, as ye say, she might hae done better, and she might hae done waur. But the warst o't is, I dinna think there is muckle love

u 3

on her side;" and uncle Adam heaved a sigh of fond remembrance.

" I'll tell you what, Mr. Ramsay, love's a very different thing now-a-days from what it was in our time. — Preserve me! I believe I would have sunk through the ground before I could have gone on as Lady Rossville does. Such a work as she makes with — Cousin Lyndsay this, and Edward that! — and what's all this work about visiting the poor, and building school-rooms, and such nonsense, but to please him ? And yet she's a sweet, modest-like creature, too, and, for as easy as she is, there's really nothing flirting in her manner neither. But just look at that! " with a jog on the elbow to her ally, as Lady Rossville entered, followed by Colonel Delmour. " Did you ever see such impudence, to be hunting her in that manner ? — Poor soul! she looks quite fluttered : I really think she has been crying."

Lady Rossville was beginning to apologize for the delay she had occasioned, when dinner was, for the second time, announced. She motioned Lady Betty, as usual, to take the lead, and looked at Colonel Delmour to offer his arm; but with one of what uncle Adam called his Prince of Wales's bows to Edward Lyndsay, he fell back, and seized the Countess's hand with a look of haughty triumph.

"I hope you observed that manoeuvre," whispered Miss Pratt, bending towards uncle Adam, as they stotted along, side by side, but a full yard asunder — for he would as soon have offered his head as his hand, or even his arm, upon these occasions;—" but there's an old byword, ' Fanned fires and forced love ne'er did weel;' and some people will maybe not crack quite so crouse by and by."

Miss Pratt's ideas were farther confirmed by Lady Rossville's manner at dinner; for she observed she paid more attention to, and seemed more at her ease with every body, than Colonel Delmour. Uncle Adam likewise remarked this — but he drew a different augury from it, as he called to mind his own shame-facedness when Lizzie Lundie was in question. He marked, too, Edward Lyndsay's thoughtful, melancholy expression, so different from that of a favoured suitor, and the more striking from being contrasted with his rival's gay exulting air. And as he revolved all these things, his mind misgave him, even in spite of Miss Pratt's confidential assurances.

"I could wager you anything you like, you're mista'en about yon," said he, with a shake of his head, to her.

"Done!" was promptly replied, — for, next to a legacy, Miss Pratt liked a wager. — " What shall it be ? "

" I could lay you a crown."

" A crown!" with contempt; " I'll take you five guineas."

" Five guineas ! — that's a wager indeed!—Weel, I dinna care though I do—* a's no tint that's in hazard.'" And uncle Adam and Miss Pratt touched thumbs upon it.

"I'm very curious to know what you and my uncle are laying not only your heads hut your hands together about ?" said the Countess, with a smile, to Miss Pratt.

Mr. Ramsay blushed up to the eyes at having been so detected; but Miss Pratt, nowise abashed, answered, with a significant look —

" Your ladyship has, perhaps, a better right to know than any body else; but there's a good time coming — all's well that ends well."

" Even when a gentleman gives his left hand to a lady ?" said Colonel Delmour. — " I thought even Miss Pratt would scarcely have ventured on such a contract."

" They say ill-doers are ill-dreaders, Colonel, " retorted his antagonist ; — " and, for my part, I would prefer an honest man's left hand to a neer-do-weel's right any day of all the year. —' There's my thumb, I'll ne'er beguile you,' was a favourite song in our day, sir," to uncle Adam, "though it's maybe little, too little in vogue now — but we have not forgot it."

This was a random shot of Miss Pratt's; but it had the effect of raising Colonel Delmour's colour as well as his anger, though he prudently suppressed the latter for the present, and dexterously managed to give the conversation a turn to Scottish songs, and from thence, by an easy transition, to Italian music and poetry, which gave him an opportunity of uttering and insinuating many a tender sentiment, and, at the same time, put him completely beyond the reach of his enemy, who had the command of no tongue but her own.

When the dessert was put upon the table, the usual bustle announced the entrance of Mrs. St. Clair ; for an extraordinary eclat now attended all that lady's movements, as she entered a room somewhat in the manner of a tragedy queen coming upon the stage. And as she was really a fine-looking woman, dressed highly, and had a good portly air, the effect was very successful.

She really looked — what she evidently intended to represent — the Dowager Countess.

Colonel Delmour rose and advanced to meet her with an air of empressement he was far from feeling; but the hand he held out to her was not accepted, and a distant inclination of the head was the only acknowledgment vouchsafed, as she moved on to the seat he had vacated by Lady Rossville, and took possession of it.

" I presume I interfere with no one's rights in taking this chair, which, to me, possesses the double attraction of being next my daughter and nearest the fire."

Lady Rossville blushed at this open display of her mother's hostility. Colonel Delmour bit his lip to repress the scornful retort which was ready to burst forth. Miss Pratt hemmed, and gave uncle Adam a jog on the elbow.

" You look fatigued, love," addressing her daughter in a fondling manner; "you have done too much to-day—why, you must have been out at least three hours this morning—Mr. Lyndsay, I shall scarcely trust my daughter with you again. I hope you ate something—Lady Betty, I hope you made a point of Gertrude taking something good ? Now, come, let me dress a little pine for you in the way you used to like it abroad;" and taking off her gloves, and displaying her large, round, white arms, all glittering in rings and bracelets, she began to cut up a pine-apple, and show her skill in this refined branch of elegant cookery.

Lady Rossville felt this display of her mother's affection was merely with a view to deceive others as to the footing they were upon; she could, therefore, only sit in silent endurance of it, and Mrs. St. Clair continued to overwhelm her with endearing epithets and tormenting assiduities, which she could neither repel nor return. The party was too small to admit of tete-a-tetes, and too dissimilar in all its parts to carry on any thing of general conversation; and the Countess, weary of the irksome and idle verbiage of the dinner-table, rose early, and retired to the drawing-room.

" Take you care of these two," whispered Miss Pratt to uncle Adam, as she was leaving the room; " for I see a certain person's ready to fight with the wind."

No sooner had the ladies left the room than Colonel Delmour, going to the already blazing fire, began to stir it so violently that it roared, and crackled, and burned, till uncle Adam felt as though he should be roasted alive sitting in his own seat. But Colonel Delmour, uttering an ejaculation about cold, rang the bell, and ordered some mulled claret, well spiced, to be got ready immediately; then, placing himself before the fire, he stood there humming an opera air, and occasionally exciting the troublesome gambols of a large French poodle, to whom he addressed a few words in its native tongue.

" It will no be possible to live in a hoose wi' that puppy," thought uncle Adam, and he began to meditate his retreat the following day; but then, as the thoughts of Guy Mannering came over him, he staggered in his resolution : leave it he could not—to borrow it he would have been ashamed—to abstract it never entered into his primitive imagination ; for, in his day, it had not been the fashion for ladies and gentlemen to take other people's books, or to lose other people's books, or, in short, to do any of the free and easy things that are the privilege of the present age. True, there were libraries in Barnford ; but to have recourse to a circulating library !—to have it through the town that he was a novelle reader !—there was distraction in the thought! Perish Dumple and Dandie Dinmont, Dominie Sampson, and the whole host of them, before he would stoop to such a measure ! But, then, not to see the end of that scoundrel Glossin, whom he could have hanged with his own hands, only that hanging was too good for him—ay, there's the rub ! To he sure, he might skip to the end ; but he never had skipped in his life, and had such a thorough contempt for skippers that he would rather have " burst in ignorance," than have submitted to so degrading a mode of heing relieved. At one time, during dinner, he had thoughts of sounding Miss Pratt as to the result, but his courage failed him—it was hazarding too much with a woman ; now he resolved whether he might not, hy going about the bush with Mr. Lyndsay, extract the catastrophe from him —hut then he never had gone about the hush all his life, and he was rather at a loss how to set about it now. Before he could make up his mind, therefore, the time came for adjourning to the drawing-room; but, instead of repairing there, uncle Adam stole away to his own apartment, to try whether another chapter would not set the matter at rest.

CHAPTER XXXV.

But, all in vain, I bolt my sentences. Euripides.

Mrs. St. Clair's generalship was exerted so ■ successfully, throughout the evening, that, without any apparent design, the lovers were effectually precluded from exchanging words with each other, except in the way of common conversation. But this could not always continue ; she felt she had committed herself with her daughter, and must now either act with decision and authority, or give up the attempt altogether. The first would be a dangerous experiment with one of the Countess's high spirit, and the other was too galling an alternative to be voluntarily emhraced. Sooner or later, she saw it must end in guardians being appointed for her daughter, and she therefore determined to put the best face she could upon it, and be the first to propose the measure herself; not without hopes that, while she thus appeared to throw up the reins, she might at the same time be enabled the more effectually to strengthen her own hands. When the party broke up for the night she took Lady Rossville's arm and led her to her own dressing-room, when, dismissing her attendant, she thus hegan —" Gertrude, as this is perhaps the last time I may have an opportunity of addressing you under your own roof "

" Oh, mamma!" exclaimed the Countess, seizing her mother's hand, " do not, I beseech you do not recur to what has passed on that subject! This house is yours—you must not leave it— I will not leave you "

" Gertrude, be calm and hear me-

" No, mamma; first hear me declare that all remonstrance

-will prove unavailing — that no earthly consideration ever can change my resolution — I will not renounce my own free choice."

Lady Rossville spoke slowly, and she pronounced the last words in a manner which showed that opposition would indeed be vain.

" My object is not to contend with you, Gertrude," said her mother, with a sigh; " for I am fully aware how little influence I now possess over you; but my wish is to see you placed under the protection and guardianship of those who, if they want a mother's love, may soon possess more than a mother's influence. Say who it is that you would choose for your guardian ? "

" I choose you, mamma, for one, and my cousin Lyndsay for another — if a third is necessary, do you and he appoint whom you please."

Mrs. St. Clair was thunderstruck at the promptitude and decision of this answer ; and she could only repeat, in a tone of amazement —

" Mr. Lyndsay your guardian ! What an idea! "

" Surely there is nothing wrong in it, mamma? — and who else could I name ? "

" It certainly is not customary to choose so very young a man for such an office."

"But Mr. Lyndsay knows how I am situated — I consider myself as having been repeatedly obliged to him beyond the possibility of my ever repaying him; and although on one point we certainly differ,"—Gertrude blushed as she spoke—"yet that dees not prevent my doing justice to his general character. I respect and esteem him as my friend — as the person who has twice saved me from insult, once from destruction ; and I would fain prove to him, in perhaps the only way I may ever have in my power, the reliance I have on him, by placing myself under his control. After the scenes he has witnessed, I owe to myself to appoint Edward Lyndsay my guardian."

Mrs. St. Clair was silent for some time, while, in her own mind, she balanced the pros and cons of this measure. In the first place, she disliked the thought of having to deal with a person of Edward Lyndsay's acute understanding, unbending principle, and high standard of rectitude — one who, besides, already knew too much of her private concerns, and, consequently, could not be impressed with a very favourable idea of her character. But, to balance these drawbacks, he was evidently no friend to Colonel Delmour, and she thought she might safely calculate on his assistance to further any scheme to preserve Gertrude from becoming the dupe of his artifices. She was aware that he took more than a common interest in her daughter, and she had no doubt but she would so manage as by that means to gain an ascendency over him, while she had little fear that he would ever succeed in supplanting his rival; she would be on her guard against that, and, at any rate, it was

worth running all risks to detach her from her present entanglement. Still, even in this view, it was a hitter pill to swallow, and she remained thoughtful and disconcerted. At last she said, " You talk of repaying your obligations to Lyndsay, as though it were a benefit you were about to confer on him, by choosing him for your guardian. Are you aware that it is an office attended with much trouble and responsibility, and that you will only be adding to the weight of that mighty debt you have already incurred ?"

" My cousin, I know, will not consider it in that light; and, even if he should, I would rather be indebted to him than to any one else."

" Yet there are others on whom you have at least equal claims, and whom the world might think rather more suitable guardians for you."

" I do not know to whom you allude, mamma."

" It is not for me to point them out to you," said Mrs. St. Clair, with affected dignity.

" If you mean my uncle Adam, he is out of the question ; he is so odd "

" I do not mean my uncle," interrupted her mother; " you have still nearer relatives."

Lady Rossville coloured at the thoughts of Mr. Alexander Black ; — there was a good-humoured vulgar familiarity about him she could scarcely brook, and to subject herself to it was more than her proud spirit could submit to. She made no reply.

" There is also another person, whom I have less scruple in naming to you; and either, or both of those, I believe, the world in general would deem perfectly unexceptionable in point of station, connection, character, experience, property—in short, all the essentials for such a trust; neither of them certainly are Werters or St. Preux, but they are both what I think fitter for the purpose — they are both men of unblemished character, respectable understanding, mature age, and good if not great families ; but to one or both of these add, if you choose, any third party, such as Lord Millbank, Sir Peter Wellwood, Lord Fairacre—all of them you have seen and know something of, and one of them, joined eitherwith Mr. Black or Major Waddell "

" Major Waddell!" exclaimed the Countess; " surely, mamma, you are not serious ? Major Waddell my guardian! No, that is too, really too humiliating."

"You assume a vast deal too much with your new dignities," said Mrs. St. Clair, warmly, " when you presume to talk in that strain of a man born and bred a gentleman, and connected, too, with the first families in the country. The time may come when you may know what degradation is ; and, much as you despise my family, you may yet But no more of this folly ; I have named to you no less than five individuals, each and all of whom I consider perfectly unexceptionable in every respect."

" Well, then, if I must be so guarded, let Mr. Lyndsay and you raise a whole regiment of guards if you will — with the exception of Major Waddell — every thing else I leave to you and my cousin"—Lady Rossville laid particular emphasis on the word cousin — " and now, mamma, pray dismiss me — I am dying for sleep."

" And I of care," said her mother, with a deep sigh.

" Do not say so, mamma; be assured we shall both be happy in our own way;" and, kissing her, Gertrude withdrew to her own apartment.

Unwilling as she was to yield, Mrs. St. Clair felt that she had no alternative. Sometimes she thought of leaving Rossville, and taking her daughter along with her. But where could they go that Colonel Delmour would not follow ? And by adopting violent measures, she found she would only drive the Countess to extremities — perhaps accelerate the very evils she was most anxious to avoid. In short, after a night of restless deliberation, the mortifying conclusion she arrived at was, that, in this instance, she must submit to her daughter's decision, and adopt the plan she had declared herself determined to pursue. It was particularly disagreeable to her too, on account of the footing she was upon with Mr. Lyndsay. She still stood pledged to him for an explanation of the mysteries he had witnessed, but that pledge she had no wish or intention to redeem. The time was past—she had nothing to fear from him, and she felt averse to recur to a subject which she wished to be for ever consigned to oblivion.

In spite of all this, however, the thing must be done; and it would be much better done were she to come boldly forward as if of her own free will, than if she waited till she was compelled to do so in compliance with her daughter's wish. The following morning, therefore, she sent at an early hour to desire Lady Rossville to attend her in her dressing-room; and Gertrude was surprised, upon obeying the summons, to find her mother already up and dressed, as, ever since Lord Rossville's death, she had indulged in late hours, and secluded herself in her own apartment during the greater part of the day.

" I wish to know, Gertrude," said she, in a solemn manner, " whether you still retain the same sentiments that you professed last night — is it still your determination to throw off the parental yoke, to publish your distrust of your mother ?"

" It is still my determination," answered the Countess, gravely, " to obey my mother in all things compatible with what is due to myself; and I proclaim my sentiments to the world when I voluntarily make choice of her as my guardian—the other must be Edward Lyndsay." Lady Rossville spoke even more firmly than she had done the preceding night; and Mrs. St. Clair found that all attempts to turn her from this resolution would prove abortive.

" Be it so, then!" cried she ; " any thing must be better than this state of things. Give me your arm. I mean to breakfast below to-day;" and they descended together to the breakfast-room, where only uncle Adam and Miss Pratt had just appeared. These two worthies were in the heat of a colloquy; but on the entrance of the ladies it suddenly ceased in a very abrupt and suspicious manner; and uncle Adam shuffled away to the window with ears pendent, while Miss Pratt, who at first was quite thrown on her beam-ends, began to rally her forces.

The mystery was simply the last night's wager, renewed, not without hopes on Pratt's side, of persuading uncle Adam to knock under at once upon the voluminous mass of evidence she was pouring out upon him, and which, she flattered herself, would finally terminate in her fingering the five guineas, as she already looked upon them as her own, and felt somewhat impatient at being kept out of her lawful property. They had, however, all the air of detected lovers; and Mrs. St. Clair's antipathy against Miss Pratt was trebled tenfold, as the idea flashed upon her that she was endeavouring to inveigle uncle Adam and his seventy thousand pounds into an alliance offensive in the highest degree. However, their loves were a secondary consideration at present, and she allowed them to pass unnoticed, in the virtuous intention of crushing them effectually at some future period.

Breakfast passed very heavily. There was an evident constraint on all present; for even Miss Pratt was more intent on watching the progress of her wager, than in dispensing the usual flow of chit-chat. Mrs. St. Clair maintained the same haughty reserve towards Colonel Delmour, which he either was or affected to appear quite unconscious of, and directed his looks and attentions solely to Lady Rossville. But Miss Pratt's abstraction seldom lasted long; and as she chanced to cast her eye on Lyndsay, she suddenly exclaimed, " Bless my heart, my dear! what makes you look so ill to-day ?"

" I was not aware that I was looking particularly ugly this morning," answered he.

" Ugly, my dear! that's a very strong word; as Anthony Whyte says, it's one thing to look ill, and another thing to look ugly; and that there's many a one it would be paying too high a compliment to to tell them they were looking ill, for that would imply that they sometimes looked well — so you see you ought to be much flattered by my telling you that you are looking ill. — Don't you think so, Lady Rossville ?"

" I suspect Mr. Lyndsay is not easily flattered," answered she; " I was trying my powers with him in that way yesterday, but I cannot flatter myself I was successful."

" A fair acknowledgment that you were only flattering me all the while," said he, forcing a smile; " I half suspected as much, and therefore, to punish you for your insincerity, I shall certainly remain where I am for this day at least."

" I suspect that will prove rather an encouragement than a corrective to the vice," said Mrs. St. Clair, gaily ; " and lest Mr. Lyndsay should next mistake the matter so far as to think of rewarding our plain-dealing by running away from us, I engage him to attend me now to the library."

Mr. Lyndsay bowed his acquiescence, not without some surprise ; and, as he rose, Mrs. St. Clair put her arm within his, and was leaving the room, when, as if recollecting something, she called her daughter to her, and contrived to converse her out of the room, and to lead her through the suite of apartments till they came to that adjoining the library.

" Wait here, my love, for a few minutes," said she ; " I would first speak with Mr. Lyndsay alone, but it will be necessary you should join us immediately."

Lady Rossville felt as if she had only been taken there to be away from Colonel Delmour, and she almost smiled in derision at her mother's petty stratagems.

" Now !" cried Miss Pratt, in an exulting tone, to uncle Adam, as the party left the room.

" Weel — what noo?" demanded he, in an undaunted tone.

" That's really speaking out," continued she, pointing after them, and, at the same time, casting a glance at Colonel Delmour, who had hitherto sat in a sort of bitter scornful silence; but, on finding himself left at table with such a group as uncle Adam, Lady Betty, and Miss Pratt, he had immediately risen, and after carelessly tossing some fragments of the breakfast to his dog, and whistling a French air to him, he sauntered away with his usual air of high-bred nonchalance.

" Sour grapes," whispered Miss Pratt to uncle Adam.

" I'm no very sure about that," was the reply, as he prepared to creep away to his turret to Lizzie Lundie and Meg Merrilees.

CHAPTER XXXVI.

For my part, I think there is nothing so secret that shall not be brought to light within the world Burnet.

Mrs. St. Clair's nerves almost failed her when she found herself alone with Lyndsay, for the first time since their meeting in the wood; but then the reflection that the secret connected with that scene was for ever buried in the deep (or, what was still deeper, her own heart), recalled her self-possession; and, without betraying any fear or hesitation, she began —

" It must doubtless appear extraordinary to you that I should have allowed so much time to elapse without giving you the eclaircissement which you must naturally have expected."

" Which I was promised," said Lyndsay, emphatically.

" True, you were so; but my own illness, the subsequent events which have taken place in the family, rendered the performance of such a promise, for a time, impracticable; since then it has become unnecessary. The person who was the cause of so much needless alarm to my daughter and myself is no more; he has perished at sea — you must have observed in a late newspaper the detail of the shipwreck, and probably drew from it the same conclusion, that the wrong-headed, infatuated man, who had caused us so much annoyance, had met his fate."

" Yes, so far I did conjecture; but the circumstances which seemed to have placed Lady Rossville and you so completely in the power of such a man — you surely do not mean to leave these to conjecture?"

" It is certainly not every one on whose candour, and liberality, and charity, I could place such reliance as to leave a shadow of doubt on their minds which it was in my power to clear away; but when I balance, on the one hand, the painful task I should have to perform in recurring to past events — in disturbing the ashes of the departed — in harrowing up my own feelings, by recalling the unmerited obloquy, the poverty, and privations my unfortunate husband was doomed to endure, in consequence of his ill-fated attachment to me — can I — ought mine to be the hand to tear aside the veil in which his errors are now for ever shrouded ? On the other, what have I to dread from a nature so honourable and candid as yours — one which I believe to be as incapable of suspecting evil as of committing it?"

" I fear you give me credit for an extent of virtue I do not possess," said Lyndsay, gravely; "for I must freely confess that I have received impressions of so unfavourable a nature that I find all my charity quite insufficient to dispel them. Surely, then, justice is due to the living, as well as tenderness to the dead."

" You say true; and rather than that my daughter should

suffer in your estimation " Mrs. St. Clair stopped and sighed.

— " Yet I flattered myself that, with the thousand opportunities I have lately afforded you of gaining a thorough insight into her character, and of witnessing the almost childish openness of her disposition, you would ere now have been enabled, from your own knowledge of her (an infinitely surer criterion than a mother's commendation), to have acquitted her of all culpability in this unfortunate occurrence, ambiguous as it may appear."

" My suspicions do not, in the least degree, attach to Lady Rossville," cried Lyndsay, warmly; " I could stake my life on the purity of her mind and conduct — but "

" But you distrust me. — Well, be it so; since my daughter does not suffer, I am satisfied. Let mine be the obloquy —

only let me screen from reproach the memory of my hus-hand."

" I am little used to disguise my sentiments," said Lyndsay;

— " and the present occasion, I think, warrants my expressing them very plainly. You must excuse me, then, when I say, that I can scarcely conceive any motive so powerful as to induce a mother to endanger her own and her daughter's reputation. I have twice seen Lady Rossville insulted — had I possessed the power, she should certainly have been under other protection before now."

Mrs. St. Clair coloured deeply, and struggled for some moments to retain her composure; but she succeeded, and resumed —

" I was aware that such must be your opinion — and, mortifying as it is, I shall make no attempt to change it at present. Hereafter, perhaps, you may do me justice; in the meantime, it is my determination to resign the guardianship of my daughter into other hands. It is my wish, and that of Lady Rossville, that Mr. Lyndsay should accept this trust — the strongest proof we can either of us give of our own self-respect, as well as our confidence and esteem for him."

Mr. Lyndsay's emotion at this proposal did not escape Mrs. St. Clair's piercing observation, and she secretly hoped he might decline the proposal; but, after a few minutes' consideration, he said —

" I accept of the trust, and hope I may be enabled to discharge it faithfully — but I cannot take the whole responsibility of such an office; there must be other guardians appointed."

" My daughter insists upon my acting also in that capacity, although it was my wish to have delegated the office entirely to others — to my brother, for instance, or my nephew, Major Waddell, or any other of the county gentlemen she would name

— but she is immoveable on that point; so we have only to consider hereafter who it will be proper to make choice of. Meanwhile, allow me to consider you as the actual guardian of my daughter, and as such anxious to co-operate with me in all that is for her advantage ;" and Mrs. St. Clair went over pretty much the same ground she had done before, in painting the anticipated miseries of her union with Colonel Delmour — aggravated, too, by his late evasive conduct — the whole concluding with, " Had his absence been prolonged but for a few months, this childish fancy would have passed away — a more rational and more enduring attachment would have taken its place. Already, I sometimes flattered myself, the work was begun;"

— and she sighed as she fixed her eyes on Lyndsay, whose changing expression and varying colour spoke the feelings he would not for worlds have uttered. — " And now what is to be done ? Separated they must be, and that without delay; for while they are suffered to remain together, his influence will

prevail over every other. — Already his ascendency is ohvious

— every day, every hour spent together, will only serve to strengthen it. — My authority singly will be of no avail to counteract it — but you possess weight and influence with Gertrude "

" Which I have neither the right nor the inclination to use at present. Rashness and violence can serve no purpose but to increase opposition. Rely upon Lady Rossville's promise not to marry" — and Lyndsay's voice faltered a little as he said it

— "till she is of age. In the meantime, treat her with openness and confidence ; these will prove firmer holds than bolts or bars with a nature such as hers — suffer her mind to expand, and her judgment to mature. Suffer the slow but gradual process of mental elucidation to go on — let her see others perhaps as gifted as Colonel Delmour, and leave her free to form her own opinions and draw her own conclusions — perhaps, when she knows him better, she will learn to value him less — but any attempt to force a mind such as hers against its own bent will never succeed. You may gall and fret her temper, but you will not change, or at least improve her nature, and I will never consent to any measures of the kind."

This was very contrary to what Mrs. St. Clair had anticipated. She had flattered herself that he would have caught eagerly at the bait thrown out, and would have been ready to assist her in any scheme she might have suggested for the separation of the lovers. But Lyndsay's mind was much too noble and generous to allow any selfish considerations for a moment to sway him, even where the temptation was most powerful. He had no base passions to gratify, — neither envy, nor jealousy, nor revenge; and, consequently, his decisions were always just and upright. But it was far otherwise with Mrs. St. Clair, and she was provoked and disappointed at having failed to stimulate him to cooperate with her in the violent measures she had projected. She was aware, however, that it would be in vain to oppose the Countess and him together, and she was therefore obliged to yield an unwilling assent for the present.

. Lady Rossville was now summoned to the conference ; and the result was, that Lord Millbank and Mr. Alexander Black should be requested to accept the office of joint guardians along with Mrs. St. Clair and Mr. Lyndsay.

" As there are now no secrets amongst us, Gertrude," said her mother, in her most ostentatious manner, waving her hand to Mr. Lyndsay, " I may inform you, that it has been agreed upon by Mr. Lyndsay aud myself that Colonel Delmour shall be permitted to remain here for the present, on the footing of any other guest — such is the confidence we both place in your good sense and propriety."

Lady Rossville blushed at this extraordinary address, and both Lyndsay and she turned away their eyes from each other.

x

" It would be a strange assumption of brief authority in me," said he, " were I to presume to interfere with Lady Rossville in the choice of her guests;" and with a slight inclination of the head, he quitted the room.

" What a load has been taken from my mind by this arrangement !" said Mrs. St. Clair, with a sigh, which rather belied her words; " and now, Gertrude, love, will you order the carriage, or shall I? We must pay some visits — in particular, we must go to my brother's. Mr. Lyndsay has promised to ride to Lord Millbank's this morning, and settle matters with him. He is a stupid man ; but it seems he is a relation of yours, and understands business, so he may do very well. As for your uncle, 'tis proper you should see him yourself. I don't think you have been at Bellevue since Lord Rossville's death ?"

" But this morning is so delightful, it would be a sin to waste it on a dull drive to Bellevue; a much worse one might serve equally well for that purpose, and there are a thousand things I have to do to-day — I must see what progress has been made with my rustic bridge — whether the terrace-walk has yet been begun — how speeds my bower — if my flower-knots are arranging according to rule — apropos, mamma, what a lack of shrubs and flowers are here ! I must have quantities immediately — not a day must be lost. I must have clouds of dropping roses to meet this ' ethereal mildness,' and do all honour to this gentlest of gentle springs."

" Don't be a fool, Gertrude ; or, at least, remember there is a time for all things — even for folly. The present belongs to more important subjects than building baby-houses, and dressing dolls."

" Well, mamma, pray manage them as you will, but leave me at liberty to have a walk to-day."

" And who, pray, is to be your escort in this important sur-vey?"

Lady Rossville blushed and hesitated, then, in a faint voice, said, " Anybody, mamma."

" But Lady Rossville is not to ramble all over the country with anybody or everybody," said her mother, sarcastically; " I will have no clandestine meetings, remember."

" Clandestine!" repeated the Countess, " no ; with my own guests and relations, why should I have recourse to clandestine measures? My intention was to walk with Colonel Delmour; but since it is your desire that I should accompany you, I will do so ;" and she rose to ring the bell and order the carriage, ▪when the movement was arrested by hearing the sound of wheels crisping the gravel, as they rolled slowly round to the grand entrance. " Ah! there are my aunts!" exclaimed Lady Rossville. " I wrote yesterday to invite them, but I scarcely looked for them so soon. I must fly to welcome them;" and in an instant she was on the outer steps of the entrance, ready to assist her aunt Mary herself.

CHAPTER XXXVII.

These Indian wives are loving fools, and may do well to keep company with the Arrias and Portias of old Rome. — Dryden.

But the carriage door being opened, there stepped out Major Waddell, having upon his back a vast military cloak, with all its various appliances of tags, and jags, and flags, and waving capes, and scarlet linings, and shining brooch, &c. &c. &c. The Major having placed himself on one side of the carriage door, black Csesar, in no less gorgeous array, stationed himself at the other ; and then, after a little feminine delay, there came forth Mrs. Major Waddell in all her bravery. A rich and voluminous satin mantle enveloped her person ; a rare and costly lace veil streamed like a meteor to the wind; muff, bonnet, feathers, boots, reticule — all were in perfect keeping ;and Mrs. Major Waddell, from the crown of the head to the sole of the foot, might have stood for the frontispiece of La Belle Assemblee.

Placing a hand upon each of her supporters, she descended the steps of the carriage with much deliberate dignity ; and then, as if oppressed with the weight of her own magnificence, she gave her muff to Csesar, while the Major gallantly seized her reticule, and assisted her to ascend the flight of steps, where stood Gertrude, provoked at herself for her precipitation in having so unwarily hastened to receive this unexpected importation.

" Well cousin, this is really kind!" exclaimed Mrs. Major: " but you see what it is to be without a lord and master. Here is mine would be in perfect agonies if I were to stand for a single moment outside the door without my bonnet."

" You ought to tell Lady Rcssville, at the same time, who it was tied two double neck-cloths round my throat yesterday, when "

But Lady Rossville could not listen to the Major's playful recrimination, and she interrupted him by saying, witm"a somewhat stately air —

" I imagined it was my aunt Mary who had arrived; acd knowing how helpless she is, I hastened out to see that she was-properly attended to. — But my friends are all welcome," added she, with her usual sweetness of manner, and she led the way to the saloon.

Mrs. Waddell was a prize to Lady Betty and Miss Pratt, who were both fond of seeing fine-dressed people ; and Mrs. Waddell had so much to look at, and her things were all so new, and so rich, and so fashionable ; and India muslin, and India shawls, and India chains, and lace, and trinkets, were heaped upon her with such an unsparing hand, that it was quite a feast to sit and scan each article individually. Miss Pratt even went farther, and anticipated, at the least, half a piece of sprigged India muslin to herself, the same as Mrs. Waddell's gown, which she forthwith began to admire with all her might. Moreover, she intended to ingratiate herself so far as to obtain a footing in the house, for, as she reasoned with herself, there was nobody knew good living better than your nabobs; they were commonly squeamish and bilious, and needed a nice bit; and, at any rate, one might depend upon genuine Mullagatawney and Madeira at their tables, and, to a used stomach, these were great restoratives, for a fortnight or so, now and then. Miss Pratt, thereupon, began to do the honours with even more than her usual activity. She made a point of taking off Mrs. Waddell's mantle with her own hands, commenting upon its beauty as she did so; she insisted upon her using a footstool, and having two additional squab-cushions to lean upon, and pressed a cup of chocolate in a manner not to be withstood. She was obliged to give back a little, however, when Mrs. St. Clair came sweeping in, with her usual authoritative air, and welcomed her relations with a patronizing grandeur of deportment that sunk Miss Pratt's nimble civilities into nothing.

Mrs. St. Clair was vulgar enough to feel gratified by the appearance made by her niece. Her equipage was handsome — her dress fashionable and expensive — she herself very pretty; the Major's rank was respectable — his connections were good — and though they were both fools, yet a fool in satin was a very different thing from a fool in sackcloth, and was treated accordingly. She therefore began, " I observe your carriage has not been put up, Isabella; surely Major Waddell and you have not come so far to pay us a mere morning visit? Gertrude, you must endeavour to persuade your cousins "

" The best of all persuasions," said Miss Pratt, " is to order the horses to be put up; that's a sure argument—is it not, Major? Let me pull the bell, Lady Rossville."

" Why, to tell you the truth, the Major and I had agreed before we set out, that if we found you living quietly here, and no company, we would have no objection to spend a day or two with you en famille; — but, as I go nowhere at present, it must be upon condition that I remain quite incog."

Mrs. St. Clair already repented of her invitation; and Gertrude could only say, " We are quite a family party."

" In that case then, Major, I think we must remain where we are. You had better speak to Robert yourself about the horses, and tell Caesar to see that every thing is taken out of the carriage. As we were quite uncertain of remaining, I did'nt think of bringing my own maid with me — and, Major, I think I must have left my vinaigrette in one of the pockets of the carriage; when one travels in their own carriage, they are so apt to litter it, you know, and leave things lying about, that really mine is almost 'ike my dressing-room."

<(

A very handsome carriage it is," said Miss Pratt, as it wheeled past the windows.

" Very plain — hut the Major and I are hoth partial to every thing plain."

This plainness consisted in a hright hlue hody, with large scarlet arms, bearing the Black and Waddell quarterings, mantle, crest, cipher, couped gules, and all appliances to hoot.

" By-the-by, I hear strange things of my poor uncle," said Mrs. Major, when the carriage was out of sight, — "I'm told, cousin, you found him all hut dead in his own house, and had him carried away in a fit. The Major and I were from home at the time; we were on a visit at Lord Fairacre's, and heard nothing of it till two days ago, that we returned, or I should certainly have made a point of seeing after him, poor man. — He is not confined to bed, I hope?—does he know we are here, I wonder ?"

"I shall let him know myself," said Lady Rossville ; who instantly conjectured, that if uncle Adam came unwarily to the knowledge of the Major and lady being under the same roof with himself, stone and lime would scarcely contain him. She, therefore (glad, at the same time, of an excuse for leaving her company), hastened to the yellow turret. She tapped several times at the door, but received no answer—she listened, all was silent —she slowly opened the door, no notice was taken—she looked in ; and there sat uncle Adam, with spectacles on nose, so intent upon a book, that all his senses seemed to be completely lapt in its pages. Gertrude coughed, but in vain — she spoke, but it was to the walls — she went close up to him, but he saw her not — at length she ventui'ed to lay her hand on his shoulder, and Guy Mannering dropt upon the floor.

"You seem to be much interested in your studies," said Lady Rossville, as she stooped to pick it up for him.

Mr. Ramsay purpled with shame, as he tried to affect a tone of indifference, and said, " Oo—I—hem—it's just a wheen idle havers there that I—just — hem — they maun hae little to do that tak up their heads writing sic nonsense."

"I never heard the author accused of idleness before," said Lady Rossville, with a smile ; " and no one need be ashamed to own the interest excited by these wonderful works of genius."

"Interest—hugh! — Folk may hae other things to interest them, I think, in this world. I wonder if there's ony o't true ? I I canna think how ae man could sit down to contrive a' that. I dinna misdoot that scoondrel Glossin at a'. I would gie a thoosand pound out o' my pocket to see that rascal hanged, if hanging wasna ower gude for him!"

"Well, you may be at ease on that head, as even worse befalls him," said Lady Rossville.

"Weel, I rejoice at that; for if that scoondrel had gotten leave to keep that property, by my troth, I believe, I would

x 3

have burnt the book ;"—then, ashamed of his ardour in such a cause, he added, in a peevish tone—"But it's a' nonsense thegither, and I'm no gaun to fash my head ony mair about it."

Lady Rossville now announced the arrival of the Waddells in the most conciliating manner she could; but in any way it was an event to rouse all uncle Adam's angry feelings, though for some minutes he said nothing, but merely walked round and round the turret, rubbing his forehead, as if at a loss how to proceed. At last he stopped and said —

"I ken weel enough what's brought them here. That creature, though she is a fule, has the cunning o' auld nick himsel'; but you may just tell her frae me she'll mak naething o' me — she shall ne'er see ae bawbee o' mine; you may just tell her that."

Gertrude here attempted a sort of vindication of her cousin from such debasing suspicions ; but she was cut short with,—

"Weel, if ye winna tell her, I'll tell her mysel'. I'm no gaun to be hunted up and down, in and out, that I canna turn mysel', but Maister and Mrs. Major Waddell maun be at my heels;" and he resumed his perambulations, as if to give the lie to his words by his actions.

"I'm just swithurin'," resumed he, " whether to quit the hoose this minute, or whether to stay still and see the creaters oot o't;" then, as his eye, in a fine frenzy rolling, glanced from Lizzie Lundie to Guy Mannering, he added, " But I'll no gie them the satisfaction o' thinking they hae driven me awa. I daursay that's just what she wants; so I'll stay still where I am."

This magnanimous resolution formed, Lady Rossville tried to prevail upon him to return to the saloon with her to meet his relatives, but in vain; he declared, that till dinner was on the table, he would not stir from where he was, and Lady Rossville, who had too much sense to attempt to combat his prejudices openly, was obliged to leave him, and make the best excuse she could for his non-appearance. No sooner had she left the room than Mr. Ramsay locked and bolted the door, to prevent any further intrusion ; and after a few glances at Lizzie, his ruffled pinions were smoothed, and he returned with unabated ardour to his studies.

Colonel Delmour and Mr. Lyndsay had both joined the party during Gertrude's absence ; and she again felt something like shame as she marked her lover's lofty bearing towards her relations, while the Major seemed to grow ten times sillier, and his lady twenty times more affected in their struggles to keep on par with him. With Lyndsay it was otherwise ; for although his manners were not less elegant, yet, as they emanated from better feelings, so they never oppressed others with the painful consciousness of their own inferiority; and even the Major and lady in his company might have become something better, had

not his benign influence been counteracted by the haughty port and humiliating condescension of the other. But his horses had been some time announced, and he set out upon his ride to Mill-bank House.

" Do you know I begin to think Mr. Lyndsay really quite handsome, and his manners extremely pleasing," said Mrs. Major, with an air as though her approbation set the seal to him at once.

" He sits his horse remarkably well," said the Major; " I wonder whether he ever was in the dragoons ? "

" Do you walk to-day, Lady Rossville ?" demanded Colonel Delmour, abruptly.

As the expedition to Bellevue was now given up, Gertrude answered in the affirmative, and invited Mrs. Waddell to be of the party.

" O, you must first get my lord and master's leave for that.— Major, what would you think of my taking a walk to-day?" looking very archly at the rest of the company.

The Major looked distressed.

" Why, you know, Isabella, the very last time you walked was to see Lord Fairacre's new pinery, and you certainly caught cold; for you may remember Lady Fairacre remarked next morning how heavy your eyes were, and I think you look a little pale to-day, my love."

" There now ! I knew how it would be. You see how completely I am under orders. However, I beg I mayn't prevent you from indulging your taste in a rural stroll—with your beau," added she in a whisper, to Lady Rossville, who, ashamed and wearied of such intolerable folly, rose and went to prepare for a walk, at the same time, in a general way, inviting such of the party as chose to accompany her.

On returning she found the party was to consist of herself and the two gentlemen. Lady Betty and Mrs. St. Clair (like Mrs. Waddell) never walked when they could help it; and Miss Pratt had attached herself so assiduously to the nabobess, and had so much to tell and to say, that, contrary to her usual practice, she was a fixture for the day.

" Major Waddell," cried Mrs. St. Clair, in her most authoritative manner, as they were leaving the room, " remember I commit Lady Rossville solely to your care—Gertrude, you will be at pains to point out to Major Waddell the beauties of Rossville, and get his opinion of the improvements you have begun."

" You see what you have brought upon yourself, Major, by your care of me," cried his lady, not much delighted with this arrangement, which she thought was rather interfering with her privileges.

Lady Rossville and Colonel Delmour were too much annoyed at this appendage to say any thing; the latter, indeed, was re-volving in his own mind how to dismiss him the moment they were out of sight, and the Countess was hesitating whether she should do more than merely take a single turn before the house under such guardianship, when, as they crossed the hall, Mrs. "Waddell's voice was heard loudly calling the Major back ; and the lady herself presently appeared, in great agitation.

" Now, Major, is it possible you were really going out without your cloak, when you know very well you was so hoarse this morning that I could scarcely hear what you said ? "

" Well, for Heaven's sake, compose yourself, my dear girl," said the Major, in a whisper.

" Now, Major, that is impossible, unless you put on your cloak."

" But, I assure you, I am much more likely to catch cold with my cloak than without it. Why, this is almost like a day in Bengal. I do assure you my cloak would be quite overcoming."

" Now, Major "

" Well, well, my dear, don't say any more. Do, I beseech you, compose yourself;—but this cloak is so confoundedly heavy — do just feel it."

" Now, Major "

" Well, no matter, my dear ; any thing to make you easy;" and the poor Major buckled on his apparatus, while the lady set up the collar, clasped the brooch, and drew the voluminous folds close round his person, already bursting at every pore.

" Now, Major, be sure you keep it close round you, and, for any sake, don't open your collar. — Do you promise? "

" But, my dear Bell "

" Well, Major, I can only say-

" Well, well," gasped the poor Major, " that is enough." " There now, I feel quite comfortable," said the lady, as she completed her operations.

"It is more than I do," thought the Major, as he slowly sallied forth, and caught a glimpse of Lady Rossville and Colonel Del-mour, who had taken advantage of this conjugal delay to make their escape. " So my companions have got the start of me ;" and he footed away as fast as his short legs and ponderous cloak permitted. But in vain, like panting Time, did he toil after the fugitives, whose light figures and elastic steps mocked his utmost exertions to overtake them ; and the provoking part of it was, that while he was puffing and blowing, and sawing the air with his arms, without ever gaining a single step upon them, they had the appearance of sauntering along quite at their ease, and deaf to his repeated calls.

END OF THE SECOND VOLUME.

THIRD VOLUME.

CHAPTER I.

Oh ! sooner shall the rose of May-Mistake her own sweet nightingale, And to some meaner minstrel's lay Open her bosom's glowing veil, Than Love shall ever doubt a tone, A breath of the beloved one ! Lalla Rookh.

Meanwhile the lovers had much to say to each other; but, for a time, the eloquence and the vehemence of Colonel Delmour bore down the softer accents of the Countess, as he pleaded his suit in all the energy of passion, and appealed to herself as a witness of the injurious treatment he met with from Mrs. St. Clair. But when he proceeded to urge an immediate union, as the only means of putting an end to the machinations against him, she stopped him by saying, " Do not renew that subject again for years to come, as you love me — I have promised my mother that I will enter into no engagement till I am twenty-one, but I promise you then "

" Then," interrupted Delmour, impetuously, — " that is a mere mockery. Gertrude, if you loved as I do, you would not talk so calmly of what may be years hence — every day seems to me an eternity, until you are mine beyond the power of fate to separate us. Years! better tell me at once that I have nothing to hope : despair itself would be almost a blessing compared to this intolerable agony of suspense."

• " Ah! Delmour, why should you be so unjust to yourself and me as to talk thus ! — I have no doubts of your faith and constancy, why should you have any of mine ?"

" Because no one can love as I do to distraction, without inquietude — passion without passion is an anomaly I cannot comprehend."

" And love without confidence in the person beloved seems to me still more inconceivable; I have no more doubt of your fidelity than I have of my own."

" But every thing will be done to destroy your confidence in me — your mother is ambitious, Gertrude; she wants a more splendid alliance for you; she thinks I am unworthy of you, and perhaps she is right."

"But in that I must judge for myself, and she knows my choice is made," said the Countess with a blush.

"But not confirmed.—Ah! Gertrude, would to Heaven you loved as I do ! —that you could conceive the miseries of separation—the worse than death it will be to me to part from you!"

" But we shall see each other frequently—you must give up the army — you must not go abroad again — indeed you must not — and then two years will soon pass away."

" And in that time what may not be effected by the misrepresentations of your mother, and the artful insinuations of that cold-blooded stoic, Lyndsay ? "

" You wrong your cousin, indeed you do, by such a supposition — he is far above any thing of the kind."

" Has he never once said any thing that had a tendency to injure me in your estimation ? " demanded Colonel Delmour, turning his eyes full upon her.

"If he had, he has certainly been very unsuccessful," said the Countess with a smile ; " but, indeed, Edward is incapable of meanly insinuating "

" What! he spoke out, then ? " exclaimed Delmour, passionately ; " he told you of the follies and the extravagances of my boyish days, in which, however, he himself went hand in hand —and exaggerated them into vices—and warned you to beware of the profligate who had lost I forget how many hundred pounds one night at cards ? "

" No, indeed, he told me nothing of all this — you wrong him — you misunderstand each other ; but you must be better friends, now that he is my guardian."

" Your guardian ! " exclaimed Delmour, as if thunderstruck ; " what, in the name of Heaven, do you mean ? "

" Even that it seems it was necessary for me to have guardians appointed, and so I have made choice of my cousin for one : he has already proved himself my friend on more occasions than one, and to him, I think, I owe my life; you cannot, therefore, wonder at my choice."

" Yet you must be aware that Lyndsay is no friend to me, nor — I confess it — am I to him: we think differently upon most subjects, and his creed is much too bigotted and intolerant for me."

" Indeed, I have not found him so ; on the contrary, I should say he was extrmeely liberal in his sentiments, and lenient in his judgments ; and, I am sure, he has a great deal more toleration than I have. I wish I saw you both better friends — why should it not be so? "

" Because I am no hypocrite, Gertrude ; and, perhaps, also, because — shall I confess my weakness to you ? — I am jealous that you should bestow so much of your regard upon him."

" Jealous of my regard for Edward Lyndsay!" exclaimed the Countess; " then you would be jealous if I had a brother whom I loved ? "

" Yes, I believe I should. "When a man loves, as I do, to adoration, he can seldom brook any interference in those affections which ought to be exclusively his own: your lukewarm sort of people, I know, make all welcome; but I am not one of those. Ah! Gertrude, -woman's heart is, indeed, a royal palace, if it admit but one guest, and then 'tis a glorious privilege to be that one!"

" Nay, you would rather turn it into a cell, I think," said Gertrude, smiling, " and become yourself a moping monk."

" No matter what it is, provided it is mine — solely and exclusively mine," returned Delmour, impatiently.

" But being yours, wholly yours," said the Countess, and she blushed at the tone of emphatic tenderness with which she said it, " surely you would not wish it to be unjust and ungrateful to all the world beside—such a thing would be no better worth having than this pebble on which I tread," as she touched one with her foot.

" Do not blame me, Gertrude, because conscious that I possess a pearl richer than all its tribe I fear to leave it open to all, lest even a part of it should be stolen from me.—Common things may be shared—but who could lose the hundredth part of a rare and costly gem, without feeling that its value was gone ? Even such a miser am I with your affections. You are all the universe to me ; day and night I think, I dream but of you—a desert island in the midst of the ocean with you would be a paradise. Gertrude, if you shared in these feelings, how little would you think or care for others in comparison."

"Alas! you little know.— but how shall I convince you, sceptic as you are, of my — folly ?" added she with a smile; " you would not have me perjured, and to my mother!—or drive from my house a friend and relation, to whom I owe so much — or retract my word passed to him, when I chose him for my guardian ? "

Colonel Delmour remained silent.

" Surely you would not have me so base as to do any of those things, nor would you value such proofs of my attachment."

Colonel Delmour found he had gone far enough for the present, and that, gentle and feminine as Gertrude was, his influence over her mind must be more gradual than he had expected. He saw that he was beloved with all the fervour and simplicity of a young confiding heart—but love "with her was yet too pure and unsullied a passion to have tainted the better feelings of her nature. These still flowed free and generous — she loved and was beloved, and her heart expanded beneath the joyous influence, and the bright rainbow hues of hope and fancy tinged every object with their own celestial colours. But no shade of suspicion or mistrust fell on the noontide of her happiness.

Even the narrow, selfish, domineering sentiments she had just heard fall from the lips of her lover, seemed to her to breathe only the quintessence of love, and she looked on him in all the calm radiance of a happy trusting heart.

" Be it as you will, Gertrude," said he, " my fate is in your hands— you know your power, for I have told you what I am — proud, jealous, vindictive, perhaps, where you are concerned ; but such as I am you have vowed to be mine—have you not?"

" When I am twenty-one — that is, unless you should change your mind," added she sportively.

"I change!" repeated he; "no, Gertrude; you will see many a strange sight before that comes to pass — this river may change its course, and these rocks may change into plains, but my heart can never change in its love for you."

Much more of the same sort passed; for lovers, it is well known, carry the art of tautology to its utmost perfection, and even the most impatient of them can both bear to hear and repeat the same things times without number, till the sound becomes the echo to the sense or the nonsense previously uttered. But lovers' walks, and lovers' vows must have an end, and Lady Rossville and Colonel Delmour found themselves at the castle ere they had uttered one hundredth part of all they had to say.

CHAPTER II.

Hot from the field, indulge not yet your limbs
In wish'd repose; nor court the fanning gale,
Nor taste the spring. Oh! by the sacred tears
Of widows, mothers, sisters, aunts, forbear! Armstrong.

"What have you done with the Major?" exclaimed his lady, as they entered the saloon, and found her and Miss Pratt with their heads together.

Gertrude was at a loss how to answer this question, as, till this moment, she had as completely forgot the Major as though no such a person were in existence.

"Where in the world is the Major?" was repeated, in a voice of alarm.

"Very snug in his cloak, probably," answered Colonel Delmour, with a disdainful smile.

"Lady Rossville — cousin, I entreat of you, say what has become of the Major?"

"I dare say he is not far off," answered the Countess; "but he did not overtake us."

"Good gracious!" exclaimed the lady, all panting with alarm, "did he not overtake you? Then the Major is lost!"

"My dear Mrs. Waddell, don't distress yourself," began Miss
Pratt; —" depend upon it he'll cast up; there's good daylight yet, and he may meet some of the work people in the woods; and we'll send out some of the servants to seek for him. Colonel Delmour, will you pull the bell? He never would think of taking the Crow-Foot Crag, and that's the only ugly turn about the banks
— Lady Rossville, I'll thank you for the smelling-bottle there
— there's not much water in the river just now — Jackson, a glass of water here as quick's you can, and send out some of the men to look for Major Waddell"

"With bells, ropes, and lanthorns," said Colonel Delmour.

"There is Major Waddell, ma'am," said the pompous Jackson, as he glanced his eye, but without turning his head, towards the window.

"Where—Oh! where?" exclaimed his lady, as she flew to the window. — "Thank Heaven!" as she again sunk upon her seat.

The Major it certainly was in propria persona, slowly and laboriously plodding his weary way, close buttoned to the chin, though evidently ready to drop with heat and fatigue. He carried a handkerchief in his hand, which he ever and anon applied to his face, which shone forth like a piece of polished yew. To add to his perturbation, Miss Pratt, throwing open a window, screeched out to him —

"Come away, Major, make haste;—here's your good lady almost in hysterics about you."

The poor Major, uttering an ejaculation of despair, did his utmost to mend his pace; and again the drooping capes, arms, sails, and tails of his cloak were all in commotion, as the inward man struggled and plunged amidst the toils of broad-cloth and timmen, till at length the whole mass came floundering into the room.

"O, Major!" exclaimed his lady faintly, as she rose to meet him.

"My sweet girl, what is all this?" cried the Major, as he cast back part of his folds, and extended his arms like claws towards her.

"I have been so frightened about you, Major! You must have met with something; you are so heated, and—do tell me what has happened—I see you have met with something!"

"My dearest girl, I do assure you I have met with nothing. I have been rather on a wild-goose chase to be sure, trying to overtake my charge, the Countess there; but," turning to Colonel Delmour and her, "I could not make you hear me at all, though I had you in sight almost all the way." At this reu ark there was a smile on Colonel Delmour's lip, and a slight blush on Lady Rossville's cheek, which Miss Pratt did not like, and a .sort of vague tremor ran through her frame.

"That was very odd," said Mrs. Major, recovering—" I never doubted you were all together.— I shall take care another time how I trust you to walk without me.— O! you have got yourself

heated to such a degree, I am sure you will catch your death of cold.— Pray, Miss Pratt, shut down that window;—now, Major, do sit away from the door, and, I beseech you, don't think of taking off your cloak till you are cooler."

"My dear Bell," gasped the almost suffocated Major.

"Now, Major, I entreat of you "

"But—'pon my soul, this is a thousand degree? hotter than ever I felt it in Bengal."

"Well—but, Major, you know very well how ill you were in consequence of throwing off your cloak suddenly one sunny day, when you had got yourself over-heated, and you promised me that you never -would do so again."

"But, my dear Bell, this is absolutely like a day in June."

"Now, Major, I can only say "

But happily for all concerned, the lady's sayings were here stopped by the sound of the dressing-bell; and half-distracted between her desire to superintend the cooling of the Major by keeping him in a hot room enveloped in his cloak, and her anxiety to dedicate the full three-quarters of an hour to the duties of her toilette and the display of her Oriental finery, she felt much at a loss which to choose—at length the woman prevailed over the wife; and the Major was allowed to betake himself to his dressing-room, while the lady repaired to hers.

CHAPTER III.

Ah! sure as Hindu legends tell, "When music's tones the bosom swell, The scenes of former life return, Ere, sunk beneath the morning star, We left our parent climes afar, Immured in mortal forms to mourn.

Or if, as ancient sages ween,
Departed spirits, half unseen,
Can mingle with the mortal throng,
'Tis when from heart to heart we roll
The deep-toned music of the soul
That warbles in our Scottish song. Leyden.

At dinner Mrs. Major reappeared in a dress which might have done honour to Cinderella's godmother; but which, even with the aid of Hyder Ally's carbuncle, had no effect in subduing uncle Adam's flinty heart towards her. He, however, received her salutations with tolerable composure, and, moreover, permitted her to touch his hands; but as for shaking them, that required an effort little short of tearing the limpet from its native rock. As for the Major, he was too much exhausted by the toils of the day to be able even to offend, being reduced to a state of perfect passiveness.

" What a pretty woman your niece, Mrs. Waddell, is," whispered Miss Pratt, as uncle Adam and she stotted along, as usual, to dinner.

" Pretty !—what makes her pretty?—wi' a face like a sooket carvy!" "

" Ah ! to he sure, she's not like Lady Rossville ; but where will you see the like of her, such a distinguished-looking creature as she is ? for you see, although she has but that bit myrtle in her hair that she brought in her hand from the greenhouse before dinner, how much better her head looks than Mrs. Wad-dell's, with that fine pearl-sprig that must have cost many a gold rupee ;—as Anthony Whyte would say, she's really very classical."

" I wish you wud nae compare them," interrupted Mr. Ramsay impatiently; as his temper was still farther irritated at seeing the haughty but graceful air with which Colonel Delmour led the Countess to the top of the table, and, as a matter of course, placed himself by her.

" There's a bold stroke for a wife playing there ; but it won't do," again responded Miss Pratt, with a slight palpitation at the heart; which she would have scorned, however, to have admitted, even to herself.

Dinners are uncommonly dull things, unless when there is some bel esprit to take the lead, and act as sauce piquante to the company ; but here was nobody (except Miss Pratt) who could or would lay themselves out to talk ; and even she was somewhat damped, as the thoughts of her five guineas came across her, now and then, with a qualm. As if to counteract that, her chief business was in calling forth, and then construing, Lady Rossviile's most common civilities towards Mr. Lyndsay, to the great annoyance of both, and the repressed indignation of Colonel Delmour.

Mrs. Waddell thought neither the Major nor she met with that attention that was their due. She, therefore, sat very stately with Hyder Ally's carbuncle, emitting dark and lurid gleams, as if it shared in her displeasure. In the evening it w r as somewhat better, though, in any way, it was difficult to get such incongruous materials as the company was composed of to hang together. But then they were more at liberty to follow their own devices; and if music has not always charms to soothe a savage breast, it has at least the merit of keeping civilized beings sometimes in order. Although Lady Rossville had little expectation of deriving any pleasure from an exhibition of Mrs. Waddell's musical powers, yet she was too polite to pass htj over.

" Pray sing me a Scotch song," said she, seeing her preparing to execute an Italian one ; " I have taken quite a fancy for Scotch songs."

" Scotch songs !" repeated Mrs. Waddell, with astonishment
and contempt; " I hope, cousin, you don't think me quite so vulgar as to sing Scotch songs. I assure you, they are quite exploded from the drawing-room now : they are called kitchen songs," with an affected giggle.

" Call them what they will," said Lady Rossville, " I shall certainly learn to sing the songs of my own country, and to sing them, too, in my own way, con amore."

" If so, you will sing them better than any mere taught singer will do," said Mr. Lyndsay.

" But, I assure you, cousin, nobody sings them now," said Mrs. Major, vehemently.

" The more shame, then, to every body," said Gertrude.

" To every body who can sing them," said Mr. Lyndsay; " but I believe it is much more difficult to sing one's national music well in their native land, than it is to ' discourse most eloquent music' in a foreign tongue : the first speaks to every one's heart and feelings ; the other merely addresses itself to the ear or the taste, or, it may be, the ignorance of the audience. To sing Scotch songs well requires great compass of voice, a clear articulation, much taste, and the very soul of feeling."

" Pray, Mr. Lyndsay, were you ever abroad ?" demanded Mrs. Waddell, abruptly.

" I spent two years on the Continent; one of them in Rome."

" Indeed!" in a manner as if she doubted the fact, and rather displeased to think that any body should have been where the Major had not been. " Well, I must say, I am rather surprised at any body who has ever been abroad being able to tolerate Scotch music. I think you say, Major, you have had little relish for it since you were in India."

" Oh ! surely," said the Major, who just knew a drum from a fife.

" I like every thing that is good of its kind," said Lyndsay.

" Some of the Scotch airs are rather pretty," said Colonel Delmour, who, but for his abhorrence of Mrs. Waddell, would have uttered an anathema against them.

" And I hope you admire the words ?" said Mrs. Waddell with an ironical air.

" Indeed I do many of them," said Lady Rossville. " Here,
for instance, is such a pretty sentiment prettily expressed;" and,
as she leant against her harp, she touched its chords, and sung
with taste and feeling —
Wilt thou be my dearie ?
When sorrow wrings thy gentle heart,
O, wilt thou let me cheer thee ?
By the treasure of my soul,
And that's the love I bear thee.

" Well, I suppose it's my want of taste, for I can't say I can discover any thing very beautiful there," said Mrs. Major, with a disdainful toss. " My dearie! what a vulgar expression ! How should I look, Major, if you were to call me your dearie?"

" Ha! ha! — very good; but that is a charming thing you sing, nay dear,' Rosina mia caro,' " said the Major, who was half asleep.

" Many of the Scotch songs are undoubtedly coarse, vulgar, and silly," said Lyndsay ; " and most of them sung from beginning to end would certainly be somewhat of a penance ; but some of them are charming, and a verse here and a verse there, in almost all of them, will be found to possess infinite beauty and »

" I thought people who were really musical cared little for the words of a song," interrupted Mrs. Major triumphantly.

" Milton thought otherwise, and few will dispute his ear for music ; but if words are not fit to be heard, they ought not to be sung. It by no means follows that because words are Scotch they must needs be vulgar ; on the contrary, I have heard good musicians say, that, from the frequent termination of the Scotch words in vowels, there is a softness in the language which renders it much better adapted to music than any other, the Italian excepted ; and then, what a superiority in the poetry of our songs ! How little nature, feeling, or variety, is there in the greater part of the Italian ariettas and Venetian canzonettes."

" Did you ever hear ' Dee tentee pellpeetee ? '" asked Mrs. Waddell, with a consequential air.

Mr. Lyndsay could scarcely restrain a smile at the question ; " Di tantipalpiti" being scarcely less hackneyed than "The Flower of Dumblane, or " From the white-blossomed sloe,"

&c.

But, without waiting an answer, the lady forthwith squared her elbows, rounded her arms, spread out her fingers, and commenced, waving her head and rolling her eyes from side to side in the manner usually practised by vulgar affected singers, who try to make up by their bodily gestures for the want of all taste, feeling, and expression.

Colonel Delmour had been talking to Lady Rossville, in a low voice, during the greater part of this colloquy, which otherwise he never would have suffered to proceed, as he seemed to look upon the Major and his lady as quite beneath his notice ; and although he might have deigned to contradict, he never would have stooped to reason with either of them. When she began he certainly would have left the room, had not Gertrude's presence restrained him ; not that her singing was more obnoxious to him than it was to Lyndsay; but the one was accustomed to consult only his own pleasure, the other to consider the feelings of others.

" What a store of pretty old Scotch songs your sister Anne has," said Lady Rossville, trying to gloss over the deficiencies of the one sister in the praises of the other.

u My sister Anne has a great store of nonsense in her head," said Mrs. Waddell, with a toss of her own ; " it is so stuffed with religion and poetry, I think, and with texts, and songs, and hymns, that there seems little room for good common sense."

"From your account, she must greatly resemble a little quaint simple sketch I have met with somewhere, and admired," said Lyndsay; "I think it is one of old Izaak Walton's. Speaking, I presume, of some such person, he says, ' To say truth, she is never alone; for she is still accompanied with old songs, honest thoughts, and prayers, but short ones.'"

"That seems to suit my cousin Anne exactly," said Lady Rossville; "she is very sweet and very pleasing, and, I am sure, very good. I wished her to .have come here with my aunts; but she writes me she cannot be spared at present, and they will not be persuaded to leave home it seems — so we must do the best we can without them."

Colonel Delmour placed some music before her, and they sung Italian and French duet + s for the rest of the evening. Miss Pratt and Mr. Ramsay battled away as usual at backgammon; but she was victorious, and again his suspicions of her recurred, and he thought —

"I wish she may be the thing after all; she kens owre weel how to shake the dice!"

CHAPTER IV.

Unless one could cure men of being fools, it is to no purpose to cure them of any folly, as it is only making room for some other. — Horace Walpole.

Mrs. Waddell did not find herself at all at home at Rossville; except Lady Betty and Miss Pratt, nobody seemed to notice her finery. The simplicity of Lady Rossville's dress was felt to be impertinent towards her, a married woman, and the Major could not stand beside Colonel Delmour's lordly port and fashionable nonchalance.

Then, except at meals, there seemed no possibility of getting hold of uncle Adam, and there was no speaking to him before so many people; it was only exposing him, poor man, to observation, and the less he was called out the better. It was inconceivable, too, what he made of himself all day, there was no getting a private word of him; and, in short, the result was a determination to depart the following day. Fortune, however, seemed to favour her design on uncle Adam, as she found herself in the breakfast room with only him and the Major; none of the others of the party having yet appeared. She therefore accosted him in her most ingratiating manner, which was met. as usual, by a very cool response.

"It is very difficult to get a word of you, uncle, except in the
midst of these fine people. You seem always engaged — you are certainly composing something."

"Maybe I'm makin' my will," was the reply, in a manner most suspiciously calm and benign.

"Indeed! but I'm sure, uncle, you have no occasion to think of that just now. The Major and I were both remarking how uncommonly well you are looking — you were just saying to me yesterday, Major, that you really thought my uncle looked twenty years younger than he did last time you saw him."

"Yes, indeed, 'pon my word I think so."

"It's a sign that change of air agrees with you, uncle; so I hope you'll take a seat with the Major and me in our carriage, and accompany us to Thornbank. I assure you, I shall be quite affronted if you don't; after staying here so long, it will have a very odd appearance in the eyes of the world, if you pass the Major and me over, and me a married woman — and, besides, you know, uncle, if you really wish to do any thing about your property, though, I'm sure, there can be no hurry about that, you know you are much nearer the law people at Thornbank than here; and, indeed, Mr. Aikinhead the advocate has promised us a visit this vacation, and perhaps you might like to advise with him before "

" I thank you, but I need naebody's advice as to the disposal o' my ain property," replied uncle Adam, still preserving a sort of horrid supernatural mildness; " my mind's made up."

" Indeed! well I really think I should be at a loss how to dispose of such a charming property as Broom Park."

" But I'm at nane — I'm just gaun to mak' a mortification* o't."

" A mortification of Broom Park! " repeated Mrs. Vfaddell, in tones well suited to the words.

" A mortification, my dear sir!" ejaculated the Major.

" Yes, just a mortification — what is there wonderful in that ? "

" Why, I must say, I think, uncle, considering " gasped Mrs. Waddell, vainly trying to preserve her unruffled dignity — " how much is done for the lower classes now, I really think the higher ranks stand quite as much in need of mortifications."

" I think sae, too; so it's lucky we're baith agreed."

" I can assure you, uncle, although it's a thing I would not choose to say to every body, the Major finds he has quite enough to do with his money."

" I dinna doot it."

" There is so much required now to support one's rank in the world, that, I assure you, it is no joke."

" Joke ! — wha said it was a joke ? "

" In short, uncle, I can assure you, in spite of the appearance we make in the eyes of the world, the Major and I both find

* In Scotland an endowment is termed a mortification.

ourselves pinched enough, and he now doubts very much about buying a place; although certainly Thornbank does not suit us in many respects — the house is very indifferent — we have only one drawing-room, and, with his connections, that is not the thing— and the garden is really a poor affair; so that, altogether, I am really anxious the Major should find another residence."

" He'll maybe find ane at Broom Park before it's lang," said uncle Adam, drily.

" O! uncle, I'm sure we never thought of that, and I thought you said you were going to make a mortification of it ?"

" So I am — but it's to be a mortification, as you say, for the rich ; — it's to be a mortification for thae miserable, unfortunate men, that are married to taupies and haverels that spend a' their substance for them."

Uncle Adam had here broke out into his natural manner; and there is no saying how much plainer he might have spoken, had he not, at that moment, been checked in his career by the entrance of Mr. Lyndsay, who was the only person (strange as it may appear) for whom he felt any thing approaching to respect; but there was so much mildness and calmness of manner, with so much manly dignity in his deportment, that even uncle Adam was ashamed to behave ill before him. The rest of the party came dropping in, and Mrs. Waddell, with her cheeks very red, was obliged to take her seat in silence; they gradually cooled, how-ever, as she began to think it was just her uncle's way; he liked a rough joke, and so on; while the Major, for some little time, sat revolving whether he should not call upon the old man to say what he meant: if there was any thing personal in his allusion, he — but the poor Major, even to himself, could not say what he would do — at last he too gulped down the affront with his last cup of tea, and by the time breakfast was over both were ready to enter the lists again with uncle Adam.

Upon hearing of the proposed departure of the Major and lady, Gertrude said all that was necessary on the occasion; but she was too sincere to be pressing in her entreaties for them to prolong their stay; she felt that her relations were ridiculous, and she saw they were despised by Colonel Delmour. It was rather a relief, therefore, to hear they were going away. Any deficiencies on her part were, however, amply atoned for by Miss Pratt, who was vehement in her remonstrances; assuring them they had seen nothing of Rossville yet, that it was really no visit at all; people scarcely knew one another's faces till they had spent at least three days together, &c.

In spite of all that could be urged by Miss Pratt, however, the Major and lady remained fixed in their purpose to return home; all they would concede was to remain part of the morning, and the carriage and Csesar were ordered to be in readiness accordingly.

The breakfast party, with the exception of Lyndsay, having lounged over then* repast to the utmost length of procrastination, read their letters and newspapers, pampered their dogs, and, in short, done all that idle people do to kill time, even at his very outset, en masse, -were severally sauntering away to try their skill individually, each their own way, when, as uncle Adam was retreating, Mrs. Waddell followed him into the ante-room, and was as usual followed hy the Major.

" Before we go, uncle, I wish to know if there is any thing I can do for you ; since you don't seem inclined to accompany us at present — any message to Broom Park ? — We shall pass close by it, you know ; and by-the-by, uncle, I really wish you would give us an order of admittance there — it has a most extraordinary appearance in the eyes of the world that the Major has never yet been within your gate."

" O, my dear Bell! you know, if your uncle has any objections to showing his grounds "

" Weel, weel, dinna plague me, since it's to be a mortification at ony rate; gi'e me pen and ink, and ye shall ha'e an order, if that's a' ye want," said Mr. Ramsay, impatiently.

Pen, ink, and paper, were speedily procured; and uncle Adam, seating himself in a most deliberate manner, produced the order.

Mrs. Major glanced her eye upon it, then reddened as she exclaimed —

" Such a way of wording it! — Good gracious! uncle, can you suppose I will go on these terms ? ' Admit Major Waddell and his wife!' — Wife! I really never met with any thing like that!"

" What is't you mean ?" demanded uncle Adam, in a voice of thunder. — " Are you no Major Waddell's wife ?"

" Why, my good sir," began the Major, " you know it is not customary to call ladies of a certain rank wives now."

" Certainly not," interposed his lady ; " I thought every body had known that! — Wife ! — what else could you have said if the Major had been a carter?"

" What are you then, if you're no his wife ? "

" Why, ' my lady,' you know, my dear sir, would have been the more proper and delicate thing."

" Your leddy !" cried uncle Adam, with a sardonic laugh, — " your leddy !"

" Certainly," said the lady, with much dignity ; " there can be no doubt about that; and I can assure you I have too much respect for Major Waddell and myself to submit to any such low vulgar appellation."

"I've met wi' mony a daft thing in my day," said uncle Adam, "but this beats them a'; a married woman that'll no submit to be called a wife! I dinna ken what's to come next. Will you be his dearie then?"

"Really, uncle, I must say, I have borne a great deal from you; but there are some things that nobody can put up with, and there is a duty we owe to ourselves, that — I must say I think neither the Major nor I have been very well used by you;" and the lady's passion grew strong, the Major looked frightened.

"Do compose yourself, my dear; I am sure your good uncle had no intention of doing any thing disrespectful. Why, my dear sir, a very little will set all to rights," offering the pen to uncle Adam; "if you will just take the trouble to write the line over again in the customary style, 'Major Waddell and lady,' all will be well."

"I'll just as soon cut off my finger," said uncle Adam, ferociously; "and if she winna gang to my hoose as your wife, she shall ne'er set her foot in't in ony other capacity."

"My dear Bell, you hear that," said the poor Major.

"Yes, Major, I do; but I have too much respect for you to give up the point; it would be lowering you indeed, in the eyes of the world, if I were to allow myself to be put on a footing with any common man's wife in the country. It is what I will not put up with!" And with much majesty she seized the order and put it into the fire.

Uncle Adam looked at her for a moment, as if he too would have burst into a blaze. Then, as if disdaining even to revile her, he walked out of the apartment, banging the door after bim in a manner enough to have raised the ghost of Lord Chesterfield.

"The old gentleman is very testy this morning," said the Major.

"I am surprised at your patience with him, Major; I have no idea of allowing one's self to be trampled upon in this manner. — Wife! I really can't think enough of it! What else could he have said, speaking of my coachman's wife?"

"It's very true, my dear, the same thing struck me; and in a political point of view, I assure you, I think it the duty of every gentleman who wishes well to the government of the country to support the standing order of things, and to keep up the existing ranks of society."

"That is exactly what I think, Major; it is quite necessary there shoidd be distinctions kept up. — Wife! — every beggar has a wife!"

"Undoubtedly, my dear; beggar-wife, in fact, means neither more nor less than the wife of a beggarman; and, in these times, when there is such a tendency to a bad spirit amongst the people, and such an evident wish to bring down the higher ranks to a level with themselves, it becomes the duty of every gentleman to guard his privileges with a jealous eye."

"I for one will certainly never give in to these liberty and equality notions, that I am determined."

"I hope not, indeed," said the Major, warmed into fervour by the spirit of his lady, — "I hope not, indeed."

"How," said the lady, "can my servants possibly look up to me with proper respect, when I am brought upon a level with themselves?"

"You are perfectly right, my dear, they cannot do it, it is impossible."

"Perfectly — wife, indeed!"

CHAPTER V.

Leath we are to diseas or hurt your persone ony wayis, and far leather to want you. — Bannatyne's Journal.

The dialogue was now at its lowest ebb, when Miss Pratt came pattering into the room full speed.

While this disturbance was going on in one room, Mrs. St. Clair was conversing with Mr. Lyndsay in another on the subject of her daughter's pupillage ; and Lady Rossville and Colonel Delmour found themselves together in the drawing-room, where they flattered themselves with enjoying an uninterrupted tete-a tele. But within the drawing-room was a small turret, containing piles of music, porte-feuilks of drawings and engravings, heaps of worsteds and sewing-silks, and, in short, a variety of miscellaneous articles, which the Countess had not yet had leisure to look over. This was a favourite haunt of Miss Pratt's, who was fond of picking and grabbing amongst other people's goods ; not that she actually stole, but that, as she expressed it, she often met with bits of things that were of no use to any body, and which, when she showed to Lady Rossville, she always made her welcome to. For some time her head had been completely immersed in a large Indian chest, containing many oriental odds and ends, a few of which she had selected for the purpose of being hinted for, and she was just shaking her ears from the cobwebs they might have contracted in their researches, when they were suddenly smote with the sound of her OAvn name pronounced by Colonel Delmour ; she heard the Countess's voice in reply, but it was too soft and low to enable her to ascertain her words.

" Since Miss Pratt is disagreeable to you and odious to me, why don't you dismiss her the house, then? "asked Colonel Delmour.— " Much as you despise her, she may do mischief — Ah, Gertrude ! " — But here Colonel Delmour's voice sunk into a tenderer strain, and its undistinguished accents only penetrated the massive door which was betwixt them. Miss Pratt had met with many a buffet in her day, but she never had met with any thing like this, and her ears tingled with rage and mortification at hearing herself talked of in such a manner.

" I wish Anthony Whyte heard him ! " was her first mental

y 4

ejaculation; though even to herself, had she considered a moment, the mortifying conviction must have heen that if Anthony Whyte did hear it, it would only be to laugh at it. She tried to make out something more, which might prove either a confirmation or a refutation of this opprobrious expression; but " love — doubts — adore — agony — suspense — unalterable heart — wholly mine," &c, were all she could pick up ; but these were too much — the sword that had just fallen upon her cut two ways, if not three : her respectability (and that was her weak side) was compromised, her footing in a house she had long looked upon as a home was endangered, and her five guineas were in the most imminent peril. In short, she found she was in a very great scrape, and the best thing she could do at present would be to take the first word of flyting and depart.

" Dismiss, indeed ! dismiss one's own blood! " and Miss Pratt's danced and bubbled at the bare thought of such a thing. There was a little back stair from the turret, by which she could emerge without going through the drawing-room and confronting her adversaries ; and to that she betook herself, and after a little searching found the Major and his lady just beginning to recover their equilibrium. When one's mind is ruffled it is always a satisfaction to meet with others in the same state, especially when the cause is somewhat similar ; and though neither party would for the world have betrayed to the other the cause of its discomposure, yet both felt that sort of secret sympathy which made it hail fellow, well met!

Miss Pratt was too experienced in the art of offering visits, securing a seat in a friend's carriage, and such like manoeuvres, to be at any loss on the present occasion; and as the Major and lady, in spite of all their finely, were not particularly sought after, they were much flattered at the compliment, and soon settled that she should accompany them, in the first instance, to Thornbank, where she insinuated she would not be allowed to remain long, as both Lady Wellwood and Lady Restall would go mad if they heard she was in their neighbourhood, till they got hold of her.

This important point settled, the next thing to be done was to give all possible bustle and importance to her departure, that she might not appear to have been driven away by any thing that insolent puppy had said;—she had no notion of sneaking away, as if her nose had been bleeding, or showing herself any way flustered, or giving him the slightest satisfaction in any way. She therefore went openly to work — rung all the bells — called to the servants — spoke loudly, but calmly, about her preparations to Lady Betty and Mrs. St. Clair; and finally repaired to the room where she had left the Countess and her lover, and where she still found them.

" Well, Lady Rossville, I am just come to apologize to you for doing what is really an ill-bred thing ; but your good friends,

the Major and his lady, have pi-evailed upon me to take a seat in their carriage ; and as there's many visits I ought to have paid long ago, our cousins the Millbanks for one, I'm just going to run away from you. I declare there's the carriage; and, by-the-by, Countess, there's a bit of Indian silk I have of yours that I got for a pattern, and have always forgot to return — but I shall bring it with me next time I come," with a look of cool defiance at Colonel Delmour.

" You are perfectly welcome to it," said Lady Rossville, in some little embarrassment what to say next — " but this is a very sudden resolution of yours."

" I'm a great enemy to your long preparations, — a long warning is just a lingering parting, as Mr. Whyte says, so farewell. God bless you, my dear! and take care of yourself," in a most emphatic and oracular tone — " take care of yourself; and," —in a loud whisper, — " if you would take an old friend's advice, you would dismiss at least one of your lovers," with a glance at Colonel Delmour, who from the moment of her entrance had been amusing himself with a musical snuff-box, which he continued to play off with the most unceasing attention, as if quite unconscious of her presence. Gertrude was leaving the room with Miss Pratt, to do the parting honour to her guests — when looking up he called, " Shall I walk to the stables now, and examine the state of your stud, or I shall wait for you?"

" I am no judge of horses," answered the Countess — " so I shall leave that department entirely to you," — and she passed on to the saloon, before Miss Pratt could find words to express her indignation at finding he had already begun to interfere in the Rossville menage. All was now leave-taking — regrets, compliments, promises and invitations, and final adieus — and the trio at length were wheeled off. Much solace they found in each other's society during the drive, for each and all of them had something to animadvert upon as to the state of affairs at Rossville.

Uncle Adam missed Miss Pratt at dinner, and the kind message she had left for him with Mrs. St. Clair was not delivered. Lyndsay was out of spirits, and Lady Rossville was inattentive; and, in short, uncle Adam began to feel himself one too many. He was also within two pages of the end of Guy Mannering ; and therefore, upon retiring to his chamber, he sent off a line to the Blue Boar desiring a chaise might be sent for him the following morning at six o'clock.

CHAPTER VI.

Ah ! what will not a woman do who loves ! What means will she refuse to keep that heart Where all her joys are placed ! Dryden.

The seeds of false shame were beginning to be sown in Lady Rossville's heart, and she was secretly pleased Avhen she heard of uncle Adam's intended departure. She felt the contrast between Colonel Delmour and him was too much ; the gulf seemed impassable that was betwixt them, and it was painful to her to feel that she was ashamed of her uncle.

" I wonder why I never felt this with Edward Lyndsay," thought she ; " it must be that he is not so refined in his ideas as Delmour," and with that answer the thought passed away from her mind. She, however, pressed her uncle to wait breakfast, and to accept of her carriage to take him home ; but he was resolute in taking his own way, which was commonly the most uncomfortable that could be contrived.

" Fare ye weel," said he, with something of softness in his look and manner; " ye want naething frae me, so you'll tak naething."

" No, indeed, my dear uncle," said Gertrude, affectionately shaking his hand, " I do not require any thing; but I shall always remember your kindness to me when I did; I only wish I could make you as happy as — as I am myself," added she, with a smile and a blush.

Mr. Ramsay shook his head, and uttered something betwixt a groan and a hem.

rt Weel, weel, I wish it may last; but ' rue and thyme grow baith in ae garden ;' but I need nae fash to gi'e ye ony o' my advice, for whan folk need naething else, they '11 no tak that; so fare ye weel;"—and with something amounting almost to a squeeze of the hand, in its own uncouth way, the uncle and niece parted. Her relief from the presence of her mother's relations was, however, of short duration.

The following days were almost entirely devoted to business; for Lord Millbank and Mr. Alexander Black came to Rossville, and long meetings and discussions ensued, at many of which Gertrude was obliged to be present, to her own and Colonel Delmour's infinite weariness and chagrin. His only solace, during the hours she was shut up from him, was in lounging about the house and grounds, devising plans of useless expense, which he longed impatiently to have put in execution. No views of beneficence or charity made any part of his schemes ; his every idea centred in self-indulgence, and luxury and magnificence were all to which he looked as his recompence.

At length the business was brought to a conclusion, and Gertrude was once more at liberty ; for Mrs. St. Clair, after several ineffectual attempts to gain the entire direction of her daughter, and the control of her every action, found it vain, and she was therefore obliged to carry the reins with a light hand, lest the Countess should have sought to free herself from them altogether.

Lyndsay alone, of all the guests, now remained; and he still lingered, as though loth to give her up entirely to the influence of Colonel Delmour. He was aware that the heart cannot be long and exclusively devoted to one object without contracting somewhat of affinity towards it; and he sighed in bitterness of spirit, when he thought how Gertrude's nature, even now, with all its faults, so pure, so lofty, so generous, so amiable, would be debased and perverted by the baser alloy with which it mingled. What a different creature might she become under other guidance, so easily managed when her affections led the way ! — what capacities of happiness for herself and others seemed now at stake! But, alas ! how misdirected, how useless, if not pernicious, might they become under such control! —and Lyndsay, unlike himself, became wavering and irresolute as to the part he ought to act. Every day seemed to increase the alienation between Colonel Delmour and him ; but on Lyndsay's part it was so calm and mild, so free from all wrath and bitterness, that it might have escaped notice altogether, but for the sort of repressed animosity which the other occasionally betrayed.

" Why is it," said Lady Rossville one day to her lover, " that Edward and you are not better friends ? — Has any misunderstanding taken place between you, for you are not even upon the same terms you were when I first saw you? — then you walked, rode, shot, conversed together; but now you seem carefully to avoid all intercourse— it is unpleasant to me to witness this."

" 'Tis you yourself are the cause of it, Gertrude," answered Colonel Delmour, warmly. — " How can you imagine I can endure the sight of a man who, knowing the terms we are upon, yet presuming upon the encouragement you give him, dares to love you, and is, at this moment, planning to undermine me in your affections ? — By Heaven, I think I am but too patient!"

" Lyndsay love me ! " exclaimed the Countess ; " what a fancy!" But, at the same moment, a confused crowd of half-formed, half-forgotten thoughts, rushed upon her mind, and raised a blush on her cheek, which did not escape Delmour's notice.

" Yes, in his own cold-blooded, methodistical way ; not in the way I love you —to madness — to idolatry: — his existence, his soul, are not bound up in you as mine are ; but he would supplant me if he could."

" His love must, indeed, be of a different nature from yours," said Lady Rossville, trying to laugh away Colonel Delmour's roused passion, " for he has scarcely ever said a civil thing to me ; and as for a compliment, I have sometimes tried whether I could not extort one from him, hut never have succeeded. Nay, don't frown so, Delmour — if Lyndsay does not natter, at least he never frowns."

This remark did not dispel the cloud from her lover's hrow ; on the contrary, he bit his lip, as if to express the rising of his anger: after a few moments he said, in a suhdued voice — " I have never flattered you, if hy flattering you mean insincerity; hut I had flattered myself that you had been above practising those paltry arts by which so many women seek to enhance their value. I flattered myself, Gertrude, that you had been superior to coquetry; but when I see you encouraging the attentions of one who presumes to love you, even in the face of him to whom you have given your vows — one, too, whom you must know to be my enemy, — can you wonder that lam sometimes driven to hate him, and almost to doubt whether you really love me?"

" Unjust, unkind !" said Lady Rossville, turning from him in displeasure.

" No, Gertrude, 'tis you who are unjust, unkind; my heart is solely yours ; its every thought and wish centre in you ; but it must have yours — yours wholly and undivided, in return : less will not satisfy love such as mine."

Lady Rossville remained silent, and Colonel Delmour's agitation increased.

" I see how it is," cried he, passionately ; " his artful insinuations have prevailed ; — but he shall answer for this."

" Ah, Delmour! if you love me as you say you do, why do you thus grieve me ? — I would not for worlds willingly afflict you."

" But you do," interrupted he ; "you torture me to agony, and when I dare to complain \'7dou reproach me."

" Tell me what it is you require of me, since all I have done and suffered for your sake is insufficient."

" All that I require of you, Gertrude, is, that you will not at least ask me to become the bosom friend of one who, I know, seeks to undermine me in your affections — I cannot be the friend of a hypocrite."

" Edward a hypocrite ! — Ah, Delmour ! how your passion misleads you!—He is all truth and openness—he is indeed "

Then, after a pause, " When I look back a few months, and think of the state of incertitude I was then in as to your faith and constancy—when at times my own was almost shaken by my doubts — at such a time, had Lyndsay been what you suppose, had he sought to ingratiate himself with me — I do not know — I cannot tell—perhaps he might have gained an influence over me. But, indeed, he never tried, he never spoke to me as a lover ; but, on every occasion, he proved himself my friend, — as such I must always consider him. Do not, then, dear Frederick, embitter my peace with any of those idle jealousies : the time is past," added she," with a smile, " for Lyndsay to think of loving me now."

" But he does love you, Gertrude — I read it in the agitation he betrayed upon my arrival — he guessed his schemes would then be frustrated — he knew that I detested all underhand plots, and would come boldly forward, and bring matters to an issue. I did so — you have promised to be mine — he knows you have, and yet he would supplant me if he could. And is it right in you, warned as you are of all this, to continue to encourage him, and lavish your attentions on him ? "

" What can I do ?" asked the Countess, beginning to give way to her lover's vehemence, and to believe that she really was doing wrong — " what would you have me do?"

" Nay, it is not for me, Gertrude, to point out the line of conduct you ought to pursue—I leave that to yourself. I would have concealed from you, if I could, all that you have made me suffer; but when you call upon me to make a friend of the man who, in spite of our mutual vows, dares to love you "

" But this is mere fancy."

" No — I speak from certainty. Gertrude, is it possible you can be so blind as not to have perceived it yourself ?"

" Would that I were both blind and deaf to all the jarring elements which are for ever threatening my peace," said Lady Bossville, sorrowfully. — " How happy, how perfectly happy might I be, but for the passions and the prejudices of others! but it is distracting to me to see all those I love thus at variance. If this is the necessary consequence of riches and grandeur, oh! how willingly would I exchange them for good-will and mutual confidence !"— and tears dropped from her eyes, as she leaned her head upon her hand.

" Gertrude, dearest, most beloved! forgive me that I have thus distressed you — were you but mine, all these doubts would vanish ; but while it is in the power of malice or treachery yet to separate us, can you wonder that it requires all your love to still the tumults of my heart? Call it suspicion — jealousy — what you will; until you are once mine, your partiality for Lyndsay will constitute the toi'ment of my life."

" And I must become unjust, ungrateful, to one to whom I owe so much ? Ah, Delmour' at what price must I satisfy you!"

CHAPTER VII.

Human faults with human grief confess
'Tis thou art changed. Prior.

From this time Gertrude's manner was wholly changed towards her cousin. Instead of the sweet smile with which she used to welcome him, her eyes were now commonly averted from him; and an air of constraint and embarrassment had succeeded the open, confiding carelessness, which had hitherto marked their intercourse.

Lyndsay felt the change, and was at no loss to guess the cause. The books they had been reading together, the songs they used to sing together, were now discarded for others of Colonel Del-mour's choice ; and she read and sung with him, and with him only. The plans they had been carrying on together were stopped or overturned, and others of a totally different nature were adopted.

" Will you walk with me to-day, Gertrude?" asked Lyndsay, one morning, when he accidentally was left alone with her. " It is long since you have seen your school-house ; should you not like to look at it, and see what progress it has made since we last saw it together ? "

" Certainly, I should like very much to see it; but the phaeton and horses Colonel Delmour ordered for me have arrived, and I promised to take a drive with him."

" Perhaps you will drive that way, and I shall meet you there ?"

" I am afraid it will not be possible." Then, after a pause, she added, " I am afraid you will think me very foolish and expensive, as you tell me I have not much money to squander; but Colonel Delmour and I discovered such a lovely little spot lately on the banks of the river, just a little below the cascade, you know, a sort of tiny Paradise, that the thought struck us both of making a sort of miniature of a ferme ornee, quite a baby-house thing, in fact — a sort of Lilliputian beau ideal of rustic life," said she, attempting by a laugh to hide her confusion ; " with a flower-garden and all sorts of prettinesses, for you know flowers are my passion; and we appointed to meet some of the people there to-day, to talk and walk over it; but I am afraid you will think "

" You did not use to be so afraid of me, Gertrude," said Lyndsay mildly, but gravely ; " what have I done to inspire you with so much dread ? "

" You know you are my guardian now," said she, with au assumed gaiety ; " of course, it is my duty to be a little afraid of you, especially when I know I deserve a scold."

" Well, you will be relieved from your fears — I shall leave you to-day."

" My dear cousin, I spoke but in jest," cried Gertrude, thrown off her guard, and relapsing into her natural manner.

" Not entirely," said Lyndsay, with a melancholy smile ; " but, whether you fear me or not, I feel you no longer look upon me as your friend."

" Indeed you wrong me," cried the Countess, in emotion; " I never can cease to regard you as my friend, would you but become the friend of those who are dear to me."

" Impossible!" exclaimed Lyndsay, while a flush passed over his face, and he was for a moment silent; he then added, in a calmer tone, " I trust I am no one's enemy — I wish well to all mankind, and so far I may style myself the friend of all; but, with some characters, farther I cannot go."

Lady Rossville coloured deeply, and remained silent; but, from her look and air, she was evidently displeased.

" You distrust me, Gertrude," said Lyndsay, at length breaking silence ; " and that is worse than being afraid of me."

" I am, perhaps, too little distrustful of any one," answered she — " it is not my nature to suspect evil — I hope it never will — surely there are other marks by which we may know those who love us than any that base suspicion can furnish us with."

" Yes, and here is one," said Lyndsay, taking a book from amongst a' mass of French novels which lay upon the sofa-table. It was the Life of Colonel Hutchinson, and Lyndsay had begun to read it to her before Colonel Delmour's arrival, since when it had lain neglected. " Here is a picture of true and faithful love; who studies that may soon learn to distinguish the real from the counterfeit;" and he read that simple description of the perfection of human attachment with an emotion which showed how deeply he felt it.

"There is this only to be recorded, that never was there a passion more ardent and less idolatrous — he loved her better than his life, with inexpressible tendernesse and kinclnesse — had a most high and obliging esteeme of her — yet still considered honour, religion, and duty above her, nor ever suffered the intrusion of such dotage as should blind him from marking her imperfections: these he looked on with such an indulgent eye as did not abate his love and esteeme of her, while it augmented his care, and blotted out all those spots which might make her appeare lesse worthy of that respect he paid her."*

He laid down the book, but Lady Rossville made no comment — she continued to busy herself arranging some fine forced flowers, which had just been brought her, in a vase, and seemed to give her whole attention to them. This continued for some minutes, and Lyndsay made no attempt to interrupt her; but,

* Life of Colonel Hutchinson.

on hearing the sound of a carriage, she raised her head, and saw the phaeton driven by Colonel Delmour, and drawn by four beautiful horses, followed by two grooms mounted on two of the same set. A throb of pride and pleasure was felt at her heart, as she looked at the elegant bauble which had stopped opposite the saloon; and as she threw open the sash with childish delight, Delmour called to her, to know if she was ready. She answered in the affirmative, and was leaving the room to put on her things, when Lyndsay said —

"Is it thus, then, we are to part, Gertrude, after all the pleasant friendly days we have passed together?"

Lady Rossville stopped, and turned towards him.—"You are not serious in thinking of leaving us to-day?"

"I am, indeed, perfectly so."

"At least, stay till to-morrow—this is such a strange hurried way of leaving us — pray, give us one day more?"

"I would give you many days if they could be of service to you, but that cannot be; forgive me, my dear cousin, if I have pained you — farewell — God bless you!"

Gertrude's heart swelled, and the tear started to her eye as she returned the affectionate pressure of her cousin's hand, but she repressed her emotion.

"You will come again soon," said she; but Lyndsay made no reply, and they parted.

"I fear I have not done as I ought," thought Gertrude with a sigh; but in another moment the thought was gone, and she was seated by her lover. The equipage was perfect, the day was beautiful, all was gaiety and brightness—Colonel Delmour was more than usually delightful, and Lyndsay was forgotten!

CHAPTER VIII.

Serment d'aimer toujours, ou de n'aimer jamais, me paroit un peu teme-raire Voltaire.

Several days passed in the same manner, and every day some new scheme of useless profusion was suggested by Colonel Delmour, and adopted by the Countess. New stables must be built to accommodate the additional number of horses he declared to be absolutely necessary; the present billiard-room was inconvenient, a new one would cost a mere trifle; there was no good music-room, and there was no living in the country without a private theatre; the present library might be turned into a conservatory; and the smooth green bank, which sloped gradually down to the river, must be changed into an Italian garden, with hanging terraces and marble fountains; and he

sketched a design of the whole so beautiful that the Countess was in ecstasies.

Mrs. St. Clair witnessed all this with very different feelings ; but she saw the ascendency Colonel Delmour had gained over her daughter was absolute, and she feared to come to extremities with either of them, lest it should prove the means of throwing her more completely into his power, and he might prevail upon her to unite herself to him, notwithstanding her promise to the contrary. She had remonstrated with both on the impropriety of Colonel Delmour continuing to reside at Rossville in the present situation of the family ; but her words produced no effect, till, at length, finding she could not dislodge him, she formed the resolution of taking Lady Rossville to London, as the best means of detaching her, in some degree, from him. She thought of Lyndsay's words too, " Let her see others no less gifted than he is,"—and she thought it was not impossible that a change might be wrought in Gertrude's sentiments; at least, there was more likelihood of its being effected amidst the novelty and variety of the metropolis, than in the romantic seclusion of Rossville.

This resolution caused infinite chagrin to the lovers. To Gertrude's young enthusiastic heart, all happiness seemed centred in the spot which contained herself and the idol of her affections ; and although the mere inanimate objects of nature,— woods, rocks, water,—are in themselves nothing, yet, combined with the associations of fancy and memory, they acquire a powerful hold upon our hearts. Every step to her was fraught with fond ideas ; for it was at Rossville her feelings had been most powerfully excited, whether to joy or sadness ; and Rossville, its trees, its banks, its flowers, seemed all entwined with her very existence. It is thus, when the heart is exclusively occupied with one object, it clings with fond tenacity to every circumstance connected with it.

" Ah, mamma!" said she, with a sigh, " how sad to think of leaving Rossville, when it is just beginning to burst forth in all its beauty ; and to immure ourselves amidst the stone, and lime, and smoke, and dust of London ! Do only look at these almond trees and poplars."

But Mrs. St. Clair put it on the footing of her health, which required change of air and scene, and a consultation of the London faculty; and her daughter could say no more.

Colonel Delmour shared in her regrets ; but his arose from a different cause : his heart was too worldly and sophisticated to participate in those pure and simple pleasures which imparted such delight to hers. But he was aware of the admiration Gertrude would excite when she made her appearance in London; and he was unwilling that she should be seen there until she should be introduced as his wife. He thought too well of himself and her to dread any rival in her affections; but

z

still the gay world was very unfavourable to the growth of sentiment ; there was a multiplicity of objects — a diversity of amusements—a glare, a glitter, and bustle, that could not fail to distract her attention, and weaken the strength of that exclusive attachment she now cherished for him ; and, selfish and engrossing as he was, he felt the charm would be diminished, were the devotion lessened.

But, in his murmurs and repinings, Gertrude heard only the same tender regrets which filled her own heart even to overflowing, and she loved him the more for this sympathy in her feelings. The day before that on which they were to set off was the Countess's birthday, but she would not have it observed.

" This day twelvemonths it shall be celebrated gaily, nobly, if you will," said she.

" And must this one pass away, like other vulgar hours," saidDelmour, "without a single memorial to distinguish it from common days ? Poor that I am! I have not even the most trifling memento worthy to lay at your feet."

" I will not tax you so unmercifully as did the ladies of old their lovers," said Gertrude, with a smile. " I want neither a dragon's scale nor a hydra's head, nor even a glass of singing-water, nor a branch of a talking-tree ; but you shall bring me, from the greenhouse, a rose unique, and that shall be my only gaud to-day."

Colonel Delmour brought the rose. Lady Rossville drew from her finger a rare and costly gem, which had belonged to the late Earl.

" Such tokens are but mere vulgar and oft-repeated emblems of an old story," said she, " from Queen Elizabeth and the Earl of Essex down to the milkmaid and her ' rush ring;' but it will mark the day, will it not ? And if you should turn rebel, or I tyrant — you must choose some more faithful messenger than poor Essex did ; and that's all the moral of my tale."

" Woe to the hand that shall ever seek to wear this while 1 live !" exclaimed Delmour, as he pressed it to his lip, and then placed it on his finger.

Lady Rossville's sole ornament when she appeared at dinner was the rose unique; but the heat of the room caused it to expand too quickly, and the leaves dropped suddenly away.

" Happily my nurse could never succeed in making me superstitious," said she, in a low voice, to Colonel Delmour ; " else I should have looked on this as some fatal omen."

" The prodigy is," answered he, with a smile, " that either the rose unique has suddenly expired of envy at finding itself so eclipsed by the wearer, or—that your gardener forces his flowers too much."

" I fear the latter is the true cause," answered the Countess, laughing; " and it is my own fault, for I never have patience to

wait the gradual growth of any thing. I am for every thing starting into full-blown perfection at once."

" Yes, yes, you say true," said Mrs. St. Clair, significantly, as she caught her daughter's last words, — " art seems to carry the day with you in all things, Gertrude ; 'tis well you are beginning to discover your own foible."

Colonel Delmour bit his lip ; and Lady Rossville blushed with wounded feeling, as she bent her head to pick up some of the scattered rose leaves.

CHAPTER IX.

Une personne a la mode n'a de prix et de beaute que ce qu'elle emprunte d'un caprice leger, qui nait et qui tombe presque dans le meme instant: au-jourd'hui elle est courue. les femmes s'en parent; demain elle est negligee, et rendue au peuple. — La Briyere.

Lady Rossville's departure from the home of her fathers called forth the regrets and the lamentations of the poor ; for although her attentions towards them had somewhat relaxed since Colonel Delmour's arrival, yet she had done enough under Lyndsay's auspices to render herself completely beloved by them. The various works-, too, which she had begun, all in the spirit of profuseness and self-gratification, contributed for the present to her popularity ; and she flattered herself that she was equally actuated by beneficence and humanity, although they had taken a different direction under her lover from what they had done under her cousin's guidance. She sent splendid rather than suitable gifts to her aunts and her cousin Anne, and directed that the former should be constantly supplied with the choicest of fruits and flowers from Rossville. She felt unwilling to depart without sending some remembrance to Lyndsay — some little token of her gratitude for all she owed him of generous interference — of time, and trouble, and kindness hitherto but ill requited ; yet she feared to mention the subject hefore Colonel Delmour, aware of the jealous irritability it might excite. At length the thought struck her, to send him a picture of his mother, which was the most admired and conspicuous of any of the family portraits. It was a

Sir Joshua, and done at a time when the subject was in all the graces of early beauty, and the artist in all the fulness of his perfection. The picture was, therefore, not merely precious as a portrait; but was valuable in itself, as most of that great master's works are, on account of its own intrinsic beauty. " There is something of Lyndsay in the half-melancholy, half-smiling expression of those dark eyes," thought Gertrude, as she looked on the picture ; " something, too, of his reproachful look," added she, with a sigh, as her heart told her he had cause to reproach her.

She wrote a few lines to accompany the picture, which was to be packed and sent after she was gone ; and then, all being arranged, she bade adieu to Rossville, and the tears stood in her eyes as she looked on its budding woods and sparkling waters, in the soft rays of vernal sunshine.

Mrs. St. Clair had peremptorily refused permission to Colonel Delmour to accompany them to London, and Gertrude had at once conceded that point to her mother. However much chagrined, he was therefore obliged to acquiesce ; and as his rate of travelling was rather more rapid than theirs, he preceded them by several days, and (apprised by a note from the Countess of their approach to the metropolis) was at the hotel ready to receive them on their arrival.

The following day he brought his mother and sisters to introduce them to Gertrude. She had anticipated the meeting with that trepidation natural to one so situated; but her timidity was soon dispelled by the pleasant easy manners of Lady Augusta, and the lively good-humoured frankness of her daughters. There was much to attract, and nothing to be afraid of; and before they had been half an hour together, Gertrude felt as though she were already one of themselves. They were pressed to dine with Lady Augusta in Brook Street; but Mrs. St. Clair declared herself too much fatigued with the journey for such an exertion, and Gertrude resisted their entreaties out of compliment to her mother. They were, however, to meet the following day, when something was to be fixed; and after much talking, and a great display of affection on both sides between the cousins, they parted. Even Mrs. St. Clair was more pleased with them than she cared to admit to herself, for they had paid her more attention than she was accustomed to receive ; and had they not been Colonel Delmour's mother and sisters, she would have been loud in her praises of them. Gertrude spoke of them to her lover with all the warmth she felt, but he appeared but little gratified by her commendations. " You do not seem sufficiently sensible how charming they are," said she ; " you did not say half enough in their praise."

" I told you you would find Lady Augusta a very good-looking, well-bred person, did I not ? " said he, with a smile ; " and the girls very gay, and good-humoured, and very like other girls."

" O more than that! Lady Augusta is very delightful, and your sisters—how much more agreeable they are, for instance, than the Miss Millbanks."

" Are they? yes, by-the-by, the Miss Millbanks are very Scotch, indeed ; but most misses, Scotch or English, are pretty much alike."

A house had been procured in Park Lane ; Mrs. St. Clair thought it too magnificent and too expensive; but Colonel

Delmour approved of it, Lady Rossville admired it, and the house was taken. Then came equipages, horses, liveries ; in short, an establishment in which taste and splendour only were consulted without any regard to the means, which indeed Gertrude herself believed to he inexhaustible, and which Delmour, with the reckless profusion of selfish extravagance, thought not about at all. Since Lady Rossville was to appear in the world, his only anxiety was that she should, at the first, take her place at the very head of the fashionable world; aware that if she once entered in an inferior grade, she might not afterwards, even as his wife, be able to attain the proud pre-eminence of ton, which, of all pre-eminences, is the one most esteemed in the great world.

" Lady Augusta has kindly offered to introduce me to her milliner and jeweller, and all sorts of useful people," said Gertrude to him one day, — " and in the evening she proposes that mamma and I should accompany her to the opera."

Colonel Delmour received this information rather dryly, and seemed to hesitate in his reply. At last he said — "I have a great respect for Lady Augusta's good sense and good intentions ; but really her tradespeople are so perfectly antediluvian, that you will oblige me by having nothing to do with them."

Gertrude was disposed to take this as a joke, but that she saw he was serious. " Lady Augusta does not dress in good taste," continued he; " and as for the girls, they can scarcely be said to have a taste at all—they stick themselves over with feathers, or flowers, or butterflies, or any thing that comes in their way. — Emily rather carries it off well; but poor Georgy looks as if her ornaments had been actually blown upon her."

" But how can I refuse so polite an offer?—and, besides, I don't know who are the people to employ."

" Leave all that to me, or rather to a friend of mine, Lady Charles Arabin, who comes to town to-morrow, and whom I shall bring to visit you immediately."—Seeing Gertrude look surprised, he added—" She is not handsome, and is rather passee; but she has the best air and taste of anybody in town—in fact, . she gives the tone at present to every thing ; and, therefore, I would rather that you took her as your guide, than Lady Augusta, that is, in all matters of mere taste and fashion."

" Bat I have a taste of my own in dress," said Lady Rossville, half-displeased at the idea of being obliged to submit to the decision of another.

" And a perfect one," said Colonel Delmour ; " but taste alone won't do without fashion. Venus herself, even attired by the Graces, would be thought maussade, were she to be introduced by a duchess who had been excluded from Almack's, or who had never supped at D House."

" Then, who can value the blind admiration of the multitude?" said Gertrude; —" not I indeed; —'tis much too paltry a triumph for me to take any trouble to acquire. I care not a straw for such empty distinctions, and would rather have the approbation of your mother than of the whole fashionable world."

" What a word for you !" said Delniour, laughing.—" Approbation is a very good thing in itself, and a very useful school-word ; but for you, Gertrude, with your charms and your graces, to be approved of! No; you must be followed, admired, adored, worshipped."

" I am afraid 'tis in your imagination alone I stand any chance for being deified," said Gertrude, smiling—" so I shall certainly not start a candidate for immortal honours. I am not ambitious, Delniour, and shall be satisfied with your homage and true affections, since you will not allow me the approbation of your family."

" But I am proud, and vain, and ambitious of and for you, dearest Gertrude," said Delmour gaily, " and must not suffer your partiality for me and my family to detract from the brilliancy of your star."

" But I would rather be introduced by them than by any one else ; — if Lady Augusta does not mix much in society, there is your aunt, the Duchess of Burlington."

" Worse and worse," cried Delmour —" I would rather you never appeared at all than have you brought out by her."

"Why so?" asked Gertrude in some surprise.—" Is she not respectable ?"

Colonel Delmour could scarcely preserve his gravity at this question, as he replied —" Respectability, like approbation, is a thing of no account here — it gives no consequence whatever to its possessor."

" Then, what precious gifts of nature, or acquirements of art, are they which do give consequence in this magic circle of yours? " said the Countess.

" That nameless je ne sai quoi which all admire, but none can define, and which unfortunately my highly respectable relations want. The Duchess is an excellent person in her way; but she is antiquated in her notions, dresses shockingly, gives parties where I should blush to be detected, and I should be undone were I to be seen offering her my arm in public."

This was said in a sportive manner, which made Gertrude look upon it as a jest.

" Then I may scarcely expect to be acknowledged by you tonight," said she, in the same tone. " Perhaps it would be your ruin also were you to be seen in Lady Augusta's box talking to, or, it may be, handing out a Scotch cousin."

Colonel Delmour looked grave.

" You will really oblige me," said he, " if you will decline going into public for a day or two ; although I have been talking mere nonsense on the subject, yet, I do assure you, a first introduction is of more consequence than you at present are aware of."

" Consequence!" repeated Gertrude, contemptuously; " if I am not entitled to be of consequence on my own account, I certainly do not wish to derive it from Lady Charles Arabin."

" You mistake the matter entirely, dearest Gertrude ; I am desirous you should appear with that effect which you are so well entitled to produce, but which you will derive much more from your beauty and your grace than from your rank. I cannot exactly make one so unsophisticated as you comprehend the arbitrary and capricious mechanism of the fashionable world."

" No, pray do not attempt it. I am sure I shall never be fashionable. Ah, Delmour ! it was not thus we talked and felt at dear Rossville ! What was the world to us there ? "

" Would to Heaven we were there now!" said Delmour, echoing her sigh; " but you mistake me, Gertrude ; it is not that I place the world in competition with you, but that I abhor the thoughts of your preference for me lowering you in the slightest degree. You have every thing that entitles you to take the first place in the best society; but, absurd as it seems, I must candidly confess to you that my family, although high in rank and fair in character, cannot do you justice in that respect. I keep clear of all that sort of thing; but if once you get into their circle, you will be shackled eternally with bad parties and acquaintances that will keep all the best people aloof: for instance, Lady Augusta would introduce the girls into the Burlington set; the consequence is, they are eternally followed by men with whom I don't associate ; in short, secondary men, whom they are forced to smile on faute de mieux; but that must not be with you, Gertrude—you have already given up too much for me ; do not, as you love me, add yet more to the self-reproach I sometimes feel for having suffered you to sacrifice so much."

" The feeling is a generous, a noble one ; but I cannot help thinking it a mistaken one," said the Countess ; " but since you are so scrupulous, I shall yield the point: make me, then, what you will, only pray don't make me a fine lady."

Colonel Delmour was all rapture and gratitude, and only left her to go and inform his mother that Lady Rossville had caught cold, and was unable to fulfil her engagements; his sisters visited her in the course of the day, and Gertrude blushed with shame as she attempted to confirm the falsehood.

" I half suspect," said Georgiana, laughing, " that Master Fred, has been telling you that mamma is not fashionable ; he is so admired and recherche himself, that we think he gives himself airs: so, pray don't encourage him, or you will spoil him entirely."

"It is so provoking," said Miss Emily, "that he won't allow you to go with us ; for I can see it is he that prevents you from going with us to Kitchener's this morning—he has some such exquisite things just now !—things really to die for !" with a deep sigh.

" Since that is the case," said Gertrude, smilingly, " I am fortunate in having escaped the danger ; hut, if you are not afraid to encounter it, you shall each of you choose something for me according to your own taste, and then I shall see how far we agree."

" How happy you must he who can afford to choose what you like !" said hoth sisters, sorrowfully.

" For to-day I devolve my happiness upon you," said Lady Rossville ; " only remember to choose exactly what you should like for yourselves."

The sisters departed, delighted with the commission, and not without some latent suspicion as to the result of their choice, which was verified by each receiving the very handsome and expensive articles of jewellery they had selected.

CHAPTER X.

The stage is pleasant, and the way seems short, All strew'd with flowers ; The days appear but hours, Being spent in time beguiling sport. Here griefs do neither press, nor doubts perplex; Here's neither fear to curb, nor care to vex. Quarles.

Perhaps no woman ever heard another highly commended by her lover without feeling at least a slight sensation of pique and jealousy, and something of this sort Gertrude had begun to cherish against Lady Charles Arabin before she saw her. She was, therefore, prepared to receive her with something of the air and manner with which a pretty spoiled child migh be supposed to welcome its governess ; and, unknown to herself, there was a tournure of the head, a colour on the cheek, a slight pout on the lip, when that Lady and Colonel Delmour were announced together. But the first glance at Lady Charles instantly dispelled all her fears and thick-coming fancies ; as she beheld (what in common life would be called) a middle-aged woman, without any pretensions to beauty, beyond a tolerably regular set of features, and a figure which, though evidently of a fine structure, was thin almost to meagreness. Her dress was striking without being singular—her manners were quiet, but perfectly elegant; and the tout ensemble conveyed that impression of high birth and high breeding, which is something too subtle and refined to be described or analysed ; something of so delicate and impalpable a nature that it might sometimes escape notice altogether, but for the effect it produces upon others.

Gertrude had never felt that her mother was vulgar, till she contrasted the florid pomposity of her manner with the ease, grace, and simplicity of Lady Charles Arabin : she spoke little, and there was nothing in her conversation beyond the frivolous chit-chat of the day ; but her voice and accent were both fine, and she skimmed over subjects with an airy lightness that would have baffled any thing like discussion, even had any one been so inclined. She invited Gertrude to take a drive with her, to which she readily acceded, notwithstanding Mrs. St. Clair's manifest displeasure, which, however, she did not venture to express.

That lady was considerably annoyed by the manners of Lady Charles, which made her feel her own as something unwieldy and overgrown — like a long train, they were both out of the way and in the way, and she did not know very well how to dispose of them. Indeed, few things can be more irritating than for those who have hitherto piqued themselves upon the abundance of their manner, to find all at once that they have a great deal too much; that no one is inclined to take it off their hands; and that, in short, it is dead stock.

Lady Charles took leave, but Gertrude stopped a moment in the drawing-room behind her companions to say a few coaxing words to her mother; then, as she hurried to overtake them, she heard Lady Charles say, as in answer to some remark of Colonel Delmour, " She is perfect!" and she blushed as she caught the meaning glance he turned to cast upon her. Much was done in the way of shopping; a variety of splendid dresses were ordered; a great deal of bijouterie was purchased ; and Gertrude was whirled from place to place, and from shop to shop, till her head was almost turned with the varied and bustling scenes in which she was acting, for the first time, a part.

It is not at first that London either astonishes or delights. It is too vast and too complicated to be taken in all at once, either by the eye or the mind ; and it requires a little schooling to enjoy even the variety and the brilliancy of its pleasures, as they .flash in rapid and never-ceasing succession on the bewildered senses. Lady Rossville, like all novices, felt something of this; and she sighed for the peaceful romantic seclusion of her own domain, where she was all in all, and where her lover was all to her. But it is not the young and admired who can stand long on the brink of pleasure, indulging their own sentimental reveries; and Gertrude, with all her feeling, and romance, and enthusiasm, was soon in the vortex of elegant dissipation.

Borne like a feather on the tide of fashionable celebrity, she was hurried along she knew not whither; while, at the same time, wherever she Avent she was hailed as the leader of every favourite folly. She was the idol of the day, and she breathed only in an atmosphere of adulation, baleful alike in its effects

•

on the head and the heart. Amidst the delusions of the senses, she forgot every thing save her lover; but even when all looks were turned upon her, as the magnet of the glittering throng, it was in his eyes only that she sought to read her triumph. Although her engagement with Colonel Delmour was pretty generally understood, and he had all the bearing of the accepted lover, still that did not prevent others from entering the lists, but, on the contrary, was rather an additional attraction ; and men far superior to himself in rank and station, and some of them not much his inferiors in personal endowments, had declared themselves her lovers. But even Delmour, jealous and irritable as he was, felt that he had no cause to dread a rival in her affections. Mr. Delmour and she had only met once, and that at a formal dinner at the Duke of Burlington's, where they had merely exchanged the common courtesies of acquaintanceship. He was evidently of the family school; the Duke and Duchess being formal, dull personages, living in a vast and stately mansion, amidst a profusion of magnificent heirlooms of every description.

" That would have been an establishment for you, Gertrude," sighed her mother, as they left the mansion, where she had felt more at home than amidst the gay unattainable ease of fashionable manners; "what madness to reject so magnificent a lot! but even yet "

" O, mamma! beware how you utter even a hope on that subject, unless you would raise the shades of the whole race of the mighty departed Delmours. I have been thinking how fortunate it is that I am destined to be a mere scion on that noble stock; —how could I ever have sustained the whole weight of the family dignity! I protest I have got a crick in my neck with only looking at and imagining the weight of the Duchess's old-fashioned diamond necklace ;" and Gertrude said to herself that Colonel Delmour was quite right in wishing to preserve her from his family circle.

She now gave herself up with greater zest than ever to the round of frivolous occupations and amusements which form the sole business of so many an immortal being's existence, and which are no less fascinating to the unreflecting mind than they are vain and unsatisfying to the eye of reason and experience. It was to no purpose that Mrs. St. Clair remonstrated, and threatened, and denounced—her power was gone;—she never had possessed the affection of the daughter, and she had now lost the control of authority. Besides, the Countess afforded her little time or opportunity to expatiate on her extravagances;—she lived in such an unceasing whirl, that Mrs. St. Clair had in vain strove to keep pace with her. She had been obliged to relinquish the attempt—their hours did not keep time, and their engagements were in opposite spheres—each had their apartments — their carriage—their society; and Gertrude felt satisfied that

her mother had all these things, and was also noticed by, and indeed in habits of intimacy "with, Colonel Delmour's family. Her own mornings were spent in sitting to half the sculptors and painters in town for busts and pictures, in all possible variety, to please the fastidious taste of her lover;—in riding in the Park with him, or in shopping with Lady Charles, or some other frivolous idler; — in the evening there were dinners, and parties, and balls, and operas, and assemblies, in such quick succession, as left her scarcely conscious of having been at one before she found herself at some other.

" Confess this is to live," said Delmour to her one evening, as he led her from one gay multitude where she had been the admired of all admirers, to another where her appearance would excite an equal sensation.

" All that is wanting," replied she, with a smile, " is time to feel one's enjoyment; but I can scarcely tell whether I chase pleasure or it chases me, or whether we are running a race, or — in short, how we go on together."

" Take a ride with me to-morrow in the Park, and we shall go at a sober foot-pace, that you may have time to find out," said Delmour.

" But to-morrow I give Lawrence another sitting "

" Take the ride first, and you will go to him with a bloom that will make him burn his palette."

CHAPTER XL

All these inconveniences are incident to love: reproaches, jealousies, quarrels, reconcilements, war — and then peace .Terence.

The Countess smiled a consent, and Colonel Delmour was at her breakfast-table the following morning. A salver stood upon it covered with cards, notes, letters, bills, petitions, and memoranda of every description. She carelessly tossed over some, opened and glanced over others, while she listened at the sam? time to her lover as he read the record of her triumphs in the Morning Post. At length, as she discovered some post letters amid the heap, she drew back her hand, and, with a shudder, exclaimed —

" Ah! these ugly letters!"

"What letters?" inquired Delmour, as be at the same time drew the stand towards him.— "O! some Scotch parish business, is that all ?"

" Lectures from my guardians, and tiresome explanations from my steward, are the best I have to expect. I had a letter from him t'other day, telling me the school-house was stopped for want of money."

" How very distressing!" said Colonel Delmour, with an ironical smile; —" then you will have no long, lean, grey, weeping-looking building, with its steep, straight roof, and its little green glass windows, and its shoals of hoddy-doddy, white-haired, blubbered boys and girls.—I hope it was to have formed a vista in the park ; it would have been what is called, I believe, a most gratifying sight."

" You are very kind to try to reconcile me to myself by treating it so slightly; but I feel I have been to blame : I have been too expensive."

" In what respect ?"

" In every thing — this service, for instance," pointing to the magnificent breakfast service of richly chased antique plate and Sevres china—" I am shocked to think how much it cost."

" Why delft, to be sure, would have been cheaper—and, to the philosophic eye, a pewter basin is as becoming, perhaps, as a silver one — 'tis a pity you did not consult me instead of Lady Charles about it! "

" Lady Charles is certainly very extravagant," said the Countess, gravely.

" Not more so than others in her rank. Lord Charles has a good fortune, and allows her to spend it, which she does in supporting her station in society.—Methodists and misers, I believe, are for abolishing all these distinctions, and building conventicles, and endowing hospitals with their money."

" One of these letters, I perceive, is from Lyndsay," said Gertrude, with another sigh.

" Which you seem afraid even to look upon.—Shall I open it for you?"

" Do; but first give Zoe a few of these strawberries."

Colonel Delmour read the letter aloud—it was short and hurried, and the purport of it was communicating the sudden death of the parish minister of Rossville, by which means the Countess would have it in her power to provide for young Leslie, who had just been with him bespeaking his good offices.

" Who is this Leslie who finds such a patron in Lyndsay ?" inquired Colonel Delmour.

" He is a very interesting young man, who is engaged to my cousin, Anne Black, and the want of a church has hitherto been the only obstacle to their marriage.—How happy it makes me to have it in my power to remove it!—Pray, reach me my writing stand, and I shall settle that sur le champ."

But, instead of obeying, Delmour took the hand she had so impatiently extended, and said—

" Is it possible, my dear Gertrude, you can be serious in this? Can you really think, for a moment, of having your relations placed so near you in so inferior a situation? Only consider, the manse is almost close by the gate—that is of little consequence with people who have no claim upon you; but really the

Countess of Rossville, and her cousin the minister's wife, thus Drought in contact,—there is confusion in the thought!"

Lady Rossville looked displeased ; then said— " My cousin is a person I never can feel ashamed of."

" Not as she is; but as she will be, when she degenerates into the -minister's wife, with her printed gown and black mittens, with a troop of half-licked cubs of children at her heels, and the minister himself, honest man ! at their bead, with his lank locks, and his customary suit of rusty blacks, all coming to visit, perchance to dine with, their cousin the Countess."

" If you are ashamed of my relations, you ought to have said so sooner," said Gertrude, struggling with her emotion; " as it is, it is not yet too late "

" Dearest Gertrude, how seriously you take my badinage ! But you must be sensible that where the difference of rank and station is so great between near relations, the local affinity had as well not be quite so close ; your own good sense and delicate perception must point out to you the inevitable disagreements that must ensue—the slights that will be felt, the offences that will be taken, the affronts that will be imagined."

" My cousin is not a person of that sort," said Gertrude ; " and, I am sure, her near vicinity would be a source of great pleasure to me. I like her society, and should have her often with me."

" You may at present; but, be assured, that could not possibly continue ; you must move in such different spheres, and must associate with such different people, that 'tis impossible you could act or think alike. For instance, you told me that the Duchess of Arlingham, the Arabins, Lady Peverley, Mrs. Beechey, and I know not all, who had promised to pay you a a visit at Rossville this summer, and to take parts in your theatricals, if you can have the theatre ready : how do you suppose the minister and his wife could relish, or be relished by, those of your friends ? "

" But I am in a manner pledged to my cousin "

" Not for this church, surely ?"

" No, not for this one in particular; but I repeatedly assured her that whenever I had it in my power I would befriend her, and now it is so "

" Dearest Gertrude, it is not in your power, that is, if I possess that influence with you I have hitherto nattered myself I did; on that faith, in the transaction I had lately with Harry Monteith relating to my exchange into the Guards, I ventured to promise that the first church that was in your gift, as the phrase is, you would—that is I w r ould—engage your interest in behalf of his old tutor—quite a charity case, as he represented it; a married man with a large family, and I forget all the particulars ; but, at the time, it struck me as a thing that would interest you."

Lady Rossville's colour rose during this speech, and for some moments she remained silent, as if struggling with her feelings: at last she said —" You have taken a strange liberty, it seems, and one which I cannot easily pardon."

At that moment a servant entered to say her ladyship's horses were at the door.

" Desire them to be put up ; I shall not ride to-day," said she; and taking up Lyndsay's letter she quitted the room, leaving Delmour too much piqued, as well as surprised at this display of spirit, to make any attempt to detain her. He, however, lounged a considerable time at the breakfast-table, expecting her return ; tossed over all the litter of new publications, and music, and expensive toys that lay scattered about; touched her harp, to ascertain whether it were in tune, and broke two of the strings ; stirred the fire, although the room was suffocating ; then threw open a window, exclaiming at the smell of a tuberose ; but still Gertrude did not return— carriage after carriage was sent from the door, and even Lady Charles was not admitted. At length his patience was exhausted: he wrote—" Dearest Gertrude, see me but for one moment, as you love me ;" and, ringing the bell, he desired it might be conveyed to Lady Rossville. A verbal answer was returned — her ladyship was sorry she was particularly engaged; and Delmour, too proud to sue any further, left the house in a transport of indignation.

CHAPTER XII.

Is Nature's course dissolved ? Doth Time's glass stand ?
Or hath some frolic heart set back the hand
Of Fate's perpetual clock ? Will't never strike ?
Is crazy Time grown lazy, faint, or sick.
With very age ? Quarles.

Gertrude, too, was proud in her way, and her feelings had been severely wounded. She had already become sufficiently fine to be able to feel, in some degree, the truth of what Delmour had said in regard to her relations; but she was piqued that he should have been the person to force so disagreeable a conviction upon her — he who had so often declared that she was all the universe to him — and whose favourite maxim it was, that love could see no defects in aught pertaining to the object beloved ! How often had he repeated to her, when she smilingly chid his flatteries—" O que les illusions de Vamour sont amiables! Les flatteries sont en un sens des verites — lejugementse tait, mais le cceur park!" Why was it, then, that he was become so clearsighted as thus to anticipate these paltry feelings of wounded vanity?—and to have presumed so far already as to have

usurped her power—to have promised away in her name, without leave asked or obtained, a gift of so much importance —one which she might have had a pleasure in conferring at his solicitation, but which it would be weakness to allow to be thus wrested from her! " Lyndsay would not have acted thus!" thought she, as she looked at his letter, and a tear dropt upon it. She leant her head upon her hand, and, for the first time since her arrival in London, fell into a train of reflection, from which she only roused herself to begin an answer to his letter. But she had only got as far as — "My dear Cousin, —7" am

happy to have it in my power " when Colonel Delmour's

billet was brought to her. She read it, and wavered. — " No, I will not see him," thought she, proudly, at this triumph over her already returning tenderness. —" But I will not finish my letter to Lyndsay till to-morrow—one day can make no difference, and 'tis almost time to go to Lawrence's." She rang, and ordered the carriage—then drove to Lady Augusta's to get one of the girls to accompany her. As they drove along, Delmour passed on horseback, and merely bowed with an air of lofty respect.

" Fred, seems to be on his high horse to-day," said Miss Georgiana, laughing; " I told you he would give himself airs ;* but"— looking after him— " he certainly is the handsomest man in town, and unquestionably the most admired and imitated. Apropos, have you seen the Duchess of St. Ives? — I hear she has already doffed her weeds, and come out in all her glory. Delmour was an admirer of hers, you must know, in her married state — at least so the ill-natured world said. I know that she is desperately in love with him, and I believe would marry him to-morrow if he would ask her; so she will be ready to poison you, or pierce you to the heart perhaps with a bodkin, as the ladies in old ballads used to do their rivals."

There certainly was nothing in this that ought to have gratified a mind in a right state of feeling—it was food for a perverted taste only; but how often are the passions and the prejudices gratified at the expense of the principles! Gertrude's vanity was pleased to hear her lover praised, and her pride was piqued to show her triumph over the Duchess of St. Ives.

These two ladies had met, exchanged cards, and graced each other's parties; but a mutual and instinctive sort of antipathy had, from the first, existed between them. They were both young, beautiful, distinguished, and independent: rivals in celebrity and extravagance, Gertrude learnt, for the first tim°, that they were also rivals in love, and a momentary pang shot across her breast at the discovery. But hers was not a nature to harbour jealous fears, and she soon dismissed them.

•' No," thought she, " whatever Delmour's faults may be, I should wrong him were I to doubt his love and truth ;" and she recollected some slighting and satirical remarks he had made

upon the Duchess the evening before. She, therefore, listeued with complacency, -while Miss Delmour rattled away ahout the Duchess — her beauty — her pride — her parties — her diamonds — her jointure —her independence of all control — and, to sum up the whole, she concluded, with a sigh —

" Do you know I never see the Duchess of St. Ives that I do not wish I had been born a widow."

When Gertrude returned home it was in the secret hope of hearing that Colonel Delmour had called during her absence.

" Has any body called since I went out ? " inquired she of her porter, as she entered the hall.

" O, surely, my lady!" replied he, in some surprise at such a question, as he pointed to a pile of cards.

" No one else ?" as she tossed them over with an air of chagrin.

" No, my lady!" in the same tone of amazement at being, for the first time, so strictly interrogated on the duties of his office.

" He may have called, although that stupid man has forgot to mention it," thought she ; " and he will probably call again — it is not very late. Those French clocks and watches are always wrong"—as they told a different tale — " it cannot be more than seven."

But just then Mrs. St. Clair entered, and the mother and the daughter exchanged their morning salutations. The former was going to the theatre, as it was one of her greatest enjoyments to patronise a large party of secondary people, by whom she was looked up to with that respect which money and consequence will always procure from one set, if not from another. She expressed her astonishment at finding her daughter seated at her harp in her morning dress ; and the Countess, hastily rising, said she was just going to commence her toilette. — " But I dine with Lady Peverley, who is always late."

" And then what else ?" asked Mrs. St. Clair.

" Then, I believe, I shall go to the opera with Lady Charles; and I shall, perhaps, just look in for half an hour at the Duchess of Arlington's."

" You are killing yourself, Gertrude—absolutely killing yourself— you look wretchedly—I must put a stop to this—we must leave this town."

" We shall talk of that to-morrow, mamma—good bye," cried the Countess, as she flew away to her dressing-room, anxious to avoid all unpleasant discussion.

She half expected to meet Colonel Delmour at dinner, but she was mistaken. At all events, there could not be a doubt of seeing him at the opera; and to the opera she went with Lady Charles, escorted by two or three fashionable men. But Delmour was not there ; and she watched the opening of every box, to see whether he would not yet enter. Her whole attention absorbed in this single point of observation, she neither saw nor heard any thing else. She "was merely conscious that her companions were amused at something, she knew not—cared not what; till at last Lady Charles, touching her on the arm, said —

" Do, Lady Rossville, take a little share of our diversion, bad as it is ; that odd little nid-nodding face is too good to be kept all to ourselves ; and 'tis so comical, all its nods and grimaces seem as if directed to our box."

" It is very savage that none of us will return the compliment," said Lord Ilfrington.

" It will be no sinecure," said Mr. Vavasour ; " there must be a prodigious arrear, and still accumulating ;" as a fresh succession of nods ensued.

" We must draw lots," said Lord Ilfrington; " but Vavasour has the strongest head of the party."

While this was going on Lady Rossville had looked to the spot indicated ; and there, in the centre of the pit, was to be seen a long small throat, with a pretty little, broad, smirking, delighted-looking face on the top of it, surmounted by a most elaborate pile of hair, dressed in all the possible varieties of style, combining Grecian braids, and Gothic bows, and Tuscan curls, which seemed to vibrate with renewed vigour, as the Countess looked in that direction.

" Surely," thought she, " that is a face I have seen somewhere;" but she still looked on it with a vacant eye, till at once it flashed upon her that the face, and the head, and the nods, were all combined in the person of her cousin, Mrs. Augustus Larkins ! As if to confirm the fact, Mr. Augustus himself, a caricature of the reigning fashions, turned round and joined his bows to his Lilly's nods. On first coming to town Gertrude had heard from Mrs. St. Clair that they were in the country, which had proved rather a relief; and from that time to the present no thought of Mr. or Mrs. Larkins had ever crossed her brain ; — and now to be recognized by them in this public manner, where they were only conspicuous to be laughed at! The Countess felt her very temples glow; and, with an exclamation at the heat of the house, she drew back, then rose and took a chair in the back of the box.

" How mean, how silly I am!" thought she to herself, " that dare not acknowledge my own relations, for fear of sharing in the pitiful ridicule of two or three people who are nothing to me ! — O, I could beat myself for my folly ! — Ah, Deknour knows me better than I know myself, and I have quarrelled with him because he does so !" and tears of mortification and disappointment rose to her eyes. —'" I will get the better of this paltry feeling," said she to herself; and again she returned to the front of the box, determined to acknowledge her cousin ; but the ballet was drawing near a close, and Mr. and Mrs. Larkins devoted their whole attention to it;—then came the bustle and confusion of

A A

"breaking up; and Gertrude began to tbink she should have her good resolutions for her pains, when again the good-humoured Lilly turned round her bright, joyous face, and Lady Rossville gave her a smile, and a bow of recognition. But the next moment she felt her cheeks glow as she beheld the whole party, as if touched by electricity, face about simultaneously with looks of eager expectation. Again sbe turned away, and only breathed freely when she found herself in her carriage.

Delmour was not at the Duchess of Arlington's. Lady Charles expressed her astonishment at not finding him in any of his usual haunts, and Gertrude disclaimed all knowledge of his proceedings with as much indifference as she could assume.

" He is probably at the Duchess of St. Ives'" said Lady Stanley, — " she has a musical party, I believe, to-night."

Again the Countess found the heat insupportable, and her easy good-humoured chaperon left the party with her as soon as her carriage could be got.

Gertrude returned home, wearied in body, and wretched in mind. All the worst qualities of her nature had been called forth and excited during the day — resentment, envy, pride, jealousy, had all been felt, and some of their leaven still wrought in her breast. " Oh, how I hate mvself! and how hideous I look!" thought she, as she glanced at herself in a mirror. — " Is this pleasure ? Ah! how different from the sweet serene days I passed at Rossville ! — but there I was not the vain, foolish, fantastic thing I am here. Lyndsay was right when he told me I should never find my happiness in what the world calls pleasure!" And the admired and envied Lady Rossville owned for the time that to be admired was but vanity — and to be envied but vexation of spirit.

CHAPTER XIII.

Perish those who have said our good things before us ! Donatus.

But a sound sleep and a bright sun have wonderful effects in dispelling solemn thoughts; and the following morning found Gertrude's mind again gay with ideas of happiness, and her beauty restored to all its native freshness. She tried to think how she ought to receive Delmour; but she never could study a part, — she must always be swayed by circumstances, or by impulses ; and to these she committed herself.

" Perhaps I shall find him already below," thought she, and, in that half-formed expectation, she hastened to breakfast. — " There may be some mistake," was the next idea that occurred; " those people are all so stupid !" and she rang the bell. — "I am at home to every body this morning."

" Every body, my lady?"

" Yes, every body."

She dawdled over her breakfast,—again murmured at the rapidity of her time-piece, while in her heart she felt the slowness of time itself. Amongst her letters was one from Anne Black to the same effect as Lyndsay's.

" I am quite resolved," said she, as she read it, " that Mr. Leslie shall have that church — all I will concede is, that I shall first convince Delmour of the propriety of it. To be sure, I may answer Lyndsay's letter now;" and she took up a pen ; " but I think I began one yesterday, which I left in my dressing-room ; I may as well finish it as begin another." The entrance of Mrs. St. Clair added another to the many excuses for procrastination.

That lady had by some means discovered that a, misunderstanding had taken place between the Countess and Colonel Delmour, though she was ignorant of the cause of it; and she deemed it more politic to take no notice of it, that she might not be suspected of any sinister design in wishing to get her daughter out of London. But, before she had an opportunity of beginning an oration on the subject, Lady RossviJle held out her cousin's letter to her, saying —

" By-the-by, mamma, do you know Mr. Bauld, the minister of Rossville, is dead, and I mean to bestow the church upon William Leslie?—Here is a letter from Anne upon the subject."

Mrs. St. Clair looked very solemn. " You forget you have guardians to consult upon these occasions, Gertrude."

" I had a letter from Edward yesterday; he is very anxious for it, and Anne says her father will not object to it. Lord Millbank, you know, is a mere name, and of course you must approve of it, mamma,"

" No — I do not approve of your being instrumental to the degrading of your uncle's daughter into the wife of your parish minister. — If she will throw herself away, let it be in some remote situation ; but don't let her bring her poverty and contempt to our very door."

" She may be poor; but I am sure she never can be despised, mamma."

" Poverty and contempt generally go hand in hand in this world," said Mrs. St. Clair. " She cannot possibly afford to dress herself even upon an occasion so as to be fit to appear at your table as your cousin, though merely as the minister's wife she might pass without observation."

" She is so gentle and ladylike in her manners, and so unr -suming in her dress, that I am sure I never could be ashamed of either."

" Then she can scarcely afford hats and shoes, certainly not stockings and gloves, to her children; and you would enjoy very much, every time you went outside your gate, to be followed by a troop of half-naked urchins staring after their fine lady cousin."

A A 2

" But, mamma, I promised-

" But at present you have no right to perform ; you are a minor, you are under pupillage ; it is your guardians you must be guided by; wait till you are of age, and then do as you think proper; by that time a much better living may be in your gift, for this, I understand, is one of the poorest."

The discussion was stopped; for just then there drew up an equipage, somewhat of a different style from those which usually graced the Countess's door. It was a very large, heavy, roomy-looking coach, evidently built to carry six, of a strong salmon colour, with grass-green hammer-cloth, and green and orange liveries. The general effect was shocking to the eye of taste, and Gertrude uttered an exclamation of horror as she caught a glance of it. It appeared to be literally as full as it could hold, as sundry bonnets were to be seen ; and it was some minutes before Mr. Larkins could extricate himself from the company within, and several more elapsed before Mrs. Larkins emerged. Then followed another lady, and another, in less time ; and all four were actually in the hall before Lady Rossville had presence of mind to take any precautions against this irruption.

Mr. and Mrs. Augustus Larkins, Miss Larkins, Miss Barbara Larkins, were now announced; and much bowing and courtesying, and introducing took place, and the good-natured simple Lilly seemed as though she never would weary of shaking hands and expressing her delight at sight of her aunt and cousin. At length they were all seated, and then apologies commenced for not having been to wait upon them sooner.

" You must have thought it very unkind," said she ; " but we have been staying at old Mr. Larkins's beautiful villa, Willow Bank, snd we only came back to town the day before yesterday,—and how odd it was that we should see each other first at the opera! I saw you didn't know me at first; but Augustus said, he daresay'd you were angry because I had not been to wait upon you; but, I assure you, it was only the day before yesterday we came to town, and yesterday we couldn't get old Mr. Larkins's coach, for he wanted it himself, but we have got it to-day; and old Mrs. Larkins came with us, but she has hurt her leg, and finds it very troublesome to get out, so she hopes you'll excuse her."

" Chawming owse this, mem," observed Mr. Augustus, surveying the apartment all round.

" Monsous nice owse, indeed," said Miss Larkins.

" Sweet purty owse it is," said Miss Barbara Larkins.

" Well, mem, you have been to our theatres of course ?" inquired Mr. Augustus.

Lady Rossville answered in the negative.

" Good la, mem, it an't possible! — Why, then, you have seen nothing! — S'pose we make a party for Drury Lane some of these nights ? "

A thundering rap at the door here proclaimed other visitors,

and Gertrude thought she should have swooned when the Duchess of St. Ives was announced. She rose to receive her in the other drawing-room ; — hut she was too late — the Duchess was already in the very heart of the Larkinses.

" How do you do, dear Lady Rossville ? I heard you were taken ill at the Duchess of Arlington's last night, and I felt quite anxious ahout you; but you seem pretty well to-day?"

This was uttered in that tone of insolent, condescending superiority, which is intended at once to convey an impression of the speaker's own triumphant happiness, and their commiseration for the person they are addressing. Gertrude tried to repel it, but she was no adept in dissimulation ; and her attempt at gaiety failed when she answered, that she had merely been fatigued by the length of the ballet at the opera, and overcome by the excessive heat of the Duchess's rooms.

"I judged wisely, theD, it seems," said the Duchess, carelessly, "in having my own little quiet party at home ; though, to own the truth, I believe I was rather wise by compulsion, as I had two or three friends dining with me, who positively would not go away, and I was forced to sing to them till I actually made myself hoarse," giving a little affected cough as she spoke.

Gertrude's colour rose, and her heart beat; but she made no reply. Mrs. St. Clair, therefore, thought it necessary to say something, if only to prevent the Larkinses from getting in a word.

"Your grace's musical powers, it seems, have greater attractions than even the wonder of the day, the celebrated Cata-lani."

"O dear no," said the Duchess, in a sort of careless, contemptuous manner, as if she disdained to be complimented; — "but 'tis pleasant to sing with those who understand one's style of singing. There is only one person I know who can sing 1 Felice chi vi mira,' that is, in the way I sing it."

That was Colonel Delmour's favourite song, and one Gertrude and he had often sung together; and she had heard him mention the Duchess of St. Ives's singing, as something fine in its way, though in a different style from hers. She felt that her agitation would betray her if she attempted to carry on the conversation, and she was glad even to turn to the Larkinses, who attracted by the splendid binding of some books which lay upon one of the tables had begun to inspect, or rather to handle them.

"This is beautiful," said Mrs. Larkins, displaying some fine engravings in one of them to her sisters-in-law ; — "I never saw this before — ' Fisk, by Mrs. Tigg,' " reading the title of it.

"Peseechye, my dear," whispered Mr. Larkins, as if a little ashamed of her mal-pronunciation.

"Dear! is that Fishie ? " said Miss Larkins ; — "a sweet purty thing it is."

Gertrude could almost have cried at this Malaprop murder of

A A 3

"Psyche, by Mrs. Tighe," while the Duchess had recourse to her little affected cough to conceal the play of her muscles.

"Apropos of music, which we are talking of," said she, "pray, is not Colonel Delmour some relation of yours ? I think he told rae you were somehow cousins — how very well he sings ' Felice chi vi mira ! ' "

"Yes, I believe Colonel Delniour is my cousin," said Lady Rossville, now wrought up to an air of haughty indifference ; "and he does sing some things very well, in particular ' Vorrei die ahnen per gioco.' "

"Ah, that, I suppose, he keeps for his particular favourites," said the Duchess, with an insolent smile — " as he has never sung it to me. I shall certainly reproach him with his treachery when I see him. Meanwhile, good morning, dear Lady Ross-ville ; I am quite happy to find you so well;" and with a squeeze of the hand to the Countess, a slight bow to Mrs. St. Clair, and a supercilious stare at the Larkinses, as they all rose and bowed and courtesyed with profound respect, she swept out of the room. Gertrude was much too wretched to know or care what passed during the remainder of the visit. She heard something said about a dinner, and about a party to the play, and about old Mr. Larkins's villa, and old Mrs. Larkins's leg; and in the inanity of despair she assented to every thing, and they at length took leave, impatient to carry the tidings of all they had seen and heard to their less noble acquaintances.

CHAPTER XIV.

My truant heart
Forgets each lesson that resentment taught, And in thy sight knows only to be happy.
Mason's Elfrida.

Like all those who are the slaves of their feelings, Lady Ross-ville found she must fly to one extreme or other — she must either shut herself up in her chamber, and refuse to he comforted, or she must plunge still deeper into the whirlpool of folly and extravagance to drown thought. As persons in a similar state of mind generally do, she chose both evils—she first wept the bitter tears of jealousy and mortification, then ordered her carriage, and, throwing on a veil, drove away to Lady Charles Arabin, to get her assistance in choosing some dresses and jewels.

" I may as well order the furniture I want for Rossville too," said she to herself— " I shall be there very soon now ; " and the tears again sprung to her eyes, as Rossville and all its tender recollections rose to her mind ; but she strove to put them down with the splendid plans she tried to busy her imagination about.

On being ushered into Lady Charles's drawing-room, she found her surrounded by gentlemen, children, and dogs ; and the bustle of her first entrance prevented her all at once from recognizing Colonel Delmour amongst the number, and when she did a mutual bow was the only acknowledgment.

One by ^ne the idlers dropped off, the children were sent to dinner, and only Lady Charles and her two friends remained. Gertrude then made her request, to which she acceded, adding—

" Though, as I have got a little cold to-day, and your carriage is open, I must wrap up — so pray don't tire to death if I should be ten minutes at my toilette ;" and, with a smile, she disappeared.

Silence ensued. Gertrude carefully avoided looking in the direction where Delmour was, lest he should construe it into an appeal to him; and she almost feared to breathe, lest he should imagine she had spokeh. She flattered herself she was the very emblem of indifference and abstraction; but even through the folds of her veil Delmour marked, with secret triumph, her quivering lip and tearful eyes. At length this state became too painful to be endured. She rose with the intention of passing into the adjoining drawing-room, when Delmour, approaching her with an air of agitation, said —

" Although I should not have presumed to seek an interview with Lady Rossville in her own house again after having been once turned from it, yet I cannot allow the present opportunity to pass without making an attempt to obtain from her justice what I have now little hope of owing to her tenderness." He stopped in emotion — but Gertrude felt her tears ready to spring forth, and made no reply. " All I ask is, that you would hear what I have to offer in excuse for my conduct, rash and unwarrantable as it must appear to you, until, in some degree, explained."

" I was wrong," said Lady Rossville, summoning all her pride to her aid; M the step you had taken was one of so extraor-. dinary a nature that I certainly ought to have heard what you had to offer in vindication of it."

This was a more prompt and spirited reply than Colonel Delmour had reckoned upon, and, for a moment or two, he was silent and disconcerted; he then said —

" I find I have mistaken your character, or rather I have judged it by my own. Had I been master of the universe, my pride, my happiness would have been, that the object of my love should, from the moment I loved, be the partner also of my power, be it what it might; but your sentiments are different from mine, it seems."

"I, too, should have had a pleasure in sharing the gifts of fortune, whatever they were," said the Countess; "but to have them wrested from me—"

"But I never sought to wrest them from you," said Delmour, with earnestness; "though, being rather rough and blunt in speech, I perhaps did not go so wooingly to work as some one more designing would have done. I told you, too briefly perhaps, the simple truth, that at your wish I had used every means to get myself exchanged into the Guards; but it was a matter of difficulty, and — why should I scruple to own it? — of expense, too, beyond my means; but this I was too proud to own to you, and I have been punished for it. — In short, not to bore you with tiresome business detail, Monteith proposed that I should engage to — to use my influence with you to provide for this old tutor of his, who is a sort of dead weight upon the family; and I, in the belief that I was — pardon my presumption — gratifying you, foolishly enough pledged myself to that effect."

"Nay, more — that you would obtain it," said Lady Rossville, still struggling against betraying her tenderness.

"Perhaps I did, in the sanguine hope that, when the time came for fulfilling my promise, I should then have acquired greater influence with you than I can flatter myself I now possess. But that hope is at an end. However disgraceful it may be to fail in my promise, disgrace itself could scarce be more intolerable than the misery I have endured under your displeasure."

"And yet you could sing with the Duchess of St. Ives?" said Gertrude, reproachfully, while her cheek flushed, and the tear swelled to the very brim.

"Did I? It may be so, for I can scarcely tell what I have done for the last four-and-twenty hours. — Yes, now I recollect Lord Westerton forcing me to her house, and being compelled to sing with her something or other — I forget what — that I used, I believe, to sing with her before the flood — that is, when I rather admired her bravura style of beauty and of singing; but these days are past— never to return!"

Gertrude's tears, hitherto with difficulty restrained, now dropped from her eyes; but they were tears of joy and tenderness. "Ah, Delmour!" said she, as she gave him her hand, "we have both been to blame;—you have been rash, and I hasty; but you shall keep your promise." She rose, and placed herself at a writing-table. "What is the name of the person you wish to befriend?" asked she, as she began to write; but she sighed as the name of William Leslie presented itself to her mind's eye. Colonel Delmour could not tell the name; but she wrote a few lines, engaging to bestow the church and living of Rossville upon , then presented the paper to her lover, who, with affected generosity, for some time refused to receive it; but at length the Countess prevailed, and he consented to keep his promise at the expense of hers.

Still Gertrude did not feel happy; but the usual panacea was applied, viz. squandering money in dissipating thought. Colonel Delmour was of the shopping party, and encouraged her in every expensive whim. The most magnificent orders were given for furnishing Rossville with all possible expedition; and, to crown her transient delusive pleasure, when they met the Duchess of St. Ives Delmour's only salutation to her was a distant bow.

"Do you go to her assembly to-night?" inquired the Countess of her lover.

"Not unless to accompany you."

"Then, pray don't, dear Lady Rossville," said Lady Charles, who was of the opposite faction to the Duchess. "Do, both of you, come and dine quietly with Arabin and me. My cold is really too bad to admit of my going out in an evening ; and, you know, we never give dinners, so we shall be a party quarre —no bad thing, sometimes." .

Gertrude consented; and the quiet evening was passed partly in arranging a ball to be given by her, and partly in losing fifty guineas to Lord Charles at ecarte.

" What an odd jumble of a day this has been !" thought she, as she laid her head on her pillow; " and yet I have had a great deal of pleasure in it too." But she sighed as she said it; for not all the delusions of her own heart, or the blandishments of her lover, could stifle the voice of conscience, or conceal from her that she had acted unjustly and unwisely.

" What shall I say to Lyndsay ?" was the first thought that presented itself the following morning ; but, by the time she was dressed, she heard Delmour's well-known knock. — "I fear I shall not have leisure to write to him to-day," said she, as she hastened to receive her lover, glad of the excuse for delaying the irksome task. Then came the " strenuous idleness " of the day, most unremittingly persevered in for many successive days, till at length it became too late to think of writing at all. — It would be better now to wait till she returned to Rossville, she could explain the matter so much better in person than she could do by letter. Alas! she took not into account (how few of the great and the gay do!) the thought of that " hope deferred " which " maketh the heart sick," and which was experienced in all its intensity, as post after post arrived, and brought no tidings for those whose happiness hung upon her word.

Anne wrote again, and a blush of shame and remorse stained Lady Rossville's cheek as she beheld her cousin's hand-writing ; but she opened all her trifling billets, and read all her cards and newspapers, and pampered her dog, and made her bullfinch pipe to her; but still she could not find leisure to break the seal of her cousin's letter! Her mind was now averse to exert itself upon any thing that did not bring some semblance of pleasure along with it; and it was not so much the want of leisure as

the utter inability to employ what she had to any useful purpose, that thus bereft her of all self-command and power of action.

The thought she takes is, how to take no thought;
an art in which she was every day becoming a greater adept.

She went, however, with her mother to return Mrs. Larkins's visit; and found the romantic Lilly settled to her heart's content in a dull, vulgar, well-furnished house in the heart of the city, talking Cockney by way of English, and overflowing with rapture at her own blissful lot. She pressed most vehemently for her aunt and cousin to fix a day to dine with them— Augustus would be so disappointed if they did not do it— he was so anxious they should meet some near relations of his, Sir Christopher and Lady Huggins — he had been lord mayor once, and was a remarkably genteel, nice man ; and Lady Huggins was such a nice woman !—but, indeed, Augustus was very petikler in his friends, and had no ideer of visiting vulgar people. — But if they would not fix it now, Augustus and she would call in Park Lane some day very soon, for she knew he would take no denial — he kept a gig, and cculd drive her there any day. At this threat, Lady Rossville promised to look over the list of her engagements when she returned home ; and if she had a day disengaged before leaving town, she would dine with them.

Mrs. St. Clair here engaged that a day should certainly be allotted for the purpose ; and at length they were permitted to depart, with much lamentation that Augustus was from home, and repeated assurances of calling again some day soon.

In hopes of averting that evil, Gertrude, upon consulting her engagements, found a day disengaged, and it was settled accordingly that it should be given to the Larkinses. Mrs. St. Clair, indeed, rather anticipated pleasure from a party there. She was sure of being of consequence, and of making and of causing a fuss and a bustle ; a thing she could by no manner of means effect in the higher circles, where she could not even shine in the reflected lustre of her daughter.

CHAPTER XV.

O, fair ladies, how plesing war this lyfe of yours, if it sould ever abyde, and
then in the end that we might pas to" hevin with all this gay gear John
Knox.

Meanwhile the day of the ball arrived, and even in the greatest of great houses a ball causes more or less of confusion and commotion. Mrs. St. Clair had in vain remonstrated against it. Her remonstrances, indeed, were rather reproaches, as the cards had been issued before she had even been consulted; and the

preparations, made upon the most splendid scale, had all been arranged by the Countess and Colonel Delmour, aided by some of their friends. They were to come early to assist her in receiving the company ; and she was dressed, and her apartments lighted in due time. She walked through them with almost childish delight. All was light, and flowers, and perfume ; and her own figure, radiant in beauty and pleasure, flashed upon her in all directions from the magnificent mirrors, as they gave back the brilliant scene in almost endless succession. She had stopped at one of them to alter something about her hair, when in the long vista she perceived a servant ushering in a gentleman, who she immediately concluded must be Delmour. She turned round to meet him with a smile ; but, to her amazement, she beheld — not her lover, but her guardian, Lyndsay !

" Mr. Lyndsay ! my dear cousin! " exclaimed she ; but there was more of surprise than pleasure in the accent in which the words were uttered ; " how — where have you dropped from ? — the moon ? "

" No, dear Gertrude," said he, as he affectionately shook her hand; " you have given me a long journey, but not quite so long a one as that — I come from Scotland."

" From Scotland ! " repeated Lady Rossville, in some confusion, as her conscience smote her at the sound; " and how long have you been in town ? "

" Only since the morning — that is, my morning, which, I suppose, is your daybreak ; for I called — such is my vulgarity ! — about noon, and was told my lady was not up. I left my card, and called again at three, when I was told my lady had just gone out; and here I am now, it seems, just in time for my ladv's ball."

" Will you, indeed, stay ? " cried Gertrude, rather at a loss to ascertain whether he were in jest or earnest; " that will add so much to my pleasure — that is, I — but, indeed, I never heard you had called, and I forgot to look over my cards this morning."

" Is that all you have forgot, Gertrude ? " inquired Lyndsay, in a somewhat reproachful tone.

. " I fear not," said she, with a smile and a blush ; but the one was forced, the other natural; " but this is not the time for me to remember all I have forgot."

" When is the time then, Gertrude ?"

" O, any time, you know, that —that — any morning "

u Any morning sometimes means no day, does it not ? " said Lyndsay. " But I have come far on purpose to see you, and to talk with you, since you will not write to me, and I must km w when you will be disengaged."

" Spoken like a guardian, indeed! " said the Countess, with ar affected laugh; " but since you must know, I must candidly confess that I really cannot, at this precise moment, recollect what my engagements are. — To morrow, I know, I made a party to go to Richmond by water to breakfast. I wish to get out of the way of the debris of to-night."

" And what follows ? "

" Why, we shall probably dine there, and return in the evening, when I have several engagements."

" And the day after to-morrow — can I see you then ? "

" What day is that ? — Friday. I rather think — yes, indeed, I remember now I engaged to give Tournerelli a sitting at a very early hour; and as I forgot once before, if I fail this time he will certainly make a Gorgon or a Medusa of me. But you will join our party to Richmond to-morrow, and then we can talk it all over — pray do."

Lyndsay sighed. " Ah, Gertrude! what changed days since those we passed at Rossville together! I little thought then you would have grudged half an hour from your pleasures to bestow upon your friend ! "

" You surely would not have me break my engagements?" said the Countess, with some pique.

" On the contrary, it was to remind you of them chiefly that brought me here," said Lyndsay, mildly but gravely ; " but I would have you choose the lesser evil—that which will give least pain to others. Your gay friends will not break their hearts, I dare say, although you should disappoint them to-morrow ; but there are others, Gertrude, with whom you have made engagements of more consequence, and whose happiness is in your hands

— it is for them I would intercede."

Lady Rossville coloured deeply, and rising said, " It will have rather a ridiculous effect for you and me to be found sitting here in grave debate, discussing our parish business in the ball-room

— the place is, at least, as ill chosen as the time," added she, somewhat haughtily, as she moved away. For a moment Lyndsay seemed too much hurt to reply ; but recollecting himself, he said —

" Upon my own account I certainly would not intrude where I am evidently so unwelcome, but I have undertaken a task which I must perform; I have engaged to remind Lady Rossville of her promise — and more, to get that promise fulfilled."

The Countess remained silent, but her countenance betrayed the agitation of her mind. At that moment the knocker sounded an alarm.

" You have refused to fix an hour to see me," said Lyndsay; " I will therefore name one to wait upon you —to-morrow at one I will be here."

Gertrude made no reply, but hurried forward to receive Lady Charles, Colonel Delmour, and a succession of friends, who now came pouring in.

Delmour's astonishment at sight of Lyndsay could only be equalled by his dissatisfaction, and the meeting on both sides was cold and distant. Mrs. St. Clair now made her appearance; Lady

Augusta and her daughters followed; and Lyndsay was soon overwhelmed with expressions of surprise and pleasure from all quarters, but he contrived to disengage himself from them, and disappeared.

" Lyndsay has been giving you a godly exhortation against the sinfulness of dancing, I suppose," said Delmour, as he led Gertrude to open the ball; " and you look almost as grave as though you had the fear of the kirk-session before your eyes."

Gertrude smiled; and the exhilarating effects of the music, and all the concomitants of a brilliant ball, soon dispelled the unpleasant thoughts which Lyndsay's appearance had excited. All was enchantment — while it lasted; and the Countess believed she was happy.

But the morrow told another tale, when she awoke to the realities of life, and found the delusion had vanished, leaving only dust and rubbish to mark where it had been. It was near the hour when LyDdsay had said he was to call, but she had not promised to receive him. It was disagreeable to see any body that morning — her head ached — her house was in confusion — her servants were all stupid with wine or sleep — nothing was as it ought to be ; then two o'clock was the hour when she was to set off for Richmond, and she should be so hurried! — No, it was impossible — quite impossible — it was unreasonable to expect that she should be able to enter on business all at once so wholly unprepared, and she resolved to send her excuse; but just then her maid entered to say that Mr. Lyndsay was below, but, as he was in no hurry, begged her ladyship might not be disturbed. There was no evading this; and, with a mixture of haste and delay, she prepared for the interview.

CHAPTER XVI.

You do imagine,
No doubt, you have talked wisely, and confuted
London past all defence. James Shirley.

If Lyndsay had parted in displeasure, as Gertrude thought he had done the night before, all traces of it had completely vanished. But there was a settled seriousness in his look and manner, which made her feel that levity would be misplaced ; and if any thing so graceful could have felt awkward, she would hu.ve done so. As it was, she was evidently embarrassed. She rung for her chocolate — caressed her dog — spoke to her bird — ordered away some flowers that were too powerful—desired her maid to fetch her some eau de Cologne — and, in short, seemed bent upon keeping up a bustle around her, as if to prevent the
possibility of any thing like settled conversation. Lyndsay sat calmly waiting till all this should be over ; and at length, her orders having been all obeyed, she began to feel ashamed of such trifling, and allowed the servants to leave the room without any more frivolous commands.

" I think I am very good-natured — am I not ?" said she, making an attempt to rally her spirits, as she sipped her chocolate, " to admit you this morning, considering how ill you used me last night in running away from my ball; and now to come thus behind the scene, only to see how ugly we look after all is over, is scarcely fair."

" The spectre of pleasure is perhaps not more beautiful than other spectres," said Lyndsay ; " but I have something of a wizard's eye in these matters, and last night's scene, brilliant as it was, could not impose upon me. — I have learnt to distinguish real from artificial happiness."

" But my happiness, I do assure you, was quite real while it lasted," said Gertrude, gaily: " the only melancholy part of it was, that it did not last quite so long as one could have wished."
" Is your happiness, then, of so evanescent a nature, Gertrude?" asked Lyndsay.

" How very literal you are become! " answered she, attempting to laugh; — " you seem to have forgot the way to jest."

u Not when there is good occasion," said Lyndsay, gravely : " but at present, I confess, I am not in a jesting mood."

" How unfortunate! for I am not in a serious one; so we shall never agree—unless, indeed, you agree to be of my party to Richmond. Come, you surely cannot refuse me that ? However you might despise my ball as an artificial pleasure, you must/by the same rule, approve of my fete champetre as a piece of real rural felicity. Now, don't be so churlish as to refuse. Do consent to be gay and happy like other people."

" Are you happy, Gertrude ?" asked Lyndsay, still more gravely.

" To be sure — why should you doubt it ?"

" Because I have always looked upon true happiness as a generous, diffusive sentiment, that sought to impart a portion of its own blessedness to all around. Such it was with you, Gertrude, at Rossville; but now you seem to confine it within narrower bounds — none of it finds its way there now ! "

Gertrude blushed, while she attempted to smile, and said —

" I am keeping it all to carry there along with me. I mean to return to Rossville very soon now, and I intend that you should all be very happy to see me."

" Some, I trust, will have good cause," said Lyndsay; " but, in the mean time, there are two young lovers who are suffering not merely the tortures of suspense, but the aggravation of an evil report; yet it seems so incredible a one that I almost hesitate to repeat it, you will think us country folks so credulous."

" Pray let me hear it," said the Countess, faintly.

" It is said that you have actually given away the living' of Rossville, which you had promised to young Leslie, to a superannuated bon vivant hanger-on of the Monteiths."

Lady Rossville's colour mounted to her very temples, and at that moment a servant entered to say her ladyship's carriage was in waiting. She rose, and stammered out something about her engagement — her party, and she knew not what, as she was moving towards the door.

" I too have an engagement to keep," said Lyndsay, calmly, but very gravely, and he took her hand and led her to her seat; " I have engaged to prove the falsity of that report from your own lips."

But Lady Rossville remained silent, evidently struggling with her feelings.

" Gertrude, you could not be so false to others, so unjust to yourself?" said Lyndsay, with emotion.

Shame, sorrow, and pride, all swelled in Lady Rossville's heart almost to suffocation, but pride prevailed ; and, even while her burning cheeks and downcast eyes betrayed her consciousness of wrong, she answered, with an air of haughty indignation —

" One part of the report you are certainly at liberty to contradict — I never promised the living of Rossville to Mr. Leslie."

" You promised to provide for him when it should be in your power."

" And I will yet do so — but, in the present instance, it is not in my power; and now, Mr. Lyndsay, excuse me if I must begone."

" No, it is not thus we must part," said Lyndsay, in a tone so firm, yet so sad, as awed the Countess, even in spite of herself, and she remained passively waiting for what was to follow. " If we part thus, we may never meet again as we have done "— he stopped in some emotion, and then proceeded — " Before I became your guardian I had learned to consider myself as your friend, and I had flattered myself the confidence you then honoured me with would have been continued, but it has not proved so; I appeal to yourself, Gertrude, has it ? "

For a moment Gertrude could not answer, but at length she said —

" My sentiments remain unchanged ; but surely you might know enough of a London life to make allowance for any omissions I may have been guilty of."

" I have — I do make allowance for them," said Lyndsay ; — " I knew all the dangers that awaited one of your ardent, confiding, susceptible, but. volatile nature — I knew that the adulation of the world would prove incense too intoxicating to be resisted by one who had not yet looked through the shallowness of earthly grandeur; I do not, therefore, reproach you with your neglect, your unkindness, your almost boundless extravagance — these are faults that may yet be repaired; but broken promises and power misused — Ah, Gertrude ! what can make up for these ? "

Lady Rossville made a gesture of impatience, as if to conceal her agitation ; then said —

" I have already disclaimed the promise — the power is my own ; I did not imagine I was accountable for it to Mr. Lyndsay."

" No, Gertrude, you are not accountable to me — you are accountable to a higher tribunal, even to God himself, for the choice you make of his ministers. I am aware that in the world the appointment of a clergyman is reckoned a slight thing, but I view it differently: it is the most solemn — the most responsible act you may ever be called upon to perform ; and, as your guardian, I protest against tbe choice you have made."

" It is too late," said Gertrude, in a faultering voice.

" No, it cannot be too late. You have been misled, betrayed into one engagement at the expense of another. If you will give me leave, I will yet extricate you from it."

" Impossible!" exclaimed the Countess, in an agitated tone, as she shrunk from the thoughts of encountering Delmour's displeasure. — " Why then teaze me by prolonging this painful and needless discussion ? — I will not, I cannot retract what I have done."

" Ah, Gertrude! do not suffer a false principle of honour thus to sway all your better feelings. If no higher motive can influence you in this, at least let me conjure you by the friendship of former days—by the affection you bear your cousin, who loves you so tenderly she will not believe in the possibility of your deceiving her "

" Oh, Edward ! do not, do not torture me ! " cried Gertrude, as she covered her face with her hand.

" It is to save you from the torture of an upbraiding conscience, dear Gertrude, that I thus afflict you. It is to save you from mocking God, from betraying the immortal interests of the people he has committed to you. The happiness of two amiable interesting beings is in your hands; you are their only earthly stay at present: should you fail them, their disappointment may be bitter, but the reproaches of your own heart will be bitterer still!"

Lady Rossville's heart heaved, and, in spite of her efforts to restrain them, tears burst from her eyes; but at that moment she thought she heard Delmour's knock. She started up, and hastily brushed away the tear from her cheek: — " Let there be an end of this," said she — "I can hear no more."

" Yes," said Lyndsay, seizing her hand to detain her, while his own shook with emotion — " you must hear yet more — you must hear me resign from henceforth the office of your guardian ; 'tis a mockery I can no longer endure."

Lady Rossville made no reply. A thousand contending feelings struggled in her breast; but she repressed them all "with that force which is the result of conscious weakness, and with the calmness of one determined to do wrong she merely bent her head in acquiescence.

" Should the time ever arrive when Lady Rossville, gay and prosperous as she now is, should want the aid or counsel of a friend," — Lyndsay's voice faltered, but the Countess remained calm and motionless — " Gertrude, will you remember me ?" — But Gertrude averted her face to hide the anguish that filled her heart. — " At least, you will say ' Farewell' to me ? "

"Farewell," said Gertrude, in an assumed tone of indifference, and without turning round. Lyndsay dropped the hand he held in his, and in another instant was gone.

It was then Gertrude's long-repressed feelings burst forth in all their violence. "Unkind, unjust, ungrateful that I am!" exclaimed she to herself, as she wept in an agony of remorse. — "I have lost the best, the truest friend ; and he thinks me — Oh, what a cold-hearted, unfeeling wretch must he think me ! — How must I have behaved, when even Lyndsay, the mild, forgiving, disinterested Lyndsay, has renounced me ! " But her sorrow and her self-reproaches were checked by the entrance of Del-mour, who, after knocking, had stopped to speak to a friend who was passing, and while so engaged Lyndsay had gone out. The cousins did not speak; but, from the expression of his countenance, Delmour at once perceived he had no cause for jealousy.

But, for the first time, the sight of her lover failed to bring pleasure to Gertrude, as she contrasted his gay triumphant mien with Lyndsay's mild pleading look and melancholy air ; and when he accosted her with an exclamation of astonishment, she turned from him, as she thought " It is he who has caused me to act thus! "

"My dear Gertrude," cried he — " what is the meaning of all this ? But I guess how it is — you have had a puritanical lecture from the Very Reverend Edward Lyndsay ; and I am not surprised you should weep at it, were it only from weariness."

But Gertrude still leant her head dejectedly upon her hand, and only sighed in answer.

"By Heaven !" cried Delmour, passionately, — " he shall answer to me for every tear he has made you shed."

"Beware how you add to the sorrow you have already brought upon me, Delmour," said Gertrude in a mournful but decided tone; — "I have forgiven much, and may forgive more, but I will never forgive insult or injury offered to Edward Lyndsay on my account."

Haughty and overbearing as Delmour was, he saw that, on the present occasion, he was not likely to obtain the mastery; and he was piqued to find that it required all his skill and elo-

B B

quence to prevail upon Lady Rossville to keep her engagement, and join the party to Richmond. At length he prevailed; hut she set out with a heavy heart. By degrees, however, the novelty and the gaiety of the scene — the heauty of the day — the succession of lovely landscapes that met the eye as they glided along — the music — the company — all combined to charm the senses ; and Lyndsay was forgotten !

CHAPTER XVII.

Something that's bitter will arise *

Even amid our jollities. Lucretius.

Penso qual ne parti, qual vi ritorno. Metastasio.

The London season was now drawing near a close, and Lady Rossville had run her full career of folly and extravagance. As hills came pouring in upon her fronr all quarters, she was startled at the magnitude of the sums she had expended, and for which she had now nothing to show hut a parcel of gewgaws, which had ceased with their novelty to afford her any pleasure. She felt almost glad that Lyndsay was no longer her guardian, that he might not see the extent of her imprudence ; for even Delmour was surprised when he heard how much she had spent in so short a time. As for Mrs. St. Clair, this discovery, joined to the disappointment of her other schemes, occasioned her a fit of the jaundice, which put a stop to the Larkinses' dinner; and, as soon as she was able to travel, she was ordered to Cheltenham for the benefit of the waters. — There they accordingly repaired, but not before it had been arranged by the lovers that Colonel Delmour should join them in a short time.

At first Gertrude was pleased with the combination of picturesque beauty and fashionable gaiety which are so happily blended at this celebrated watering-place ; but a short time sufficed to dispel the illusion. The amusements wanted the life, splendour, and variety of the London parties, and the walks and rides were little resorted to ; the supreme bon-ton of the idlers being to drive or walk backwards and forwards for about the space of a quarter of a mile of dusty street, without intermission for two or three hours, day after day, and week after week, and that with as much settled seriousness as though they were actually fulfilling the high destinies of immortal beings.

O, how canst thou renounce the boundless store Of charms which nature to her votary yields I

But in vain would the minstrel have attempted to sing the beaux and belles of Cheltenham off the burning pavement, even while the dog-star raged, provided the libraries, and confectioners, and toy-shops kept their places. What to them

The warbling woodland, the resounding shore, The pomp of groves, and garniture of fields ; All that the genial ray of morning gilds, And all that echoes to the song of even !

But it was otherwise with Lady Rossville ; her taste was not yet so vitiated as to take pleasure in the vapid pastimes of a watering-place ; which, however they may amuse and relax the minds of the sick and the studious, can only tend to enfeeble those of the healthy and the gay. She sighed as she thought of her own fair domain — its woods and its waters — its flowers blooming unseen — herself a queen there ; while here she was one of a motley throng, with nought to recompense her but stare, and heat, and dust, and pressure. To add to her weariness and chagrin, Delmour had been detained in London on some regimental business, and was not likely to join her before her return to Rossville.

Mrs. St. Clair's aversion to Colonel Delmour had by no means diminished : but she found her opposition so perfectly vain, and her attempts to lead her daughter now so futile, that she had almost abandoned both ; though not without many severe struggles, and some dark mysterious threats, which, however, the Countess had now learnt to disregard.

At length they bade adieu to Cheltenham ; but summer was far advanced, or rather autumn had commenced, before they returned to Rossville. It was with mingled feelings of pleasure and pain that Gertrude beheld it again. Even while her heart bounded at sight of every well-known object, they seemed to reproach her with having lavished her thoughts, her affections, her money, upon worthless baubles and heartless pleasures. Her conscience smote her as she passed some old cottages which she had planned pulling down, and building new and more commodious ones in their place. " Half of what my opera-box cost me would have done that," sighed she. " And that bridge ! " as she caught a glimpse of one half-finished; " the poor people must still go two miles round, till my diamond necklace is paid; " and tears of contrition dropped from her eyes.

But it was not so at the castle ; for Delmour's orders had superseded Lyndsay's schemes, and, however the poor might suffer, nothing had been left undone there. The conservatory and the garden had been completed, and stocked at an immense expense; the apartments were superbly and tastefully furnished ; the theatre was almost finished ; and again Gertrude's volatile heart throbbed with pride and pleasure, as she looked on this new creation of taste and fancy, and anticipated the joys yet to come. But, as the novelty abated, again the voice of conscience

was heard, and the thoughts of Lyndsay recurred. She wondered whether he would come to visit her upon her return, and she "both wished and dreaded the meeting; but day after day passed on, and Lyndsay came not. Her cousin Anne, too, how could she behold her without shame and confusion of face! But her apprehensions on that score were partly relieved by receiving the following note a few days after her arrival: —

" My dear Lady Rossville, "lam very sure it will give you pleasure to hear that William has at length been provided for, as I know how much it must have pained you to be unable to fulfil your kind intentions in his favour. But what you could not do yourself your kind friend Mr. Lyndsay has done for you. He has so generously interested himself in this affair, that he has got William appointed to the living of Whinbrae ; and Mr. Turner, who was to have succeeded to that church, he has secured in a secular office of greater emolument, and better suited to his views and sentiments. The only obstacle to our union is therefore now removed ; and as we are to have immediate possession of the manse, it is to take place very soon — perhaps in the course of next week. It is to you, under Heaven, that we owe our happiness, by interesting so kind and generous a patron in our behalf. Accept, therefore, my dear Lady Rossville, the united thanks and prayers of

" Your affectionate Anne Black,
" and obliged and grateful William Leslie."

" Kind and generous, indeed! " exclaimed Lady Rossville, as she read this billet, and a blush of shame burned on her cheek. "He has saved me as far as he could from the disgrace of— at best, I fear—equivocation, and from the wretchedness of having disappointed the hopes of those whom I had taught to put their trust in me."

In the overflowing of her heart she wrote to Anne, expressing her participation in her happiness, and giving the sole credit of it to Mr. Lyndsay. She could not bring herself to tell her exactly how matters stood; but she assured her again and again that it was to him, and to him only, they were indebted.

She thought she ought also to write to Lyndsay, to thank him for his kindness to her relations; and she took up the pen for that purpose, but she could not write any thing to please herself: one style was too cold and formal for the warmth of her feelings; another too humble and penitential for her pride to stoop to, and Delmour might be displeased. — " No!" exclaimed she, as she threw down the pen, " I cannot write what I feel — I must either say too much or too little. It would be otherwise were we to meet; a few words would set all to rights, and how I wish he would afford me an opportunity of making

my peace "with him! — I cannot be happy -while I think I have forfeited his good opinion. — Surely he will come, and he will he pleased to find I have not forgot all his good lessons ;" and she tried to resume the studies and occupations she had begun at his suggestion ; but it would not do—the illusions of passion and the vanities of life still maintained their sway over her, and all was dull and joyless that did not administer to one or other. " I shall never be good," sighed she, " according to Lyndsay's notions, so 'tis in vain to try—and perhaps Delmour would not like me so well if I were ; " and that argument was conclusive against all farther attempts of the kind.

Colonel Delmour's absence had been protracted much beyond the period assigned by the alarming illness of his brother, whose life at one time had been in imminent danger from a pleuretic attack ; the consequence, it was said (as every thing of the kind must either have or be a consequence), of cold caught at a late sitting of a committee of which he was chairman. He was now better, and as soon as he was sufficiently recovered for his brother to leave him the impatient lover was to set off for Rossville ; meanwhile he implored Gertrude to write to him every day, every hour, if possible, as the only alleviation to the tortures of separation. Such was

Colonel Delmour's way of telling the story ; and, as usual, it contained a portion of truth and falsehood. It was true that his brother had been dangerously ill while he was in London, but it was not true that he was still detained there from that cause. The fact was, he rather dreaded a dull family party at Rossville ; for, lover as he was, he was too much a man of the world, too much accustomed to be amused, to be able to devote himself entirely to one object, however much beloved, — and Gertrude was as much beloved by him as any thing could be ; but he felt himself now so secure in her affections, that there was not even the stimulants of jealousy or uncertainty to give a zest to their intercourse. In short, Colonel Delmour's heart and affections were so jaded and sophisticated, that simple feelings and simple pleasures had now become stale and insipid. He rather liked the country for two or three months in the autumn with a good party; but to be constantly enacting the sentimental lover, and with no greater variety than Lady Betty and Mrs. St. Clair, or an interchange of neighbourly visits with some agricultural lord or raw-boned squire—to be bored about county politics or county races — it was more than either his love or his philosophy could endure. At length his brother's convalescence left him no excuse, and he wrote to Gertrude that he would have set off instantly ; but as the Arabins, Peverleys, and his friend Ilfrington were preparing to storm Rossville, he had been prevailed upon to wait a day or two, and join the party. A postscript added, that they should probably go by the Lakes, as Lady Charles had taken a fancy for sketching, and Lord Charles wished to eat char.

B B 3

Lady Rossville was deeply mortified at this letter. It contained even more than the usual quantity of love superlatives, was eloquent on the miseries of separation, and the anticipated happiness of their meeting; hut still he did not fly to her—he could suhmit to wait on the movements of a capricious fine lady, and the taste of an indolent gourmand — and, for the first time, a douht of the reality of his attachment struck upon her heart. The supposition was too dreadful to be endured, and she shrunk from it as she would have done from the stroke of a dagger. " At least he does not love as I do!" thought she, as she tried to dispel the fast gathering tears that, in spite of herself, rushed to her eyes ; " but I was a fool to expect it. Who ever loved so fondly, so truly, as I have done ? — and men never love with the devotion of women. But I would have Delmour different from every one else — I would be his all, as he is mine." Then to wounded tenderness succeeded pride. He had besought her to write to him as usual, and mentioned the places where he should expect to find letters from her; but she determined to punish him by her silence, though the punishment would, in the first instance, fall upon herself, as the forbearance of not writing was, probably, at least equal to the disappointment of not receiving her letters.

Gertrude was naturally of an open communicative temper, and the want of a confidant had often been severely felt by her; but she had never met with any one whom she thought perfectly suited to act even that subordinate part. Lady Charles was too much a woman of the world to enter into her enthusiastic notions, the Miss Delmours were too deep in flirtations themselves to be able to listen to any thing of the kind at second-hand, and she had formed no other particular intimacy in London. Her cousin Anne might have done, for she was patient and attentive ; but then she was so good, and so flat, and so matter-of-fact in her ideas on the subject, that it was in vain to expect any congeniality there. Hitherto she had contrived to exist without one; but now the want was felt, as sooner or later it must be, in all its loneliness. It would have been such a luxury to have complained of her lover to some considerate friend, who would have defended him, and proved to her that he was right, and she was wrong! Her mother was out of the question — she was the last person to whom she would have uttered a complaint of Delmour,

-whose name, by a sort of tacit agreement, was seldom mentioned between them. Lady Rossville was mortified, and ashamed too, at discovering what advantage had been taken of her in the appointment of a minister. True, there was nothing positively immoral to be laid to his charge, but an unholy pastor makes an immoral people ; and the effects were soon but too visible in the deserted church, the frequented alehouse, the neglected school, the careless because uncared-for people. In this state of restless displeasure, it was a relief to have something to do, however disagreeable in itself; and she therefore acceded to Mrs. St. Clair's proposal that she should go and visit some of the members of her family, she herself being confined with a cold. Lady Rossville then ordered her carriage, and set forth to try the effects of rapid driving and change of company in dispelling chagrin and ennui.

CHAPTER XVIII.

, Fair seemly pleasance each to other makes,
With goodly purposes there as they sit. Fairy Queen.

A name unmusical to Volscian ears,
And harsh in sound to thine. Shakespeare.

Bellevue svas her first destination ; for she could now endure to meet Anne, since she found her conduct was not viewed in the fight she feared it would have been. She was welcomed by Mrs. Black with even more than her wonted cordiality; and having dismissed the children, who were in the room with her, she immediately started the subject of Anne's marriage, prefacing her observations with a deep sigh, or rather groan.

" I'm sure we were all much obliged to you, my lady, for refusing to give them your church. I was in great hopes that might have put an end to the thing altogether, and I really believe it would, if it had not been for Mr. Lyndsay. — Folk are really ill employed sometimes when they think they're doing good, and it woidd maybe be just as well if there was less of that kind of interference in the world. As Mr. Black says,' Let ilka sheep hang by its ain shank ;' and it might have been long enough before William Leslie would have got a kirk, and in that time there's no saying what might have happened ; but now her father's just weary and sick of the subject, and he has given his consent—and what could he do else? — so it will be all over soon now;" and Mrs. Black heaved another sigh.

" I trust they will both be very happy," said Gertrude.

" It may be so," said Mrs. Black coldly ; " but it will be but a waiff kind of happiness — very different from her two sisters', who want for nothing, and both keep their own carriages — but I must always think her family are little obliged to Mr. Lyndsay."

Anne's entrance put a stop to her mother's lamentation?, and Gertrude was then strictly questioned as to all she had seen or heard of Mrs. Larkins, who, Mrs. Black seemed to think, must, from her own account, be a very distinguished personage in London. Lady Rossville made no attempts to undeceive her, but gave as flattering a picture as she could of the Larkinses' prosperity.

Upon hearing that her cousin was going to walk to Barnford to visit her aunts, the Countess offered her a seat in her barouche, which she willingly accepted of. While Anne went to get ready, Mrs. Black again returned to the charge, and again expressed her own and Mr. Black's gratitude for the friendly part she had acted in refusing the kirk. " As for this marriage," said she, " I have no heart to make any ploy of it, so I shall ask nobody. The lads may come out to it if they like, but I'm very doubtful if the Major and his lady will countenance it."

Gertrude was upon the point of offering to attend, but just then Anne returned, and they set off. No sooner were they alone than Anne began to repeat her acknowledgments for what had been done. " Had it not been for Mr. Lyndsay," said she, " I know not what would have become of us, for my mother had resolved upon sending me to London to live with my sister, in hopes that a change might have been wrought in my sentiments ; but it would have served no purpose but to render us both unhappy, for the love that is founded in religion and virtue cannot change."

" No," said Gertrude ; " I do not think the love could have been true that any circumstances could ever change."

" It is perhaps sometimes difficult to distinguish false from true," said Anne ; " but I am sure whoever Mr. Lyndsay loves he will love truly, and whoever loves him will love for ever and aye."

" He has made a warm advocate in you," said Lady Rossville, smiling.

" Ah, he deserves much more than I can say of him ! Had you but seen with what, warmth and kindness he entered into our affairs, and how feelingly he sympathized in our disappointment, and how vexed he seemed upon your account too •"

" Upon my account!" exclaimed Gertrude, while a glow of conscious shame suffused her cheek.—" How! — what could he say for me ? "

" He did not say much ; but when my father and mother argued from your having otherwise disposed of the church that you were opposed to our union, he disclaimed that idea altogether, and said, that although you had inadvertently made an engagement which you thought you could not break, yet he was sure you suffered more than any of us did; and he said it in a way that showed how much he felt for you."

" It is in sorrow then, and not in anger, that he thinks of me!" thought Gertrude; but there was something more humiliating in the one than the other. She could have made overtures to be reconciled, but she could not sue to be forgiven; and she sought to steel herself against the repentance that her cousin's recital had awakened in her breast.

As Anne was about to renew the grateful theme, the Countess abruptly changed the conversation; and as they "were then in sight of uncle Adam's mansion, she proposed to pay him a visit, to which Anne timidly assented, not having had the courage to encounter him since her marriage had been made known to him.

They were received, as usual, in a very doubtful sort of -way by Mr. Ramsay. Gertrude's looks commonly softened his asperities by recalling the image of his Lizzie ; and it was so long since he had seen her, that he would have almost hailed her appearance, had not the rumour of her engagement with Colonel Delmour reached his ears, and caused them to tingle to the very drums with indignation. She looked pale, and out of spirits too, and less like Lizzie than usual; so that he was ready to take the field against her, especially as he saw she had got a new and still more fashionable equipage, and her dress was something he was not accustomed to see pass his windows every day.

" I canna say London has improved you," said he, scarcely looking at her. " I dinna think I wad hae kent you if I had met you. If that's a' you have made by it, I think you would have been just as weel at hame."

" Much "better, I believe," said Lady Rossville, with a sigh she did not intend. " London is not the place for either light heads or light purses like mine."

Uncle Adam thought this savoured of an attack upon his hoards, and he resented it accordingly. —. "Ay, light heads mak light purses, and it's best they should keep company wi' ane anither."

Lady Rossville only smiled at this rebuff; then said, " Well, as you don't seem to make my light head and my light purse very welcome, here is a light heart that I hope will please you better," — pointing to Anne, whose happy, blooming face, and little simply dressed figure, formed quite a contrast to the Countess's pale complexion, dissatisfied expression, and elegant but fanciful style of dress.

" Oo ay, sweet hearts are aye light hearts ; but maybe that's ower light a word for you and your dominie. I dinna ken what you religious folk ca' yoursels. Hae ye ony godly name that you carry on your courtships wi' ?"

Poor Anne blushed, as she answered, in some confusion, that her uncle might call her what he pleased.

" And if I should ca' you twa great fules?" demanded he.

Perhaps you will only call us by our right names," said Anne, with a smile.

" There's some modesty at least in that," said uncle Adam, more benignly ; " but what did you mean by carrying on this hiddlin' coortship o' yours sae lang ? I never heard a word o't till I heard it frae your father last week."

" I thought it unnecessary to trouble you upon a subject which did not interest you," said Anne.

" How did you ken whether it would interest me or no ? I suppose if I had had a kirk in my gift, you wad hae thought it very interestin'." Then, as his attention was attracted to the carriage moving forward, " That's a fine ootset for a minister's wife, or else no, to be riding up and down the country in a phyeton and fower, and her twa flunkies!" — But at that moment the Wad-dell carriage took the place of the Rossville one, and Mrs. Major herself appeared in all her pomp and bustle. — " This is very hard," muttered Mr. Ramsay, as he turned to and fro, " that I canna ca' my hoose my ain."

But Mrs. Major now entered in a very' slow, solemn, interesting manner ; and, as if much fatigued by the exertion of walking from her carriage to the house, she seated herself immediately on her entrance, and then held out her hand, first to uncle Adam, who would not take it; next to Lady Rossville, with an affectionate shake; and, lastly, to Anne, whom she scarcely touched.

" This is the second time I have been out," said she, speaking in a languid affected tone, and applying a smelling-bottle to her nose ; " and I feel quite fatigued with the exertion of walking from the carriage here."

" I am sorry to hear you have been unwell," said Lady Rossville ; " nothing serious, I hope ?"

" Good gracious, Lady Rossville !" exclaimed Mrs. Waddeil, roused into energy, " have you forgot that I have been confined?"

" O — I — I beg pardon," said Gertrude, as some confused notion darted across her brain of having heard of some such event when in London.

" The Major announced it to Mrs. St. Clair, I know," said the lady.

" Yes — very true — I had forgot, but I "

" And you must have seen it in the papers — I know the Major sent it to all the papers."

"4He had very little to do," observed uncle Adam.

"What paper do you get?" demanded Mrs. Major, determined to dive to the bottom of this mystery.

" I seldom read any but the Morning Post."

" And was it not there ?"

"Perhaps — very likely — I dare say it was — but "

"You know, if it had been thei'e you must have seen it, and it wasn't a thing to overlook. I must let the Major know that, and have it inquired into. I know he sent it to evei'y one of the papers — 1 know that perfectly."

Rady Rossville now thought she recollected Mrs. St. Clair mentioning an heir to the race of Waddells ; and, by way of atoning for her lapse, she said, " I hope your little boy is quite well?"

" Boy!" exclaimed the still more exasperated lady; " it happens to be a girl! and, I assure you, the Major and I were much better pleased — we were both very anxious for a girl; for although, where there is a title in the family, it is natural to wish for a son, yet we both think it is of the greatest consequence the eldest should be a girl, so it was a great gratification to us — it was just what we wanted."

" Very true — I beg your pardon."

But the outraged mother turned towards Mr. Ramsay — "I am come, uncle, to make a request in the name of my little miss, who we must really think of having christened some of these days. As the Major is an Episcopalian, we will, of course, have it done according to that service, and we hope you will kindly officiate as godfather upon the occasion."

At this proposal uncle Adam looked " black as night, fierce as ten furies ;" and he seemed on the point of uttering some awful anathema, when, suddenly checking himself, he said, in one of his alarmingly mild tones, " I've nae great objections — provided I'm to hae the bairn called after me."

Mrs. Waddell was confounded. On the one hand, that was all but declaring the child his heir; on the other, Adam Waddell was rather an uncouth appellation for a young lady. But then a moveable tail might be tacked to Adam; — she might be Adam to him, and Adamine or Adamella, or Adamintha, to the rest of the world; and Mrs. Major inwardly chuckled at the proposal, though she resolved, at the same time, to enhance the value of the concession. She therefore said — " Why, to tell you the truth, uncle, I had fixed in my own mind to have our little miss called after the Major, although he declares she must be named after me ; but I think Andromache is such a beautiful name, and so off the common "

" Andrew Mackaye's a very gude name for her, to be sure," said uncle Adam gravely.

" Good gracious, uncle! such a way of pronouncing Andromache ! However, I shall give up all thoughts of that, since you are so anxious to have our missy named after you "

" Weel," said uncle Adam, with a savage smile — " that's a' settled, for you'll no object to a bit trifling addition to the name, for it's rather short and pookit — isna't ? "

" Why, to tell you the truth, I think it is, and an addition would certainly be an improvement—Adamintha, for instance?"

" I like a name that has some meaning in't, and the name that ye're to ca' your bairn after me maun be Adamant; for I can tell baith you and her that Adamant you'll find me to the last generation o' you."

The natural man here broke out, and Adam was himself again.

" Really, uncle, you have the oddest ways," began the lady, affecting to laugh, in order to cover her confusion ; ; ' so we shall say no more about it at present. I shall leave it to the Major and you to settle it; and," addressing Lady Rossville, " -when it does take place, we hope, cousin, you will be one of the godmothers, and favour us with your company on the occasion*— and, I natter myself, your god-daughter will not discredit you. Dr. Bambleton says she is, without exception, the largest and finest child he ever beheld, and just her father's picture."

Lady Rossville bowed; then rose to take her leave, and motioned Anne to accompany her.

"Bless me!" exclaimed Mrs. Waddell, " is it possible, Anne, that you are flaunting about in a fine open carriage ? I had no idea you would have done any thing so dissipated — what will the synod say to that ?" in an affected whisper.

Anne was too meek to retort, but uncle Adam was always ready to take up the cudgels for the oppressed.

"Are you no satisfied wi' ha'in a chaise o' your ain, but you maun envye your sister, puir thing ! a ride in other folk's ? "

"Envy!" repeated Mrs. Major, with a toss; "I'm sure I don't know what I should envy her or any one else for. As for four horses, I could have them whenever I choose, but I greatly prefer a pair; so what I have to envy I'm sure I don't know "—with an affected laugh of contempt.

"It's a pity you should be at a loss for something to rack your envye upon," said uncle Adam, as he opened his little old bureau, and took out the identical 500Z. bill he had received from Lady Rossville, and which had lain there ever since. " Hae, my dear," to Anne, " there's something for you to begin the world wi' — see what it is."

Anne looked at the bill, and was too much overwhelmed to be able to speak ; but the glow that overspread her face, and the tears of joy that stood in her soft blue eyes, spoke volumes. Uncle Adam saw her vainly attempting to thank him, and, patting her on the shoulder, said, " You needna fash to say ony thing about it, so gang your ways. — Hae you a pocket to pit it in ? " and he almost thrust her out at the door.

Mrs. Waddell was now past speaking. She was to have waited for the Major, whom she had permitted to go to a meeting in the County Hall, but to wait was impossible. She instantly drove off, and called the Major away from his business to attend to her injuries, and consult whether it would not be possible to cognosce uncle Adam, and get the editor of the Morning Post put in the pillory.

So much time had been-spent at Bellevue and uncle Adam's, that Lady Rossville found she had little to bestow upon her aunts. She had pleasure, however, in seeing them, and in seeing that in many things she had contributed to their enjoyment. Their rooms were filled with the choicest flowers and plants from Rossville. Some beautiful scriptural engravings, which she had sent them, decorated their walls ; and she had filled an empty space at one end of the room with a pretty bookcase

filled with well-chosen books. All these things her aunts were at pains to point out to her, and to tell her what pleasure her kind considerate gifts had afforded them. She pressed them to come to Rossville for a few days, while her mother and she were quite alone, for even Lady Betty was absent on a visit; but aunt Mary was too much of an invalid to leave home, and her sister never quitted her ; so, with many thanks, the kind offer was declined, and they parted still more favourably impressed with each other.

CHAPTER XIX.

This is the state of man: in prosperous fortune A shadow passing light throws to the ground Joy's baseless fabric ; in adversity Comes malice with a sponge moisten'd in gall, .And wipes each beauteous character away. /Eschylus.

The weather had now set in wet — every thing without was cheerless, within was dull; and, surrounded with all that wealth and luxury could furnish, Lady Rossville felt that neither could protect their possessors against weariness and satiety. Delmour had taught her to despise the society of the neighbourhood, and since her return she had kept rather aloof from any intercourse ; but she would now have been glad of any one to break the tedium of the maternal tete-a-tete. Her reading — her music — her drawing—her embroidery — were all tried, and all failed to interest or amuse ; for her ardent but ill-regulated mind sought in every occupation, not the medicine to cure, but the aliment to feed her distempered fancy. Delmour voluntarily absent from her, was the idea that haunted her day and night. To look at his picture — to shed tears over it—to begin letters of reproach only to be torn—to think of whether she ought ever to see him again — were the chief resources against the weariness of existence.

The third day of incessant rain was drawing to a close. The mother and daughter were together in the saloon, when the Countess rose and opened a window, for the fifth time within the last hour, to see whether the rain was not abating; but it fell thicker than ever—everything was dripping, but there was not a breath of wind to relieve the surcharged trees of their moisture — no living thing to be seen, except now and th n a bird, which shot silently past — not a sound was to be heard, except the sullen roar of the river, as it was urged along beyond its natural course.

Lady Rossville in despair was about to shut the window, when, dimly discernible through the mist and rain, she descried a carriage approaching.

" It is Delmour, after all," thought she, with a throb of delight — " he has meant to take me by surprise!" and all sadness and ennui fled at that idea.

" Mamma — it is — he is — there is a carriage," cried she, in all the flutter of joy, as a hack chaise-and-four, with one gentleman inside, wheeled rapidly round to the enhance, and was lost to sight.

In a second the door was thrown open — no name was announced ; but, preceded by the groom of the chambers, there entered — Lewiston!

At sight of him Gertrude stood immoveable ; while Mrs. St. Clair, uttering a shriek, clapped her hands before her eyes, as if to shut out the dreadful apparition. He only smiled at this salutation, and, approaching the Countess, held out his hand to her with the freedom of an old acquaintance; but her cheeks glowed w T ith indignation while she turned from him with an air of lofty disdain. He looked at her for a moment with an expression half menacing, half ironical; then turned to Mrs. St. Clair, who, trembling and convulsed, rested her head upon a table, as if not daring to look up.

" This intrusion is too much," said the Countess, as she moved towards the bell; but in passing her mother caught her gown with almost frantic energy, and, without raising her head, exclaimed, in alow gasping tone, "Gertrude—Gertrude — have mercy upon me !" Then, making a violent effort, she rose and tottered, rather than walked, a few steps towards Lewiston, and extending her hands tried to welcome him ; but her face was ghastly, and the words died upon her lips.

" Why, what is all this ? " said he in his usual tone of familiar assurance, as he took her hands in his. — " You look as though you had seen a ghost, my good lady, instead of an old friend — but don't be afear'd—I am not from the other world, only from the right side of this one, a rovin' here and there, with my honest Trudge here," patting a great sneaking lurcher, which stuck to him like a bur ; — and he.laughed.

" Pardon me," said Mrs. St. Clair; " but the surprise — I
believed you — I " But her lips seemed parched, and her
tongue as though it clove to the roof of her mouth — she could not proceed.

" It must be apparent to you, sir," said Lady Rossville, haughtily, while yet her heart trembled within her —" that your presence was unlooked for — is unwelcome," added she, as, even while she spoke, he seated himself, and smiled saucily.

Her indignation got the better of her fear.

" I know not who you are," said she, again approaching the bell — " and I receive no visitors who are unknown to me."

Again Mrs. St. Clair caught her — " Gertrude — dearest Gertrude, be quiet — all will be well ! "

" The Countess was a goin' to order her servants to show me to the door, was she ? " demanded Lewiston, in the same insulting tone of irony ; — " but her ladyship may spare herself the trouble — I have paid off the chaise—this will be my home for some pretty considerable time, won't it ? " to Mrs. St. Clair.

Lady Rossville disengaged herself from her mother, and rang the bell with violence.

" Gertrude, wilTyou destroy me ? " exclaimed Mrs. St. Clair, in a voice of agony that thrilled to her daughter's heart, and made her pause. When the summons was answered, "Nothing — nothing, Thompson," cried Mrs. St. Clair eagerly to the servant; " shut the door — that's all."

Gertrude's face was in a glow with the emotions that struggled in her breast. To be thus braved in her own house — her resentment mocked — her power, as it were, annihilated — her mother trembling before a menial, or at least one whom she herself only recognized as the husband of a menial — her brain felt as on fire, and she stood speechless from excess of agitation.

" So you thought, I s'pose, I had gone to Davy's Locker?" said Lewiston, addressing Mrs. St. Clair. " I read the account of the shipwreck of the Dauntless — by-the-by, it was in the same paper with the old squire's death, for these things are sometimes a long while of reaching us on t'other side the Atlantic—so, when I saw how the land lay, thinks I, 'tis time I was off to pay my respects to the Countess. She has'nt given me a very kind reception though. But was'nt it a luckiness that I had changed my ship ? Some poor devil of a Jack Lapslie it was, I think, was in a hurry to be off, and I gave up my berth to him, and waited for the next, the Hebe — wasn't I good-natured ? But I am very good-natured, and vartue, you know, is always its own reward — eh ? "

" If such are your friends," said Lady Rossville, addresssing her mother, in a voice almost inarticulate, " this house is no longer a residence for me ;" and again ringing the bell, which was instantly answered (probably from Mr. Thompson having stationed himself outside the door), she desired her carriage to be got ready immediately ; then rushing past the servant, she flew to her own apartment. There her exasperated spirit gave way to tears, and she wept in uncontrollable agony. In a few minutes she was followed by Mrs. St. Clair ; but on her entrance Gertrude turned away her head from her, as if determined to listen to nothing she could say.

" Gertrude ! " said her mother, in a deep and agitated voice ; but she made no answer.

" Gertrude ! " cried she again, as she would have taken her hand ; but the Countess withdrew it.

" Gertrude ! " repeated she, and she sank on her knees at her daughter's feet.

Lady Rossville started up in horror; but her mother clung to her gown.

" Do not turn from me," cried she wildly ; — u but tell me can I do more to soften you ? — On my knees I beg of you to have mercy upon me ! "

" Oh ! " exclaimed Gertrude, with a shudder, as she sought to raise her mother.

" No — I have to beg for my life — for my fame — at your hands "

" This is too dreadful! " exclaimed the Countess. — " If you would not drive me to distraction, rise."

" Will you then hear me ? "

" I will — I will — any thing but this."

Mrs. St. Clair rose. — " Gertrude, you may bring me yet lower than you have now seen me — you may bring me to my grave. — Oh that I were already there ! " cried she, with a burst of tears.

" Tell me — only tell me — the meaning of this horrid mystery," said Gertrude, trying to speak calmly ; — " tell me why that man dares to treat me as he does ? "

" Oh do not — in mercy to yourself and me do not ask me "

Lady Rossville stood for some moments with her eyes bent upon the ground, while her colour gradually rose till her very brow was crimsoned; then, in a voice of assumed calmness, which only spoke repressed agony, she said, speaking slowly — ^Z " Am I the daughter of Thomas St. Clair ? " Then, raising her clasped hands to her forehead, she pressed them upon it, as if to still the throbbings of her brain.

Mrs. St. Clair looked upon her with a wild and ghastly stare — her very lips turned white, and she seemed as if bereft of all power of reply ; but by a sudden revulsion the blood flew to her face, and she said in a tone of bitterness —

" Even this humiliation I will endure — as I hope to be saved, I was ever a true and faithful wife— so judge me, Heaven ! " There was a fervour and solemnity in the appeal which carried conviction.

Lady Rossville uncovered her eyes, and fetched her breath; and a pause ensued, which, after some minutes, Mrs. St. Clair gathered courage to break —

" It is in vain that you would seek to penetrate the mysterious tie which links my fate with that of Lewiston, and which extends even to you — and it will be no less vain to attempt to free yourself from his power. — Hear me, Gertrude — hear me! — you promised you would. — If it were possible, if it were in human endeavour, can you for a moment imagine that I would submit to what you have witnessed?" and tears of passion dropt from her eyes.

" Still less can I imagine any cause which can make you

submit to it," said the Countess ; " and it is impossible tbat I should — I will not — I cannot do it, be the consequences "what they may."

At that moment her maid entered, to say her ladyship's carriage was waiting, and while she spoke the rain fell like a waterspout.

" That is enough — let it wait," said her mistress, who, in the tumult of her mind, forgot all feelings of humanity for man or beast. The abigail withdrew, to agree with Mr. Thompson that something strange was certainly going on, but what they could not divine — the gentleman in the saloon had ordered up some luncheon for himself, and was eating and drinking to his heart's content, while the ladies were above stairs all in tears. " 'Twas strange, 'twas passing strange ! "

No sooner was this interruption over, than Mrs. St. Clair exclaimed, " Go — go then — but I will also go — not in my carriage, attended as you are, but even as I am, on foot and alone, — a wretched, homeless outcast.— Yes — it is no idle threat — I here solemnly swear, that if you this day leave your house, I, too, leave it — never to return ! "

It required no very high feelings of filial duty to turn with horror from such an alternative, aggravated as it was by every circumstance which could give effect to the picture — her mother but lately recovered from a severe illness, and yet far from well, driven from her daughter's house — exposed to the inclemency of the weather — it was too dreadful to be dwelt upon. Lady Rossville felt as though her senses would forsake her; and she said, in a vacant dejected manner, " Do what you will." Mrs. St. Clair seized her daughter's hands, and pressed them repeatedly to her lips, calling her at the same time by every endearing epithet; but Gertrude sat in passive endurance, and as if scarcely conscious of the caresses lavished upon her. Her mother then rung for her maid to dismiss the carriage, and ordered her to bring some drops from her dressing-room for the Countess, who had been overcome, she said, at sight of an old friend of her father's ; and having both administered and partaken of them, she saw her laid upon a couch to rest, and, leaving her in charge of Masham, she returned to the saloon to her guest.

CHAPTER XX.

But that shall gall thee most,
Will be the wortless and vile company
With whom thou must be thrown into these straits. Dante.

O doux momens d'borreur empoisonnes ! Alzike.

The hour of dinner came ; and when Mrs. St. Clair returned to her daughter's dressing-room, she found her as she had left her,

c c

extended upon a couch, and deaf to all Miss Masham's hints of dressing. Mrs. St. Clair dismissed the maid, and then, in a soothing voice, said, " Gertrude, my dearest, you will come to dinner — I have had a long conversation with Lewiston — he has promised not to offend you with the hluntness of his American manners ; but you ought to make allowance for them — he is an independent citizen of a republican state, where all, you know, is liberty and equality — but he means no offence, and will endeavour to adapt himself more to our notions of propriety while he remains, which I expect will be for a very short time."

" While he remains I shall keep my own apartment," said Gertrude, without raising her head.

" Impossible! " exclaimed Mrs. St. Clair, in agitation; "he will never consent — that is, I cannot consent — dearest Gertrude, if you would not have me on my knees again, rise and come with me."

Lady Rossville sighed heavily, and rose.

" You will suffer Masham, my love, to dress you-

" No — I will not be dressed to-day," said the Countess in an absolute manner.

" At least you will have your hair arranged a little, my love?"

" I will go as I am," said Lady Rossville, in the same self-willed tone, " or not at all."

Mrs. St. Clair saw it would not do to contend; she gave up the point, and, accompanied by her daughter, descended to the dining-room.

Lady Rossville's appearance certainly was not in unison with the pomp, and order, and high-keeping of every tbing that surrounded her; she still wore her morning dress — her hair was dishevelled — the cheek on which she had rested was of a crimson hue, while the other was of a deadly pale; and though she passed on with an even loftier mien than usual, it was with an abstracted air, and without once lifting her eyes from the ground.

" I hope your ladyship feels recruited," said Lewiston, as she took her place at table. He evidently meant to be polite, but there was something in the tone that grated on her ear.— She started at the sound of his voice, and a faint flush overspread her whole face, as she slightly bent her head in reply. .

" I found the Countess fast asleep when I went to her," said Mrs. St. Clair, quickly, as if answering for her daughter; " but she has not slept away that vile headach, it seems; however, we are such a little quiet party, that I persuaded her to appear. 1 — We shall not expect you to talk, my love, but do eat something — the soup is very good — I think Brumeau has even surpassed himself to-day."

" You keep a French cook?" demanded Lewiston ; " that's a confounded expense, is it not ? "

" Not for Lady Rossville, said Mrs. St. Clair, with a Hush at the vulgarity of her friend, as she saw a sneer on the faces even of the well-bred gentlemen of the second table.

" Ah, but there are better ways and worse of spending money; however, another plateful of it, if you please, my lady— you may give me two spoonfuls—there—that's it — now, will you do me the favour to drink a glass of wine ?"

" The Countess is so poor a wine-drinker," again interposed Mrs. St. Clair, " that you had better accept of me as her substitute."

" Come — we shall all drink together — come, my lady, take a glass to drive away the blue devils this bad day — your good health and better spirits, my lady."

Gertrude's agony was scarcely endurable ; but she still sat immoveable, with her eyes bent upon her plate, though without even attempting to taste what Mrs. St. Clair had put upon it.

" What have we got here ?" said Lewiston, as he uncovered one of the dishes, and looked at it as at something he had never seen before.

" Blanquette de poularde, sir," said the maitre d'hotel.

" Blankate day pollard! " repeated he ; " shall I help your ladyship to some of them ? — come, let me persuade you."

Gertrude with difficulty made out a " No —thank you ;" but Mrs. St. Clair was ready, as usual, to atone for her deficiencies.

" You seldom eat, I think, my love, till the second course. I hope there is something coming that you like. What was it you liked so much t'other day — do you remember ? "

" I don't know," said the Countess, with a sigh, and an absent look.

" Jourdain, you ought to observe what Lady Rossville likes.— How stupid, that I can't think what it was you said was so good —was it perdreau saute au truffes ? "

" Perhaps — I can't tell," said Lady Rossville, with an air that showed she was rather oppressed than gratified with this show of attention.

Meanwhile Lewiston was eating and drinking with all the ardour of a hungry man, and the manners of a vulgar one. — He tasted of every thing, evidently from curiosity ; and, though it was apparent that the style was something he had not been accustomed to, yet he maintained the same forward ease, as though he were quite at home.

" Well, that may do for once," said he, after having finished; " but, in America, we should scarcely call this a dinner — e^, Trudge ? " to his dog. " Why, another such as myself would have looked silly here — I like to see a good joint or two."

Mrs. St. Clair tried to laugh, but she coloured again, as she said — u Lady Rossville and I make such poor figures by ourselves at any thing of a substantial repast, that our dinners have, indeed, dwindled away into very fairy-like entertainments ; but, Jour-

dain, you will remember to let us have something more solid to-moiTow." .

" What do you think, for instance, of a fine, jolly, juicy, thirty pound round of well-corned beef and parsnips; or a handsum leg of pork and pease-pudding, and a couple of fat geese, well stuffed with sage and onions, swimming in apple-sauce ? — Ah! these are the dishes for me!" and he rubbed his hands with horrid glee.

It was a relief when dinner was over, and the servants had withdrawn ; for although the degradation was not lessened, at least there was no one to witness it, unless it were the portraits of the Rossville family, as they frowned from their frames on the rude plebeian who seemed thus to have usurped their place. Gertrude had wrought herself up to a pitch of forbearance which it required all her powers of mind to maintain — a thousand times she was on the point of giving way to her feelings and ending this hateful scene ; but as she caught her mother's eye fixed on her with a look of imploring agony she checked herself— " No," thought she, " I will bear all for this night; but worlds shall not tempt me to submit to such another;" and she sat in a sort of marble endurance, while yet every nerve and fibre were stretched as upon a rack. Like all vulgar people Lewiston told so many good stories of and about himself, and talked so very loud, and laughed so very heartily, reason or none, that he completely deadened every other sound. A slight commotion in the hall, caused by an arrival, had not therefore been heard by any of the party; when suddenly a servant entered, and approaching the Countess said, " Colonel Delmour, your ladyship;" and scarcely had he spoken, when Delmour himself advanced with eager step. Gertrude rose to welcome him with a rush of delight, which, for the moment, absorbed every other consideration. But the first rapturous emotion over, it was instantly succeeded by the painful consciousness of the strange and unaccountable situation in which he found her.

" Mr. Lewiston, — Colonel Delmour," said Mrs. St. Clair, in almost breathless agitation; " a friend of the family," added she, as she marked the haughty condescending bow with which Delmour acknowledged the introduction. But before Lewiston had opened his lips, his assumed overdone air of nonchalance — his vulgar but confident deportment — the very cut of his clothes — all at a single glance betrayed to Colonel Delmour's practised eye and refined tact that this friend of the family was no gentleman. There was something so commanding in his own presence, such a decided air of superiority about him, that even the American, coarse and blunt as he was in feeling and perception, seemed for the moment overawed, or, at least, was silenced. Gertrude began to breathe, as she thought her lover had come to deliver her from the hateful bondage in which she was held by this man and her mother, who were both, in the jockey phrase.

evidently thrown out by his arrival. It was not till he saw the Countess seated at table that Delmour was struck with her appearance, as contrasted with all around her : she, who was always so gay and splendid in her evening dress, was now in a morning deshabille; her hair was beautiful even in disorder, but still it was in disorder; and although nothing could bereave her of her loveliness and her grace, yet she looked ill, and was embarrassed, and altogether unlike herself.

" You have been ill, Gertrude," said Delmour, in a low voice, and speaking in Italian, while he gazed upon her with looks of the deepest interest.

" No—nothing—only since the morning," answered she.

" And what has happened since the morning?" inquired he, still speaking in the same language, while he turned a quick glance upon the stranger.

" Of all them there pickters," said Lewiston, throwing himself back in his chair, as he pointed to the family portraits, " which do you reckon would fetch most money ? "

Mrs. St. Clair's face crimsoned while she replied she was no judge of pictures, and Gertrude already wished Delmour had not come. She could not answer his question; but, scarcely knowing what she said, she asked whether he had dined.

" Yes — I was detained at Darleton for want of horses, and was obliged to have recourse to a greasy mutton-chop, and a bottle of bad port, by way of pastime—and after all I could only get one wretched pair, who "

" I had the advantage of you there, sir," said the American, rudely interrupting him; " I had four horses from Darleton ; —by gosh ! how one does go with four horses!" and he chucked and made a gesture as though he were driving.

This was too much — Lady Rossville started up, and, forgetting all her mother's cautions, said to Delmour, " Since you have dined there is no occasion to remain here;" and taking his offered arm, she led the way to the drawing-room, leaving Mrs. St. Clair and Lewiston confounded at her temerity ; but as they passed on Mrs. St. Clair's voice was heard in accents of entreaty to her guest.

" In the name of Heaven, what does all this mean?" said Colonel Delmour, when the Countess and he were alone. But pride, shame, indignation checked Gertrude's utterance, and she could not answer.

" Something is wrong—tell me what it is—who is that man ?"

Gertrude tried to repress her feelings while she answered—

" He is an American."

" That maybe—but certainly not an American gentleman."

" He is an old acquaintance of my father's, it seems."

" Then you have seen him before ?"

" Yes—but he only arrived to-day, and, I trust, will depart

cc 3

to-morrow; it is unfortunate that you should have come at the very time -when we are encumbered with such a guest."

" You don't think I have come too soon, I hope ? " said Del-mour, with a smile.

" Sooner certainly than I had reason to expect you," said Gertrude, roused to recollection of the slight put upon her by her lover,—"considering what interesting pursuits you were engaged in."

Delmour coloured slightly, and in some confusion said —

" So you really were taken in by excuses, lame as they were ? The fact was, I was rather unwell at the time I wrote, and not caring to say so to you, I wrote—I forget what—something about a fishing party with Arabin, was it not ?"

" No matter what it was," cried Gertrude, " since it was not so—though I would rather you had told me the truth at once." But the fact was even so as he had first stated it; but, whether he had taken the alarm at receiving no letter from the Countess, or that he had tired of his company, or that some sudden freak had seized him, he suddenly left his party, and set off by himself for Rossville, leaving them to follow at their own time. Gertrude's heart felt lightened of half its load. Delmour loved her as much as ever, and he was there to protect her—what had she to fear ? and again her sanguine buoyant spirit danced in her heart, and sparkled in her eyes.

" Well, you will endure this odious American for to-night," said she, " and to-morrow will surely rid us of him ; but he is so rude and overbearing in his manners, that I fear you will scarcely be able to tolerate him : promise me, then, that you won't notice him—I am so afraid of your quarrelling."

" Quarrelling !" repeated Delmour, with a smile of contempt; " no, I expect to be much amused with him—but as for quarrelling with such a person "

" O ! he is not a person to be amused with," said Gertrude, in alarm; " he is coarse and violent, and must not be provoked. — Do not, for Heaven's sake, attempt to make game of him!"

" What has brought such a person here ? "

" I cannot tell—but promise me that you will, for this night, bear with him such as he is?"

Delmour promised—but smiled, at the same time, at the importance she attached to so insignificant a being. Nothing more was said; for just then Mrs. St. Clair entered, with traces of agitation still visible on her countenance. Gertrude expected that her mother would have taken notice of her abrupt retreat from the dining-room, but she did not speak ; she seated herself with assumed calmness, and began stringing some pearls belonging to one of her bracelets—but her hand shook, and her thoughts were evidently otherwise employed. In a few minutes she rose and rang the bell—when it was answered, " Have you got the segars for Mr. Lewiston?" inquired she of the servant.

" I do not know, ma'am," replied Mr. Thompson, whose business it was to adjust chairs, not to furnish pipes, and who seemed to resent the question by the cold pomposity of his reply.

" Inquire, then, and let me know immediately."

" So, in addition to his other agreeable qualities, Mr. Lewiston is a smoker," said Lady Rossville, provoked at this pollution of her beautiful apartment. But she was sorry she had said it; for Mrs. St. Clair only answered with a sigh, so profound that it seemed to come from the very bottom of her heart. Some minutes elapsed, and again she rang—"Have the segars been taken to Mr. Lewiston ?" and she seemed relieved when an affirmative was returned.

" While Mr. Lewiston is indulging his taste, then," said the Countess, " I must go and dress — the old adage of 'better late than never,' is certainly illustrative of my case to-night;" and she turned from the mirror, ashamed, for the first time, of the image it reflected.

" And the best apology I can make for my boots," said Colonel Delmour, " is to take them off as fast as possible ;" and the Countess and her lover severally retired to their toilettes.

CHAPTER XXL

What he did amiss was rather through rudeness and want of judgment than any malicious meaning. — Hayward.

Upon returning to the drawing-room, Gertrude found her mother and Colonel Delmour seated at opposite sides of the room—he lounging over some books of engravings, she with her head resting on her hands as if buried in thought. Upon her daughter's entrance she looked up. " Have we had coffee?" inquired she, in a way which betrayed the wandering of her mind; but at that moment Lewiston came into the room, in the loud, noisy manner of an under-bred man who had taken rather too much wine, and she seemed instantly roused to recollection. She pointed to a seat on the sofa where she was sitting; but his eyes were rivetted on the Countess, whom he did not at first recognise in her change of dress. When he did he exclaimed, "By Jove! I didn't know you, you're so rigged out—why what's going to be acted now ? The deuce ! I was almost thinking of my bed," and he yawned. Lady Rossville crimsoned; but she caught her mother's eye, and she said in a low voice to Delmour, " Take no notice ;" and she began to talk earnestly to him about some of the engravings he 8 was looking at, while Mrs. St. Clair said—

c c 4

" We have brought London hours to the country with us, but we must make a reform."

" Ha, reform! yes, that's a very good word. I like the word reform," interrupted the American. " Reform, reform," repeated he, " yes, it's a good thing, is it not, my lady ? And I will reform your fire in the first place ;" and he began to stir and beat it in the most annoying manner — then threw down the poker with a horrid clang, and drawing his chair close to the fire, he put his feet actually within the fender, and rasped and crunched the ashes which he had scattered all over the hearth. Lady Rossville was on the point of rising and leaving the room, when Mrs. St.

Clair crossed to where she was sitting, and, under pretence of looking at one of the pictures, she pressed her daughter's hand in a significant manner, while, in a low voice, and speaking very rapidly to Delmour in French, she said —

" I must beg your forbearance for American manners — you will oblige me by it."

This was the first time Mrs. St. Clair had ever addressed Colonel Delmour on easy or friendly terms — their intercourse hitherto had been marked either by constraint or enmity, and now, all of a sudden, she condescended to sue to him. Gertrude could scarcely credit her senses, and even Delmour looked surprised, while he answered with a bow.

After sitting two or three minutes whistling, with his hands clasping one of his knees, Lewiston started up, and pushing back his chair in the same rude violent manner that marked his every action, he planted himself directly before the fire, so as to screen it from every one else. All this was excruciating to Lady Rossville and Colonel Delmour, both so elegantly quiet and refined in all their habits and movements; and they exchanged looks with each other, as much as to say, ought this to be endured ?

Mrs. St. Clair perceived it, and hastily said —

" How shall we pass the evening ? Gertrude, my dear, will you give us some music ? — Mr. Lewiston, are you fond of music — or should you prefer cards ? "

" Quite agreeable to either, ma'am — I like a song — none of your Italian gibberish though — and have no objections to a game ; — but, by-the-by, my lady, can you play at draughts ? that's the game for me !"

" No, sir," was the Countess's cold laconic reply.

" That's a pity — but I'll teach you — you have a draughtboard, surely ? Ah! there's a table — still better.— Come, my lady," and he touched her arm.

Colonel Delmour looked as if he would have shot him.

" Excuse me, sir," said lady Rossville, drawing back, and colouring with indignation.

" No, no, come away — don't be afear'd — you'll soon lam;" and again he took hold of her.

" Lady Rossville is not accustomed to be so importuned, sir," said Delmour, while his lip quivered with passion.

" Is Lady Rossville, sir, accustomed to have you for her prompter ?" demanded Lewiston, sneeringly.

" Colonel Delmour — Mr. Lewiston !" exclaimed Mrs. St. Clair, in violent agitation, " I entreat — I beg — Mr. Lewiston, I shall be happy to play at draughts with you — Lady Rossville cannot play — indeed she cannot."

" So much the better — so much the better — I like to lam people their t duty," added he, with an insolent smile, and looking at Colonel Delmour.

" Another time, then," said Mrs. St. Clair; " but, for this evening, accept of me."

" No, no, I will have my lady," said the American, with all the determination of unconquerable obstinacy.

" He is either mad or drunk!" exclaimed Delmour, passionately, " and no company for you;" and, rising, he took Gertrude's hand to lead her away.

" No, sir, I am neither mad nor drunk, as you will find," cried Lewiston, placing himself before them; "but I have something to say— "

" Mr. Lewiston !" cried Mrs. St. Clair, with almost a shriek, " for Heaven's sake — Gertrude — Colonel Delmour — what is all this ? How childish! — Gertrude, I command you as a daughter to sit down to draughts with Mr. Lewiston."

" That's it—that's right " said Lewiston, with exultation.

Lady Rossville's cheeks glowed, and tears of pride and anger stood in her eyes — she hesitated.

" You must not," said Delmour, impetuously. — " You shall not."

" For mercy's sake, obey me!" whispered her mother, in a voice of agony; and taking her hand she led her to the table. — " Sit down, my love," whispered she, " and I will play for you — Gertrude, have mercy upon me!" and she wrung her daughter's hand as the Countess would have drawn back.

" Do you submit to be so compelled ?" cried Delmour, almost frantic with rage at the idea of his beautiful Countess sitting down to play at draughts with a rude low-bred unknown.

" Yes, yes," said Gertrude, moved to pity at her mother's appeal— " I will try for once;" and she seated herself, and Mrs. St. Clair took a chair close by her.

Lewiston, satisfied with having carried his point of getting Lady Rossville to sit down with him, allowed Mrs. St. Clair to play the game for her daughter. He entered into it himself with loud boyish delight — rubbed his hands — snapped his fingers — swore by Jove ! and by Jingo ! — and when he came to the castling or crowning, always insisted that the Countess should perform that ceremony.

" I will have all my honours from you," said he, laughing ; all — all — you shall crown me — you shall castle me — shan't she?" to Mrs. St. Clair, who looked the picture of wretchedness, though she strove to keep up with his intemperate mirth.

..

He is certainly mad," thought Lady Rossville, and she began to feel afraid — she wished for Delmour; but Delmour, in displeasure, had left the apartment, and she heard him knocking about the billiard balls by himself in the billiard-room. Game after game was played, and won by Lewiston with unabated energy and delight, till at last Gertrude's patience could endure no longer, and she rose with an exclamation of weariness.

" Well, you have had a good lesson for one night, my lady — let us see how much it has cost you;" and he began to count over his winnings; then, putting them between his hands, he rattled them with a glee that, under other circumstances, would have been ludicrous.

" Now, give us a song, my lady, do — come, mamma," to Mrs. St. Clair, " exert your authority — I must have a song. Why, I haven't heard you sing yet, and I've something of a pipe myself."

" Lady Rossville has done so much for me, that I am sure she will not refuse me this request," said her mother, in an imploring manner, as she took her daughter's hand and pressed it tenderly in hers.

" I cannot sing," said Gertrude, almost choking with the conflict of her feelings.

" What's the matter ? not in tune ? Never mind, you'll do very well."

" The night is nearly over," said Mrs. St. Clair soothingly, but in a whisper, as Lewiston, tired of chucking his money, was busy transferring it to a large silk purse; " your compliance may prevent a quarrel."

" Never again will I submit to what I have this day endured!" said Gertrude, with emotion, as her mother took her arm and led her into the music-room.

" What!—you seem rather piano, my lady," said Lewiston, looking at her with a smile; " well, I'll give you a song, since you won't give me one, and one of your own Scotch ones too — I'm half a Scotchman now, you know," with a wink to Mrs. St. Clair; "so here's for your glorious Robert Bruce!" And he burst out with " Scots wha hae wi' Wallace bled," in a key that made the very walls reverberate the sound. Yet, to own the truth, he had a fine, deep, clear voice, and sung well in a very vulgar style, with a great deal of gesticulation, clenching of hands, stamping of feet, and suiting of the action to the words. To that succeeded an American song, and another, and another, in rapid succession, for his lungs seemed inexhaustible; and he sung volumes of odious political songs with the same vehemence and enthusiasm, till both Mrs. St. Clair and Lady Rossville were ready to faint with the fatigue of listening to him. The former, indeed, encouraged him to go on by her applause, while, at the same time, she held her daughter's hand, and by her looks and gestures constrained her, in spite of herself, to remain. To add to the mortification, Delmour, attracted by the noise, had entered the room; but, -with a look expressive of his indignation and contempt, had instantly quitted it.

" Now, my lady, I've done my part, haven't I? — I have a right to your song now — come, I must have it — I never gave up a point in my life — I'v e got a square head; and square heads as well as square toes are all obstinate ; at least some people call it obstinacy — I call it firmness — and I'm firm for your song."

" This insolence is not to be borne!" exclaimed Lady Ross-ville, starting up, and endeavouring to wrest her hand from her mother's grasp, that she might leave the room; but she clung to her with fear and agony in every lineament.

" Gertrude — Gertrude! — hear me but this once — this is my last attempt. — For such a trifle would you drive me to destruction ? — It will come soon enough, but not now — spare me

— oh ! spare me now !"

" There's a pretty daughter for you, by jingo!" exclaimed Lewiston, as the Countess stood with her face averted from her mother, who still held her hands in spite of her efforts to liberate them.

Lady Rossville's passion rose. " Come what may I care not," cried she ; " I command that man to leave my house."

" That's easier said than done, my lady," returned he with the most provoking coolness — " is it not, my good Trudge ? " as he pulled his dog by the ear. — " But, come now, give us the song, the night's wearing on;" and he was going to have taken her arm to lead her to the instrument, when, by a sudden effort, she freed herself from her mother's grasp, and rushed into the adjoining room, where, throwing herself on a seat, she almost sobbed in the bitterness of her feelings. Lewiston's voice, loud as if in argument, and Mrs. St. Clair's as if in entreaty, were distinctly heard; but they added nothing to Lady Rossville's emotion. In a few minutes her mother joined her in the wildest and most violent agitation.

" Gertrude," cried she, " I no longer ask your forbearance

— your mercy — I see it cannot be!" And she wrung her hands in agony. — " To-morrow must end it — Oh that the earth would cover me before to-morrow !"

Violent passion has always the effect of absorbing or annihilating all inferior degrees of excitement, and Lady Rossville was gradually composed at sight of her mother's real despair. She would even have tried to soothe her, but at that mom mt Lewiston entered as if nothing had happened.

" Well, you have made a fine row," said he, addressing Gertrude— "and all for what? Because I asked you to sing a song ? You must be deucedly thin-skinned, my lady, to fly off like a witch in a storm for that — you've something to larn yet, I can tell ye, and that's a fact."

" She will learn all soon enough," said Mrs. St. Clair, gloomily; " to-morrow — but let this night pass over "

"Not without some supper, I hope — for your blankates lie very light upon me, I can tell you," and he laughed heartily at his own witticism.

Mrs. St. Clair rang the bell for some refreshments, eager to end this hateful evening, and, at the same time, Delmour made his appearance, with evident traces of ill-humour visible on his countenance. But she felt too happy to see him, on any terms, to resent his behaviour — there was protection — there seemed even a propriety in his presence; and her looks brightened, and her tears passed away, when he came and placed himself by her in a manner to screen Lewiston from her sight, who was on the opposite side of the room making a noise with his dog.

"You have passed a gay, and, of course, a pleasant evening," said he in a bitter ironical tone; "one of your guests, at least, has no cause to complain of lack of courtesy."

"Oh, Delmour!" said Gertrude, in a tone of wretchedness, "do not add to my unhappiness by your reproaches — it is unkind when you see me thus " and her heart swelled almost to suffocation.

"It is degrading to you and myself to suffer this," cried he, passionately. —" This instant I will end it by ordering that fellow from your presence." And he made a movement towards Lewiston — Gertrude caught his arm.

■?'

"No — not now. — Suffer him for a little longer — to-morrow G^ is to end it — if he does not leave this house to-morrow "

She stopped — a faint red tinged her cheek as she gave her hand to Delmour, and said — " You shall take me from it."

"Pray Heaven he may remain then," said Delmour, earnestly, " if upon these terms you will indeed be mine!"

Gertrude only sighed; but it was her firm determination, unless this mystery was cleared up, and Lewiston left the house, to throw herself on the protection of her guardian, Lord Millbank — and, holding herself absolved from her promise to her mother, there to have her marriage with Colonel Delmour solemnized.

On Delmour's side the suspicion was, that Mrs. St. Clair was privately married to Lewiston; and much as his pride revolted from such a connection, still his interest might benefit by it. Lady Rossville would instantly emancipate herself from her mother's authority, and give him a legal right to protect her; and it would be easy to get rid of the couple by agreeing to settle something upon them, provided they retired to America for life. A tray with refreshments, such as Lady Rossville and Mrs. St. Clair had been in the habit of taking, was now brought in ; but at which the American expressed great dissatisfaction.

"Why, them here are what we give to our porkers on t'other side the water," said he, contemptuously taking up a peach — " and as for your French wines and liquors, by jingo! I wouldn't give a glass of good grog for a dozen of 'em. Hark ye, my good friend," to one of the servants, " you'll please to lay a bit of a cloth for me ; and order your cook to send me up a good rasher of bacon, and a brace or two of eggs — a Virginian if you have him, and cut at least as thick as my finger; and, Mr. Butler, I'll trouble you for a bottle of your best Hollands — that's the thing; — but faith I'll go down and see the porker cut myself—where does your kitchen lie?" And away he marched.

"Let us to bed," said Mrs. St. Clair, in a tone of suppressed torture, and as if taking advantage of his absence to leave the room; her daughter rose to accompany her, but she lingered behind a moment to say to Delmour — " You will not remain here I hope ? "

" No, I shall leave the butcher to use his knife upon his porker, and go to my own apartment — I pray he may make a good supper here for some nights to come," added he, with a smile.

But Lady Rossville shook her head and sighed, then followed her mother to her dressing-room.

" I will say nothing to-night," cried Mrs. St. Clair, as she entered, — " leave me, then—leave me."

" At least, mamma, suffer me to stay with you a little."

" Not an instant — leave me, I say," cried she impatiently. " What would you have more than my ruin and your own? — that, I have told you, you have nearly accomplished.

" Be it so then," said Gertrude with emotion; " there can no ruin surpass the disgrace and ignominy "

" Peace!" exclaimed Mrs. St. Clair; " you will drive me mad!" and she put her hand distractedly to her forehead.

Gertrude would have embraced her as usual at parting for the night, but she repelled her.

" To-morrow your embrace may be of some value to me — to-night it is of none — it is worse than none — I will not have it," and she pushed her daughter from her. —" Leave me, I command you," cried she, violently ; and Gertrude was obliged to obey. No sooner was she outside the door than she heard the lock turned upon her, and when Mrs. St. Clair's maid came she was refused admittance. Lady Rossville was terrified; and she lingered long at her mother's door, and heard her walk backwards and forwards, and groan as if in anguish; but when she tapped or spoke to her, she was instantly silent, and would make no reply. As her apartment communicated with her mother's, several times in the course of the night she rose and listened, but the same thing went on; and the morning was far advanced before, exhausted as she was, she could compose her self to sleep.

CHAPTER XXII.

O visions ill foreseen ! Better had I
Lived ignorant of future ! so had borne
My part of evil only ! Milton. !

When Lady Rossville awoke, one subject naturally engrossed her mind to the utter exclusion of every other. This was the day of her cousin Anne's marriage, and she had promised to be present; but the thoughts of that never once occurred to her — every thing was absorbed in the intense interest she felt as to the disclosure that was to take place—or failing that, the strong measure which she had determined upon as to her own disposal. Upon leaving her own apartment she hastened to her mother's, but the door was still fastened — she knocked repeatedly, but no answer was returned — she listened, all was silent — her heart trembled within her, and she was on the point of calling out, when she bethought her of a back-stair communicating with the dressing-room, by which she might probably gain access. She was not disappointed — the door was open, and she entered her mother's bed-room; but it was dark, except here and there where a bright ray of sunshine chequered the floor, and the candles, which had been burning all night, cast a sickly gleam as they died away in their sockets. Gertrude hastily withdrew a window-curtain and opened a shutter, and there discovered her mother asleep in an arm-chair, in the dress she had worn the preceding evening, and which formed an unnatural contrast with her situation and appearance.

A phial marked " laudanum" stood on a table by her; and it was evident that she owed her sleep to medicine, not to nature. Such as it was, it was certainly not rest that she enjoyed; for she was disturbed and agitated — sighed heavily, and muttered some unintelligible words, as if in an agony, and Gertrude's name was once or twice pronounced with a kind of shriek. Shocked beyond expression at beholding her mother thus haunted by her sense of wretchedness even in sleep, Lady Rossville felt it would be humanity to rouse her from such a state, and after a while she succeeded. Mrs. St. Clair opened her eyes; but it was some time before she came to her recollection, or that her daughter could make her comprehend perfectly how and where she was.

" I fear, mamma, you have taken too much of this hateful drug," said she, in alarm, as she looked at the bottle.

" Too much — and yet not enough," answered her mother, with a sigh.

" Allow me to send for Doctor Bruce," cried the Countess, in increasing agitation — "you are ill, mamma, indeed you are," ; s she pressed her mother's burning hand in hers.

" I shall soon be better," said Mrs. St. Clair, with a still deeper sigh. — " "What time is it ? — I have been asleep, I believe — shall we sup?" as she looked upon her dress with a bewildered eye.

" O, mamma, suffer yourself to be undressed, and put to bed."

" No — I will go to — to breakfast, is it?—yes, I remember now, to breakfast," as she looked up to a blazing sun; then turned to a mirror — " Will my dress do, Gertrude?"

Lady Rossville was too much shocked to reply; for the contrast was frightful between her mother's gay handsome dress and her parched lips, haggard cheeks, and distended eyeballs.

" The air will revive you, mamma," said she, as she led her mother to the window, and threw it open; but the lovely landscape seemed as though it smiled in scorn upon her, for all things looked fresh, and renovated, and happy. Mrs. St. Clair sat for some time with her head resting on her hand; at length she suddenly looked up, and said abruptly—" You are very fond of Rossville, are you not, Gertrude ? "

" O! it is Paradise to me," said the Countess, as she looked on her towering woods and far-spreading domain ; " but why do you ask, mamma?"

" Then you will never part with it ?" cried Mrs. St. Clair, in a tone of wild interrogation.

" Never — never!" exclaimed Lady Rossville, emphatically; then recalled to her mother's situation, she said in a soothing voice, "Do, mamma, allow me to ring for Lisle to undress you — it will refresh you."

" And what then ?" interrupted Mrs. St. Clair ; " but I know what I have to do—yet I would see that man once more before —perhaps—yes—I will—ring for Lisle then;" and she began impatiently to tear rather than to take off her ornaments. " Now go — leave me — why do you stand there looking upon me?" cried she, angrily.

Lady Rossville burst into tears. " It is distracting to me to see you thus, mamma, and to think I am perhaps the cause "

" Perhaps!" repeated Mrs. St. Clair, bitterly; " there is no perhaps — you are the cause."

" Only say in what way — tell me how—trust me, and I will do aU f

" All but the very thing I require of you," interrupted Mrs. St. Clair impatiently, — " all but obedience and forbearance — all but duty and patience — all but love and tenderness. Answer me then, once for all—'tis for the last time I put the question — its consequences be upon your own head — Can you — will you be guided by me in your behaviour to Lewiston ?"

"I cannot!" said Lady Rossville, in an agony of grief.

"Then go," cried her mother, ringing the bell violently for her maid — M not another word — if your fate is sealed, do not blame me;" then, as her maid entered, she waved her hand for her daughter to leave her, and Gertrude withdrew, afraid to irritate her hy farther opposition.

"What can this dreadful mystery he ?" was the question that had naturally presented itself at every turning of her mind, till thought had been lost in the mazes of conjecture. The idea which most frequently occurred was, that her mother must have been previously married to Lewiston, and, in the belief of his death, had become the wife of St. Clair. But then his youthful appearance ill accorded with such a supposition —indeed, seemed to render it altogether impossible ; and again the idea was rejected for others which were no less improbable. "Be it what it may," thought she, " this day must end it;" and at that moment, in crossing the hall, she suddenly encountered the object of her dread and her wonder. He looked heated and ruffled, and as if he had been engaged in a squabble. "So," said he, seizing her hand before she was aware, and looking earnestly in her face, which bore traces of her agitation — " so you have been with the old lady, I see! — Well, has she let the cat out of the bag, or has she left it to me ? "

Some of the servants just then entered the hall, and Lady Rossville, without answering, passed on to the saloon, where she hoped to find Delmour; but he was not there. Lewiston followed, and again began —

"What! all in the dark yet ?—what's the old-lady about ? — But, by Jove! I'll not wait another day to be treated as I have been by you and your confounded rapscallions. But I've given one of your grooms, as you call them, a settler. I've given him a bit of a knob on the side of his head, to keep him in mind of his duty — and I'll have them all broke in for you by and by ; a set of lazy, insolent, eating and drinking scoundrels that you keep about you! — and one of these low-lived rascals to pretend to pass off his airs to a gentleman like me "

"This is past all bearing!" cried Lady Rossville, as her face flushed with shame and indignation at having been thus disgraced to her servants — "I command you instantly to quit my house " and she stretched out her hand to ring the bell.

Lewiston hastily snatched it, and looked at her with an expression which made her tremble even in spite of her resentment.

"Do you know who it is you are a speakin' to ?" said he.

"I neither know nor care," said Lady Rossville, while her heart beat as though it would have burst. Lewiston was silent for a minute ; he then said abruptly, but in some agitation —

« No ? —hem — why what if I am your father ? "

Gertrude gazed upon him with a look almost bordering on idiotcy—her lips were apart, but no sound came from them.

"It's a fact though—ask the old lady, her you call your mother, if it arn't — she'll confess it, that she will! She'll tell you you're no more Countess of Rossville than I am —take it as you will, that's a fact—you're the daughter of your nurse, Marian La Motte ; and I, Jacob Ruxton Lewiston— I say — I'm your father."

Like a flash of lightning, the horrible conviction darted across Gertrude's mind for an instant. The next beheld her senseless ; and she would have fallen to the ground had not Lewiston caught her in his arms and placed her on a sofa.

"The deuce!" exclaimed he, in some consternation at this unlooked-for result. "Why, I'd better have let the old one manage it her own way, after all;" and, ringing the bell, he desired the servant to fetch Mrs. St. Clair cleverly, for that her ladyship the Countess was in a fit. The alarm was instantly communicated, and the whole house was presently in commotion.

CHAPTER XXIII.

What! shall such traces of my birth appear,
And I not follow them ? It may not be ! Sophocles.

Long ere Gertrude had power to unclose her eyes the frantic exclamations of her lover had pierced her ear, as he hung over her in an agony of apprehension — and joy sent the first faint blush to her cheek, and spoke in the look with which she met his anxious gaze. For a moment all was forgot by her, or rather seemed as a hideous dream ; and Delmour, kneeling by her side in all the agitation of love and fear, was the only image that presented itself.

" I hope, my lady, your ladyship feels a something better," said Lewiston, thrusting himself forward; but at the sound of of his voice a deadly paleness again overspread her face, and her senses forsook her.

" Will none of you drag that madman away?" cried Delmour, passionately, to some of the servants, who were bustling pompously about with glasses and decanters.

" No — no—no," shrieked Mrs. St. Clair, throwing herself between Lewiston and them, as they approached him; " Marshall—Jourdain—on your peril touch him."

" Send instantly for advice," cried Delmour, wildly, as Gertrude's lifeless hand grew colder even in his grasp — " make haste —bring Bruce—Smith—all of them—why do you stand there ? — By Heaven she will be gone ! " and snatching every restorative offered by the housekeeper and ladies' maids, he would administer them himself. Once more Gertrude slowly opened her eyes, and again they rested on her lover.

'i It was—all—a dream — was it not?" said she, in a low gasping voice.

" Ah! our Countess is corned to herself again," cried Lewiston,

D D

i

in a loud significant tone, as much as to say, " Keep your own secret."

" Protect me!" murmured she, as she convulsively held Del-mour's hand, and again relapsed into a deathlike swoon.

" For Heaven's sake retire !" cried Mrs. St. Clair to Lewiston, dreading some scene of violence when Delmour should extricate himself from Gertrude's unconscious grasp—" only to the next room, till this is over.—If," added she, in a whisper — " if you

would prevent discovery, go " and she led him to an adjoining

room, and shut the door. Once more Gertrude's marble features showed signs of returning life ; but she neither spoke nor opened her eyes—she remained motionless, as if unwilling to be scared by sight or sound, or aught that could break the deathlike repose in which she lay.

" Lady Rossville—dearest " exclaimed Mrs. St. Clair, as

she would have lifted her hand; but when she spoke a tremor shook Gertrude's whole frame, and she recoiled from her touch with a shudder.

" Gertrude—my life ! suffer Mrs. Roberts and Masham to assist you to your dressing-room— you will be quieter there — no one shall enter but those you wish to see—they shall not, indeed, my angel!"

But a low convulsive sigh was Gertrude's only answer.

" Gertrude—speak to me — say what is it that has alarmed you? — tell me what you wish, and it shall be done," cried Delmour, in an accent of grief and tenderness which seemed to thrill to her heart. " Shall I order the carriage to take you to Lord Millbank's ?" added he, in a low voice.

" O — no — no," cried she, putting her hands to her face.

" Colonel Delmour, I must entreat that you will not thus agitate Lady Rossville," cried Mrs. St. Clair; " this is neither a time nor a place for such questions ; when she has had a little quiet repose in her own apartment "

" I will not lose sight of her again," interrupted Delmour passionately, " till I see her in safer hands than any here."

" This is too much," cried Mrs. St. Clair, struggling to preserve her composure, and dreading every instant lest the disclosure (which she at once perceived had taken place) should burst, from Gertrude's lips, if Delmour persisted in talking to her; " but I submit — suffer her to be removed to her own apartment, with Mrs. Roberts and Masham to attend upon her till this nervous attack has subsided, and I consent to remain here till the arrival of Dr. Bruce."

Delmour could not object to this arrangement, for Mrs. Roberts was a discreet and respectable person in her way, and both she and Masham were devoted to their lady—he therefore consented, and she was accordingly conveyed there, and left to the care of her two faithful attendants, who received the strictest injunctions upon no account to speak to her. Mrs. St. Clair felt secure that,

unless in a fit of delirium, she would not betray herself to them ; and if, in that state, she did drop any thing of the truth, it would all pass for the raving of fever. Gertrude was therefore left to silence and to darkness ; while Mrs. St. Clair and Colonel Del-mour, by a sort of mutual understanding, seemed resolved not to lose sight of each other. He, indeed, was bent upon more than that—he was determined that instant to force an explanation of the mystery which involved such a person as Lewiston (and that in no common way) in the family concerns of Lady Rossville; and, ringing the bell, he ordered the servant to inform Mr. Lewiston, who was in the next room, that his presence was desired in the saloon.

At this message Mrs. St. Clair turned pale and trembled — she rose from her seat — she would have stopped the servant, but she knew not what to say; and before she could summon recollection Lewiston entered, and her confidence returned at sight of his free unabashed air.

" Well," said he, accosting Mrs. St. Clair with an air of freedom, " you see I am yours to go and to come, ma'am — but what have you made of my lady ?"

" You are not here to ask questions, but to answer them, sir," said Delmour, his lip quivering with passion. " I insist upon knowing by what right you have intruded yourself into this house ? "

" Perhaps it would be as well if I first know'd what right you have to ask the question," retorted the other, boldly.

" Colonel Delmour," exclaimed Mrs. St. Clair, eagerly, as she saw his flashing eyes, and dreading some act of violence — " Mr. Lewiston is a friend of the family — he is my friend, that is enough "

" Your friend !" repeated Delmour, contemptuously — " that is indeed enough, quite enough, to warrant Lady Rossville seeking other protection." He rang the bell furiously — " Desire Lady Rossville's travelling-carriage and my riding-horses to be ready at a minute's warning," called he to the servant.

" Hark ye, my man, there's no hurry about the first," cried the intolerable Lewiston —" we shall have two words about that

yet."

But the servant, evidently disregarding him, bowed his acquiescence to Delmour, and withdrew.

" What is the meaning of all this, Colonel Delmour ?" cried Mrs. St. Clair in the most violent agitation.

Delmour endeavoured to speak coolly, while he said —

" It was settled last night, by Lady Rossville, that while Mrs. St. Clair's unknown friend remained here, this was no fit residence for her. — She leaves it, therefore, for the protection of her guardian, Lord Millbank ; and when Dr. Bruce arrives, I intend that he shall accompany her." And he looked with the sort of resolute indifference of one whose determination could not be affected by any circumstances.

" This is the most extraordinary proceeding, Colonel Del-niour," said Mrs. St. Clair, pale and trembling. — " You can have no authority for such interference in my in Lady Rossville's situation, to take her from her own house—from my protection —it shall not be."

" No — by Jove ! she shall not stir a foot from this house today," cried Lewiston, " nor any day, without the leave of them who have somethin' of a better right to dictate to her ladyship than you have, sir ;" and he nodded to Mrs. St. Clair, as if to encourage her.

Delmour's passion was at its climax, and he could no longer suppress it.

" What is this infernal mystery," cried he to Mrs. St, Clair, " which allows such a person to dare to talk in this manner ? —

I will know it—something is fat the bottom of all this—if " and he seemed almost choked to utter it — " if this man is, as I suspect, your husband "

" No — oh no!;" shrieked Mrs. St. Clair, wildly.

" Well, and if I am the lady's husband, sir, or likely to be so, sir, what then? What is your objection to me, sir? My lady Countess's proud stomach, it seems, can't put up with me for her father — but what is that to you ? You're not my lord yet, and one gentleman's as good's another, and that's a fact."

" Colonel Delmour — oh no — help me — I am not — I "

exclaimed Mrs. St. Clair, in a state of distraction, at finding herself caught in such horrible toils. But again Lewiston interposed.— "Come, come — 'tis of no use to deny it now— the thing's over, and my lady will come to herself by and by, when she finds she can't make a better of it — there, I told you "

as a servant entered, to say that his lady wished to see Mrs. St. Clair immediately.

Delmour, who had been pacing the room in a perfect tumult of passion, stopt short at this, and demanded of the servant who had brought this message ?

" Miss Mash am, sir," was the reply.

" Then desire Miss Masham to come and deliver it herself, sir," cried he, fiercely; and Masham, not without fear and trembling, confirmed the fact. He then abruptly quitted the room to traverse the gallery opposite the Countess's apartment, and see that no one else obtained entrance.

At sight of Mrs. St. Clair all Gertrude's tremors returned upon her, and again she relapsed into successive fainting-fits, from which her attendants with difficulty recovered her. At length she became more composed, whether from strength or weakness, and, in a faint voice, inquired for Mrs. St. Clair, who, conscious of the impression she made upon the -victim of her guilt, had retired out of sight.

" Mrs. St. Clair is there, my lady," whispered Mrs. Roberts.

" Then leave me, Roberts. Masham, go — I will ring when I want you."

But they still lingered.

" Colonel Delmour, my lady, forbade that we should lose sight of your ladyship, upon no account, till the doctor's arrival."

" Colonel Delmour !" repeated Gertrude. — " Ah !" — and tears, the first she had shed, burst from her eyes; they gave her a temporary relief, and she, with some difficulty, dismissed her faithful attendants, and Mrs. St. Clair once more approached her. Many and bitter were the tears shed on both sides before either had power to utter a syllable. At length Mrs. St. Clair said —

" Can you forgive me, Gertrude ?"

But Gertrude only turned away her head and wept the more — then suddenly looking up, by a violent effort she stopt her tears ; and, while they yet hung round her eyes, and her pale lips quivered, she said —

" Tell me aU "

" Oh, not now — spare yourself— spare me," cried Mrs. St. Clair, with a fresh burst of weeping.

" No, no — there is nothing to spare — say that it is not —
that he " and again she seemed as though she would have
fainted, as the thoughts of Lewiston, her father, rushed upon her.

" Oh tell me all — I must — I will know all!" And Mrs. St. Clair was obliged to commence a broken and weeping narrative of the events of her early days.

CHAPTER XXIV.

O, Light! thy beams no more
Let me behold; for I derive my birth
From those to whom my birth I should
Not owe. Sophocles.

She dwelt upon the injurious and exasperating treatment she had received from the Rossville family, as though she sought in their conduct an excuse, or at least a palliation, for her own. She spoke of the exile and the poverty in which she had for so many years dragged out a joyless existence—of her husband's disinheritance — of the utter hopeless insignificance of their lot, as outcast, childless annuitants, on the one hand — or the brilliant destiny which seemed to court them on the other, where riches and honours awaited them in the person of their offspring.

" It was at this time," continued the wretched narrator of her own guilt, " that accident brought me acquainted with—with Marian La Motte "

" With my mother—was she not ?" interrupted Gertrude, in a voice of repressed agony. Mrs. St. Clair's only answer was a burst of tears. Gertrude hid her face on the cushion of the couch on which she lay, and, without looking up, in the same tone said, " Go on — tell me all."

" In her I discovered the daughter of Lizzie Lundie, whose name and history had been familiar to me in my younger days. She had emigrated to America with her husband, and upon his death had married a French Canadian. Marian was the child of that union ; but at this time her parents were both dead, and she was the wife of Jacob Lewiston, an American trader, whom she had accompanied to Bourdeaux. She was then in absolute want, for his vessel had been wrecked, and the whole cargo lost; but at the time I became acquainted with them he obtained a situation on board a merchantman, and went to sea again, leaving his wife in delicate health to earn her livelihood as she best could till his return. To complete her wretchedness, she looked forward to giving birth to a child "

Here Mrs. St. Clair stopped, overcome with her feelings; then suddenly seizing Gertrude's hands —

" Gertrude! Gertrude! God knows I had then no evil thoughts! I had not, indeed ; but when she besought me on her knees that if she should die a stranger in a strange land, and leave an orphan baby, I would be as a mother to it. — Oh! then the tempter assailed me!"

" Would that I had died ere I saw the light!" exclaimed Gertrude, in an agony of grief.

" Oh, Gertrude! do not tear my heart by forcing me to retrace what can be of no avail — what can it signify now to tell you of the thoughts — the fears — the struggles I endured myself— of the arguments and entreaties I used with her and my husband to induce them to co-operate in my schemes ? It is enough to tell you that it was done — that we quitted Bourdeaux on pretence of returning to Scotland, and that at Bagnolet you were brought into the world as the heiress of Rossville ; and such you still are, Gertrude — the secret is known but to yourself, and those who "

" Hush! " exclaimed Gertrude, wildly, and with a shudder.

" There cannot be the possibility of discovery if you will but "

*' You have not told me all," cried Gertrude, hurriedly.

" Gertrude, I will not survive the shame — the infamy—"

" Tell me all — all quickly. — Why did he leave her ? — Why has he so long — it is about him," gasped she, " I would know ? "

" From the day that he left her his wife never heard any tidings of him, and we at last naturally concluded he had perished at sea. Still there was no positive certainty of this being the case, and she always cherished the hope of seeing him again; for she loved him, Gertrude — indeed she did." But Gertrude only wept the more, to think that she could not love her father.

" Your mother — Oh, Gertrude! how dreadful is it to me to call another by that title ! " And again Mrs. St. Clair wept long and bitterly; then went on —" Your mother had been long threatened with a consumption, and when she found herself dying she had, it seems, unknown to me, written a letter containing the secret of your birth, which she had attested by her priest (for you know she was a Catholic); this she confided to his care, receiving his solemn promise, in return, never to divulge its contents, or part with it to another than Jacob Ruxton Lewiston, of Perth-Amboy, New Jersey."

" Years after this man went to America as a missionary ; and there, alas ! it was our evil fortune that he should find your father ! — I need not tell you that he came immediately to Britain to claim you. — You must well remember our first meeting, and the mysterious interviews that followed. He would even then have made himself known to you, that he might have established his authority over you ; but I prevailed upon him to forego his claims, at least till the Earl's death. — Oh ! had he known you as I do, he would never have dared the disclosure ; but you will not, Gertrude — you cannot be so infatuated! — he is your father, — as such he is entitled to your duty, your obedience •"

" Now — now — no more," cried Gertrude, covering her face with her hands.

" Gertrude, only say you will not be so mad — for Heaven's sake, promise me you will not! — Gertrude, he threatens to carry you off to America, should you drop a hint of Oh ! for the love of Heaven, be calm! — think of your mother. You loved her, Gertrude, for her sake then "

"My mother!—how could she sell her child! " exclaimed Gertrude, wringing her hands in an agony.

" She did not sell you, Gertrude.— Never mother loved her child as she doated upon you. — While she lived, you may remember, you were never out of her sight — worlds would not have bribed her to have parted with you ; and now could she see you thus great, and "

" Oh ! that she had suffered me to remain the beggar I was born ! "

" Do not talk thus, dearest Gertrude, if you would not kill me — compose yourself, and all will yet be well—it will indeed — your father "

" Do not — do not call him — Oh God ! forgive me, wretch that I am! " exclaimed she, almost frantic with horror at herself for so abhorring his name.

" Well, your mother, my dearest — think of her — think how you loved her — had she lived, you would not have shamed her with this disclosure ? — You will not bring disgrace upon her memory ?" — And Gertrude wept softer tears, as she called to mind the well-remembered proofs of her mother's love.

" How could she do it ?" cried she again, roused to agony.

" Ah, Gertrude! can you wonder the temptation was too strong to be resisted ? — Consider how we were both situated— you could bring nothing but additional care and poverty to her —to me you would ensure riches and honour—do not condemn us — Gertrude, say you forgive me ?"

Gertrude's whole frame shook with emotion, but she remained silent.

" Gertrude — Gertrude ! " cried Mrs. St. Clair, seizing her hands, "have I not been as a mother to you — will you not say you forgive me?"

"I cannot!" gasped Gertrude, in a wild suffocating voice, and she turned shuddering away.

Her maid now entered to announce the arrival of Dr. Bruce; adding, that Colonel Delmour hoped her ladyship would see the Doctor without delay.

" Lady Rossville will ring when she is ready," said Mrs. St. Clair, in violent agitation ; then when Masham withdrew, she cried, " Gertrude, you will not betray yourself to Dr. Bruce! promise me — promise me that, for the love of Heaven! " and she wrung her hand.

" To him ! " repeated Gertrude. — " No—I will not see him at all—why should I ? — 'tis a mockery— leave me—leave me to myself," cried she, with a fresh burst of grief.

But just then Masham returned to say that Colonel Delmour was very impatient for her ladyship to see the Doctor ; and as she spoke, Delmour's voice was heard outside the door. At the dear loved sound, again Gertrude's pale cheek glowed for a moment, and her eyes brightened; but in another instant she dropped her head with an air of hopeless dejection — and Dr. Bruce was now ushered in.

Mrs. St. Clair anticipated all questions by taking the Doctor apart, and telling him candidly, as she called it, that the Countess was suffering under a severe nervous attack, and that something of a composing nature was what was wanting. Gertrude was, therefore, spared answering any questions; and having felt her pulse, administered some di'ops, and recommended quietness, the Doctor withdrew to make his report to Delmour, who was impatiently waiting for him. Mrs. St. Clair at the same time hastened to Lewiston to prevent him, if possible, from doing more mischief; and Gertrude was once more left to the care of her attendants, who imagined she slept, from the still and silent state in which she lay.

CHAPTER XXV.

O, Fortune ! with what weight
Of misery dost thou crush me !
This is a stain fixed by some vengeful power,
Surpassing thought; all th.it remains of life
Must waste away in anguish : such a sea
Of woe swells o'er me, that never can I rise
Again, or stem the surge of this affliction. Euripides.

But sleep was far from Gertrude's eyelids; and in the multitude of her thoughts within her, she felt as though she should never know repose again. Her very soul sickened and her Drain whirled at the horrible destiny just opened to her. To fall from her high estate to a condition so vile and abject! Instead of the heiress of a mighty house, the daughter of a noble line, to be a beggar — an impostor—the child of one against whom her whole being revolted! Yet voluntarily to proclaim this to the world — to stand forth a mark for the finger of scorn to point at — to be laughed at by some, despised by others — to leave each thing beloved most dearly — to become an outcast, an alien! Could she do this and live ? No, she would pass away in secret — she would consume her days in grief and in penitence— she would abjure, renounce, fly all that she had loved and enjoyed — she would dwell in darkness and in solitude — few and sad would be her days, but she would go down to the grave as Countess of Rossville—her " soul was ready to choose strangling rather than life," for what had life now to offer to her of good or fair? Delmour— ah ! there her heart trembled within her — this day she had promised to be his! At that instant a note was delivered to her, which Colonel Delmour himself had brought to the door of her apartment, and insisted on its being instantly delivered.

" I claim your promise, dearest Gertrude. — Dr. Bruce is of opinion you may be removed to Millbank with perfect safety — if you wish it, he and Masham will accompany you in the carriage, and I shall attend it. — Say but yes, my angel, to your adoring F.D."

Here was a fresh wave of misery to overwhelm the unhappy Gertrude! The cup of happiness was held to her lips by the hand she loved, and she herself must dash it to the ground for ever! Poor — low-born >— degraded as she was, what a bri le for the proud, high-minded Delmour !

"And Delmour — would even Delmour despise and reject me if he knew all!"—thought she, as for a moment she covered her face with her hands, and bowed beneath the humiliation. But soon a loftier feeling succeeded. " No," thought she, " he will not — I know he will not." Then, as a bitter pang

shot through her heart, " But if— if we must part, it shall be in the face of day — he shall learn all from myself. — He loved me, and he will love me still—but he loved me as Countess of

Rossville—he must now love me as an outcast—a beggar

If he respected me as Countess of Rossville, he shall still respect me, low-born—beggar as I am!"

She desired her maid to say to Colonel Delmour that she would see him in the library ; then, rising, she bathed her eyes and adjusted her hair, and endeavoured to dispel, as much as possible, the traces of grief and agitation from her face.

" I will not go to him a weeping supplicant!" thought she — " I will owe nothing to his pity;" and she repressed each rising emotion, and with a calm and noble air entered the apartment where her lover awaited her. But what a change had a few hours of intense suffering made upon her! Her mutable countenance had now all the fixedness and the paleness of marble; and those eyes—those lovely eyes, which had so often met him with smiles, and which always " seemed to love whate'er they looked upon," now heavy and brimful, drooped beneath the weight of their swollen eyelids.

" Gertrude! — my own!—my adored!" cried Delmour, as he took her passive hand, and led her to a seat—"speak to me, dearest! —it is death to me to see you thus."

Gertrude opened her lips and vainly tried to articulate ; but her tongue seemed to cleave to her mouth.

" This is dreadful—it will kill you to remain in this house — you must leave it, indeed you must, my love — your carriage is ready—suffer me to order it;" and he was going to ring the bell, when Gertrude laid her hand upon his arm. Again she strove to speak; but a sigh, so deep, so sad, burst from her heart, as told the unutterable anguish of her soul.

"Gertrude!—my love ! my life!"—exclaimed Delmour, terror-struck, as he felt her hand grow colder, and saw her features gradually becoming more rigid—"for God's sake speak to me!"

Gertrude spoke ; but her voice was so changed that Delmour started at the sound.

" You love me, Frederick, I know you do—and I—but no matter—I never can be yours now.— Delmour, I have a strange, a frightful tale to tell you—I — I am not what I seem — I am not Countess of Rossville — I am a beggar!" She hid her face for a moment; while Delmour, too much amazed to answer, remained silent.

" It is true—they have told me all — all—all — I am fas daughter— he is my father!" And her voice grew wilder in her attempts to speak calmly and firmly.

" My dearest Gertrude, you take this matter too violently; although your mother has made a degrading marriage, that ought not to affect you in this manner—it does not interfere with your rights, or diminish my attachment to you— why then "

'• Ah, Delmour! you are deceived—she is not my mother— I am his daughter—the daughter of Jacob Lewiston—I have been an usurper, but I did not know it!"

The dreadful truth now flashed upon Delmour with the force and the rapidity of a stroke of lightning, and he remained horror-struck beneath its shock. For some minutes neither of them spoke; but Gertrude's breast heaved with agitation she would not betray, and her eyes were distended in endeavours to retain her tears within the brim.

" Good God!" at length exclaimed Delmour, striking his forehead in a distracted manner — " Gertrude — dearest!" and he seized her hands. " No—it cannot be—you are mine—my own "

" I was —but not now," said Gertrude; and her heart almost broke in the effort to appear calm in resigning him. — " Not now — you are free !" added she, in an accent of despair.

" Free ! — Oh, Gertrude ! my life !" and he paced the room with disordered steps; then suddenly stopping, " No — you must — you shall be mine — I will not believe it — by Heaven 'tis false!—you—you the daughter of that "

" Oh ! he is my father !" cried Gertrude, shuddering.

" No — there is some infernal plot at the bottom of this — it shall be cleared up;" and he was hurrying towards the door, when Gertrude called to him —

" Stay, Delmour, 'tis from me you shall hear it all — I will not that you should hear it from another that you have loved an impostor — a beggar!" And with desperate energy she recapitulated to him the evidence of her birth, as detailed by Mrs. St. Clair. When she had ended, Delmour said nothing; but he buried his face in his handkerchief in an agony of grief, and Gertrude's high-wrought fortitude almost forsook her as she beheld her lover thus overcome. She felt she could not long sup-poit the continuance of the scene ; and she said —

" Now I have told you all, Delmour—I am no longer what I have been. From this hour let my shame—my disgrace be proclaimed, and—let us part!"

" Gertrude, if you would not drive me mad, do not — Oh! you know not how I love—how I adore you !" And he pressed her hands to his lips, and Gertrude felt his burning tears fall upon them, and every drop was as a life-drop from her heart.

" Gertrude !" exclaimed he, passionately, " you have never loved as I do, or you could not be thus unmoved."

A faint smile of anguish quivered on Gertrude's pale lip, a.nd a single tear rolled slowly down her bloodless cheek.

Again a long and bitter pause ensued. Delmour still held her hands in his, while he seemed to struggle with contending emotions. Suddenly Lewiston's loud voice was heard, as if issuing some orders in his usual authoritative tone. The blood rushed to Delmour's face—he started up, and dropped the bands

he had but a moment before clasped in his own. Gertrude, too, rose—cold drops were upon her brow, and she shook in every joint; but, by a desperate effort, she gained the door, She thought she heard her name pronounced by her lover in an accent of tenderness and despair; but a thousand sounds were ringing in her ears — a thousand figures were before her eyes—■ and she only reached her own apartment when all sights and sounds had vanished ; for she fainted.

CHAPTER XXVI.

"What greater gryefe may come to any Iyfe Than after sweete to taste the bitter sower ? Or, after peace, to fall at warre and stryfe ? Or, after myrth, to have a cause to lower ? Upon such "props false Fortune buylds her tower; On sodayne chaunge her flitting frames be set, Where is no way for to escape her net.

Thomas Churchyard.

Delmour's whole mind was a chaos of conflicting passions. That he loved was undoubted ; but his love was compounded of many ingredients — pride, vanity, ambition, self-interest; and now all these were up in arms to oppose each purer or more generous sentiment that might have found place in his heart. In this state of excitation he sought Mrs. St. Clair, who was yet ignorant of what had passed in her absence; but Delmour's disordered looks and wild incoherent expressions soon proclaimed that all was disclosed. To deny or prevaricate she felt would be in vain — the terrors of guilt and of shame were upon her— infamy and ruin had overtaken her. There was nothing left to suspicion or conjecture — the evidence was infallible — it was her own. Still, while her very soul sank beneath the weight of her crime, her proud spirit refused to humble itself before the man she hated; and her only reply to his reproaches and invectives was, that he would now have an opportunity of proving the sincerity and the disinterestedness of his attachment.

More than ever exasperated, Delmour hastened from her to shut himself up in his own apartment. Distracted at the thoughts of the evil which had come upon him, his soul was tossed in a whirlwind of contending passions. To resign Gertrude — his own beautiful, his betrothed Gertrude! — there was despair in the thought; but to marry the descendant of the huntsman—the daughter of Lewiston — it was madness to dream of such degradation ! Innocent as she was in herself, there was a stigma affixed to her name which never could be effaced — a changeling !

the child of wretchedness and imposture! No!—he never could dishonour himself and his family by such an alliance. Then the image of Gertrude, rich in native loveliness — the tender, confiding, noble-minded Gertrude, rose to view, as if to mock the littleness of that pride that would have spurned her.

Delmour passed a sleepless night, and the morning found him resolved to renounce Gertrude for ever ! But how to do it was the difficulty — to see her again was impossible. — He attempted to write to her, but could not.— He felt that he was about to pierce a heart which beat but for him, and his hand shrunk from the barbarous task. But something must be done — it was impossible that Lewiston and he could remain under one roof— he shuddered at the thoughts of meeting him — meeting him as the father of Gertrude — the man who, but for her disclosure, might even now have been his father-in-law — yet to send him from the house would be to turn Gertrude also from the home which but yesterday she had held as her own, and that was too cruel even for Delmour's selfish heart. The result of his deliberations was, that he would leave things as they were, and repair to London to consult with his brother upon what ought to be done ; and having formed this resolution, he wrote as follows to Gertrude : —

"Dearest, adored Gertrude, "I will not attempt to paint to you what I have suffered since that sad disclosure took place ; — would to Heaven it were in my power to raise you to that height from which you have fallen, or rather from which you have so nobly cast yourself! — but, alas, my beloved ! by uniting your fate with mine at present, I should only involve you in deeper ruin. I have neither wealth nor power to bear you through this overwhelming tide of misfortune ; and yet to lose you — voluntary to renounce one a thousand times dearer to me than my own existence! — No, Gertrude, I cannot — I will not resign you! — mine you are in soul and in love — are you not, Gertrude ? You never can love another — and what other ever could love you as I have done ? My brain is on fire — I scarcely know what I write; but you will understand me, dearest, most beloved! — It is better that we should not meet. I will depart, but you shall remain here as mistress for the present. I will see my brother; but, until then, let nothing more be said on this heartrending disclosure. Farewell, dearest! — Pity your distracted, but adoring, F. H. D."

Meanwhile Gertrude had remained in a state of morbid woe, infinitely more alarming than the wildest ebullitions of grief. She neither spoke nor wept, but remained silent and passive — her glassy eyes fixed on vacancy, and her ear unconscious of every sound.

When Delmour's note was brought to her she closed her eyes, and turned away her head from it — while she thought, " It is all over — he has cast me from him!"

" It is from Colonel Delmour, my lady," said Masham, soothingly, who concluded there was a lover's quarrel in the case. " He is most petiklarly anxious to hear how your ladyship is this morning."

Still her lady remained motionless.

" The Colonel looks so ill, my lady — I'm sure it will break his heart entirely if your ladyship does not take his letter."

A deep sigh burst from Gertrude's heart; but Masham hailed it as a happy omen, and went on —

" Dear, my lady! if you did but see the Colonel, I don't think you'd have known him — his face, my lady, is as white as your handkerchief; and his beautiful eyes, my lady, quite red, for all the world, as he had been crying — indeed, my lady, I could scarce keep from crying myself to look at him." And, upon the faith of this pathetic appeal, Masham made another attempt to prevail upon her mistress to take his letter ; but again Gertrude rejected it.

" Dear, my lady ! what shall I do ? I could no more tell the Colonel that you would not look at his letter, than I could put a knife into his heart, my lady—just the same thing. — Oh! my lady, Smith says he hasn't been in bed all night; but has been walking up and down his room, tearing his hair, and taking on so, that he says he's sure he'll lose his senses unless something is done, my lady." And Masham ended with a sob ; for Delmour's gaiety, his good looks, and his liberality had completely won Masham's favour. " I'm sure, my lady, he'll either kill himself or somebody else, if your ladyship refuses him, for "

But at the horrid idea of Delmour and her father engaged in mortal strife, Gertrude shuddered; then, taking the letter, she tore it open, and, as she read it, tears again found their way to her eyes.

" Rash — unjust — misjudging that I am!" thought she —" he does not—he will not renounce me! — Involve me in deeper ruin by uniting my fate with his!—Ah!—no — no — 'tis I who would involve him in ruin !— Yes — I am his in soul and in love !" and the hard unnatural tension of mind under which she had laboured gradually melted into softer feelings. " But he loves me — why — why then does he leave me ?" and again her doubts and her fears returned ; but then there was so much delicacy in wishing to have the discovery of her disgrace kept secret until he could have made arrangements for her, she had no doubt, to soften the blow as much as possible, that again her sanguine spirit exulted in the truth and honour of her lover. Had she followed the dictates of her own feelings, she would instantly have declared herself to her whole household ; but Delmour had besought her not, and, painful as it was, she thought, for his sake, she would submit for a while to carry on the deception.

But she would not appear—she would not see the light — she would pass the time in darkness and in solitude ; and her soul sickened at the very idea of ever again beholding Mrs. St. Clair and Lewiston. That lady and she had not met since the disclosure had been made — she had then hastened to her own apartment; and there, under the influence of guilt, shame, and passion, had swallowed the remainder of the laudanum contained in the phial, which, although not sufficient to make her sleep the sleep of death, had the effect of throwing her into a convulsive stupor, from which she could not be roused. Dr. Bruce had taken leave-after prescribing for Gertrude, whose disorder he soon discovered was altogether of a mental nature, and as such beyond his skill. Lewiston had, therefore, been left to carouse by himself, and to be his own master of the revels. He was a man of much too coarse a mind to conceive the delicacy of such a character as Gertrude's, and had always laughed at the idea of her being such a fool as to betray her own secret; he, therefore, remained quite unconscious of the storm which was ready to burst upon him. Being always on the watch to spy every thing that was going on, he soon came to the knowledge of Colonel Delmour's intended departure, which he heard of with great exultation, and thought the field was now his own. His vulgar curiosity, therefore, led him, as usual, into the midst of the preparations, and he lounged about the carriage while it was packing—questioned the servants — examined and patted the horses — and waited till Delmour appeared ; when he briskly accosted him with —

" So, you're for the road, sir—fine mornin' — my lady's four bays will carry you at a famous rate—you only have them as far as Barnford, I guess. — I had some thoughts of taking them out myself to-day to give the ladies a ride ; but you're welcome to them, sir—quite welcome—the greys will do for us."

Delmour with difficulty refrained from spurning him ; but he repressed his rage, and, as he passed, said in a low voice— " Beware how you abuse the indulgence shown you in the name of the Earl of Rossville, for the sake of one " He could not finish, but, throwing himself into the carriage, drove off.

There was something so stern and commanding in his eye and voice, and yet so melancholy and subdued in his manner, that Lewiston felt alarmed.—" The Earl of Rossville,who the deuce is he!" was his exclamation as he turned quickly round, and entered the house.— Could any body have blabbed ? not Mrs. St. Clair — not Gertrude, for it was the interest of both to conceal it—no, the thing was impossible, but he must see them ; and he immediately sent a message to Mrs. St. Clair, demanding an interview. But it was answered by her maid in great agitation, to report that her lady had with the utmost difficulty been roused fro?n her stupor—and that she was not herself, her mind was wandering—the doctor must be sent for.

" Come—come — I'm for none of your doctors," cried Lewis-ton — "a prying, useless, swindling pack ! — Why, what did that pompous fellow do for my lady Countess yesterday ? Felt her pulse, and gave her a glass of water — eh— and for that he pockets his five guineas ! Why a man would he ruined in this country if he were to give way to women's nonsensical vagaries. — Come, I'm something of a docter myself, I'll go and see your lady— come along. " And drawing Mrs. Lisle's arm within his, he marched along, and, in spite of her remonstrances, made his way to Mrs. St. Clair.

But she was, as her maid had represented her, in no condition to answer questions or receive company—there was a total aberration of intellect, and even Lewiston's presence made no impression on her. He was so far relieved to find she was not in the way of endangering the secret, as she merely muttered to herself a few unintelligible words about, her daughter, then repeated the word " daughter " to herself many times over without ceasing.

" She'll come to herself by and by if you'll let her alone," said Lewiston, as he left her, with the resolution of next seeing his daughter.

CHAPTER XXVII.

Non, je ne serai point complice de ses crimes ! Racine.

Gertrude's restored confidence in her lover had given an impulse to her mind; and she was beginning to recover in some degree from the dreadful shock she had sustained, when Lewis-ton's message, desiring to see her again, deprived her of the little composure she had regained. Her agitation was so excessive, that Masham, in alarm, summoned Mrs. Roberts; and both agreed that it would be as much as their lady's life was worth to see any body that was not particularly agreeable to her at present; and this opinion Mrs. Roberts delivered in person to Lewiston, who, from some hints he had thrown out that morning to the servants, was generally considered as the husband of Mrs. St. Clair, and consequently the stepfather of their lady. This idea "was farther confirmed by Colonel Del-mour's sudden departure ; and in that capacity he found himself feared and obeyed, -where he would otherwise have been ridiculed and despised. After swearing a little at Mrs. Roberts's communication, he said—

" Well, mistress, take you care of your lady—feed her well — give her plenty of good stout meat and drink—none of your slip-slops — none of your meal and water, your gruels and panadas.—Why I'd have a fit of hysterics myself, if I was to be fed upon such stuff; and, hark ye, if there's such a thing as a nice plump little sucking pig to be had, now's the time — have it killed directly, and it will be prime for my lady's dinner; and, do you hear, tell that French fellow of a cook to take care to have the ears crisp, or I'll slit his own for him! — Stop, Goody," as Mrs. Roberts was retiring in silent horror—and he pulled out his watch —" Now, go you to my lady Countess, and say, that, as I'm a reasonable good-natured man, and always behave handsumly when I'm a treated handsumly, I shall allow her twenty-four hours to settle her brains, or her spirits, or whatever is wrong — and then I shall expect her to wait upon me here, with a merry face—as much sooner as she likes—she'll be welcome, but not a minute after the twenty-four hours — now trot, Goody—don't forget the pig—a three weeks old -will serve my lady Countess," — and he went off singing a vulgar sea song. He then went to order out all the horses, which he made the servants parade before the house, while he tried some of them himself; next ordered a chaise-and-four, and two outriders, as if he had been going a journey; but he merely drove up and down the avenue, till, tired of that, he fell to quoits with the servants; and, in short, completely illustrated the homely adage of, " Set a beggar on horseback," &c.

Gertrude felt grateful for the respite allowed her, and she resolved, if possible, to prove her obedience by meeting her father, and at the same time declaring to him what she bad done, even although she trembled to think of all she would have to encounter. Should he persist in his threat of carrying her off to America, what would become of her ? — who could interpose between a father and his child? — who could—alas ! who would save her ? There was no one to whom she could appeal — for there was no one being with whom she could claim any kindred, save him to whom she owed her being. Where was Delmour at this trying moment ? — why had he deserted her ? His was the voice to have whispered peace to her soul — his the arm to have supported and protected her; but he, her only earthly prop, had left her !

She was roused from the overwhelming conviction of her own utter helplessness, and the frightful destiny that perhaps awaited her, by the indefatigable Masham, who, in her softest accents, besought her ladyship's pardon. But there was a box of new dresses just arrived for her ladyship from Madame Delacour—such beauties! they were fit for a princess!—would her ladyship be pleased only just to take a look of them. — " See what a deshabille, my lady!—when you please to rise, how charming it will be!"

Time was when Gertrude's eyes would have sparkled with pleasure at sight of the beautiful dresses now displayed; but she turned away from them with a shudder, and desired they might be taken away.

" These were for the Countess of Rossville," thought she, with a bitter pang; " and I, impostor—beggar that I am! — shall

E E

I ever again dare to appear as such ?" She covered her face with her hands, and groaned in spirit; then, as if struck with some sudden thought, she called her maid.

" Masham, I would have a dress very different from any of these—I would have one made of the coarsest of stuffs, such as poor people or charity children wear." She stopped to wipe away the tears which covered her face, while Masham stood in speechless amazement. " It must he very coarse and quite plain, Masham ; and you must set about getting such a one for me directly."

" Sure, my lady, you don't mean it for yourself?" cried the amazed Masham, doubting either her own or her lady's senses had gone astray. But her lady repeated her commands in so peremptory a manner, that Masham dared not expostulate on the subject, but set about obeying the order, strange and unseemly as it appeared.

Gertrude had inquired for Mrs. St. Clair, and she was told she was keeping her room ; and she asked no farther, for the mention of her name was an effort almost too much for her, associated as it was in her mind with all the degradation and ruin she had brought upon her.

Heavily as the time wore away in tears and solitude, the hour appointed by Lewiston drew near too soon. In the interval he had sent many messages, which, rough and wayward as they were, yet showed a species of kindness in their way ; but his ideas of affection seemed to be of the lowest description, and the only way in which he testified his was through the medium of meat and drink ; and many was the savoury mess he despatched to Gertrude, who turned with loathing from such coarse demonstrations of paternal regard.

Gertrude clothed herself in the sordid garb which had been prepared for her ; but her beauty was of too noble and decided a character to be dependent upon adventitious aid: the regularity of her features — their touching expression — the sadness of her dove-like eyes—the paleness of her complexion contrasted with the dark ringlets which fell negligently around her face — the exquisite form of her head and throat — her distinguished air, even in humility — all these only appeared the more pre-eminent in the absence of aught to distract the attention. Averse to having the appearance of being compelled to meet her father, she repaired to the saloon rather before the appointed time — she entered, with downcast eyes and a throbbing heart, unconscious of every thing but that she was to meet, for the first time as her father, him who had so long been the object of her fear and her abhorrence. But what was her surprise when, upon entering, the person who sprung forward to meet and to welcome her, and to press her hands in his — was Lyndsay !

" Gertrude, ^ear Gertrude ! " exclaimed he, as he gazed upon her sad and colourless countenance, " how ill you look! Something is wrong." But as the recollection of their last meeting rushed upon Gertrude's mind, her heart swelled at the thoughts of her abasement, and the blush of shame rose almost to her brow.

" I have heard — and it is that report has brought me here now — that the man whom you have such cause to dread is an inmate^of your house — at least I guess it is the same — tell me, Gertrude, is it so ? "

" You will hear all soon enough," said Gertrude, in a low suffocating voice. — " Leave me — Oh! leave me now! "

" No, never, till I see you safe and happy," cried Lyndsay, with emotion. " Gertrude, I am your cousin — your friend — your brother if you will — speak to me then as such — say, what can I do to serve you ?"

But Gertrude only answered with her tears ; then repeated —

" Leave me — Oh ! leave me !"

"I will, if there is any one here to protect—to save you "

At that instant Lewiston entered with the swagger of a man who wished to show he was quite at home. At sight of Lyndsay he started, and was evidently disconcerted ; but quickly recovering, he said, with his usual assurance —

" So squire, I didn't expect to find you here — I've just been seeing some young puppies have their ears cropped— sit down, sir; " then approaching Gertrude, who rose to meet him, and bowed her head towards him, he took her hand and shook it. — " Well, my lady Countess, how goes it now? — By jingo! " as he surveyed her dress, " you women are always in extremes. — Why, to-day you're dressed like a charity-school girl!"

Lyndsay was too much confounded to speak— he had heard, in a vague way, that a foreigner, whom no one knew any thing about, was living at Rossville with the ladies — and that Colonel Delmour had left it abruptly in consequence of a quarrel — with various other particulai'S, some true, some false, which had been circulated by the servants, and soon reached the ears of their masters and mistresses. No sooner had Lyndsay heard them, than, forgetting all Gertrude's unkindness and ingratitude, he thought only of how he could serve her, and instantly set off for that purpose.

He had only arrived the moment before she appeared, and the first glance at her had told him a tale of woe and suffering that filled him with grief and amazement The gay, proud, brilliant Countess of Rossville, was gone; and there stood the sad, humble, downcast Gertrude, in passive endurance of, if not actually inviting familiarity, which formerly her high spirit would have spurned. He looked at her for a moment in silence, and again the deadly paleness which had overspread her face at Lewiston's

entrance "was succeeded by a deep flush, and she raised her hand as if to hide it from his view.

" Well, sir," said Lewiston, seating himself on a sofa, and placing Gertrude beside him, while he still held her hand, " this is not our first meeting — but let that pass — you're my lady Countess's cousin, I understand, eh? — that's enough—sit down."

" You"have the advantage of me, sir," said Lyndsay, bridling his indignation for Gertrude's sake ; " it seems you know who I am — who you are I have yet to learn."

" All in good time, sir Would you choose to take a glass of any thing after your ride, or a bit of cold meat ? There's a nice little fellow of a pig that I ordered for my lady's dinner yesterday, and she wouldn't look at him it seems ; so I've ordered him for my lunch to-day — as fat as an eel and as tender as a chicken, I'll answer for him — I saw him scalded myself."

Agony was painted in every feature of Gertrude's face — Lyndsay saw it; and, wishing to end this strange scene, he said calmly to Lewiston —

" Lady Rossville seems too unwell to take an interest in such discussions — if you will accompany me to another room "

" With all my heart," cried Lewiston, jumping up. — " You say true, my lady is a little narvous or so ; but she'll soon get over it," with a wink to her.

Gertrude rose too — her colour changed from white to red, and from red to white, and she gasped as though she were suffocating ; at length, by a violent effort, she said —

" Go then ; but, Lyndsay, remember he is — my father! "

Lyndsay stood speechless, and for a moment Lewiston was thrown into consternation; but, quickly recovering himself, he said — " Aye — come along, it shall all be explained," and he moved impatiently towards the door. But Lyndsay saw only Gertrude standing motionless in shame and anguish — her head bent beneath her humiliation, and the cold drops of agony on her brow — he flew towards her.

" Gertrude," cried he, " what do you mean ? Your father! speak, tell me "

" Well, since the cat's out of the bag," cried Lewiston, " you may as well catch it at once— I'm married to my lady Countess's mother, so I am — that's all—what is there so dreadful wonderful in that ?" And again he cast a fierce and threatening look at Gertrude.

" Is it even so, Gertrude?" said Lyndsay. " Then this can be no home for you at present "

" What right have you to meddle between a father and his daughter ? " said Lewiston, fiercely. — "I am her stepfather, and I have the best right to manage her;" and he would have taken her hand, but Lyndsay placed himself between them. — " Lady Rossville once chose me for her guardian — she will yet ac-

knowledge me as such—-will you not, Gertrude?—you will trust yourself with me, and I will place you in safety."

" Oh ! he is my father — my own father!" cried Gertrude, in an accent of despair.

"Surely—surely!" exclaimed Lewiston, hastily— "I am the husband of her mother—her own father—you say true — I am

— I am."

"No—no—no — she is not my mother — she told me all

— he is my father!" and Gertrude almost shrieked as she uttered it.

"She is a ravin," cried Lewiston —"I say she is mad."

"'Tis you have made her so, then," said Lyndsay, passionately ; then, turning to Gertrude, " Dearest Gertrude, try to compose yourself—retire — I will "

He is my father!" repeated Gertrude, convulsively—"hut save me from him!" and she clung to Lyndsay's arms.

"I will, dearest Gertrude — do not be afraid." Then, turning to Lewiston, he said, in a voice of forced calmness, but with an air of the most resolute determination — " You are mistaken if you suppose that, as the husband of Mrs. St. Clair, you have acquired any lawful authority over this lady. — If you claim it by any other tie, you must first bring forward your evidence, and have it recognised, before it can be acknowledged—in the meantime, Lady Rossville is under my protection — I am her guardian, and from her own lips only will I listen to what has passed. — You will do well, then, to leave this room without altercation, otherwise it may be unpleasant for you."

"Oh! no — no," cried Gertrude, in an agony of terror — " he is my father, — do not use him ill!"

"Don't you hear her acknowledge my authority ?" cried Lewiston ; " and what title have you, then, to interfere, you "

"Gertrude, will you go into the next room for a few minutes ?" said Lyndsay, and he would have led her to the door.

"Aye, do—go along," cried Lewiston ; " women are always better out of the way when there's business on hand."

"I will not leave you," said Gertrude, as pale and trembling she still held by Lyndsay.

"But I order you to "

"Speak but another syllable to this lady," interrupted Lynd-say, on the point of losing all self-command, " and I will instantly call the servants to force you from her presence."

"Coward !" cried Lewiston, furiously.

The blood rushed to Lyndsay's brow.

"Edward, Edward !" cried Gertrude,— " he is my father !"

"Gertrude, I know you only as Lady Rossville, and as such I will speak to you alone," said Lyndsay. He rang the bell, and when the servant answered it, desired him, in a calm but firm manner, to show that gentleman to the library; then, waving his hand to Lewiston, in a way that showed he would be obeyed,

lie said, " I "will join you there in half an hour;" and Lewiston, easting a threatening look at Gertrude, and muttering imprecations on Lyndsay, was thus compelled to withdraw.

CHAPTER XXVIII.

He whose mind
Is virtuous is alone of noble kind ;
Though poor in fortune, of celestial race;
And he commits the crime who calls him base. Dryden.

But it was with difficulty Gertrude could be brought to repeat to Lyndsay all that she had already recapitulated to Delmour. She had then been under an excitement of mind, to which every thing had given way— she had felt as though she were then about to cast the die for life or death; and, in the energy of desperation, she had told all with the eloquence of feelings which mocked control. But here there was no such stimulus, and she shrank from repeating the hateful and ignominious detail of her disgrace. It was throwing herself too much upon the sympathy and the commiseration of one on -whom she had no claim — one whom, in the hey-day of her prosperity, she had treated with coldness and ingratitude ; and she leant her burning brow on her hand, and strove to steel herself against the kind and affectionate entreaties Lyndsay used to gain her confidence. At length, he gathered from her such particulars as enabled him to trace out the whole of the dark transaction which had involved her in ruin. For a time his emotion kept him silent; while Gertrude sat with her elbows resting on a table, and her face buried in her hands. But Lyndsay was ever more intent on allaying the afflictions of others than in indulging his own feelings ; and he soon mastered his own agitation, that he might be the better able to calm Gertrude's ; but his voice faltered as he spoke.

"Dearest Gertrude," said he, " I know it will be in vain to talk of comfort to you in the first anguish of your mind ; but— ah, Gertrude ! could you discern the hand that has thus smitten y OU j—could you look up to heaven and say, it is my Father's will! "

" I do," cried Gertrude, in a low suffocating voice. But, alas! the feeling burnt feebly in her breast. — " And any thing but this 1 could have borne ; but disgrace — infamy " her emotion choked her utterance.

" No, Gertrude, you are unjust to yourself—ungrateful to God — if you attach such ideas of personal degradation to what has befallen you. — 'Tis true you have no longer a title, a vain empty title—or wealth to spend perhaps to satiety—but how much

nobler a being are you now, thus dignified by voluntary self-abasement, and rich in all the native gifts of your Creator, than ever you were, or would have been, as the mere favoured child of this world ! —Ah, Gertrude! — dear Gertrude ! could you but view yourself with my eyes !"

" To have been an impostor — an usurper !" exclaimed she.

" How perverse sorrow has made you, Gertrude!—You are neither — you have been the victim of imposture, but your own name is pure and spotless — it is more — to those who can appreciate virtue it will carry a nobler sound along with it than any that heraldry could have bestowed. — How poor is the boast of ancestry, compared with that lofty sense of honour which has made you trample under foot all those allurements to which your soul still cleaves even in renouncing! — This is greatness!"

" Who but you will judge me thus ?"

" All who love virtue—all who love you, Gertrude "

" Love me!" repeated she, relapsing into an agony of grief— " Oh ! who could love me — base — vile—abject as I am ?"

" Gertrude!" cried Lyndsay, in emotion almost equal to her own, " do you, indeed, ask who could love you ?"

But Gertrude was silent, for her thoughts were all of Delmour. Lyndsay's agitation increased.

" You ask me who could love you, Gertrude ? He who has once loved you truly will love you still—will love you more

than ever — I " He stopped, then took two or three turns

about the room in great disorder ; while Gertrude, absorbed in grief, and thinking only of his words as applied to her lover, was little aware of what was passing in Lyndsay's generous heart. In a few minutes he regained his usual calmness, and, approaching her, took her hand and said—

" Gertrude, you are unable to stand this storm which has come upon you—you must retire to your own apartment, and allow me to act for you—I promise you that nothing shall provoke me to violence — I promise you that I will bear every thing."

" Oh! you have borne too much already for me," cried Gertrude with a burst of weeping. — " My best — my only friend!" added she in a voice choked with emotion.

" You will then look upon me as your friend — your guardian — your brother — will you not, Gertrude ? — Such and all will I be to you, so help me God!"

Gertrude could not speak, but she pressed the hand which still held hers in grateful acknowledgment; and relying on Lyndsay's promise, as she knew she well might, she, at last, consented that he should see her father alone, and that she should await the result of the conference.

After seeing her mind somewhat strengthened, and her spirits more composed, Lyndsay then repaired to the library, where he found Lewiston vainly attempting to hide his rage by affecting

e e 4

to busy himself in coolly turning over the hooks, while it was evident he was only exercising his fury upon them. He took no notice of Lyndsay's entrance, but went on tossing over the leaves of a splendid folio in a maDner enough to have made a biblio-polist faint; then began to whistle with an air of unconcern, which, however, did not sit very easily upon him.

Lyndsay waited for a few minutes in silence, then said—

" I have been hearing a strange tale, sir, from one "

" Have you so, squire ?" rudely interrupted Lewiston, looking at an engraving in the book, as if deeply interested in it; " have you so ? — and what then ? "

" Then I would have your account, sir, of the same story."

" You would ? —Then I must trouble you, sir, to let me know what your story is in the first place, that we may onderstand each other, sir."

Lyndsay repeated what Gertrude had communicated to him, and added —

" It is, therefore, in vain to attempt to carry on any farther concealment — the truth must be proclaimed; but for the sake of one whom hitherto I have only known as a dearly loved relative, I would fain have it softened, as "

" Idiot!" exclaimed Lewiston furiously, as he hurled the book from him with violence, and pushed over an inkstand — then kicked back his chair, and drove every thing aside, while he took two or three strides across the room, biting his thumb in the manner of one who must have something, no matter what, on which to wreak his passion.

Lyndsay was too judicious to interrupt him ; disgusting as the spectacle of coarse uncontrolled passion was, for Gertrude's sake he submitted to it in silence. At length Lewiston stopped, and said abruptly—

" Has the fool blabbed to any body else, or is it you that's her only father confessor ?"

" I cannot tell whether the disclosure has been made known to any one else," said Lyndsay, for Delmour's name had not been mentioned between them; " but it can signify little, since it must soon be made public."

" Well, she deserves to suffer for her folly — but — you seem to have a liking for her, fool as she is !" Then, as if communing with himself, " She is handsum — oncommon handsum

— I've seen nothing like her — she'll make a splendid figire in New Jersey — she'll go well off there. She's a lovely critter ! stump the universe, if I ever see a lovelier ! "

Lyndsay tried to be calm, even at the idea of the beautiful high-souled Gertrude taken to America to be bartered—sold— by such a savage; and said, " Even if you are the person you give out, it does not necessarily follow that this unfortunate lady must be compelled to reside with you."

" Why what's to become of her ?"

" It is unnecessary to discuss that question at present; but be assured sbe possesses friends, whose influence and fortune — neither of them inconsiderable—will be devoted to her service."

" That is to say, you would marry her such as she is ? Well, as you seem to have a likin' for her, I'll tell you what — if the thing has gone no farther, and I don't think it has, or t'other spark wouldn't have set off as he did — why, since you're fond of her, I'll give my consent that you shall have her, upon condition that it's all to be kept snug — she'll come to her senses by and by, and be sorry that she's played the fool this way. — And more than that, if you'll agree to settle handsum upon me, I'll engage to go back to my own country, which is the best after all; and, since we don't put up together, let us keep on different sides of the Atlantic. — What do you say to that, sir ?"

" I say you are a villain," burst from Lyndsay's lips; " and I must have the most clear undeniable evidence that you are the person you profess to be, before I will give credit to it— I do not believe you are the father of Gertrude ;" and he fixed his eyes upon him, as though he would have searched his very soid.

The blood rushed to Lewiston's face, and for some minutes he was silent; then recovering himself, he said, in his usual manner—

" I'm all you'll have for him though, sir, whether you believe it or nof— I'm Jacob Ruxton Lewiston, of Perth-Amboy, New Jersey; and that you'll find, if you'll be so good as step over the way and inquire, that you may depend."

" That may be ; but there may have been more Jacob Ruxton Lewistons than one."

" Why, haven't I got my wife's letter here?" taking out a pocket-book, and holding it up with triumph — " haven't I the testimony of the priest who witnessed it — and he still alive too, and forthcoming if wanted, and who swore to her never to give it into any hand but her husband's ? And isn't there Mrs. St.Clair aready to swear to me when she comes to herself? — What the plague would you have, sir ?"

" All that is insufficient "

" Perhaps you judge by my looks — I've wore well, I grant you — but I'm intir'd in my forties for all that — married at nineteen — the more fool "

" Nothing you can now say will have the slightest effect in removing my doubts," said Lyndsay.

" Faith I'm a carin' very little about it," said Lewiston, with affected coolness; " you may keep your doubts, and welcome, for me."

" That I shall certainly do, till I have obtained better evidence than your own. I will send a person, on whose fidelity and prudence I can perfectly rely, to the place from whence you say you came, to procure proofs of your identity — when he returns with these you may then claim your daughter, but not

till then. — I am her guardian, and will he answerahle for her safety "

Here Lewiston burst out in a strain of the coarsest invective and imprecations ; hut

Lyndsay remained calm and resolute, and only said —

" In these circumstances, you must he aware this can he no residence for you. You will do well, therefore, to prepare to leave it as soon as you can make your arrangements; and, if the means are wanting, I am ready to furnish you with what is necessary."

He then left the room, and hastened to Gertrude, who was waiting him in an agony of apprehension.

CHAPTER XXIX.

Tout se sait tot ou tard et la verite perce. Gresset.

It was with caution Lyndsay communicated to Gertrude the suspicions which he entertained; but, to one of her sanguine spirit, the slightest surmise was sufficient to kindle hope in her breast. It was certain she was no longer Countess of Rossville ; but not to be the daughter of this man — not to loathe and shudder at him to whom she owed her being, even this seemed almost happiness. But then, as she thought of the difficulty of procuring evidence from so distant a quarter of the world, her spirit sunk; and she exclaimed, —" But how impossible for me to obtain information, and how vague and unsatisfactory must it be!"

" Trust that to me, dear Gertrude," said Lyndsay. " I will send, by the first ship, a person who will thoroughly investigate into this man's history, and on whose testimony you may safely rely. I would go myself if that would be more satisfactory to you, and if I saw you in a place of safety."

" Oh, Edward!" cried Gertrude, with a burst of tears which, for a moment, choked her utterance; then passionately exclaimed, " You protect and save me, while he " She uttered a sob, as though her heart had broke, then remained silent.

Blinded as Gertrude was by romantic passion, she could not but be struck with the contrast between her lover's conduct and that of Lyndsay ; and the conviction rushed upon her heart with a bitterness which, for a time, absorbed every other consideration. With emotion scarcely less than her own, Lyndsay now inquired whether she had divulged the secret to any one else. Gertrude struggled for a few moments to regain her composure; then said, "Yes — to one whom it more nearly concerned than any other — and now I wait hut to hear from him to make known my disgrace to the whole world."

" How false — how worldly are your notions of disgrace, dear Gertrude !" said Lyndsay. " But I will not stop to comhat them now; tell me what you wish to have done—what are your plans?"

" It is Colonel Delmour's wish that I should remain here until I hear from him," said Gertrude, in a faltering voice.

" Be it so, then," said Lyndsay, with emotion; " but remember, Gertrude, you have a home, if you will design to accept of it; my house is yours to command. My aunt, Mrs. Lyndsay, whom you have heard me mention, is now in Scotland, and will reside there with you. You would love her if you knew her—for she is good and gentle, and knows what suffering is : for myself, I shall possibly go abroad for a time — or — but, in short, I can be at no loss — so promise that if "

" No — no, I never will be a pensioner on your bounty," cried Gertrude, in violent agitation — "I will work — beg — Oh, Edward! how you wring my heart!"— and she leaned her head on a table, and wept bitterly.

" Forgive me, dearest Gertrude, if I have hurt you — it was far from my thoughts! — Now, let me recommend to you to retire to your own apartment — you will there be safe from intrusion— leave every thing to me, and rest assured there shall no violence be used — he shall be treated as your father, though not recognized as such."

" But ought I not to see him once more ? — and — Oh, Lyndsay! — if I should have turned my father from the house! no — I cannot. — Suffer him to remain — he is — he must be my father — he could not have imposed upon her !"

" At such a distance of time it is quite possible he might; but, dear Gertrude, confide in me, I will do nothing harshly — but you cannot remain under the same roof—it will kill you — he shall go to my house — he shall be well treated — indeed he shall." And Gertrude, calmed by these assurances, at length consented to shut herself up in her own apartment, and even to refuse to see Lewiston if he should attempt it. Lyndsay's next business was to visit Mrs. St. Clair, in hopes of elucidating something from her; but he was shocked at the situation in which he found her, and immediately sent off for medical assistance; and also to Mr. and Miss Black, requesting them to come to Rossville as soon as possible. He had scarcely done all this, when Lewiston entered the room where he was, with a minted air of confusion and effrontery.

" So, sir, you're a goin' to raise the country, it seems—two men on horseback a gallopin' away there as if the deuce were in them. —"What's the meanin' of all this ? — I must see my own daughter," added he, abruptly.

" When you have established your claim to that title you shall
see her—till then, I have already told you, I act as her guardian ; and, as such, I will not consent to your meeting — if you had the feelings of a parent, you would see the propriety of this."

" Feelins!" exclaimed Lewiston; " hy Jove ! my feelins have been prettily treated since I came amongst you — may I be flayed if ever I met with such usage! — I say my feelins have been consummately ill-used — and I feel it too!" and he walked up and down in great discomposure.

" She whom you call your daughter is not unmindful of your feelings," said Lyndsay; " although, by my advice, she declines a meeting, which could serve no purpose but to agitate and distress her. She is very desirous that you should be treated with consideration—that you should have every comfort and indulgence which you may require, and I shall therefore make a point of seeing you properly accommodated."

"What does she mean by all this botheration? — does she mean by comfort and indulgences, and so forth, a round sum of money ? — If she does, I comprehend that—give me money, and faith I'll soon find comforts and indulgences for myself."

" You must be conscious that, as your daugher, she can have nothing to bestow," said Lyndsay; " but I possess the means; and when assured that you have told me the truth, one way or other — for the truth is all I require from you—we shall then perhaps be able to come to an agreement."

Lewiston remained thoughtful for a few minutes ; then said, " Has the goose quacked to any but yourself? — I want to know."

" Colonel Delmour has been made acquainted with all the particulars, and is gone to consult with his brother, now Earl of Rossville, as to what is to be done. — Be assured at their hands you will meet with little indulgence."

Here Lewiston broke out into an execration against Delmour, and against Gertrude, both of whom he denounced in the bitterest terms ; then suddenly changing his tone, he said, " It will cost you something, I can tell you, to send to New Jersey, that it will — a few dollars, I can tell you."

" I have already told you I am ready to pay a good price for the knowledge of the truth, be it what it may," said Lyndsay.

"What! even supposing — only supposing you know that I ar'nt the girl's father ?"

" Perhaps I should be inclined to pay more for that discovery than for any other," said Lyndsay, trying to hide his emotion ; " but I again repeat it is the truth, and the truth only, I require —and that, sooner or later, I am sure of arriving at—a few months will bring me the knowledge of that."

" I tell you it will cost you an awful of money !"

" And I have told you I am ready to pay it."

" Why how much do you reckon upon? —what lengths are you ready to go—eh?"

" I am "willing to go any lengths to detect fraud and villany, but not to reward it — I am perhaps wrong in offering to come to any compromise with you; but regard for the peace of one who is suffering from your villany induces me "

" Will you give a thousand pound ?" interrupted Lewiston, abruptly.

" No—I will give more, if necessary, to discover the truth; but I will not reward falsehood in the same measure."

" Confound your distinctions! Will you give five hundred?

— I swear I won't bate a halfpenny."

" Upon condition that you swear solemnly to tell the whole truth," said Lyndsay, " I will do more for you than I am perhaps justified in doing — I will pay your expenses from America and back to it; and I will settle an annuity upon you of fifty pounds per annum, upon condition that you give up that letter and never set foot in Britain again."

" I'd rather have a good round sum at once — I want "

" It is in vain to say more on the subject," said Lyndsay; " if you wish to have an hour to reflect upon it, you may — but that must be all. I shall immediately set about the necessary steps to be taken in this affair, and it is likely you will repent having refused my offer when too late."

He was moving away, when Lewiston caught his arm.

" Well — will you put in black and white what you have agreed to give, and—and then—we shall see?"

Lyndsay immediately took up a pen and wrote his offer. Lewiston took it — looked at it — hemmed — coloured — and became confused; at last, plucking up effrontery, he said —

" Well then — I am not the girl's father, and that's as true as that I stand here."

At this acknowledgment Lyndsay's heart thrilled with rapture, and he could scarcely refrain from flying to Gertrude with the joyful tidings. Lewiston went on — " But I am of the same blood — the only one, by-the-by, remaining; and the same name — I was her father's cousin; and when the old dotard of a priest came to Perth-Amboy, and inquired for Jacob Ruxton Lewiston, to be sure, he found me — 'twas by way of humbug at first that I passed myself off for the man who had been drowned nearly twenty years before ; but when I found what his business was — but that's enough — I hate your long skim-milk stories

— and so, as soon as you can let me have this on a proper bit of parchment," pointing to the paper Lyndsay had given him, " then I'll wish you a good afternoon and vanish in a wink."

" But how came you to impose yourself so easily upon Mrs. St. Clair ?" inquired Lyndsay, anxious for Gertrude's sake to ascertain every thing. " She had seen the person you represented?"

" She had so, but it was near twenty years ago — and there was a strong family likeness, it seems; besides, I had the letter to shut her mouth; and since I was master of her secret, it signified little to her whether I were the girl's father or not — I had got the upper hand of her any how."

Having got all the information that was wanted. Lyndsay was now only desirous of being rid of so worthless an inmate; and after admonishing him upon the iniquity of his ways, he gave him a letter to his agent, directing the money to be paid, and the bond to be made out for his annuity, then only waited to see him fairly out of the house before he communicated to Gertrude the happy result.

CHAPTER XXX.

Plus nous etions jeunes, moins nous avions de resignation ; car dans la jeu-nesse, surtout l'on s'attend au bonheur, Ton croit en avoir le droit; et Ton se revoke a l'idee de ne pas l'obtenir. — Madame de Stael.

For a time Gertrude felt as though she were again restored to all she had lost, in her joy at finding she was not the daughter of the man whom her very soul abhorred; and, at the moment, all other evils seemed light compared to that ^he had just escaped.

She could not find words to thank Lyndsay for his generous interference (though that was only known to her in part); but her looks — her tears — her broken exclamations, spoke more forcibly the feelings of her heart. But the first flush of joy over, many a bitter thought arose. She was still the fallen, degraded, dependant being, — without a home — without a friend save one—him to whom she owed all—and Delmour! — but on Delmour she would not think — she would wait in all the unnatural calmness of patience which knew not resignation till she heard from him — and then! — and her heart heaved in agony as she thought what might then be the result.

Lyndsay seemed to guess something of what was passing in her mind; for he said, with some emotion —

" Those who like yourself have been imposed upon in this fraud, ought they not also to be undeceived?—shall I perform that duty for you?—shall I write " he stopped; but Gertrude knew to whom he alluded, and, for a moment, she wished that Delmour were indeed apprised of the discovery which had been made — that she was not the daughter of the horrid Lew-iston ; but in another instant she rejected the idea.

"No," thought she — "I will not seem to court his notice — as heiress of Rossville I gloried in avowing my preference for him; but as the poor homeless Gertrude, 'tis he must now seek me — my heart may break, but it will not bend — I will wait—I will be to him all or nothing!" But she almost gasped as she repeated to Lyndsay, " I will wait " Then, after a pause, she added, with a deep blush, " But do you what you think right for me."

And Lyndsay's generous disinterested spirit, guided upon every occasion by that heavenly principle, " Do unto others even as you would that others should do unto you," prompted him to write and acquaint Delmour with the truth. As the daughter of Lewiston, he was certain he would never have stooped to an alliance with Gertrude; but whether, as she was now situated, he would still fulfil his engagement, was a doubtful question. At any rate, it was due to him to be undeceived; and though he comprehended and approved of the delicacy which kept Gertrude silent, he deemed it but the more incumbent on him to declare the truth. He therefore wrote a simple and brief statement of what had passed, without noticing or alluding to any thing else; and having despatched his letter, he awaited the answer in an agitation of mind little inferior to Gertrude's.

Meanwhile Dr. Bruce and Mr. and Miss Black had successively arrived, and it was Lyndsay's painful task to make the two latter acquainted with the guilty transaction, which he did in the gentlest and most delicate manner. But, however desirous he was of sparing their feelings, it was impossible to soften the disgraceful fact, which fell upon them like a thunderbolt, and affected them each according to the difference of their mind and feelings. When the first shock had been surmounted, it was settled that Miss Black should remain at Rossville for the present in attendance upon Mrs. St. Clair, whose situation was such as to disarm every hostile feeling, even could such have found harbour in her sister's breast. But it was in sorrow, not in anger, that she acknowledged the disgrace which had fallen upon them; and Lyndsay hoped that her soft unupbraiding spirit might tend to calm Gertrude's wilder grief—but Gertrude refuse to see her.

M Do not," said she to Lyndsay, with an agitation that shook her whole frame — " do not ask me to see any one at present— never ask me to see the sister of " she stopped, shuddering.

" But you forgive her, Gertrude ? " said Lyndsay.

Gertrude was silent for some moments; then exclaimed with a burst of emotion —

" Oh ! it is dreadful to have been thus striving against nature —striving to love as my mother her who was my bitterest enemy — she has broken bands which God himself had knit—my mother ! and I knew her not as such! — gentle and uncomplaining, I treated her as my servant—Oh ! may God forgive me—but do not ask me to forgive her!"

" Ah, Gertrude ! it was not thus we were taught to pray by Him who forgave us !"

But Gertrude only wept in bitterness of heart.

" Dear Gertrude! you have been heroic—will you not be for-giving ?—Bo not let me think you find it easier to be great than to be good."

" For you I would do much," said Gertrude, in increasing emotion—" I would do even this, if I could—but I cannot —do not, then—do not name her to me," cried she passionately, while she pressed her hands on her bosom, as if to still the tumult of her soul.—"She it is who has made me the lost, degraded, wretched being that I am, and ever must remain !"— and again her tears burst forth.

" How you disappoint me, Gertrude !" said Lyndsay, with a sigh. —" I had flattered myself that the same greatness of mind which led you to cast far from you all that you most prized upon earth, would at the same time have taught you the worthlessness of those mere worldly objects.—Ungrateful that you are!—which of all the gifts a liberal Creator has endowed you with would you exchange for those empty distinctions which one creature bestows upon another? — Would you exchange your beauty for rank — your talents for wealth—your greatness of mind for extended power — for all of them would you exchange your immortal soul? — Ah, Gertrude! what avails it by what name we are called for the few short years of our earthly pilgrimage ? — If to be made fit partakers of immortal life is, as I believe it is, the sole end of existence, all that we are called upon to endure here are but m.eans for that end. Do not impute your trials, then, severe as they are, to a being such as yourself—but look upon them as instruments in the hand of God, it may be to bring you unto Him. Even in this world, Gertrude, you may yet live to reap in smiles what has been sown in tears, if you will look for happiness where it is only to be found."

Gertrude shook her head, and still wept; but her tears were softer, and her agitation less violent.

Lyndsay's was not that indiscreet zeal which would break the bruised reed, and quench the smoking flax, in its blind misjudging enthusiasm. He looked not that the soil should be harrowed, and the seed sown, and the harvest reaped, at one and the same time; but he trusted that the influence of Divine truth would bring peace to the soul, still fainting with agony beneath the load assigned it; and that the heart which God had stricken would yet, in prostrating itself at the throne of grace, and acknowledging Him in all His ways, rise superior to the changes of this passing world. " O, virtue ! when this solemn pageantry of earthly grandeur shall be no more ; when all distinctions but moral and religious shall vanish ; when this earth shall be dissolved; when the moon shall be no more a light by night, neither the sun by day ;—thou shalt still survive, thy votary's immortal friend—thou shalt appear like thy great Author in perfect beauty; thy lustre undiminished, thy glory imperishable !" *

* Jeremiah Seed.

CHAPTER XXXI.

Whilst skies are blue and bright,
"Whilst flowers are gay, Whilst eyes that change ere night
Make glad the day; Whilst yet the calm hours creep, Dream thou —and from thy sleep
Then wake to weep. Shelly.

Gertrude now experienced the agony of suspense in all its intensity. Restless and unquiet she walked ahout her own apartment, or starting at every sound stopped to listen with suspended "breath—then pressed her throbbing heart, as though she could have stilled its tumults by the touch of her hand.

"Why do I submit to this—why do I endure it?" inquired she of herself, as she bent her burning brow in shame at the tears that had fallen in showers on her lover's picture, on which she had been gazing,— 4i He left me, and at what a time ! — No, I will not wait to be rejected—cast off like something vile — I will go, if it were to beg;" and for a moment she formed the desperate resolution of leaving Rossville secretly—of flying she knew not, cared not where — she would find some spot on which to lay her aching head till death should close her eyes. But then the madness of the scheme struck her—she felt she could not mingle with the vulgar throng :—young, distinguished, and delicately bred, where could she find a shelter ? Lyndsay, 'tis true, had offered her a home—but her spirit already bowed beneath the load of gratitude she owed to him. Then, with that ebb and flow of mind which is ever the effect of powerful excitement, returned her faith in Delmour — yes—it was—it must be his love for her which had hurried him from her. — His was not that selfish passion—he had said so a thousand times—which would plunge the object he loved in all the wretchedness of poverty ; and she knew that he was poor—that he was even in debt—that it was impossible he could support her as he would have his wife appear ; but he had gone to prevail upon his brother to provide for them, and he would come—Oh yes! he would come and claim her as his own!

It was thus Gertrude communed with herself—her mind either a prey to despair, or busied in vain fantastic dreams, which, even if they were destined to be realized, it was idleness to indulge. Her agitation was not lessened when, on the thh I morning after her lover's departure, intelligence arrived of the death of Mr. Delmour !

Gertrude was not so callous to right feeling as not to hear of this event with mingled grief and awe ; and the moral was too striking not to fall with conviction on her heart. With tears she acknowledged the vanity—the emptiness of worldly distinction ;

F F

and, kneeling, prayed—for the moment fervently, devoutly prayed, in all the humiliation of a contrite spirit and an awakened heart.

Lyndsay did not omit the opportunity of enforcing the solemn lesson which came to shed its calming influence on her ruffled breast. It, indeed, required no very high sense of religion, at such a time, to feel the utter insignificance of mere worldly greatness, and to acknowledge that its grandeurs are vapours —its pleasures illusions—its promises falsehoods — when he on whom it seemed to have lavished all that it had to bestow was now, as if in mockery —

A thing, at thought of which
The roused soul swells boundless and sublime !

But alas! these wholesome thoughts were yet strangers in Gertrude's heart; and the first sudden shock over, bright thoughts began to spring up even from the ashes of the dead.

Even in this hour of grief and fears, "When awful Truth unveil'd appears, Some pow'r unknown usurps my breast; Back to the world my thoughts are led, My feet in folly's lab'rinth tread, And fancy dreams that life is blest.

Again Gertrude's heart bounded, as she thought her lover was now Earl of Rossville — able, and — could she doubt?—willing to restore her to all she had lost. She would have renounced all for him — she had stood the test, and a thousand, aye, ten thousand times, had he wished that it were in his power to prove to her the disinterestedness of his love in return.

There was*no longer room for uncertainty; although he might not choose to involve her in the hardships and privations of poverty, yet how would he exult in raising her to the height from which she had descended! And again gay and vainglorious visions began to swim before those eyes still wet with tears of penitence for former follies.

Suspense was now changed into impatience scarcely less supportable, as she counted the days and hours which must elapse before she could receive the assurance of her lover's faith ; but at length the time came when she might hear from him — but no letter was there. Another—and another—and another day passed on, every instant of which was as an age of agony to Gertrude's throbbing heart, as again it was overwhelmed with a sea of doubts, and again the sickness of hope deferred crept like poison through her veins. But who can count the beatings of the lonely heart? Once more she had watched from her window the arrival of the post — again she had held her breath to listen for the footstep that was to bring her the letter on which her existence seemed to depend ; but a long and dreary pause followed. At length it was broken by a message from Lyndsay, requesting to see her.

" Something is wrong!" thought she ; " he is dead—01

she could not finish the sentence, even in imagination ; but pale, trembling, gasping for breath, she repaired to the library, where she was told he awaited her.

Her own agitation was too great to permit her to notice Lyndsay's, as he advanced to meet her, and would have spoken, but the words died on his lips. Then Gertrude looked on him; but it was not grief that was depicted in his countenance — yet neither was it joy, but a strange mingled expression agitated his usually serene features, which she in vain strove to construe. He took her hand ; but it was in a manner more respectful and with an air more embarrassed than he was wont to testify towards her, with whom he had hitherto been on the familiar footing of a friend.

" You have heard—you have heard"—cried Gertrude ; but she could say no more.

" I have," said Lyndsay, with an emotion he vainly tried to

master ; " Gertrude — dearest Gertrude ! " he turned from

her for a moment, and paced the chamber in disorder; while Gertrude, bereft of all motion, stood pale and speechless. — Suddenly he approached her; and putting a letter into her hands, he held them locked in his, while he said in a voice choked with agitation —

" Gertrude — I cannot now say what I feel; but if, at this time, you can think of me at all, think of me as your truest, your firmest friend—as one who sbares your every feeling." He then quitted the apartment; but Gertrude was scarcely conscious he had spoken, for a glance of her eye had told her the letter was from Delmour. It was an opened one, and addresssed to Lyndsay. With desperate courage she unfolded it—she began to read it with a beating heart and a trembling hand ; but as she went on, every nerve and fibre felt as though they were hardening into stone. It was as follows : —

*G

" Dear Lyndsay, . " The melancholy intelligence of my lamented brother's death would reach you some days ago — that, together with the heartrending scene I went through at Rossville, was almost too much for me, and must be my excuse for having so long delayed acknowledging your letter. Perhaps another motive, still more powerful, has also influenced me, which I know I need not hesitate to avow to you. — It is the earnest heartfelt desk "e I have to do every justice to one, who, though still dearer to me than life, and whom it is distraction to me even to think of relinquishing — yet, at present, I fear I may not venture to call mine — yet mine I know she is, and ever will be in heart, as Heaven knows how wholly I am hers! — But, circumstanced as we both are, it would be folly, madness — in short, you must be aware of the difficulties with which I have to contend. — You

F F 2

know, and I do not hesitate to acknowledge, that I consider birth as the most important of all distinctions; and, I believe, I am not singular in my sentiments upon this subject, at least I find my uncle the Duke (whom I ventured to sound upon this matter) is still more decided in his opinion ; and as he is now in a very declining state, and has much in his own power, I own I am unwilling to come to extremities with him at present. You are aware that the Rossville property did not prove sufficient, during the last year, to support the dignity of the family, and that debts to a large amount have in consequence been incurred. — I am far from intending to convey the most distant insinuation against the dear object of my affections; for if any blame was imputable, it would be, perhaps, more justly due to me. But she only lived as her rank demanded, and as I should choose my wife to do; and I merely mention this to prove to you that I am, at present, far from independent — as my own debts (that to yourself amongst others, dear Lyndsay) are of considerable magnitude, and both together leave me little choice as to what, in common prudence, I am called upon to do. Distressing as it is, I consider myself therefore compelled, for the present, to relinquish those hopes which have so long formed the happiness of my life, and which I will still cherish even in spite of fate — a time may, and, I trust, will yet come, when no such heartrending alternative will be necessary. Meanwhile, it is my most anxious wish that every thing should be done that can possibly contribute to the peace and comfort of my adored Gertrude, and I entreat you will therefore prevail upon her to remain at Rossville. It is my intention to go abroad for a year or two, and it will materially contribute to my tranquillity to know that she is still mistress there, and in possession of all those enjoyments which I know she prizes so much. I must therefore entreat your good offices to have every thing arranged on this point. Let her choose whom she will to reside with her; or, should she persist in choosing another residence, let every thing be arranged in the most liberal manner. I inclose you an order upon Coutts, that you may draw on my account for whatever is requisite — let nothing be wanting that can, in any degree, tend to embellish an existence which, alas! like my own, will I fear from henceforth be but a wretched one. Dear Lyndsay, to your hands I commit my treasure — on your friendship I place the utmost reliance. I know her affections are mine

— wholly mine— and I but who that has loved Gertrude

could ever love another?—I will endeavour to write to her myself when my nerves have regained some firmness; but at present you may judge of the state of my mind from this distracted scrawl. Write to me, I entreat of you, dear Lyndsay — tell me how my dearest love bears herself—write by return of post—tell me all;— every thing ; and believe me your affectionate

" Rossville.

** P. S. — The law people are taking the necessary steps to have my rights recognized. Contrive to save my adored Ger trude's feelings as much as possible on this occasion."

CHAPTER XXXIL

Go to ! hath life

A blessing yet for me ? I have no country,

I have no house, a refuge from my ills. Euripides.

Such was the letter ; and when Gertrude had read it her head sank on her breast, as she murmured —

" For him I would have abandoned all — all!"

She could not have found a name for the wretchedness which wrung her heart, and for a moment her spirit felt as if crushed beneath the weight — but by one desperate effort she seemed to cast it from her; and instantly rising, with a mien outwardly calm, save for her burning cheek and quivering lip, she passed to the adjoining room, where Lyndsay was waiting with the most intense anxiety the effect which this communication would produce. As Gertrude returned the letter, she merely bent her head to him; but he saw that her eyes were tearless, and under the influence of high-wrought but repressed feeling there was something more than usually calm and noble in her air and bearing. She moved on towards a door, at the opposite end of the room, which communicated with her own suite of apartments, and Lyndsay made no attempt to detain her; but when her hand was upon the lock she turned round, and, approaching him, took his hand, and pi'essed it between hers —

" My dear — my only friend!" said she, " may God bless you!"

" Why do you say so now, dearest Gertrude ?" cried Lyndsay, fearing, he knew not what, from the unnatural calmness of her manner.

" Because — because I feel it!" said Gertrude, with a sigh, as though her heart had broke.

" And I — may I too say all I feel for you ?" said Lyndsay, with emotion.

" No — why should you feel for me? — I am well — quite well," said she, with the same sort of wild calmness; "but I will never forget your kindness to me!"

A tear gleamed in her eye as she turned away. Lyndsay made an effort to detain her, as he exclaimed, " Speak, then — tell me what you would have me do to serve you—to save you, if I can, from "

Gertrude gently disengaged herself from him, while she said

FF3

in a firm voice, " I will not remain here —but I have arrange-ments to make before I go : — do not seek to detain me !"

" Where, will you go, dearest Gertrude ? — my house is yours, and my aunt "

" I will not go to your house, Edward," said Gertrude, and her voice began to falter: — then, making an effort to regain her composure, she quickly added, " I know not yet where I shall go — I must have time — I have arrangements to make — but I cannot breathe here " — and she gasped as she spoke; then, waving her hand to Lyndsay, she hastily entered her own apartment.

Still Gertrude's energy did not forsake her, as she set about her preparations ; but she mistook for fortitude what in reality was only fever of mind, and it was under that false excitement that she acted. She was alive but to one feeling—she had been deserted by him for whom she would have sacrificed the world itself—him whom she loved sufficiently even to have renounced

— him whom every hallowed obligation, every principle of honour, every feeling of tenderness, had bound to her by ties she had considered as indissoluble! He had dared to insult her by supposing she would choose to be indebted to his bounty for her support — he deemed her unworthy of being his wife — and he would have her submit to become his pensioner! — to live upon his alms ! — to be clothed and fed by him! — to drag out a life of dependence amid those very scenes which had witnessed her in the full meridian of her prosperity ! She could not — she would not consider what she was to do — whither she was to go : it mattered not what became of her were she but away from Rossville — she would work — beg — starve — but she would not sink into a base stipendiary.

But, alas ! Gertrude knew nothing of life and its ways, when she reasoned thus — she knew nothing of those various manners and degrees in which every human being — even those possessed of the loftiest feelings of independence—are bound more or less to one another. She only panted to escape from the degradation she felt she was enduring, and every other idea was absorbed in that single one.

But when her arrangements were completed, then the dreadful sense of her own utter loneliness came upon her; and she pressed her throbbing temples in agony, as she leant her head upon her hand, and vainly strove to think of whither and to whom she would go. But " the world seem'd all before her where to choose," for she had no claim upon any one being in it; and who would claim her— abject—degraded — fallen as she was?

— No one but the generous noble-minded Lyndsay, and he was the last person she would have recourse to — she could not bear that he should look upon her in her humiliation— he knew that she had been rejected—forsaken—he had seen that heart which had been so fondly sought, so proudly won, now cast back upon her as a thing of nought !

She was roused from this agony of thought by the entrance of her maid to announce that Mr. Ramsay was in the saloon, and wished to see her.

" I will not see him — I will not see any one that " and

again the horror which she felt for all connected with the author of her misery rushed upon her.

" My lady !" exclaimed Miss Masham.

" I am not your lady — I am — but no matter — you will know all when I am gone Gone ! — Where, whither?" repeated she to herself. Then the sudden resolution seized her that she would see Mr. Ramsay — he would take her from Rossville — no matter what became of her after that; and not daring to deliberate, she hastily passed on to the apartment, still under the excitement of feelings strained to their utmost stretch.

Mr. Ramsay had been made acquainted by Mr. Black with the discovery which had taken place, and for some time indignation against Mrs. St. Clair was the only feeling that found place in his breast; then, as that somewhat abated, his heart began to yearn with pity towards the victim of her guilt, and at length that stranger sentiment (for uncle Adam was not prone to the indulgence of such weakness) gradually grew into something almost akin to joy at the thought that she, whom he had always loved for her resemblance to his first and only love, was indeed her descendant. The resemblance, even in his mind's eye, grew twenty times stronger; and he felt that he should look upon her with greater • delight as the granddaughter of Lizzie Lundie than ever he had done as Countess of Rossville. She was his own nearest relation, too; for Lizzie and he had been cousins-german—brother and sister's children ; while his connection with the Blacks was only by half-blood. All this uncle Adam had revolved over and over again, as he paced his little chamber irresolute how to act. At length, unable to come to any fixed determination, he took chaise from the Blue Boar, and set off for Rossville, where he arrived, as if heaven-directed, at the very moment when his appearance seemed, indeed, an interposition of Providence. For the first time, he voluntarily extended his hand, and grasped Gertrude's in it with a vehemence which was indicative of the warmth and sincerity of his goodwill. Both were silent for some moments, for even uncle Adam, for the time, seemed overcome ; but, at length, he said —

" It is needless to say ony thing aboot it — I dinna want to hear ony mair — just tell me whether I can do you ony gude.— Will you gang wi' me ? "

" Oh! yes — yes," cried Gertrude — " take me from this — oh! take me now "

"But stay now — are you sure you're ready?" said Mr. Ramsay, who was not quite so rapid in his movements ; and who, although perfectly sincere in his offer, had not expected it

F f 4

to be so promptly acted upon. Moreover, he was not quite sure that they perfectly understood each other, and he thought some explanation necessary before they set off together. He would fain have put the question in a delicate form, but he had never been accustomed to sounding, and delicacy was not his fort; he was, therefore, fain to have recourse to his own method of gaining information, which was, to put the question in the most direct manner ; and he said, with his usual bluntness —

" Do you ken whar it is you're gawin ?"

The question struck like a dagger to Gertrude's heart; and, smote with the consciousness of her own desolation, she could not speak — she turned away her head to hide the burning drops that forced their way from her eyes.

" I have no home," said she, in a voice choking with emotion ; " I am a beggar! "

" I'm very glad to hear't," said uncle Adam, warmly ; " that's just the very thing I wanted— I rejoice that you're to owe nae-thing to that prood thrawn pack — so come wi' me, my dawtie, and ye's no want for ony thing that I hae to gie you — Lizzie Lundie's bairn will be my bairn — so come your ways. — ' The bird maun flichter that flees wi' ae wing'— but ye's haud up your head yet in spite o' them a'."

In the tumult of her mind Gertrude had entirely overlooked the ties which bound her, the daughter of Jacob Lewiston, to him whom she had only known as the uncle of Mrs. St. Clair ; but now it glanced upon her that in uncle Adam she beheld a relation of her own — the only being with whom she might claim kindred. But she was too wretched even to feel pleasure at the discovery; she only considered that he would take her away — that he would give her a shelter, and there she would die, and be heard of no more.

" Is there naebody here you wad see before you gang ? " said Mr. Ramsay, as she was hurrjdng wildly away.

" No — no," cried she, impatiently; then suddenly stopping, " Yes, I have one kind friend to whom I will say farewell once more," as the thought glanced upon her that Lyndsay would be glad to see her so protected, and she sent to say she wished to see him. He instantly hastened to her, and was made acquainted with the arrangement which had been made, though he was still left in ignorance of the relationship which subsisted between them ; for Gertrude, in the fervour of her mind, had already ceased to think of it, and uncle Adam, from certain tender feelings, was unwilling to enter into particulars.

Although he was not exactly the person to whose hands Lyndsay would have chosen to commit Gertrude ; yet, situated as she was, even uncle Adam's home was better than none, especially as he most cordially invited him to come to it as often as he pleased.

" There is one person you wished me to see, and I would not,"

said Gertrude, in agitation, to Lyndsay, as she was almost on the threshold to depart; " but now I would see her sister before I go."

And the wish was no sooner signified to Miss Black than she hastened to comply with it. At sight of her a slight tremor shook Gertrude's frame ; but she neither wept nor spoke — she merely kissed her twice with fervour, then turned away, and bade a long farewell to Rossville. The same day Mrs. St. Clair was removed to the house of her sisters.

CHAPTER XXXIII.

Sorrows are well allow'd, and sweeten nature,
Where they express no more than drops on lilies ;
But when they fall in storms they bruise our hopes, —
Make us unable, though our comforts meet us,
To hold our heads up. Massinger.

But this state of high-wrought feeling could not long continue. In vain Gertrude struggled against the burning sense of her wrongs and her wretchedness — in vain she repressed each rising sigh and starting tear, with lofty scorn at the weakness they would have betrayed—in vain she repeated to herself a thousand times that she was calm — she was well. Her throbbing head and aching heart told another tale ; and she was at length compelled to yield to the fever which, for some time, had been preying upon her. Then reason fled, and for many days her life was doubtful; and, during that time, poor uncle Adam, like some faithful mastiff, hung round the bed which contained this new-found treasure, in all the stern woe of rigid old age. Lyndsay was the only person (excepting the medical attendants) whom he would see ; but to him he would utter the grief which filled his heart even to overflowing, long closed as it had been against each softer feeling ; and Lyndsay, even in the midst of his own anguish, strove to cheer and support the disconsolate old man. But the object of all this solicitude was once more restored to them— the crisis of the fever was past, and Gertrude again woke to consciousness. It was only then she was aware of the danger she had passed; she had walked unconsciously through the valley of the shadow of death — the gates, of eternity had been before her, but she had not descried them. It was then, while still hovering on the confines of this world, that she felt all the emptiness and the vanity of its pleasures: her dreams of greatness — her hopes of happiness — her gay-spent days — her festive nights, where were they now ?—Gone ; and where they had been was marked but with shame—disappointment—remorse ! All earthly distinctions had been hers — and

what was the account which she had now to render to God for the use of these His gifts ? On which of these was it that she would now build her hopes of acceptance with Him?—on which of them would she now rest her hopes of eternal happiness ? Alas ! miserable comforters were they all!

A deep melancholy now took possession of Gertrude's mind. Like all persons of an ardent and enthusiastic temperament, she flew from from one extreme to the other; and what had formerly " whispered as faults now roared as crimes," only to be expiated by a life of penitence and sorrow. She kept her own apartment—refused to see any body, even Lyndsay, and passed her time in solitude and woe. In vain did uncle Adam attempt to stem the tide of affliction which had thus broken in upon her shattered heart. She acknowledged his kindness with tears and with gratitude ; but when he attempted to remonstrate with her, or urged her to see any one, she became violently agitated; and her only answer was, " If you love me, suffer me — oh! suffer me to die in peace!"

The indulgence of her grief had now become a sort of strange unnatural luxury to her; she loved to sit for hours brooding on her sorrows — to hoard them, as it were, in her own heart —she could not have borne that another should have shared in them ; she loved to think that no one could share in them—that she stood alone in the world — a wretched, forsaken, lonely thing. To a heart such as hers the existence of some powerful sentiment was necessary—she had strove to tear from her heart every root, every fibre of her once cherished tenderness ; but no flower had arisen to fill the void they had left. All was dreariness and desolation.

Lyndsay had written to her repeatedly, urging and imploring her to see him, and using every argument to rouse her from this wasteful excess of grief; but she only wept when she read his letters, and wished that he would cease to think of one so wretched, so degraded as she was.

Poor uncle Adam was almost heartbroken at this pertinacity of suffering ; all that he possessed, he had told her again and again, should be hers—she should go to Broom Park — she should be mistress there—she should have every thing that gold and goodwill could procure to make her happy ; but Gertrude would only exclaim, " No—no — once I had wealth and power and how did I abuse them ! — leave me then, the beggar that I am—that I deserve to be !"

She was in this state of mind, when one day the door of her apartment was gently opened, and Anne Leslie slowly entered. At sight of her Gertrude turned away her head in displeasure at the intrusion; but Anne caught her hand, and, as she respectfully kissed it, her tears dropt upon it. Gertrude stood some moments irresolute; then, throwing herself on Anne's neck, she exclaimed, with a burst of anguish—

" You trusted in God, and He has not deceived you—while I " she stopped, overcome with the acuteness of remembrance.

" But you will trust in Him, and He will yet put gladness in your heart," said Anne, wiping away the tears from her own sweet serene face, where shone the peaceful calm of a heavenly mind.

" No—never! I do not desire to be happy!" said Gertrude — " I do not deserve to be happy!" added she, in an accent of despair.

" Ah! — who has ever deserved that happiness which we owe to a Saviour's love ?' If

Thou, Lord shouldest mark iniquities, who shall stand?' Guilty and frail as we all are, which of us would dare to lift up our eyes to Heaven, and say we merited its favour ? "

"But I had power, and I misused it—I had wealth, and I squandered it—I had an idol, and "

" Alas !" said Anne, meekly, " who can weigh even their own actions in the balance ? If your errors were more glaring than mine, so were your temptations greater. He only who made the heart can judge it, for He only knows what have been its trials."

" He knows," said Gertrude, bitterly, " that, in the day of prosperity, mine was far from Him."

" And therefore He has deprived you of those vain delights which would have separated your soul from Himself. Do not then turn away from God as from an offended Judge, whose anger you fear; but look to Him as to a tender Father reconciled to his erring child through the merits and mediation of One who has borne our sins, and who invites you and me and all of us to come and receive from Him the pardon and the blessing He has purchased for us."

" The pardon may be mine, for God is merciful!" said Gertrude. " But what blessing is now left for me ?" added she in an accent of despair.

" The blessing of God — if you will but open your heart to receive it," said Anne, tenderly. " Ah! think of those blessed words, 'Come unto me, all ye that are weary and heavy laden, and I will give you rest!' "

" Aye," said Gertrude, in the same sad tone ; " there is a place where the weary are at rest!"

" But that is not the rest which God has provided for His children," said Anne; " that would indeed be a gloomy prospect, if we looked but to the grave as the end of our trials. Remember these were words uttered in the agony of a soul struggling with the powers of darkness, but afterwards repented of in the dust and ashes of a heart enlightened and renewed by divine grace."

A low convulsive sigh was Gertrude's only answer; and Anne continued her efforts to administer consolation and encourage-ment to the heart "whose only aliment seemed its own intense wretchedness.

" Even on this side of the grave, dear Gertrude ! there is a rest for those who will accept it— a rest from the dominion of sin and worldly sorrow, and a happy rest; not the rest of oblivion, but the rest of unalloyed enjoyment beyond the grave "

" The grave is now the only possession I covet," said Gertrude, as she bent her head, and shaded her face with her hand, as if to hide the anguish it would have betrayed.

Poor Anne's gentle heart was filled to overflowing at this pertinacity in wretchedness in one so young, so fair, so gifted, and for some moment tears choked her utterance. " No, no," said she earnestly, " you must not give way to such gloomy despairing thoughts. You take to yourself the words of Job in the hour of tribulation and strong temptation; but you forget how the soul which had looked but to death for deliverance, which had even prayed to be cut off from the presence of its Maker, yet lived to bless the mercy and goodness of God, and to rejoice even in this world in the rest which it found in the knowledge of its Redeemer."

" I pray that I may be enabled to endure existence," said Gertrude : " as to ever again enjoying it "

" Not in the same manner or kind," said her friend; " but be assured God would not have taken away your enjoyments, but to give you something better and more enduring; you know that He who stilled the tempest with a word can also speak peace to the troubled heart — a peace which the world can neither give nor take away."

But Gertrude only sighed, for the promise afforded no consolation to her. To the young and imaginative nothing seems less desirable than a state of calm ; and while the heart is still heaving beneath the influence of the storm that has swept over it, it yet shrinks from the prospect of the deathlike stillness that must succeed.

But young as Anne was in years, she was experienced in heavenly wisdom, and, in the character of the faithful minister's wife, well-skilled in the angel art of administering consolation to the afflicted ; of cheering the downcast mourner; of pouring balm into the wounded spirit; of binding up the broken heart. Day after day she devoted herself to the task, regardless of all selfish considerations, till at length Gertrude's feelings were touched by such unwearying love and tenderness, and she began to evince something like pleasure at sight of her; then to listen to her conversation with somewhat of interest; and at length she consented to receive a visit from Mr. Lyndsay.

That was an act of humiliation, and she felt it as such ;—thus to meet in her low and fallen state, as an object of pity, those whom in the days of her pride and prosperity she had despised and deceived! But these painful feelings passed away in the

soothing intercourse and respectful sympathy of those truly Christian friends. By degrees Gertrude's heart opened to the holy influence of those divine truths they so earnestly yet gently sought to impress upon it; and gradually her soul emerged from the dreary stupor in which it had so long been buried, and her mind became soothed and composed beneath the calming influence of that religion whose very essence is love and peace. She saw that her heart bad gone astray in its own delusions, but these were now dispelled. She had received a new impulse ; and she had awakened, if not to happiness, at least to something less perishable — less fatal. Hers had been " a young fancy, which could convert the sound of common things to something exquisite;" but now she bowed her heart in quietness — she knew "her blighted prospects could revive no more; yet was she calm, for she had heaven in view."

Be thence encouraged more, when tried,
On the best Father to confide ;
O ! my too blind but nobler part,
Be moved ! Be won by these, my heart!
See of how rich a lot, how bless'd,
The true believer stands possess'd!
Come, backward soul, to God resign ;
Peace, his best blessing, shall be thine:
Boldly recumbent on His care,
Cast thy full burden only there. Luther.

CHAPTER XXXIV.

Forgiveness to the injur'd does belong ;
But they ne'er pardon who commit the wrong. Dryden.

It was with emotion that Gertrude and Lyndsay met once more, and both were struck with the change in each other's appearance ; for Lyndsay, too, looked as though he had indeed borne a part in all her sufferings — and she was smote with the selfishness which had caused her so long to indulge her sorrow, unmindful of the generous heart which had shared in it. But if the brilliancy of her beauty was dimmed by the blight which had fallen upon her, it had acquired a character of still deeper interest in the eyes of those who loved her.

Her pale cheek,

Like a white rose on which the sun hath look'd
Too wildly warm (is not this passion's legend ?) —
The drooping lid whose lash is wet with tears —
A lip which has the sweetness of a smile,
But not its gaiety — do not these bear
The scorched foot-prints sorrow leaves in passing
O'er the clear brow of youth ?

" I would first see you to acknowledge the boundless gratitude I owe for all your kindness to me," said Gertrude, who was the first to speak; " and then once you asked me to forgive her who had injured me, and I would not, for then I was proud, passionate, revengeful; but now I would go to her— I would forgive her, even as I trust I have been forgiven !"

" Dearest Gertrude!" said Lyndsay, with emotion, " how happy this makes me! But do not humble me by talking of your gratitude to me—to have done less than I have done, when the means were in my power, would have been criminal—if I have been enabled to serve you, that is recompence more than sufficient. — I have borne a selfish part in your welfare, for your happiness was mine — in vain my heart has tried to create a separate interest — it cannot "

" Do not talk thus, my dear friend," said Gertrude, in agitation.

" Ah, Gertrude! since the same true and immortal passion has touched our hearts, suffer me now to avow the sentiments which I have so long cherished for you "

" No, no—not now," cried Gertrude, in increasing emotion ; " be to me all that you have hitherto been — a friend, a guardian, a brother — but "

She sighed, and, in spite of herself, a tear rolled slowly down her cheek.

" I will, then," said Lyndsay; for he feared that the ties which bound them might be broken in the effort to draw them closer.

Gertrude went to the house of the Miss Blacks, and was received by them with tears of tenderness and thankfulness.

Mrs. St. Clair had recovered from the effects of the laudanum she had swallowed, and it was now her determination to go abroad for the remainder of her life, and in a few days she was to depart.

" She talked much of you for some time," said Miss Black, " and said she could not die in peace till she had obtained your forgiveness;, but of late — alas ! since her health has been restored she has thought, I fear, less seriously—and she has not spoken of you at all — perhaps she may even be averse to see you." And she went to acquaint her that Gertrude was there.

Some time elapsed before she returned, and she said her sister had been violently agitated at the thoughts of seeing Gertrude, and had at first refused to do it; but that she was now more composed, and had consented to receive her, upon condition that she came alone. The room was darkened to which Gertrude was conducted; but there was a studied arrangement — an air of elegant seclusion about it, which at once indicated that the inmate was unchanged. No symptom of penitence was there, amidst a display of frivolous, heartless selfishness. She was attired in an elegant deshabille; and her fa uteuil —her cushions — her footstool — her screen — her flowers — her perfumes — her toys, were all collected around her in the manner Gertrude had been so long accustomed to see them, and on the arrangement of which Mrs. St. Clair had been wont to pique herself, as a combination of French elegance and English comfort.

For a moment Gertrude's agitation almost overpowered her at again beholding one whom she had hitherto been accustomed to look upon as the author of her being—but whom she could now only view as the author of all her woe. But she repressed her feelings ; and, extending her hand, said mildly —

" I am come to offer that forgiveness which I once refused ; but God has softened my heart and humbled my pride — I can now forgive, as I hope to be forgiven."

" I too have something to forgive," said Mrs. St. Clair, vehemently ; " I have to forgive the cruel disregard—the unnatural, unrelenting violence, with which you treated one who had ever been as a mother to you in all but the natural tie. — I had done all for your aggrandizement — I had raised you from beggary and obscurity to wealth and greatness; and it is you who have brought me to shame, and misery, and poverty — and am I to have nothing to forgive ? I humbled myself in the dust to you, and you were deaf to my prayers—I told you that my life was in your hands: that it did not pay the forfeit of your rash and inhuman conduct is no merit of yours—have I then nothing to forgive ? — But I do forgive," said she, extending the hand she had hitherto refused, but with an air and manner of haughty condescension : " my wrongs and injuries have been great, but I forgive them."

Gertrude almost recoiled with horror from the touch of one whose mind was still so perverted, and whose soul seemed to have been corroded instead of purified by the judgment that had fallen upon her ; but she meekly took her hand, and said —

" Yes — you have also wrongs to forgive me, and I thank you from my heart that you do so. — Mere human forgiveness is, indeed, a thing of nought, more blessed to them who give than to those who receive — may that blessing be yours and mine! and oh ! may the forgiveness of God be vouchsafed to us both! "

She would have kissed her in token of reconcilement, but Mrs. St. Clair turned her head haughtily away ; and Gertrude, after lingering a few moments in deep emotion, quitted the apartment. She did not wound her sisters by repeating what had passed ; but her own heart felt lighter that she had been enabled to pray in sincerity of heart for heavenly forgiveness, even for her who had wrought all her woe.

CHAPTER XXXV.

Good the beginning, good the end shall be,
And transitory evil only makes
The good end happier. Southey.

The following day a plain but handsome carriage, -with suitable attendants, stood at uncle Adam's door, which he at first seemed ashamed of; but after a little coyness and confusion he let Gertrude understand it was for her accommodation, and proposed that they should together make trial of it.

Gertrude had never appeared abroad (except in her visit to Mrs. St. Clair) from the time of her. arrival at Mr. Ramsay's, and a thousand painful feelings rushed upon her at the thoughts of exposing herself to the public gaze — and the public gaze of a small, idle, gossipping, impertinent country town. She was, therefore, on the point of expressing her repugnance; but she thought it would be unkind, ungrateful, when he had sacrificed his feelings so far as to keep a carriage for her, if she did not appear to be gratified by this proof of his affection. She therefore accepted of his proposal, and they set off together. She was not yet sufficiently mistress of her thoughts to bestow much observation on the shifting scenes as they passed along; and she was scarcely aware of where she was, or on what she looked, when she found herself at the very door of Broom Park. They entered ; and a respectable-looking housekeeper and butler, with inferiors, stood ready to receive them.

"There's your leddy," said uncle Adam, giving Gertrude a slight push, by way of introducing her; "see that you a' behave discreetly, an' when ye want ony thing ye maun gang to her, for she kens mair about thae things than me."

This was quite an oration for uncle Adam; and having made it, he stotted into one of the public rooms, and Gertrude followed him.

"My dear uncle," said she, for she still continued that appellation, "how your kindness overpowers me!>—I cannot express how much I feel it."

"Hoot, it's naething," said he, impatiently; "so dinna gang to fash yourself aboot that — the best thanks you can gi'e me is to let me see the red on your cheek, and the smile in your e'e that used to be there, and then I'll believe that I've done you some gude — but no till then." And he affectionately patted her shoulder, which was going great lengths for uncle Adam.

Every thing had evidently been done with a view to gratify Gertrude's ta?te and feelings; and there was good taste and elegance in the arrangements that had recently been made, for which, with all his good intentions, she could scarcely give uncle Adam credit. — It must be Lyndsay's doing — Lyndsay, who knew so well all her habits and pursuits, had provided every indulgence and facility for both; and that, too, merely in a general way, without descending to all the little minutice which it is woman's prerogative to arrange.

The news of Mr. Ramsay's establishment at Broom Park soon circulated in the neighbourhood, and was not long of reaching the ears of Mrs. Major Waddell, and caused them to tingle with indignation and envy. In the midst of all her finery she was not happy; for Gertrude, as uncle Adam's heiress, was the thorn in her side — the bitter drop in her cup — the black man in her closet — the Mordecai at her gate! Such is ever the effect of any baleful passion, especially when operating on a weak mind, and so difficult is it to form an estimate of worldly enjoyment by the symbols of outward prosperity. Her only hope was that she would be able to prove uncle Adam in his dotage; and, for that purpose, she would fain have established a system of espionage betwixt Thornbank and Broom Park; but all her schemes were counteracted by uncle Adam's sagacity. The only way in which she could therefore give vent to her malice was when in company with Gertrude, by taking, or rather making, every opportunity of resting all claim to distinction solely on the ground of birth — family — connections, and other such adventitious circumstances, as the weak vulgar mind lays hold of to exalt itself in the eyes of those who must be weaker than itself to be so dazzled. But in this she was met by uncle Adam, who guarded Gertrude, in aught that in any way concerned her, as a faithful shepherd's colly does the lamb committed to his charge, and he was now too happy to be discomposed even by Mrs. Waddell — he had found something to love, which had long been the desideratum in his life, and he was gradually getting more benign and mellow beneath Gertrude's gentle influence. The first inconveniences of a change of residence and habits fairly over, he even began to take some interest in rural avocations; only stipulating, that he was never to be spoken to on any of the numerous evils inseparable from extensive property, and which not unfrequently embitter the peace of the possessor; such as bad tenants—bad crops—bad weather—bad servants—poachers— robbers — trespassers — and all the thousand ills that wealth is heir to, and which, perhaps, bring happiness more upon a par between the rich and the poor than is generally supposed.

One of the first to pay her respects to the new heiress of Broom Park was Miss Pratt. That lady's absence, or at least her silence, for so long a period, remains to be accounted for to such as take an interest in her fate. But the simple matter of fact was, that she had been refreshing and invigorating herself at Harrowgate, at the expense of her friend and ally, Sir Peter Wellwood, and had but just returned to give the lie direct to the current report of Gertrude's having been rejected by her lover on the discovery of her birth. This, she roundly asserted, was so far from being the case, that she had, with her own ears, heard her refuse him again and again — it was consistent with her knowledge that she had been long engaged to Edward Lyndsay; and, although the little episode of the turret scene was somewhat of a staggerer, yet even that Miss Pratt contrived to bolt, and settled the matter with herself by her having had a great cold and ringing in her ears all that day, which had prevented her hearing exactly what passed. She therefore boldly claimed her five guineas from uncle Adam, though how far she was entitled to them was a doubtful question, and might have borne a dispute; and time was when uncle Adam would as soon have given her his five fingers as his five guineas upon such debateable ground ; but now he was not disposed to cavil at trifles, and he paid her the money at the first suggestion, only taking every possible precaution against the possibility of his giving her a note more than enough.

" Well, my dear," said she, displaying her winnings to Gertrude, "you see I can sing a blithe note at your wedding—ha! ha ! ha! — And, by-the-by, do you know the news is, that a certain cast-off lover of yours is on the top of his marriage with his old flame, the Duchess of St. Ives ? They're both together at Paris, it seems, and it's all settled. I wish them good of one another, for I fancy they're well met; but whether they'll hang long together is another story."

Gertrude could not hear of this event without some degree of emotion, but it soon passed away; and when, at the end of some months, she read a pompous detail of it in the newspapers, it was with feelings far removed from either envy or regret. Still less would they have been called for, could she have foreseen the termination which a few years brought round. Without the cement of one virtuous principle, vice soon dissolved the tie which united them. Injured and betrayed by a faithless wife, the Earl of Rossville fought to avenge his honour, and fell in the cause. But long before then Lyndsay's virtues, and the fervour and disinterestedness of his attachment, had insensibly created for him a warm interest in Gertrude's affections. As has been truly said, " In considering the actions of the mind, it should never be forgotten that its affections pass into each other like the tints of the rainbow ; though we can easily distinguish them when they have assumed a decided colour, yet we can never determine where each hue begins." *

The bewildering glare of romantic passion no longer shed its

r Quarterly Review.

fair but perishable lustre on the horizon of her existence ; but the calm radiance of piety and virtue rose with steady ray, and brightened the future course of a happy and a useful life ; and Gertrude, as the wife of Edward Lyndsay, lived to bless the day that had deprived her of her earthly Inheritance. Thus,

All our ill
May, if directed well, find happy end.
THE END.

Printed in Great
Britain
by Amazon